WAVERLEY

broadview editions
series editor: L.W. Conolly

"Sir Walter Scott," 1822, by Sir Henry Raeburn.
Reprinted by permission of the Scottish National Portrait Gallery.

WAVERLEY

Sir Walter Scott

edited by Susan Kubica Howard

broadview editions

Library and Archives Canada Cataloguing in Publication

Scott, Walter, Sir, 1771-1832
    Waverley / Sir Walter Scott ; edited by Susan Kubica Howard.

(Broadview editions)
Originally published under title: Waverley, or, 'Tis sixty years since.
Includes bibliographical references.
ISBN 978-1-55111-895-6

    1. Jacobite Rebellion, 1745-1746—Fiction.   I. Howard, Susan Kubica, 1958-
II. Title.   III. Series: Broadview editions

PR5322.W4 2010   823'.7   C2010-902293-9

Broadview Editions
The Broadview Editions series represents the ever-changing canon of literature in English by bringing together texts long regarded as classics with valuable lesser-known works.

Advisory editor for this volume: Martin Boyne

Broadview Press is an independent, international publishing house, incorporated in 1985.

We welcome comments and suggestions regarding any aspect of our publications—please feel free to contact us at the addresses below or at broadview@broadviewpress.com.

North America
Post Office Box 1243, Peterborough, Ontario, Canada K9J 7H5
2215 Kenmore Avenue, Buffalo, NY, USA 14207
Tel: (705) 743-8990; Fax: (705) 743-8353
email: customerservice@broadviewpress.com

UK, Europe, Central Asia, Middle East, Africa, India, and Southeast Asia
Eurospan Group, 3 Henrietta St., London WC2E 8LU, United Kingdom
Tel: 44 (0) 1767 604972; Fax: 44 (0) 1767 601640
email: eurospan@turpin-distribution.com

Australia and New Zealand
NewSouth Books
c/o TL Distribution, 15-23 Helles Ave., Moorebank, NSW, Australia 2170
Tel: (02) 8778 9999; Fax: (02) 8778 9944
email: orders@tldistribution.com.au

www.broadviewpress.com

This book is printed on paper containing 30% post-consumer fibre.

Typesetting and assembly: True to Type Inc., Claremont, Canada.

PRINTED IN CANADA

For my children—Ben, Amy, and Lena

Contents

Acknowledgements

I wish to thank Duquesne University for granting me a reduced course load for one semester and for two internal NEH summer grants that helped fund the work of research assistants Jessica Jost-Costanzo, Lee Ann Glowzenski, Michelle Gaffey, and Melissa Jones. Jess's research skills and editorial acumen were especially helpful to this project. I very much appreciate the support of my family and friends for their help in making my research a great source of satisfaction in a balanced life. Thanks too are owed to Helen Holliday and her family for introducing me to the Highlands of Scotland—to their romance and their reality.

Introduction

Biographical Context; the Composition, Publication, and Early Reception of *Waverley*; the *Magnum Opus Waverley*

Walter Scott was born on 15 August 1771 in Edinburgh, Scotland, to Anne Rutherford Scott and Walter Scott, a lawyer. His early childhood was spent at his grandfather's home, Sandy-Knowe, in rural Scotland, where he convalesced from polio. At the age of eight, he began school in Edinburgh, and at twelve he entered Edinburgh University where he studied law. At fifteen, Scott began a five-year apprenticeship in his father's law office, though he continued to read widely in European and British literature. In the "General Preface" to his *Magnum Opus* edition of the Waverley Novels, published between 1829 and 1833, Scott described his very earliest experiences as a "tale-teller," going back to his boyhood in Edinburgh where he reveled in the "romances, old plays, and epic poetry" he found in the city's circulating library, passing his enthusiasm for these, as well as the stories he found in "histories, memoirs, voyages and travels, and the like" (vi) along to his classmates; and he makes the comparison between his own education and that of Edward Waverley, the hero of his first novel (vii).

Scott's interest in ballads and British folklore inspired him to collect and publish *Minstrelsy of the Scottish Border* in 1802-03, his first major literary work. He followed this with such significant poetic works as *The Lay of the Last Minstrel* in 1805, *Marmion* in 1808, and *The Lady of the Lake* in 1810, as well as with an edition of Dryden's works. Also in the early years of the nineteenth century, he began what he calls in the "General Preface" a "tale of chivalry, which was to be in the style of the *Castle of Otranto*,[1] with plenty of Border characters, and supernatural incident" (ix). This work—the fragment, "Thomas the Rhymer," which he includes in the Appendix to the *Magnum Opus* edition of the Waverley Novels—was put aside, and while Scott never finished this piece, he notes that he "did not abandon the idea of fictitious composition in prose, though I determined to give another turn to the style of the work" (ix-x). He turned to his childhood remembrances of the Highlands, of the "old warriors of 1745" that he'd met on his visits to Sandy-Knowe: "it naturally occurred to me, that the ancient traditions and high spirit of a people, who, living in a civilized age and country, retained so strong a tincture of manners belonging to an early period of society, must afford a subject favourable for

---

1 Horace Walpole's *Castle of Otranto* (1765) is viewed as the first Gothic novel.

romance ..." (x), and so, he tells us, in 1805, he wrote the first third of Volume I of *Waverley*.[1] He might have gone on with the work, he writes, if a friend he showed it to had not given an unfavorable opinion of it; discouraged, he put the novel aside and only found the manuscript when, a number of years later, he was looking for fishing equipment in an old writing desk in the attic of his home. Although by then deemed a phenomenally successful poet, Scott was inspired to take up the telling of this tale once again by two circumstances. One was the example of Maria Edgeworth, whose novel *The Absentee* Scott had read in 1812, and whom he credits with doing more through her writing for the success of the union between Ireland and Britain than any lawmaker:

> Without being so presumptuous as to hope to emulate the rich humour, pathetic tenderness, and admirable tact, which pervade the works of my accomplished friend, I felt that something might be attempted for my own country, of the same kind with that which Miss Edgeworth so fortunately achieved for Ireland—something which might introduce her natives to those of the sister kingdom, in a more favourable light than they had been placed hitherto, and tend to procure sympathy for their virtues and indulgence for their foibles. (xiii)

In addition to the example and inspiration that Edgeworth's Irish novels offered him, Scott comments on his experience with an unfinished romance by Joseph Strutt (1749-1802), called *Queen-Hoo Hall*, for which he had written a conclusion; the work had not been well received. While he viewed this work as "a step in my advance towards romantic composition" (xvi), his experience with it also made clear to him that neither he nor his audience had much affinity for a work set in the Middle Ages; he was "led to form the opinion that a romance, founded on a Highland story, and more modern events,

---

1 In his introduction to the Estes and Lauriat edition of *Waverley*, published in 1893, Andrew Lang notes that the manuscript of the novel offers clear proof that the first seven chapters were written in 1805 and the rest of the first volume in 1813 because the watermarks on the paper correspond to those dates (xc). More recently, Lamont, in her introduction to the Oxford University Press edition of *Waverley*, and Millgate, in *Walter Scott: The Making of a Novelist*, posit that the first seven chapters might have been written in 1805 but that additions were made to the first volume in 1810 and the last two volumes were written in 1814. Peter Garside looks at internal and material evidence, including watermarks, to suggest that 1810 is a more likely date for the novel's initial composition ("Dating *Waverley*'s Early Chapters," 75).

would have a better chance of popularity than a tale of chivalry" (xvii), that "in the historical novel, it is necessary ... that the subject assumed should be ... translated into the manners, as well as the language, of the age in which we live" (qtd. in Buzard, 34). Scott wanted *Waverley* as an historical novel to be accessible and relevant as Strutt's work was not.

Having found the manuscript of *Waverley*, and armed with Edgeworth's positive and Strutt's negative examples, Scott set to work on the novel and completed Volume I in 1813. Lockhart, Scott's biographer and son-in-law, writes that Scott showed the first volume of the novel to his friend Erskine, who declared it potentially Scott's best work to date; on that recommendation, the volume was given to another friend, James Ballantyne, who copied it and sent it on to be printed. Once printed, it was sent to Constable, the publisher, who apparently knew it was Scott's work, though it had been presented to him as an anonymous work. He offered £700 for the copyright, which Lockhart declares a "liberal" offer, given that the most respected novelist of the time, Maria Edgeworth, had never received more than a tenth of that for any of her works (I, 237).[1] Scott told Constable that £700 was "too much in case the novel should not be successful, and too little if it should" (Lockhart I, 237).[2] The upshot was that Constable did not offer more, so he and Scott agreed to split the profits on the novel, all of this based on seeing only the first volume. The second and third volumes, according to Scott in an 1830 letter to his friend Morritt, were "begun and finished between the 4th June and the first July" of 1814 (qtd. in Lockhart I, 238). The quick pace of composition is indicative of Scott's practice throughout his years as a fiction writer: as Andrew Lang points out in the introduction to his 1893 edition of *Waverley*, there is little blotting on the manuscript to be seen, but much revision at the proof stage (lxxxiii).

Waverley was published on 7 July 1814, in three volumes, anonymously, since Scott was unsure of how the novel would be received by a public that saw him primarily as a poet and still somewhat distrusted novels. He persisted in this anonymity even after the novel had gone into many editions, and copies numbering, according to Scott, "to the

---

1 Edgeworth's own reckoning of her earnings over her lifetime, dated September 1842, suggests otherwise. She notes there that she was paid £100 for *Castle Rackrent* (1800), for instance (*Maria Edgeworth: A Literary Biography*, 492).

2 Harvie writes that the only time Scott wasn't pressured by economic and political concerns was during the period between 1810 and 1820 when he wrote his historical fiction (177). This could explain his willingness to decline Constable's offer and take a risk on readers liking *Waverley*.

amount of betwixt eleven and twelve thousand" (General Preface, xxi) had been sold.[1] Explaining his anonymous publication as "the author's humour or caprice for the time," Scott only admitted authorship in 1827 in the introduction to his novel *Chronicles of the Canongate*, where he notes that his original intention was to have his authorship revealed posthumously and his decision to own the Waverley Novels as his own work came as a result of the need to publish them in a collected form that would raise money to pay off the huge debts he had incurred when his publishers and printer were bankrupted in 1826.

After a slow start, *Waverley* did well. According to Lockhart, the whole impression of 1,000 copies was gone within five weeks—"an occurrence then unprecedented in the case of an anonymous novel, put forth at what is called among publishers *the dead season*"[2] (I, 243)—and he goes on to note that a second edition of 2,000 copies was decided upon by the end of July and was available to the public by the end of August. It too vanished from the bookstalls, so that a third edition of 1,000 copies had to be published in October, and in November plans for a fourth edition got under way. Scott made revisions to the second and third editions and added a preface to the third. There were subsequent editions published in 1815, 1816, 1817, and 1821. In 1819, *The Novels and Tales of the Author of Waverley* was published. An American edition of *Waverley* came out in 1815, and the novel was translated into French in 1818, German in 1821-22, Italian

---

1   James Raven points out that "the overwhelming majority of the English novels of the eighteenth and early nineteenth centuries were published without attribution of authorship" on the title page, preface or elsewhere in the text (441). However, during the first decade of the nineteenth century, "the public admission of authorship continued to increase, and the total of anonymously issued novels fell for the first time to under half of all new novels published. After about 1810, however, anonymity advanced again ..." (441). He explains this phenomenon as resulting from the "popularity and savagery of the published critical reviews" (442). Given the still poor opinion of novel writing in general at this time, many novels were published anonymously—Edgeworth's *Castle Rackrent*, for instance—so Scott's decision to do so was not without precedent. Still, author and publisher maintained this secrecy over the years by resorting to rather extreme precautions, to the point of printing off double proof-sheets so that Scott could correct his set of proofs and send them back to Ballantyne, who would copy Scott's alterations onto the other set of proofs and send these on to the printer; thus the "corrected proofs of the author were never seen in the printing-office" (General Preface, xxi).

2   In publishing, the dead season was traditionally the summer months.

in 1823, Hungarian in 1823, Swedish in 1824-26, Danish in 1826, and Russian in 1827.[1]

Critical reception of *Waverley* when it was first published was generally positive and reviews were substantive, despite the publication's anonymity,[2] though critics made negative comments about the many errors in the text—grammatical, historical, structural[3]—the verbosity, the difficulty of comprehending the Scots dialect and the many Latin passages, and the choice of the Jacobite Rebellion as subject matter. *Waverley* gained critical acceptance, however, for its inclusion of strong characters from many classes and its depiction of Scotland (which was almost a foreign land to many of the novel's readers), as well as for its mingling of history and romance. In an unsigned review in the *British Critic* August 1814 (Appendix A3), the reviewer sees *Waverley* as a didactic text, a cautionary tale meant to remind readers of the "civil

---

1 The success of *Waverley* in terms of sales of the novel set the stage for the success of the subsequent Waverley novels: 4,000 copies of *Old Mortality*, published in 1816, were sold in the first month and a half, and in 1818, 10,000 copies of *Rob Roy* were sold in the first two weeks of sales; *The Fortunes of Nigel*, which arrived by ship at the London wharf on a Sunday morning in May 1822, had sold 7,000 copies by the next day (Hayden, 3). Lockhart suggests that by 1822, Scott was realizing somewhere between £10,000 and £15,000 per year from sales of his novels (II, 397). (In 1814, £10,000 would have had the purchasing power of roughly £500,000 in today's economy.)

2 Most reviews of this period, especially those dealing with anonymous publications, if they went beyond basic notices of publication, offered only plot summaries. Most reviewers guessed the identity of the novel's author (which may explain to some extent why *Waverley* received substantive critical commentary), but they went along with Scott's insistence on anonymity throughout his early career as a novelist by giving him such complimentary titles as "the Great Unknown," "the Enchanter of the North," "the Northern Magician," "the Scottish Prospero," and "the Pet of the Public" (Hayden, 4). See Appendix A for excerpts from selected reviews of the first edition of *Waverley* and of the *Magnum Opus Waverley*.

3 Critics continued to write negatively about the number of errors in Scott's novels, but neither Scott nor his publishers rectified the situation, since the reading public continued to buy his novels despite their errors; nor did he respond to this criticism, except to emphasize the historical veracity of his novels (see especially the preface to the third edition of *Waverley* included in this edition, and Scott's Notes). In fact, in his "Introductory Epistle" to *The Fortunes of Nigel*, Scott answers critics' charges against his verbosity, errors in grammar and spelling, and his historical errors by blaming his prolixity on enthusiasm for his subject: "there is a demon who seats himself on the feather of my pen when I begin to write, and leads it astray from the purpose. Characters expand under my hand; incidents are multiplied; the story lingers, while the materials increase ..." (qtd. in Abbey and Mullane, 265).

commotion" caused by the political unrest of the previous 150 years: "if the history of those bloody days, which is embodied in this tale, shall by an early and awful warning inspire the nation with a jealous vigilance against the very first symptoms of their recurrence, we shall consider that not even the light pages of fiction have trifled in vain." This critic is "unwilling to consider this publication in the light of a common novel" because of the amount of information it contains about

> the history and manners of a very, very large and renowned portion of the inhabitants of these islands; of a race who, within these few years, have vanished from the face of their native land, but have left their names and their actions behind them as monuments of spirited independence....

This critic applauds the characterization of major and minor players in the novel and notes the ease and credibility with which *Waverley*'s author has managed to incorporate "feigned characters as actors in those real scenes" of history, finding that the time elapsed since 1745 has made it possible for the reader to suspend his or her disbelief. The reviewer marks the humor of the novel, the blend of serious and pathetic scenes, and the novel's inclusion of poetry.

In one of the few signed reviews of *Waverley* upon its publication, Francis Jeffrey, literary reviewer for the *Edinburgh Review*, wrote in November 1814 that

> one great source of the interest which the volumes before us undoubtedly possess, is to be sought in the surprise that is excited by discovering, that in our own country, and almost in our own age, manners and characters existed, and were conspicuous, which we had been accustomed to consider as belonging to remote antiquity, or extravagant romance. (Appendix A6)

He credits Scott with having given readers characters of all classes that they can believe in, credible because "made from actual experience and observation," with the exception of the Baron of Bradwardine or Baillie Macwheeble, whom he sees as caricatures; in addition, he praises the descriptions, not only of the Highlands, but also of the Border region between Scotland and England, and the poetry within the novel, though he notes the errors therein that detract from his experience of the novel, as well as the problematic use of an intrusive first-person narrator. In a March 1817 review, Jeffrey develops his ideas on Scott's methods of characterization, noting especially the ways in which he made his readers "present to the times in which he has placed ... [his characters], less by his direct notices of the great transactions by which they were distinguished, than by his casual intimations of their effects on private persons, and by the very contrast which their temper and occupations often appear to furnish to the colour of the national story." For Scott, says Jeffrey, "all public events are important only as they ultimately concern individuals" (qtd. in Hayden, 9-10).

The reviewer for the *Quarterly Review*, John Wilson Croker, writing in July 1814, immediately after the novel's publication, recognizes in *Waverley* a "Scotch Castle Rackrent, [though in] ... a much higher strain" (Appendix A1);[1] this seeming praise is mitigated by his open hostility toward historical romances, Scott's as well as Edgeworth's. Edgeworth herself wrote to "The Author of *Waverley*" in 1814 after she and her family had read a borrowed copy of the novel, not being able to buy one anywhere in Dublin, in praise of the novel's characterization, use of Scots dialect, humor, and credibility of action, but admits that she and her family "could not endure the occasional addresses from the author to the reader" because the resemblance of this narrative technique to that of Fielding's[2] problematized the novel's authenticity needlessly; and they found Flora's actions at times overly dramatic (qtd. in Abbey, 258). She ends her letter by voicing her gratitude for Scott's acknowledgement of her in the novel's final chapter.

Other literary figures of the period also weighed in with their opinions of *Waverley*. In a letter dated 1815, William Wordsworth lauds "the pictures of Highland manners at Mac Ivor's castle, and the delineation of his character, which are done with great spirit," though he finds the caricatures of the Baron and other characters to be overdone, "too peculiar and *outre*" (qtd. in Abbey, 259). Tongue in cheek, Jane Austen declares in a letter to her niece Anna in September 1814 that Scott "has no business to write novels, especially good ones.—It is not fair.—He has Fame and Profit enough as a Poet, and should not be taking the bread out of other people's mouths.—I do not like him, & do not mean to like *Waverley* if I can help it—but fear I must" (qtd. in Abbey, 257). William Hazlitt's essay on Scott, dated 1824, offers praise for the freshness of Scott's writing: "by going a century or two back

---

1 As Ina Ferris notes, most reviews of *Waverley* "locate [the novel] ... in some relation to Edgeworth's Irish fictions" (*The Achievement of Literary Authority*, 106).

2 Henry Fielding (1707-54), English novelist and dramatist, author of *The History of Tom Jones, a Foundling* (1749) and *The Adventures of Joseph Andrews* (1742), both of which use the narrative technique of directly addressing the reader.

and laying the scene in a remote and uncultivated district, all becomes new and startling in the present advanced period" (qtd. in Abbey, 267). For Scott, says Hazlitt, "there is no romance like the romance of real life," and he finds Scott's rendering of human life exhilarating: "What a world of thought and feeling rescued (almost) from oblivion!'" he exclaims. In a more specific vein, Hazlitt finds Scott's political emphasis in the "Scotch Novels" a "relief to the mind, rarified as it has been with modern philosophy, and heated with ultra-radicalism." Scott is a writer who "reconciles ... all the diversities of human nature to the reader," treating of vices and virtues "as they are to be found blended in the whole race of mankind" (qtd. in Abbey, 268). Joanna Baillie, the dramatist, sums up the significance of Scott's work as a novelist when she writes that "The Scotch novels put poetry out of fashion" and make the novel respectable (Lang, lxxxiv).

It can be said that the *Magnum Opus* edition in forty-eight volumes of the complete, revised Waverley Novels, with Scott's introductions to the novels and his notes, would not have come into existence if *Waverley*, the first of the novels Scott wrote that had as their subjects Scottish and English history and culture, had not remained popular with the public. Indeed, because this latter edition required "a large outlay on drawings and engravings, and otherwise" (Lockhart II, 539), Scott and the publisher of this edition, Cadell, had been anxious about its viability; they need not have been. While reviews of the *Magnum Opus Waverley*, and more particularly, the entire *Magnum Opus* edition, were mixed, this did not hurt sales. In fact, Cadell sold an estimated 78,270 sets of the *Magnum Opus* edition of the Waverley Novels from 1827 through 1849, according to William St. Clair in *The Reading Nation in the Romantic Period*. Certainly, the number of buyers of the individual volumes and sets attests to the greater accessibility of Scott's works in the cheaper *Magnum Opus* edition, an occurrence that some critics commented positively upon. And the added introductions and annotations, which were problematic for some critics, seemed not to discourage readers from buying the volumes. Indeed, Millgate suggests that the *Magnum Opus* edition of the Waverley Novels put Scott's works into "standard form and provided [them] with the apparatus of introductions and annotations that proclaimed [their] classic status for the decades that were to follow" (*Scott's Last Edition*, 107); such an edition, she asserts, gave "a new dignity to the novel as a genre" (114). As St. Clair contends, and as sales of the *Magnum Opus* edition confirm, "with novels as with poems, by sales as well as by reputation, the dominant author of the romantic period, and indeed of the Victorian period which followed was Walter Scott" (221).

Literary Context

Scott suggests, in the first chapter of *Waverley*, the nature of the literary landscape in the early nineteenth century as he was writing the novel: *Waverley* took shape amidst the traditions of the chivalrous romance, the sentimental novel, the gothic tale, and the novel of manners. It is none of these, but it borrows from them all; while Scott was critical of the various subgenres of the novel for their lack of credibility, their formulaic nature, their artificiality, and their dearth of innovation, he nonetheless recognized the power of Radcliffe's gothic, Mackenzie's sentiment, Fielding's comedy, and Burney's social satire, and learned much from these successful novelists.[1] But as he himself notes, his main inspiration for *Waverley* came from Edgeworth's Irish novels, especially *Castle Rackrent* (1800), *The Absentee* (1812), and *Ennui* (1809). Gary Kelly writes that Edgeworth was "the best-known novelist in Britain from 1800 until the publication of Scott's *Waverley* in 1814" (78) and credits her with developing the twin subgenres of the novel of manners and the sentimental novel as practiced in the late eighteenth century by Burney, Mackenzie, and others, into the national novel.[2]

But Scott was also inspired by lesser-known writers of the national tale, especially the Scottish national tale. In the last chapter of *Waverley*, "A Postscript, Which Should Have Been a Preface," Scott acknowledges the works of Scottish authors, Elizabeth Hamilton (1756-1816), whose *The Cottagers of Glenburnie* was published in 1810 (see Appendix D2), and Anne Grant (1755-1838) whose *Essays on the Superstitions of the Highlanders of Scotland* was published in 1811 (see Appendix D3). While he sees himself following in their wake in his efforts to write of his nation, he distinguishes his work from the work of these "female authors, whose genius is highly creditable to their country," when he writes:

---

1 Ann Radcliffe (1764-1823), English novelist specializing in the Gothic novel. Her best-known novel is *The Mysteries of Udolpho* (1794). Henry Mackenzie (1745-1831), Scottish novelist, author of the popular sentimental novel, *The Man of Feeling* (1771); Scott dedicated his first novel to Mackenzie. Frances Burney (1752-1840), English novelist and dramatist, whose very popular *Evelina* (1778) was followed by three additional novels and several plays.
2 Katie Trumpener in *Bardic Nationalism* notes that while Scott acknowledges "only Edgeworth as a precedent," he actually owes much also to other contemporary writers, including Charlotte Smith (1749-1806), Jane West (1758-1852), Sydney Owenson (c. 1776-1859), and Charles Maturin (1782-1824), who were also writing national and historical novels (138-42).

... the first is confined to the rural habits of Scotland, of which it has given a picture with striking and impressive fidelity; and the traditional records of the respectable and ingenious Mrs. Grant of Laggan, are of a nature distinct from the fictitious narrative which I have here attempted. (452)

His national tale is broader than Hamilton's, and it is a novel, unlike Grant's work, but like both of them Scott was seen by his contemporaries and by later critics as "a Scottish writer, whose perceptions only made sense when placed in the context of a specific national experience" (Harvie, 173).

Certainly, *Waverley* shares much with works by other Scottish authors of the eighteenth and early nineteenth centuries. Like Hamilton's *Glenburnie*, Scott's first novel owes much to the novels written by Tobias Smollett (1721-71), especially his final novel, *Humphry Clinker* (1771), which, like *Waverley*, launches a journey from the south of Britain to the north and allows for the examination and dismantling of national prejudices.[1] As Robert Crawford notes, it is sympathy that breaks down prejudice in Smollett's novel, which suggests that Smollett, like Scott, owed much also to fellow Scottish novelist Henry Mackenzie's sentimental novels, in particular *The Man of Feeling* (1771), which was both a powerful and popular novel in its time, though out of favor with the audience of Scott's own day.[2] Crawford also notes Scott's debts to eighteenth-century Scottish social philosophers Adam Ferguson (1723-1816) and Alexander Fraser Tytler (1747-1813), to Scottish poet James Macpherson's *The Poems of Ossian* (1762),[3] and to James Boswell's writings—his *Life of Johnson* (1791) and his travelog, *Journal of a Tour of the Hebrides* (1785), the latter of which, like Grant's essays, chronicles the manners of people in rural Scotland. These writers, as Crawford points out, recognize and celebrate the elements of Scottish culture that empower the British nation (117).

But Scott does this in a genre that before *Waverley* did not exist: the historical novel, a form that blended fiction with fact. What about the historical novel was so important to the period in which it was created that only this genre could answer that period's needs? Like the national

---

1 For Smollett's poem "Tears of Scotland," see Appendix C1.
2 Cognizant of changing literary tastes, Lady Louisa Stuart, Lady Mary Wortley Montagu's granddaughter, wrote to Scott in 1826 to say that while she remembered crying over *The Man of Feeling* when it first came out, reading it aloud now brought only giggles from the audience (Millgate, *Scott's Last Edition*, 106). Still, it is to Henry Mackenzie that Scott dedicates *Waverley*.
3 See Appendix D1 for Macpherson's poem "The Battle of Lora."

tale, historical novels are mediating texts, but they mediate time as well as, in the case of historical national novels such as *Waverley*, cultures. *Waverley*'s narrator is described by Buzard as "a genial, intrusive narrator, an anonymous metropolitan, lowland Scot, firmly situated in the readers' present and speaking their language" (34); he translates the Britain of 1745 for the British of 1805, 1814, and 1829. He represents a present very different from the past he narrates, one seemingly more economically and politically stable. Yet, as Ferris notes, his "insistent dating of the change (sixty years since) calls attention as much to loss and disorientation as to success and achievement" ("Melancholy," 82). The historical novel, she writes, "emerged out of the tension" between the recognition of the positive changes progress had brought and the acknowledgement of the costs of those changes (83). The extent to which *Waverley* is an accurate depiction of the past is in question, according to James Kerr, who argues that the historical novel is an "evasion of history" because it is a fictional reworking of the past (4), but other critics, including Richard Stein, argue that in *Waverley* "the past is not an end in itself" (219).[1] While Lukacs sees Scott as the originator of historical realism, whose work was full of realistic, convincing detail, Scott learned his lesson from Strutt's mishandling of history and instead, according to Stein, "parodies the triviality of merely antiquarian historians who can't live in the present for their consumption of the past" (219) in his depiction of Edward Waverley. The Edward Waverley of the early chapters, at home in his library, teaches us how not to read history as separate from the meaningful, engaged present, and it is Scott's intent that the historical novel invite us into the past so that we might bring something of it back to the present to live by. It was Scott's ability to bring in aspects of real life that history books left out, the "social and personal relationships, manners and mores, costumes and customs, and the individual lives of ordinary people," writes St. Clair, that distinguished *Waverley* as an historical novel from Strutt's *Queen-Hoo Hall* (220) and made the Waverley Novels "virtually the only novels that were universally recommended, without reservation, to be read by men, women, and young people" (160).

Scott envisaged *Waverley*'s audience to be both Scottish and English—Scottish because he wished to give the people of his own

---

1   Kerr suggests that Scott's effort in *Waverley* to balance the "loss of the past with the progress of the present" is problematic (12). Additionally, David Craig is critical of Scott for not chronicling Scottish people's real situations at the turn of the nineteenth century. He charges that Scott's fiction did not respond to the situations experienced by working-class Scots as a result of industrialization and population growth, and contends that Scott's understanding of history did not "lead on ... into the life of his own time" (149).

country a past they could be proud of, and English because he desired to further the union between the two countries, and, on a more pragmatic level, because good sales of the novel would only be assured if English readers bought the book.[1] Of these English readers, he sought particularly to entice educated men, rather than only female romance readers. To this end, notes Peter Garside, Scott carefully dropped "markers"—for instance, the mention of Edgeworth and Elizabeth Hamilton, the allusions to Fielding's novel *Tom Jones*, and the dedication to Henry Mackenzie—alerting those more literary-minded readers that *Waverley*, like the established, respected authors noted, was not to be seen as popular or transitory literature, but as the stuff of which canonical literature is made ("Popular Fiction and National Tale," 32). Scott's references to Mackenzie also suggest his desire for a sympathetic reader, someone open to romance and to being enthralled as novel readers are by the worlds such works imagine.[2]

Historical Context

Scott was writing *Waverley* between 1805 and 1813; for much of this period Britain was at war with France. While there was some movement for reform in Britain in the 1790s, no doubt impelled by the example of the early days of the French Revolution, the end of the century and the early decades of the nineteenth century saw Britain fighting united against an ambitious and serious foe. Scott himself joined the Edinburgh Light Dragoons during this period and was promoted to quartermaster, and Scotland was finally allowed the militia that the government in London had not granted in the mid-eighteenth century, in order that the country be ready for attacks from France. Historians agree that Scotland prospered as the eighteenth century wore on, but they disagree about the extent to which this prosperity was owing to the Union or to the Scots' abilities to exploit that Union. Yet, despite the outward sense of unity during the latter part of the eighteenth century and the early nineteenth, Scotland, and especially the Highlands, experienced a period of distress as a result of poor har-

---

1 Peter Garside suggests that his need to involve English readers in *Waverley* from the start accounts for the long opening section set at Waverley-Honour in the South of England ("Popular Fiction and National Tale," 47). James Buzard contends that Scott envisioned *Waverley*'s audience as "either English or Englishing, as Lowlanders were assiduously doing" (36).

2 Scott himself wrote of Mackenzie that his novels "are rather the history of effects produced on the human mind by a series of events, than the narrative of those events themselves" (qtd. in Williams, 80), and that Mackenzie "aimed at being the historian of feeling" (83); one can see the similarity between Scott's own work in *Waverley* and that of the novelist he admired.

vests, overpopulation, enclosure laws, and greedy landlords that caused many to leave the Highlands for urban areas or to emigrate abroad, and bred a sense of alienation among Scots. And while industrial expansion brought wealth to factory owners, and to the government in London, many Scots lived in squalor in the cities of Glasgow and Edinburgh. J.D. Mackie contends that "there was both good and evil in the economic situation in Scotland during the early decades of the nineteenth century. The good, however, lay mainly in the promise for the future and the evil in present distress" (320).[1]

Scott's own financial situation was stable as he wrote *Waverley*: he had succeeded as a lawyer and as a poet, had been offered the poet-laureateship, and he had bought Abbotsford, the home on which he would lavish much attention and money over the coming years. He firmly believed from his conservative political stance that the Union with England had done and would do Scotland good, but his written assessment of the Union was complex. In an 1825 letter to Edgeworth, for instance, Scott calls the Union of 1707 "an event which had I lived in that day I would have resigned my life to have prevented but which being done before my day I am sensible was a wise turn" (qtd. in Vakil, 413). In his *Letters from Malachi Malagrowther* (1826), he acknowledges the need for Scotland to

> remain in union with England ... as far as national consequence is concerned ... But there is no harm in wishing Scotland to have just so much national spirit as may determine her to stand by her own rights, conducting her assertion of them with every feeling of respect and amity towards England. (qtd. in P. Scott, 81)

The conciliatory realist, Scott is at once concerned, as Paul Scott notes, with maintaining "peace and stability," but insists on Scotland's right to a national identity within the Union, for "... if you unscotch us you will find us damned mischievous Englishmen" (84). In "A Second Letter to the Editor of the Edinburgh Weekly Journal from Malachi Malagrowther Esq.," Scott stresses the negative consequences for both Scotland and England if the characteristics that make Scotland unique were to be denied:

> We would not become better subjects, or more valuable members of the common empire, if we all resembled each other like so many

---

1 J.D. Mackie, *A History of Scotland*, 288; for more on the economic situation of Scotland at the end of the eighteenth century, see also Bruce Lenman, *An Economic History of Modern Scotland 1660-1976*, 67; Paul Scott, *Walter Scott and Scotland*, 83; and Richard Finlay, "'Caledonia or North Britain?' ...,"145.

smooth shillings.... The degree of national diversity between different countries, is but an instance of that general variety which Nature seems to have adopted as a principle through all her works, as anxious, apparently, to avoid, as modern statesmen to enforce, anything like an approach to absolute 'uniformity.' (147)

Even given his pragmatically pro-Union stance, still Scott could see that people within his country were suffering. And while Mackie points out that the real causes of the distress felt by those in the Highlands and elsewhere in Scotland's impoverished areas had deep roots, and often arose from an unwillingness to "abandon the old methods" and were not a result of the Union, it was the Union, and the vengeance taken by the Hanoverian government in the aftermath of the Jacobite Rebellion, that many blamed for their suffering. In difficult times, the government in London seemed insensible to Scotland's needs, and old animosities resurfaced. Scott addresses this tension between Scotland and England in his "General Preface" to the *Magnum Opus Waverley* when he writes that *Waverley* was his effort to bring Scotland and England to a better understanding of one another (xiii). He saw that these two nations, officially, legally, politically one, were as yet not united in feeling. England did not really know Scotland's people, history, or culture; to the English, Scotland was a foreign land, and this was especially true of the Highland region. And to Scotland, the English were still not to be trusted, their motives and actions suspect, those of a colonizer, not a sister. Scott's task is the difficult one of "celebrating the Union while respecting Scotland's past," Murray Pittock writes in *The Invention of Scotland* (86),[1] translating Scotland into what James Buzard aptly describes as "something at once alien and English—that is to say, into something 'British'" (37).[2] Thus, while Scott does not deal at any great length with the Union of 1707, it is present as a necessary precondition to the events of the 1745 Jacobite Rebellion and as the situation from which the narrator

---

1   Colin Kidd goes even further to suggest that Scott "aimed to complete the Union by educating the English nation in Scottish history, by way of the Waverley Novels" (266), though in general, historians find that the history in these novels, especially in *Waverley*, is garbled. As Lenman notes, "reconciling national animosities" requires some creative recasting of history ("Union, Jacobitism, and Enlightenment," 71).

2   Franco Moretti argues that the nation-forming project of the historical novel is to voice regional difference, to "represent internal unevenness ... and then, to abolish it" (40). The extent to which Scott succeeds in integrating Scotland into Britain is a matter for debate among critics of the novel.

of the tale speaks, sixty years after the Rebellion, and one hundred years after the Union itself.[1]

The Union of 1707 was brought about by a number of factors. Ireland, England, and Scotland had been joined by a dynastic "Union of the Crowns" since 1603, when James VI of Scotland came to the throne of England and Ireland as James I. The three countries had coexisted uneasily since then, but with some autonomy. At various points in their history together, England had been willing to consider a parliamentary union with Scotland, but not if it meant allowing Scotland trade rights with the American colonies, a condition upon which Scotland would not compromise. On Scotland's side, union did not appear an option because the powerful Presbyterian Church feared an Anglican takeover by the Church of England. Scott himself sums up the situation in *Tales of a Grandfather* (1829), published at around the same time as the *Magnum Opus Waverley*, when he writes that while many in England found the idea of a connection with the "rude and savage tribes of the North" repugnant:

> the more enlightened part of the nation, remembering the bloody wars which had so long desolated Britain in its divided state, dated from the Union an era of peace and happiness to both countries; and looking far into futurity, foresaw a time when the national prejudices, which for the present ran so high, would die out, or be eradicated, like the weeds which deface the labours of the agriculturist, and give place to plenty and peace. (9)

Devine and Mackie both suggest that what happened in the two countries to bring about a union has to do to a large extent with the aftermath of the Revolution of 1688, with the diminishment of monarchical control of Parliament, and with William III's fear that Scotland, severely disgruntled over England's role in the failure of the Darien expedition,[2] could not be "governed within the existing context of the

---

1 Several critics have noted the same, including Brian Hollingsworth in "'Completing the Union.'"

2 In an attempt to open trade routes to Africa and the Indies, and as an alternative to the East India Company's monopoly on such trade, Scotland decided to launch a colony on the Isthmus of Darien (i.e., in Panama) at the end of the seventeenth century. Originally, England was supposed to contribute equally to this colony, but pulled out, leaving Scotland to go it alone. Mackie writes that "fever, dissension, and English opposition [as well as bloody confrontations with the Spanish, who also claimed the land] ruined the venture, and the colony was abandoned after great loss of life" (256)—2,000 men, as well as monetary losses of £200,000.

Union of the Crowns and that a union of the Edinburgh and West-minster parliaments was vital to national [i.e., British] stability and security" (Devine, 6)—and this at a time when William was also keen to win the war against France. The English parliament at Westminster finally got on board with this plan during Queen Anne's reign, after the 1703 session of the Scottish parliament in which that body asserted its autonomy from England by refusing to vote for money to fund the government in London unless it gave Scotland trade rights to the North American colonies and France. The Scottish parliament also asserted its "right to declare war and make peace [even] if the two nations continued to share a sovereign after Anne's death" (Devine, 7).

While acknowledging the Scottish parliament's power to make things difficult, England's parliament also recognized that Scotland's economy had been suffering from what Bruce Lenman in *An Economic History of Modern Scotland 1660-1976* terms a "major subsistence crisis" since the 1690s (45). In addition, wars, "trade prohibition or rising tariff barriers all over the Atlantic world," and the Darien scheme all made Scotland's economic situation vulnerable (Lenman, *Economic History*, 48-49). With these present realities, as well as Scot-land's potential to benefit England's economy in the future, England struck out for an "incorporating union," one that required the disso-lution of the Edinburgh parliament and allowed for the creation of a United Kingdom legislature; it also assured a Protestant line of suc-cession in all three kingdoms, one economic market, one set of sub-jects, and a civil basis to the Church (Robertson, 244). Public opinion in general in Scotland was against such an "entire union" (Devine, 8), and in particular, this full union was opposed by conservative members of the Presbyterian Church and by the Jacobites, who saw it as an end to the chance for a return of the Stuart monarchy. Indeed, anti-union sentiments were preached from the pulpit, and anti-union demonstrations, even riots, occurred in most cities in Scotland throughout 1706 and into 1707. England sent in ready troops to intimidate the anti-unionist activists and employed such propagan-dists as Daniel Defoe, who has been viewed as "England's primary pro-union pamphleteer" (Penovich, 232) and whose writings "grossly exaggerated the benefits of the English trade for Scotland" (Lenman, *Economic History*, 56).[1] Such strategies were apparently enough to engender a positive vote for union; in 1707, the Scottish parliament in Edinburgh, in voting for the Union, essentially dissolved itself and accepted the Westminster parliament's authority over Scotland, but only after it had received assurances of power to trade with the Amer-

---

1 For an excerpt from Defoe's *Tour* see Appendix B2.

ican colonies and to maintain religious freedom. Indeed, John Robertson suggests that it was Scotland's sense of itself against the backdrop of the Spanish Succession crisis and other problems in Europe that made union with England seem like a wise move (237); those Scots who supported the Union felt "the terms were reasonable" and they looked forward to economic benefits from it (Lenman, *Economic History*, 61).

The several Jacobite uprisings occurred as the result of a number of factors, chief of which were dissatisfaction with the Union—to the point where a motion was introduced into the House of Lords in 1713 to "rescind" the Act of Union. The motion failed, but only barely. This dissatisfaction was based mostly on a sense of economic injustice, a belief that the government in London was using Scottish resources to benefit England, not Scotland. This sense was buttressed by the recognition that a legitimate heir to the English and Scottish throne did exist, and the belief that the difficult times that followed the exile of James VII, king of Scotland, who was also James II of England in 1688—the famines, the War of Spanish Succession, the Massacre of Glencoe,[1] the failure of the Darien expedition—were a sign from God that denying the divine right of kings could only result in disaster. However, as Mackie writes, the Scottish Jacobite attempts in 1708, 1715, 1719, and 1745 to resuscitate Stuart rule

> were founded upon false hopes. While the Jacobites were justified in counting upon discontent in Scotland, they and their agents deceived themselves and deceived others as to the extent to which this discontent would express itself in arms. The growing economic prosperity inclined men, especially the wealthier men, to accept with complacency a rule of which perhaps, in theory, they did not approve. (269)

All of these attempts, for various reasons, failed; the last, in 1745, in which Charles Edward Stuart (Bonnie Prince Charlie), with the promise of French aid, came nearer to success than any other exiled Jacobite leader, might be viewed as a last hurrah for a dying cause. As Paul Scott writes, "the prevalent mood in Scotland at [the time of the rebellion] was Whig, Presbyterian, and egalitarian and could not

---

1 The Massacre of Glencoe of 1692 occurred because the Macdonald clan were not quick enough in forcing the Jacobites to support King William III. William's secretary of state ordered all Macdonalds to be killed; many were, which certainly aided the Jacobite cause. The War of Spanish Succession was fought between 1695 and 1715 by England and France for control of the American colonies and those in the Indies.

accept a cause which was inevitably associated with Catholicism, Episcopalianism, and arbitrary royal power" (71). By 1745, the Highlands had been disarmed, but regular companies of Highlanders had been formed by the British government into the highly regarded Black Watch, which fought at Fontenoy[1] with great credit. In addition, Charles had little backing from European powers, since Louis XV had decided to stall an invasion of England after word of his plans was leaked to the Royal Navy, whose actions pre-empted France's strike, so Charles arrived in Scotland with only seven men, a little money, and a few guns.[2] The Highland chiefs were not keen to risk their people's lives for a man they did not know. Charles's charisma managed to attract some of the clans to his cause, and this cause was enhanced by the fact that the government forces were fighting in Flanders when he landed and began his advance. Some success took him to Derby, in central England, a fact that alarmed anti-Jacobite writers such as Henry Fielding, who recognized the extent of the threat that Charles's army posed.[3] Indeed, Charles would have gone on to London, but he would have done so alone, as by that time he had lost much of his Highland support, and his officers advised retreat in the face of a lack of any European involvement or any significant support within England for the Jacobite cause. However, on his retreat, he managed to pick up more recruits, and went on fighting his way north, taking Stirling Castle, Falkirk, and stumbling only when he got to Inverness, where on 16 April 1746, 1,000 Jacobite soldiers died on the field of Culloden; Charles himself escaped to France after many months in hiding in Scotland and was never recognized again as king by any European power.[4] He died without legitimate heirs in 1788, his

---

1 The Battle of Fontenoy was fought in 1745 during the War of the Austrian Succession by the French, aided by Irish Jacobites, against the Duke of Cumberland and his English army. The French were able to vanquish the English, thus encouraging Charles Edward Stuart to launch the Jacobite Rebellion, aided by French and Irish troops (*OCBH*, 382).

2 The plan hatched by Charles Edward Stuart and Louis XV had Charles invading the south coast of England at the head of an army of 10,000 men, forcing a battle between them and the Hanoverian army. This plan had to be scuttled once the Royal Navy got wind of it. The Scottish Jacobites then advised Charles to wait until he had "at least 6,000 French troops, arms for 10,000 more and a war chest of 30,000 *louis d'or*" (Devine, 42). Charles ignored their advice.

3 See Appendix C4 for an excerpt from Fielding's *History of the Present Rebellion in Scotland*.

4 Scott published his novel *Redgauntlet* ten years after *Waverley*. In its last chapter he describes Charles Edward Stuart's departure from Scotland in a tone that is much bleaker than the ending of his first novel. See Appendix C5 for an excerpt from the final chapter of *Redgauntlet*.

brother Henry, cardinal of York, living on until 1807. Of the men left behind to face the government's wrath, 120 were executed, 1,150 were transported, and what happened to another 700 prisoners remains unclear; the lands of anyone marked as a traitor to the Crown were forfeited. The Disarming Act was again enacted, with the addition that the kilt and the pipes were also banned.[1]

The Jacobite Rebellion of 1745, the historical event Scott uses as his backdrop for *Waverley,* was the last of many Jacobite rebellions in Britain, and it was the one that captured the imaginations of nationalists in Scotland even many years after the event itself had occurred. Indeed, the song that the blacksmith's wife, Mrs. Mucklewrath, sings on that Sunday in 1745 when Edward Waverley stops in Cairnvreckan to have his horse's shoe fixed—"Charlie Is My Darling"—was not even written until many years after Prince Charles Edward Stuart came to the shores of Scotland for a brief period of time, and then left for France, never to return again to lead Stuart supporters.[2] But he was remembered, and he caught the imagination of not only the Scots but the English as well, in ways his father and grandfather, in their abortive Jacobite uprisings earlier in the century, had not. Perhaps it was his youth, perhaps his near success, but Bonnie Prince Charlie continued to serve as an imaginative, sentimental marker for Scotland's fight for independence until the end of the twentieth century

---

1 As Linda Colley notes, after the defeat at Culloden, Parliament "devised legislation to undermine the cultural, political and economic distinctiveness of the Scottish Highlands"; in addition to the banning of the plaid and pipes, oaths were administered that required the Scots to pledge allegiance to a Hanoverian king, not a Stuart. But Colley contends that while traditional affiliations were being undermined, channels between the Scots and the English were being created: many industries necessary to the economic well-being of Scotland were subsidized, schools were opened, Scottish soldiers were highly sought after for positions within the British army, and Scotsmen were promised equal opportunities to succeed in London's business and government (119-20). Richard Finlay agrees that it is "perhaps more appropriate to date the beginning of the Anglo-Scottish Union as a tangible entity from 1746 rather than 1707" ("Caledonia or North Britain?," 146). See also McCrone, Morris and Kiely, 192.

2 Claire Lamont suggests this song was probably written by Robert Burns. He included it in the fifth volume of *The Scots Musical Museum* late in 1796. Lamont posits that though the song was written long after the Jacobite Rebellion of 1745 failed, it offered late eighteenth- and early nineteenth-century Scots "a way of asserting value in the face of defeat" (111). For this reason, folk groups such as the Corries made Jacobite songs part of their repertoire in the 1960s and 1970s when nationalism came to the forefront once again in Scotland. See Pittock, *The Invention of Scotland,* 164, and see Appendices C2 and C3 for other Jacobite songs.

when Scotland regained control of its parliament. Scott himself admitted in 1813 that "I am very glad I did not live in 1745 for though as a lawyer I could not have pleaded Charles's right and as a clergyman I could not have prayed for him, yet as a soldier I would I am sure against the convictions of my better reason have fought for him even to the bottom of the gallows" (qtd. in Daiches, 68). It is the romance of this effort to regain past glory that suffuses *Waverley* the novel and carries Waverley the character into the Rebellion along with the warriors fighting for Scotland.

Interestingly, it was Scott who found and opened the chest in Edinburgh Castle in 1818 that contained Scotland's royal regalia, the crown and mantle that had been used by Scottish kings on "formal occasions, as at the riding of Parliament, to represent the royal presence" (Mackie, 232), and which had been saved from Dunottar Castle in 1652 when the castle fell to Cromwell's forces. After the Union of 1707, the regalia had been placed in a chest in a closet of Edinburgh Castle where it had remained. In an 8 June 1823 letter about her visit to Scott in Edinburgh, Maria Edgeworth tells her aunt the story as Scott told it to her:

> A commission was sent down to search ... [for the old crown and regalia]—He told us that the room which had not been opened for 110 years was 9 inches thick with dust on the floor—It was like walking on snow he says—The crown is now placed in a sort of iron cage—with lamps *lighted* round it, when visitors go to see it—in a small room hung with scarlet—With bad taste I think—they have burnished up the crown &c—& have substituted a new ermine frontlet for the old—which moth eaten as it is looks much more respectable—Scott disapproved much of this gewgaw taste—but some of the English Lords of the bedchamber in the Commission wld have it so— (qtd. in R.F. Butler, 30)

This experience must have reminded Scott of the novel he'd published nine years before: while the dust wasn't quite as thick as in that closet in Edinburgh Castle, he was still moving back through a substantial amount of time in trying to capture the authentic feel of the '45 for his readers, but in *Waverley*, as contemporary and modern readers of the novel attest, we aren't aware of the dust of ages, only the events and the people who acted them, as if it were yesterday.

Unions

A consideration of family structures and the relationship of the family to the estate in *Waverley* suggests Scott's concern with how personal unions on a smaller scale come into being and serve as bridges to national unions. In this respect, Edward Waverley functions as a mediating figure as he journeys from his home, Waverley-Honour in the south of England, to the Baron of Bradwardine's estate, Tully-Veolan, and finally to the Highlands and the country of Fergus Mac-Ivor, connecting the various perspectives of those English and Scots he meets to one another. Additionally, as James Buzard notes, Edward's "relative colorlessness is licensed by the degree to which he is expected to function as vessel for a host of unknown readers"—English readers especially, who would be ignorant of the Scottish culture, language, and society (42, 38). Many of these readers, like Edward himself, may have read romances, heroic tales, and adventure stories; his journey, and theirs, is as much a journey away from romance and into a more realistic understanding of Scottish culture as it is a physical journey into a country into which he has never crossed, despite the fact that it has technically been part of his own for thirty-eight years.

Edward discovers his role as mediator early in life, as his upbringing is shared by his father and uncle; while these two men do not see eye to eye, politically or as parents, Edward connects them to each other. His family at Waverley-Honour is an extended one, including his aunt, his tutor, and various servants and tenants, several of whom he leads off to serve in the king's army under his command. In many ways, the Baron of Bradwardine's family, inhabiting an estate in the border region between England and Scotland, is similar to Edward's in the south of England in that it too incorporates many disparate individuals, few of whom are related to him by blood, including his daughter, Rose; his steward, Baillie McWheeble; Davie Gellately and his mother; and various servants and retainers. And Fergus's role as clan chief ensures that Glennaquoich in the Highlands of Scotland will also harbor an extended family group, including Fergus's sister, Flora, as well as members of the clan Mac-Ivor.

Each of these family groupings requires loyalty of its members and responsible leadership of its head. Each takes issues of name, ancestry, family lineage, and honor seriously; most in these extended family configurations are willing to sacrifice themselves in defense of the honor of their family unit. And to the extent that these values have positive consequences, Scott supports them. But when family loyalty and honor and heroic self-sacrifice become immoderate, they are judged dangerous, both to the individuals involved and to larger national interests, as Scott shows in his depictions of the three families at the moment of a political crisis that occurs at least in part as a result of these very values, in particular the Jacobites' support of the Stuart family as rulers of Scotland.

As the novel begins, it is Edward Waverley who is the outsider to the Jacobite cause embraced by these three families, more because he is young, inexperienced in life, Romantic in his sensibilities, and without political opinions or convictions, than because he has considered and rejected the Jacobite position. His Romantic nature takes fire from the Scottish scenery as he travels to the baron's home in the border region between England and Scotland, from the family legends and superstitions Rose tells him as they stand in her room, looking out at St. Swithin's seat, and from Flora's grand sentiments as she and Edward stand in the picturesque bower near the waterfall in the Highlands. He is drawn to the Jacobite cause through the fine feelings it has engendered in the men and women he meets: his uncle's commitment to his fellow rebel, the baron, in the aftermath of the 1715 uprising; the baron's past sacrifices for the cause and his still vibrant fervor for an old cause; Fergus's personal and political respect for Charles Edward Stuart; and Charles's seeming embodiment of the moral justness of his cause and stalwart conviction in his ability to accomplish it. These motives seem much more compelling than maintaining the status quo for the Hanoverian government, as Edward and his regiment are supposed to be doing. And because he has enlisted in the king's army, not out of any deeply held convictions but because his father feels he needs to see more of the world than the library of Waverley-Honour, it is understandable to the reader when Edward stops being a soldier and lets his prolonged visit to the baron, and his excursions into the Highlands, segue into involvement in the rebellion on the side of the rebel forces. The narrator explains Edward's actions as arising from "the prejudices of education and the political principles of his family" (284), but it is more than this that is responsible for Edward's seemingly rash actions: he has been charmed by Scotland and its people.

And yet, as taken as Edward is with the commitment of Fergus, the baron, and his uncle to the cause of bringing back the Stuart monarchy, and with the principles of loyalty, honor, and justice that seem to impel the rebellion, he keeps—almost unconsciously—one foot in the Hanoverian camp, despite the fact that he resigns his commission in the Hanoverian army. For all his participation in Fergus's hunting parties, the court life of Prince Charles, and the camp life once the armed rebellion begins, Edward Waverley remains something of an outsider. He is wounded at the stag hunt because he doesn't understand the signal, given in Gaelic, to duck; he is fitted for Highland garb by the commands of none other than Charles Edward Stuart himself, and yet he rejects Charles's offer to make him an officer and determines to serve Fergus as a volunteer instead; while the wearing of the tartan no doubt allows him to lose his social inhibitions and shine at the Prince's ball at Holyrood Palace, it is there that Flora rejects him as a lover; and finally, in camp, he seems to exist on the margins, actually losing his regiment at a crucial point during the Battle of Clifton as the forces retreat from Derby with the Duke of Cumberland's army behind them. Edward's ability to relinquish the Jacobite cause is even more understandable after he is confronted with the dying Houghton and his recriminations against Edward's abandonment, not simply of his duty to the king, but to the men who had followed him into the army from his uncle's estate, men for whom he was responsible as their commanding officer, representative of their employer, and friend.

Along with Houghton's death, Edward confronts other realities of war that further loosen the grip that romance has had on him. He is made aware of the disparity in arms and equipment between the commanders of the Jacobite forces and those who serve under them as the consequences of the The Disarming Act decreed after the 1715 Jacobite uprising become clear: it is the lower class, the impoverished Highlanders, who are worst off, having no weapons to speak of except those they have improvised from farm implements, no food, and poor clothing. They terrify the Lowlanders fighting alongside them, who view them as savages. If Edward were entrenched in the Jacobite mindset, caught as many were, including Fergus and Charles Edward Stuart, by ambition and those very principles that in the private sphere of family lead to positive ends, he would not be aware of these inequalities that make for disunity and that ultimately lead to the failure of the Prince's intent to reach London.

When the Jacobite army confronts the government troops under General Cope at Preston, Edward comes face to face with the Hanoverian army in which he had served. The death of Colonel Gardiner, his former commanding officer, as well as the capture of Colonel Talbot; the lack of support among the citizenry for the uprising, evident after the Jacobites take Carlisle as they move southward to England; and the breakdown of discipline within the Jacobite ranks as Callum Beg tries to kill Edward for his supposed affront to Flora, and Fergus challenges Edward to a duel—all of these force Edward to further consider the justness of this war and the consequences of his actions as a participant in it.

Before he can make a decision to abandon the cause, word comes to Edward that his father is dead, that his own treasonable actions are responsible for this event, and that they could cause harm to his uncle if Edward does not return to England to answer charges. With the help of a number of disguises and the goodwill and aid of a Scots farmer and his family, as well as Colonel Talbot, Edward Waverley gets back to London, looks in on his uncle, allows Colonel Talbot to intercede with the king on his behalf, and returns to Scotland, still in disguise, despite the danger, to aid the baron in the aftermath of Charles Edward Stuart's defeat at Culloden and the end of the rebellion.

The final pages of *Waverley* establish a permanent bond between Waverley-Honour and Tully-Veolan in Edward's marriage to Rose Bradwardine and the restoration of Tully-Veolan, ruined by the Hanoverian troops, to its past glory, though "lighter and more picturesque" (443).[1] But the novel also ends with Fergus's death, Flora's self-exile to a French convent, and the end of the Jacobite cause. Some critics question whether Edward Waverley deserves such a happy ending. Bruce Beiderwell suggests that justice in *Waverley* is "uneven ... [which] makes the final happiness of Waverley so unconvincing or even unseemly" (16-17). And Alexander Ross sees Edward's settling at Tully-Veolan as a somewhat self-serving embrace of the benefits of the Act of Union of 1707, a "retreat from commitment to service to the sentiment and safety of picturesque vision" (58). Robert Kiely questions whether the hero's return to Tully-Veolan is a "pathetic compromise or a triumph of reason and virtue" (153). Others find the ending sentimental, Mackenziesque, simplistic, and pat. Certainly, after Fergus's heroic death, Edward's domestic arrangements don't seem all that important to the reader, and perhaps his happiness does strike us as a little "unseemly," but only in the immediate moment. Scott, however, offers a plan for the future, and as such the ending seems a legitimate, rational yet romantic, progressively oriented resolution to a difficult situation. Edward's marriage to Rose accomplishes a union between England and Scotland. As Georg Lukacs notes in his influential study of *Waverley* as a historical novel, Edward's role is "to bring the extremes whose struggle fills the novel, whose clash expresses artistically a great crisis in society, into contact with one another" (36). Scott, Lukacs writes, recognized the significance of those in the middle class as the people who keep the daily routines going amidst the civil wars (36-37). Edward's wavering may have arisen from a lack of certitude or an inability to commit, but it becomes an attitude of flexibility, an ability to occupy the border, to leave neither side out of the equation: while Edward does not have the reach to completely understand the Highlander, he does admire and respect Evan Dhu's loyalty to Fergus at the last, and while London's world of political influence is as foreign to him as the Highlands once were, he appreciates Colonel Talbot's effectiveness in this arena. This open-minded, democratic stance seems to be what Scott proposes in 1814 as a solution to the English desire for control and the Scots'

---

1 It is a resolution reminiscent of Fielding's *Tom Jones*, where Tom and Sophia, and their families, unite as a "family of love" and retire to the countryside to live in isolation from the rest of society.

impulse to rebellion. Edward and Rose are border personalities, and to end with their marriage suggests the fertility of the union between Scotland and England as it yields a dual subjectivity or the creation of a third national identity, neither English nor Scottish, but (possibly) British, a viable, alternative community that is future-oriented yet rests on the memory of the past, captured in the portrait of Edward and Fergus in their Highland dress hanging in Tully-Veolan's hall or the baron's toasts in the Bear goblet.

The narrator of *Waverley*, positioned in 1805, leaves Edward and Rose at this moment of possibility, on the brink of great change, sixty years in the past; from his vantage point, it is clear that he looks back on this period not with nostalgia, exactly, because Scott was a progressive who accepted change as a necessary accompaniment to forward movement, but with respect for those people who did fight in 1745 for a cause out of "attachment to the principles of loyalty which they received from their fathers, and of old Scottish faith, hospitality, worth, and honour" (450). It would be difficult not to locate in this passage from the final chapter of *Waverley* a clear sense of who the heroes of the novel were for Scott. Thus, while it is the border personality with whom the success of the union rests, and on whom the narrator places the burden of the future, Edward Waverley's Romantic self-centeredness distances us from him and allows other competing perspectives to have their say. Finally, it is the Jacobite rebels who capture the reader's attention, imaginations, and sympathy in *Waverley*. They help us to understand the importance of the past even as we commit to a present that recognizes a definition of union incorporating difference rather than denying it,[1] and to consider a future for Scotland that seems bound for independence.

---

1 Richard Finlay explains the lack of national fervor in Scotland after the '45, even into the 1990s, as a result of the fact that the Union allowed the Scottish identity to flourish to such an extent that independence was not necessary ("Controlling the Past," 128); this could also explain the failure of the 1979 Devolution Referendum, despite the help of Jacobite rallying songs. But something shifted in the 1990s to bring about a vote for limited parliamentary independence in 1998.

Sir Walter Scott: A Brief Chronology

1771   Born on 15 August in Edinburgh.

1772-73   Recuperates from polio at his grandfather's home at Sandy-Knowe.

1775   Death of grandfather and return to Edinburgh.

1779-83   Attends high school in Edinburgh.

1783-86   Attends Edinburgh University.

1792-95   Receives law degree; practices law in Edinburgh.

1797   Marries Charlotte Charpentier (or Carpenter), with whom he will have four children.

1802-03   Publishes *Minstrelsy of the Scottish Border*.

1805   Publishes *The Lay of the Last Minstrel*. Begins *Waverley*.

1808   Publishes *Marmion*; edits *The Works of John Dryden*; finishes Joseph Strutt's *Queen-Hoo Hall*.

1810   Publishes *The Lady of the Lake*; resumes *Waverley*.

1811   Buys a farm on the River Tweed; begins to build Abbotsford.

1813   Publishes *Rokeby* and *The Bridal of Triermain* (anonymously); refuses poet laureateship.

1814   Publishes *Waverley* (anonymously); edits *The Works of Jonathan Swift*.

1815   Publishes *The Field of Waterloo*, *The Lord of the Isles*, and *Guy Mannering*.

1816   Publishes *The Antiquary* and *Tales of My Landlord*, First Series (*The Black Dwarf* and *Old Mortality*).

1817   Publishes *Harold the Dauntless* and *Rob Roy*.

1818   Publishes *Tales of My Landlord*, Second Series (*The Heart of Midlothian*).

1819   Publishes *Tales of My Landlord*, Third Series (*The Bride of Lammermoor* and *A Legend of Montrose*) and *Ivanhoe*.

1820   Publishes *The Monastery* and *The Abbot*, its sequel.

1821   Publishes *Kenilworth*.

1822   Organizes George IV's state visit to Edinburgh; publishes *The Pirate*, *The Fortunes of Nigel*, and *Peveril of the Peak*.

1823   Publishes *Quentin Durward* and *St. Ronan's Well*.

1824   Publishes *Redgauntlet*.

1825   Publishes *Tales of the Crusaders* (*The Betrothed* and *The Talisman*).

1826   Financial ruin of Scott's publisher, Constable, and printer Ballantyne, leading to a debt of £130,000 for Scott, who had been Ballantyne's silent partner. Publishes *The Letters of Malachi Malagrowther* and *Woodstock*.

1827   Publicly acknowledges authorship of Waverley Novels. Publishes *Life of Napoleon* and *Chronicles of the Canongate*, First Series ("The Highland Widow," "The Two Drovers," and *The Surgeon's Daughter*).

1828   Publishes *Chronicles of the Canongate*, Second Series (*The Fair Maid of Perth*) and *Tales of a Grandfather* (1818-31), which was written for his grandson, John Lockhart, who died in 1831, aged 10.

1829   Publishes the *Magnum Opus* edition of *Waverley*, along with *Anne of Geierstein*. The *Magnum Opus* edition of the Waverley Novels was published over the course of the next four years, one volume per month.

1830   Publishes *Letters of Demonology and Witchcraft*; suffers two strokes.

1832   Dies on 21 September at Abbotsford, leaving *The Siege of Malta* unfinished; buried at Dryburgh Abbey; *Tales of My Landlord*, Fourth Series (*Count Robert of Paris* and *Castle Dangerous*) published posthumously.

A Note on the Text

This edition uses as its copy-text the *Magnum Opus* edition of *Waverley*. The forty-eight volumes of the *Magnum Opus* edition of Scott's Waverley Novels, with revisions, notes, and introductions by Scott, were published by Robert Cadell in Edinburgh, each month from 1829 until 1833, at the cost of five shillings per volume. *Waverley* accounts for the first two volumes, published in 1829. This was the last edition of *Waverley* revised by Scott.

In 1823, Scott's publisher, Constable, suggested that Scott consider preparing an annotated edition of the Waverley Novels. Scott agreed, thinking it would be a posthumous publication that would benefit his family, and began work on the edition in 1825. He worked sporadically over the next two years on notes for *Waverley*, even through the financial crisis involving his publisher and printer, but stopped altogether when the ownership of copyright to the novels became unclear (Scott had sold these to Constable, but Constable owed him money). Only after the publisher, Cadell, and Scott's trustees bought the copyrights to the Waverley Novels at auction in 1827 did Scott again consider the idea of publishing an annotated edition of the novels, attracted by Cadell's plan to market the inexpensive volumes to a much broader readership. At this point, then, the work Scott had begun for Constable using the 1822 second edition of *Waverley* from *Novels and Tales of the Author of Waverley* as a copy-text to revise from and add notes to continued. Scott used the first twelve volumes of the 1822 edition, those that Constable had prepared with "blank pages inserted or interleaved between each pair of pages for his notes" (Millgate, "The Interleaved Waverley Novels," 5), and then other editions for the remaining thirty-six volumes to work on. These volumes eventually became Scott's *Magnum Opus* edition; Jane Millgate, in her comprehensive study, "The Interleaved Waverley Novels," notes that "by the time the last of the forty-eight volumes appeared, more than 30,000 copies of each of the early titles had been produced" (4).

The changes Scott made to the 1822 edition of *Waverley* to create his *Magnum Opus* edition of the novel were extensive. As Millgate notes, for all of the volumes in the edition, except the last two, Scott "not only revised the text, composed the new introductions and notes, and sought out the information and documentation required for the notes, but he also wrote out the vast majority of these new materials in his own hand" ("The Interleaved Waverley Novels," 9). The new edition also included a dedication, advertisement, and General Preface, as well as three appendices to the entire series (which appear in Volume I, before *Waverley*), and a glossary in which Scott gives definitions of relevant Scots words.[1] In addition, as noted above, Cadell contracted for new engravings for the edition; Millgate notes that Scott chose the subjects of the engravings and ensured "their accuracy and appropriateness" (*Scott's Last Edition*, 17). Scott wrote an "Advertisement" for the *Magnum Opus* edition in the fall of 1828, after revising *Waverley* and writing its introduction and notes; the advertisement assures readers that he has not "altered, in the slightest degree, either the story or the mode of telling it," but has rather "taken this opportunity to correct errors of the press and slips of the pen." He hopes that "the present edition will be found free from errors of that accidental kind," but he also notes that he has "ventured to make some emendations of a different character, which, without being such apparent deviations from the original stories as to disturb the reader's old associations, will ... add something to the spirit of the dialogue, narrative, or description" (qtd. in Millgate, *Scott's Last Edition*, 71).

In order to create what he and Cadell called "the improved edition" of *Waverley* for the *Magnum Opus* edition, Scott "intermingled revision with annotation, breaking off to enter at least those notes that would fit on to the interleaves as he came to the appropriate point in the text" (Millgate, *Scott's Last Edition*, 61).[2] After finishing the introduction and the notes, Scott gave Cadell the interleaved *Waverley*. Cadell and his wife, Anne, then transcribed Scott's emendations and additions onto another copy of the 1822 edition of *Waverley*, before sending the novel to the printer, Ballantyne, who then set the work in type and had it proofed by a printer's reader; in addition, Cadell read the proofs of the novel, since he was especially concerned about the stereotype plates that were being used to produce the edition. Finally, Scott proofed the copy. On 8 October 1828, he wrote to Cadell that he had revised the set of proofs of *Waverley* and sent them on to Ballantyne: "It is needless to say the utmost must be done for correctness" (qtd. in Millgate, *Scott's Last Edition*, 67).

Scott's work on the interleaved *Waverley* attests to his concern to achieve consistency, clarity, and correctness in the text. For instance, he changed "Stuart" to "Stewart" throughout, D— became Dundee and G— became Gardiner, and "boots" became "jackboots." He inserted more paragraph breaks, added tags to enable the reader to know which character is speaking, and brought in many more commas

---

1 Marilyn Butler notes that Scott was indebted to Edgeworth's example in *Castle Rackrent*, and in her glossary for Leadbetter's *Cottage Dialogues Among the Irish Poor*, of providing extra materials for a text (*Castle Rackrent*, 351).

2 Scott's notes are included in the present edition immediately following the text of the novel.

for greater ease of reading the novel aloud. He also made simple corrections to typos: "mask" replaced "mark" and "Amhurst" replaced "Amherst," for instance.

But Scott also uses the new edition for more substantive ends. For instance, he uses it as an opportunity to respond on several occasions to criticisms that had been launched at *Waverley* over the years. To those critics who had censured the introductory chapters of the novel as "tedious and unnecessary," Scott justifies their inclusion by noting that "there are circumstances recorded in them which the author has not been able to persuade himself to retract or cancel."[1] He is clearly taking the upper hand, suggesting that the reader must trust the author to know his creation. He does however admit to anachronisms in the text, as in his admission that the agricultural process of "bottom dressing" was indeed "unknown to the Scotch sixty years since" (note s), as readers had pointed out to him.

In a similar vein, he answers the charge made by critics that he had been "accused of confounding fiction with reality" with the insistence that, as far as he knows the hunting scene that precedes the "insurrection of 1745" is "entirely imaginary," but he goes on to note that "it is well known such a great hunting was held in the Forest of Brae-Mar ... preparatory to the Rebellion of 1745" (note aaa). This note upholds the fictional nature of his tale, but it also claims Scott's right to use historical events for his own purposes, to enhance the essential verisimilitude of his historical novel. In addition, Scott wants credit for his creative abilities; it is to his benefit as a novelist that his readers recognize both the difference between history and fiction, as well as their interdependence within the genre of the historical novel.

In fleshing out notes he had included earlier, as well as adding new notes that inform readers through personal anecdote or researched specifics, Scott is concerned to enhance the reader's experience on many levels. For example, where in the first edition of the novel he had simply given the words to the song Davie Gellately sings, in the interleaved *Waverley*, and subsequently in the *Magnum Opus* edition, he provides the name of the tune the words are sung to. Similarly, the note on Colonel Gardiner informs the reader of the biography of this historical personage in a fair and balanced manner. In the notes Scott includes in the interleaved *Waverley* he is careful to document the sources he uses to enhance information, suggesting a concern that he appear objective and informed. This is true of the note on Nicholas Amhurst, for instance, which explores Amhurst's significance according to *Lord Chesterfield's Characters Revered*, a respected authority on

---

1   See Scott's note g, below. All subsequent references to the present edition will be cited parenthetically within the text by note or page number.

political figures of the day (note i). But Scott uses his own eyewitness accounts to validate information as well, especially with regard to Highland culture, as in his note on Highland military prowess, which he writes he himself had witnessed as a boy (note ll). It is his personal knowledge of the Highlands that perhaps compels him to add notes that together establish a positive view of Scotland for his English readers in particular, but also for the Lowland Scots who would find the Highlands foreign territory as well. His note on Scottish hospitality, for instance, assures readers that Scotland was not and is not a land of savages; it emphasizes similarity while it chronicles differences in customs and language: his note on the stirrup-cup, for instance, given via anecdote, illustrates the "ancient hospitality of Scotland" while still explaining on a basic level what a stirrup cup is and what its significance is to Scottish culture (note r).

In his "Descriptive Guide to the Interleaved Set," J.H. Alexander suggests that "one of the more frequent types of revision [in the interleaved *Waverley*] is intended to clarify the original version: perhaps Scott felt that the new readership envisaged for the *Magnum Opus* needed rather more help than his original readers had done" (11). I would agree that this is the case: that Scott recognizes that the reader of the *Magnum Opus* edition, especially the English reader, separated from the events *Waverley* depicts by eighty-five years, may need help to bridge the gap in knowledge that such a span of time brings with it. An example of that kind of information occurs in the note on Charles Edward Stuart (note gggg), where Scott takes the opportunity to address the criticism that he had painted Charles as more amiable than he deserved. In the note, Scott brings in other sources to document Charles Edward Stuart's strength of character, his personal presence, and his amiability. The effect of giving expanded coverage of historical events and figures in the notes is that the flow of the narrative is allowed to continue, while the details that anchor the plot of the historical fiction are safely available in the notes.

Most of the subsequent editions of *Waverley* until the Clarendon Press edition of 1981 were based on the 1829 edition, though the Penguin edition of *Waverley*, edited by Andrew Hook and published in 1972, uses the Centenary edition of 1870-71 as its copy-text. Claire Lamont's 1986 Oxford University Press edition is based on the 1981 Clarendon Press edition, which is based on the first edition of *Waverley* published in 1814. The Edinburgh edition of *Waverley*, published in 2007 and edited by Peter Garside, is also based on the first edition.

In this edition, I have retained inconsistencies in spelling as they occur in *Waverley*. Also, I have maintained the 1829 edition's two-volume format. I have silently emended the copy-text of the novel in the following cases: when there is an obvious printing or spelling error;

when keeping the punctuation as it is would cause confusion for the reader, such as when no end punctuation follows a hyphen, but an upper-case letter does, indicating the beginning of a new sentence. In such cases, I have added end punctuation, unless the situation occurs in a piece of dialogue where the breathless quality suggested by a hyphen, and no end punctuation between the hyphen and the beginning of the next sentence, is appropriate. Also, I have moved punctuation outside parentheses. Single quotation marks become double because of the necessity of being able to follow the dialogue. For the sake of consistency, I have italicized all foreign phrases in the text. In addition, I have capitalized the first letter of a word when it follows end punctuation; I have also regularized capitalization of all honorifics such as "Sir," "Lady," etc. I have left "Mr" "Dr" "Mrs" "St" without punctuation, as these were contractions in the eighteenth century (as they still are, even though they are commonly treated as abbreviations). It should also be noted that I have attempted to simulate particular stylistic aspects of the copy-text where possible (for instance, the script type used for certain poem titles or phrases in *Waverley*). I have regularized the length of the long dash used between and at the end of sentences, and in place of names in the novel.

I do not include Scott's "General Preface" or his "Appendices," "Advertisement," and "Dedication" to the *Magnum Opus Waverley* in this edition. I do include the "Introduction" to the edition, which was placed before the beginning of *Waverley*, as well as the "Preface to the Third Edition" of *Waverley*, which Scott included in the *Magnum Opus* edition immediately after the title page for *Waverley* and before the beginning of the novel. I used the glossary Scott included at the end of Volume XLVIII of the *Magnum Opus* edition of the Waverley novels in annotating the text of *Waverley*; I did not replicate it in this edition because it glosses the Scots terms that appear throughout the *Magnum Opus* edition's forty-eight volumes. Scott placed his notes to the *Magnum Opus Waverley* at the bottom of the page and, if the note were quite lengthy, at the end of the chapter. In this edition, his notes follow the novel. If an item in the novel appears in Scott's notes, this is indicated in the novel with a lower-case letter.

I have annotated the novel, Scott's notes, and the appendices with an eye to providing an undergraduate reader with the tools to read this edition as easily and fully as possible, and a more advanced reader the sources to go further in-depth with his or her inquiries. To that end, I have translated foreign phrases (Latin, French, and Scots); attempted to identify the many poems included in the text; and suggested ways in which the allusions in the novels illuminate themes and concerns within the work. My annotations are given as footnotes so that they may more immediately and accessibly clarify aspects of the text that might be confusing for a modern reader. In completing the annotations, I have consulted a number of reference works and editions of the novels; a list of these sources, with abbreviations, follows. I wish to note my gratitude to the modern editors of *Waverley*, especially Claire Lamont and Andrew Hook; their work significantly informs this edition.

There are four appendices following the text of the novel and Scott's notes. They include reviews of *Waverley* published between 1814 and 1831; contemporary poems and prose on the topic of the Union of 1707; eighteenth- and early-nineteenth-century works on the Jacobite Rebellion of 1745; and selections of Scottish folklore and legend from the works of Anne MacVicar Grant, Elizabeth Hamilton, and James Macpherson.

Abbreviations for Works Consulted for Annotations

AHD   *The American Heritage Dictionary*, 3rd ed. (Boston: Houghton Mifflin, 1992)

BH   J.P. Brooke-Little, ed., *Boutell's Heraldry* (London: Frederick Warne, 1970)

CBD   J.O. Thorne and T.C. Collocott, eds., *Chambers Biographical Dictionary*, rev. ed. (Edinburgh: Chambers, 1986)

CCE   *Concise Columbia Encyclopedia*, 3rd ed. (New York: Columbia UP, 1994)

CGBD   Alexander Chalmers, ed. *General Biographical Dictionary*, new ed., 32 vols. (New York: AMS, 1969)

EB   *New Encyclopedia Britannica*, 15th ed., 29 vols. (Chicago: Encyclopedia Britannica, 2003)

GW   *The Project Gutenberg Etext of Waverley, by Sir Walter Scott* <http://www.gutenberg.org/files/5998>

HEP   John Greene, *History of the English People*, 4 vols. (New York: Harper, 1880)

LCD   Frances Illingworth, et al., eds., *Larousse Compact French-English Dictionary*, 2nd ed. (New York: Larousse, 2001)

LED   John C. Traupman, *Latin and English Dictionary*, rev. ed. (New York: Bantam, 1995)

LW   Andrew Lang, ed., *Waverley* (Boston: Estes and Lauriat, 1893)

NA   M.H. Abrams, et al., eds., *The Norton Anthology of English Literature*, 7th ed., vol. I. (New York: W.W. Norton, 2000)

OCBH   John Cannon, ed., *Oxford Companion to British History*, rev. ed. (Oxford: Oxford UP, 2002)

OCEL   Margaret Drabble, ed. *Oxford Companion to English Literature*, rev. ed. (Oxford: Oxford UP, 1998)

OED   *Oxford English Dictionary*, 2nd ed., 20 vols. (Oxford: Clarendon P, 1989)

OW   Claire Lamont, ed. *Waverley* (Oxford: Oxford UP, 1986)

PW   Andrew Hook, ed. *Waverley* (London: Penguin, 1985)

RE   William Rose Benet, *Reader's Encyclopedia*, 2nd ed. (New York: Thomas Y. Crowell, 1965)

RS   G. Blakemore Evans, et al., eds., *The Riverside Shakespeare* (Boston: Houghton Mifflin, 1974)

WD   *Webster's College Dictionary* (New York: Random House, 1991)

WSG   Sir Walter Scott, "Glossary" in *Waverley Novels*, vol. XLVIII (Edinburgh: Robert Cadell, 1833)

Waverley

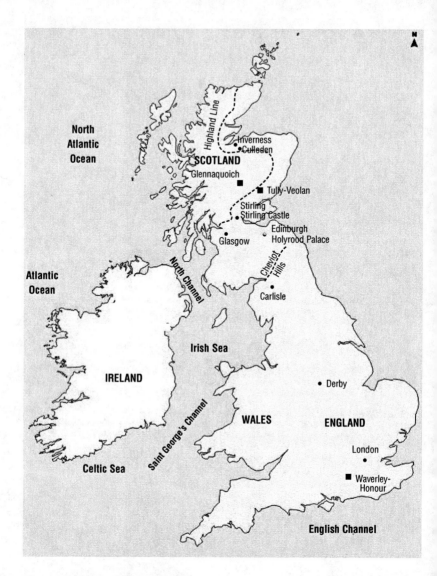

Map of Britain and Ireland, 1745

WAVERLEY NOVELS,
VOL. I
WAVERLEY.

PRINTED FOR CADELL & COMPANY, EDINBURGH
AND SIMPKIN AND MARSHALL, LONDON.
1829

WAVERLEY;
OR,
'TIS SIXTY YEARS SINCE

Under which King, Bezonian? speak, or die!

Henry IV, Part II.[1]

---

1 Shakespeare's *Henry IV, Part II*, V.iii.112. Shallow, whom Pistol calls "beson-ian" or scoundrel, responds to this question with "Harry the Fourth"; Pistol reveals that Henry V is now king; this information sends Falstaff off to find King Hal in order to remind him of their past friendship, at which Henry V, acting as king, not drinking buddy, disowns Falstaff, noting that he—Hal—is not what he once was. Scott may be using the quotation to suggest the similar confusion British citizens might have felt during the Jacobite rebellions, being reminded of the monarchical upheaval of the past 100 years. It also registers the shifting nature of alliances during a time of change.

INTRODUCTION.

THE plan of this edition leads me to insert in this place some account of the incidents on which the Novel of WAVERLEY is founded. They have been already given to the public, by my late lamented friend, William Erskine, Esq., (afterwards Lord Kinneder), when reviewing the Tales of My Landlord for the Quarterly Review, in 1817. The particulars were derived by the critic from the author's information. Afterwards they were published in the preface to the Chronicles of the Canongate. They are now inserted in their proper place.

The mutual protection afforded by Waverley and Talbot to each other, upon which the whole plot depends, is founded upon one of those anecdotes which soften the features even of civil war; and as it is equally honourable to the memory of both parties, we have no hesitation to give their names at length. When the Highlanders, on the morning of the battle of Preston, 1745, made their memorable attack on Sir John Cope's army, a battery of four field-pieces was stormed and carried by the Camerons and the Stewarts of Appine. The late Alexander Stewart of Invernahyle was one of the foremost in the charge, and observing an officer of the King's forces, who, scorning to join the flight of all around, remained with his sword in his hand, as if determined to the very last to defend the post assigned to him, the Highland gentleman commanded him to surrender, and received for reply a thrust, which he caught in his target. The officer was now defenceless, and the battle-axe of a gigantic Highlander (the miller of Invernahyle's mill) was uplifted to dash his brains out, when Mr Stewart with difficulty prevailed on him to yield. He took charge of his enemy's property, protected his person, and finally obtained him liberty on his parole.[1] The officer proved to be Colonel Whitefoord, an Ayrshire gentleman of high character and influence, and warmly attached to the House of Hanover; yet such was the confidence existing between these two honourable men, though of different political principles, that while the civil war was raging, and straggling officers from the Highland army were executed without mercy, Invernahyle hesitated not to pay his late captive a visit, as he returned to the Highlands to raise fresh recruits, on which occasion he spent a day or two in Ayrshire among Colonel Whitefoord's Whig friends, as pleasantly and as good-humouredly as if all had been at peace around him.

---

1 On his word.

After the battle of Culloden[1] had ruined the hopes of Charles Edward, and dispersed his proscribed adherents, it was Colonel Whitefoord's turn to strain every nerve to obtain Mr Stewart's pardon. He went to the Lord Justice Clerk, to the Lord Advocate, and to all the officers of state, and each application was answered by the production of a list, in which Invernahyle (as the good old gentleman was wont to express it) appeared "marked with the sign of the beast!" as a subject unfit for favour or pardon.

At length Colonel Whitefoord applied to the Duke of Cumberland in person. From him, also, he received a positive refusal. He then limited his request, for the present, to a protection for Stewart's house, wife, children, and property. This was also refused by the Duke; on which Colonel Whitefoord, taking his commission from his bosom, laid it on the table before his Royal Highness with much emotion, and asked permission to retire from the service of a sovereign who did not know how to spare a vanquished enemy. The Duke was struck, and even affected. He bade the Colonel take up his commission, and granted the protection he required. It was issued just in time to save the house, corn, and cattle at Invernahyle from the troops, who were engaged in laying waste what it was the fashion to call "the country of the enemy." A small encampment of soldiers was formed on Invernahyle's property, which they spared while plundering the country around, and searching in every direction for the leaders of the insurrection, and for Stewart in particular. He was much nearer them than they suspected; for, hidden in a cave (like the Baron of Bradwardine), he lay for many days so near the English sentinels, that he could hear their muster-roll called. His food was brought to him by one of his daughters, a child of eight years old, whom Mrs Stewart was under the necessity of intrusting with this commission; for her own motions, and those of all her elder inmates, were closely watched. With ingenuity beyond her years, the child used to stray about among the soldiers, who were rather kind to her, and thus seize the moment when she was unobserved, and steal into the thicket, when she deposited whatever small store of provisions she had in charge, at some marked spot, where her father might find it. Invernahyle supported life for several weeks by means of these precarious supplies; and as he had been wounded in the battle of Culloden, the hardships which he endured were aggravated by great bodily pain. After the soldiers had removed their quarters, he had another remarkable escape.

1 The battle of Culloden, fought on 16 April 1746, just south-east of Inverness, was the final battle of the 1745 Jacobite Rebellion in which the 5,000 Jacobites were overwhelmed by the king's army under the command of the duke of Cumberland (*OCBH*, 267).

As he now ventured to his own house at night, and left it in the morning, he was espied during the dawn by a party of the enemy who fired at and pursued him. The fugitive being fortunate enough to escape their search, they returned to the house, and charged the family with harbouring one of the proscribed traitors. An old woman had presence of mind enough to maintain that the man they had seen was the shepherd. "Why did he not stop when we called to him?" said the soldier.—"He is as deaf, poor man, as a peat-stack," answered the ready-witted domestic.—"Let him be sent for directly." The real shepherd accordingly was brought from the hill, and as there was time to tutor him by the way, he was as deaf when he made his appearance, as was necessary to sustain his character. Invernahyle was afterwards pardoned under the Act of Indemnity.[1]

The author knew him well, and has often heard these circumstances from his own mouth. He was a noble specimen of the old Highlander, far descended, gallant, courteous, and brave, even to chivalry. He had been *out*, I believe, in 1715 and 1745, was an active partaker in all the stirring scenes which passed in the Highlands, betwixt these memorable eras; and I have heard, was remarkable, among other exploits, for having fought a duel with the broadsword with the celebrated Rob Roy MacGregor, at the Clachan of Balquidder.

Invernahyle chanced to be in Edinburgh when Paul Jones came into the Frith[2] of Forth, and though then an old man, I saw him in arms, and heard him exult (to use his own words), in the prospect of "drawing his claymore once more before he died." In fact, on that memorable occasion, when the capital of Scotland was menaced by three trifling sloops or brigs, scarce fit to have sacked a fishing village, he was the only man who seemed to propose a plan of resistance. He offered to the magistrates, if broadswords and dirks[3] could be obtained, to find as many Highlanders among the lower classes, as would cut off any boat's crew who might be sent into a town, full of narrow and winding passages, in which they were like to disperse in quest of plunder. I know not if his plan was attended to; I rather think it seemed too hazardous to the constituted authorities, who might not, even at that time, desire to see arms in Highland hands. A steady and powerful west wind settled the matter, by sweeping Paul Jones and his vessels out of the Frith.

---

1 In 1660, Charles II granted general amnesty to "bury all seeds of future discords" (*OCBH*, 505).

2 "An indentation of the seacoast" (*WD*). The more usual modern spelling is "firth."

3 "The dagger of a Highlander" (*OED*).

If there is something degrading in this recollection, it is not unpleasant to compare it with those of the last war, when Edinburgh, besides the regular forces and militia, furnished a volunteer brigade of cavalry, infantry, and artillery, to the amount of six thousand men and upwards, which was in readiness to meet and repel a force of a far more formidable description, than was commanded by the adventurous American. Time and circumstances change the character of nations, and the fate of cities; and it is some pride to a Scotchman to reflect, that the independent and manly character of a country, willing to intrust its own protection to the arms of its children, after having been obscured for half a century, has, during the course of his own lifetime, recovered its lustre.

Other illustrations of WAVERLEY will be found in the Notes at the foot of the pages[1] to which they belong. Those which appeared too long to be so placed are given at the end of the chapters to which they severally relate.

---

1   Scott added sometimes quite lengthy notes to his 1829 edition of *Waverley*. They appeared as footnotes and as notes at the end of chapters (if particularly lengthy). As the "Note on the Text" indicates, all of Scott's notes are indicated by lower case letters of the alphabet in the text and appear immediately following the novel. Footnotes are supplied by the editor of the present edition.

PREFACE
TO THE THIRD EDITION.

TO this slight attempt at a sketch of ancient Scottish manners, the public have been more favourable than the author durst have hoped or expected. He has heard, with a mixture of satisfaction and humility, his work ascribed to more than one respectable name. Considerations, which seem weighty in his particular situation, prevent his releasing those gentlemen from suspicion by placing his own name in the title-page; so that, for the present at least, it must remain uncertain, whether WAVERLEY be the work of a poet or a critic, a lawyer or a clergyman, or whether the writer, to use Mrs Malaprop's phrase, be, "like Cerberus—three gentlemen at once." The Author, as he is unconscious of any thing in the work itself (except perhaps its frivolity) which prevents its finding an acknowledged father, leaves it to the candor of the public to choose among the many circumstances peculiar to different situations in life, such as may induce him to suppress his name on the present occasion. He may be a writer new to publication, and unwilling to avow a character to which he is unaccustomed; or he may be a hackneyed author, who is ashamed of too frequent appearance, and employs this mystery, as the heroine of the old comedy used her mask, to attract the attention of those to whom her face had become too familiar. He may be a man of a grave profession, to whom the reputation of being a novel-writer might be prejudicial; or he may be a man of fashion, to whom writing of any kind might appear pedantic. He may be too young to assume the character of an author, or so old as to make it advisable to lay it aside.

The Author of Waverley has heard it objected to this novel, that, in the character of Callum Beg, and in the account given by the Baron of Bradwardine of the petty trespasses of the Highlanders upon trifling articles of property, he has borne hard, and unjustly so, upon their national character. Nothing could be farther from his wish or intention. The character of Callum Beg is that of a spirit naturally turned to daring evil, and determined, by the circumstances of his situation, to a particular species of mischief. Those who have perused the curious Letters from the Highlands, published about 1726,[1] will find

---

1   [Edward J. Burt,] *Letters from a Gentleman in the North of Scotland to his Friend in London Containing the Description of a Capital Town in that* (continued)

instances of such atrocious characters which fell under the writer's own observation, though it would be most unjust to consider such villains as representatives of the Highlanders of that period, any more than the murderers of Marr and Williamson[1] can be supposed to represent the English of the present day. As for the plunder supposed to have been picked up by some of the insurgents in 1745, it must be remembered, that although the way of that unfortunate little army was neither marked by devastation nor bloodshed, but, on the contrary, was orderly and quiet in a most wonderful degree, yet *no* army marches through a country in a hostile manner without committing some depredations; and several, to the extent, and of the nature, jocularly imputed to them by the Baron, were really laid to the charge of the Highland insurgents; for which many traditions, and particularly one respecting the Knight of the Mirror, may be quoted as good evidence.[a]

Northern Country. With an Account of Some Uncommon Customs of the Inhabitants...., 2 vols. (Dublin: Peter Wilson, 1726; London, 1754).
1   The murders of the Marr family and the Williamson family took place during December 1811, in the Ratcliffe-highway area of London (now known as St. George's Street East), twelve days apart from one another. The only suspect, Mr. Williams, hanged himself while in prison. The murders caused great panic among the populace (<http://www.victorianlondon.org>).

CHAPTER I.
Introductory.

THE title of this work has not been chosen without the grave and solid deliberation, which matters of importance demand from the prudent. Even its first or general denomination, was the result of no common research or selection, although, according to the example of my predecessors, I had only to seize upon the most sounding and euphonic surname that English history or topography affords, and elect it at once as the title of my work, and the name of my hero. But alas! what could my readers have expected from the chivalrous epithets of Howard, Mordaunt, Mortimer, or Stanley, or from the softer and more sentimental sounds of Belmour, Belville, Belfield, and Belgrave, but pages of inanity, similar to those which have been so christened for half a century past? I must modestly admit I am too diffident of my own merit to place it in unnecessary opposition to preconceived associations; I have, therefore, like a maiden knight with his white shield, assumed for my hero, WAVERLEY, an uncontaminated name, bearing with its sound little of good or evil, excepting what the reader shall hereafter be pleased to affix to it. But my second or supplemental title was a matter of much more difficult election, since that, short as it is, may be held as pledging the author to some special mode of laying his scene, drawing his characters, and managing his adventures. Had I, for example, announced in my frontispiece, "Waverley, a Tale of other Days," must not every novel-reader have anticipated a castle scarce less than that of Udolpho,[1] of which the eastern wing had long been uninhabited, and the keys either lost, or consigned to the care of some aged butler or housekeeper, whose trembling steps, about the middle of the second volume, were doomed to guide the hero, or heroine, to the ruinous precincts? Would not the owl have shrieked and the cricket cried in my very title page? And could it have been possible for me, with a moderate attention to decorum, to introduce any scene more lively than might be produced by the jocularity of a clownish but faithful valet, or the garrulous narrative of the heroine's fille-de-chambre, when rehearsing the stories of blood and horror which she had heard in the servants' hall? Again, had my title borne, "Waverley, a Romance from the German," what head

---

1   Castle in the Apennine region of Europe in Ann Radcliffe's gothic novel *The Mysteries of Udolpho* (1794).

so obtuse as not to image forth a profligate abbot, an oppressive duke, a secret and mysterious association of Rosycrucians and Iluminati,[1] with all their properties of black cowls, caverns, daggers, electrical machines, trap-doors, and dark-lanterns? Or if I had rather chosen to call my work a "Sentimental Tale," would it not have been a sufficient presage of a heroine with a profusion of auburn hair, and a harp, the soft solace of her solitary hours, which she fortunately finds always the means of transporting from castle to cottage, although she herself be sometimes obliged to jump out of a two-pair-of-stairs window, and is more than once bewildered on her journey, alone and on foot, without any guide but a blowzy peasant girl, whose jargon she hardly can understand? Or again, if my Waverley had been entitled "A Tale of the Times," wouldst thou not, gentle reader, have demanded from me a dashing sketch of the fashionable world, a few anecdotes of private scandal thinly veiled, and if lusciously painted, so much the better? A heroine from Grosvenor Square, and a hero from the Barouche club or the Four-in-Hand,[2] with a set of subordinate characters from the elegantes of Queen Anne Street East, or the dashing heroes of the Bow-Street Office?[3] I could proceed in proving the importance of a title-page, and displaying at the same time my own intimate knowledge of the particular ingredients necessary to the composition of romances and novels of various descriptions: but it is enough, and I scorn to tyrannize longer over the impatience of my reader, who is doubtless already anxious to know the choice made by an author, so profoundly versed in the different branches of his art.

By fixing, then, the date of my story Sixty Years before this present 1st November 1805, I would have my readers understand, that they will meet in the following pages neither a romance of chivalry, nor a tale of modern manners; that my hero will neither have iron on his shoulders, as of yore, nor on the heels of his boots, as is the present fashion of Bond Street; and that my damsels will neither be clothed "in purple and in pall,"[4] like the Lady Alice of an old ballad, nor reduced to the primitive nakedness of a modern fashionable at a rout. From this my choice of an era the understanding critic may farther presage, that the object of my tale is more a description of men than

---

1 Secret societies believing in the occult, magic, alchemy, etc.
2 The Barouche club and the Four-in-Hand were fashionable clubs in 1805. Likewise, Grosvenor Square was an elegant and popular address among the affluent and well-established of London society.
3 The "dashing heroes" of Bow Street were the Bow Street Runners, London police officers whose organization was formed originally by Sir John Fielding in the mid-eighteenth century.
4 Costly purple robe (*OED*).

manners. A tale of manners, to be interesting, must either refer to antiquity so great as to have become venerable, or it must bear a vivid reflection of those scenes which are passing daily before our eyes, and are interesting from their novelty. Thus the coat-of-mail of our ancestors, and the triple-furred pelisse of our modern beaux, may, though for very different reasons, be equally fit for the array of a fictitious character; but who, meaning the costume of his hero to be impressive, would willingly attire him in the court dress of George the Second's reign, with its no collar, large sleeves, and low pocket-holes? The same may be urged, with equal truth, of the Gothic hall, which, with its darkened and tinted windows, its elevated and gloomy roof, and massive oaken table garnished with boars-head and rosemary, pheasants and peacocks, cranes and cygnets, has an excellent effect in fictitious description. Much may also be gained by a lively display of a modern fête, such as we have daily recorded in that part of a newspaper entitled the Mirror of Fashion, if we contrast these, or either of them, with the splendid formality of an entertainment given Sixty Years since; and thus it will be readily seen how much the painter of antique or of fashionable manners gains over him who delineates those of the last generation.

Considering the disadvantages inseparable from this part of my subject, I must be understood to have resolved to avoid them as much as possible, by throwing the force of my narrative upon the characters and passions of the actors;—those passions common to men in all stages of society, and which have alike agitated the human heart, whether it throbbed under the steel corslet of the fifteenth century, the brocaded coat of the eighteenth, or the blue frock and white dimity waistcoat of the present day.[b] Upon these passions it is no doubt true that the state of manners and laws casts a necessary colouring; but the bearings, to use the language of heraldry, remain the same, though the tincture may be not only different, but opposed in strong contradistinction. The wrath of our ancestors, for example, was coloured *gules*; it broke forth in acts of open and sanguinary violence against the objects of its fury. Our malignant feelings, which must seek gratification through more indirect channels, and undermine the obstacles which they cannot openly bear down, may be rather said to be tinctured *sable*. But the deep-ruling impulse is the same in both cases; and the proud peer, who can now only ruin his neighbor according to law, by protracted suits, is the genuine descendant of the baron, who wrapped the castle of his competitor in flames, and knocked him on the head as he endeavored to escape from the conflagration. It is from the great book of Nature, the same through a thousand editions, whether of black-letter, or wire-wove and hot-pressed, that I have venturously essayed to read a chapter to the public. Some favourable opportunities of contrast have been afforded me, by the state of society in the northern part of the island at the period of my history, and may serve at once to vary and to illustrate the moral lessons, which I would willingly consider as the most important part of my plan; although I am sensible how short these will fall of their aim, if I shall be found unable to mix them with amusement,—a task not quite so easy in this critical generation as it was "Sixty Years since."

CHAPTER II.
Waverley-Honour.—A Retrospect.

IT is, then, sixty years since Edward Waverley, the hero of the following pages, took leave of his family, to join the regiment of dragoons in which he had lately obtained a commission. It was a melancholy day at Waverley-Honour when the young officer parted with Sir Everard, the affectionate old uncle to whose title and estate he was presumptive heir.

A difference in political opinions had early separated the Baronet from his younger brother Richard Waverley, the father of our hero. Sir Everard had inherited from his sires the whole train of Tory or High-church predilections and prejudices, which had distinguished the house of Waverley since the Great Civil War. Richard, on the contrary, who was ten years younger, beheld himself born to the fortune of a second brother, and anticipated neither dignity nor entertainment in sustaining the character of Will Wimble. He saw early, that, to succeed in the race of life, it was necessary he should carry as little weight as possible. Painters talk of the difficulty of expressing the existence of compound passions in the same features at the same moment: it would be no less difficult for the moralist to analyze the mixed motives which unite to form the impulse of our actions. Richard Waverley read and satisfied himself from history and sound argument that, in the words of the old song,

> Passive obedience was a jest,
> And pshaw! was non-resistance;

yet reason would have probably been unable to combat and remove hereditary prejudice could Richard have anticipated that his elder brother, Sir Everard, taking to heart an early disappointment, would have remained a bachelor at seventy-two. The prospect of succession, however remote, might in that case have led him to endure dragging through the greater part of his life as "Master Richard at the Hall, the baronet's brother," in the hope that ere its conclusion he should be distinguished as Sir Richard Waverley of Waverley-Honour, successor to a princely estate, and to extended political connexions as head of the county interest in the shire where it lay. But this was a consummation of things not to be expected at Richard's outset, when Sir Everard was in the prime of life, and certain to be an acceptable suitor in almost any family, whether wealth or beauty should be the object of his pursuit, and when, indeed, his speedy marriage was a report which regularly amused the neighbourhood once a-year. His younger brother[1] saw no practicable road to independence save that of relying upon his own exertions, and adopting a political creed more consonant both to reason and his own interest than the hereditary faith of Sir Everard in High-church and in the house of Stewart. He therefore read his recantation at the beginning of his career, and entered life as an avowed Whig, and friend of the Hanover succession.

The ministry of George the First's time were prudently anxious to diminish the phalanx of opposition. The Tory nobility, depending for their reflected lustre upon the sunshine of a court, had for some time been gradually reconciling themselves to the new dynasty. But the wealthy country gentlemen of England, a rank which retained, with much of ancient manners and primitive integrity, a great proportion of obstinate and unyielding prejudice, stood aloof in haughty and sullen opposition, and cast many a look of mingled regret and hope to Bois le Duc, Avignon, and Italy.[c] The accession of the near relation of one of those steady and inflexible opponents was considered as a means of bringing over more converts, and therefore Richard Waverley met with a share of ministerial favour, more than proportioned to his talents or his political importance. It was, however, discovered that he had respectable talents for public business, and the first admittance to the minister's levee being negotiated, his success became rapid. Sir Everard learned from the public News-Letter, first, that Richard Waverley, Esquire, was returned for the ministerial borough of Barterfaith; next, that Richard Waverley, Esquire, had taken a distinguished part in the debate upon the Excise bill[2] in the support of government; and, lastly, that Richard Waverley, Esquire, had been honoured with a seat at one of those boards, where the pleasure of serving the country is combined with other important gratifications, which, to render them the more acceptable, occur regularly once a-quarter.

---

1 In his revisions for the *Magnum Opus Waverley*, Scott added "elder" and "younger" to describe Sir Everard and Richard in this paragraph, in order to emphasize family hierarchies.

2 Sir Robert Walpole, George II's prime minister, introduced the Excise Bill in 1733. The bill was meant to bring in revenues and curry favor with landowners. It proposed to substitute a tax on tobacco and wine for one on property. It was met by substantial opposition by Tories in Parliament led by William Pulteney, 1st Earl of Bath, and Walpole withdrew it, regaining his footing in the government.

Although these events followed each other so closely that the sagacity of the editor of a modern newspaper would have presaged the two last even while he announced the first, yet they came upon Sir Everard gradually, and drop by drop, as it were, distilled through the cool and procrastinating alembic of Dyer's Weekly Letter.[d] For it may be observed in passing, that instead of those mail-coaches, by means of which every mechanic at his six-penny club may nightly learn from twenty contradictory channels the yesterday's news of the capital, a weekly post brought, in those days, to Waverley-Honour, a Weekly Intelligencer, which, after it had gratified Sir Everard's curiosity, his sister's, and that of his aged butler, was regularly transferred from the Hall to the Rectory, from the Rectory to Squire Stubbs's at the Grange, from the Squire to the Baronet's steward at his neat white house on the heath, from the steward to the bailiff, and from him through a huge circle of honest dames and gaffers, by whose hard and horny hands it was generally worn to pieces in about a month after its arrival.

This slow succession of intelligence was of some advantage to Richard Waverley in the case before us; for, had the sum total of his enormities reached the ears of Sir Everard at once, there can be no doubt that the new commissioner would have had little reason to pique himself on the success of his politics. The Baronet, although the mildest of human beings, was not without sensitive points in his character; his brother's conduct had wounded these deeply; the Waverley estate was fettered by no entail[1] (for it had never entered into the head of any of its former possessors that one of their progeny could be guilty of the atrocities laid by Dyer's Letter to the door of Richard), and if it had, the marriage of the proprietor might have been fatal to a collateral heir. These various ideas floated through the brain of Sir Everard, without, however, producing any determined conclusion.

He examined the tree of his genealogy, which, emblazoned with many an emblematic mark of honour and heroic achievement, hung upon the well-varnished wainscot of his hall. The nearest descendants of Sir Hildebrand Waverley, failing those of his eldest son Wilfred, of whom Sir Everard and his brother were the only representatives, were, as this honoured register informed him (and, indeed, as he himself well knew), the Waverleys of Highley Park, com. Hants;[2] with whom

---

1 "The settlement of the succession of a landed estate, so that it cannot be bequeathed at pleasure by any one possessor; the rule of descent settled for any estate; the fixed or prescribed line of devolution" (*OED*).

2 "In the *comitatus* of" Hants, i.e., in the county of Hampshire. This side of the family has the same heraldic arms as John Bradshaw (1602-59), member of the court that sentenced Charles I to death under the government of Oliver

the main branch, or rather stock, of the house had renounced all connexion, since the great law-suit in 1670.

This degenerate scion had committed a farther offence against the head and source of their gentility, by the intermarriage of their representative with Judith, heiress of Oliver Bradshawe, of Highley Park, whose arms, the same with those of Bradshawe the regicide, they had quartered with the ancient coat of Waverley. These offences, however, had vanished from Sir Everard's recollection in the heat of his resentment; and had Lawyer Clippurse, for whom his groom was dispatched express, arrived but an hour earlier, he might have had the benefit of drawing a new settlement of the lordship and manor of Waverley-Honour, with all its dependencies. But an hour of cool reflection is a great matter, when employed in weighing the comparative evil of two measures, to neither of which we are internally partial. Lawyer Clippurse found his patron involved in a deep study, which he was too respectful to disturb, otherwise than by producing his paper and leathern ink-case, as prepared to minute his honour's commands. Even this slight manoeuvre was embarrassing to Sir Everard, who felt it as a reproach to his indecision. He looked at the attorney with some desire to issue his fiat, when the sun, emerging from behind a cloud, poured at once its chequered light through the stained window of the gloomy cabinet in which they were seated. The Baronet's eye, as he raised it to the splendour, fell right upon the central scutcheon, impressed with the same device which his ancestor was said to have borne in the field of Hastings; three ermines, passant, argent, in a field of azure, with its appropriate motto, *sans tache*. "May our name rather perish," exclaimed Sir Everard, "than that ancient and loyal symbol should be blended with the dishonoured insignia of a traitorous Roundhead!"

All this was the effect of the glimpse of a sunbeam, just sufficient to light Lawyer Clippurse to mend his pen. The pen was mended in vain. The attorney was dismissed, with directions to hold himself in readiness on the first summons.

The apparition of Lawyer Clippurse at the Hall occasioned much speculation in that portion of the world to which Waverley-Honour formed the centre: But the more judicious politicians of this microcosm augured yet worse consequences to Richard Waverley from a movement which shortly followed his apostacy. This was no less than an excursion of the Baronet in his coach-and-six, with four attendants

---

Cromwell's Roundheads, Puritans so named because they wore their hair close to their heads. Sir Everard chooses to keep Waverley-Honour in his immediate family, despite his brother Richard's "enormities," rather than bequeath it to more distant relatives who had taken part in the overthrow of the monarchy and the death of the king.

in rich liveries, to make a visit of some duration to a noble peer on the confines of the shire, of untainted descent, steady Tory principles, and the happy father of six unmarried and accomplished daughters.

Sir Everard's reception in this family was, as it may be easily conceived, sufficiently favourable; but of the six young ladies, his taste unfortunately determined him in favour of Lady Emily, the youngest, who received his attentions with an embarrassment, which showed, at once, that she durst not decline them, and that they afforded her any thing but pleasure.

Sir Everard could not but perceive something uncommon in the restrained emotions which the young lady testified at the advances he hazarded; but, assured by the prudent Countess that they were the natural effects of a retired education, the sacrifice might have been completed, as doubtless has happened in many similar instances, had it not been for the courage of an elder sister, who revealed to the wealthy suitor that Lady Emily's affections were fixed upon a young soldier of fortune, a near relation of her own. Sir Everard manifested great emotion on receiving this intelligence, which was confirmed to him, in a private interview, by the young lady herself, although under the most dreadful apprehensions of her father's indignation.

Honour and generosity were hereditary attributes of the house of Waverley. With a grace and delicacy worthy the hero of a romance, Sir Everard withdrew his claim to the hand of Lady Emily. He had even, before leaving Blandeville Castle, the address to extort from her father a consent to her union with the object of her choice. What arguments he used on this point cannot exactly be known, for Sir Everard was never supposed strong in the powers of persuasion; but the young officer, immediately after this transaction, rose in the army with a rapidity far surpassing the usual pace of unpatronised professional merit, although, to outward appearance, that was all he had to depend upon.

The shock which Sir Everard encountered upon this occasion, although diminished by the consciousness of having acted virtuously and generously, had its effect upon his future life. His resolution of marriage had been adopted in a fit of indignation; the labour of courtship did not quite suit the dignified indolence of his habits; he had but just escaped the risk of marrying a woman who could never love him, and his pride could not be greatly flattered by the termination of his amour, even if his heart had not suffered. The result of the whole matter was his return to Waverley-Honour without any transfer of his affections, notwithstanding the sighs and languishments of the fair tell-tale, who had revealed, in mere sisterly affection, the secret of Lady Emily's attachment, and in despite of the nods, winks, and innuendoes of the officious lady mother, and the grave eulogiums which the Earl pronounced successively on the prudence, and good sense, and admirable dispositions, of his first, second, third, fourth, and fifth daughters. The memory of his unsuccessful amour was with Sir Everard, as with many more of his temper, at once shy, proud, sensitive, and indolent, a beacon against exposing himself to similar mortification, pain, and fruitless exertion for the time to come. He continued to live at Waverley-Honour in the style of an old English gentleman, of an ancient descent and opulent fortune. His sister, Miss Rachel Waverley, presided at his table; and they became, by degrees, an old bachelor and an ancient maiden lady, the gentlest and kindest of the votaries of celibacy.

The vehemence of Sir Everard's resentment against his brother was but short-lived; yet his dislike to the Whig and the placeman,[1] though unable to stimulate him to resume any active measures prejudicial to Richard's interest, in the succession to the family estate, continued to maintain the coldness between them. Richard knew enough of the world, and of his brother's temper, to believe that by any ill-considered or precipitate advances on his part, he might turn passive dislike into a more active principle. It was accident, therefore, which at length occasioned a renewal of their intercourse. Richard had married a young woman of rank, by whose family interest and private fortune he hoped to advance his career. In her right, he became possessor of a manor of some value, at the distance of a few miles from Waverley-Honour.

Little Edward, the hero of our tale, then in his fifth year, was their only child. It chanced that the infant with his maid had strayed one morning to a mile's distance from the avenue of Brere-wood Lodge, his father's seat. Their attention was attracted by a carriage drawn by six stately long-tailed black horses, and with as much carving and gilding as would have done honour to my lord mayor's. It was waiting for the owner, who was at a little distance inspecting the progress of a half-built farm-house. I know not whether the boy's nurse had been a Welsh or a Scotch-woman, or in what manner he associated a shield emblazoned with three ermines with the idea of personal property, but he no sooner beheld this family emblem, than he stoutly determined on vindicating his right to the splendid vehicle on which it was displayed. The Baronet arrived while the boy's maid was in vain endeavoring to make him desist from his determination to appropriate the gilded coach and six. The rencontre was at a happy moment for

---

1   "One who holds an appointment in the service of the sovereign or state; almost always with depreciatory or hostile connotation; one who is appointed (or who desires to be appointed) to such a position from motives of interest, without regard to fitness" (*OED*).

Edward, as his uncle had been just eyeing wistfully with something of a feeling like envy, the chubby boys of the stout yeoman whose mansion was building by his direction. In the round-faced rosy cherub before him, bearing his eye and his name, and vindicating a hereditary title to his family, affection, and patronage, by means of a tie which Sir Everard held as sacred as either Garter or Blue-mantle,[1] Providence seemed to have granted to him the very object best calculated to fill up the void in his hopes and affections. Sir Everard returned to Waverley-Hall upon a led horse, which was kept in readiness for him, while the child and his attendant were sent home in the carriage to Brerewood Lodge, with such a message as opened to Richard Waverley a door of reconciliation with his elder brother.

Their intercourse, however, though thus renewed, continued to be rather formal and civil, than partaking of brotherly cordiality; yet it was sufficient to the wishes of both parties. Sir Everard obtained, in the frequent society of his little nephew, something on which his hereditary pride might found the anticipated pleasure of a continuation of his lineage, and where his kind and gentle affections could at the same time fully exercise themselves. For Richard Waverley, he beheld in the growing attachment between the uncle and nephew the means of securing his son's, if not his own, succession to the hereditary estate which he felt would be rather endangered than promoted by any attempt on his own part towards a closer intimacy with a man of Sir Everard's habits and opinions.

Thus, by a sort of tacit compromise, little Edward was permitted to pass the greater part of the year at the Hall, and appeared to stand in the same intimate relation to both families, although their mutual intercourse was otherwise limited to formal messages, and more formal visits. The education of the youth was regulated alternately by the taste and opinions of his uncle and of his father. But more of this in a subsequent chapter.

CHAPTER III.
Education.

THE education of our hero, Edward Waverley, was of a nature somewhat desultory. In infancy, his health suffered, or was supposed to

---

1 In 1348, Edward III founded the Order of the Garter, modeled on the knights of King Arthur; the Order consisted of the King, the Prince of Wales, and 24 knights. In 1786, George III's seven sons were given "supernumerary status" (*OCBH*, 400). It is "the highest order of knighthood in Great Britain." The Blue Mantle refers to the "English pursuivant-at-arms, a heraldic officer, who wears a blue cloak" (*PW*, 573).

suffer (which is quite the same thing), by the air of London. As soon, therefore, as official duties, attendance on Parliament, or the prosecution of any of his plans of interest or ambition, called his father to town, which was his usual residence for eight months in the year, Edward was transferred to Waverley-Honour, and experienced a total change of instructors and of lessons, as well as of residence. This might have been remedied, had his father placed him under the superintendence of a permanent tutor. But he considered that one of his choosing would probably have been unacceptable at Waverley-Honour, and that such a selection as Sir Everard might have made, were the matter left to him, would have burdened him with a disagreeable inmate, if not a political spy, in his family. He, therefore, prevailed upon his private secretary, a young man of taste and accomplishments, to bestow an hour or two on Edward's education while at Brere-wood Lodge, and left his uncle answerable for his improvement in literature while an inmate at the Hall.

This was in some degree respectfully provided for. Sir Everard's chaplain, an Oxonian, who had lost his fellowship for declining to take the oaths at the accession of George I.,[1] was not only an excellent classical scholar, but reasonably skilled in science, and master of most modern languages. He was, however, old and indulgent, and the recurring interregnum, during which Edward was entirely freed from his discipline, occasioned such a relaxation of authority, that the youth was permitted, in a great measure, to learn as he pleased, what he pleased, and when he pleased. This slackness of rule might have been ruinous to a boy of slow understanding, who, feeling labour in the acquisition of knowledge, would have altogether neglected it, save for the command of a task-master; and it might have proved equally dangerous to a youth whose animal spirits were more powerful than his imagination or his feelings, and whom the irresistible influence of Alma[2] would have engaged in field-sports from morning till night. But the character of Edward Waverley was remote from either of these. His powers of apprehension were so uncommonly quick, as almost to resemble intuition, and the chief care of his preceptor was to prevent him, as a sportsman would phrase it, from over-running his game, that is, from acquiring his knowledge in a slight, flimsy, and inadequate manner. And here the instructor had to combat another propensity too often united with brilliancy of fancy and vivacity of talent,—that

---

1   Oxonian: member of the University of Oxford. Jacobite supporters saw Queen Anne's death as an opportunity to bring back the Stuart line, and they were unwilling to take an oath of allegiance recognizing the validity of the Hanoverian monarchy.

2   "Alma: the Vital Principle" by Matthew Prior (1664-1721).

indolence, namely, of disposition, which can only be stirred by some strong motive of gratification, and which renounces study as soon as curiosity is gratified, the pleasure of conquering the first difficulties exhausted, and the novelty of pursuit at an end. Edward would throw himself with spirit upon any classical author of which his preceptor proposed the perusal, make himself master of the style so far as to understand the story, and, if that pleased or interested him, he finished the volume. But it was in vain to attempt fixing his attention on critical distinctions of philology, upon the difference of idiom, the beauty of felicitous expression, or the artificial combinations of syntax. "I can read and understand a Latin author," said young Edward, with the self-confidence and rash reasoning of fifteen, "and Scaliger or Bentley[1] could not do much more." Alas! while he was thus permitted to read only for the gratification of his amusement, he foresaw not that he was losing for ever the opportunity of acquiring habits of firm and assiduous application, of gaining the art of controlling, directing, and concentrating the powers of his mind for earnest investigation,—an art far more essential than even that intimate acquaintance with classical learning which is the primary object of study.

I am aware I may be here reminded of the necessity of rendering instruction agreeable to youth, and of Tasso's[2] infusion of honey into the medicine prepared for a child; but an age in which children are taught the driest doctrines by the insinuating method of instructive games, has little reason to dread the consequences of study being rendered too serious or severe. The history of England is now reduced to a game at cards,—the problems of mathematics to puzzles and riddles,—and the doctrines of arithmetic may, we are assured, be sufficiently acquired, by spending a few hours a-week at a new and complicated edition of the Royal Game of the Goose. There wants but one step further, and the Creed and Ten Commandments may be taught in the same manner, without the necessity of the grave face, deliberate tone of recital, and devout attention, hitherto exacted from the well-governed childhood of this realm. It may, in the meantime, be subject of serious consideration, whether those who are accustomed only to acquire instruction through the medium of amusement, may not be brought to reject that which approaches under the aspect of study; whether those who learn history by the cards, may not be led to prefer the means to the end; and whether, were we to teach religion in the

---

1 Joseph Justus Scalinger (1540-1609), Renaissance scholar, known also for his critical editions of classical authors; Richard Bentley (1662-1742), classical scholar, especially of Horace and Manilius (*OCEL*, 88, 865-66).

2 Torquato Tasso (1544-95), Italian philosopher and poet, author of the epic poem *Gerusalemme liberata* (1581).

way of sport, our pupils may not thereby be gradually induced to make sport of their religion. To our young hero, who was permitted to seek his instruction only according to the bent of his own mind, and who, of consequence, only sought it so long as it afforded him amusement, the indulgence of his tutors was attended with evil consequences, which long continued to influence his character, happiness, and utility.

Edward's power of imagination and love of literature, although the former was vivid, and the latter ardent, were so far from affording a remedy to this peculiar evil, that they rather inflamed and increased its violence. The library at Waverley-Honour, a large Gothic room, with double arches and a gallery, contained such a miscellaneous and extensive collection of volumes as had been assembled together, during the course of two hundred years, by a family which had been always wealthy, and inclined, of course, as a mark of splendour, to furnish their shelves with the current literature of the day, without much scrutiny, or nicety of discrimination. Throughout this ample realm Edward was permitted to roam at large. His tutor had his own studies; and church politics and controversial divinity, together with a love of learned ease, though they did not withdraw his attention at stated times from the progress of his patron's presumptive heir, induced him readily to grasp at any apology for not extending a strict and regulated survey towards his general studies. Sir Everard had never been himself a student, and, like his sister Miss Rachel Waverley, held the common doctrine, that idleness is incompatible with reading of any kind, and that the mere tracing the alphabetical characters with the eye, is in itself a useful and meritorious task, without scrupulously considering what ideas or doctrines they may happen to convey. With a desire of amusement, therefore, which better discipline might soon have converted into a thirst for knowledge, young Waverley drove through the sea of books, like a vessel without a pilot or a rudder. Nothing perhaps increases by indulgence more than a desultory habit of reading, especially under such opportunities of gratifying it. I believe one reason why such numerous instances of erudition occur among the lower ranks is, that, with the same powers of mind, the poor student is limited to a narrow circle for indulging his passion for books, and must necessarily make himself master of the few he possesses ere he can acquire more. Edward, on the contrary, like the epicure who only deigned to take a single morsel from the sunny side of a peach, read no volume a moment after it ceased to excite his curiosity or interest; and it necessarily happened, that the habit of seeking only this sort of gratification rendered it daily more difficult of attainment, till the passion for reading, like other strong appetites, produced by indulgence a sort of satiety.

Ere he attained this indifference, however, he had read, and stored in a memory of uncommon tenacity, much curious, though ill-arranged and miscellaneous information. In English literature he was master of Shakspeare and Milton, of our earlier dramatic authors, of many picturesque and interesting passages from our old historical chronicles, and was particularly well acquainted with Spenser, Drayton, and other poets who have exercised themselves on romantic fiction, of all themes the most fascinating to a youthful imagination, before the passions have roused themselves, and demand poetry of a more sentimental description. In this respect his acquaintance with Italian opened him yet a wider range. He had perused the numerous romantic poems, which, from the days of Pulci, have been a favourite exercise of the wits of Italy, and had sought gratification in the numerous collections of *novelle*, which were brought forth by the genius of that elegant though luxurious nation, in emulation of the Decameron.[1] In classical literature, Waverley had made the usual progress, and read the usual authors; and the French had afforded him an almost exhaustless collection of memoirs, scarcely more faithful than romances, and of romances so well written as hardly to be distinguished from memoirs. The splendid pages of Froissart, with his heart-stirring and eye-dazzling descriptions of war and of tournaments, were among his chief favourites; and from those of Brantome and De la Noue[2] he learned to compare the wild and loose yet superstitious character of the nobles of the League, with the stern, rigid, and sometimes turbulent disposition of the Huguenot party. The Spanish had contributed to his stock of chivalrous and romantic lore. The earlier literature of the northern nations did not escape the study of one who read rather to awaken the imagination than to benefit the understanding. And yet, knowing much that is known but to few, Edward Waverley might justly be considered as ignorant, since he knew little of what adds dignity to man, and qualifies him to support and adorn an elevated situation in society.

The occasional attention of his parents might indeed have been of service, to prevent the dissipation of mind incidental to such a desul-

---

1 Luigi Pulci (1432-84), Italian poet, author of the epic *Il Morgante Maggiore* (1481); comic novelist and sonneteer. *The Decameron* (1358) by Giovanni Boccaccio (1313-75) consisted of 100 prose tales and is viewed as a precursor to the novel.

2 Jean Froissart (1337-1410?), French poet, chronicled western European life during the first half of the Hundred Years' War; Pierre de Bourdeille Brantome (c. 1530-1614), soldier and French author of several works depicting life at the Valois court; Francois De la Noue (1531-91), "Huguenot leader, author of a series of *Discours politiques et militaires*" (*OW*, 413).

tory course of reading. But his mother died in the seventh year after the reconciliation between the brothers, and Richard Waverley himself, who, after this event, resided more constantly in London, was too much interested in his own plans of wealth and ambition, to notice more respecting Edward, than that he was of a very bookish turn, and probably destined to be a bishop. If he could have discovered and analyzed his son's waking dreams, he would have formed a very different conclusion.

CHAPTER IV.
Castle-Building.

I HAVE already hinted, that the dainty, squeamish, and fastidious taste acquired by a surfeit of idle reading, had not only rendered our hero unfit for serious and sober study, but had even disgusted him in some degree with that which he had hitherto indulged.

He was in his sixteenth year, when his habits of abstraction and love of solitude became so much marked, as to excite Sir Everard's affectionate apprehension. He tried to counterbalance these propensities, by engaging his nephew in field-sports, which had been the chief pleasure of his own youthful days. But although Edward eagerly carried the gun for one season, yet when practice had given him some dexterity, the pastime ceased to afford him amusement.

In the succeeding spring, the perusal of old Isaac Walton's fascinating volume[1] determined Edward to become "a brother of the angle." But of all diversions which ingenuity ever devised for the relief of idleness, fishing is the worst qualified to amuse a man who is at once indolent and impatient; and our hero's rod was speedily flung aside. Society and example, which, more than any other motives, master and sway the natural bent of our passions, might have had their usual effect upon the youthful visionary. But the neighborhood was thinly inhabited, and the home-bred young squires whom it afforded, were not of a class fit to form Edward's usual companions, far less to excite him to emulation in the practice of those pastimes which composed the serious business of their lives.

There were a few other youths of better education, and a more liberal character, but from their society also our hero was in some degree excluded. Sir Everard had, upon the death of Queen Anne, resigned his seat in Parliament, and, as his age increased and the number of his contemporaries diminished, had gradually withdrawn

---

1 Isaac Walton (1593-1683), author of the pastoral *The Compleat Angler or the Contemplative Man's Recreation* (1653); also, biographer of Donne, Herbert, and other seventeenth-century men of letters.

himself from society; so that when, upon any particular occasion, Edward mingled with accomplished and well-educated young men of his own rank and expectations, he felt an inferiority in their company, not so much from deficiency of information, as from the want of skill to command and to arrange that which he possessed. A deep and increasing sensibility added to this dislike of society. The idea of having committed the slightest solecism in politeness, whether real or imaginary, was agony to him; for perhaps even guilt itself does not impose upon some minds so keen a sense of shame and remorse, as a modest, sensitive, and inexperienced youth feels from the consciousness of having neglected etiquette, or excited ridicule. Where we are not at ease, we cannot be happy; and therefore it is not surprising, that Edward Waverley supposed that he disliked and was unfitted for society, merely because he had not yet acquired the habit of living in it with ease and comfort, and of reciprocally giving and receiving pleasure.

The hours he spent with his uncle and aunt were exhausted in listening to the oft-repeated tale of narrative old age. Yet even there his imagination, the predominant faculty of his mind, was frequently excited. Family tradition and genealogical history, upon which much of Sir Everard's discourse turned, is the very reverse of amber, which, itself a valuable substance, usually includes flies, straws, and other trifles; whereas these studies, being themselves very insignificant and trifling, do nevertheless serve to perpetuate a great deal of what is rare and valuable in ancient manners, and to record many curious and minute facts which could have been preserved and conveyed through no other medium. If, therefore, Edward Waverley yawned at times over the dry deduction of his line of ancestors, with their various intermarriages, and inwardly deprecated the remorseless and protracted accuracy with which the worthy Sir Everard rehearsed the various degrees of propinquity between the house of Waverley-Honour and the doughty barons, knights, and squires, to whom they stood allied; if (notwithstanding his obligations to the three ermines passant) he sometimes cursed in his heart the jargon of heraldry, its griffins, its moldwarps, its wyverns, and its dragons, with all the bitterness of Hotspur[1] himself, there were moments when these communications interested his fancy and rewarded his attention.

The deeds of Wilibert of Waverley in the Holy Land, his long absence and perilous adventures, his supposed death, and his return on the evening when the betrothed of his heart had wedded the hero

---

1 *Henry IV, Part I*, III.I.148f. Here Hotspur tells Mortimer why Glendower's prophecies and interest in animals such as the griffin, moldwarp, and dragon (all animals out of heraldry) frustrate him.

who had protected her from insult and oppression during his absence; the generosity with which the Crusader relinquished his claims, and sought in a neighbouring cloister that peace which passeth not away;^e—to these and similar tales he would hearken till his heart glowed and his eye glistened. Nor was he less affected, when his aunt, Mrs Rachel, narrated the sufferings and fortitude of Lady Alice Waverley during the Great Civil War. The benevolent features of the venerable spinster kindled into more majestic expression, as she told how Charles had, after the field of Worcester, found a day's refuge at Waverley-Honour, and how, when a troop of cavalry were approaching to search the mansion, Lady Alice dismissed her youngest son with a handful of domestics, charging them to make good with their lives an hour's diversion, that the king might have that space for escape. "And, God help her," would Mrs Rachel continue, fixing her eyes upon the heroine's portrait as she spoke, "full dearly did she purchase the safety of her prince with the life of her darling child. They brought him here a prisoner, mortally wounded; and you may trace the drops of his blood from the great hall door along the little gallery, and up to the saloon, where they laid him down to die at his mother's feet. But there was comfort exchanged between them; for he knew, from the glance of his mother's eye, that the purpose of his desperate defence was attained. Ah! I remember," she continued, "I remember well to have seen one that knew and loved him. Miss Lucy St Aubin lived and died a maid for his sake, though one of the most beautiful and wealthy matches in this country; all the world ran after her, but she wore widow's mourning all her life for poor William, for they were betrothed though not married, and died in—I cannot think of the date; but I remember, in the November of that very year, when she found herself sinking, she desired to be brought to Waverley-Honour once more, and visited all the places where she had been with my grand-uncle, and caused the carpets to be raised that she might trace the impression of his blood, and if tears could have washed it out, it had not been there now; for there was not a dry eye in the house. You would have thought, Edward, that the very trees mourned for her, for their leaves dropt around her without a gust of wind; and, indeed, she looked like one that would never see them green again."

From such legends our hero would steal away to indulge the fancies they excited. In the corner of the large and sombre library, with no other light than was afforded by the decaying brands on its ponderous and ample hearth, he would exercise for hours that internal sorcery, by which past or imaginary events are presented in action, as it were, to the eye of the muser. Then arose in long and fair array the splendour of the bridal feast at Waverley-Castle; the tall and emaciated form of its real lord, as he stood in his pilgrim's weeds, an unnoticed spectator of the festivities of his supposed heir and intended bride; the electrical shock occasioned by the discovery; the springing of the vassals to arms; the astonishment of the bridegroom; the terror and confusion of the bride; the agony with which Wilibert observed, that her heart as well as consent was in these nuptials; the air of dignity, yet of deep feeling with which he flung down the half-drawn sword, and turned away for ever from the house of his ancestors. Then would he change the scene, and fancy would at his wish represent Aunt Rachel's tragedy. He saw the Lady Waverley seated in her bower, her ear strained to every sound, her heart throbbing with double agony, now listening to the decaying echo of the hoofs of the king's horse, and when that had died away, hearing in every breeze that shook the trees of the park, the noise of the remote skirmish. A distant sound is heard like the rushing of a swoln stream; it comes nearer, and Edward can plainly distinguish the galloping of horses, the cries and shouts of men, with straggling pistol-shots between, rolling forwards to the hall. The lady starts up—a terrified menial rushes in—but why pursue such a description!

As living in this ideal world became daily more delectable to our hero, interruption was disagreeable in proportion. The extensive domain that surrounded the Hall, which, far exceeding the dimensions of a park, was usually termed Waverley-Chase, had originally been forest ground, and still, though broken by extensive glades, in which the young deer were sporting, retained its pristine and savage character. It was traversed by broad avenues, in many places half grown up with brushwood, where the beauties of former days used to take their stand to see the stag coursed with greyhounds, or to gain an aim at him with the cross-bow. In one spot, distinguished by a moss-grown Gothic monument, which retained the name of Queen's Standing, Elizabeth herself was said to have pierced seven bucks with her own arrows. This was a very favourite haunt of Waverley. At other times, with his gun and his spaniel, which served as an apology to others, and with a book in his pocket, which perhaps served as an apology to himself, he used to pursue one of these long avenues, which, after an ascending sweep of four miles, gradually narrowed into a rude and contracted path through the cliffy and woody pass called Mirkwood Dingle, and opened suddenly upon a deep, dark, and small lake, named, from the same cause, Mirkwood-Mere. There stood, in former times, a solitary tower upon a rock almost surrounded by the water, which had acquired the name of the Strength of Waverley, because, in perilous times, it had often been the refuge of the family. There, in the wars of York and Lancaster,[1] the last adherents of the Red Rose who dared to maintain her cause, carried on a harassing and predatory warfare, till the strong-hold was reduced by the celebrated Richard of Gloucester. Here, too, a party of cavaliers long maintained themselves under Nigel Waverley, elder brother of that William whose fate Aunt Rachel commemorated. Through these scenes it was that Edward loved to "chew the cud of sweet and bitter fancy,"[2] and, like a child among his toys, culled and arranged, from the splendid yet useless imagery and emblems with which his imagination was stored, visions as brilliant and as fading as those of an evening sky. The effect of this indulgence upon his temper and character will appear in the next chapter.

CHAPTER V.
Choice of a Profession.

FROM the minuteness with which I have traced Waverley's pursuits, and the bias which these unavoidably communicated to his imagination, the reader may perhaps anticipate, in the following tale, an imitation of the romance of Cervantes.[3] But he will do my prudence injustice in the supposition. My intention is not to follow the steps of that inimitable author, in describing such total perversion of intellect as misconstrues the objects actually presented to the senses, but that more common aberration from sound judgement, which apprehends occurrences indeed in their reality, but communicates to them a tincture of its own romantic tone and colouring. So far was Edward Waverley from expecting general sympathy with his own feelings, or concluding that the present state of things was calculated to exhibit the reality of those visions in which he loved to indulge, that he dreaded nothing more than the detection of such sentiments as were dictated by his musings. He neither had nor wished to have a confi-

---

1 The dynastic wars between the Houses of Lancaster and York, known as the Wars of the Roses: the Lancastrians were associated with the red rose, the Yorkists with the white. The wars ended in 1485 when Henry Tudor, purported descendent of the Lancastrian line, married Edward IV's daughter, Elizabeth of York (*OCBH*, 1012, 557).

2 "Chewing the food of sweet and bitter fancy," from Shakespeare's *As You Like It*, IV.iii.103.

3 Miguel de Cervantes Saavedra (1547-1616), Spanish novelist and dramatist, author of *Don Quixote* (Part 1, 1605; Part 2, 1615), which burlesques the romance of chivalry (*OCEL*, 180-281) while suggesting the value of such a perspective.

dant, with whom to communicate his reveries; and so sensible was he of the ridicule attached to them, that, had he been to choose between any punishment short of ignomy, and the necessity of giving a cold and composed account of the ideal world in which he lived the better part of his days, I think he would not have hesitated to prefer the former infliction. This secrecy became doubly precious, as he felt in advancing life the influence of the awakening passions. Female forms of exquisite grace and beauty began to mingle in his mental adventures; nor was he long without looking abroad to compare the creatures of his own imagination with the females of actual life.

The list of the beauties who displayed their hebdomadal finery at the parish church of Waverley was neither numerous nor select. By far the most passable was Miss Sissly, or, as she rather chose to be called, Miss Cecilia Stubbs, daughter of Squire Stubbs at the Grange. I know not whether it was by the "merest accident in the world," a phrase which, from female lips, does not always exclude *malice prepense*,[1] or whether it was from a conformity of taste, that Miss Cecilia more than once crossed Edward in his favourite walks through Waverley-Chase. He had not as yet assumed courage to accost her on these occasions; but the meeting was not without its effect. A romantic lover is a strange idolater, who sometimes cares not out of what log he frames the object of his adoration; at least, if nature has given that object any passable proportion of personal charms, he can easily play the Jeweller and Dervise[2] in the Oriental tale,[f] and supply her richly, out of the stores of his own imagination, with supernatural beauty, and all the properties of intellectual wealth.

But ere the charms of Miss Cecilia Stubbs had erected her into a positive goddess, or elevated her at least to a level with the saint her namesake, Mrs Rachel Waverley gained some intimation which determined her to prevent the approaching apotheosis. Even the most simple and unsuspicious of the female sex have (God bless them!) an instinctive sharpness of perception in such matters, which sometimes goes the length of observing partialities that never existed, but rarely misses to detect such as pass actually under their observation. Mrs Rachel applied herself with great prudence, not to combat, but to elude, the approaching danger, and suggested to her brother the necessity that the heir of his house should see something more of the world than was consistent with constant residence at Waverley-Honour.

Sir Everard would not at first listen to a proposal which went to separate his nephew from him. Edward was a little bookish, he admit-

---

1 Deliberate malice or mischief (*OED*).
2 Characters in John Hoppner's *Oriental Tales, trans. into English Verse* (1805), pp. 41-55.

ted; but youth, he had always heard, was the season for learning, and, no doubt, when his rage for letters was abated, and his head fully stocked with knowledge, his nephew would take to field-sports and country business. He had often, he said, himself regretted that he had not spent some time in study during his youth: he would neither have shot nor hunted with less skill, and he might have made the roof of St Stephen's echo to longer orations than were comprised in those zealous Noes, with which, when a member of the House during Godolphin's administration,[1] he encountered every measure of government.

Aunt Rachel's anxiety, however, lent her address to carry her point. Every representative of their house had visited foreign parts, or served his country in the army, before he settled for life at Waverley-Honour, and she appealed for the truth of her assertion to the genealogical pedigree; an authority which Sir Everard was never known to contradict. In short, a proposal was made to Mr Richard Waverley, that his son should travel, under the direction of his present tutor, Mr Pembroke, with a suitable allowance from the Baronet's liberality. The father himself saw no objection to this overture; but upon mentioning it casually at the table of the minister, the great man looked grave. The reason was explained in private. The unhappy turn of Sir Everard's politics, the minister observed, was such as would render it highly improper that a young gentleman of such hopeful prospects should travel on the Continent with a tutor doubtless of his uncle's choosing, and directing his course by his instructions. What might Mr Edward Waverley's society be at Paris, what at Rome, where all manner of snares were spread by the Pretender and his sons—these were points for Mr Waverley to consider. This he could himself say, that he knew his Majesty had such a just sense of Mr Richard Waverley's merits, that if his son adopted the army for a few years, a troop, he believed, might be reckoned upon in one of the dragoon regiments lately returned from Flanders.

A hint thus conveyed and enforced was not to be neglected with impunity; and Richard Waverley, though with great dread of shocking his brother's prejudices, deemed he could not avoid accepting the commission thus offered him for his son. The truth is, he calculated much, and justly, upon Sir Everard's fondness for Edward, which made him unlikely to resent any step that he might take in due submission to parental authority. Two letters announced this determina-

---

1 Refers to the state of impasse Parliament experienced under the administration of Sidney Godolphin, first earl of Godolphin (1645-1712), Queen Anne's prime minister, 1702-10, when the Whigs took gradual control of the government (*OCBH*, 424).

tion to the Baronet and his nephew. The latter barely communicated the fact, and pointed out the necessary preparations for joining his regiment. To his brother, Richard was more diffuse and circuitous. He coincided with him, in the most flattering manner, in the propriety of his son's seeing a little more of the world, and was even humble in expressions of gratitude for his proposed assistance; was, however, deeply concerned that it was now, unfortunately, not in Edward's power exactly to comply with the plan which had been chalked out by his best friend and benefactor. He himself had thought with pain on the boy's inactivity, at an age when all his ancestors had borne arms; even Royalty itself had deigned to inquire whether young Waverley was not now in Flanders, at an age when his grandfather was already bleeding for his king in the Great Civil War. This was accompanied by an offer of a troop of horse. What could he do? There was no time to consult his brother's inclinations, even if he could have conceived there might be objections on his part to his nephew's following the glorious career of his predecessors. And, in short, that Edward was now (the intermediate steps of cornet and lieutenant being overleapt with great agility) Captain Waverley, of Gardiner's regiment of dragoons, which he must join in their quarters at Dundee in Scotland, in the course of a month.[1]

Sir Everard Waverley received this intimation with a mixture of feelings. At the period of the Hanoverian succession he had withdrawn from parliament, and his conduct, in the memorable year 1715, had not been altogether unsuspected. There were reports of private musters of tenants and horses in Waverley-Chase by moonlight, and of cases of carbines and pistols purchased in Holland, and addressed to the Baronet, but intercepted by the vigilance of a riding officer of the excise, who was afterwards tossed in a blanket on a moonless night, by an association of stout yeomen, for his officiousness. Nay, it was even said, that at the arrest of Sir William Wyndham, the leader of the Tory party, a letter from Sir Everard was found in the pocket of his night-gown. But there was no overt act which an attainder could be founded on, and government, contented with suppressing the insurrection of 1715, felt it neither prudent nor safe to push their vengeance farther than against those unfortunate gentlemen[2] who actually took up arms.

---

1 Earlier editions of *Waverley* refer only to "the — regiment of dragoons" and to "D—." Scott's revisions to the *Magnum Opus Waverley* bring greater specificity to the text, as in this case where Gardner's regiment and Dundee make for a more concrete reality for the reader.

2 The insertion of "unfortunate" to describe the rebels is a *Magnum Opus* revision and certainly suggests Scott's sympathetic judgment of these men.

Nor did Sir Everard's apprehensions of personal consequences seem to correspond with the reports spread among his Whig neighbours. It was well known that he had supplied with money several of the distressed Northumbrians and Scotchmen, who, after being made prisoners at Preston in Lancashire, were imprisoned in Newgate and the Marshalsea,[1] and it was his solicitor and ordinary counsel who conducted the defence of some of these unfortunate gentlemen at their trial. It was generally supposed, however, that, had ministers possessed any real proof of Sir Everard's accession to the rebellion, he either would not have ventured thus to brave the existing government, or at least would not have done so with impunity. The feelings which then dictated his proceedings were those of a young man, and at an agitating period. Since that time Sir Everard's jacobitism had been gradually decaying, like a fire which burns out for want of fuel. His Tory and High-church principles were kept up by some occasional exercise at elections and quarter-sessions; but those respecting hereditary right were fallen into a sort of abeyance. Yet it jarred severely upon his feelings, that his nephew should go into the army under the Brunswick dynasty;[2] and the more so, as, independent of his high and conscientious ideas of paternal authority, it was impossible, or at least highly imprudent, to interfere authoritatively to prevent it. This suppressed vexation gave rise to many poohs and pshaws, which were placed to the account of an incipient fit of gout, until, having sent for the Army List,[3] the worthy Baronet consoled himself with reckoning the descendants of the houses of genuine loyalty, Mordaunts, Granvilles, and Stanleys, whose names were to be found in that military record; and, calling up all his feelings of family grandeur and warlike glory, he concluded, with logic something like

1 At Preston in Lancashire in 1715, the Jacobite forces under Thomas Forster were "bottled up" by the Hanoverian soldiers, defeated, and sent to prison. Forster escaped from Newgate and followed the Pretender to Europe. Marshalsea Prison in Southwark (London) was established in the thirteenth century as a state prison. After 1660, the Marshalsea became a debtors' prison; it was closed in 1849. Newgate Prison was established during Henry I's reign in the city of London's west gatehouse. It handled serious criminals and, after 1783, served as a place for public executions. Conditions there were squalid and harsh; it was closed in 1902 (OCBH, 678, 622).
2 The Welf family owned Brunswick or Braunschweig in Germany, a district in southeast Lower Saxony, northern Germany. "One of the Welf Lines, the House of Calenberg-Gottingen (Hanover), became dominant in the seventeenth century because of its marriage connections with the English royal family and succeeded to the throne of Great Britain and Ireland in 1714 as the House of Hanover" (EB, 2: 485-86).
3 "An official list of all the commissioned officers of the Army" (OED).

Falstaff's,[1] that when war was at hand, although it were shame to be on any side but one, it were worse shame to be idle than to be on the worst side, though blacker than usurpation could make it. As for Aunt Rachel, her scheme had not exactly terminated according to her wishes, but she was under the necessity of submitting to circumstances; and her mortification was diverted by the employment she found in fitting out her nephew for the campaign, and greatly consoled by the prospect of beholding him blaze in complete uniform.

Edward Waverley himself received with animated and undefined surprise this most unexpected intelligence. It was, as a fine old poem expresses it, "like a fire to heather set,"[2] that covers a solitary hill with smoke, and illumines it at the same time with dusky fire. His tutor, or, I should say, Mr Pembroke, for he scarce assumed the name of tutor, picked up about Edward's room some fragments of irregular verse, which he appeared to have composed under the influence of the agitating feelings occasioned by this sudden page being turned up to him in the book of life. The doctor, who was a believer in all poetry which was composed by his friends, and written out in fair straight lines, with a capital at the beginning of each, communicated this treasure to Aunt Rachel, who, with her spectacles dimmed with tears, transferred them to her common-place book, among choice receipts[3] for cookery and medicine, favourite texts, and portions from High-church divines, and a few songs, amatory and jacobitical, which she had caroll'd in her younger days, from whence her nephew's poetical *tentamina*[4] were extracted when the volume itself, with other authentic records of the Waverley family, were exposed to the inspection of the unworthy editor of this memorable history. If they afford the reader no higher

---

1   In *Henry IV, Parts I and II,* Falstaff is the old man whose friendship with Prince Hal allows Hal to keep his finger on the pulse of the people; Falstaff is unscrupulous and self-serving, a liar and braggart, and his usefulness to Hal ends once Hal becomes King Henry V. Falstaff's death is related at the beginning of *Henry V.*

2   Lady Elizabeth Wardlaw's 1719 poem "Hardyknute," which she claimed to have found in bits and pieces stuck to the bottoms of yarn spools. "Its authenticity as ancient heroic poetry was quickly questioned. Today it is generally accepted as Wardlaw's own composition, possibly based on her hearing of oral versions of the tale" of old Hardyknute's defeat of Norse invaders in the thirteenth century (<http://www.auburn.edu/~downejm/hardyknute.html>).

3   Favorite cooking recipes were often found in a lady's commonplace book: "A book in which 'commonplace' or passages important for reference were collected, usually under general heads; hence, a book in which one records passages or matters to be especially remembered or referred to, with or without arrangement" (*OED*).

4   Efforts.

amusement, they will serve, at least, better than narrative of any kind, to acquaint him with the wild and irregular spirit of our hero:—

Late, when the Autumn evening fell
On Mirkwood-Mere's romantic dell,
The lake return'd, in chasten'd gleam,
The purple cloud, the golden beam:
Reflected in the crystal pool,
Headland and bank lay fair and cool;
The weather-tinted rock and tower,
Each drooping tree, each fairy flower,
So true, so soft, the mirror gave,
As if there lay beneath the wave,
Secure from trouble, toil, and care,
A world than earthly world more fair.

But distant winds began to wake,
And roused the Genius of the Lake!
He heard the groaning of the oak,
And donn'd at once his sable cloak,
As warrior, at the battle-cry,
Invests him with his panoply:
Then as the whirlwind nearer press'd,
He 'gan to shake his foamy crest
O'er furrow'd brow and blacken'd cheek,
And bade his surge in thunder speak.
In wild and broken eddies whirl'd
Flitted that fond ideal world,
And to the shore in tumult tost,
The realms of fairy bliss were lost.

Yet, with a stern delight and strange,
I saw the spirit-stirring change.
As warr'd the wind with wave and wood,
Upon the ruin'd tower I stood,
And felt my heart more strongly bound,
Responsive to the lofty sound,
While, joying in the mighty roar,
I mourn'd that tranquil scene no more.

So, on the idle dreams of youth,
Breaks the loud trumpet-call of truth,
Bids each fair vision pass away,
Like landscape on the lake that lay,
As fair, as flitting, and as frail,
As that which fled the Autumn gale—
For ever dead to fancy's eye

Be each gay form that glided by,
While dreams of love and lady's charms
Give place to honour and to arms!

In sober prose, as perhaps these verses intimate less decidedly, the transient idea of Miss Cecilia Stubbs passed from Captain Waverley's heart amid the turmoil which his new destinies excited. She appeared, indeed, in full splendour in her father's pew upon the Sunday when he attended service for the last time at the old parish church, upon which occasion, at the request of his uncle and Aunt Rachel, he was induced (nothing loth, if the truth must be told) to present himself in full uniform.

There is no better antidote against entertaining too high an opinion of others, than having an excellent one of ourselves at the very same time. Miss Stubbs had indeed summoned up every assistance which art could afford to beauty; but, alas! hoop, patches, frizzled locks, and a new mantua of genuine French silk, were lost upon a young officer of dragoons, who wore, for the first time, his gold-laced hat, jack-boots, and broadsword. I know not whether, like the champion of an old ballad,[1]

His heart was all on honour bent,
  He could not stoop to love;
No lady in the land had power
  His frozen heart to move;

or whether the deep and flaming bars of embroidered gold, which now fenced his breast, defied the artillery of Cecilia's eyes; but every arrow was launched at him in vain.

Yet did I mark where Cupid's shaft did light;
  It lighted not on little western flower,
But on bold yeoman, flower of all the west,
  Hight Jonas Culbertfield, the steward's son.

Craving pardon for my heroics (which I am unable in certain cases to resist giving way to), it is a melancholy fact, that my history must here take leave of the fair Cecilia, who, like many a daughter of Eve, after the departure of Edward, and the dissipation of certain idle

---

1 According to Lamont, Scott noted that these lines were from "the second verse of an old ballad in Ramsay's *Tea table Miscellany*," specifically "Lord Henry and Katharine" II, p. 221 (*OW*, 415).

visions which she had adopted, quietly contented herself with a *pis-aller*,[1] and gave her hand, at the distance of six months, to the aforesaid Jonas, son of the Baronet's steward, and heir (no unfertile prospect) to a steward's fortune; besides the snug probability of succeeding to his father's office. All these advantages moved Squire Stubbs, as much as the ruddy brow and manly form of the suitor influenced his daughter, to abate somewhat in the article of their gentry; and so the match was concluded. None seemed more gratified than Aunt Rachel, who had hitherto looked rather askance upon the presumptuous damsel (as much so, peradventure, as her nature would permit), but who, on the first appearance of the new-married pair at church, honoured the bride with a smile and a profound courtesy, in presence of the rector, the curate, the clerk, and the whole congregation of the united parishes of Waverley *cum* Beverley.

I beg pardon, once and for all, of those readers who take up novels merely for amusement, for plaguing them so long with old-fashioned politics, and Whig and Tory, and Hanoverians and Jacobites. The truth is, I cannot promise them that this story shall be intelligible, not to say probable, without it. My plan requires that I should explain the motives on which its action proceeded; and these motives necessarily arose from the feelings, prejudices, and parties, of the times. I do not invite my fair readers, whose sex and impatience give them the greatest right to complain of these circumstances, into a flying chariot drawn by hippogriffs, or moved by enchantment. Mine is a humble English post-chaise,[2] drawn upon four wheels, and keeping his majesty's highway. Such as dislike the vehicle may leave it at the next halt,[3] and wait for the conveyance of Prince Hussein's tapestry, or Malek the Weaver's flying sentry-box.[4] Those who are contented to remain with me will be occasionally exposed to the dulness inseparable from heavy roads, steep hills, sloughs, and other terrestrial retardations; but, with tolerable horses and a civil driver, (as the advertisements have it), I engage to get as soon as possible into a more pic-

---

1 Last resort.
2 "A travelling carriage, either hired from stage to stage, or drawn by horses so hired: used in the eighteenth century and the earlier half of the nineteenth century" (*OED*).
3 "A temporary stoppage on a march or journey" (*OED*).
4 A sentry box is "a small wooden structure in which a sentry may stand at his post in bad weather" (*OED*). Hook notes that Prince Hussein's tapestry is in *The Arabian Nights*, in "The Story of Prince Ahmed and the Fairy Pari Banou" (*PW*, 575). Malek appears in a Persian tale, "The History of Malek and the Princess Schirine." Hook suggests that Scott read these two in Henry Weber's *Tales of the East*, volumes one and two, published in Edinburgh, 1812.

turesque and romantic country, if my passengers incline to have some patience with me during my first stages.[g]

CHAPTER VI.
The Adieus of Waverley.

IT was upon the evening of this memorable Sunday that Sir Everard entered the library, where he narrowly missed surprising our young hero as he went through the guards of the broadsword with the ancient weapon of old Sir Hildebrand, which, being preserved as an heirloom, usually hung over the chimney in the library, beneath a picture of the knight and his horse, where the features were almost entirely hidden by the knight's profusion of curled hair, and the Bucephalus[1] which he bestrode concealed by the voluminous robes of the Bath[2] with which he was decorated. Sir Everard entered, and after a glance at the picture and another at his nephew, began a little speech, which, however, soon dropt into the natural simplicity of his common manner, agitated upon the present occasion by no common feeling. "Nephew," he said; and then, as mending his phrase, "My dear Edward, it is God's will, and also the will of your father, whom, under God, it is your duty to obey, that you should leave us to take up the profession of arms, in which so many of your ancestors have been distinguished. I have made such arrangements as will enable you to take the field as their descendant, and as the probable heir of the house of Waverley; and, sir, in the field of battle you will remember what name you bear. And, Edward, my dear boy, remember also that you are the last of that race, and the only hope of its revival depends upon you; therefore, as far as duty and honour will permit, avoid danger—I mean unnecessary danger—and keep no company with rakes, gamblers, and Whigs, of whom, it is to be feared, there are but too many in the service into which you are going. Your colonel, as I am informed, is an

---

1 Horse, after the wild horse given to Philip II. His son, Alexander, then twelve, said he'd tame the horse, when all other attempts to ride it had failed. If Alexander failed, his father would punish his audacity and disrespect by having Alexander pay for the horse. Seeing the horse's fear of his shadow, Alexander led him into the sun, vanquished the shadow, and successfully rode the horse, causing his father to think on Alexander's future greatness (<http://faq.macedonia.org>).

2 Though the idea of honoring the knight for his moral purity was long lived in Britain, in 1725 the Order of the Bath was officially recognized and was "extended in 1815 and 1847. It has a military and civilian division, with three categories in each: Knights Grand Cross (GCB), Knights Commander (KCB), and Companions (CB). The women members are dames" (*OCBH*, 84).

excellent man—for a Presbyterian; but you will remember your duty to God, the Church of England, and the"—(this breach ought to have been supplied, according to the rubrick, with the word *king*; but as, unfortunately, that word conveyed a double and embarassing sense, one meaning *de facto*, and the other *de jure*,[1] the knight filled up the blank otherwise)—"the Church of England, and all constituted authorities." Then, not trusting himself with any further oratory, he carried his nephew to his stables to see the horses destined for his campaign. Two were black (the regimental colour), superb chargers both; the other three were stout active hacks, designed for the road, or for his domestics, of whom two were to attend him from the Hall; an additional groom, if necessary, might be picked up in Scotland.

"You will depart with but a small retinue," quoth the Baronet, "compared to Sir Hildebrand, when he mustered before the gate of the Hall a larger body of horse than your whole regiment consists of. I could have wished that these twenty young fellows from my estate, who have enlisted in your troop, had been to march with you on your journey to Scotland. It would have been something, at least; but I am told their attendance would be thought unusual in these days, when every new and foolish fashion is introduced to break the natural dependence of the people upon their landlords."

Sir Everard had done his best to correct this unnatural disposition of the times; for he had brightened the chain of attachment between the recruits and their young captain, not only by a copious repast of beef and ale, by way of parting feast, but by such a pecuniary donation to each individual, as tended rather to improve the conviviality than the discipline of their march. After inspecting the cavalry, Sir Everard again conducted his nephew to the library, where he produced a letter, carefully folded, surrounded by a little stripe of flox-silk, according to ancient form, and sealed with an accurate impression of the Waverley coat-of-arms. It was addressed, with great formality, "To Cosmo Comyne Bradwardine, Esq. of Bradwardine, at his principal mansion of Tully-Veolan, in Perthshire, North Britain. These—By the hands of Captain Edward Waverley, nephew of Sir Everard Waverley, of Waverley-Honour, Bart."

The gentleman to whom this enormous greeting was addressed, of whom we shall have more to say in the sequel, had been in arms for the exiled family of Stewart in the year 1715, and was made prisoner at Preston in Lancashire. He was of a very ancient family, and somewhat embarrassed fortune; a scholar, according to the scholarship of Scotchmen, that is, his learning was more diffuse than accurate, and

---

1   In fact, and by right. George II is in fact king, despite Sir Everard's feeling that the "Old Pretender, James II's son, should by right be King" (*PW*, 575).

he was rather a reader than a grammarian. Of his zeal for the classic authors he is said to have given an uncommon instance. On the road between Preston and London he made his escape from his guards; but being afterwards found loitering near the place where they had lodged the former night, he was recognised, and again arrested. His companions, and even his escort, were surprised at his infatuation, and could not help inquiring, why, being once at liberty, he had not made the best of his way to a place of safety; to which he replied, that he had intended to do so, but, in good faith, he had returned to seek his Titus Livius, which he had forgot in the hurry of his escape.[h] The simplicity of this anecdote struck the gentleman, who, as we before observed, had managed the defence of some of those unfortunate persons, at the expense of Sir Everard, and perhaps some others of the party. He was, besides, himself a special admirer of the old Patavinian,[1] and though probably his own zeal might not have carried him such extravagant lengths, even to recover the edition of Sweynheim and Pannartz[2] (supposed to be the princeps), he did not the less estimate the devotion of the North Briton,[3] and in consequence exerted himself to so much purpose to remove and soften evidence, detect legal flaws, *et cetera*, that he accomplished the final discharge and deliverance of Cosmo Comyne Bradwardine from certain very awkward consequences of a plea before our sovereign lord the king in Westminster.

The Baron of Bradwardine, for he was generally so called in Scotland (although his intimates, from his place of residence, used to denominate him Tully-Veolan, or, more familiarly, Tully), no sooner stood *rectus in curia*,[4] than he posted down to pay his respects and make his acknowledgments at Waverley-Honour. A congenial passion for field-sports, and a general coincidence in political opinions, cemented his friendship with Sir Everard, notwithstanding the difference of their habits and studies in other particulars; and, having spent several weeks at Waverley-Honour, the Baron departed with many expressions of regard, warmly pressing the Baronet to return his visit, and partake of the diversion of grouse-shooting upon his moors in

---

1 Livy, in full Titus Livius (b. 59/60 BCE in Patavium, Venetia, Italy, and d. 17 CE, also in Patavium), Roman historian, author of a history of Rome.

2 Konrad Sweynheim of Frankfurt, in Germany, and Arnold Pannartz of Prague were the first printers in Italy; both ecclesiastics, they put out an edition of Livy's *History*.

3 A Scot; possibly a derisive term, after John Wilkes's *The North Briton*, a weekly periodical begun in 1762 in response to Smollett's *Briton*, and offering satiric portraits of Scots.

4 "One who stood at the bar, but against whom no charge was made; or one whose outlawry had been reversed" (*PW*, 575).

Perthshire next season. Shortly after, Mr Bradwardine remitted from Scotland a sum in reimbursement of expenses incurred in the King's High Court of Westminster, which, although not quite so formidable when reduced to the English denomination, had, in its original form of Scotch pounds, shillings, and pence, such a formidable effect upon the frame of Duncan Macwheeble, the laird's confidential factor, baron-bailie,[1] and man of resource, that he had a fit of the cholic which lasted for five days, occasioned, he said, solely and utterly by becoming the unhappy instrument of conveying such a serious sum of money out of his native country into the hands of the false English. But patriotism, as it is the fairest, so it is often the most suspicious mask of other feelings; and many who knew Bailie Macwheeble, concluded that his professions of regret were not altogether disinterested, and that he would have grudged the moneys paid to the *loons* at Westminster much less had they not come from Bradwardine estate, a fund which he considered as more particularly his own. But the Bailie protested he was absolutely disinterested—

"Woe, woe, for Scotland, not a whit for me!"

The laird was only rejoiced that his worthy friend, Sir Everard Waverley of Waverley-Honour, was reimbursed of the expenditure which he had outlaid on account of the house of Bradwardine. It concerned, he said, the credit of his own family, and of the kingdom of Scotland at large, that these disbursements should be repaid forthwith, and, if delayed, it would be a matter of national reproach. Sir Everard, accustomed to treat much larger sums with indifference, received the remittance of £294, 13s. 6d., without being aware that the payment was an international concern, and, indeed, would probably have forgot the circumstance altogether, if Bailie Macwheeble had thought of comforting his cholic by intercepting the subsidy. A yearly intercourse took place, of a short letter, and a hamper or a cask or two, between Waverley-Honour and Tully-Veolan, the English exports consisting of mighty cheeses and mightier ale, pheasants, and venison, and the Scottish returns being vested in grouse, white hares, pickled salmon, and usquebaugh.[2] All which were meant, sent, and received, as pledges of constant friendship and amity between two important houses. It followed as a matter of course, that the heir-apparent of Waverley-Honour could not with propriety visit Scotland without being furnished with credentials to the Baron of Bradwardine.

---

1 Factor: estate manager, steward, agent. Baron-bailie: "a baillie or magistrate appointed by the lord-superior in a burgh or barony" (*OED*).
2 Water of life (*OED*); the Gaelic name for whisky.

When this matter was explained and settled, Mr Pembroke expressed his wish to take a private and particular leave of his dear pupil. The good man's exhortations to Edward to preserve an unblemished life and morals, to hold fast the principles of the Christian religion, and to eschew the profane company of scoffers and latitudinarians,[1] too much abounding in the army, were not unmingled with his political prejudices. It had pleased Heaven, he said, to place Scotland (doubtless for the sins of their ancestors in 1642) in a more deplorable state of darkness than even this unhappy kingdom of England. Here, at least, although the candlestick of the Church of England had been in some degree removed from its place, it yet afforded a glimmering light; there was a hierarchy, though schismatical, and fallen from the principles maintained by those great fathers of the church, Sancroft and his brethren;[2] there was a liturgy, though wofully perverted in some of the principal petitions. But in Scotland it was utter darkness; and, excepting a sorrowful, scattered, and persecuted remnant, the pulpits were abandoned to Presbyterians, and, he feared, to sectaries of every description. It should be his duty to fortify his dear pupil to resist such unhallowed and pernicious doctrines in church and state, as must necessarily be forced at times upon his unwilling ears.

Here he produced two immense folded packets, which appeared each to contain a whole ream of closely written manuscript. They had been the labour of the worthy man's whole life; and never were labour and zeal more absurdly wasted. He had at one time gone to London, with the intention of giving them to the world, by the medium of a bookseller in Little Britain, well known to deal in such commodities, and to whom he was instructed to address himself in a particular phrase, and with a certain sign, which, it seems, passed at that time current among the initiated Jacobites. The moment Mr Pembroke had uttered the Shibboleth,[3] with the appropriate gesture, the bibliopolist greeted him, notwithstanding every disclamation, by the title of Doctor, and conveying him into his back shop, after inspecting every possible and impossible place of concealment, he commenced: "Eh, doctor!—Well—all under the rose—snug—I keep no holes here even

---

1   Informed by the ideas of Cudworth and the Cambridge Platonists, Latitudinarians supported religious toleration and the efficacy of good works.

2   William Sancroft (1617-93), Archbishop of Canterbury, dean of St. Paul's, he worked to strengthen Anglicanism in the country through the education of clerics. He crowned James II but refused to sit on his Court of Ecclesiastical Commission, and he was one of the seven bishops who petitioned James II against the Declaration of Indulgence in 1688. He refused to take the oath of allegiance to William III in 1690 and was deprived of his office (*OCBH*, 836).

3   Password.

for a Hanoverian rat to hide in. And, what—eh! any good news from our friends over the water?—And how does the worthy King of France?—Or perhaps you are more lately from Rome? It must be Rome will do it at last—the church must light its candle at the old lamp.—Eh—what, cautious? I like you the better; but no fear."

Here Mr Pembroke with some difficulty stopt a torrent of interrogations, eked out with signs, nods, and winks; and, having at length convinced the bookseller that he did him too much honour in supposing him an emissary of exiled royalty, he explained his actual business.

The man of books with a much more composed air proceeded to examine the manuscripts. The title of the first was "A Dissent from Dissenters, or the Comprehension confuted; showing the Impossibility of any Composition between the Church and Puritans, Presbyterians, or Sectaries of any Description; illustrated from the Scriptures, the Fathers of the Church, and the soundest Controversial Divines." To this work the bookseller positively demurred. "Well meant," he said, "and learned, doubtless; but the time had gone by. Printed on small-pica it would run to eight hundred pages, and could never pay. Begged therefore to be excused.—Loved and honoured the true church from his soul, and, had it been a sermon on the martyrdom, or any twelve-penny touch[1]—why I would venture something for the honour of the cloth.—But come, let's see the other. 'Right Hereditary righted!'—Ah! there's some sense in this. Hum—hum—hum—pages so many, paper so much, letter-press.—Ah—I'll tell you, though, doctor, you must knock out some of the Latin and Greek; heavy, doctor, damn'd heavy—(beg your pardon) and if you throw in a few grains more pepper.—I am he that never peached my author—I have published for Drake and Charlwood Lawton, and poor Amhurst.[i]— Ah, Caleb! Caleb! Well, it was a shame to let poor Caleb starve, and so many fat rectors and squires among us. I gave him a dinner once a-week; but, Lord love you, what's once a-week, when a man does not know where to go the other six days?—Well, but I must show the manuscript to little Tom Alibi the solicitor, who manages all my law affairs—must keep on the windy side—the mob were very uncivil the last time I mounted in the Old Palace Yard—all Whigs and Roundheads every man of them, Williamites and Hanover rats."

The next day Mr Pembroke again called on the publisher, but found Tom Alibi's advice had determined him against undertaking the work. "Not but what I would go to—(what was I going to say?) to the Plantations for the church with pleasure—but, dear doctor, I have a wife and family; but, to show my zeal, I'll recommend the job to my

---

1 Twelve pence or a shilling.

neighbor Trimmel—he is a bachelor, and leaving off business, so a voyage in a western barge would not inconvenience him." But Mr Trimmel was also obdurate, and Mr Pembroke, fortunately perchance for himself, was compelled to return to Waverley-Honour with his treatise in vindication of the real fundamental principles of church and state safely packed in his saddle-bags.

As the public were thus likely to be deprived of the benefit arising from his lucubrations by the selfish cowardice of the trade, Mr Pembroke resolved to make two copies of these tremendous manuscripts for the use of his pupil. He felt that he had been indolent as a tutor, and, besides, his conscience checked him for complying with the request of Mr Richard Waverley, that he would impress no sentiments upon Edward's mind inconsistent with the present settlement in church and state.—But now, thought he, I may, without breach of my word, since he is no longer under my tuition, afford the youth the means of judging for himself, and have only to dread his reproaches for so long concealing the light which the perusal will flash upon his mind.—While he thus indulged the reveries of an author and a politician, his darling proselyte, seeing nothing very inviting in the title of the tracts, and appalled by the bulk and compact lines of the manuscript, quietly consigned them to a corner of his travelling trunk.

Aunt Rachel's farewell was brief and affectionate. She only cautioned her dear Edward, whom she probably deemed somewhat susceptible, against the fascination of Scottish beauty. She allowed that the northern part of the island contained some ancient families, but they were all Whigs and Presbyterians except the Highlanders; and respecting them she must needs say, there could be no great delicacy among the ladies, where the gentlemen's usual attire was, as she had been assured, to say the least, very singular, and not at all decorous. She concluded her farewell with a kind and moving benediction, and gave the young officer, as a pledge of her regard, a valuable diamond ring (often worn by the male sex at that time), and a purse of broad gold pieces, which also were more common Sixty Years since than they have been of late.

CHAPTER VII.
A Horse-Quarter in Scotland.

THE next morning, amid varied feelings, the chief of which was a predominant, anxious, and even solemn impression, that he was now in a great measure abandoned to his own guidance and direction, Edward Waverley departed from the Hall amid the blessings and tears of all the old domestics and the inhabitants of the village, mingled with some sly petitions for sergeantcies and corporalships, and so forth, on the part of those who professed that "they never thoft to ha' seen Jacob, and Giles, and Jonathan, go off for soldiers, save to attend his honour, as in duty bound." Edward, as in duty bound, extricated himself from the supplicants with the pledge of fewer promises than might have been expected from a young man so little accustomed to the world. After a short visit to London, he proceeded on horseback, then the general mode of travelling, to Edinburgh, and from thence to Dundee, a seaport on the eastern coast of Angus-shire, where his regiment was then quartered.

He now entered upon a new world, where, for a time, all was beautiful because all was new. Colonel Gardiner, the commanding officer of the regiment, was himself a study for a romantic, and at the same time an inquisitive, youth. In person he was tall, handsome, and active, though somewhat advanced in life. In his early years, he had been what is called, by manner of palliative, a very gay young man, and strange stories were circulated about his sudden conversion from doubt, if not infidelity, to a serious and even enthusiastic turn of mind. It was whispered that a supernatural communication, of a nature obvious even to the exterior senses, had produced this wonderful change; and though some mentioned the proselyte as an enthusiast, none hinted at his being a hypocrite. This singular and mystical circumstance gave Colonel Gardiner a peculiar and solemn interest in the eyes of the young soldier.[j] It may be easily imagined that the officers of a regiment, commanded by so respectable a person, composed a society more sedate and orderly than a military mess always exhibits; and that Waverley escaped some temptations to which he might otherwise have been exposed.

Meanwhile his military education proceeded. Already a good horseman, he was now initiated into the arts of the manege,[1] which, when carried to perfection, almost realize the fable of the Centaur, the guidance of the horse appearing to proceed from the rider's mere volition, rather than from the use of any external and apparent signal of motion. He received also instructions in his field of duty; but I must own, that when his first ardour was past, his progress fell short in the latter particular of what he wished and expected. The duty of an officer, the most imposing of all others to the inexperienced mind, because accompanied with so much outward pomp and circumstance, is in its essence a very dry and abstract task, depending chiefly upon arithmetical combinations, requiring much attention, and a cool and reasoning head to bring them into action. Our hero was liable to fits of absence, in which his blunders excited some mirth, and called down some reproof. This circumstance impressed

---

1   The arts of the manège: horsemanship.

him with a painful sense of inferiority in those qualities which appeared most to deserve and obtain regard in his new profession. He asked himself in vain, why his eye could not judge of distance or space so well as those of his companions; why his head was not always successful in disentangling the various partial movements necessary to execute a particular evolution; and why his memory, so alert upon most occasions, did not correctly retain technical phrases, and minute points of etiquette or field discipline. Waverley was naturally modest, and therefore did not fall into the egregious mistake of supposing such minuter rules of military duty beneath his notice, or conceiting himself to be born a general, because he made an indifferent subaltern. The truth was, that the vague and unsatisfactory course of reading which he had pursued, working upon a temper naturally retired and abstracted, had given him that wavering and unsettled habit of mind, which is most averse to study and riveted attention. Time, in the meanwhile, hung heavy on his hands. The gentry of the neighbourhood were disaffected, and showed little hospitality to the military guests; and the people of the town, chiefly engaged in mercantile pursuits, were not such as Waverley chose to associate with. The arrival of summer, and a curiosity to know something more of Scotland than he could see in a ride from his quarters, determined him to request leave of absence for a few weeks. He resolved first to visit his uncle's ancient friend and correspondent, with the purpose of extending or shortening the time of his residence according to circumstances. He travelled of course on horseback, and with a single attendant, and passed his first night at a miserable inn, where the landlady had neither shoes nor stockings, and the landlord, who called himself a gentleman, was disposed to be rude to his guest, because he had not bespoke the pleasure of his society to supper.[k] The next day, traversing an open and uninclosed country, Edward gradually approached the Highlands of Perthshire, which at first had appeared a blue outline in the horizon, but now swelled into huge gigantic masses, which frowned defiance over the more level country that lay beneath them. Near the bottom of this stupendous barrier, but still in the Lowland country, dwelt Cosmo Comyne Bradwardine of Bradwardine; and, if grey-haired eld can be in aught believed, there had dwelt his ancestors, with all their heritage, since the days of the gracious King Duncan.[1]

---

1 Duncan I (d. 1040), king of Strathclyde, and of Scotland (1034-40). Macbeth challenged his throne while Duncan was campaigning in Northumbria. He was killed in battle at Pitgaveny.

CHAPTER VIII.

A Scottish Manor-House Sixty Years since.

IT was about noon when Captain Waverley entered the straggling village, or rather hamlet, of Tully-Veolan, close to which was situated the mansion of the proprietor. The houses seemed miserable in the extreme, especially to an eye accustomed to the smiling neatness of English cottages. They stood, without any respect for regularity, on each side of a straggling kind of unpaved street, where children, almost in a primitive state of nakedness, lay sprawling, as if to be crushed by the hoofs of the first passing horse. Occasionally, indeed, when such a consummation seemed inevitable, a watchful old grandam, with her close cap, distaff, and spindle, rushed like a sibyl in frenzy out of one of these miserable cells, dashed into the middle of the path, and snatching up her own charge from among the sun-burnt loiterers, saluted him with a sound cuff, and transported him back to his dungeon, the little white-headed varlet screaming all the while from the very top of his lungs, a shrilly treble to the growling remonstrances of the enraged matron. Another part in this concert was sustained by the incessant yelping of a score of idle useless curs, which followed, snarling, barking, howling, and snapping at the horses' heels; a nuisance at that time so common in Scotland, that a French tourist, who, like other travellers, longed to find a good and rational reason for every thing he saw, has recorded, as one of the memorabilia of Caledonia, that the state maintained in each village a relay of curs, called *collies*, whose duty it was to chase the *chevaux de poste*[1] (too starved and exhausted to move without such a stimulus) from one hamlet to another, till their annoying convoy drove them to the end of their stage. The evil and remedy (such as it is) still exist: but this is remote from our present purpose, and is only thrown out for consideration of the collectors under Mr Dent's dog-bill.[2]

As Waverley moved on, here and there an old man, bent as much by toil as years, his eyes bleared with age and smoke, tottered to the door of his hut, to gaze on the dress of the stranger and the form and motions of the horses, and then assembled, with his neighbours, in a little group at the smithy, to discuss the probabilities of whence the stranger came, and where he might be going. Three of four village girls, returning from the well or brook with pitchers and pails upon

---

1 Stagecoach horses used to transport the mail.
2 "An allusion to a dog-tax Act of 1796. Mr. John Dent was M.P. for Lancaster 1790-1800" (*PW*, 576). One section of the bill, according to Lamont, was "much criticized [because it] exempted the lower classes from paying the tax" (*OW*, 417).

their heads, formed more pleasing objects, and, with their thin short-gowns and single petticoats, bare arms, legs, and feet, uncovered heads and braided hair, somewhat resembled Italian forms of landscapes. Nor could a lover of the picturesque have challenged either the elegance of their costume, or the symmetry of their shape; although, to say the truth, a mere Englishman, in search of the *comfortable*, a word peculiar to his native tongue, might have wished the clothes less scanty, the feet and legs somewhat protected from the weather, the head and complexion shrouded from the sun, or perhaps might even have thought the whole person and dress considerably improved, by a plentiful application of spring water, with a *quantum sufficit* of soap. The whole scene was depressing; for it argued, at the first glance, at least a stagnation of industry, and perhaps of intellect. Even curiosity, the busiest passion of the idle, seemed of a listless cast in the village of Tully-Veolan: the curs aforesaid alone showed any part of its activity; with the villagers it was passive. They stood and gazed at the handsome young officer and his attendant, but without any of those quick motions and eager looks, that indicate the earnestness with which those who live in monotonous ease at home, look out for amusement abroad. Yet the physiognomy of the people, when more closely examined, was far from exhibiting the indifference of stupidity; their features were rough, but remarkably intelligent; grave, but the very reverse of stupid; and from among the young women, an artist might have chosen more than one model, whose features and form resembled those of Minerva.[1] The children also, whose skins were burnt black, and whose hair was bleached white, by the influence of the sun, had a look and manner of life and interest. It seemed, upon the whole, as if poverty, and indolence, its too frequent companion, were combining to depress the natural genius and acquired information of a hardy, intelligent, and reflecting peasantry.

Some such thoughts crossed Waverley's mind as he paced his horse slowly through the rugged and flinty street of Tully-Veolan, interrupted only in his meditations by the occasional caprioles which his charger exhibited at the reiterated assaults of those canine Cossacks, the *collies* before mentioned. The village was more than half a mile long, the cottages being irregularly divided from each other by gardens, or yards, as the inhabitants called them, of different sizes, where (for it is Sixty Years since) the now universal potatoe was unknown, but which were stored with gigantic plants of *kale* or cole-wort, encircled with groves of nettles, and exhibited here and there a huge hemlock, or the national thistle, overshadowing a quarter of the petty inclosure. The broken ground on which the village was built had

---

1 Roman goddess of handicrafts, professions, arts, and later, war. Minerva was also the Goddess of wisdom.

never been levelled; so that these inclosures presented declivities of every degree, here rising like terraces, there sinking like tan-pits. The dry-stone walls which fenced, or seemed to fence (for they were sorely breached), these hanging gardens of Tully-Veolan, were intersected by a narrow lane leading to the common field, where the joint labour of the villagers cultivated alternate ridges and patches of rye, oats, barley, and pease, each of such minute extent, that at a little distance the unprofitable variety of the surface resembled a tailor's book of patterns. In a few favoured instances, there appeared behind the cottages a miserable wigwam, compiled of earth, loose stones, and turf, where the wealthy might perhaps shelter a starved cow or sorely gailed horse. But almost every hut was fenced in front by a huge black stack of turf on one side of the door, while on the other the family dunghill ascended in noble emulation.

About a bowshot from the end of the village appeared the inclosures, proudly denominated the Parks of Tully-Veolan, being certain square fields, surrounded and divided by stone walls five feet in height. In the centre of the exterior barrier was the upper gate of the avenue, opening under an archway, battlemented on the top, and adorned with two large weather-beaten mutilated masses of upright stone, which, if the tradition of the hamlet could be trusted, had once represented, at least had been once designed to represent, two rampant Bears, the supporters of the family of Bradwardine. This avenue was straight, and of moderate length, running between a double row of very ancient horse-chestnuts, planted alternately with sycamores, which rose to such huge height, and flourished so luxuriantly, that their boughs completely over-arched the broad road beneath. Beyond these venerable ranks, and running parallel to them, were two high walls, of apparently the like antiquity, overgrown with ivy, honey-suckle, and other climbing plants. The avenue seemed very little trodden, and chiefly by foot-passengers; so that being very broad, and enjoying a constant shade, it was clothed with grass of a deep and rich verdure, excepting where a foot-path, worn by occasional passengers, tracked with a natural sweep the way from the upper to the lower gate. This nether portal, like the former, opened in front of a wall ornamented with some rude sculpture, with battlements on the top, over which were seen, half-hidden by the trees of the avenue, the high steep roofs and narrow gables of the mansion, with lines indented into steps, and corners decorated with small turrets. One of the folding leaves of the lower gate was open, and as the sun shone full into the court behind, a long line of brilliancy was flung upon the aperture up the dark and gloomy avenue. It was one of those effects which a painter loves to represent, and mingled well with the struggling light which found its way between the boughs of the shady arch that vaulted the broad green alley.

The solitude and repose of the whole scene seemed almost monastic; and Waverley, who had given his horse to his servant on entering the first gate, walked slowly down the avenue, enjoying the grateful and cooling shade, and so much pleased with the placid ideas of rest and seclusion excited by this confined and quiet scene, that he forgot the misery and dirt of the hamlet he had left behind him. The opening into the paved court-yard corresponded with the rest of the scene. The house, which seemed to consist of two or three high, narrow, and steep-roofed buildings, projecting from each other at right angles, formed one side of the inclosure. It had been built at a period when castles were no longer necessary, and when the Scottish architects had not yet acquired the art of designing a domestic residence. The windows were numberless, but very small; the roof had some nondescript kind of projections, called bartizans, and displayed at each frequent angle a small turret, rather resembling a pepper-box than a Gothic watch-tower. Neither did the front indicate absolute security from danger. There were loop-holes for musketry, and iron stancheons on the lower windows, probably to repel any roving band of gipsies, or resist a predatory visit from the Caterans of the neighbouring Highlands.[1] Stables and other offices occupied another side of the square. The former were low vaults, with narrow slits instead of windows, resembling, as Edward's groom observed, "rather a prison for murderers, and larceners, and such like as are tried at 'sizes,[2] than a place for any Christian cattle." Above these dungeon-looking stables were granaries, called girnels, and other offices, to which there was access by outside stairs of heavy masonry. Two battlemented walls, one of which faced the avenue, and the other divided the court from the garden, completed the enclosure.

Nor was the court without its ornaments. In one corner was a tun-bellied pigeon-house, of great size and rotundity, resembling in figure and proportion the curious edifice called Arthur's Oven,[3] which would have turned the brains of all the antiquaries in England, had not the worthy proprietor pulled it down for the sake of mending a neighbouring dam-dyke. This dovecot, or *columbarium*,[4] as the owner called

---

1 "Common people of the Highlands in a troop or band, fighting men.... One of a Highland band; a Highland irregular fighting man, reiver, or marauder" (*OED*).

2 I.e., assizes: "The sessions held periodically in each county of England [and Ireland and Scotland], for the purpose of administering civil and criminal justice, by judges acting under certain special commissions...." (*OED*).

3 "A Roman shrine on the river Carron just north of Falkirk. It was pulled down by the owner, Sir Michael Bruce, in 1743, to furnish material for repairing a mill-dam," according to Lamont (*OW*, 417).

4 "Pigeonhole; niche in a sepulcher" (*LED*).

it, was no small resource to a Scottish laird of that period, whose scanty rents were eked out by the contributions levied upon the farms by these light foragers, and the conscriptions exacted from the latter for the benefit of the table.

Another corner of the court displayed a fountain, where a huge bear, carved in stone, predominated over a large stone-basin, into which he disgorged the water. This work of art was the wonder of the country ten miles round. It must not be forgotten, that all sorts of bears, small and large, demi or in full proportion, were carved over the windows, upon the ends of the gables, terminated the spouts, and supported the turrets, with the ancient family motto, "𝔅𝔢𝔴𝔞𝔯 𝔱𝔥𝔢 𝔅𝔞𝔯," cut under each hyperborean form. The court was spacious, well paved, and perfectly clean, there being probably another entrance behind the stables for removing the litter. Every thing around appeared solitary, and would have been silent, but for the continued plashing of the fountain; and the whole scene still maintained the monastic illusion which the fancy of Waverley had conjured up.—And here we beg permission to close a chapter of still life.[1]

CHAPTER IX.
More of the Manor-House and its Environs.

AFTER having satisfied his curiosity by gazing around him for a few minutes, Waverley applied himself to the massive knocker of the hall-door, the architrave of which bore the date 1594. But no answer was returned, though the peal resounded through a number of apartments, and was echoed from the court-yard walls without the house, startling the pigeons from the venerable rotunda which they occupied, and alarming anew even the distant village curs, which had retired to sleep upon their respective dunghills. Tired of the din which he created, and the unprofitable responses which it excited, Waverley began to think that he had reached the castle of Orgoglio, as entered by the victorious Prince Arthur,[1]

> When 'gan he loudly through the house to call,
> But no man cared to answer to his cry;
> There reign'd a solemn silence over all,
> Nor voice was heard, nor wight was seen in bower or hall.

Filled almost with expectation of beholding some "old, old man, with beard as white as snow," whom he might question concerning

---

1 Spenser's *Faerie Queene* (Book 1, canto viii, stanzas 29 and 30).

this deserted mansion, our hero turned to a little oaken wicket-door, well clenched with iron-nails, which opened in the court-yard wall at its angle with the house. It was only latched, notwithstanding its fortified appearance, and, when opened, admitted him into the garden, which presented a pleasant scene.[m] The southern side of the house, clothed with fruit-trees, and having many evergreens trained upon its walls, extended its irregular yet venerable front, along a terrace, partly paved, partly gravelled, partly bordered with flowers and choice shrubs. This elevation descended by three several flights of steps, placed in its centre and at the extremities, into what might be called the garden proper, and was fenced along the top by a stone parapet with a heavy balustrade, ornamented from space to space with huge grotesque figures of animals seated upon their haunches, among which the favourite bear was repeatedly introduced. Placed in the middle of the terrace, between a sashed-door opening from the house and the central flight of steps, a huge animal of the same species supported on his head and fore-paws a sun-dial of large circumference, inscribed with more diagrams than Edward's mathematics enabled him to decipher.

The garden, which seemed to be kept with great accuracy, abounded in fruit-trees, and exhibited a profusion of flowers and evergreens, cut into grotesque forms. It was laid out in terraces, which descended rank by rank from the western wall to a large brook, which had a tranquil and smooth appearance, where it served as a boundary to the garden; but, near the extremity, leapt in tumult over a strong dam, or wear-head, the cause of its temporary tranquility, and there forming a cascade, was overlooked by an octangular summer-house, with a gilded bear on the top by way of vane. After this feat, the brook, assuming its natural rapid and fierce character, escaped from the eye down a deep and wooded dell, from the copse of which arose a massive, but ruinous tower, the former habitation of the Barons of Bradwardine. The margin of the brook, opposite to the garden, displayed a narrow meadow, or haugh, as it was called, which formed a small washing-green; the bank, which retired behind it, was covered by ancient trees.

The scene, though pleasing, was not quite equal to the gardens of Alcina;[1] yet wanted not the "*due donzelette garrule*"[2] of that enchanted paradise, for upon the green aforesaid two bare-legged damsels, each standing in a spacious tub, performed with their feet the office of a patent washing-machine. These did not, however, like the maidens of

---

1   "Alcina, a witch in Ariosto's *Orlando Furioso* and *Orlando Innamorato*, had an enchanted garden" (*PW*, 576).

2   Two talkative maidens (*PW*, 576).

Armida,[1] remain to greet with their harmony the approaching guest, but, alarmed at the appearance of a handsome stranger on the opposite side, dropped their garments (I should say garment, to be quite correct) over their limbs, which their occupation exposed somewhat too freely, and, with a shrill exclamation of "Eh, sirs!" uttered with an accent between modesty and coquetry, sprung off like deer in different directions.

Waverley began to despair of gaining entrance into this solitary and seemingly enchanted mansion, when a man advanced up one of the garden alleys, where he still retained his station. Trusting this might be a gardener, or some domestic belonging to the house, Edward descended the steps in order to meet him; but as the figure approached, and long before he could descry its features, he was struck with the oddity of its appearance and gestures. Sometimes this mister wight held his hands clasped over his head, like an Indian Jogue[2] in the attitude of penance; sometimes he swung them perpendicularly, like a pendulum, on each side; and anon he slapped them swiftly and repeatedly across his breast, like the substitute used by a hackney-coachman for his usual flogging exercise, when his cattle are idle upon the stand, in a clear frosty day. His gait was as singular as his gestures, for at times he hopp'd with great perseverance on the right foot, then exchanged that supporter to advance in the same manner on the left, and then putting his feet close together, he hopp'd upon both at once. His attire also was antiquated and extravagant. It consisted in a sort of grey jerkin, with scarlet cuffs and slash'd sleeves, showing a scarlet lining; the other parts of the dress corresponded in colour, not forgetting a pair of scarlet stockings, and a scarlet bonnet, proudly surmounted with a turkey's feather. Edward, whom he did not seem to observe, now perceived confirmation in his features of what the mien and gestures had already announced. It was apparently neither idiocy nor insanity which gave that wild unsettled, irregular expression to a face which naturally was rather handsome, but something that resembled a compound of both, where the simplicity of the fool was mixed with the extravagance of a crazed imagination. He sung with great earnestness, and not without some taste, a fragment of an old Scottish ditty:[n]

> False love, and hast thou play'd me this
>   In summer among the flowers?
> I will repay thee back again
>   In winter among the showers.

---

1 "Armida, in Tasso's *Gerusalemme liberata*, lures her victims into a delicious garden where they are overcome by indolence" (*PW*, 576).

2 "An Indian devotee or ascetic who practices the system of Yoga" (*OED*).

Unless again, again, my love,
  Unless you turn again;
As you with other maidens rove,
  I'll smile on other men.[1]

Here lifting up his eyes, which had hitherto been fixed in observing how his feet kept time to the tune, he beheld Waverley, and instantly doff'd his cap, with many grotesque signals of surprise, respect, and salutation. Edward, though with little hope of receiving an answer to any constant question, requested to know whether Mr Bradwardine were at home, or where he could find any of the domestics. The questioned party replied,—and, like the witch of Thalaba,[2] "still his speech was song,"—

The Knight's to the mountain
  His bugle to wind;
The Lady's to greenwood
  Her garland to bind.
The bower of Burd Ellen
  Has moss on the floor,
That the step of Lord William
  Be silent and sure.

This conveyed no information, and Edward, repeating his queries, received a rapid answer, in which, from the haste and peculiarity of the dialect, the word "butler" was alone intelligible. Waverley then requested to see the butler; upon which the fellow, with a knowing look and nod of intelligence, made a signal to Edward to follow, and began to dance and caper down the alley up which he had made his approaches.—A strange guide this, thought Edward, and not much unlike one of Shakspeare's roynish clowns. I am not over prudent to trust to his pilotage; but wiser men have been led by fools.—By this time he reached the bottom of the alley, where, turning short on a little parterre of flowers, shrouded from the east and north by a close yew hedge, he found an old man at work without his coat, whose appearance hovered between that of an upper servant and gardener; his red nose and ruffled shirt belonging to the former profession; his hale and sun-burnt visage, with his green apron, appearing to indicate

Old Adam's likeness, set to dress this garden.[3]

---

1 See David Herd, *Ancient and Modern Scottish Songs* (1776), II, p. 6.
2 In Robert Southey's *Thalaba the Destroyer* (1801), Book VIII, stanza 26.
3 *Richard II*, III.v.73.

The major domo, for such he was, and indisputably the second officer of state in the barony (nay, as chief minister of the interior, superior even to Bailie Macwheeble, in his own department of the kitchen and cellar),—the major domo laid down his spade, slipped on his coat in haste, and with a wrathful look at Edward's guide, probably excited by his having introduced a stranger while he was engaged in this laborious, and, as he might suppose it, degrading office, requested to know the gentleman's commands. Being informed that he wished to pay his respects to his master, that his name was Waverley, and so forth, the old man's countenance assumed a great deal of respectful importance. "He could take it upon his conscience to say, his honour would have exceeding pleasure in seeing him. Would not Mr Waverley choose some refreshment after his journey? His honour was with the folk who were getting doon the dark hag; the twa gardener lads (an emphasis on the word *twa*) had been ordered to attend him; and he had been just amusing himself in the mean time with dressing Miss Rose's flower-bed, that he might be near to receive his honour's orders, if need were: he was very fond of a garden, but had little time for such divertisements."

"He canna get it wrought in abune twa days in the week at no rate whatever," said Edward's fantastic conductor.

A grim look from the butler chastised his interference, and he commanded him, by the name of Davie Gellatley, in a tone which admitted no discussion, to look for his honour at the dark hag, and tell him there was a gentleman from the south had arrived at the Ha'.[1]

"Can this poor fellow deliver a letter?" asked Edward.

"With all fidelity, sir, to any one whom he respects. I would hardly trust him with a long message by word of mouth—though he is more knave than fool."

Waverley delivered his credentials to Mr Gellatley, who seemed to confirm the butler's last observation, by twisting his features at him, when he was looking another way, into the resemblance of the grotesque face on the bole of a German tobacco-pipe; after which, with an odd congé to Waverley, he danced off to discharge his errand.

"He is an innocent, sir," said the butler; "there is one such in almost every town in the country, but ours is brought far ben. He used to work a day's turn weel eneugh; but he help'd Miss Rose when she was flemit[2] with the Laird of Killancureit's new English bull, and since that time we ca' him Davie Do-little; indeed we might ca' him Davie Do-naething, for since he got that gay clothing, to please his honour and my young mistress (great folks will have their fancies), he has done

---

1 Hall (*WSG*).
2 Frightened (*WSG*).

naething but dance up and down about the *toun*, without doing a single turn, unless trimming the laird's fishing-wand or busking his flies, or may be catching a dish of trouts at an orra-time.[1] But here comes Miss Rose, who, I take burden upon me for her, will be especial glad to see one of the house of Waverley at her father's mansion of Tully-Veolan."

But Rose Bradwardine deserves better of her unworthy historian, than to be introduced at the end of a chapter.

In the meanwhile it may be noticed, that Waverley learned two things from this colloquy; that in Scotland a single house was called a *town*, and a natural fool an *innocent*.°

CHAPTER X.
Rose Bradwardine and her Father.

MISS Bradwardine was but seventeen; yet, at the last races of the county town of —, upon her health being proposed among a round of beauties, the Laird of Bumperquaigh, permanent toast-master and croupier of the Bautherwhillery Club, not only said *More* to the pledge in a pint bumper of Bourdeaux, but, ere pouring forth the libation, denominated the divinity to whom it was dedicated, "the Rose of Tully-Veolan"; upon which festive occasion, three cheers were given by all the sitting members of that respectable society, whose throats the wine had left capable of such exertion. Nay, I am well assured, that the sleeping partners of the company snorted applause, and that although strong bumpers and weak brains had consigned two or three to the floor, yet even these, fallen as they were from their high estate, and weltering—I will carry the parody no farther—uttered divers inarticulate sounds, intimating their assent to the motion.

Such unanimous applause could not be extorted but by acknowledged merit; and Rose Bradwardine not only deserved it, but also the approbation of much more rational persons than the Bautherwhillery Club could have mustered, even before discussion of the first *magnum*. She was indeed a very pretty girl of the Scotch cast of beauty, that is, with a profusion of hair of paley gold, and a skin like the snow of her own mountains in whiteness. Yet she had not a pallid or pensive cast of countenance; her features, as well as her temper, had a lively expression; her complexion, though not florid, was so pure as to seem transparent, and the slightest emotion sent her whole blood at once to her face and neck. Her form, though under the common size, was remarkably elegant, and her motions light, easy, and unembarrassed. She came from another part of the garden to receive Captain Waverley, with a manner that hovered between bashfulness and courtesy.

---

1 Time that "may be spared" (*WSG*).

The first greetings past, Edward learned from her that the *dark hag*, which had somewhat puzzled him in the butler's account of his master's avocations, had nothing to do either with a black cat or a broomstick, but was simply a portion of oak copse which was to be felled that day. She offered, with diffident civility, to show the stranger the way to the spot, which, it seems, was not far distant; but they were prevented by the appearance of the Baron of Bradwardine in person, who, summoned by David Gellatley, now appeared, "on hospitable thoughts intent," clearing the ground at a prodigious rate with swift and long strides, which reminded Waverley of the seven-league boots of the nursery fable.[1] He was a tall, thin, athletic figure, old indeed and grey-haired, but with every muscle rendered as tough as whip-cord by constant exercise. He was dressed carelessly, and more like a Frenchman than an Englishman of the period, while, from his hard features and perpendicular rigidity of stature, he bore some resemblance to a Swiss officer of the guards, who had resided some time at Paris, and caught the *costume*, but not the ease or manner, of its inhabitants. The truth was, that his language and habits were as heterogeneous as his external appearance.

Owing to his natural disposition to study, or perhaps to a very general Scottish fashion of giving young men of rank a legal education, he had been bred with a view to the bar. But the politics of his family precluding the hope of his rising in that profession, Mr Bradwardine travelled with high reputation for several years, and made some campaigns in foreign service. After his démêlée with the law of high treason in 1715,[2] he had lived in retirement, conversing almost entirely with those of his own principles in the vicinage. The pedantry of the lawyer, superinduced upon the military pride of the soldier, might remind a modern of the days of the zealous volunteer service, when the bar-gown of our pleaders was often flung over a blazing uniform. To this must be added the prejudices of ancient birth and Jacobite politics, greatly strengthened by habits of solitary and secluded authority,

---

1 The wearer of such boots can cover seven leagues in a stride. In "Sleeping Beauty," the dwarf's seven-league boots help him to quickly cover the distance between Sleeping Beauty's castle and the home of the good Fairy when Sleeping Beauty pricks her finger; in "Little Poucet," the ogre who kills his seven daughters thinking they are seven male visitors also has a pair of seven-league boots (Peter and Iona Opie, *The Classic Fairy Tales* [Oxford UP, 1974], pp. 86, 135).

2 His contest with the law of high treason: "a crime against the state which meant, in practice, against the monarch" (*OCBH*, 930). Punishment was hanging, and until 1814, cutting down the traitor while still alive and disemboweling him, and then quartering and beheading him.

which, though exercised only within the bounds of his half-cultivated estate, was there indisputable and undisputed. For, as he used to observe, "the lands of Bradwardine, Tully-Veolan, and others, had been erected into a free barony by a charter from David the First, *cum liberali potest. habendi curias et justicias, cum fossa et furca* (LIE pit and gallows) *et saka et soka, et thol et theam, et infang-thief et outfang-thief, sive hand-habend. sive bak-barand.*" The peculiar meaning of all these cabalistical words few or none could explain; but they implied, upon the whole, that the Baron of Bradwardine might, in case of delinquency, imprison, try, and execute his vassals at his pleasure. Like James the First, however, the present possessor of this authority was more pleased in talking about prerogative than in exercising it; and excepting that he imprisoned two poachers in the dungeon of the old tower of Tully-Veolan, where they were sorely frightened by ghosts, and almost eaten by rats, and that he set an old woman in the *jougs* (or Scottish pillory)[1] for saying "there were mair fules in the laird's ha' house than Davie Gellatley," I do not learn that he was accused of abusing his high powers. Still, however, the conscious pride of possessing them gave additional importance to his language and deportment.

At his first address to Waverley, it would seem that the hearty pleasure he felt to behold the nephew of his friend had somewhat discomposed the stiff and upright dignity of the Baron of Bradwardine's demeanor, for the tears stood in the old gentleman's eyes, when, having first shaken Edward heartily by the hand in the English fashion, he embraced him *a-la-mode Françoise*, and kissed him on both sides of his face; while the hardness of his gripe, and the quantity of Scotch snuff which his *accolade* communicated, called corresponding drops of moisture to the eyes of his guest.

"Upon the honour of a gentleman," he said, "but it makes me young again to see you here, Mr Waverley! A worthy scion of the old stock of Waverley-Honour—*spes altera*, as Maro[2] hath it—and you have the look of the old line, Captain Waverley; not so portly yet as my old friend Sir Everard—*mais cela viendra avec le tems*, as my Dutch acquaintance, Baron Kikkitbroeck, said of the *sagesse* of *Madame son epouse.*[3]—And so ye have mounted the cockade? Right, right; though I could have wished

---

1   "A contrivance for the punishment of offenders, consisting usually of a wooden framework erected on a post or pillar, and formed like the stocks, of two movable boards which, when brought together at their edges, leave holes through which the head and hands of an offender were thrust, in which state he was exposed to public ridicule, insult, and molestation" (*OED*). Abolished in Great Britain in 1837.

2   "'Another hope,' as Virgil puts it" (*PW*, 577)

3   But that comes with time, as my Dutch acquaintance, Baron Kikkitbroeck, said of the wisdom of Madam, his wife.

the colour different, and so I would ha' deemed might Sir Everard. But no more of that; I am old, and times are changed.—And how does the worthy knight baronet, and the fair Mrs Rachel?—Ah, ye laugh, young man! In troth she was the fair Mrs Rachel in the year of grace seventeen hundred and sixteen; but time passes—*et singula prædantur anni*[1]—that is most certain. But once again ye are most heartily welcome to my poor house of Tully-Veolan!—Hie to the house, Rose, and see that Alexander Saunderson looks out the old Chateau Margoux, which I sent from Bourdeaux to Dundee in the year 1713."

Rose tripped off demurely enough till she turned the first corner, and then ran with the speed of a fairy, that she might gain leisure, after discharging her father's commission, to put her own dress in order, and produce all her little finery, an occupation for which the approaching dinner-hour left but limited time.

"We cannot rival the luxuries of your English table, Captain Waverley, or give you the *epulæ lautiores*[2] of Waverley-Honour—I say *epulæ* rather than *prandium*,[3] because the latter phrase is popular; *Epulæ ad senatum, prandium vero ad populum attinet*, says Suetonius Tranquillus.[4] But I trust ye will applaud my Bourdeaux; *c'est des deux oreilles*,[5] as Captain Vinsauf used to say—*Vinum primæ notæ*,[6] the Principal of St Andrews denominated it. And, once more, Captain Waverley, right glad am I that ye are here to drink the best my cellar can make forthcoming."

This speech, with the necessary interjectional answers, continued from the lower alley where they met, up to the door of the house, where four or five servants in old-fashioned liveries, headed by Alexander Saunderson, the butler, who now bore no token of the sable stains of the garden, received them in grand *costume*,

> In an old hall hung round with pikes and with bows,
> With old bucklers and corslets that had borne many shrewd
> blows.[7]

---

1 "The years rob us of our joys, one by one" (Horace, *Epistles* II, ii, 55) (*PW*, 577).

2 "Complimentary feasts" (*PW*, 577).

3 Meal.

4 "Feasts for the senate, but an ordinary meal is more suitable for the people"—Suetonius Tranquilus (75-150 CE), Roman historian (*PW*, 577).

5 Hook and Lamont both note that the phrase should have been "vin d'une oreille."

6 An excellent wine.

7 Hook suggests this may be Scott's work (*PW*, 577); Lamont says it belongs to "a song about a courtier of Queen Elizabeth who survived into the reign of James I": "Of an Old Courtier and a New," in Joseph Ritson's *A Select Collection of English Songs* (1783), II, p. 140 (*OW*, 419).

With much ceremony, and still more real kindness, the Baron, without stopping in any intermediate apartment, conducted his guest through several into the great dining parlour, wainscotted with black oak, and hung round with the pictures of his ancestry, where a table was set forth in form for six persons, and an old-fashioned beaufet displayed all the ancient and massive plate of the Bradwardine family. A bell was now heard at the head of the avenue; for an old man, who acted as porter upon gala days, had caught the alarm given by Waverley's arrival, and, repairing to his post, announced the arrival of other guests.

These, as the Baron assured his young friend, were very estimable persons. "There was the young Laird of Balmawhapple, a Falconer by surname, of the house of Glenfarquhar, given right much to field-sports—*gaudet equis et canibus*[1]—but a very discreet young gentleman. Then there was the Laird of Killancureit, who had devoted his leisure *untill* tillage and agriculture, and boasted himself to be possessed of a bull of matchless merit, brought from the county of Devon (the Damnonia of the Romans, if we can trust Robert of Cirencester[2]). He is, as ye may well suppose from such a tendency, but of yeoman extraction—*servabit odorem testa diu*[3]—and I believe, between ourselves, his grandsire was from the wrong side of the Border—one Bullsegg, who came hither as a steward, or bailiff, or ground-officer, or something in that department, to the last Girnigo of Killancureit, who died of an atrophy. After his master's death, sir,—ye would hardly believe such a scandal,—but this Bullsegg, being portly and comely of aspect, inter-married with the lady dowager, who was young and amorous, and pos-sessed himself of the estate, which devolved on this unhappy woman by a settlement of her umwhile husband, in direct contravention of an unrecorded taillie, and to the prejudice of the disponer's own flesh and blood, in the person of his natural heir and seventh cousin, Girnigo of Tipperhewit, whose family was so reduced by the ensuing law-suit, that his representative is now serving as a private gentleman-sentinel in the Highland Black Watch. But this gentleman, Mr Bullsegg of Kil-lancureit that now is, has good blood in his veins by the mother and grandmother, who were both of the family of Pickletillim, and he is well liked and looked upon, and knows his own place. And God forbid, Captain Waverley, that we of irreproachable lineage should

---

1 Rejoicing in horses and dogs.
2 Lamont contends "it should be Richard of Cirencester, a fourteenth-century monk and chronicler" and the work alluded to as his in the passage is a forgery, not disproved until after Scott's death (*OW*, 419).
3 "'The cask will long retain the smell' (of what was once in it)," Horace, *Epis-tles* I, ii, 69-70 (*OW*, 419).

exult over him, when it may be, that in the eighth, ninth, or tenth generation, his progeny may rank, in a manner, with the old gentry of the country. Rank and ancestry, sir, should be the last words in the mouths of us of unblemished race—*vix ea nostra voco*, as Naso[1] saith.—There is, besides, a clergyman of the true (though suffering) Episcopal church of Scotland. He was a confessor in her cause after the year 1715, when a Whiggish mob destroyed his meeting-house, tore his surplice, and plundered his dwelling-house of four silver spoons, intromitting also with his mart and his meal-ark,[2] and with two barrels, one of single, and one of double ale, besides three bottles of brandy.P My Baron-Bailie and doer, Mr Duncan Macwheeble, is the fourth on our list. There is a question, owing to the incertitude of ancient orthography, whether he belongs to the clan of Wheedle or of Quibble, but both have produced persons eminent in the law."—

> As such he described them by person and name,
> They enter'd, and dinner was served as they came.

CHAPTER XI.
The Banquet.

THE entertainment was ample, and handsome, according to the Scotch ideas of the period, and the guests did great honour to it. The Baron ate like a famished soldier, the Laird of Balmawhapple like a sportsman, Bullsegg of Killancureit like a farmer, Waverley himself like a traveller, and Bailie Macwheeble like all four together; though, either out of more respect, or in order to preserve that proper declination of person which showed a sense that he was in the presence of his patron, he sat upon the edge of his chair, placed at three feet distance from the table, and achieved a communication with his plate by projecting his person towards it in a line which obliqued from the bottom of his spine, so that the person who sat opposite to him could only see the foretop of his riding periwig.[3]

This stooping position might have been inconvenient to another person; but long habit made it, whether seated or walking, perfectly easy to the worthy Bailie. In the latter posture, it occasioned, no doubt, an unseemly projection of the person towards those who hap-

---

1 I.e., Ovid, Roman poet (43 BCE-17 CE) (*PW*, 577): "I can hardly claim them as ours" (*LED*).

2 Intromitting: "interfering with" (*OED*); "mart" concerns "the fatted cow, or whatever animal is slaughtered at Martinmas for winter provisions" (*WSG*); meal-ark: "meal-chest" (*OED*).

3 A wig or half-wig.

pened to walk behind; but those being at all times his inferiors (for Mr Macwheeble was very scrupulous in giving place to all others), he cared very little what inference of contempt or slight regard they might derive from the circumstance. Hence, when he waddled across the court to and from his old grey pony, he somewhat resembled a turnspit walking upon its hind legs.

The nonjuring clergyman was a pensive and interesting old man, with much the air of a sufferer for conscience sake. He was one of those,

> Who, undeprived, their benefice forsook.[1]

For this whim, when the Baron was out of hearing, the Bailie used sometimes gently to rally Mr Rubrick, upbraiding him with the nicety of his scruples. Indeed, it must be owned, that he himself, though at heart a keen partisan of the exiled family, had kept pretty fair with all the different turns of state in his time; so that Davie Gellatley once described him as a particularly good man, who had a very quiet and peaceful conscience, *that never did him any harm.*

When the dinner was removed, the Baron announced the health of the King, politely leaving to the consciences of his guests to drink to the sovereign *de facto* or *de jure*, as their politics inclined. The conversation now became general; and, shortly afterwards, Miss Bradwardine, who had done the honours with natural grace and simplicity, retired, and was soon followed by the clergyman. Among the rest of the party, the wine, which fully justified the encomiums of the landlord, flowed freely round, although Waverley, with some difficulty, obtained the privilege of sometimes neglecting the glass. At length, as the evening grew more late, the Baron made a private signal to Mr Saunders Saunderson, or, as he facetiously denominated him, *Alexander ab Alexandro*, who left the room with a nod, and soon after returned, his grave countenance mantling with a solemn and mysterious smile, and placed before his master a small oaken casket, mounted with brass ornaments of curious form. The Baron, drawing out a private key, unlocked the casket, raised the lid, and produced a golden goblet of a singular and antique appearance, moulded into the shape of a rampant bear, which the owner regarded with a look of mingled reverence, pride, and delight, that irresistibly reminded Waverley of Ben Jonson's Tom Otter,[2] with his Bull, Horse, and Dog, as that wag wittily denominated his chief carousing cups. But Mr Bradwardine,

---

1 From John Dryden's "The Character of a Good Parson," ln. 126.
2 In *The Silent Woman* (IV, ii) by Ben Jonson (1572-1637).

turning towards him with complacency, requested him to observe this curious relic of the olden time.

"It represents," he said, "the chosen crest of our family, a bear, as ye observe, and *rampant*; because a good herald will depict every animal in its noblest posture; as a horse *salient*,[1] a greyhound *currant*,[2] and, as may be inferred, a ravenous animal *in actu ferociori*, or in a voracious, lacerating, and devouring posture. Now, sir, we hold this most honourable achievement by the wappen-brief, or concession of arms, of Frederick Red-beard,[3] Emperor of Germany, to my predecessor, Godmund Bradwardine, it being the crest of a gigantic Dane, whom he slew in the lists in the Holy Land, on a quarrel touching the chastity of the emperor's spouse or daughter, tradition saith not precisely which, and thus, as Virgilius hath it—

Mutemus clypeos, Danaumque insignia nobis
Aptemus.[4]

Then for the cup, Captain Waverley, it was wrought by the command of St Duthac, Abbot of Aberbrothock, for behoof of another baron of the house of Bradwardine, who had valiantly defended the patrimony of that monastery against certain encroaching nobles. It is properly termed the Blessed Bear of Bradwardine, (though old Dr Doubleit used jocosely to call it Ursa Major), and was supposed, in old and Catholic times,[5] to be invested with certain properties of a mystical and supernatural quality. And though I give not in to such *anilia*,[6] it is certain it has always been esteemed a solemn standard cup and heirloom of our house; nor is it ever used but upon seasons of high festival, and such I hold to be the arrival of the heir of Sir Everard under my roof; and I devote this draught to the health and prosperity of the ancient and highly-to-be-honoured house of Waverley."

During this long harangue, he carefully decanted a cobwebbed bottle of claret into the goblet, which held nearly an English pint; and, at the conclusion, delivering the bottle to the butler, to be held carefully in the same angle with the horizon, he devoutly quaffed off the contents of the Blessed Bear of Bradwardine.

Edward, with horror and alarm, beheld the animal making his

---

1 Leaping, jumping (*OED*).
2 Running, flowing (*OED*).
3 Frederick Red-beard or Barbarossa (1152-89).
4 Virgil, *Aeneid*, II, 389-90.
5 Catholicism was the state religion until Henry VIII embraced Protestantism and denied the authority of the Pope in 1536.
6 Old wives' tales.

rounds, and thought with great anxiety upon the appropriate motto, "Beware the Bear"; but, at the same time, plainly foresaw, that, as none of the guests scrupled to do him this extraordinary honour, a refusal on his part to pledge their courtesy would be extremely ill received. Resolving, therefore, to submit to this last piece of tyranny, and then to quit the table, if possible, and confiding in the strength of his constitution, he did justice to the company in the contents of the Blessed Bear, and felt less inconvenience from the draught than he could possibly have expected. The others, whose time had been more actively employed, began to show symptoms of innovation,—"the good wine did its good office."q The frost of etiquette, and pride of birth, began to give way before the genial blessings of this benign constellation, and the formal appellatives with which the three dignitaries had hitherto addressed each other, were now familiarly abbreviated into Tully, Bally, and Killie. When a few rounds had passed, the two latter, after whispering together, craved permission (a joyful hearing for Edward) to ask the grace-cup.[1] This, after some delay, was at length produced, and Waverley concluded the orgies of Bacchus[2] were terminated for the evening. He was never more mistaken in his life.

As the guests had left their horses at the small inn, or *change-house*, as it was called, of the village, the Baron could not, in politeness, avoid walking with them up the avenue, and Waverley, from the same motive, and to enjoy, after this feverish revel, the cool summer evening, attended the party. But when they arrived at Luckie Macleary's the Lairds of Balmawhapple and Killancureit declared their determination to acknowledge their sense of the hospitality of Tully-Veolan, by partaking, with their entertainer and his guest Captain Waverley, what they technically called *deoch an doruis*, a stirrup-cup,[3] to the honour of the Baron's roof-tree.r

It must be noticed, that the Bailie, knowing by experience that the day's jovialty, which had been hitherto sustained at the expense of his patron, might terminate partly at his own, had mounted his spavined grey pony, and, between gaiety of heart, and alarm for being hooked into a reckoning, spurred him into a hobbling canter (a trot was out of the question), and had already cleared the village. The others entered the change-house, leading Edward in unresisting submission; for his landlord whispered him, that to demur to such an overture would be construed into a high misdemeanour against the *leges conviviales*, or regulations of genial compotation. Widow Macleary seemed to have

---

1 "The last cup of liquor drunk before retiring, a parting draught" (*OED*).

2 Bacchus was the Roman god of intoxication and licentiousness.

3 "A cup of wine or other drink handed to a man when already on horseback setting out for a journey; a parting glass" (*OED*).

expected this visit, as well she might, for it was the usual consummation of merry bouts, not only at Tully-Veolan, but at most other gentlemen's houses in Scotland, Sixty Years since. The guests thereby at once acquitted themselves of their burden of gratitude for their entertainer's kindness, encouraged the trade of his change-house, did honour to the place which afforded harbour to their horses, and indemnified themselves for the previous restraints imposed by private hospitality, by spending, what Falstaff calls the sweet of the night, in the genial license of a tavern.

Accordingly, in full expectation of these distinguished guests, Luckie Macleary had swept her house for the first time this fortnight, tempered her turf-fire to such a heat as the season required in her damp hovel even at Midsummer, set forth her deal table newly washed, propped its lame foot with a fragment of turf, arranged four or five stools of huge and clumsy form upon the sites which best suited the inequalities of her clay floor; and having, moreover, put on her clean toy, rokelay,[1] and scarlet plaid, gravely awaited the arrival of the company, in full hope of custom and profit. When they were seated under the sooty rafters of Luckie Macleary's only apartment, thickly tapestried with cobwebs, their hostess, who had already taken her cue from the Laird of Balmawhapple, appeared with a huge pewter measuring-pot, containing at least three English quarts, familiarly denominated *a Tappit Hen*, and which, in the language of the hostess, reamed (*i.e.*, mantled) with excellent claret just drawn from the cask.

It was soon plain that what crumbs of reason the Bear had not devoured, were to be picked up by the Hen; but the confusion which appeared to prevail favoured Edward's resolution to evade the gaily circling glass. The others began to talk thick and at once, each performing his own part in the conversation, without the least respect to his neighbour. The Baron of Bradwardine sung French *chansons-à-boire*,[2] and spouted pieces of Latin; Killancureit talked, in a steady unalterable dull key, of top-dressing and bottom-dressing,[s] and year-olds, and gimmers, and dinmonts, and stots, and runts, and kyloes,[3] and a proposed turnpike-act;[4] while Balmawhapple, in notes exalted above both,

---

1 Toy: "a close cap or head-dress, of linen or wool, with flaps coming down to the shoulders, formerly worn by women of the lower classes in Scotland" (*OED*); rokelay: "a short cloak worn by women in the eighteenth century" (*OED*).

2 Drinking songs.

3 Year olds are one-year-old sheep; dinmonts are "wethers between one and two years old, or that have not yet been shorn" (*WSG*); gimmers are two-year-old ewes (*WSG*); a stot is a "bullock between two and three years old" (*WSG*); a runt is "an old cow; also the stalk of a colewort or cabbage" (*WSG*); kyloes are Highland cattle (*WSG*).

4 "A private act of parliament authorizing a turnpike or toll road" (*PW*, 578).

extolled his horse, his hawks, and a greyhound called Whistler. In the middle of this din, the Baron repeatedly implored silence; and when at length the instinct of polite discipline so far prevailed, that for a moment he obtained it, he hastened to beseech their attention "unto a military ariette, which was a particular favourite of the Marechal Duc de Berwick";[1] then, imitating, as well as he could, the manner and tone of a French musquetaire, he immediately commenced,—

> Mon coeur volage,[2] dit elle,
>   N'est pas pour vous, garçon;
> Est pour un homme de guerre,
>   Qui a barbe au menton.
>   Lon, Lon, Laridon.
>
> Qui port chapeau à plume,
>   Soulier à rouge talon,
> Qui joue de la flute,
>   Aussi de violon.
>   Lon, Lon, Laridon.

Balmawhapple could hold no longer, but broke in with what he called a d—d good song, composed by Gibby Gaethroughwi't, the piper of Cupar; and, without wasting more time, struck up,—

> It's up Glenbarchan's braes I gaed,
> And o'er the bent of Killiebraid,
> And mony a weary cast I made,
> To cuittle the moor-fowl's tail.[3]

The Baron, whose voice was drowned in the louder and more obstreperous strains of Balmawhapple, now dropped the competition, but continued to hum, Lon, Lon, Laridon, and to regard the successful candidate for the attention of the company with an eye of disdain, while Balmawhapple proceeded,—

---

1 James Fitzjames (1670-1734) was the illegitimate son of James II and VII and Arabella Churchill, sister of the Duke of Marlborough; he was a soldier, marshal in the French army (*PW*, 578).

2 "Old French chanson accommodated," writes Scott (*OW*, 420).

3 Andrew Macdonald (c. 1755-88), author of this ballad, according to Scott's note, was a Scottish Episcopalian clergyman. His *Vimonda* was staged but did not keep him from dying in poverty. "Bent" is "a kind of grass, metaphorically the hill or the moor"; "cast" is "got over; recovered from lot; fate" (*WSG*); "cuittle" is "tickle" (*WSG*).

If up a bonny black-cock should spring,
To whistle him down wi' a slug in his wing,
And strap him on to my lunzie string,[1]
    Right seldom would I fail.

After an ineffectual attempt to recover the second verse, he sung the first over again; and, in prosecution of his triumph, declared there was "more sense in that than in all the *derry-dongs* of France, and Fifeshire to the boot of it." The Baron only answered with a long pinch of snuff, and a glance of infinite contempt. But those noble allies, the Bear and the Hen, had emancipated the young laird from the habitual reverence in which he held Bradwardine at other times. He pronounced the claret *shilpit*,[2] and demanded brandy with great vociferation. It was brought; and now the Demon of Politics envied even the harmony arising from this Dutch concert, merely because there was not a wrathful note in the strange compound of sounds which it produced. Inspired by her, the Laird of Balmawhapple, now superior to the nods and winks with which the Baron of Bradwardine, in delicacy to Edward, had hitherto checked his entering upon political discussion, demanded a bumper, with the lungs of a Stentor,[3] "to the little gentleman in black velvet who did such service in 1702, and may the white horse break his neck over a mound of his making!"[4]

Edward was not at that moment clear-headed enough to remember that King William's fall, which occasioned his death, was said to be owing to his horse stumbling at a mole-hill; yet felt inclined to take umbrage at a toast, which seemed, from the glance of Balmawhapple's eye, to have a peculiar and uncivil reference to the Government which he served. But, ere he could interfere, the Baron of Bradwardine had taken up the quarrel. "Sir," he said, "whatever my sentiments, *tanquam privatus*,[5] may be in such matters, I shall not tamely endure your saying any thing that may impinge upon the honourable feelings of a gentleman under my roof. Sir, if you have no respect for the laws of urbanity, do ye not respect the military oath, the *sacramentum militare*, by which every officer is bound to the standards under which he

---

1 "Lunzie string" is "the cord of a knapsack hung at the hip" or loin (*OW*, 421).
2 "Weak, washy, and insipid" (*WSG*).
3 "The name of a Greek warrior in the Trojan war, 'whose voice was as powerful as fifty voices of other men'; applied allusively to a man of powerful voice" (*OED*).
4 Lamont notes that the white horse was "the cognizance of the House of Hanover" (*OW*, 421).
5 In private.

is enrolled? Look at Titus Livius, what he says of those Roman soldiers who were so unhappy as *exuere sacramentum*,[1]—to renounce their legionary oath; but you are ignorant, sir, alike of ancient history and modern courtesy."

"Not so ignorant as ye would pronounce me," roared Balmawhapple. "I ken weel that you mean the Solemn League and Covenant;[2] but if a' the Whigs in hell had taken the"—

Here the Baron and Waverley both spoke at once, the former calling out, "Be silent, sir! Ye not only show your ignorance, but disgrace your native country before a stranger and an Englishman"; and Waverley, at the same moment, entreating Mr Bradwardine to permit him to reply to an affront which seemed levelled at him personally. But the Baron was exalted by wine, wrath, and scorn, above all sublunary considerations.

"I crave you to be hushed, Captain Waverley; you are elsewhere, peradventure, *sui juris*,[3]—foris-familiated, that is, and entitled, it may be, to think and resent for yourself; but in my domain, in this poor Barony of Bradwardine, and under this roof, which is *quasi* mine, being held by tacit relocation by a tenant at will, I am *in loco parentis*[4] to you, and bound to see you scathless.—And for you, Mr Falconer of Balmawhapple, I warn ye, let me see no more aberrations from the paths of good manners."

"And I tell you, Mr Cosmo Comyne Bradwardine, of Bradwardine and Tully-Veolan," retorted the sportsman, in huge disdain, "that I'll make a moor-cock of the man that refuses my toast, whether it be a crop-eared English Whig wi' a black ribband at his lug, or ane wha deserts his ain friends to claw favour wi' the rats of Hanover."

In an instant both rapiers were brandished, and some desperate passes exchanged. Balmawhapple was young, stout, and active; but the Baron, infinitely more master of his weapon, would, like Sir Toby Belch,[5] have tickled his opponent other gates than he did, had he not been under the influence of Ursa Major.

Edward rushed forward to interfere between the combatants, but the prostrate bulk of the Laird of Killancureit, over which he stumbled, intercepted his passage. How Killancureit happened to be in this

---

1 Livy's *History of Rome*, Vols. II, 24; IV, 53; XXV, 5; and XLI, 5, mentions the military oath (*OW*, 421). *Exuere sacramentum* is to cast off the oath.

2 Hook points out that Balmawhapple, in his drunkenness, "confuses the Baron of Bradwardine's reference to the sacred oaths of the Roman legionaries with the Solemn League and Covenant of 1643" (*PW*, 578).

3 Legally one's own master (*LCD*).

4 In place of your parents.

5 In Shakespeare's *Twelfth Night*, Belch is Olivia's uncle.

recumbent posture at so interesting a moment, was never accurately known. Some thought he was about to ensconce himself under the table; he himself alleged that he stumbled in the act of lifting a joint-stool, to prevent mischief, by knocking down Balmawhapple. Be that as it may, if readier aid than either his or Waverley's had not inter-posed, there would certainly have been bloodshed. But the well-known clash of swords, which was no stranger to her dwelling, aroused Luckie Macleary as she sat quietly beyond the hallan, or earthen par-tition of the cottage, with eyes employed on Boston's Crook of the Lot,[1] while her ideas were engaged in summing up the reckoning. She boldly rushed in, with the shrill expostulation, "Wad their honours slay ane another there, and bring discredit on an honest widow-woman's house, when there was a' the lee-land in the country to fight upon?" a remonstrance which she seconded by flinging her plaid with great dexterity over the weapons of the combatants. The servants by this time rushed in, and being, by great chance, tolerably sober, sepa-rated the incensed opponents, with the assistance of Edward and Kil-lancureit. The latter led off Balmawhapple, cursing, swearing, and vowing revenge against every Whig, Presbyterian, and fanatic in England and Scotland, from John-o'-Groat's to the Land's End, and with difficulty got him to horse. Our hero, with the assistance of Saun-ders Saunderson, escorted the Baron of Bradwardine to his own dwelling, but could not prevail upon him to retire to bed until he had made a long and learned apology for the events of the evening, of which, however, there was not a word intelligible, except something about the Centaurs and the Lapithæ.[2]

CHAPTER XII.
Repentance and a Reconciliation.

WAVERLEY was unaccustomed to the use of wine, excepting with great temperance. He slept therefore soundly till late in the succeed-ing morning, and then awakened to a painful recollection of the scene of the preceding evening. He had received a personal affront,—he, a gentleman, a soldier, and a Waverley. True, the person who offered it was not, at the time it was given, possessed of the moderate share of sense which nature had allotted him; true also, in resenting this insult, he would break the laws of Heaven, as well as of his country; true, in

---

1 *The Crook of the Lock or the Wisdom and Sovereignty of God Displayed in the Afflictions of Men,* by Thomas Boston (1676/7-1732), a Scottish Calvinist.
2 Centaurs in Greek mythology were creatures who were half men, half horse. The Lapithae were a mythical race in Thessaly, who, according to legend, fought the Centaurs.

doing so, he might take the life of a young man who perhaps respectably discharged the social duties, and render his family miserable; or he might lose his own;—no pleasant alternative even to the bravest, when it is debated coolly and in private.

All this pressed on his mind; yet the original statement recurred with the same irresistible force. He had received a personal insult; he was of the house of Waverley; and he bore a commission. There was no alternative; and he descended to the breakfast parlour with the intention of taking leave of the family, and writing to one of his brother officers to meet him at the inn mid-way between Tully-Veolan and the town where they were quartered, in order that he might convey such a message to the Laird of Balmawhapple as the circumstances seemed to demand. He found Miss Bradwardine presiding over the tea and coffee, the table loaded with warm bread, both of flour, oatmeal, and barleymeal, in the shape of loaves, cakes, biscuits, and other varieties, together with eggs, rein-deer ham, mutton and beef ditto, smoked salmon, marmalade, and all the other delicacies which induced even Johnson[1] himself to extol the luxury of a Scotch breakfast above that of all other countries. A mess of oatmeal porridge, flanked by a silver jug, which held an equal mixture of cream and butter-milk, was placed for the Baron's share of this repast; but Rose observed he had walked out early in the morning, after giving orders that his guest should not be disturbed.

Waverley sat down almost in silence, and with an air of absence and abstraction, which could not give Miss Bradwardine a favourable opinion of his talents for conversation. He answered at random one or two observations which she ventured to make upon ordinary topics; so that feeling herself almost repulsed in her efforts at entertaining him, and secretly wondering that a scarlet coat should cover no better breeding, she left him to his mental amusement of cursing Dr Doubleit's favourite constellation of Ursa Major, as the cause of all the mischief which had already happened, and was likely to ensue. At once he started, and his colour heightened, as, looking toward the window, he beheld the Baron and young Balmawhapple pass arm in arm, apparently in deep conversation; and he hastily asked, "Did Mr Falconer sleep here last night?" Rose, not much pleased with the abruptness of the first question which the young stranger had addressed to her, answered drily in the negative, and the conversation again sunk into silence.

---

1 Samuel Johnson (1709-84) wrote *A Journey to the Western Isles of Scotland* in 1775 after a tour of Scotland and the Hebrides during which some of his negative opinions of Scots were confirmed, but others were modified. One can read *Waverley* as a corrective to Johnson's travelog.

At this moment Mr Saunderson appeared, with a message from his master, requesting to speak with Captain Waverley in another apartment. With a heart which beat a little quicker, not indeed from fear, but from uncertainty and anxiety, Edward obeyed the summons. He found the two gentlemen standing together, an air of complacent dignity on the brow of the Baron, while something like sullenness or shame, or both, blanked the bold visage of Balmawhapple. The former slipped his arm through that of the latter, and thus seeming to walk with him, while in reality he led him, advanced to meet Waverley, and, stopping in the midst of the apartment, made in great state the following oration: "Captain Waverley,—my young and esteemed friend, Mr Falconer of Balmawhapple, has craved of my age and experience, as of one not wholly unskilled in the dependencies and punctilios of the duello or monomachia,[1] to be his interlocutor in expressing to you the regret with which he calls to remembrance certain passages of our symposion last night, which could not but be highly displeasing to you, as serving for the time under this present existing government. He craves you, sir, to drown in oblivion the memory of such solecisms against the laws of politeness, as being what his better reason disavows, and to receive the hand which he offers you in amity; and I must needs assure you that nothing less than a sense of being *dans son tort*,[2] as a gallant French chevalier, Mons. Le Bretailleur, once said to me on such an occasion, and an opinion also of your peculiar merit, could have extorted such concessions; for he and all his family are, and have been, time out of mind, *Mavortia pectora*,[3] as Buchanan[4] saith, a bold and warlike sept, or people."

Edward immediately, and with natural politeness, accepted the hand which Balmawhapple, or rather the Baron in his character of mediator, extended towards him. "It was impossible," he said, "for him to remember what a gentleman expressed his wish he had not uttered; and he willingly imputed what had passed to the exuberant festivity of the day."

"That is very handsomely said," answered the Baron; "for undoubtedly, if a man be *ebrius*, or intoxicated, an incident which on

---

1 "A single combat"; a duel (*OED*).

2 In the wrong (*LCD*).

3 Warlike beasts.

4 George Buchanan (1506-82), Scottish teacher and scholar, poet, a "critic of corruption and inefficiency in church and state during the period of the Reformation in Scotland" (*EB* 2: 595). He left his view of the Scots in *Rerum Scoticarum historia* (1582) from their origins with Fergus to his own day; he also wrote *Epithalamium* (1558), a poem on the occasion of Mary, Queen of Scots' marriage to the French dauphin.

solemn and festive occasions may and will take place in the life of a man of honour; and if the same gentleman, being fresh and sober, recants the contumelies which he hath spoken in his liquor, it must be held *vinum locutum est;*[1] the words cease to be his own. Yet would I not find this exculpation relevant in the case of one who was *ebriosus,* or an habitual drunkard; because, if such a person choose to pass the greater part of his time in the predicament of intoxication, he hath no title to be exeemed from the obligations of the code of politeness, but should learn to deport himself peaceably and courteously when under influence of the vinous stimulus.—And now let us proceed to breakfast, and think no more of this daft business."

I must confess, whatever inference may be drawn from the circumstance, that Edward, after so satisfactory an explanation, did much greater honour to the delicacies of Miss Bradwardine's breakfast-table than his commencement had promised. Balmawhapple, on the contrary, seemed embarrassed and dejected; and Waverley now, for the first time, observed that his arm was in a sling, which seemed to account for the awkward and embarrassed manner with which he had presented his hand. To a question from Miss Bradwardine, he muttered, in answer, something about his horse having fallen; and, seeming desirous to escape both from the subject and the company, he arose as soon as breakfast was over, made his bow to the party, and, declining the Baron's invitation to tarry till after dinner, mounted his horse and returned to his own home.

Waverley now announced his purpose of leaving Tully-Veolan early enough after dinner to gain the stage at which he meant to sleep; but the unaffected and deep mortification with which the good-natured and affectionate old gentleman heard the proposal, quite deprived him of courage to persist in it. No sooner had he gained Waverley's consent to lengthen his visit for a few days, than he laboured to remove the grounds upon which he conceived he had meditated a more early retreat. "I would not have you opine, Captain Waverley, that I am by practice or precept an advocate of ebriety, though it may be that, in our festivity of last night, some of our friends, if not perchance altogether *ebrii,* or drunken, were, to say the least, *ebrioli,* by which the ancients designed those who were fuddled, or, as your English vernacular and metaphorical phrase goes, half-seas-over. Not that I would so insinuate respecting you, Captain Waverley, who, like a prudent youth, did rather abstain from potation; nor can it be truly said of myself, who, having assisted at the tables of many great generals and marechals at their solemn carousels, have the art to carry my

---

1 "It was the wine that spoke" (*OW*, 422).

wine discreetly, and did not, during the whole evening, as ye must have doubtless observed, exceed the bounds of a modest hilarity."

There was no refusing assent to a proposition so decidedly laid down by him, who undoubtedly was the best judge; although, had Edward formed his opinion from his own recollections, he would have pronounced that the Baron was not only *ebriolus*, but verging to become *ebrius*; or, in plain English, was incomparably the most drunk of the party, except perhaps his antagonist the Laird of Balmawhapple. However, having received the expected or rather the required, compliment on his sobriety, the Baron proceeded—"No, sir, though I am myself of a strong temperament, I abhor ebriety, and detest those who swallow wine *gulæ causa*, for the oblectation of the gullet;[1] albeit I might deprecate the law of Pittacus of Mitylene, who punished doubly a crime committed under the influence of *Liber Pater*;[2] nor would I utterly accede to the objurgation of the younger Plinius, in the fourteenth book of his 'Historia Naturalis.'[3] No, sir, I distinguish, I discriminate, and approve of wine so far only as it maketh glad the face, or, in the language of Flaccus, *recepto amico*."[4]

Thus terminated the apology which the Baron of Bradwardine thought it necessary to make for the superabundance of his hospitality; and it may be easily believed that he was neither interrupted by dissent, nor any expression of incredulity.

He then invited his guest to a morning ride, and ordered that Davie Gellatley should meet them at the *dern path* with Ban and Buscar. "For, until the shooting season commence, I would willingly show you some sport, and we may, God willing, meet with a roe. The roe, Captain Waverley, may be hunted at all times alike; for never being in what is called *pride of grease*,[5] he is also never out of season, though it be a truth that his venison is not equal to that of either the red or fallow deer.^u But he will serve to show how my dogs run; and therefore they shall attend us with David Gellatley."

Waverley expressed his surprise that his friend Davie was capable of such trust; but the Baron gave him to understand that this poor simpleton was neither fatuous, *nec naturaliter idiota*,[6] as is expressed in

---

1 For the enjoyment of the gullet.
2 Pittacus of Mitylene (650-570 BCE) was one of the seven wise men of Greece (*CGBD*, 1167). *Liber Pater* refers to Bacchus, god of wine (*PW*, 579).
3 It was actually Pliny the Elder (23-79 CE) who wrote *The Natural History*.
4 Horace (Flaccus), *Odes* II, vii, 27: "recepto dulce mihi furere est amico," which Hook translates as "Sweet to me is revelry when a friend is regained" (*PW*, 579).
5 "Fat and fit for killing" (*OED*).
6 Not naturally an idiot, not so from birth (*LED*).

the brieves of furiosity,[1] but simply a crack-brained knave, who could execute very well any commission which jumped with his own humour, and made his folly a plea for avoiding every other. "He has made an interest with us," continued the Baron, "by saving Rose from a great danger with his own proper peril; and the roguish loon must therefore eat of our bread and drink of our cup, and do what he can, or what he will; which, if the suspicions of Saunderson and the Baillie are well founded, may perchance in his case be commensurate terms."

Miss Bradwardine then gave Waverley to understand, that this poor simpleton was dotingly fond of music, deeply affected by that which was melancholy, and transported into extravagant gaiety by light and lively airs. He had in this respect a prodigious memory, stored with miscellaneous snatches and fragments of all tunes and songs, which he sometimes applied, with considerable address, as the vehicles of remonstrance, explanation, or satire. Davie was much attached to the few who showed him kindness; and both aware of any slight or ill usage which he happened to receive, and sufficiently apt, where he saw opportunity, to revenge it. The common people, who often judge hardly of each other, as well as of their betters, although they had expressed great compassion for the poor *innocent* while suffered to wander in rags about the village, no sooner beheld him decently clothed, provided for, and even a sort of favourite, than they called up all the instances of sharpness and ingenuity, in action and repartee, which his annals afforded, and charitably bottomed thereupon a hypothesis, that David Gellatley was no farther fool than was necessary to avoid hard labour. This opinion was not better founded than that of the Negroes, who, from the acute and mischievous pranks of the monkeys, suppose that they have the gift of speech, and only suppress their powers of elocution to escape being set to work. But the hypothesis was entirely imaginary; David Gellatley was in good earnest the half-crazed simpleton which he appeared, and was incapable of any constant and steady exertion. He had just so much solidity as kept on the windy side of insanity; so much wild wit as saved him from the imputation of idiocy; some dexterity in field sports (in which we have known as great fools excel), great kindness and humanity in the treatment of animals intrusted to him, warm affections, a prodigious memory, and an ear for music.

The stamping of horses was now heard in the court, and Davie's voice singing to the two large deer greyhounds,

---

1   A brieve is a "writ or precept issued from chancery in the sovereign's name, directing trial to be made of certain points specified" (*OED*). A brieve of furiosity is "a brieve directing an inquiry as to a person's sanity" (*OED*).

Hie away, hie away,
Over bank and over brae,
Where the copsewood is the greenest,
Where the fountains glisten sheenest,
Where the lady-fern grows strongest,
Where the morning dew lies longest,
Where the black-cock sweetest sips it,
Where the fairy latest trips it:
Hie to haunts right seldom seen,
Lovely, lonesome, cool and green,
Over bank and over brae,
Hie away, hie away.

"Do the verses he sings," asked Waverley, "belong to old Scottish poetry, Miss Bradwardine?"

"I believe not," she replied. "This poor creature had a brother, and Heaven, as if to compensate to the family Davie's deficiencies, had given him what the hamlet thought uncommon talents. An uncle contrived to educate him for the Scottish kirk, but he could not get preferment because he came from our *ground*.[1] He returned from college hopeless and broken-hearted, and fell into a decline. My father supported him till his death, which happened before he was nineteen. He played beautifully on the flute, and was supposed to have a great turn for poetry. He was affectionate and compassionate to his brother, who followed him like his shadow, and we think that from him Davie gathered many fragments of songs and music unlike those of this country. But if we ask him where he got such a fragment as he is now singing, he either answers with wild and long fits of laughter, or else breaks into tears of lamentation; but was never heard to give any explanation, or to mention his brother's name since his death."

"Surely," said Edward, who was readily interested by a tale bordering on the romantic, "surely more might be learned by more particular inquiry."

"Perhaps so," answered Rose; "but my father will not permit any one to practise on his feelings on this subject."

By this time the Baron, with the help of Mr Saunderson, had indued a pair of jack-boots of large dimensions, and now invited our hero to follow him as he stalked clattering down the ample staircase, tapping each huge balustrade as he passed with the but of his massive horse-whip, and humming, with the air of a chasseur of Louis Quatorze,[2]

---

1 Davie's brother is not promoted within the Church of Scotland because "he was a tenant of a family of Episcopal persuasion" and because that family was also Jacobite (*OW*, 422; *PW*, 579).

2 Hunter at the court of Louis XIV in France.

Pour la chasse ordonnée il faut preparer tout,
Ho la ho! Vite! Vite debout.[1]

CHAPTER XIII.
A more rational Day than the last.

THE Baron of Bradwardine, mounted on an active and well-managed horse, and seated on a demi-pique saddle, with deep housings[2] to agree with his livery, was no bad representative of the old school. His light-coloured embroidered coat, and superbly barred waistcoat, his brigadier wig, surmounted by a small gold-laced cocked-hat, completed his personal costume; but he was attended by two well-mounted servants on horseback, armed with holster-pistols.

In this guise he ambled forth over hill and valley, the admiration of every farm-yard which they passed in their progress, till, "low down in a grassy vale," they found David Gellatley leading two very tall deer greyhounds, and presiding over half a dozen curs, and about as many bare-legged and bare-headed boys, who, to procure the chosen distinction of attending on the chase, had not failed to tickle his ears with the dulcet appellation of *Maister Gellatley*, though probably all and each had hooted him on former occasions in the character of *daft Davie*. But this in no uncommon strain of flattery to persons in office, nor altogether confined to the bare-legged villagers of Tully-Veolan; it was in fashion Sixty Years since, is now, and will be six hundred years hence, if this admirable compound of folly and knavery, called the world, shall be then in existence.

These *gillie-wet-foots*,[v] as they were called, were destined to beat the bushes, which they performed with so much success, that, after half an hour's search, a roe was started, coursed, and killed; the Baron following on his white horse, like Earl Percy[3] of yore, and magnanimously flaying and embowelling the slain animal (which, he observed, was called by the French chasseurs, *faire la curée*) with his own baro-

---

1   It is necessary to prepare for the ordered hunt. Ho la ho! Quick! Get out of bed.
2   Half-peaked saddle with "a cloth covering put on a horse ... for defense or ornament;... trappings" (*OED*).
3   Henry Percy (1364-1403), also known as "Hotspur." Eldest son of the Earl of Northumberland, he fought against the Scottish army as warden of the east and then west march on the border between England and Scotland, an action captured in the ballad "Chevy Chase." Lamont suggests that it was not Percy who rode "the milke-white steede" but Douglas, according to F.J. Child, *The English and Scottish Popular Ballads* (1882-98), no. 162B, stanza 17 (*OW*, 422). Douglas: Archibald Douglas, fourth earl of Douglas (c. 1372-1424), fought at Shrewsbury alongside Henry Percy against the forces of Henry IV in 1403 (*OCBH*, 304).

nial *couteau de chasse*.[1] After this ceremony, he conducted his guest homeward by a pleasant and circuitous route, commanding an extensive prospect of different villages and houses, to each of which Mr Bradwardine attached some anecdote of history or genealogy, told in language whimsical from prejudice and pedantry, but often respectable for the good sense and honourable feelings which his narrative displayed, and almost always curious, if not valuable, for the information they contained.

The truth is, the ride seemed agreeable to both gentlemen, because they found amusement in each other's conversation, although their characters and habits of thinking were in many respects totally opposite. Edward, we have informed the reader, was warm in his feelings, wild and romantic in his ideas and in his taste of reading, with a strong disposition towards poetry. Mr Bradwardine was the reverse of all this, and piqued himself upon stalking through life with the same upright, starched, stoical gravity which distinguished his evening promenade upon the terrace of Tully-Veolan, where for hours together—the very model of old Hardyknute—

> Stately stepp'd he east the wa',
> And stately stepp'd he west.

As for literature, he read the classic poets, to be sure, and the Epithalamium of Georgius Buchanan, and Arthur Johnstone's Psalms,[2] of a Sunday; and the *Deliciæ Poetarum Scotorum*, and Sir David Lindsay's Works, and Barbour's Bruce, and Blind Harry's Wallace, and the Gentle Shepherd, and the Cherry and the Slae.[3] But though he thus

---

1 Hunting knife.

2 Arthur Johnstone (1587-1641), Scottish doctor and scholar, translated the Psalms (*PW*, 579).

3 *Deliciae Poetarum Scotorum* (1637) was "an anthology of contemporary Latin verse by Scottish poets compiled by Arthur Johnstone" (*PW*, 579); Sir David Lindsay (1486-1555), Scottish political poet and dramatist, author of *Ane Pleasant Satyre of the Thrie Estaitis*, which was performed in 1540 at the court of James V (*OCEL*, 574); John Barbour (c. 1320-95), a Scottish poet, wrote *The Bruce (The Actes and Life of the Most Victorious Conqueror, Robert Bruce King of Scotland)* (1376); Blind Harry, or Henry the Minstrel (1440?-1492?), Scottish poet ("half legendary") wrote *The Wallace* (*OCEL*, 453), which chronicles William Wallace's life and death at the hands of the English in 1305 (c. 1460); Allan Ramsay (1686-1758) was a Scottish poet whose "pastoral comedy, *The Gentle Shepherd* (1725) was very popular" (*OCEL*, 809); Alexander Montgomerie (c. 1545-c. 1598) was a Scottish poet whose principal work was *The Cherry and the Slae*, an allegory contrasting the cherry and the sloe (1597) (*OCEL*, 664).

far sacrificed his time to the Muses, he would, if the truth must be spoken, have been much better pleased had the pious or sapient apothegms, as well as the historical narratives, which these various works contained, been presented to him in the form of simple prose. And he sometimes could not refrain from expressing contempt of the "vain and unprofitable art of poem-making," in which, he said, "the only one who had excelled in his time was Allan Ramsay, the periwig-maker."[w]

But although Edward and he differed *toto cœlo*,[1] as the Baron would have said, upon this subject, yet they met upon history as on a neutral ground, in which each claimed an interest. The Baron, indeed, only cumbered his memory with matters of fact; the cold, dry, hard outlines which history delineates. Edward, on the contrary, loved to fill up and round the sketch with the colouring of a warm and vivid imagination, which gives light and life to the actors and speakers in the drama of past ages. Yet with tastes so opposite, they contributed greatly to each other's amusement. Mr Bradwardine's minute narratives and powerful memory supplied to Waverley fresh subjects of the kind upon which his fancy loved to labour, and opened to him a new mine of incident and of character. And he repaid the pleasure thus communicated, by an earnest attention, valuable to all story-tellers, more especially to the Baron, who felt his habits of self-respect flattered by it; and sometimes also by reciprocal communications, which interested Mr Bradwardine, as confirming or illustrating his own favourite anecdotes. Besides, Mr Bradwardine loved to talk of the scenes of his youth, which had been spent in camps and foreign lands, and had many interesting particulars to tell of the generals under whom he had served, and the actions he had witnessed.

Both parties returned to Tully-Veolan in great good-humour with each other; Waverley desirous of studying more attentively what he considered as a singular and interesting character, gifted with a memory containing a curious register of ancient and modern anecdotes; and Bradwardine disposed to regard Edward as *puer* (or rather *juvenis*) *bonæ spei et magnæ indolis*,[2] a youth devoid of that petulant volatility, which is impatient of, or vilipends, the conversation and advice of his seniors, from which he predicted great things of his future success and deportment in life. There was no other guest except Mr Rubrick, whose information and discourse, as a clergyman and a scholar, harmonized very well with that of the Baron and his guest.

Shortly after dinner, the Baron, as if to show that his temperance was not entirely theoretical, proposed a visit to Rose's apartment, or,

---

1 Wholly.
2 "A ... youth ... of high promise and great ability" (*PW*, 580).

as he termed it, her *Troisieme Etage*. Waverley was accordingly conducted through one or two of those long awkward passages with which ancient architects studied to puzzle the inhabitants of the houses which they planned, at the end of which Mr Bradwardine began to ascend, by two steps at once, a very steep, narrow, and winding stair, leaving Mr Rubrick and Waverley to follow at more leisure, while he should announce their approach to his daughter.

After having climbed this perpendicular corkscrew until their brains were almost giddy, they arrived in a little matted lobby, which served as an anteroom to Rose's *sanctum sanctorum*, and through which they entered her parlour. It was a small, but pleasant apartment, opening to the south, and hung with tapestry; adorned besides with two pictures, one of her mother, in the dress of a shepherdess, with a bell-hoop; the other of the Baron, in his tenth year, in a blue coat, embroidered waistcoat, laced hat, and bag-wig, with a bow in his hand. Edward could not help smiling at the costume, and at the odd resemblance between the round, smooth, red-cheeked, staring visage in the portrait, and the gaunt, bearded, hollow-eyed, swarthy features, which travelling, fatigues of war, and advanced age, had bestowed on the original. The Baron joined in the laugh. "Truly," he said, "that picture was a woman's fantasy of my good mother's (a daughter of the Laird of Tulliellum, Captain Waverley; I indicated the house to you when we were on the top of the Shinnyheuch; it was burnt by the Dutch auxiliaries[1] brought in by the Government in 1715); I never sate for my pourtraicture but once since that was painted, and it was at the special and reiterated request of the Marechal Duke of Berwick."

The good old gentleman did not mention what Mr Rubrick afterwards told Edward, that the Duke had done him this honour on account of his being the first to mount the breach of a fort in Savoy during the memorable campaign of 1709, and his having there defended himself with his half-pike for nearly ten minutes before any support reached him. To do the Baron justice, although sufficiently prone to dwell upon, and even to exaggerate his family dignity and consequence, he was too much a man of real courage ever to allude to such personal acts of merit as he had himself manifested.

Miss Rose now appeared from the interior room of her apartment, to welcome her father and his friends. The little labours in which she had been employed obviously showed a natural taste, which required only cultivation. Her father had taught her French and Italian, and a few of the ordinary authors in those languages ornamented her

---

1   "Six thousand Dutch auxiliaries were brought in to suppress the rising of 1715" (*OW*, 423).

shelves. He had endeavoured also to be her preceptor in music; but as he began with the more abstruse doctrines of the science, and was not perhaps master of them himself, she had made no proficiency farther than to be able to accompany her voice with the harpsichord; but even this was not very common in Scotland at that period. To make amends, she sung with great taste and feeling, and with a respect to the sense of what she uttered that might be proposed in example to ladies of much superior musical talent. Her natural good sense taught her, that if, as we are assured by high authority, music be "married to immortal verse," they are very often divorced by the performer in a most shameful manner. It was perhaps owing to this sensibility to poetry, and power of combining its expression with those of the musical notes, that her singing gave more pleasure to all the unlearned in music, and even to many of the learned, than could have been communicated by a much finer voice and more brilliant execution, unguided by the same delicacy of feeling.

A bartizan, or projecting gallery, before the windows of her parlour, served to illustrate another of Rose's pursuits; for it was crowded with flowers of different kinds, which she had taken under her special protection. A projecting turret gave access to this Gothic balcony, which commanded a most beautiful prospect. The formal garden, with its high bounding walls, lay below, contracted, as it seemed, to a mere parterre; while the view extended beyond them down a wooded glen, where the small river was sometimes visible, sometimes hidden in copse. The eye might be delayed by a desire to rest on the rocks, which here and there rose from the dell with massive or spiry fronts, or it might dwell on the noble, though ruined tower, which was here beheld in all its dignity, frowning from a promontory over the river. To the left were seen two or three cottages, a part of the village; the brow of the hill concealed the others. The glen, or dell, was terminated by a sheet of water, called Loch Veolan, into which the brook discharged itself, and which now glistened in the western sun. The distant country seemed open and varied in surface, though not wooded; and there was nothing to interrupt the view until the scene was bounded by a ridge of distant and blue hills, which formed the southern boundary of the strath or valley. To this pleasant station Miss Bradwardine had ordered coffee.

The view of the old tower, or fortalice,[1] introduced some family anecdotes and tales of Scottish chivalry, which the Baron told with great enthusiasm. The projecting peak of an impending crag which rose near it, had acquired the name of St Swithin's Chair. It was the scene of a peculiar superstition, of which Mr Rubrick mentioned some

---

1 A defensive structure or position; a fortress (*AHD*).

curious particulars, which reminded Waverley of a rhyme quoted by Edgar in King Lear;[1] and Rose was called upon to sing a little legend, in which they had been interwoven by some village poet,

> Who, noteless as the race from which he sprung,
> Saved others' names, but left his own unsung.

The sweetness of her voice, and the simple beauty of her music, gave all the advantage which the minstrel could have desired, and which his poetry so much wanted. I almost doubt if it can be read with patience, destitute of these advantages; although I conjecture the following copy to have been somewhat corrected by Waverley, to suit the taste of those who might not relish pure antiquity.

St Swithin's Chair.[2]

> On Hallow-Mass Eve, ere ye boune ye to rest,
> Ever beware that your couch be bless'd;
> Sign it with cross, and sain it with bead,
> Sing the Ave, and say the Creed.

> For on Hallow-Mass Eve the Night-Hag will ride,
> And all her nine-fold sweeping on by her side,
> Whether the wind sing lowly or loud,
> Sailing through moonshine or swath'd in the cloud.

> The Lady she sat in St Swithin's Chair,
> The dew of the night has damp'd her hair:
> Her cheek was pale—but resolved and high
> Was the word of her lip and the glance of her eye.

> She mutter'd the spell of Swithin bold,
> When his naked foot traced the midnight wold,
> When he stopp'd the Hag as she rode the night,
> And bade her descend, and her promise plight.

> He that dare sit on St Swithin's Chair,
> When the Night-Hag wings the troubled air,
> Questions three, when he speaks the spell,
> He may ask, and she must tell.

---

1 Lamont and Hook both identify this as "probably III.iv.118ff, 'Swithold footed thrice the wold'" (*OW*, 423; *PW*, 580).

2 The poem is an original work by Scott.

The Baron has been with King Robert his liege,
These three long years in battle and siege;
News are there none of his weal or his woe,
And fain the Lady his fate would know.

She shudders and stops as the charm she speaks;—
Is it the moody owl that shrieks?
Or is it that sound, betwixt laughter and scream,
The voice of the Demon who haunts the stream?

The moan of the wind sunk silent and low,
And the roaring torrent has ceased to flow;
The calm was more dreadful than raging storm,
When the cold grey mist brought the ghastly Form!

***

"I am sorry to disappoint the company, especially Captain Waverley, who listens with such laudable gravity; it is but a fragment, although I think there are other verses, describing the return of the Baron from the wars, and how the lady was found 'clay-cold upon the grounsill ledge.'"

"It is one of those figments," observed Mr Bradwardine, "with which the early history of distinguished families was deformed in the times of superstition; as that of Rome, and other ancient nations, had their prodigies, sir, the which you may read in ancient histories, or in the little work compiled by Julius Obsequens, and inscribed by the learned Scheffer,[1] the editor, to his patron, Benedictus Skytte, Baron of Dudershoff."

"My father has a strange defiance of the marvellous, Captain Waverley," observed Rose, "and once stood firm when a whole synod of Presbyterian divines were put to the rout by a sudden apparition of the foul fiend."

Waverley looked as if desirous to hear more.

"Must I tell my story as well as sing my song?—Well—Once upon a time there lived an old woman, called Janet Gellatley, who was suspected to be a witch, on the infallible grounds that she was very old, very ugly, very poor, and had two sons, one of whom was a poet, and the other a fool, which visitation, all the neighbourhood agreed, had

---

1 Julius Obsequens (fl. 395), Roman author, wrote *De Prodigiis*. Scheffer published an edition of this work in 1679 which correctly teased out the original work from the supplement, which had been written in the sixteenth century by Conrad Lycosthenes (1518-61) and conflated with the original (*CGBD*, 23: 287).

come upon her for the sin of witchcraft. And she was imprisoned for a week in the steeple of the parish church, and sparely supplied with food, and not permitted to sleep until she herself became as much persuaded of her being a witch as her accusers; and in this lucid and happy state of mind was brought forth to make a clean breast, that is, to make open confession of her sorceries, before all the Whig gentry and ministers in the vicinity, who were no conjurors themselves. My father went to see fair play between the witch and the clergy; for the witch had been born on his estate. And while the witch was confessing that the Enemy appeared, and made his addresses to her as a handsome black man,—which, if you could have seen poor old bleareyed Janet, reflected little honour on Apollyon's[1] taste,—and while the auditors listened with astonished ears, and the clerk recorded with a trembling hand, she, all of a sudden, changed the low mumbling tone with which she spoke into a shrill yell, and exclaimed, 'Look to yourselves! Look to yourselves! I see the Evil One sitting in the midst of ye.' The surprise was general, and terror and flight its immediate consequences. Happy were those who were next the door; and many were the disasters that befell hats, bands, cuffs, and wigs, before they could get out of the church, where they left the obstinate prelatist to settle matters with the witch and her admirer, at his own peril or pleasure."

"*Risu solvuntur tabulæ*,"[2] said the Baron; "when they recovered their panic trepidation, they were too much ashamed to bring any wakening of the process against Janet Gellatley."[x]

This anecdote led into a long discussion of

> All those idle thoughts and fantasies,
>   Devices, dreams, opinions unsound,
>   Shows, visions, soothsays, and prophecies,
> And all that feigned is, as leasings, tales, and lies.[3]

With such conversation, and the romantic legends which it introduced, closed our hero's second evening in the house of Tully-Veolan.

CHAPTER XIV.
A Discovery—Waverley becomes domesticated at Tully-Veolan.

THE next day Edward arose betimes, and in a morning walk around the house and its vicinity, came suddenly upon a small court in front

---

1   Revelation 9:11: the angel of the bottomless pit, "The Destroyer" in Bunyan's *Pilgrim's Progress* (1678) (*OCEL*, 34).
2   "Charge dismissed with ridicule": Horace, *Satires*, II.i.86 (*PW*, 580).
3   *The Faerie Queene* II, ix, 51-54.

of the dog-kennel, where his friend Davie was employed about his four-footed charge. One quick glance of his eye recognised Waverley, when, instantly turning his back, as if he had not observed him, he began to sing part of an old ballad:

> Young men will love thee more fair and more fast;
> *Heard ye so merry the little bird sing?*
> Old men's love the longest will last,
> *And the throstle-cock's[1] head is under his wing.*
>
> The young man's wrath is like light straw on fire;
> *Heard ye so merry the little bird sing?*
> But like red-hot steel is the old man's ire,
> *And the throstle-cock's head is under his wing.*
>
> The young man will brawl at the evening board;
> *Heard ye so merry the little bird sing?*
> But the old man will draw at the dawning the sword,
> *And the throstle-cock's head is under his wing.[2]*

Waverley could not avoid observing that Davie laid something like a satirical emphasis on these lines. He therefore approached, and endeavoured, by sundry queries, to elicit from him what the innuendo might mean; but Davie had no mind to explain, and had wit enough to make his folly cloak his knavery. Edward could collect nothing from him, excepting that the Laird of Balmawhapple had gone home yesterday morning, "wi' his boots fu' o' bluid." In the garden, however, he met the old butler, who no longer attempted to conceal, that, having been bred in the nursery line with Sumack and Co. of Newcastle, he sometimes wrought a turn in the flower-borders to oblige the Laird and Miss Rose. By a series of queries, Edward at length discovered, with a painful feeling of surprise and shame, that Balmawhapple's submission and apology had been the consequence of a rencontre[3] with the Baron before his guest had quitted his pillow, in which the younger combatant had been disarmed and wounded in the sword arm.

Greatly mortified at this information, Edward sought out his friendly host, and anxiously expostulated with him upon the injustice he had done him in anticipating his meeting with Mr Falconer, a circumstance, which, considering his youth and the profession of arms which he had just adopted, was capable of being represented much to his prejudice. The Baron justified himself at greater length than I

---

1 The male song-thrush.
2 Poem by Scott.
3 Meeting (*LED*); in this case, a duel.

choose to repeat. He urged, that the quarrel was common to them, and that Balmawhapple could not, by the code of honour, *evite*[1] giving satisfaction to both, which he had done in his case by an honourable meeting, and in that of Edward by such a *palinode*[2] as rendered the use of the sword unnecessary, and which, being made and accepted, must necessarily *sopite*[3] the whole affair.

With this excuse, or explanation, Waverley was silenced, if not satisfied; but he could not help testifying some displeasure against the Blessed Bear, which had given rise to the quarrel, nor refrain from hinting, that the sanctified epithet was hardly appropriate. The Baron observed, he could not deny that "the Bear, though allowed by heralds as a most honourable ordinary, had, nevertheless, somewhat fierce, churlish, and morose in his disposition (as might be read in Archibald Simson, pastor of Dalkeith's *Hieroglyphica Animalium*[4]), and had thus been the type of many quarrels and dissensions which had occurred in the house of Bradwardine; of which," he continued, "I might commemorate mine own unfortunate dissension with my third cousin by the mother's side, Sir Hew Halbert, who was so unthinking as to deride my family name, as if it had been *quasi Bear-Warden*; a most uncivil jest, since it not only insinuated that the founder of our house occupied such a mean situation as to be a custodier of wild beasts, a charge which, ye must have observed, is only intrusted to the very basest plebeians; but, moreover, seemed to infer that our coat-armour had not been achieved by honourable actions in war, but bestowed by way of *paranomasia*, or pun, upon our family appellation,—a sort of bearing which the French call *armoires parlantes*; the Latins *arma cantantia*; and your English authorities, canting heraldry; being indeed a species of emblazoning more befitting canters, gaberlunzies, and such like mendicants,[5] whose gibberish is formed upon playing upon the word, than the noble, honourable, and useful science of heraldry, which assigns armorial bearings as the reward of noble and generous actions, and not to tickle the ear with vain quodlibets,[6] such as are

---

1 Avoid, escape (*LED*).
2 "An ode or song in which the author retracts something said in a former poem; hence, generally a recantation" (*OED*).
3 Put to sleep (*LED*).
4 Archibald Simpson (c. 1564-1628), Presbyterian pastor and naturalist, author of *Hieroglyphia Animalium, Reptilium, Insectorum* ... (1622-24).
5 Canters: vagabonds; gaberlunzies: strolling beggars; mendicants: beggars (esp. friars).
6 "Any question in philosophy or theology proposed as an exercise in argument or disputation; hence, a scholastic debate, thesis, or exercise on a question of this kind" (*OED*).

found in jest-books."[y] Of his quarrel with Sir Hew he said nothing more, than that it was settled in a fitting manner.

Having been so minute with respect to the diversions of Tully-Veolan, on the first days of Edward's arrival, for the purpose of introducing its inmates to the reader's acquaintance, it becomes less necessary to trace the progress of his intercourse with the same accuracy. It is probable that a young man, accustomed to more cheerful society, would have tired of the conversation of so violent an assertor of the "boast of heraldry" as the Baron; but Edward found an agreeable variety in that of Miss Bradwardine, who listened with eagerness to his remarks upon literature, and showed great justness of taste in her answers. The sweetness of her disposition had made her submit with complacency, and even pleasure, to the course of reading prescribed by her father, although it not only comprehended several heavy folios of history, but certain gigantic tomes in high-church polemics. In heraldry he was fortunately contented to give her only such a slight tincture as might be acquired by perusal of the two folio volumes of Nisbet.[1] Rose was indeed the very apple of her father's eye. Her constant liveliness, her attention to all those little observances most gratifying to those who would never think of exacting them, her beauty, in which he recalled the features of his beloved wife, her unfeigned piety, and the noble generosity of her disposition, would have justified the affection of the most doting father.

His anxiety on her behalf did not, however, seem to extend itself in that quarter, where, according to the general opinion, it is most efficiently displayed; in labouring, namely, to establish her in life, either by a large dowry or a wealthy marriage. By an old settlement, almost all the landed estates of the Baron went, after his death, to a distant relation; and it was supposed that Miss Bradwardine would remain but slenderly provided for, as the good gentleman's cash matters had been too long under the exclusive charge of Bailie Macwheeble, to admit of any great expectations from his personal succession. It is true, the said Bailie loved his patron and his patron's daughter next (though at an incomparable distance) to himself. He thought it was possible to set aside the settlement on the male line, and had actually procured an opinion to that effect (and, as he boasted, without a fee) from an eminent Scottish counsel, under whose notice he contrived to bring the point while consulting him regularly on some other business. But the Baron would not listen to such a proposal for an instant. On the contrary, he used to have a perverse pleasure in boasting that the barony

---

1 Alexander Nisbet (1657-1725) published his *System of Heraldry, Speculative and Practical* in 1722.

of Bradwardine was a male fief, the first charter having been given at that early period when women were not deemed capable to hold a feudal grant; because, according to *Les coustusmes de Normandie, c'est l'homme ki se bast et ki conseille;*[1] or, as is yet more ungallantly expressed by other authorities, all of whose barbarous names he delighted to quote at full length, because a woman could not serve the superior, or feudal lord, in war, on account of the decorum of her sex, nor assist him with advice, because of her limited intellect, nor keep his counsel, owing to the infirmity of her disposition. He would triumphantly ask, how it would become a female, and that female a Bradwardine, to be seen employed *in servitio exuendi, seu detrahendi, caligas regis post battaliam?* that is, in pulling off the king's boots after an engagement, which was the feudal service by which he held the barony of Bradwardine. "No," he said, "beyond hesitation, *procul dubio,*[2] many females, as worthy as Rose, had been excluded, in order to make way for my own succession, and Heaven forbid that I should do aught that might contravene the destination of my forefathers, or impinge upon the right of my kinsman, Malcolm Bradwardine of Inchgrabbit, an honourable, though decayed branch of my own family."

The Bailie, as prime minister, having received this decisive communication from his sovereign, durst not press his own opinion any farther, but contented himself with deploring, on all suitable occasions, to Saunderson, the minister of the interior, the Laird's selfwilledness, and with laying plans for uniting Rose with the young Laird of Balmawhapple, who had a fine estate, only moderately burdened, and was a faultless young gentleman, being as sober as a saint—if you keep brandy from him, and him from brandy—and who, in brief, had no imperfection but that of keeping light company at a time; such as Jinker, the horse-couper, and Gibby Gaethroughwi't, the piper o' Cupar; "o' whilk follies, Mr Saunderson, he'll mend, he'll mend,"—pronounced the Bailie.

"Like sour ale in simmer," added Davie Gellatley, who happened to be nearer the conclave than they were aware of.

Miss Bradwardine, such as we have described her, with all the simplicity and curiosity of a recluse, attached herself to the opportunities of increasing her store of literature which Edward's visit afforded her. He sent for some of his books from his quarters, and they opened to her sources of delight of which she had hitherto had no idea. The best English poets, of every description, and other works on belles lettres,[3]

---

1 "According to the customs of Normandy, it is the man who serves in the field and at the council board" (*PW*, 581).

2 Undoubtedly.

3 Literature.

made a part of this precious cargo. Her music, even her flowers, were neglected, and Saunders not only mourned over, but began to mutiny against the labour for which he now scarce received thanks. These new pleasures became gradually enhanced by sharing them with one of a kindred taste. Edward's readiness to comment, to recite, to explain difficult passages, rendered his assistance invaluable; and the wild romance of his spirit delighted a character too young and inexperienced to observe its deficiencies. Upon subjects which interested him, and when quite at ease, he possessed that flow of natural, and somewhat florid eloquence, which has been supposed as powerful even as figure, fashion, fame, or fortune, in winning the female heart. There was, therefore, an increasing danger, in this constant intercourse, to poor Rose's peace of mind, which was the more imminent, as her father was greatly too much abstracted in his studies, and wrapped up in his own dignity, to dream of his daughter's incurring it. The daughters of the house of Bradwardine were, in his opinion, like those of the house of Bourbon or Austria, placed high above the clouds of passion which might obfuscate the intellects of meaner females; they moved in another sphere, were governed by other feelings, and amenable to other rules, than those of idle and fantastic affection. In short, he shut his eyes so resolutely to the natural consequences of Edward's intimacy with Miss Bradwardine, that the whole neighbourhood concluded that he had opened them to the advantages of a match between his daughter and the wealthy young Englishman, and pronounced him much less a fool than he had generally shown himself in cases where his own interest was concerned.

If the Baron, however, had really meditated such an alliance, the indifference of Waverley would have been an insuperable bar to his project. Our hero, since mixing more freely with the world, had learned to think with great shame and confusion upon his mental legend of Saint Cecilia,[1] and the vexation of these reflections was likely, for some time at least, to counterbalance the natural susceptibility of his disposition. Besides, Rose Bradwardine, beautiful and amiable as we have described her, had not precisely the sort of beauty or merit, which captivates a romantic imagination in early youth. She was too frank, too confiding, too kind; amiable qualities, undoubtedly, but destructive of the marvellous, with which a youth of imagination delights to dress the empress of his affections. Was it possible to bow, to tremble, and to adore, before the timid, yet playful little girl, who now asked Edward to mend her pen, now to construe a stanza in Tasso, and now how to spell a very—very long word in her version of

---

1 St. Cecilia (d. 230) was a Christian martyr, patron saint of music. Scott may also be referring to Waverley's earlier potential love-interest, Cecilia Stubbs.

it? All these incidents have their fascination on the mind at a certain period of life, but not when a youth is entering it, and rather looking out for some object whose affection may dignify him in his own eyes, than stooping to one who looks up to him for such distinction. Hence, though there can be no rule in so capricious a passion, early love is frequently ambitious in choosing its object; or, which comes to the same, selects her (as in the case of Saint Cecilia aforesaid) from a situation that gives fair scope for *le beau ideal*, which the reality of intimate and familiar life rather tends to limit and impair. I knew a very accomplished and sensible young man cured of a violent passion for a pretty woman, whose talents were not equal to her face and figure, by being permitted to bear her company for a whole afternoon. Thus, it is certain, that had Edward enjoyed such an opportunity of conversing with Miss Stubbs, Aunt Rachel's precaution would have been unnecessary, for he would as soon have fallen in love with the dairy-maid. And although Miss Bradwardine was a very different character, it seems probable that the very intimacy of their intercourse prevented his feeling for her other sentiments than those of a brother for an amiable and accomplished sister; while the sentiments of poor Rose were gradually, and without her being conscious, assuming a shade of warmer affection.

I ought to have said that Edward, when he sent to Dundee for the books before mentioned, had applied for, and received permission, extending his leave of absence. But the letter of his commanding-officer contained a friendly recommendation to him, not to spend his time exclusively with persons, who, estimable as they might be in a general sense, could not be supposed well affected to a government, which they declined to acknowledge by taking the oath of allegiance. The letter further insinuated, though with great delicacy, that although some family connexions might be supposed to render it necessary for Captain Waverley to communicate with gentlemen who were in this unpleasant state of suspicion, yet his father's situation and wishes ought to prevent his prolonging those attentions into exclusive intimacy. And it was intimated, that while his political principles were endangered by communicating with laymen of this description, he might also receive erroneous impressions in religion from the prelatic clergy, who so perversely laboured to set up the royal prerogative in things sacred.

This last insinuation probably induced Waverley to set both down to the prejudices of his commanding officer. He was sensible that Mr Bradwardine had acted with the utmost scrupulous delicacy, in never entering upon any discussion that had the most remote tendency to bias his mind in political opinions, although he was himself not only a decided partizan of the exiled family, but had been trusted at different times with important commissions for their service. Sensible, therefore, that there was no risk of his being perverted from his allegiance, Edward felt as if he should do his uncle's old friend injustice in removing from a house where he gave and received pleasure and amusement, merely to gratify a prejudiced and ill-judged suspicion. He therefore wrote a very general answer, assuring his commanding officer that his loyalty was not in the most distant danger of contamination, and continued an honoured guest and inmate of the house of Tully-Veolan.

CHAPTER XV.
A Creagh,[z] *and its consequences.*

WHEN Edward had been a guest at Tully-Veolan nearly six weeks, he descried, one morning, as he took his usual walk before the breakfast-hour, signs of uncommon perturbation in the family. Four bare-legged dairy-maids, with each an empty milk-pail in her hand, ran about with frantic gestures, and uttering loud exclamations of surprise, grief, and resentment. From their appearance, a pagan might have conceived them a detachment of the celebrated Belides,[1] just come from their baleing penance. As nothing was to be got from this distracted chorus, excepting "Lord guide us!" and "Eh sirs!" ejaculations which threw no light upon the cause of their dismay, Waverley repaired to the fore-court, as it was called, where he beheld Bailie Macwheeble cantering his white pony down the avenue with all the speed it could muster. He had arrived, it would seem, upon a hasty summons, and was followed by half a score of peasants from the village, who had no great difficulty in keeping pace with him.

The Bailie, greatly too busy, and too important, to enter into explanations with Edward, summoned forth Mr Saunderson, who appeared with a countenance in which dismay was mingled with solemnity, and they immediately entered into close conference. Davie Gellatley was also seen in the group, idle as Diogenes at Sinope,[2] while his countrymen were preparing for a siege. His spirits always rose with any thing, good or bad, which occasioned tumult, and he continued frisking, hopping, dancing, and singing the burden of an old ballad,—

---

1 According to Lang, these were the Danaids, daughters of Danaus, son of Belus. They were punished by being forced to carry water in a sieve (*LW*, 297).

2 Diogenes (c. 400-c. 325 BCE), Greek philosopher who rolled the tub he lived in about so that he might be seen to be employed—even if ineffectually—while others around him prepared for battle.

"Our gear's a' gane,"

until, happening to pass too near the Bailie, he received an admonitory hint from his horse-whip, which converted his songs into lamentation.

Passing from thence towards the garden, Waverley beheld the Baron in person, measuring and re-measuring, with swift and tremendous strides, the length of the terrace; his countenance clouded with offended pride and indignation, and the whole of his demeanor such as seemed to indicate, that any inquiry concerning the cause of his discomposure would give pain at least, if not offence. Waverley therefore glided into the house, without addressing him, and took his way to the breakfast-parlour, where he found his young friend Rose, who, though she neither exhibited the resentment of her father, the turbid importance of Bailie Macwheeble, nor the despair of the handmaidens, seemed vexed and thoughtful. A single word explained the mystery. "Your breakfast will be a disturbed one, Captain Waverley. A party of Caterans have come down upon us last night, and have driven off all our milch cows."

"A party of Caterans?"

"Yes; robbers from the neighbouring Highlands. We used to be quite free from them while we paid black-mail to Fergus Mac-Ivor Vich Ian Vohr; but my father thought it unworthy of his rank and birth to pay it any longer, and so this disaster has happened. It is not the value of the cattle, Captain Waverley, that vexes me; but my father is so much hurt at the affront, and is so bold and hot, that I fear he will try to recover them by the strong hand; and if he is not hurt himself, he will hurt some of these wild people, and then there will be no peace between them and us perhaps for our lifetime; and we cannot defend ourselves as in old times, for the government have taken all our arms; and my dear father is so rash—O what will become of us!"—Here poor Rose lost heart altogether, and burst into a flood of tears.

The Baron entered at this moment, and rebuked her with more asperity than Waverley had ever heard him use to any one. "Was it not a shame," he said, "that she should exhibit herself before any gentleman in such a light, as if she shed tears for a drove of horned nolt and milch kine, like the daughter of a Cheshire yeoman!—Captain Waverley, I must request your favourable construction of her grief, which may, or ought to proceed, solely from seeing her father's estate exposed to spulzie[1] and depredation from common thieves and sornars,[aa] while we are not allowed to keep half a score of muskets, whether for defence or rescue."

1 Spoils (WSG).

Bailie Macwheeble entered immediately afterwards, and by his report of arms and ammunition confirmed this statement, informing the Baron, in a melancholy voice, that though the people would certainly obey his honour's orders, yet there was no chance of their following the gear to ony guid purpose, in respect there were only his honour's body servants who had swords and pistols, and the depredators were twelve Highlanders, completely armed after the manner of their country.—Having delivered this doleful annunciation, he assumed a posture of silent dejection, shaking his head slowly with the motion of a pendulum when it is ceasing to vibrate, and then remained stationary, his body stooping at a more acute angle than usual, and the latter part of his person projecting in proportion.

The Baron, meanwhile, paced the room in silent indignation, and at length fixing his eye upon an old portrait, whose person was clad in armour, and whose features glared grimly out of a huge bush of hair, part of which descended from his head to his shoulders, and part from his chin and upper-lip to his breast-plate,—"That gentleman, Captain Waverley, my grandsire," he said, "with two hundred horse, whom he levied within his own bounds, discomfited and put to the rout more than five hundred of these Highland reivers, who have been ever *lapis offensionis, et petra scandali,* a stumbling-block and a rock of offence to the Lowland vicinage—he discomfited them, I say, when they had the temerity to descend to harry this country, in the time of the civil dissensions, in the year of grace, sixteen hundred forty and two. And now, sir, I, his grandson, am thus used at such unworthy hands!"

Here there was an awful pause; after which all the company, as is usual in cases of difficulty, began to give separate and inconsistent counsel. Alexander ab Alexandro proposed they should send some one to compound with the Caterans, who would readily, he said, give up their prey for a dollar a-head. The Bailie opined that this transaction would amount to theft-boot, or composition of felony; and he recommended that some *canny hand* should be sent up to the glens to make the best bargain he could, as it were for himself, so that the Laird might not be seen in such a transaction. Edward proposed to send off to the nearest garrison for a party of soldiers and a magistrate's warrant; and Rose, as far as she dared, endeavoured to insinuate the course of paying the arrears of tribute money to Fergus Mac-Ivor Vich Ian Vohr, who, they all knew, could easily procure restoration of the cattle, if he were properly propitiated.

None of these proposals met the Baron's approbation. The idea of composition, direct or implied, was absolutely ignominious; that of Waverley only showed that he did not understand the state of the country, and of the political parties which divided it; and, standing matters as they did with Fergus Mac-Ivor Vich Ian Vohr, the Baron would make no concession to him, were it, he said, "to procure restitution *in integrum*[1] of every stirk and stot that the chief, his forefathers, and his clan, had stolen since the days of Malcolm Canmore."[2]

In fact, his voice was still for war, and he proposed to send expresses to Balmawhapple, Killancureit, Tulliellum, and other lairds, who were exposed to similar depredations, inviting them to join in the pursuit; "and then, sir, shall these *nebulones nequissimi*, as Leslæus[3] calls them, be brought to the fate of their predecessor Cacus,[4]

> "*Elisos oculos, et siccum sanguine guttur.*"

The Bailie, who by no means relished these warlike counsels, here pulled forth an immense watch, of the colour, and nearly of the size, of a pewter warming-pan, and observed it was now past noon, and that the Caterans had been seen in the pass of Ballybrough soon after sun-rise; so that before the allied forces could assemble, they and their prey would be far beyond the reach of the most active pursuit, and sheltered in those pathless deserts, where it was neither advisable to follow, nor indeed possible to trace them.

This proposition was undeniable. The council therefore broke up without coming to any conclusion, as has occurred to councils of more importance; only it was determined that the Bailie should send his own three milk cows down to the Mains for the use of the Baron's family, and brew small ale, as a substitute for milk, in his own. To this arrangement, which was suggested by Saunderson, the Bailie readily assented, both from habitual deference to the family, and an internal consciousness that his courtesy would, in some mode or other, be repaid tenfold.

The Baron having also retired to give some necessary directions, Waverley seized the opportunity to ask, whether this Fergus, with the unpronounceable name, was the chief thief-taker of the district?

"Thief-taker!" answered Rose, laughing; "he is a gentleman of great honour and consequence; the chieftan of an independent branch of a powerful Highland clan, and is much respected, both for his own power, and that of his kith, kin, and allies."

"And what has he to do with the thieves, then? Is he a magistrate, or in the commission of the peace?" asked Waverley.

---

1 In full.
2 Malcolm III (c. 1031-93), king of Scotland.
3 "Irremediable scoundrels" (*OW*, 424); John Leslie (1527-96), bishop and historian.
4 Cacus was a monster who stole cattle and strangled them "till their eyes start out and their throats are dry of blood"; he was killed by Hercules (Virgil, *Aeneid*, VIII, 261) (*OW*, 424).

"The commission of war rather, if there be such a thing," said Rose; "for he is a very unquiet neighbour to his un-friends, and keeps a greater *following* on foot than many that have thrice his estate. As to his connexion with the thieves, that I cannot well explain; but the boldest of them will never steal a hoof from any one that pays black-mail to Vich Ian Vohr."

"And what is black-mail?"

"A sort of protection-money that Low-country gentlemen and heritors, lying near the Highlands, pay to some Highland chief, that he may neither do them harm himself, nor suffer it to be done to them by others; and then if your cattle are stolen, you have only to send him word, and he will recover them; or it may be, he will drive away cows from some distant place, where he has a quarrel, and give them to you to make up your loss."

"And is this sort of Highland Jonathan Wild[1] admitted into society, and called a gentleman?"

"So much so," said Rose, "that the quarrel between my father and Fergus Mac-Ivor began at a county meeting, where he wanted to take precedence of all the Lowland gentlemen then present, only my father would not suffer it. And then he upbraided my father that he was under his banner, and paid him tribute; and my father was in a towering passion, for Bailie Macwheeble, who manages such things his own way, had contrived to keep this black-mail a secret from him, and passed it in his account for cess-money.[2] And they would have fought; but Fergus Mac-Ivor said, very gallantly, he would never raise his hand against a grey head that was so much respected as my father's.—O I wish, I wish they had continued friends!"

"And did you ever see this Mr Mac-Ivor, if that be his name, Miss Bradwardine?"

"No, that is not his name; and he would consider *master* as a sort of affront, only that you are an Englishman, and know no better. But the Lowlanders call him, like other gentlemen, by the name of his estate, Glennaquoich; and the Highlanders call him Vich Ian Vohr, that is, the son of John the Great; and we upon the braes here call him by both names indifferently."

---

1 Jonathan Wild (c. 1682-1725) was a thief taker and "fence" who organized criminal activity by groups of thieves and returned the stolen goods to their owners for a reward. Hanged at Tyburn (*OCBH*, 981-82). Henry Fielding's novel *The Life of Jonathan Wild the Great* (1743) paints him as an insidious villain whose corruption threatened the very fabric of society and was mirrored in the government of the day.

2 The land tax (*OED*).

"I am afraid I shall never bring my English tongue to call him by either one or the other."

"But he is a very polite, handsome man," continued Rose; "and his sister Flora is one of the most beautiful and accomplished young ladies in this country: she was bred in a convent in France, and was a great friend of mine before this unhappy dispute. Dear Captain Waverley, try your influence with my father to make matters up. I am sure this is but the beginning of our troubles; for Tully-Veolan has never been a safe or quiet residence when we have been at feud with the Highlanders. When I was a girl about ten, there was a skirmish fought between a party of twenty of them, and my father and his servants, behind the Mains; and the bullets broke several pains in the north windows, they were so near. Three of the Highlanders were killed, and they brought them in wrapped in their plaids, and laid them on the stone floor of the hall; and next morning, their wives and daughters came, clapping their hands, and crying the coronach,[1] and shrieking, and carried away the dead bodies, with the pipes playing before them. I could not sleep for six weeks without starting, and thinking I heard these terrible cries, and saw the bodies lying on the steps, all stiff and swathed up in their bloody tartans. But since that time there came a party from the garrison at Stirling, with a warrant from the Lord Justice Clerk, or some such great man, and took away all our arms; and now, how are we to protect ourselves if they come down in any strength?"

Waverley could not help starting at a story which bore so much resemblance to one of his own day-dreams. Here was a girl scarce seventeen, the gentlest of her sex, both in temper and appearance, who had witnessed with her own eyes such a scene as he had used to conjure up in his imagination, as only occurring in ancient times, and spoke of it coolly, as one very likely to recur. He felt at once the impulse of curiosity, and that slight sense of danger which only serves to heighten its interest. He might have said with Malvolio,[2] "'I do not now fool myself, to let imagination jade me!' I am actually in the land of military and romantic adventures, and it only remains to be seen what will be my own share in them."

The whole circumstances now detailed concerning the state of the country, seemed equally novel and extraordinary. He had indeed often heard of Highland thieves, but had no idea of the systematic mode in which their depredations were conducted; and that the practice was

---

1 "A funeral song or lamentation in the Highlands of Scotland and in Ireland; a dirge" (*OED*).
2 Shakespeare, *Twelfth Night*, II.v.176; Malvolio is a character of ill will who is in the course of the play fooled.

connived at, and even encouraged, by many of the Highland chieftains, who not only found the creaghs, or forays, useful for the purpose of training individuals of their clan to the practice of arms, but also of maintaining a wholesome terror among their Lowland neighbours, and levying, as we have seen, a tribute from them, under colour of protection-money.

Bailie Macwheeble, who soon afterwards entered, expatiated still more at length upon the same topic. This honest gentleman's conversation was so formed upon his professional practice, that Davie Gellatley once said his discourse was like a "charge of horning." He assured our hero, that "from the maist ancient times of record, the lawless thieves, limmers,[1] and broken men of the Highlands, had been in fellowship together by reason of their surnames, for the committing of divers thefts, reifs,[2] and herships[3] upon the honest men of the Low Country, when they not only intromitted with their whole goods and gear, corn, cattle, horse, nolt, sheep, outsight and insight plenishing, at their wicked pleasure, but moreover made prisoners, ransomed them, or concussed them into giving borrows (pledges) to enter into captivity again: all which was directly prohibited in divers parts of the Statute Book, both by the act one thousand five hundred and sixty-seven, and various others; the whilk statutes, with all that had followed and might follow thereupon, were shamefully broken and vilipended by the said sornars, limmers, and broken men, associated into fellowships, for the aforesaid purposes of theft, stouthreef,[4] fire-raising, murther *raptus mulierum*, or forcible abduction of women, and such like as aforesaid."

It seemed like a dream to Waverley that these deeds of violence should be familiar to men's minds, and currently talked of, as falling within the common order of things, and happening daily in the immediate vicinity, without his having crossed the seas, and while he was yet in the otherwise well-ordered island of Great Britain.[bb]

CHAPTER XVI.
An unexpected Ally appears.

THE Baron returned at the dinner-hour, and had in a great measure recovered his composure and good-humour. He not only confirmed the stories which Edward had heard from Rose and Bailie Macwheeble, but added many anecdotes from his own experience, concerning

---

1 Rogues, scoundrels (*OED*).
2 Robberies.
3 Plunderings.
4 Robbery and arson.

the state of the Highlands and their inhabitants. The chiefs, he pronounced to be, in general, gentlemen of great honour and high pedigree, whose word was accounted as a law by all those of their own sept, or clan. "It did not indeed," he said, "become them, as had occurred in late instances, to propone their *prosapia*,[1] a lineage which rested for the most part on the vain and fond rhymes of their Seannachies or Bhairds, as æquiponderate with the evidence of ancient characters and royal grants of antiquity, conferred upon distinguished houses in the Low Country by divers Scottish monarchs; nevertheless, such was their *outrecuidance*[2] and presumption, as to undervalue those who possessed such evidents, as if they held their lands in a sheep's skin."

This, by the way, pretty well explained the cause of quarrel between the Baron and his Highland ally. But he went on to state so many curious particulars concerning the manners, customs, and habits of this patriarchal race, that Edward's curiosity became highly interested, and he inquired whether it was possible to make with safety an excursion into the neighbouring Highlands, whose dusky barrier of mountains had already excited his wish to penetrate beyond them. The Baron assured his guest that nothing would be more easy, providing this quarrel were first made up, since he could himself give the letters to many of the distinguished Chiefs, who would receive him with the utmost courtesy and hospitality.

While they were on this topic, the door suddenly opened, and, ushered by Saunders Saunderson, a Highlander, fully armed and equipped, entered the apartment. Had it not been that Saunders acted the part of master of the ceremonies to this martial apparition, without appearing to deviate from his usual composure, and that neither Mr Bradwardine nor Rose exhibited any emotion, Edward would certainly have thought the intrusion hostile. As it was, he started at the sight of what he had not yet happened to see, a mountaineer in his full national costume. The individual Gael was a stout, dark, young man, of low stature, the ample folds of whose plaid added to the appearance of strength which his person exhibited. The short kilt, or petticoat, showed his sinewy and clean-made limbs; the goatskin purse, flanked by the usual defences, a dirk and steel-wrought pistol, hung before him; his bonnet had a short feather, which indicated his claim to be treated as a Duinhé-wassel, or sort of gentleman; a broadsword dangled by his side, a target hung upon his shoulder, and a long Spanish fowling-piece occupied one of his hands. With the other hand he pulled off his bonnet, and the Baron, who well knew

---

1   Put forth their lineage.
2   Presumptuousness (*LCD*).

their customs, and the proper mode of addressing them, immediately said, with an air of dignity, but without rising, and much, as Edward thought, in the manner of a prince receiving an embassy, "Welcome, Evan Dhu Maccombich; what news from Fergus Mac-Ivor Vich Ian Vohr?"

"Fergus Mac-Ivor Vich Ian Vohr," said the ambassador, in good English, "greets you well, Baron of Bradwardine and Tully-Veolan, and is sorry there has been a thick cloud interposed between you and him, which has kept you from seeing and considering the friendship and alliances that have been between your houses and forebears of old; and he prays you that the cloud may pass away, and that things may be as they have been heretofore between the clan Ivor and the house of Bradwardine, when there was an egg between them for a flint, and a knife for a sword. And he expects you will also say, you are sorry for the cloud, and no man shall hereafter ask whether it descended from the hill to the valley, or rose from the valley to the hill; for they never struck with the scabbard who did not receive with the sword, and woe to him who would lose his friend for the stormy cloud of a spring morning."

To this the Baron of Bradwardine answered with suitable dignity, that he knew the chief of clan Ivor to be a well-wisher to the *King*, and he was sorry there should have been a cloud between him and any gentleman of such sound principles, "for when folks are banding together, feeble is he who hath no brother."

This appearing perfectly satisfactory, that the peace between these august persons might be duly solemnized, the Baron ordered a stoup of usquebaugh, and, filling a glass, drank to the health and prosperity of Mac-Ivor of Glennaquoich; upon which the Celtic ambassador, to requite his politeness, turned down a mighty bumper of the same generous liquor, seasoned with his good wishes to the house of Bradwardine.

Having thus ratified the preliminaries of the general treaty of pacification, the envoy retired to adjust with Mr Macwheeble some subordinate articles with which it was not thought necessary to trouble the Baron. These probably referred to the discontinuance of the subsidy, and apparently the Bailie found means to satisfy their ally, without suffering his master to suppose that his dignity was compromised. At least, it is certain, that after the plenipotentiaries had drunk a bottle of brandy in single drams, which seemed to have no more effect upon such seasoned vessels, than if it had been poured upon the two bears at the top of the avenue, Evan Dhu Maccombich having possessed himself of all the information which he could procure respecting the robbery of the preceding night, declared his intention to set off immediately in pursuit of the cattle, which he pronounced to be "no that far off;—they have broken the bone," he observerd, "but they have had no time to suck the marrow."

Our hero, who had attended Evan Dhu during his perquisitions, was much struck with the ingenuity which he displayed in collecting information, and the precise and pointed conclusions which he drew from it. Evan Dhu, on his part, was obviously flattered with the attention of Waverley, the interest he seemed to take in his inquiries, and his curiosity about the customs and scenery of the Highlands. Without much ceremony he invited Edward to accompany him on a short walk of ten or fifteen miles into the mountains, and see the place where the cattle were conveyed to; adding, "If it be as I suppose, you never saw such a place in your life, nor ever will, unless you go with me or the like of me."

Our hero, feeling his curiosity considerably excited by the idea of visiting the den of a Highland Cacus, took, however, the precaution to inquire if his guide might be trusted. He was assured, that the invitation would on no account have been given had there been the least danger, and that all he had to apprehend was a little fatigue; and as Evan proposed he should pass a day at his Chieftain's house in returning, where he would be sure of good accommodation and an excellent welcome, there seemed nothing very formidable in the task he undertook. Rose, indeed, turned pale when she heard of it; but her father, who loved the spirited curiosity of his young friend, did not attempt to damp it by an alarm of danger which really did not exist, and a knapsack, with a few necessaries, being bound on the shoulders of a sort of deputy gamekeeper, our hero set forth with a fowling-piece in his hand, accompanied by his new friend Evan Dhu, and followed by the gamekeeper aforesaid, and by two wild Highlanders, the attendants of Evan, one of whom had upon his shoulder a hatchet at the end of a pole, called a Lochaber-axe,[cc] and the other a long ducking-gun. Evan, upon Edward's inquiry, gave him to understand that this martial escort was by no means necessary as a guard, but merely, as he said, drawing up and adjusting his plaid with an air of dignity, that he might appear decently at Tully-Veolan, and as Vich Ian Vohr's foster-brother ought to do. "Ah!" said he, "if you Saxon Duinhé-wassel (English gentleman) saw but the Chief with his tail on!"

"With his tail on?" echoed Edward, in some surprise.

"Yes—that is, with all his usual followers, when he visits those of the same rank. There is," he continued, stopping and drawing himself proudly up, while he counted upon his fingers the several officers of his chief's retinue; "there is his *hanchman*, or right-hand man; then his *bàrd*, or poet; then his *bladier*, or orator, to make harangues to the great folks whom he visits; then his *gilly-more*, or armour-bearer, to carry his sword, and target, and his gun; then his *gilly-casfliuch*, who carries him on his back through the sikes and brooks; then his *gilly-comstrian*, to lead his horse by the bridle in steep and difficult paths, then his *gilly-trushharnish*, to carry his knapsack; and the piper and the piper's man, and it may be a dozen young lads beside, that have no business, but are just boys of the belt, to follow the laird, and do his honour's bidding."

"And does your Chief regularly maintain all these men?" demanded Waverley.

"All these?" replied Evan; "ay, and many a fair head beside, that would not ken where to lay itself, but for the mickle[1] barn at Glennaquoich."

With similar tales of the grandeur of the Chief in peace and war, Evan Dhu beguiled the way till they approached more closely those huge mountains which Edward had hitherto only seen at a distance. It was towards evening as they entered one of the tremendous passes which afford communication between the high and low country; the path, which was extremely steep and rugged, winded up a chasm between two tremendous rocks, following the passage which a foaming stream, that brawled far below, appeared to have worn for itself in the course of ages. A few slanting beams of the sun, which was now setting, reached the water in its darksome bed, and showed it partially, chafed by a hundred rocks, and broken by a hundred falls. The descent from the path to the stream was a mere precipice, with here and there a projecting fragment of granite, or a scathed tree, which had warped its twisted roots into the fissures of the rock. On the right hand, the mountain rose above the path with almost equal inaccessibility; but the hill on the opposite side displayed a shroud of copsewood, with which some pines were intermingled.

"This," said Evan, "is the pass of Bally-Brough, which was kept in former times by ten of the clan Donnochie against a hundred of the Low Country carles.[2] The graves of the slain are still to be seen in that little corri, or bottom, on the opposite side of the burn[3]—if your eyes are good, you may see the green specks among the heather.—See, there is an earn, which you Southrons call an eagle—you have no such birds as that in England—he is going to fetch his supper from the Laird of Bradwardine's braes,[4] but I'll send a slug after him."

He fired his piece accordingly, but missed the superb monarch of the feathered tribes, who, without noticing the attempt to annoy him, continued his majestic flight to the southward. A thousand birds of

1 Great, large (*WSG*).
2 Gruff old man, churl (*WSG*).
3 "A small stream or brook" (*OED*).
4 Rising ground (*WSG*); "the steep bank bounding a river valley" (*OED*).

prey, hawks, kites, carrion-crows, and ravens, disturbed from the lodgings which they had just taken up for the evening, rose at the report of the gun, and mingled their hoarse and discordant notes with the echoes which replied to it, and with the roar of the mountain cataracts. Evan, a little disconcerted at having missed his mark, when he meant to have displayed peculiar dexterity, covered his confusion by whistling part of a pibroch[1] as he reloaded his piece, and proceeded in silence up the pass.

It issued in a narrow glen, between two mountains, both very lofty, and covered with heath.[2] The brook continued to be their companion, and they advanced up its mazes, crossing them now and then, on which occasions Evan Dhu uniformly offered the assistance of his attendants to carry over Edward; but our hero, who had been always a tolerable pedestrian, declined the accommodation, and obviously rose in his guide's opinion, by showing that he did not fear wetting his feet. Indeed he was anxious, so far as he could without affectation, to remove the opinion which Evan seemed to entertain of the effeminacy of the Lowlanders, and particularly of the English.

Through the gorge of this glen they found access to a black bog, of tremendous extent, full of large pit-holes, which they traversed with great difficulty and some danger, by tracks which no one but a Highlander could have followed. The path itself, or rather the portion of more solid ground on which the travellers half walked, half waded, was rough, broken, and in many places quaggy and unsound. Sometimes the ground was so completely unsafe, that it was necessary to spring from one hillock to another, the space between being incapable of bearing the human weight. This was an easy matter to the Highlanders, who wore thin-soled brogues fit for the purpose, and moved with a peculiar springing step; but Edward began to find the exercise, to which he was unaccustomed, more fatiguing than he expected. The lingering twilight served to show them through this Serbonian bog,[3] but deserted them almost totally at the bottom of a steep and very stony hill, which it was the traveller's next toilsome task to ascend. The night, however, was pleasant, and not dark; and Waverley, calling up mental energy to support personal fatigue, held on his march gallantly, though envying in his heart his Highland attendants, who con-

---

1 "In the Scotch Highlands, a series of variations for the bagpipe, founded on a theme called the *urlar*. They are generally of a martial character, but include dirges" (*OED*).

2 "Open uncultivated ground; an extensive tract of waste land; a wilderness ..." (*OED*).

3 From Milton's *Paradise Lost*, the name he gives Lake Serbonis in Egypt, "a marshy tract covered with shifting sand" (*PW*, 582).

tinued, without a symptom of abated vigour, the rapid and swinging pace, or rather trot, which, according to his computation, had already brought them fifteen miles upon their journey.

After crossing this mountain, and descending on the other side towards a thick wood, Evan Dhu held some conference with his Highland attendants, in consequence of which Edward's baggage was shifted from the shoulders of the gamekeeper to those of one of the gillies, and the former was sent off with the other mountaineer in a direction different from that of the three remaining travellers. On asking the meaning of this separation, Waverley was told that the Lowlander must go to a hamlet about three miles off for the night; for unless it was some very particular friend, Donald Bean Lean, the worthy person whom they supposed to be possessed of the cattle, did not much approve of strangers approaching his retreat. This seemed reasonable, and silenced a qualm of suspicion which came across Edward's mind, when he saw himself, at such a place and such an hour, deprived of his only Lowland companion. And Evan immediately afterwards added, "that indeed he himself had better get forward, and announce their approach to Donald Bean Lean, as the arrival of a *sidier roy*[1] (red soldier) might otherwise be a disagreeable surprise." And without waiting for an answer, in jockey phrase, he trotted out, and putting himself to a very round pace, was out of sight in an instant.

Waverley was now left to his own meditations, for his attendant with the battle-axe spoke very little English. They were traversing a thick, and, as it seemed, an endless wood of pines, and consequently the path was altogether indiscernible in the murky darkness which surrounded them. The Highlander, however, seemed to trace it by instinct, without the hesitation of a moment, and Edward followed his footsteps as close as he could.

After journeying a considerable time in silence, he could not help asking, "Was it far to the end of their journey?"

"Ta cove was tree, four mile; but as Duinhé-wassel was a wee taiglit, Donald could, tat is, might—would—should send ta curragh."[2]

This conveyed no information. The *curragh* which was promised might be a man, a horse, a cart, or chaise; and no more could be got

---

1 In the interleaved *Waverley* Scott added the following note, which was not included in the *Magnum Opus Waverley*: The words *sidier roy* or red soldier was used to distinguish the regular regiments from the independent companies used to protect the peace of the Highlands. These _____ were called *sidier dhu* i.e., black soldiers and the _____ regiment which was formed out of these independent companies is still called the Black Watch from the dark colour of their tartans.

2 "A corackle, or small skiff; boat of wicker-work, covered with hides" (*WSG*).

from the man with the battle-axe, but a repetition of "Aich ay! ta curragh."

But in a short time Edward began to conceive his meaning, when, issuing from the wood, he found himself on the banks of a large river or lake, where his conductor gave him to understand they must sit down for a little while. The moon, which now began to rise, showed obscurely the expanse of water which spread before them, and the shapeless and indistinct forms of mountains with which it seemed to be surrounded. The cool, and yet mild air of the summer night, refreshed Waverley after his rapid and toilsome walk; and the perfume which it wafted from the birch trees,^{dd} bathed in the evening dew, was exquisitely fragrant.

He had now time to give himself up to the full romance of his situation. Here he sate on the banks of an unknown lake, under the guidance of a wild native, whose language was unknown to him, on a visit to the den of some renowned outlaw, a second Robin Hood, perhaps, or Adam o' Gordon,[1] and that at deep midnight, through scenes of difficulty and toil, separated from his attendant, left by his guide:— What a variety of incidents for the exercise of a romantic imagination, and all enhanced by the solemn feeling of uncertainty, at least, if not of danger! The only circumstance which assorted ill with the rest, was the cause of his journey—the Baron's milk cows! This degrading incident he kept in the back ground.

While wrapt in these dreams of imagination, his companion gently touched him, and, pointing in a direction nearly straight across the lake, said, "Yon's ta cove." A small point of light was seen to twinkle in the direction in which he pointed, and, gradually increasing in size and lustre, seemed to flicker like a meteor upon the verge of the horizon. While Edward watched this phenomenon, the distant dash of oars was heard. The measured sound approached near and more near, and presently a loud whistle was heard in the same direction. His friend with the battle-axe immediately whistled clear and shrill, in reply to the signal, and a boat, manned with four or five Highlanders, pushed for a little inlet, near which Edward was sitting. He advanced to meet them with his attendant, was immediately assisted into the boat by the officious attention of two stout mountaineers, and had no sooner seated himself than they resumed their oars, and began to row across the lake with great rapidity.

---

1   "The villain of the ballad 'Captain Carr, or, Edom O Gordon,' F.J. Child, *The English and Scottish Popular Ballads* 1882-98, no. 178" (*OW*, 426).

CHAPTER XVII.
The Hold of a Highland Robber.

THE party preserved silence, interrupted only by the monotonous and murmured chant of a Gaelic song, sung in a kind of low recitative by the steersman, and by the dash of the oars, which the notes seemed to regulate, as they dipped to them in cadence. The light, which they now approached more nearly, assumed a broader, redder, and more irregular splendour. It appeared plainly to be a large fire, but whether kindled upon an island or the main land, Edward could not determine. As he saw it, the red glaring orb seemed to rest on the very surface of the lake itself, and resembled the fiery vehicle in which the Evil Genius of an Oriental tale[1] traverses land and sea. They approached nearer, and the light of the fire sufficed to show that it was kindled at the bottom of a huge dark crag or rock, rising abruptly from the very edge of the water; its front, changed by the reflection to dusky red, formed a strange, and even awful contrast to the banks around, which were from time to time faintly and partially illuminated by pallid moonlight.

The boat now neared the shore, and Edward could discover that this large fire, amply supplied with branches of pine-wood by two figures, who, in the red reflection of its light, appeared like demons, was kindled in the jaws of a lofty cavern, into which an inlet from the lake seemed to advance; and he conjectured, which was indeed true, that the fire had been lighted as a beacon to the boatmen on their return. They rowed right for the mouth of the cave, and then, shipping their oars, permitted the boat to enter in obedience to the impulse which it had received. The skiff passed the little point or platform of rock, on which the fire was blazing, and running about two boats' length farther, stopped where the cavern (for it was already arched overhead) ascended from the water by five or six broad ledges of rocks, so easy and regular that they might be termed natural steps. At this moment a quantity of water was suddenly flung upon the fire, which sunk with a hissing noise, and with it disappeared the light it had hitherto afforded. Four or five active arms lifted Waverley out of the boat, placed him on his feet, and almost carried him into the recesses of the cave. He made a few paces in darkness, guided in this manner; and advancing towards a hum of voices, which seemed to sound from the centre of the rock, at an acute turn Donald Bean Lean and his whole establishment were before his eyes.

The interior of the cave, which here rose very high, was illuminated by torches made of pine-tree, which emitted a bright and bickering

---

1   The villain of a tale set in the Middle or Far East, popular in the second half of the eighteenth century and early nineteenth century (*OCEL*, 719).

light, attended by a strong, though not unpleasant odour. Their light was assisted by the red glare of a large charcoal fire, round which were seated five or six armed Highlanders, while others were indistinctly seen couched on their plaids, in the more remote recesses of the cavern. In one large aperture, which the robber facetiously called his *spence* (or pantry), there hung by the heels the carcasses of a sheep, or ewe, and two cows lately slaughtered. The principal inhabitant of this singular mansion, attended by Evan Dhu as master of the ceremonies, came forward to meet his guest, totally different in appearance and manner from what his imagination had anticipated. The profession which he followed—the wilderness in which he dwelt—the wild warrior forms that surrounded him, were all calculated to inspire terror. From such accompaniments, Waverley prepared himself to meet a stern, gigantic, ferocious figure, such as Salvator would have chosen to be the central object of a group of banditti.[ee][1]

Donald Bean Lean was the very reverse of all these. He was thin in person and low in stature, with light sandy-coloured hair, and small pale features, from which he derived his agnomen of *Bean* or white; and although his form was light, well-proportioned, and active, he appeared, on the whole, rather a diminutive and insignificant figure. He had served in some inferior capacity in the French army, and in order to receive his English visitor in great form, and probably meaning, in his way, to pay him a compliment, he had laid aside the Highland dress for the time, to put on an old blue and red uniform, and a feathered hat, in which he was far from showing to advantage, and indeed looked so incongruous, compared with all around him, that Waverley would have been tempted to laugh, had laughter been either civil or safe. The robber received Captain Waverley with a profusion of French politeness and Scottish hospitality, seemed perfectly to know his name and connexions, and to be particularly acquainted with his uncle's political principles. On these he bestowed great applause, to which Waverley judged it prudent to make a very general reply.

Being placed at a convenient distance from the charcoal fire, the heat of which the season rendered oppressive, a strapping Highland damsel placed before Waverley, Evan, and Donald Bean, three cogues, or wooden vessels composed of staves and hoops, containing *eanaruich*[ff] a sort of strong soup, made out of a particular part of the inside of the beeves.[2] After this refreshment, which, though coarse, fatigue and hunger rendered palatable, steaks, roasted on the coals,

---

1   Salvator Rosa (c. 1615-73) painted landscapes in which banditti, or "lawless desperate marauders" (*OED*), figured; he is associated with the advent of the picturesque aesthetic in painting.

2   "Oxen, cattle" (*OED*).

were supplied in liberal abundance, and disappeared before Evan Dhu and their host with a promptitude that seemed like magic, and astonished Waverley, who was much puzzled to reconcile their voracity with what he had heard of the abstemiousness of the Highlanders. He was ignorant that this abstinence was with the lower ranks wholly compulsory, and that, like some animals of prey, those who practise it were usually gifted with the power of indemnifying themselves to good purpose, when chance threw plenty in their way. The whisky came forth in abundance to crown the cheer. The Highlanders drank it copiously and undiluted; but Edward, having mixed a little with water, did not find it so palatable as to invite him to repeat the draught. Their host bewailed himself exceedingly that he could offer him no wine: "Had he but known four-and-twenty hours before, he would have had some, had it been within the circle of forty miles round him. But no gentleman could do more to show his sense of the honour of a visit from another, than to offer him the best cheer his house afforded. Where there are not bushes there can be no nuts, and the way of those you live with is that you must follow."

He went on regretting to Evan Dhu the death of an aged man, Donnacha an Amrigh, or Duncan with the Cap, "a gifted seer," who foretold, through the second sight, visitors of every description who haunted their dwelling, whether as friends or foes.

"Is not his son Malcolm *taishatr* (a second-sighted person)?" asked Evan.

"Nothing equal to his father," replied Donald Bean. "He told us the other day we were to see a great gentleman riding on a horse, and there came nobody that whole day but Shemus Beg, the blind harper, with his dog. Another time he advertised us of a wedding, and behold it proved a funeral; and on the creagh, when he foretold to us we should bring home a hundred head of horned cattle, we gripped nothing but a fat bailie of Perth."

From this discourse he passed to the political and military state of the country; and Waverley was astonished, and even alarmed, to find a person of this description so accurately acquainted with the strength of the various garrisons and regiments quartered north of the Tay. He even mentioned the exact number of recruits who had joined Waverley's troop from his uncle's estate, and observed they were *pretty men*, meaning, not handsome, but stout warlike fellows. He put Waverley in mind of one or two minute circumstances which had happened at a general review of the regiment, which satisfied him that the robber had been an eye-witness of it; and Evan Dhu having by this time retired from the conversation, and wrapped himself up in his plaid to take some repose, Donald asked Edward, in a very significant manner, whether he had nothing particular to say to him.

Waverley, surprised and somewhat startled at this question from such a character, answered he had no motive in visiting him but curiosity to see his extraordinary place of residence. Donald Bean Lean looked him steadily in the face for an instant, and then said, with a significant nod, "You might as well have confided in me; I am as much worthy of trust as either the Baron of Bradwardine, or Vich Ian Vohr:—But you are equally welcome to my house."

Waverley felt an involuntary shudder creep over him at the mysterious language held by this outlawed and lawless bandit, which, in despite of his attempts to master it, deprived him of the power to ask the meaning of his insinuations. A heath pallet, with the flowers stuck uppermost, had been prepared for him in a recess of the cave, and here, covered with such spare plaids as could be mustered, he lay for some time watching the motions of the other inhabitants of the cavern. Small parties of two or three entered or left the place without any other ceremony than a few words in Gaelic to the principal outlaw, and, when he fell asleep, to a tall Highlander who acted as his lieutenant, and seemed to keep watch during his repose. Those who entered, seemed to have returned from some excursion, of which they reported the success, and went without farther ceremony to the larder, where cutting with their dirks their rations from the carcasses which were there suspended, they proceeded to broil and eat them at their own pleasure and leisure. The liquor was under strict regulation, being served out either by Donald himself, his lieutenant, or the strapping Highland girl aforesaid, who was the only female that appeared. The allowance of whisky, however, would have appeared prodigal to any but Highlanders, who, living entirely in the open air, and in a very moist climate, can consume great quantities of ardent spirits without the usual baneful effects either upon the brain or constitution.

At length the fluctuating groups began to swim before the eyes of our hero as they gradually closed; nor did he re-open them till the morning sun was high on the lake without, though there was but a faint and glimmering twilight in the recesses of Uaimh an Ri, or the King's Cavern, as the abode of Donald Bean Lean was proudly denominated.

CHAPTER XVIII.
Waverley proceeds on his Journey.

WHEN Edward had collected his scattered recollection, he was surprised to observe the cavern totally deserted. Having arisen and put his dress in some order, he looked more accurately round him; but all was still solitary. If it had not been for the decayed brands of the fire, now sunk into grey ashes, and the remnants of the festival, consisting of bones half burnt and half gnawed, and an empty keg or two, there remained no traces of Donald and his band. When Waverley sallied forth to the entrance of the cave, he perceived that the point of rock, on which remained the marks of last night's beacon, was accessible by a small path, either natural, or roughly hewn in the rock, along the little inlet of water which ran a few yards up into the cavern, where, as in a wet-dock, the skiff which brought him there the night before, was still lying moored. When he reached the small projecting platform on which the beacon had been established, he would have believed his farther progress by land impossible, only that it was scarce probable but what the inhabitants of the cavern had some mode of issuing from it otherwise than by the lake. Accordingly, he soon observed three or four shelving steps, or ledges of rock, at the very extremity of the little platform; and, making use of them as a stair-case, he clambered by their means around the projecting shoulder of the crag on which the cavern opened, and, descending with some difficulty on the other side, he gained the wild and precipitous shores of a Highland loch, about four miles in length, and a mile and a half across, surrounded by heathy and savage mountains, on the crests of which the morning mist was still sleeping.

Looking back to the place from which he came, he could not help admiring the address which had adopted a retreat of such seclusion and secrecy. The rock, round the shoulder of which he had turned by a few imperceptible notches, that barely afforded place for the foot, seemed, in looking back upon it, a huge precipice, which barred all farther passage by the shores of the lake in that direction. There could be no possibility, the breadth of the lake considered, of descrying the entrance of the narrow and low-browed cave from the other side, so that, unless the retreat had been sought for with boats, or disclosed by treachery, it might be a safe and secret residence to its garrison as long as they were supplied with provisions. Having satisfied his curiosity in these particulars, Waverley looked around for Evan Dhu and his attendant, who, he rightly judged, would be at no great distance, whatever might have become of Donald Bean Lean and his party, whose mode of life was, of course, liable to sudden migrations of abode. Accordingly, at the distance of about half a mile, he beheld a Highlander (Evan apparently) angling in the lake, with another attending him, whom, from the weapon which he shouldered, he recognised for his friend with the battle-axe.

Much nearer to the mouth of the cave he heard the notes of a lively Gaelic song, guided by which, in a sunny recess, shaded by a glittering birch-tree, and carpeted with a bank of firm white sand, he found the damsel of the cavern, whose lay had already reached him, busy, to the best of her power, in arranging to advantage a morning repast of milk, eggs, barley-bread, fresh butter, and honey-comb. The poor girl had already made a circuit of four miles that morning in search of the eggs, of the meal which baked her cakes, and of the other materials of the breakfast, being all delicacies which she had to beg or borrow from distant cottagers. The followers of Donald Bean Lean used little food except the flesh of the animals which they drove away from the Lowlands; bread itself was a delicacy seldom thought of, because hard to be obtained, and all the domestic accommodations of milk, poultry, butter, &c., were out of the question in this Scythian camp.[1] Yet it must not be omitted, that although Alice had occupied a part of the morning in providing those accommodations for her guest which the cavern did not afford, she had secured time also to arrange her own person in her best trim. Her finery was simple. A short russet-coloured jacket, and a petticoat, of scanty longitude, was her whole dress; but these were clean, and neatly arranged. A piece of scarlet embroidered cloth, called the *snood*, confined her hair, which fell over it in a profusion of rich dark curls. The scarlet plaid, which formed part of her dress, was laid aside, that it might not impede her activity in attending the stranger. I should forget Alice's proudest ornament, were I to omit mentioning a pair of gold ear-rings, and a golden rosary, which her father (for she was the daughter of Donald Bean Lean) had brought from France, the plunder, probably, of some battle or storm.

Her form, though rather large for her years, was very well proportioned, and her demeanour had a natural and rustic grace, with nothing of the sheepishness of an ordinary peasant. The smiles, displaying a row of teeth of exquisite whiteness, and the laughing eyes, with which, in dumb show, she gave Waverley that morning greeting which she wanted English words to express, might have been interpreted by a coxcomb, or perhaps by a young soldier, who, without being such, was conscious of a handsome person, as meant to convey more than the courtesy of an hostess. Nor do I take it upon me to say, that the little wild mountaineer would have welcomed any staid old gentleman advanced in life, the Baron of Bradwardine, for example, with the cheerful pains which she bestowed upon Edward's accommodation. She seemed eager to place him by the meal which she had so sedulously arranged, and to which she now added a few bunches of cran-berries, gathered in an adjacent morass. Having had the satisfaction of seeing him seated at his breakfast, she placed herself demurely

---

1 Scythians were nomadic people who migrated from Central Asia to Southern Russia in the eighth and seventh centuries BCE. They were known for their skill in battle, their horsemanship, and the *comitatus* relationship that bound them.

upon a stone at a few yards' distance, and appeared to watch with great complacency for some opportunity of serving him.

Evan and his attendant now returned slowly along the beach, the latter bearing a large salmon-trout, the produce of the morning's sport, together with the angling-rod, while Evan strolled forward, with an easy, self-satisfied, and important gait, towards the spot where Waverley was so agreeably employed at the breakfast-table. After morning greetings had passed on both sides, and Evan, looking at Waverley, had said something in Gaelic to Alice, which made her laugh, yet colour up to her eyes, through a complexion well embrowned by sun and wind, Evan intimated his commands that the fish should be prepared for breakfast. A spark from the lock of his pistol produced a light, and a few withered fir branches were quickly in flame, and as speedily reduced to hot embers, on which the trout was broiled in large slices. To crown the repast, Evan produced from the pocket of his short jerkin, a large scallop shell, and from under the folds of his plaid, a ram's horn full of whisky. Of this he took a copious dram, observing, he had already taken his *morning* with Donald Bean Lean, before his departure; he offered the same cordial to Alice and to Edward, which they both declined. With the bounteous air of a lord, Evan then proffered the scallop to Dugald Mahony, his attendant, who, without waiting to be asked a second time, drank it off with great gusto. Evan then prepared to move towards the boat, inviting Waverley to attend him. Meanwhile, Alice had made up in a small basket what she thought worth removing, and flinging her plaid around her, she advanced up to Edward, and with the utmost simplicity, taking hold of his hand, offered her cheek to his salute, dropping, at the same time, her little courtesy. Evan, who was esteemed a wag[1] among the mountain fair, advanced, as if to secure a similar favour; but Alice, snatching up her basket, escaped up the rocky bank as fleetly as a roe, and, turning round and laughing, called something out to him in Gaelic, which he answered in the same tone and language; then, waving her hand to Edward, she resumed her road, and was soon lost among the thickets, though they continued for some time to hear her lively carol, as she proceeded gaily on her solitary journey.

They now again entered the gorge of the cavern, and stepping into the boat, the Highlander pushed off, and, taking advantage of the morning breeze, hoisted a clumsy sort of sail, while Evan assumed the helm, directing their course, as it appeared to Waverley, rather higher up the lake than towards the place of his embarkation on the preceding night. As they glided along the silver mirror, Evan opened the con-

---

1 A joker, mischief maker (*OED*).

versation with a panegyric upon Alice, who, he said, was both *canny*[1] and *fendy*;[2] and was, to the boot of all that, the best dancer of a strathspey[3] in the whole strath.[4] Edward assented to her praises so far as he understood them, yet could not help regretting that she was condemned to such a perilous and dismal life.

"Oich! for that," said Evan, "there is nothing in Perthshire that she need want, if she ask her father to fetch it, unless it be too hot or too heavy."

"But to be the daughter of a cattle-stealer—a common thief!"

"Common thief!—No such thing: Donald Bean Lean never *lifted* less than a drove in his life."

"Do you call him an uncommon thief, then?"

"No—he that steals a cow from a poor widow, or a stirk from a cottar,[5] is a thief; he that lifts a drove from a Sassenach laird,[6] is a gentleman-drover. And, besides, to take a tree from the forest, a salmon from the river, a deer from the hill, or a cow from a Lowland strath, is what no Highlander need ever think shame upon."

"But what can this end in, were he taken in such an appropriation?"

"To be sure he would *die for the law*, as many a pretty man has done before him."

"Die for the law!"

"Ay; that is, with the law, or by the law; be strapped up on the *kind* gallows of Crieff,[gg] where his father died, and his goodsire died, and where I hope he'll live to die himsell, if he's not shot, or slashed, in a creagh."

"You *hope* such a death for your friend, Evan?"

"And that do I e'en; would you have me wish him to die on a bundle of wet straw in yon den of his, like a mangy tyke?"

"But what becomes of Alice, then?"

"Troth, if such an accident were to happen, as her father would not need her help ony langer, I ken nought to hinder me to marry her mysell."

---

1 "Skillful; prudent; lucky; in a superstitious sense, good-conditioned and safe to deal with; trustworthy" (*WSG*).

2 "Clever in providing" (*WSG*).

3 "A lively dance or reel for two dancers" (*OED*).

4 "A stretch of flat land by the waterside" (*OED*).

5 "A young steer or heifer between one and two years old" from a cottager (*WSG*).

6 A herd or flock from an English laird ("Sassenach" is the "name given by the Gaelic inhabitants of Great Britain and Ireland to their 'Saxon or English neighbours'" [*OED*]).

"Gallantly resolved," said Edward;—"but, in the meanwhile, Evan, what has your father-in-law (that shall be, if he have the good fortune to be hanged) done with the Baron's cattle?"

"Oich," answered Evan, "they were all trudging before your lad and Allan Kennedy before the sun blinked ower Ben-Lawers[1] this morning; and they'll be in the pass of Bally-Brough by this time, in their way back to the parks of Tully-Veolan, all but two, that were unhappily slaughtered before I got last night to Uaimh an Ri."

"And where are we going, Evan, if I may be so bold as to ask?" said Waverley.

"Where would you be ganging, but to the laird's ain house of Glennaquoich? Ye would not think to be in his country, without ganging to see him? It would be as much as a man's life's worth."

"And are we far from Glennaquoich?"

"But five bits of miles; and Vich Ian Vohr will meet us."

In about half an hour they reached the upper end of the lake, where, after landing Waverley, the two Highlanders drew the boat into a little creek among thick flags and reeds, where it lay perfectly concealed. The oars they put in another place of concealment, both for the use of Donald Bean Lean probably, when his occasions should next bring him to that place.

The travellers followed for some time a delightful opening into the hills, down which a little brook found its way to the lake. When they had pursued their walk a short distance, Waverley renewed his questions about their host of the cavern.

"Does he always reside in that cave?"

"Out, no! it's past the skill of man to tell where he's to be found at a' times; there's not a dern nook, or cove, or corri,[2] in the whole country, that he's not acquainted with."

"And do others beside your master shelter him?"

"My master?—*My* master is in Heaven," answered Evan, haughtily; and then immediately assuming his usual civility of manner, "but you mean my Chief;—no, he does not shelter Donald Bean Lean, nor any that are like him; he only allows him (with a smile) wood and water."

"No great boon, I should think, Evan, when both seem to be very plenty."

"Ah! but ye dinna see through it. When I say wood and water, I mean the loch and the land; and I fancy Donald would be put till't if the laird were to look for him wi' threescore men in the wood of Kailychat yonder; and if our boats, with a score or twa mair, were to come

---

1   "Ben" is used with the names of Scottish mountains.
2   "A hollow recess in a mountain open only on one side" (*WSG*).

down the loch to Uaimh an Ri, headed by mysell, or ony other pretty man."

"But suppose a strong party came against him from the Low Country, would not your Chief defend him?"

"Na, he would not ware the spark of a flint for him—if they came with the law."

"And what must Donald do, then?"

"He behoved to rid this country of himsell, and fall back, it may be, over the mount upon Letter Scriven."[1]

"And if he were pursued to that place?"

"I'se warrant he would go to his cousin's at Rannoch."

"Well, but if they followed him to Rannoch?"

"That," quoth Evan, "is beyond all belief; and, indeed, to tell you the truth, there durst not a Lowlander in all Scotland follow the fray a gun-shot beyond Bally-Brough, unless he had the help of the *Sidier Dhu*."

"Whom do you call so?"

"The *Sidier Dhu*? the black soldier; that is what they call the independent companies that were raised to keep peace and law in the Highlands. Vich Ian Vohr commanded one of them for five years, and I was sergeant myself, I shall warrant ye. They call them *Sidier Dhu*, because they wear the tartans, as they call your men—King George's men,—*Sidier Roy*, or red soldiers."

"Well, but when you were in King George's pay, Evan, you were surely King George's soldiers?"

"Troth, and you must ask Vich Ian Vohr about that; for we are for his king, and care not much which o' them it is. At ony rate, nobody can say we are King George's men now, when we have not seen his pay this twelvemonth."

This last argument admitted of no reply, nor did Edward attempt any: he rather chose to bring back the discourse to Donald Bean Lean. "Does Donald confine himself to cattle, or does he *lift*, as you call it, any thing else that comes in his way?"

"Troth, he's nae nice body, and he'll just tak ony thing, but most readily cattle, horse, or live Christians; for sheep are slow of travel, and inside plenishing is cumbrous to carry, and not easy to put away for siller in this country."

"But does he carry off men and women?"

"Out, ay. Did not ye hear him speak o' the Perth bailie? It cost that body five hundred merks[2] ere he got to the south of Bally-Brough.— And ance Donald played a pretty sport.[hh] There was to be a blythe

---

1   In the West Highlands, near Rannoch Moor.
2   13 1/3 d. of English money.

bridal between the Lady Cramfeezer, in the howe o' the Mearns (she was the auld laird's widow, and no sae young as she had been hersell), and young Gilliewhackit, who had spent his heirship and movables, like a gentleman, at cock-matches, bull-baitings, horse-races, and the like. Now, Donald Bean Lean, being aware that the bridegroom was in request, and wanting to cleik the cunzie (that is, to hook the siller), he cannily carried off Gilliewhackit ae night when he was riding *dovering* hame[1] (wi' the malt rather abune the meal), and with the help of his gillies he gat him into the hills with the speed of light, and the first place he wakened in was the cove of Uaimh an Ri. So there was old to do about ransoming the bridegroom; for Donald would not lower a farthing of a thousand punds"—

"The devil!"

"Punds Scottish, ye shall understand. And the lady had not the siller if she had pawned her gown; and they applied to the governor o' Stirling castle, and to the major o' the Black Watch;[2] and the governor said, it was ower far to the northward, and out of his district; and the major said, his men were gane hame to the shearing, and he would not call them out before the victual[3] was got in for all the Cramfeezers in Christendom, let alane the Mearns, for that it would prejudice the country. And in the meanwhile ye'll no hinder Gilliewhackit to take the small-pox. There was not the doctor in Perth or Stirling would look near the poor lad; and I cannot blame them, for Donald had been misguggled by ane of these doctors about Paris, and he swore he would fling the first into the loch that he catched beyond the Pass. However, some cailliachs (that is, old women), that were about Donald's hand, nursed Gilliewhackit sae weel, that between the free open air in the cove and the fresh whey, deil an he did not recover may be as weel as if he had been closed in a glazed chamber and a bed with curtains, and fed with red wine and white meat. And Donald was sae vexed about it, that when he was stout and weel, he even sent him free home, and said he would be pleased with ony thing they would like to gie him for the plague and trouble which he had about Gilliewhackit to an unkenn'd degree. And I cannot tell you precisely how they sorted; but they agreed sae right that Donald was invited to dance at the wedding in his Highland trews,[4] and they said that there was never sae meikle siller clinked in his purse either before or since. And to the

---

1 "Walking or riding half asleep as if from the effects of liquor"; home (*WSG*).
2 Prestigious Highland regiment.
3 "Food or provisions of any kind" (*OED*).
4 "Close-fitting trousers, or breeches combined with stockings, formerly worn by Irishmen and Scottish Highlanders and still by certain Scottish regiments" (*OED*).

boot of all that, Gilliewhackit said, that, be the evidence what it liked, if he had the luck to be on Donald's inquest, he would bring him in guilty of nothing whatever, unless it were wilful arson, or murder under trust."

With such bald and disjointed chat Evan went on illustrating the existing state of the Highlands, more perhaps to the amusement of Waverley than that of our readers. At length, after having marched over bank and brae, moss and heather, Edward, though not unacquainted with the Scottish liberality in computing distance, began to think that Evan's five miles were nearly doubled. His observation on the large measure which the Scottish allowed of their land, in comparison to the computation of their money, was readily answered by Evan, with the old jest, "The deil take them wha have the least pint stoup."[ii]

And now the report of a gun was heard, and a sportsman was seen, with his dogs and attendant, at the upper end of the glen. "Shough," said Dugald Mahony, "tat's ta Chief."

"It is not," said Evan, imperiously. "Do you think he would come to meet a Sassenach Duinhé-wassel in such a way as that?"

But as they approached a little nearer, he said, with an appearance of mortification, "And it is even he, sure enough; and he has not his tail[1] on after all;—there is no living creature with him but Callum Beg."

In fact, Fergus Mac-Ivor, of whom a Frenchman might have said, as truly as of any man in the Highlands, "*Qu'il connoit bien ses gens*,"[2] had no idea of raising himself in the eyes of an English young man of fortune, by appearing with a retinue of idle Highlanders disproportioned to the occasion. He was well aware that such an unnecessary attendance would seem to Edward rather ludicrous than respectable; and while few men were more attached to ideas of chieftainship and feudal power, he was, for that very reason, cautious of exhibiting external marks of dignity, unless at the time and in the manner when they were most likely to produce an imposing effect. Therefore, although, had he been to receive a brother chieftain, he would probably have been attended by all that retinue which Evan described with so much unction, he judged it more respectable to advance to meet Waverley with a single attendant, a very handsome Highland boy, who carried his master's shooting-pouch and his broadsword, without which he seldom went abroad.

When Fergus and Waverley met, the latter was struck with the peculiar grace and dignity of the Chieftain's figure. Above the middle

---

1   "A train or band of followers; a following; a retinue" (*OED*).

2   That he knows people well.

size, and finely proportioned, the Highland dress, which he wore in its simplest mode, set off his person to great advantage. He wore the trews, or close trowsers, made of tartan, chequed scarlet and white; in other particulars, his dress strictly resembled Evan's, excepting that he had no weapon save a dirk, very richly mounted with silver. His page, as we have said, carried his claymore;[1] and the fowling-piece,[2] which he held in his hand, seemed only designed for sport. He had shot in the course of his walk some young wild-ducks, as, though *close-time* was then unknown, the broods of grouse were yet too young for the sportsman. His countenance was decidedly Scottish, with all the peculiarities of the northern physiognomy, but yet had so little of its harshness and exaggeration, that it would have been pronounced in any country extremely handsome. The martial air of the bonnet, with a single eagle's feather as a distinction, added much to the manly appearance of his head, which was besides ornamented with a far more natural and graceful cluster of close black curls than ever were exposed to sale in Bond-Street.[3]

An air of openness and affability increased the favourable impression derived from this handsome and dignified exterior. Yet a skilful physiognomist[4] would have been less satisfied with the countenance on the second than on the first view. The eye-brow and upper lip bespoke something of the habit of peremptory command and decisive superiority. Even his courtesy, though open, frank, and unconstrained, seemed to indicate a sense of personal importance; and, upon any check or accidental excitation, a sudden, though transient lour of the eye, showed a hasty, haughty, and vindictive temper, not less to be dreaded because it seemed much under its owner's command. In short, the countenance of the Chieftain resembled a smiling summer's day, in which, notwithstanding, we are made sensible by certain, though slight signs, that it may thunder and lighten before the close of evening.

It was not, however, upon their first meeting that Edward had an opportunity of making these less favourable remarks. The Chief received him as a friend of the Baron of Bradwardine, with the utmost expression of kindness and obligation for the visit; upbraided him gently with choosing so rude an abode as he had done the night before; and entered into a lively conversation with him about Donald Bean's housekeeping, but without the least hint as to his predatory habits, or the immediate occasion of Waverley's visit, a topic which, as

---

1   "The two-edged broadsword of the ancient Scottish Highlanders" (*OED*).
2   "A light gun for shooting wild fowl" (*OED*).
3   Where wigs are sold.
4   One who studies the physical form of the body and head to ascertain character.

the Chief did not introduce it, our hero also avoided. While they walked merrily on towards the house of Glennaquoich, Evan, who now fell respectfully into the rear, followed with Callum Beg and Dugald Mahony.

We shall take the opportunity to introduce the reader to some particulars of Fergus Mac-Ivor's character and history, which were not completely known to Waverley till after a connexion, which, though arising from a circumstance so casual, had for a length of time the deepest influence upon his character, actions, and prospects. But this, being an important subject, must form the commencement of a new chapter.

CHAPTER XIX.
The Chief and his Mansion.

THE ingenious licentiate Francisco de Ubeda,[1] when he commenced his history of La Picara Justina Diez,—which, by the way, is one of the most rare books of Spanish literature,—complained of his pen having caught up a hair, and forthwith begins, with more eloquence than common sense, an affectionate expostulation with that useful implement, upbraiding it with being the quill of a goose,—a bird inconstant by nature, as frequenting the three elements of water, earth, and air, indifferently, and being, of course, "to one thing constant never." Now I protest to thee, gentle reader, that I entirely dissent from Francisco de Ubeda in this matter, and hold it the most useful quality of my pen, that it can speedily change from grave to gay, and from description and dialogue to narrative and character. So that if my quill display no other properties of its mother-goose than her mutability, truly I shall be well pleased; and I conceive that you, my worthy friend, will have no occasion for discontent. From the jargon, therefore, of the Highland gillies,[2] I pass to the character of their Chief. It is an important examination, and therefore, like Dogberry,[3] we must spare no wisdom.

The ancestor of Fergus Mac-Ivor, about three centuries before, had set up a claim to be recognised as chief of the numerous and powerful clan to which he belonged, the name of which it is unnecessary to mention. Being defeated by an opponent who had more justice, or at least more force, on his side, he moved southwards, with those who

---

1 Francisco Lopez de Ubeda, author of *La Picara Justina* (1605), a Spanish picaresque.
2 A Highland manservant (*WSG*).
3 Constable in Shakespeare's *Much Ado About Nothing*, known for his misapplication of terms.

adhered to him, in quest of new settlements, like a second Æneas.[1]
The state of the Perthshire Highlands favoured his purpose. A great
baron in that country had lately become traitor to the crown; Ian,
which was the name of our adventurer, united himself with those who
were commissioned by the king to chastise him, and did such good
service, that he obtained a grant of the property, upon which he and
his posterity afterwards resided. He followed the king also in war to
the fertile regions of England, where he employed his leisure hours so
actively in raising subsidies among the boors of Northumberland and
Durham, that upon his return he was enabled to erect a stone tower,
or fortalice, so much admired by his dependents and neighbours, that
he, who had hitherto been called Ian Mac-Ivor, or John the son of
Ivor, was thereafter distinguished, both in song and genealogy, by the
high title of *Ian nan Chaistel*, or John of the Tower. The descendants of
this worthy were so proud of him, that the reigning chief always bore
the patronymic title of Vich Ian Vohr, *i.e.*, the son of John the Great;
while the clan at large, to distinguish them from that from which they
had seceded, were denominated *Sliochd nan Ivor*, the race of Ivor.

The father of Fergus, the tenth in direct descent from John of the
Tower, engaged heart and hand in the insurrection of 1715, and was
forced to fly to France, after the attempt of that year in favour of the
Stewarts had proved unsuccessful. More fortunate than other fugitives, he obtained employment in the French service, and married a
lady of rank in that kingdom, by whom he had two children, Fergus
and his sister Flora. The Scottish estate had been forfeited and
exposed to sale, but was repurchased for a small price in the name of
the young proprietor, who in consequence came to reside upon his
native domains.[jj] It was soon perceived that he possessed a character
of uncommon acuteness, fire, and ambition, which, as he became
acquainted with the state of the country, gradually assumed a mixed
and peculiar tone, that could only have been acquired Sixty Years
since.

Had Fergus Mac-Ivor lived Sixty Years sooner than he did, he
would, in all probability, have wanted the polished manner and knowledge of the world which he now possessed; and had he lived Sixty
Years later, his ambition and love of rule would have lacked the fuel
which his situation now afforded. He was indeed, within his little
circle, as perfect a politician as Castruccio Castrucani[2] himself. He
applied himself with great earnestness to appease all the feuds and dis-

---

1   Aeneas was a Trojan, according to classical legend, who escaped the fall of
    Troy for Italy, where his progeny built Rome.
2   Castruccio Castrucani Degli Antelminelli (1281-1328), soldier, then Duke of
    Lucca, who was aggressive in conquering neighboring kingdoms.

sensions which often arose among other clans in his neighbourhood, so that he became a frequent umpire in their quarrels. His own patriarchal power he strengthened at every expense which his fortune would permit, and indeed stretched his means to the uttermost to maintain the rude and plentiful hospitality, which was the most valued attribute of a chieftain. For the same reason, he crowded his estate with a tenantry, hardy indeed, and fit for the purposes of war, but greatly outnumbering what the soil was calculated to maintain. These consisted chiefly of his own clan, not one of whom he suffered to quit his lands if he could possibly prevent it. But he maintained, besides, many adventurers from the mother sept, who deserted a less warlike, though more wealthy chief, to do homage to Fergus Mac-Ivor. Other individuals, too, who had not even that apology, were nevertheless received into his allegiance, which indeed was refused to none who were, like Poins,[1] proper men of their hands, and were willing to assume the name of Mac-Ivor.

He was enabled to discipline these forces, from having obtained command of one of the independent companies, raised by government to preserve the peace of the Highlands. While in this capacity he acted with vigour and spirit, and preserved great order in the country under his charge. He caused his vassals to enter by rotation into his company, and serve for a certain space of time, which gave them all in turn a general notion of military discipline. In his campaigns against the banditti, it was observed that he assumed and exercised to the utmost the discretionary power, which, while the law had no free course in the Highlands, was conceived to belong to the military parties who were called in to support it. He acted, for example, with great and suspicious lenity to those freebooters who made restitution on his summons, and offered personal submission to himself, while he rigorously pursued, apprehended, and sacrificed to justice, all such interlopers as dared to despise his admonitions or commands. On the other hand, if any officers of justice, military parties, or others, presumed to pursue thieves or marauders through his territories, and without applying for his consent and concurrence, nothing was more certain than that they would meet with some notable foil or defeat; upon which occasions Fergus Mac-Ivor was the first to condole with them, and, after gently blaming their rashness, never failed deeply to lament the lawless state of the country. These lamentations did not exclude suspicion, and matters were so represented to government, that our Chieftain was deprived of his military command.[kk]

---

1   In Shakespeare's *Henry IV, Parts I and II*, he is one of Prince Hal's drinking companions.

Whatever Fergus Mac-Ivor felt on this occasion, he had the art of entirely suppressing every appearance of discontent; but in a short time the neighbouring country began to feel bad effects from his disgrace. Donald Bean Lean, and others of his class, whose depredations had hitherto been confined to other districts, appeared from thenceforward to have made a settlement on this devoted border; and their ravages were carried on with little opposition, as the Lowland gentry were chiefly Jacobites, and disarmed. This forced many of the inhabitants into contracts of black-mail with Fergus Mac-Ivor, which not only established him their protector, and gave him great weight in all their consultations, but, moreover, supplied funds for the waste of his feudal hospitality, which the discontinuance of his pay might have otherwise essentially diminished.

In following this course of conduct, Fergus had a further object than merely being the great man of his neighbourhood, and ruling despotically over a small clan. From his infancy upward, he had devoted himself to the cause of the exiled family, and had persuaded himself, not only that their restoration to the crown of Britain would be speedy, but that those who assisted them would be raised to honour and rank. It was with this view that he laboured to reconcile the Highlanders among themselves, and augmented his own force to the utmost, to be prepared for the first favourable opportunity of rising. With this purpose also he conciliated the favour of such Lowland gentlemen in the vicinity as were friends to the good cause; and for the same reason, having incautiously quarrelled with Mr Bradwardine, who, notwithstanding his peculiarities, was much respected in the country, he took advantage of the foray of Donald Bean Lean to solder up the dispute in the manner we have mentioned. Some, indeed, surmised that he caused the enterprise to be suggested to Donald, on purpose to pave the way to a reconciliation, which, supposing that to be the case, cost the Laird of Bradwardine two good milch cows. This zeal in their behalf the House of Stewart repaid with a considerable share of their confidence, an occasional supply of louis d'or,[1] abundance of fair words, and a parchment, with a huge waxen seal appended, purporting to be an earl's patent, granted by no less a person than James the Third King of England, and Eighth King of Scotland, to his right feal, trusty, and well-beloved Fergus Mac-Ivor of Glennaquoich, in the county of Perth, and kingdom of Scotland.

With this future coronet glittering before his eyes, Fergus plunged deeply into the correspondence and plots of that unhappy period; and, like all such active agents, easily reconciled his conscience to going

---

1 "A gold coin issued in the reign of Louis XIII and subsequently till the time of Louis XVI" (*OED*).

certain lengths in the service of his party, from which honour and pride would have deterred him, had his sole object been the direct advancement of his own personal interest. With this insight into a bold, ambitious, and ardent, yet artful and politic character, we resume the broken thread of our narrative.

The Chief and his guest had by this time reached the house of Glennaquoich, which consisted of Ian nan Chaistel's mansion, a high rude-looking square tower, with the addition of a *lofted* house, that is, a building of two stories, constructed by Fergus's grandfather when he returned from that memorable expedition, well remembered by the western shires, under the name of the Highland Host. Upon occasion of this crusade against the Ayrshire Whigs and Covenanters, the Vich Ian Vohr of the time had probably been as successful as his predecessor was in harrying Northumberland, and therefore left to his posterity a rival edifice, as a monument of his magnificence.

Around the house, which stood on an eminence in the midst of a narrow Highland valley, there appeared none of that attention to convenience, far less to ornament and decoration, which usually surrounds a gentleman's habitation. An inclosure or two, divided by drystone walls, were the only part of the domain that was fenced; as to the rest, the narrow slips of level ground which lay by the side of the brook exhibited a scanty crop of barley, liable to constant depredations from the herds of wild ponies and black cattle that grazed upon the adjacent hills. These ever and anon made an incursion upon the arable ground, which was repelled by the loud, uncouth, and dissonant shouts of half a dozen Highland swains, all running as if they had been mad, and every one hallooing a half-starved dog to the rescue of the forage. At a little distance up the glen was a small and stunted wood of birch; the hills were high and heathy, but without any variety of surface; so that the whole view was wild and desolate, rather than grand and solitary. Yet, such as it was, no genuine descendant of Ian nan Chaistel would have changed the domain for Stow or Blenheim.[1]

There was a sight, however, before the gate, which perhaps would have afforded the first owner of Blenheim more pleasure than the finest view in the domain assigned to him by the gratitude of his country. This consisted of about a hundred Highlanders, in complete dress and arms; at sight of whom the Chieftain apologized to Waverley in a sort of negligent manner. "He had forgot," he said, "that he had ordered a few of his clan out, for the purpose of seeing that they were in a fit condition to protect the country, and prevent such accidents as, he was sorry to learn, had befallen the Baron of Bradwar-

---

1 Two stately homes in England.

dine. Before they were dismissed, perhaps Captain Waverley might choose to see them go through a part of their exercise."

Edward assented, and the men executed with agility and precision some of the ordinary military movements. They then practised individually at a mark, and showed extraordinary dexterity in the management of the pistol and firelock. They took aim, standing, sitting, leaning, or lying prostrate, as they were commanded, and always with effect upon the target. Next, they paired off for the broadsword exercise; and, having manifested their individual skill and dexterity, united in two bodies, and exhibited a sort of mock encounter, in which the charge, the rally, the flight, the pursuit, and all the current of a heady fight, were exhibited to the sound of the great war bagpipe.

On a signal made by the Chief, the skirmish was ended. Matches were then made for running, wrestling, leaping, pitching the bar,[1] and other sports, in which this feudal militia displayed incredible swiftness, strength, and agility; and accomplished the purpose which their Chieftain had at heart, by impressing on Waverley no light sense of their merit as soldiers, and of the power of him who commanded them by his nod.[II]

"And what number of such gallant fellows have the happiness to call you leader?" asked Waverley.

"In a good cause, and under a chieftain whom they loved, the race of Ivor have seldom taken the field under five hundred claymores. But you are aware, Captain Waverley, that the disarming act, passed about twenty years ago, prevents their being in the complete state of preparation as in former times; and I keep no more of my clan under arms than may defend my own or my friends' property, when the country is troubled with such men as your last night's landlord; and government, which has removed other means of defence, must connive at our protecting ourselves."

"But with your force, you might soon destroy, or put down, such gangs as that of Donald Bean Lean."

"Yes, doubtless; and my reward would be a summons to deliver up to General Blakeney, at Stirling, the few broadswords they have left us: there were little policy in that, methinks.—But come, captain, the sound of the pipes informs me that dinner is prepared. Let me have the honour to show you into my rude mansion."

CHAPTER XX.
A Highland Feast.

ERE Waverley entered the banqueting hall, he was offered the patriarchal refreshment of a bath for the feet, which the sultry weather, and

---

1   A field sport.

the morasses he had traversed, rendered highly acceptable. He was not, indeed, so luxuriously attended upon this occasion as the heroic travellers in the Odyssey;[1] the task of ablution and abstersion being performed, not by a beautiful damsel, trained

> To chafe the limb, and pour the fragrant oil,

but by a smoke-dried skinny old Highland woman, who did not seem to think herself much honoured by the duty imposed on her, but muttered between her teeth, "Our father's herds did not feed so near together, that I should do you this service." A small donation, however, amply reconciled this ancient handmaiden to the supposed degradation; and, as Edward proceeded to the hall, she gave him her blessing, in the Gaelic proverb, "May the open hand be filled the fullest."

The hall, in which the feast was prepared, occupied all the first story of Ian nan Chaistel's original erection, and a huge oaken table extended through its whole length. The apparatus for dinner was simple, even to rudeness, and the company numerous, even to crowding. At the head of the table was the Chief himself, with Edward, and two or three Highland visitors of neighbouring clans; the elders of his own tribe, wadsetters and tacksmen, as they were called, who occupied portions of his estate as mortgagers or lessees, sat next in rank; beneath them, their sons and nephews, and foster-brethren; then the officers of the Chief's household, according to their order; and, lowest of all, the tenants who actually cultivated the ground. Even beyond this long perspective, Edward might see upon the green, to which a huge pair of folding doors opened, a multitude of Highlanders of a yet inferior description, who, nevertheless, were considered as guests, and had their share both of the countenance of the entertainer, and of the cheer of the day. In the distance, and fluctuating round this extreme verge of the banquet, was a changeful group of women, ragged boys and girls, beggars, young and old, large greyhounds, and terriers, and pointers, and curs of low degree; all of whom took some interest, more or less immediate, in the main action of the piece.

This hospitality, apparently unbounded, had yet its line of economy. Some pains had been bestowed in dressing the dishes of fish, game, &c., which were at the upper end of the table, and immediately under the eye of the English stranger. Lower down stood

---

1 Homer's epic poem *The Odyssey* (c. 8th century BCE) chronicles the long journey home of Odysseus, king of Ithaca. He undergoes many trials and tribulations, but after twenty years reaches home to pass a test set by his wife, Penelope, slay her suitors, and reveal himself as her husband.

immense clumsy joints of mutton and beef, which, but for the absence of pork,[mm] abhorred in the Highlands, resembled the rude festivity of the banquet of Penelope's suitors. But the central dish was a yearling lamb, called "a hog in har'st," roasted whole. It was set upon its legs, with a bunch of parsley in its mouth, and was probably exhibited in that form to gratify the pride of the cook, who piqued himself more on the plenty than the elegance of his master's table. The sides of this poor animal were fiercely attacked by the clansmen, some with dirks, others with the knives which were usually in the same sheath with the dagger, so that it was soon rendered a mangled and rueful spectacle. Lower down still, the victuals seemed of yet coarser quality, though sufficiently abundant. Broth, onions, cheese, and the fragments of the feast, regaled the sons of Ivor who feasted in the open air.

The liquor was supplied in the same proportion, and under similar regulations. Excellent claret and champaigne were liberally distributed among the Chief's immediate neighbours; whisky, plain or diluted, and strong-beer, refreshed those who sat near the lower end. Nor did this inequality of distribution appear to give the least offence. Every one present understood that his taste was to be formed according to the rank which he held at table; and, consequently, the tacksmen and their dependents always professed the wine was too cold for their stomachs, and called, apparently out of choice, for the liquor, which was assigned to them from economy.[nn] The bagpipers, three in number, screamed during the whole time of dinner, a tremendous war-tune; and the echoing of the vaulted roof, and clang of the Celtic tongue, produced such a Babel of noises, that Waverley dreaded his ears would never recover it. Mac-Ivor, indeed, apologized for the confusion occasioned by so large a party, and pleaded the necessity of his situation, on which unlimited hospitality was imposed as a paramount duty. "These stout idle kinsmen of mine," he said, "account my estate as held in trust for their support; and I must find them beef and ale, while the rogues will do nothing for themselves but practise the broadsword, or wander about the hills, shooting, fishing, hunting, drinking, and making love to the lasses of the strath. But what can I do, Captain Waverley? Every thing will keep after its kind, whether it be a hawk or a Highlander." Edward made the expected answer, in a compliment upon his possessing so many bold and attached followers.

"Why, yes," replied the Chief, "were I disposed, like my father, to put myself in the way of getting one blow on the head, or two on the neck, I believe the loons would stand by me. But who thinks of that in the present day, when the maxim is,—'Better an old woman with a purse in her hand, than three men with belted brands?'"[1] Then,

---

1   Men with branded cattle to be sold.

turning to the company, he proposed the "Health of Captain Waverley, a worthy friend of his kind neighbour and ally, the Baron of Bradwardine."

"He is welcome hither," said one of the elders, "if he come from Cosmo Comyne Bradwardine."

"I say nay to that," said an old man, who apparently did not mean to pledge the toast; "I say nay to that;—while there is a green leaf in the forest, there will be fraud in a Comyne."

"There is nothing but honour in the Baron of Bradwardine," answered another ancient; "and the guest that comes hither from him should be welcome, though he came with blood on his hand, unless it were blood of the race of Ivor."

The old man, whose cup remained full, replied, "There has been blood enough of the race of Ivor on the hand of Bradwardine."

"Ah! Ballenkeiroch," replied the first, "you think rather of the flash of the carbine at the Mains of Tully-Veolan, than the glance of the sword that fought for the cause at Preston."

"And well I may," answered Ballenkeiroch; "the flash of the gun cost me a fair-haired son, and the glance of the sword has done but little for King James."

The Chieftain, in two words of French, explained to Waverley, that the Baron had shot this old man's son in a fray near Tully-Veolan about seven years before; and then hastened to remove Ballenkeiroch's prejudice, by informing him that Waverley was an Englishman, unconnected by birth or alliance with the family of Bradwardine; upon which the old gentleman raised the hitherto-untasted cup, and courteously drank to his health. This ceremony being requited in kind, the Chieftain made a signal for the pipes to cease, and said, aloud, "Where is the song hidden, my friends, that Mac-Murrough cannot find it?"

Mac-Murrough, the family *bhairdh*,[1] an aged man, immediately took the hint, and began to chant, with low and rapid utterance, a profusion of Celtic verses, which were received by the audience with all the applause of enthusiasm. As he advanced in his declamation, his ardour seemed to increase. He had at first spoken with his eyes fixed on the ground; he now cast them around as if beseeching, and anon as if commanding, attention, and his tones rose into wild and impassioned notes, accompanied with appropriate gestures. He seemed to Edward, who attended to him with much interest, to recite many proper names, to lament the dead, to apostrophize the absent, to exhort, and entreat, and animate those who were present. Waverley thought he even discerned his own name, and was convinced his con-

---

1 Poet, chronicler of family exploits, bard.

jecture was right, from the eyes of the company being at that moment turned towards him simultaneously. The ardour of the poet appeared to communicate itself to the audience. Their wild and sun-burnt countenances assumed a fiercer and more animated expression; all bent forward towards the reciter, many sprung up and waved their arms in ecstasy, and some laid their hands on their swords. When the song ceased, there was a deep pause, while the aroused feelings of the poet and of the hearers gradually subsided into their usual channel.

The Chieftain, who, during this scene, had appeared rather to watch the emotions which were excited, than to partake their high tone of enthusiasm, filled with claret a small silver cup which stood by him. "Give this," he said to an attendant, "to Mac-Murrough nan Fonn (*i.e.*, of the songs), and when he has drank the juice, bid him keep, for the sake of Vich Ian Vohr, the shell of the gourd which contained it." The gift was received by Mac-Murrough with profound gratitude; he drank the wine, and, kissing the cup, shrouded it with reverence in the plaid which was folded on his bosom. He then burst forth into what Edward justly supposed to be an extemporaneous effusion of thanks, and praises of his Chief. It was received with applause, but did not produce the effect of his first poem. It was obvious, however, that the clan regarded the generosity of their Chieftain with high approbation. Many approved Gaelic toasts were then proposed, of some of which the Chieftain gave his guest the following versions:— "To him that will not turn his back on friend or foe." "To him that never forsook a comrade." "To him that never bought or sold justice." "Hospitality to the exile, and broken bones to the tyrant." "The lads with the kilts." "Highlanders, shoulder to shoulder,"—with many other pithy sentiments of the like nature.

Edward was particularly solicitous to know the meaning of that song which appeared to produce such effect upon the passions of the company, and hinted his curiosity to his host. "As I observe," said the Chieftain, "that you have passed the bottle during the last three rounds, I was about to propose to you to retire to my sister's tea-table, who can explain these things to you better than I can. Although I cannot stint my clan in the usual current of their festivity, yet I neither am addicted myself to exceed in its amount, nor do I," added he, smiling, "keep a Bear to devour the intellects of such as can make good use of them."

Edward readily assented to this proposal, and the Chieftain, saying a few words to those around him, left the table, followed by Waverley. As the door closed behind them, Edward heard Vich Ian Vohr's health invoked with a wild and animated cheer, that expressed the satisfaction of the guests, and the depth of their devotion to his service.

CHAPTER XXI.
The Chieftain's Sister.

THE drawing-room of Flora Mac-Ivor was furnished in the plainest and most simple manner; for at Glennaquoich every other sort of expenditure was retrenched as much as possible, for the purpose of maintaining, in its full dignity, the hospitality of the Chieftain, and retaining and multiplying the number of his dependents and adherents. But there was no appearance of this parsimony in the dress of the lady herself, which was in texture elegant, and even rich, and arranged in a manner which partook partly of the Parisian fashion, and partly of the more simple dress of the Highlands, blended together with great taste. Her hair was not disfigured by the art of the friseur,[1] but fell in jetty ringlets on her neck, confined only by a circlet, richly set with diamonds. This peculiarity she adopted in compliance with the Highland prejudices, which could not endure that a woman's head should be covered before wedlock.

Flora Mac-Ivor bore a most striking resemblance to her brother Fergus; so much so, that they might have played Viola and Sebastian with the same exquisite effect produced by the appearance of Mrs Henry Siddons and her brother, Mr William Murray, in these characters.[2] They had the same antique and regular correctness of profile; the same dark eyes, eye-lashes, and eye-brows; the same clearness of complexion, excepting that Fergus's was embrowned by exercise, and Flora's possessed the utmost feminine delicacy. But the haughty, and somewhat stern regularity of Fergus's features, was beautifully softened in those of Flora. Their voices were also similar in tone, though differing in the key. That of Fergus, especially while issuing orders to his followers during their military exercise, reminded Edward of a favourite passage in the description of Emetrius:

——whose voice was heard around,
Loud as a trumpet with a silver sound.[3]

---

1 Hairdresser.
2 Viola and Sebastian are twins in Shakespeare's *Twelfth Night*. Harriet Siddons (Mrs. Henry Siddons) (1783-1844), and her brother, William Murray, were actors; she played the role of Flora and he of Balmawhapple in a dramatic version of *Waverley*.
3 Emetrius was "the King of Inde in Chaucer's *Knight's Tale*. The quotation is from Dryden's version" of this story, "Palamon and Arcite," III, 84-85 (*OW*, 429).

That of Flora, on the contrary, was soft and sweet,—"an excellent thing in woman"; yet, in urging any favourite topic, which she often pursued with natural eloquence, it possessed as well the tones which impress awe and conviction, as those of persuasive insinuation. The eager glance of the keen black eye, which, in the Chieftain, seemed impatient even of the material obstacles it encountered, had, in his sister, acquired a gentle pensiveness. His looks seemed to seek glory, power, all that could exalt him above others in the race of humanity; while those of his sister, as if she were already conscious of mental superiority, seemed to pity, rather than envy, those who were struggling for any farther distinction. Her sentiments corresponded with the expression of her countenance. Early education had impressed upon her mind, as well as on that of the Chieftain, the most devoted attachment to the exiled family of Stewart. She believed it the duty of her brother, of his clan, of every man in Britain, at whatever personal hazard, to contribute to that restoration which the partizans of the Chevalier St George[1] had not ceased to hope for. For this she was prepared to do all, to suffer all, to sacrifice all. But her loyalty, as it exceeded her brother's in fanaticism, excelled it also in purity. Accustomed to petty intrigue, and necessarily involved in a thousand paltry and selfish discussions, ambitious also by nature, his political faith was tinctured, at least, if not tainted, by the views of interest and advancement so easily combined with it; and at the moment he should unsheathe his claymore, it might be difficult to say whether it would be most with the view of making James Stewart a king, or Fergus Mac-Ivor an earl. This, indeed, was a mixture of feeling which he did not avow even to himself, but it existed, nevertheless, in a powerful degree.

In Flora's bosom, on the contrary, the zeal of loyalty burnt pure and unmixed with any selfish feeling; she would have as soon made religion the mask of ambitious and interested views, as have shrouded them under the opinions which she had been taught to think patriotism. Such instances of devotion were not uncommon among the followers of the unhappy race of Stewart, of which many memorable proofs will recur to the mind of most of my readers. But peculiar attention on the part of the Chevalier de St George and his princess to the parents of Fergus and his sister, and to themselves, when orphans, had riveted their faith. Fergus, upon the death of his parents, had been for some

---

1   James Francis Edward Stuart (1688-1766), son of James II of Britain, who had been deposed during the Glorious Revolution of 1688 and replaced by William of Orange, was known as both the Chevalier de St. George and the Old Pretender, and led the failed 1715 Jacobite Rebellion. His son, Charles Edward Stuart, known as the Young Pretender, led the 1745 Jacobite Rebellion (*OCBH*, 896).

time a page of honour in the train of the Chevalier's lady, and, from his beauty and sprightly temper, was uniformly treated by her with the utmost distinction. This was also extended to Flora, who was maintained for some time at a convent of the first order, at the princess's expense, and removed from thence into her own family, where she spent nearly two years. Both brother and sister retained the deepest and most grateful sense of her kindness.

Having thus touched upon the leading principle of Flora's character, I may dismiss the rest more slightly. She was highly accomplished, and had acquired those elegant manners to be expected from one who, in early youth, had been the companion of a princess; yet she had not learned to substitute the gloss of politeness for the reality of feeling. When settled in the lonely regions of Glennaquoich, she found that her resources in French, English, and Italian literature, were likely to be few and interrupted; and, in order to fill up the vacant time, she bestowed a part of it upon the music and poetical traditions of the Highlanders, and began really to feel the pleasure in the pursuit, which her brother, whose perceptions of literary merit were more blunt, rather affected for the sake of popularity than actually experienced. Her resolution was strengthened in these researches, by the extreme delight which her inquiries seemed to afford those to whom she resorted for information.

Her love of her clan, an attachment which was almost hereditary in her bosom, was, like her loyalty, a more pure passion than that of her brother. He was too thorough a politician, regarded his patriarchal influence too much as the means of accomplishing his own aggrandizement, that we should term him the model of a Highland Chieftain. Flora felt the same anxiety for cherishing and extending their patriarchal sway, but it was with the generous desire of vindicating from poverty, or at least from want and foreign oppression, those whom her brother was by birth, according to the notions of the time and country, entitled to govern. The savings of her income, for she had a small pension from the Princess Sobieski, were dedicated, not to add to the comforts of the peasantry, for that was a word which they neither knew nor apparently wished to know, but to relieve their absolute necessities, when in sickness or extreme old age. At every other period, they rather toiled to procure something which they might share with the Chief, as a proof of their attachment, than expected other assistance from him save what was afforded by the rude hospitality of his castle, and the general division and subdivision of his estate among them. Flora was so much beloved by them, that when Mac-Murrough composed a song, in which he enumerated all the principal beauties of the district, and intimated her superiority by concluding, that "the fairest apple hung on the highest bough," he received, in donatives from the individuals of the clan, more seed-barley than would have sowed his Highland Parnassus, the *Bard's croft*, as it was called, ten times over.

From situation, as well as choice, Miss Mac-Ivor's society was extremely limited. Her most intimate friend had been Rose Bradwardine, to whom she was much attached; and when seen together, they would have afforded an artist two admirable subjects for the gay and the melancholy muse. Indeed Rose was so tenderly watched by her father, and her circle of wishes was so limited, that none arose but what he was willing to gratify, and scarce any which did not come within the compass of his power. With Flora it was otherwise. While almost a girl, she had undergone the most complete change of scene, from gaiety and splendour to absolute solitude and comparative poverty; and the ideas and wishes which she chiefly fostered, respected great national events, and changes not to be brought round without both hazard and bloodshed, and therefore not to be thought of with levity. Her manner, consequently, was grave, though she readily contributed her talents to the amusement of society, and stood very high in the opinion of the old Baron, who used to sing along with her such French duets of Lindor and Cloris,[1] &c. as were in fashion about the end of the reign of old Louis le Grand.[2]

It was generally believed, though no one durst have hinted it to the Baron of Bradwardine, that Flora's intreaties had no small share in allaying the wrath of Fergus upon occasion of their quarrel. She took her brother on the assailable side, by dwelling first upon the Baron's age, and then representing the injury which the cause might sustain, and the damage which must arise to his own character in point of prudence, so necessary to a political agent, if he persisted in carrying it to extremity. Otherwise it is probable it would have terminated in a duel, both because the Baron had, on a former occasion, shed blood of the clan, though the matter had been timely accommodated, and on account of his high reputation for address at his weapon, which Fergus almost condescended to envy. For the same reason she had urged their reconciliation, which the Chieftain the more readily agreed to, as it favoured some ulterior projects of his own.

To this young lady, now presiding at the female empire of the tea-table, Fergus introduced Captain Waverley, whom she received with the usual forms of politeness.

---

1   Names given to shepherds in pastoral poetry.
2   Louis XIV (1638-1715), king of France.

CHAPTER XXII.
Highland Minstrelsy.

WHEN the first salutations had passed, Fergus said to his sister, "My dear Flora, before I return to the barbarous ritual of our forefathers, I must tell you that Captain Waverley is a worshipper of the Celtic muse, not the less so perhaps that he does not understand a word of her language. I have told him you are eminent as a translator of Highland poetry, and that Mac-Murrough admires your version of his songs upon the same principle that Captain Waverley admires the original,—because he does not comprehend them. Will you have the goodness to read or recite to our guest in English, the extraordinary string of names which Mac-Murrough has tacked together in Gaelic?—My life to a moor-fowl's feather, you are provided with a version, for I know you are in all the bard's councils, and acquainted with his songs long before he rehearses them in the hall."

"How can you say so, Fergus? You know how little these verses can possibly interest an English stranger, even if I could translate them as you pretend."

"Not less than they interest me, lady fair. Today your joint composition, for I insist you had a share in it, has cost me the last silver cup in the castle, and I suppose will cost me something else next time I hold *cour plénière*,[1] if the muse descends on Mac-Murrough; for you know our proverb,—When the hand of the chief ceases to bestow, the breath of the bard is frozen in the utterance.—Well, I would it were even so: there are three things that are useless to a modern Highlander,—a sword which he must not draw,—a bard to sing of deeds which he dare not imitate,—and a large goat-skin purse without a louis-d'or to put into it."

"Well, brother, since you betray my secrets, you cannot expect me to keep yours.—I assure you, Captain Waverley, that Fergus is too proud to exchange his broadsword for a marechal's[2] baton; that he esteems Mac-Murrough a far greater poet than Homer, and would not give up his goat-skin purse for all the louis-d'or which it could contain."

"Well pronounced, Flora; blow for blow, as Conan°° said to the devil. Now do you two talk of bards and poetry, if not of purses and claymores, while I return to do the final honours to the senators of the tribe of Ivor." So saying, he left the room.

The conversation continued between Flora and Waverley; for two well-dressed young women, whose character seemed to hover between

---

1 Full court.
2 French for field marshal.

that of companions and dependents, took no share in it. They were both pretty girls, but served only as foils to the grace and beauty of their patroness. The discourse followed the turn which the Chieftain had given it, and Waverley was equally amused and surprised with the account which the lady gave him of Celtic poetry.

"The recitation," she said, "of poems, recording the feats of heroes, the complaints of lovers, and the wars of contending tribes, forms the chief amusement of a winter fire-side in the Highlands. Some of these are said to be very ancient, and if they are ever translated into any of the languages of civilized Europe, cannot fail to produce a deep and general sensation. Others are more modern, the composition of those family bards whom the chieftains of more distinguished name and power retain as the poets and historians of their tribes. These, of course, possess various degrees of merit; but much of it must evaporate in translation, or be lost on those who do not sympathize with the feelings of the poet."

"And your bard, whose effusions seemed to produce such effect upon the company to-day, is he reckoned among the favourite poets of the mountains?"

"That is a trying question. His reputation is high among his countrymen, and you must not expect me to depreciate it."pp

"But the song, Miss Mac-Ivor, seemed to awaken all those warriors, both young and old."

"The song is little more than a catalogue of names of the Highland clans under their distinctive peculiarities, and an exhortation to them to remember and to emulate the actions of their forefathers."

"And am I wrong in conjecturing, however extraordinary the guess appears, that there was some allusion to me in the verses which he recited?"

"You have a quick observation, Captain Waverley, which in this instance has not deceived you. The Gaelic language, being uncommonly vocalic, is well adapted for sudden and extemporaneous poetry; and a bard seldom fails to augment the effects of a premeditated song, by throwing in any stanzas which may be suggested by the circumstances attending the recitation."

"I would give my best horse to know what the Highland bard could find to say of such an unworthy Southron as myself."

"It shall not even cost you a lock of his mane.—Una, *Mavourneen!* [1] (She spoke a few words to one of the young girls in attendance, who instantly curtsied, and tripped out of the room.)—I have sent Una to learn from the bard the expressions he used, and you shall command my skill as dragoman." [2]

---

1 Irish for "my dear."
2 Interpreter.

Una returned in a few minutes, and repeated to her mistress a few lines in Gaelic. Flora seemed to think for a moment, and then, slightly colouring, she turned to Waverley—"It is impossible to gratify your curiosity, Captain Waverley, without exposing my own presumption. If you will give me a few moments for consideration, I will endeavour to engraft the meaning of these lines upon a rude English translation, which I have attempted, of a part of the original. The duties of the tea-table seem to be concluded, and, as the evening is delightful, Una will show you the way to one of my favourite haunts, and Cathleen and I will join you there."

Una, having received instructions in her native language, conducted Waverley out by a passage different from that through which he had entered the apartment. At a distance he heard the hall of the Chief still resounding with the clang of bagpipes and the high applause of his guests. Having gained the open air by a postern door, they walked a little way up the wild, bleak, and narrow valley in which the house was situated, following the course of the stream that winded through it. In a spot, about a quarter of a mile from the castle, two brooks, which formed the little river, had their junction. The larger of the two came down the long bare valley, which extended, apparently without any change or elevation of character, as far as the hills which formed its boundary permitted the eye to reach. But the other stream, which had its source among the mountains on the left hand of the strath, seemed to issue from a very narrow and dark opening betwixt two large rocks. These streams were different also in character. The larger was placid, and even sullen in its course, wheeling in deep eddies, or sleeping in dark blue pools; but the motions of the lesser brook were rapid and furious, issuing from between precipices, like a maniac from his confinement, all foam and uproar.

It was up the course of this last stream that Waverley, like a knight of romance, was conducted by the fair Highland damsel, his silent guide. A small path, which had been rendered easy in many places for Flora's accommodation, led him through scenery of a very different description from that which he had just quitted. Around the castle, all was cold, bare, and desolate, yet tame even in desolation; but this narrow glen, at so short a distance, seemed to open into the land of romance. The rocks assumed a thousand peculiar and varied forms. In one place, a crag of huge size presented its gigantic bulk, as if to forbid the passenger's farther progress; and it was not until he approached its very base, that Waverley discerned the sudden and acute turn by which the pathway wheeled its course around this formidable obstacle. In another spot, the projecting rocks from the opposite sides of the chasm had approached so near to each other, that two pine-trees laid across, and covered with turf, formed a rustic bridge at the height of at least one hundred and fifty feet. It had no ledges, and was barely three feet in breadth.

While gazing at this pass of peril, which crossed, like a single black line, the small portion of blue sky not intercepted by the projecting rocks on either side, it was with a sensation of horror that Waverley beheld Flora and her attendant appear, like inhabitants of another region, propped, as it were, in mid air, upon this trembling structure. She stopped upon observing him below, and, with an air of graceful ease, which made him shudder, waved her handkerchief to him by way of signal. He was unable, from the sense of dizziness which her situation conveyed, to return the salute; and was never more relieved than when the fair apparition passed on from the precarious eminence which she seemed to occupy with so much indifference, and disappeared on the other side.

Advancing a few yards, and passing under the bridge which he had viewed with so much terror, the path ascended rapidly from the edge of the brook, and the glen widened into a silvan amphitheatre, waving with birch, young oaks, and hazels, with here and there a scattered yew-tree. The rocks now receded, but still showed their grey and shaggy crests rising among the copse-wood. Still higher, rose eminences and peaks, some bare, some clothed with wood, some round and purple with heath, and others splintered into rocks and crags. At a short turning, the path, which had for some furlongs lost sight of the brook, suddenly placed Waverley in front of a romantic waterfall. It was not so remarkable either for great height or quantity of water, as for the beautiful accompaniments which made the spot interesting. After a broken cataract of about twenty feet, the stream was received in a large natural basin filled to the brim with water, which, where the bubbles of the fall subsided, was so exquisitely clear, that although it was of great depth, the eye could discern each pebble at the bottom. Eddying round this reservoir, the brook found its way as if over a broken part of the ledge, and formed a second fall, which seemed to seek the very abyss; then, wheeling out beneath from among the smooth dark rocks, which it had polished for ages, it wandered murmuring down the glen, forming the stream up which Waverley had just ascended.qq The borders of this romantic reservoir corresponded in beauty; but it was beauty of a stern and commanding cast, as if in the act of expanding into grandeur. Mossy banks of turf were broken and interrupted by huge fragments of rock, and decorated with trees and shrubs, some of which had been planted under the direction of Flora, but so cautiously, that they added to the grace, without diminishing the romantic wildness of the scene.

Here, like one of those lovely forms which decorate the landscapes of Poussin,[1] Waverley found Flora gazing on the waterfall. Two paces farther back stood Cathleen, holding a small Scottish harp, the use of which had been taught to Flora by Rory Dall, one of the last harpers of the Western Highlands. The sun, now stooping in the west, gave a rich and varied tinge to all the objects which surrounded Waverley, and seemed to add more than human brilliancy to the full expressive darkness of Flora's eye, exalted the richness and purity of her complexion, and enhanced the dignity and grace of her beautiful form. Edward thought he had never, even in his wildest dreams, imagined a figure of such exquisite and interesting loveliness. The wild beauty of the retreat, bursting upon him as if by magic, augmented the mingled feeling of delight and awe with which he approached her, like a fair enchantress of Boiardo or Ariosto,[2] by whose nod the scenery around seemed to have been created, an Eden in the wilderness.

Flora, like every beautiful woman, was conscious of her own power, and pleased with its effects, which she could easily discern from the respectful, yet confused address of the young soldier. But, as she possessed excellent sense, she gave the romance of the scene, and other accidental circumstances, full weight in appreciating the feelings with which Waverley seemed obviously to be impressed; and, unacquainted with the fanciful and susceptible peculiarities of his character, considered his homage as the passing tribute which a woman of even inferior charms might have expected in such a situation. She therefore quietly led the way to a spot at such a distance from the cascade, that its sound should rather accompany than interrupt that of her voice and instrument, and, sitting down upon a mossy fragment of rock, she took the harp from Cathleen.

"I have given you the trouble of walking to this spot, Captain Waverley, both because I thought the scenery would interest you, and because a Highland song would suffer still more from my imperfect translation, were I to introduce it without its own wild and appropriate accompaniments. To speak in the poetical language of my country, the seat of the Celtic Muse is in the mist of the secret and solitary hill, and her voice in the murmur of the mountain stream. He who woos

---

1 Nicholas Poussin (1594-1665), French landscape painter who lived most of his life in Italy. His classical landscapes were marked by "mathematical precision" (*CCE*, 707).

2 Matteo Boiardo (1434-94), Italian Romantic author of *Orlando Innamorato*; Ludovico Ariosto (1474-1533), Italian epic poet, wrote *Orlando Furioso* (1532) on the subject of the story of Roland, and thereby proved a great influence on such writers as Shakespeare, Milton, and Byron (*CCE*, 43).

her must love the barren rock more than the fertile valley, and the solitude of the desert better than the festivity of the hall."

Few could have heard this lovely woman make this declaration,
with a voice where harmony was exalted by pathos, without exclaiming that the muse whom she invoked could never find a more appropriate representative. But Waverley, though the thought rushed on his
mind, found no courage to utter it. Indeed, the wild feeling of romantic delight with which he heard the few first notes she drew from her
instrument, amounted almost to a sense of pain. He would not for
worlds have quitted his place by her side; yet he almost longed for solitude, that he might decipher and examine at leisure the complication
of emotions which now agitated his bosom.

Flora had exchanged the measured and monotonous recitative of
the bard for a lofty and uncommon Highland air, which had been a
battle-song in former ages. A few irregular strains introduced a
prelude of a wild and peculiar tone, which harmonized well with the
distant waterfall, and the soft sigh of the evening breeze in the rustling
leaves of an aspen which overhung the seat of the fair harpress. The
following verses convey but little idea of the feelings with which, so
sung and accompanied, they were heard by Waverley:

> There is mist on the mountain, and night on the vale,
> But more dark is the sleep of the sons of the Gael.
> A stranger commanded—it sunk on the land,
> It has frozen each heart, and benumb'd every hand!
>
> The dirk and the target lie sordid with dust,
> The bloodless claymore is but redden'd with rust;
> On the hill or the glen if a gun should appear,
> It is only to war with the heath-cock or deer.
>
> The deeds of our sires if our bards should rehearse,
> Let a blush or a blow be the meed of their verse!
> Be mute every string, and be hush'd every tone,
> That shall bid us remember the fame that is flown.
>
> But the dark hours of night and of slumber are past,
> The morn on our mountains is dawning at last;
> Glenaladale's peaks are illumed with the rays,
> And the streams of Glenfinnan[rr] leap bright in the blaze.
>
> O high-minded Moray![ss]—the exiled—the dear!—
> In the blush of the dawning the STANDARD uprear!
> Wide, wide on the winds of the north let it fly,
> Like the sun's latest flash when the tempest is nigh!

Ye sons of the strong, when that dawning shall break,
Need the harp of the aged remind you to wake?
That dawn never beam'd on your forefathers' eye,
But it roused each high chieftain to vanquish or die.

O, sprung from the Kings who in Islay kept state,
Proud chiefs of Clan Ranald, Glengarry, and Sleat!
Combine like three streams from one mountain of snow,
And resistless in union rush down on the foe!

True son of Sir Evan, undaunted Lochiel,
Place thy targe on thy shoulder and burnish thy steel!
Rough Keppoch, give breath to thy bugle's bold swell,
Till far Coryarrick resound to the knell!

Stern son of Lord Kenneth, high chief of Kintail,
Let the stag in thy standard bound wild in the gale!
May the race of Clan Gillean, the fearless and free,
Remember Glenlivat, Harlaw, and Dundee!

Let the clan of grey Fingon, whose offspring has given
Such heroes to earth, and such martyrs to heaven,
Unite with the race of renown'd Rorri More,
To launch the long galley, and stretch to the oar.

How Mac-Shimei will joy when their chief shall display
The yew-crested bonnet o'er tresses of grey!
How the race of wrong'd Alpine and murder'd Glencoe
Shall shout for revenge when they pour on the foe!

Ye sons of brown Dermid, who slew the wild boar,
Resume the pure faith of the great Callum-More!
Mac-Neil of the Islands, and Moy of the Lake,
For honour, for freedom, for vengeance awake!

Here a large greyhound, bounding up the glen, jumped upon Flora, and interrupted her music by his importunate caresses. At a distant whistle, he turned, and shot down the path again with the rapidity of an arrow. "That is Fergus's faithful attendant, Captain Waverley, and that was his signal. He likes no poetry but what is humorous, and comes in good time to interrupt my long catalogue of the tribes, whom one of your saucy English poets[1] calls

---

1 Unidentified.

Our bootless host of high-born beggars,
Mac-Leans, Mac-Kenzies, and Mac-Gregors."

Waverley expressed his regret at the interruption.

"O you cannot guess how much you have lost! The bard, as in duty bound, has addressed three long stanzas to Vich Ian Vohr of the Banners, enumerating all his great properties, and not forgetting his being a cheerer of the harper and bard—'a giver of bounteous gifts.' Besides, you should have heard a practical admonition to the fair-haired son of the stranger, who lives in the land where the grass is always green—the rider on the shining pampered steed, whose hue is like the raven, and whose neigh is like the scream of the eagle for battle. This valiant horseman is affectionately conjured to remember that his ancestors were distinguished by their loyalty, as well as by their courage.—All this you have lost; but, since your curiosity is not satisfied, I judge, from the distant sound of my brother's whistle, I may have time to sing the concluding stanzas before he comes to laugh at my translation."

Awake on your hills, on your islands awake,
Brave sons of the mountain, the frith, and the lake!
'Tis the bugle—but not for the chase is the call;
'Tis the pibroch's shrill summons—but not to the hall.

'Tis the summons of heroes for conquest or death,
When the banners are blazing on mountain and heath:
They call to the dirk, the claymore, and the targe,[1]
To the march and the muster, the line and the charge.

Be the brand of each Chieftain like Fin's in his ire!
May the blood through his veins flow like currents of fire!
Burst the base foreign yoke as your sires did of yore,
Or die like your sires, and endure it no more!

CHAPTER XXIII.
Waverley continues at Glennaquoich.

AS Flora concluded her song, Fergus stood before them. "I knew I should find you here, even without the assistance of my friend Bran. A simple and unsublimed taste now, like my own, would prefer a *jet d'eau*[2] at Versailles to this cascade, with all its accompaniments of rock

---

1 Shield.
2 Fountain.

and roar; but this is Flora's Parnassus, Captain Waverley, and that fountain her Helicon.[1] It would be greatly for the benefit of my cellar if she could teach her coadjutor, Mac-Murrough, the value of its influence: he has just drunk a pint of usquebaugh to correct, he said, the coldness of the claret. Let me try its virtues." He sipped a little water in the hollow of his hand, and immediately commenced, with a theatrical air,—

> "O Lady of the desert, hail!
> That lovest the harping of the Gael,
> Through fair and fertile regions borne,
> Where never yet grew grass or corn.

But English poetry will never succeed under the influence of a Highland Helicon—*Allons, courage*—

> O vous, qui buvez, à tasse pleine,
> A cette heureuse fontaine,
> Ou on ne voit, sur le rivage,
>   Que quelques vilains troupeaux,
> Suivis de nymphes de village,
>   Qui les escortent sans sabots"—[2]

"A truce, dear Fergus! spare us those most tedious and insipid persons of all Arcadia.[3] Do not, for Heaven's sake, bring down Coridon[4] and Lindor upon us."

"Nay, if you cannot relish *la houlette et le chalumeau*,[5] have with you in heroic strains."

"Dear Fergus, you have certainly partaken of the inspiration of Mac-Murrough's cup, rather than of mine."

"I disclaim it, *ma belle demoiselle*, although I protest it would be the more congenial of the two. Which of your crack-brained Italian romancers is it that says,

---

1 Parnassus is a mountain in central Greece, in ancient times sacred to Apollo, Dionysus, and the Muses; Mt. Helicon in Greece was thought by ancient Greeks to be the home of the Muses.

2 Scott noted that this "was a parody but of what I cannot w[ell] remember" (*OW*, 431).

3 A region of ancient Greece known for its pastoral beauty.

4 Like Lindor, Coridon is a typical name of a shepherd in pastoral poetry.

5 Shepherd's crook and pipe, "symbols of the pastoral world" (*OW*, 431).

Io d'Elicona niente
Mi curo, in fe de Dio, che'l bere d'acque
(Bea chi ber ne vuol) sempre mi spiacque!^{tt1}

But if you prefer the Gaelic, Captain Waverley, here is little Cathleen shall sing you Drimmindhu.[2]—Come, Cathleen, *astore* (*i.e.*, my dear), begin; no apologies to the *Cean-kinné*."[3]

Cathleen sung with much liveliness a little Gaelic song, the burlesque elegy of a countryman on the loss of his cow, the comic tones of which, though he did not understand the language, made Waverley laugh more than once.^{uu}

"Admirable, Cathleen!" cried the Chieftain; "I must find you a handsome husband among the clansmen one of these days."

Cathleen laughed, blushed, and sheltered herself behind her companion.

In the progress of their return to the castle, the Chieftain warmly pressed Waverley to remain for a week or two, in order to see a grand hunting party, in which he and some other Highland gentlemen proposed to join. The charms of melody and beauty were too strongly impressed in Edward's breast to permit his declining an invitation so pleasing. It was agreed, therefore, that he should write a note to the Baron of Bradwardine, expressing his intention to stay a fortnight at Glennaquoich, and requesting him to forward by the bearer (a *gilly* of the Chieftain's) any letters which might have arrived for him.

This turned the discourse upon the Baron, whom Fergus highly extolled as a gentleman and soldier. His character was touched with yet more discrimination by Flora, who observed he was the very model of the old Scottish cavalier, with all his excellencies and peculiarities. "It is a character, Captain Waverley, which is fast disappearing; for its best point was a self-respect which was never lost sight of till now. But, in the present time, the gentlemen whose principles do not permit them to pay court to the existing government, are neglected and degraded, and many conduct themselves accordingly; and, like some of the persons you have seen at Tully-Veolan, adopt habits and companions inconsistent with their birth and breeding. The ruthless proscription of party seems to degrade the victims whom it brands, however unjustly. But let us hope a brighter day is approaching, when a Scottish country-gentleman may be a scholar without the pedantry

---

1 From canto 1 of *Orlandino* by Teofilo Folengo (1491-1544). See Scott's note for translation.
2 Lamont points out that this song had "Jacobite associations; ... for Jacobites, its true subject was King James, not the cow" (*OW*, 431).
3 The Chief.

of our friend the Baron, a sportsman without the low habits of Mr Falconer, and a judicious improver of his property without becoming a boorish two-legged steer like Killancureit."

Thus did Flora prophecy a revolution, which time indeed has produced, but in a manner very different from what she had in her mind.

The amiable Rose was next mentioned, with the warmest encomium on her person, manners, and mind. "That man," said Flora, "will find an inestimable treasure in the affections of Rose Bradwardine, who shall be so fortunate as to become their object. Her very soul is in home, and in the discharge of all those quiet virtues of which home is the centre. Her husband will be to her what her father now is, the object of all her care, solicitude, and affection. She will see nothing, and connect herself with nothing, but by him and through him. If he is a man of sense and virtue, she will sympathize in his sorrows, divert his fatigue, and share his pleasures. If she becomes the property of a churlish or negligent husband, she will suit his taste also, for she will not long survive his unkindness. And, alas! how great is the chance that some such unworthy lot may be that of my poor friend!— O that I were a queen this moment, and could command the most amiable and worthy youth of my kingdom to accept happiness with the hand of Rose Bradwardine!"

"I wish you would command her to accept mine *en attendant*,"[1] said Fergus, laughing.

I don't know by what caprice it was that this wish, however jocularly expressed, rather jarred on Edward's feelings, notwithstanding his growing inclination to Flora, and his indifference to Miss Bradwardine. This is one of the inexplicabilities of human nature, which we leave without comment.

"Yours, brother?" answered Flora, regarding him steadily. "No; you have another bride—Honour; and the dangers you must run in pursuit of her rival would break poor Rose's heart."

With this discourse they reached the castle, and Waverley soon prepared his dispatches for Tully-Veolan. As he knew the Baron was punctilious in such matters, he was about to impress his billet[2] with a seal on which his armorial bearings were engraved, but he did not find it at his watch, and thought he must have left it at Tully-Veolan. He mentioned his loss, borrowing at the same time the family seal of the Chieftain.

"Surely," said Miss Mac-Ivor, "Donald Bean Lean would not"—

"My life for him, in such circumstances," answered her brother;— "besides, he would never have left the watch behind."

---

1   Meanwhile.
2   Letter.

"After all, Fergus," said Flora, "and with every allowance, I am surprised you can countenance that man."

"I countenance him?—This kind sister of mine would persuade you, Captain Waverley, that I take what the people of old used to call 'a steakraid,' that is, a 'collop of the foray,' or, in plainer words, a portion of the robber's booty, paid by him to the Laird, or Chief, through whose grounds he drove his prey. O, it is certain, that unless I can find some way to charm Flora's tongue, General Blakeney will send a sergeant's party from Stirling (this he said with haughty and emphatic irony) to seize Vich Ian Vohr, as they nickname me, in his own castle."

"Now, Fergus, must not our guest be sensible that all this is folly and affectation? You have men enough to serve you without enlisting banditti, and your own honour is above taint. Why don't you send this Donald Bean Lean, whom I hate for his smoothness and duplicity, even more than for his rapine, out of your country at once? No cause should induce me to tolerate such a character."

"*No* cause, Flora?" said the Chieftain, significantly.

"No cause, Fergus! not even that which is nearest to my heart. Spare it the omen of such evil supporters!"

"O but, sister," rejoined the Chief, gaily, "you don't consider my respect for *la belle passion*. Evan Dhu Maccombich is in love with Donald's daughter, Alice, and you cannot expect me to disturb him in his amours. Why, the whole clan would cry shame on me. You know it is one of their wise sayings, that a kinsman is part of a man's body, but a foster-brother is a piece of his heart."

"Well, Fergus, there is no disputing with you; but I would all this may end well."

"Devoutly prayed, my dear and prophetic sister, and the best way in the world to close a dubious argument.—But hear ye not the pipes, Captain Waverley? Perhaps you will like better to dance to them in the hall, than to be deafened with their harmony without taking part in the exercise they invite us to."

Waverley took Flora's hand. The dance, song, and merry-making proceeded, and closed the day's entertainment at the castle of Vich Ian Vohr. Edward at length retired, his mind agitated by a variety of new and conflicting feelings, which detained him from rest for some time, in that not unpleasing state of mind in which fancy takes the helm, and the soul rather drifts passively along with the rapid and confused tide of reflections, than exerts itself to encounter, systematize, or examine them. At a late hour he fell asleep, and dreamed of Flora Mac-Ivor.

CHAPTER XXIV.
A Stag-hunt and its Consequences.

SHALL this be a long or a short chapter?—This is a question in which you, gentle reader, have no vote, however much you may be interested in the consequences; just as you may (like myself) probably have nothing to do with the imposing a new tax, excepting the trifling circumstance of being obliged to pay it. More happy surely in the present case, since, though it lies within my arbitrary power to extend my materials as I think proper, I cannot call you into Exchequer[1] if you do not think proper to read my narrative. Let me therefore consider. It is true, that the annals and documents in my hands say but little of this Highland chase; but then I can find copious materials for description elsewhere. There is old Lindsay of Pitscottie[2] ready at my elbow, with his Athole hunting, and his "lofted and joisted palace of green timber; with all kind of drink to be had in burgh and land, as ale, beer, wine, muscadel, malvaise, hippocras, and aquavitæ; with wheat-bread, main-bread, ginge-bread, beef, mutton, lamb, veal, venison, goose, grice, capon, coney, crane, swan, partridge, plover, duck, drake, brissel-cock, pawnies, black-cock, muir-fowl, and capercailzies"; not forgetting the "costly bedding, vaiselle, and napry," and least of all the "excelling stewards, cunning baxters, excellent cooks, and pottingars,[3] with confections and drugs for the desserts." Besides the particulars which may be thence gleaned for this Highland feast (the splendour of which induced the Pope's legate to dissent from an opinion which he had hitherto held, that Scotland, namely, was the—the—the latter end of the world)—besides these, might I not illuminate my pages with Taylor the Water Poet's[4] hunting in the braes of Mar, where,

---

1 Court of law responsible for collecting revenues.
2 Robert Lindsay (c. 1500-65) of Pitscottie, Fife, wrote *The Chronicles of Scotland.*
3 Muscadel: wine made of muscadine grapes, smelling like musk; malvaise: a wine of Madeira; hippocras: a wine flavored with spices; aquavitae: whisky; grice: a suckling pig; coney: rabbit; brissel-cock: a turkey-cock; capercailzie: the wood grouse; vaiselle: French for table service; napry: table linens; baxters: women bakers; pottingars: cooks.
4 John Taylor (1580-1654), called "the water poet" because in addition to being a poet, and later a publican, he was a waterman on the Thames River in London. Author of poetry characterized by its topicality, and its "low jingling wit" (*CGBD*, 29:175-77). The passage quoted is from one of his poems about a walking trip from England to Scotland (*PW*, 584).

"Through heather, mosse, 'mong frogs, and bogs, and fogs,
 'Mongst craggy cliffs and thunder-batter'd hills,
Hares, hinds, bucks, roes, are chased by men and dogs,
 Where two hours' hunting fourscore fat deer kills.
Lowland, your sports are low as is your seat;
 The Highland games and minds are high and great."

But without further tyranny over my readers, or display of the
extent of my own reading, I shall content myself with borrowing a
single incident from the memorable hunting at Lude, commemorated
in the ingenious Mr Gunn's Essay on the Caledonian Harp,[1] and so
proceed in my story with all the brevity that my natural style of composition, partaking of what scholars call the periphrastic and ambagi-
tory, and the vulgar and circumbendibus, will permit me.

The solemn hunting was delayed, from various causes, for about
three weeks. The interval was spent by Waverley with great satisfaction
at Glennaquoich; for the impression which Flora had made on his
mind at their first meeting grew daily stronger. She was precisely the
character to fascinate a youth of romantic imagination. Her manners,
her language, her talents for poetry and music, gave additional and
varied influence to her eminent personal charms. Even in her hours of
gaiety, she was in his fancy exalted above the ordinary daughters of
Eve, and seemed only to stoop for an instant to those topics of amusement and gallantry which others appear to live for. In the neighbourhood of this enchantress, while sport consumed the morning, and
music and dance led on the hours of evening, Waverley became daily
more delighted with his hospitable landlord, and more enamoured of
his bewitching sister.

At length, the period fixed for the grand hunting arrived, and
Waverley and the Chieftain departed for the place of the rendezvous,
which was a day's journey to the northward of Glennaquoich. Fergus
was attended on this occasion by about three hundred of his clan, well
armed, and accoutred in their best fashion. Waverley complied so far
with the custom of the country as to adopt the trews (he could not be
reconciled to the kilt), brogues, and bonnet, as the fittest dress for the
exercise in which he was to be engaged, and which least exposed him
to be stared at as a stranger when they should reach the place of rendezvous. They found, on the spot appointed, several powerful Chiefs,
to all of whom Waverley was formally presented, and by all cordially
received. Their vassals and clansmen, a part of whose feudal duty it

---

1 In 1807, John Gunn published "An Historical Enquiry Respecting the Performance of the Harp in the Highlands of Scotland from the Earliest Time, Until
   it was Discontinued, about the Year 1734."

was to attend on these parties, appeared in such numbers as amounted to a small army. These active assistants spread through the country far and near, forming a circle, technically called the *tinchel*, which, gradually closing, drove the deer in herds together towards the glen where the Chiefs and principal sportsmen lay in wait for them. In the meanwhile, these distinguished personages bivouacked among the flowery heath, wrapped up in their plaids; a mode of passing a summer's night which Waverley found by no means unpleasant.

For many hours after sun-rise, the mountain ridges and passes retained their ordinary appearance of silence and solitude, and the Chiefs, with their followers, amused themselves with various pastimes, in which the joys of the shell, as Ossian[1] has it, were not forgotten. "Others apart sate on a hill retired";[2] probably as deeply engaged in the discussion of politics and news, as Milton's spirits in metaphysical disquisition. At length signals of the approach of the game were descried and heard. Distant shouts resounded from valley to valley, as the various parties of Highlanders, climbing rocks, struggling through copses, wading brooks, and traversing thickets, approached more and more near to each other, and compelled the astonished deer, with the other wild animals that fled before them, into a narrower circuit. Every now and then the report of muskets was heard, repeated by a thousand echoes. The baying of the dogs was soon added to the chorus, which grew ever louder and more loud. At length the advanced parties of the deer began to show themselves; and as the stragglers came bounding down the pass by two or three at a time, the Chiefs showed their skill by distinguishing the fattest deer, and their dexterity in bringing them down with their guns. Fergus exhibited remarkable address, and Edward was also so fortunate as to attract the notice and applause of the sportsmen.

But now the main body of the deer appeared at the head of the glen, compelled into a very narrow compass, and presenting such a formidable phalanx, that their antlers appeared at a distance, over the ridge of the steep pass, like a leafless grove. Their number was very great, and from a desperate stand which they made, with the tallest of the red-deer stags arranged in front, in a sort of battle-array, gazing on the group which barred their passage down the glen, the more experi-

---

1 A Gaelic poet of legend, purported to be the son of Finn Mac Cumhail. One "cycle of Ossianic poetry" deals with the third-century Finn, and the other with Cuchulain. James Macpherson claimed to have discovered Ossian's poetry in the 1760s, but the poetry was eventually discovered to be Macpherson's own (*CCE*, 651). See Appendix D1 for an excerpt from Macpherson's *Poems of Ossian*.

2 Refers to the fallen angels in hell, Milton's *Paradise Lost*, Book II, ln. 557.

enced sportsmen began to augur danger. The work of destruction, however, now commenced on all sides. Dogs and hunters were at work, and muskets and fusees resounded from every quarter. The deer, driven to desperation, made at length a fearful charge right upon the spot where the more distinguished sportsmen had taken their stand. The word was given in Gaelic to fling themselves upon their faces; but Waverley, on whose English ears the signal was lost, had almost fallen a sacrifice to his ignorance of the ancient language in which it was communicated. Fergus, observing his danger, sprung up and pulled him with violence to the ground, just as the whole herd broke down upon them. The tide being absolutely irresistible, and wounds from a stag's horn highly dangerous,[vv] the activity of the Chieftain may be considered, on this occasion, as having saved his guest's life. He detained him with a firm grasp until the whole herd had fairly run over them. Waverley then attempted to rise, but found that he had suffered several very severe contusions, and, upon a further examination, discovered that he had sprained his ankle violently.

This checked the mirth of the meeting, although the Highlanders, accustomed to such incidents, and prepared for them, had suffered no harm themselves. A wigwam was erected almost in an instant, where Edward was deposited on a couch of heather. The surgeon, or he who assumed the office, appeared to unite the characters of a leech and a conjuror. He was an old smoke-dried Highlander, wearing a venerable grey beard, and having for his sole garment a tartan frock, the skirts of which descended to the knee, and, being undivided in front, made the vestment serve at once for doublet and breeches.[ww] He observed great ceremony in approaching Edward; and though our hero was writhing with pain, would not proceed to any operation which might assuage it until he had perambulated his couch three times, moving from east to west, according to the course of the sun. This, which was called making the *deasil*,[xx] both the leech and the assistants seemed to consider as a matter of the last importance to the accomplishment of a cure; and Waverley, whom pain rendered incapable of expostulation, and who indeed saw no chance of its being attended to, submitted in silence.

After this ceremony was duly performed, the old Esculapius[1] let his patient's blood with a cupping-glass with great dexterity, and proceeded, muttering all the while to himself in Gaelic, to boil on the fire certain herbs, with which he compounded an embrocation. He then fomented the parts which had sustained injury, never failing to murmur prayers or spells, which of the two Waverley could not distin-

---

1 Ancient Greek god of medicine.

guish, as his ear only caught the words *Gasper-Melchior-Balthazar-max-prax-fax*, and similar gibberish. The fomentation had a speedy effect in alleviating the pain and swelling, which our hero imputed to the virtue of the herbs, or the effect of the chafing, but which was by the bystanders unanimously ascribed to the spells with which the operation had been accompanied. Edward was given to understand, that not one of the ingredients had been gathered except during the full moon, and that the herbalist had, while collecting them, uniformly recited a charm, which, in English, ran thus:

> Hail to thee, thou holy herb,
> That sprung on holy ground!
> All in the Mount Olivet
> First wert thou found:
> Thou art boot for many a bruise,
> And healest many a wound;
> In our Lady's blessed name,
> I take thee from the ground.[yy][1]

Edward observed, with some surprise, that even Fergus, notwithstanding his knowledge and education, seemed to fall in with the superstitious ideas of his countrymen, either because he deemed it impolitic to affect scepticism on a matter of general belief, or more probably because, like most men who do not think deeply or accurately on such subjects, he had in his mind a reserve of superstition which balanced the freedom of his expressions and practice upon other occasions. Waverley made no commentary, therefore, on the manner of the treatment, but rewarded the professor of medicine with a liberality beyond the utmost conception of his wildest hopes. He uttered, on the occasion, so many incoherent blessings in Gaelic and English, that Mac-Ivor, rather scandalized at the excess of his acknowledgments, cut them short, by exclaiming, *Ceud mile mhalloich ort!* *i.e.*, "A hundred thousand curses on you!" and so pushed the helper of men out of the cabin.

After Waverley was left alone, the exhaustion of pain and fatigue,—for the whole day's exercise had been severe,—threw him into a profound, but yet a feverish sleep, which he chiefly owed to an opiate draught administered by the old Highlander from some decoction of herbs in his pharmacopeia.

Early the next morning, the purpose of their meeting being over, and their sports damped by the untoward accident, in which Fergus

---

1 From Reginald Scott (c. 1538-99), *The Discoverie of Witchcraft* (1584); Mount Olivet in Jerusalem was the place of Jesus' Ascension (*CCE*, 642).

and all his friends expressed the greatest sympathy, it became a question how to dispose of the disabled sportsman. This was settled by Mac-Ivor, who had a litter prepared, of "birch and hazel grey,"[zz] which was borne by his people with such caution and dexterity as renders it not improbable that they may have been the ancestors of some of those sturdy Gael, who have now the happiness to transport the belles of Edinburgh, in their sedan-chairs, to ten routs in one evening. When Edward was elevated upon their shoulders, he could not help being gratified with the romantic effect produced by the breaking up of this silvan camp.[aaa]

The various tribes assembled, each at the pibroch of their native clan, and each headed by their patriarchal ruler. Some, who had already begun to retire, were seen winding up the hills, or descending the passes which led to the scene of the action, the sound of their bagpipes dying upon the ear. Others made still a moving picture upon the narrow plain, forming various changeful groups, their feathers and loose plaids waving in the morning breeze, and their arms glittering in the rising sun. Most of the Chiefs came to take farewell of Waverley, and to express their anxious hope they might again, and speedily, meet; but the care of Fergus abridged the ceremony of taking leave. At length, his own men being completely assembled and mustered, Mac-Ivor commenced his march, but not towards the quarter from which they had come. He gave Edward to understand, that the greater part of his followers, now on the field, were bound on a distant expedition, and that when he had deposited him in the house of a gentleman, who he was sure would pay him every attention, he himself should be under the necessity of accompanying them the greater part of the way, but would lose no time in rejoining his friend.

Waverley was rather surprised that Fergus had not mentioned this ulterior destination when they set out upon the hunting-party; but his situation did not admit of many interrogatories. The greater part of the clansmen went forward under the guidance of old Ballenkeiroch, and Evan Dhu Maccombich, apparently in high spirits. A few remained for the purpose of escorting the Chieftain, who walked by the side of Edward's litter, and attended him with the most affectionate assiduity. About noon, after a journey which the nature of the conveyance, the pain of his bruises, and the roughness of the way, rendered inexpressibly painful, Waverley was hospitably received into the house of a gentleman related to Fergus, who had prepared for him every accommodation which the simple habits of living then universal in the Highlands, put in his power. In this person, an old man about seventy, Edward admired a relic of primitive simplicity. He wore no dress but what his estate afforded; the cloth was the fleece of his own sheep, woven by his own servants, and stained into tartan by the dyes produced from the herbs and lichens of the hills around him. His linen was spun by his daughters and maid-servants, from his own flax, nor did his table, though plentiful, and varied with game and fish, offer an article but what was of native produce.

Claiming himself no rights of clanship or vassalage, he was fortunate in the alliance and protection of Vich Ian Vohr, and other bold and enterprising chieftains, who protected him in the quiet unambitious life he loved. It is true, the youth born on his grounds were often enticed to leave him for the service of his more active friends; but a few old servants and tenants used to shake their grey locks when they heard their master censured for want of spirit, and observed, "When the wind is still, the shower falls soft." This good old man, whose charity and hospitality were unbounded, would have received Waverley with kindness, had he been the meanest Saxon peasant, since his situation required assistance. But his attention to a friend and guest of Vich Ian Vohr was anxious and unremitted. Other embrocations were applied to the injured limb, and new spells were put in practice. At length, after more solicitude than was perhaps for the advantage of his health, Fergus took farewell of Edward for a few days, when, he said, he would return to Tomanrait, and hoped by that time Waverley would be able to ride one of the Highland ponies of his landlord, and in that manner return to Glennaquoich.

The next day, when his good old host appeared, Edward learned that his friend had departed with the dawn, leaving none of his followers except Callum Beg, the sort of foot-page who used to attend his person, and who had now in charge to wait upon Waverley. On asking his host, if he knew where the Chieftain was gone, the old man looked fixedly at him, with something mysterious and sad in the smile which was his only reply. Waverley repeated his question, to which his host answered in a proverb,—

> "What sent the messengers to hell,
> Was asking what they knew full well."[bbb]

He was about to proceed, but Callum Beg said, rather pertly, as Edward thought, that "Ta Tighearnach (*i.e.*, the Chief) did not like ta Sassenagh Duinhé-wassel to be pingled[1] wi' mickle speaking, as she was na tat weel." From this Waverley concluded he should disoblige his friend by enquiring of a stranger the object of a journey which he himself had not communicated.

It is unnecessary to trace the progress of our hero's recovery. The sixth morning had arrived, and he was able to walk about with a staff,

---

1 "Pained; put to difficulty" (*WSG*).

when Fergus returned with about a score of his men. He seemed in the highest spirits, congratulated Waverley on his progress towards recovery, and finding he was able to sit on horseback, proposed their immediate return to Glennaquoich. Waverley joyfully acceded, for the form of its fair mistress had lived in his dreams during all the time of his confinement.

> Now he has ridden o'er moor and moss,
> O'er hill and many a glen,[1]

Fergus, all the while, with his myrmidons,[2] striding stoutly by his side, or diverging to get a shot at a roe or a heath-cock. Waverley's bosom beat thick when they approached the old tower of Ian nan Chaistel, and could distinguish the fair form of its mistress advancing to meet them.

Fergus began immediately, with his usual high spirits, to exclaim, "Open your gates, incomparable princess, to the wounded Moor Abindarez, whom Rodrigo de Narvez, constable of Antiquera, conveys to your castle; or open them, if you like it better, to the renowned Marquis of Mantua, the sad attendant of his half-slain friend, Baldovinos of the mountain.—Ah, long rest to thy soul, Cervantes! without quoting thy remnants, how should I frame my language to befit romantic ears!"[3]

Flora now advanced, and welcoming Waverley with much kindness, expressed regret for his accident, of which she had already heard particulars, and her surprise that her brother should not have taken better care to put a stranger on his guard against the perils of the sport in which he engaged him. Edward easily exculpated the Chieftain, who, indeed, at his own personal risk, had probably saved his life.

This greeting over, Fergus said three or four words to his sister in Gaelic. The tears instantly sprung to her eyes, but they seemed to be tears of devotion and joy, for she looked up to heaven, and folded her hands as in a solemn expression of prayer or gratitude. After the pause of a minute, she presented to Edward some letters which had been forwarded from Tully-Veolan during his absence, and, at the same time, delivered some to her brother. To the latter she likewise gave three or four numbers of the Caledonian Mercury, the only newspaper which was then published to the north of the Tweed.

---

1 From *Hardyknute* by Lady Wardlaw, st. 15.
2 Bodyguards.
3 From Cervantes, *Don Quixote, Part I*, Chapter 5; spoken by Don Quixote after his first adventure (*OW*, 432).

Both gentlemen retired to examine their dispatches, and Edward speedily found that those which he had received contained matters of very deep interest.

CHAPTER XXV.
News from England.

THE letters which Waverley had hitherto received from his relations in England, were not such as required any particular notice in this narrative. His father usually wrote to him with the pompous affectation of one who was too much oppressed by public affairs to find leisure to attend to those of his own family. Now and then he mentioned persons of rank in Scotland to whom he wished his son should pay some attention; but Waverley, hitherto occupied by the amusements which he had found at Tully-Veolan and Glennaquoich, dispensed with paying any attention to hints so coldly thrown out, especially as distance, shortness of leave of absence, and so forth, furnished a ready apology. But latterly the burden of Mr Richard Waverley's paternal epistles consisted in certain mysterious hints of greatness and influence which he was speedily to attain, and which would ensure his son's obtaining the most rapid promotion, should he remain in the military service. Sir Everard's letters were of a different tenor. They were short; for the good Baronet was none of your illimitable correspondents, whose manuscript overflows the folds of their large post paper, and leaves no room for the seal; but they were kind and affectionate, and seldom concluded without some allusion to our hero's stud, some question about the state of his purse, and a special enquiry after such of his recruits as had preceded him from Waverley-Honour. Aunt Rachel charged him to remember his principles of religion, to take care of his health, to beware of Scotch mists, which, she had heard, would wet an Englishman through and through; never to go out at night without his great-coat; and, above all, to wear flannel next to his skin.

Mr Pembroke only wrote to our hero one letter, but it was of the bulk of six epistles of these degenerate days, containing, in the moderate compass of ten folio pages, closely written, a precis of a supplementary quarto manuscript of *addenda, delenda, et corrigenda,*[1] in reference to the two tracts with which he had presented Waverley. This he considered as a mere sop in the pan to stay the appetite of Edward's curiosity, until he should find an opportunity of sending down the volume itself, which was much too heavy for the post, and which he proposed to accompany with certain interesting pamphlets, lately pub-

---

1 Additions, deletions, and corrections.

lished by his friend in Little Britain, with whom he had kept up a sort of literary correspondence, in virtue of which the library shelves of Waverley-Honour were loaded with much trash, and a good round bill, seldom summed in fewer than three figures, was yearly transmitted, in which Sir Everard Waverley of Waverley-Honour, Bart., was marked Dr to Jonathan Grubbet, bookseller and stationer, Little Britain. Such had hitherto been the style of the letters which Edward had received from England; but the packet delivered to him at Glennaquoich was of a different and more interesting complexion. It would be impossible for the reader, even were I to insert the letters at full length, to comprehend the real cause of their being written, without a glance into the interior of the British Cabinet at the period in question.

The ministers of the day happened (no very singular event) to be divided into two parties; the weakest of which, making up by assiduity of intrigue their inferiority in real consequence, had of late acquired some new proselytes, and with them the hope of superseding their rivals in the favour of their sovereign, and overpowering them in the House of Commons. Amongst others, they had thought it worth while to practise upon Richard Waverley. This honest gentleman, by a grave mysterious demeanor, an attention to the etiquette of business, rather more than to its essence, a facility in making long dull speeches, consisting of truisms and common-places, hashed up with a technical jargon of office, which prevented the inanity of his orations from being discovered, had acquired a certain name and credit in public life, and even established, with many, the character of a profound politician; none of your shining orators, indeed, whose talents evaporate in tropes of rhetoric and flashes of wit, but one possessed of steady parts for business, which would wear well, as the ladies say in choosing their silks, and ought in all reason to be good for common and every-day use, since they were confessedly formed of no holiday texture.

This faith had become so general, that the insurgent party in the cabinet of which we have made mention, after sounding Mr Richard Waverley, were so satisfied with his sentiments and abilities, as to propose, that, in case of a certain revolution in the ministry, he should take an ostensible place in the new order of things, not indeed of the very first rank, but greatly higher, in point both of emolument and influence, than that which he now enjoyed. There was no resisting so tempting a proposal, notwithstanding that the Great Man, under whose patronage he had enlisted, and by whose banner he had hitherto stood firm, was the principal object of the proposed attack by the new allies. Unfortunately this fair scheme of ambition was blighted in the very bud, by a premature movement. All the official gentlemen concerned in it, who hesitated to take the part of a voluntary resignation, were informed that the king had no farther occasion for their services; and, in Richard Waverley's case, which the minister considered as aggravated by ingratitude, dismissal was accompanied by something like personal contempt and contumely. The public, and even the party of whom he shared the fall, sympathized little in the disappointment of this selfish and interested statesman; and he retired to the country under the comfortable reflection, that he had lost, at the same time, character, credit, and,—what he at least equally deplored,—emolument.

Richard Waverley's letter to his son upon this occasion was a masterpiece of its kind. Aristides[1] himself could not have made out a harder case. An unjust monarch, and an ungrateful country, were the burden of each rounded paragraph. He spoke of long services, and unrequited sacrifices; though the former had been overpaid by his salary, and nobody could guess in what the latter consisted, unless it were in his deserting, not from conviction, but for the lucre of gain, the Tory principles of his family. In the conclusion, his resentment was wrought to such an excess by the force of his own oratory, that he could not repress some threats of vengeance, however vague and impotent, and finally acquainted his son with his pleasure that he should testify his sense of the ill-treatment he had sustained, by throwing up his commission as soon as the letter reached him. This, he said, was also his uncle's desire, as he would himself intimate in due course.

Accordingly, the next letter which Edward opened was from Sir Everard. His brother's disgrace seemed to have removed from his well-natured bosom all recollection of their differences, and, remote as he was from every means of learning that Richard's disgrace was in reality only the just, as well as natural consequence, of his own unsuccessful intrigues, the good, but credulous Baronet at once set it down as a new and enormous instance of the injustice of the existing government. It was true, he said, and he must not disguise it even from Edward, that his father could not have sustained such an insult as was now, for the first time, offered to one of his house, unless he had subjected himself to it by accepting of an employment under the present system. Sir Everard had no doubt that he now both saw and felt the magnitude of this error, and it should be his (Sir Everard's) business, to take care that the cause of his regret should not extend itself to pecuniary consequences. It was enough for a Waverley to have sustained the public disgrace; the patrimonial injury could easily be obviated by the head of their family. But it was both the opinion of Mr Richard Waverley and his own, that Edward, the representative of the

---

1 Aristides the Just, fl. 5th century BCE, Athenian statesman and general, created the Delian League that led to the creation of the Athenian state (*EB*, 1:554).

family of Waverley-Honour, should not remain in a situation which subjected him also to such treatment as that with which his father had been stigmatized. He requested his nephew therefore to take the fittest, and, at the same time, the most speedy opportunity, of transmitting his resignation to the War-Office, and hinted, moreover, that little ceremony was necessary where so little had been used to his father. He sent multitudinous greetings to the Baron of Bradwardine.

A letter from Aunt Rachel spoke out even more plainly. She considered the disgrace of brother Richard as the just reward of his forfeiting his allegiance to a lawful, though exiled sovereign, and taking the oaths to an alien; a concession which her grandfather, Sir Nigel Waverley, refused to make, either to the Round-head Parliament or to Cromwell, when his life and fortune stood in the utmost extremity. She hoped her dear Edward would follow the footsteps of his ancestors, and as speedily as possible get rid of the badge of servitude to the usurping family, and regard the wrongs sustained by his father as an admonition from Heaven, that every desertion of the line of loyalty becomes its own punishment. She also concluded with her respects to Mr Bradwardine, and begged Waverley would inform her whether his daughter, Miss Rose, was old enough to wear a pair of very handsome ear-rings, which she proposed to send as a token of her affection. The good lady also desired to be informed whether Mr Bradwardine took as much Scotch snuff, and danced as unweariedly, as he did when he was at Waverley-Honour about thirty years ago.

These letters, as might have been expected, highly excited Waverley's indignation. From the desultory style of his studies, he had not any fixed political opinion to place in opposition to the movements of indignation which he felt at his father's supposed wrongs. Of the real cause of his disgrace, Edward was totally ignorant; nor had his habits at all led him to investigate the politics of the period in which he lived, or remark the intrigues in which his father had been so actively engaged. Indeed, any impressions which he had accidentally adopted concerning the parties of the times, were (owing to the society in which he had lived at Waverley-Honour) of a nature rather unfavourable to the existing government and dynasty. He entered, therefore, without hesitation, into the resentful feeling of the relations who had the best title to dictate his conduct; and not perhaps the less willingly, when he remembered the tædium of his quarters, and the inferior figure which he had made among the officers of his regiment. If he could have had any doubt upon the subject, it would have been decided by the following letter from his commanding officer, which, as it is very short, shall be inserted verbatim:

"SIR,

"Having carried somewhat beyond the line of my duty, an indulgence which even the lights of nature, and much more those of Christianity, direct towards errors which may arise from youth and inexperience, and that, altogether without effect, I am reluctantly compelled, at the present crisis, to use the only remaining remedy which is in my power. You are, therefore, hereby commanded to repair to —, the head-quarters of the regiment, within three days after the date of this letter. If you shall fail to do so, I must report you to the War-Office as absent without leave, and also take other steps, which will be disagreeable to you, as well as to,

"Sir,
"Your obedient Servant,
"J. GARDINER, Lieut.-Col.
"Commanding the — Regt. Dragoons."

Edward's blood boiled within him as he read this letter. He had been accustomed from his very infancy to possess, in a great measure, the disposal of his own time, and thus acquired habits which rendered the rules of military discipline as unpleasing to him in this as they were in some other respects. An idea that in his own case they would not be enforced in a very rigid manner, had also obtained full possession of his mind, and had hitherto been sanctioned by the indulgent conduct of his lieutenant-colonel. Neither had any thing occurred, to his knowledge, that should have induced his commanding officer, without any other warning than the hints we noticed at the end of the fourteenth chapter, so suddenly to assume a harsh, and, as Edward deemed it, so insolent a tone of dictatorial authority. Connecting it with the letters he had just received from his family, he could not but suppose, that it was designed to make him feel, in his present situation, the same pressure of authority which had been exercised in his father's case, and that the whole was a concerted scheme to depress and degrade every member of the Waverley family.

Without a pause, therefore, Edward wrote a few cold lines, thanking his lieutenant-colonel for past civilities, and expressing regret that he should have chosen to efface the remembrance of them, by assuming a different tone towards him. The strain of his letter, as well as what he (Edward) conceived to be his duty, in the present crisis, called upon him to lay down his commission; and he therefore inclosed the formal resignation of a situation which subjected him to so unpleasant a correspondence, and requested Colonel Gardiner would have the goodness to forward it to the proper authorities.

Having finished this magnanimous epistle, he felt somewhat uncertain concerning the terms in which his resignation ought to be expressed, upon which subject he resolved to consult Fergus Mac-Ivor. It may be observed in passing, that the bold and prompt habits of thinking, acting, and speaking, which distinguished this young Chieftain, had given him a considerable ascendency over the mind of Waverley. Endowed with at least equal powers of understanding, and with much finer genius, Edward yet stooped to the bold and decisive activity of an intellect which was sharpened by the habit of acting on a preconceived and regular system, as well as by extensive knowledge of the world.

When Edward found his friend, the latter had still in his hand the newspaper which he had perused, and advanced to meet him with the embarrassment of one who has unpleasing news to communicate. "Do your letters, Captain Waverley, confirm the unpleasing information which I find in this paper?"

He put the paper into his hand, where his father's disgrace was registered in the most bitter terms, transferred probably from some London journal. At the end of the paragraph was this remarkable innuendo:

"We understand that 'this same *Richard* who hath done all this,' is not the only example of the *Wavering Honour* of W-v-r-ly H-n-r. See the Gazette of this day."

With hurried and feverish apprehension our hero turned to the place referred to, and found therein recorded, "Edward Waverley, captain in — regiment dragoons, superseded for absence without leave"; and in the list of military promotions, referring to the same regiment, he discovered this farther article, "Lieut. Julius Butler, to be captain, *vice* Edward Waverley superseded."[1]

Our hero's bosom glowed with the resentment which undeserved and apparently premeditated insult was calculated to excite in the bosom of one who had aspired after honour, and was thus wantonly held up to public scorn and disgrace. Upon comparing the date of his colonel's letter with that of the article in the Gazette, he perceived that his threat of making a report upon his absence had been literally fulfilled, and without inquiry, as it seemed, whether Edward had either received his summons, or was disposed to comply with it. The whole, therefore, appeared a formed plan to degrade him in the eyes of the public; and the idea of its having succeeded filled him with such bitter emotions, that, after various attempts to conceal them, he at length threw himself into Mac-Ivor's arms, and gave vent to tears of shame and indignation.

---

1 Discharged.

It was none of this Chieftain's faults to be indifferent to the wrongs of his friends; and for Edward, independent of certain plans with which he was connected, he felt a deep and sincere interest. The proceeding appeared as extraordinary to him as it had done to Edward. He indeed knew of more motives than Waverley was privy to for the peremptory order that he should join his regiment. But that, without farther inquiry into the circumstances of a necessary delay, the commanding officer, in contradiction to his known and established character, should have proceeded in so harsh and unusual a manner, was a mystery which he could not penetrate. He soothed our hero, however, to the best of his power, and began to turn his thoughts on revenge for his insulted honour.

Edward eagerly grasped at the idea. "Will you carry a message for me to Colonel Gardiner, my dear Fergus, and oblige me for ever?"

Fergus paused; "It is an act of friendship which you should command, could it be useful, or lead to the righting of your honour; but in the present case, I doubt if your commanding officer would give you the meeting on account of his having taken measures, which, however harsh and exasperating, were still within the strict bounds of his duty. Besides, Gardiner is a precise Huguenot, and has adopted certain ideas about the sinfulness of such rencontres, from which it would be impossible to make him depart, especially as his courage is beyond all suspicion. And besides, I—I, to say the truth—I dare not at this moment, for some very weighty reasons, go near any of the military quarters or garrisons belonging to this government."

"And am I," said Waverley, "to sit down quiet and contented under the injury I have received?"

"That will I never advise my friend," replied Mac-Ivor. "But I would have vengeance to fall on the head, not on the hand; on the tyrannical and oppressive government which designed and directed these premeditated and reiterated insults, not on the tools of office which they employed in the execution of the injuries they aimed at you."

"On the government!" said Waverley.

"Yes," replied the impetuous[1] Highlander, "on the usurping House of Hanover, whom your grandfather would no more have served than he would have taken wages of red-hot gold from the great fiend of hell!"

"But since the time of my grandfather two generations of this dynasty have possessed the throne," said Edward, coolly.

"True," replied the Chieftain; "and because we have passively given them so long the means of showing their native character,—because

---

1 Scott added this adjective to the revised *Magnum Opus Waverley* to further emphasize Mac-Ivor's lack of self-control.

both you and I myself have lived in quiet submission, have even truck-led to the times so far as to accept commissions under them, and thus have given them an opportunity of disgracing us publicly by resuming them, are we not on that account to resent injuries which our fathers only apprehended, but which we have actually sustained? Or is the cause of the unfortunate Stewart family become less just, because their title has devolved upon an heir who is innocent of the charges of misgovernment brought against his father?—Do you remember the lines of your favourite poet?—

> Had Richard unconstrain'd resign'd the throne,
> A king can give no more than is his own;
> The title stood entail'd had Richard had a son.[1]

You see, my dear Waverley, I can quote poetry as well as Flora and you. But come, clear your moody brow, and trust to me to show you an honourable road to a speedy and glorious revenge. Let us seek Flora, who perhaps has more news to tell us of what has occurred during our absence. She will rejoice to hear that you are relieved of your servi-tude. But first add a postscript to your letter, marking the time when you received this calvinistical Colonel's[2] first summons, and express your regret that the hastiness of his proceedings prevented your antic-ipating them by sending your resignation. Then let him blush for his injustice."

The letter was sealed accordingly, covering a formal resignation of the commission, and Mac-Ivor dispatched it with some letters of his own by a special messenger, with charge to put them into the nearest post-office in the Lowlands.

CHAPTER XXVI.
An Eclaircissement.[3]

THE hint which the Chieftain had thrown out respecting Flora was not unpremeditated. He had observed with great satisfaction the growing attachment of Waverley to his sister, nor did he see any bar to their union, excepting the situation which Waverley's father held in the

---

1 Lamont suggests Dryden's "The Character of a Good Parson," II.112-14, but notes the similarity between the lines Fergus utters and those in Shakespeare's *Henry VI Part III*, I.i.143ff, as does Hook (*PW*, 585; *OW*, 432).

2 Calvinism was the "national creed [of Scotland] and recognized as the estab-lished Church in 1690" (*OCBH*, 153); it was, to many during the eighteenth century, an "austere and harsh" religion.

3 Explanation.

ministry, and Edward's own commission in the army of George II. These obstacles were now removed, and in a manner which apparently paved the way for the son's becoming reconciled to another allegiance. In every other respect the match would be most eligible. The safety, happiness, and honourable provision of his sister, whom he dearly loved, appeared to be ensured by the proposed union; and his heart swelled when he considered how his own interest would be exalted in the eyes of the ex-monarch to whom he dedicated his service, by an alliance with one of those ancient, powerful, and wealthy English families of the steady cavalier[1] faith, to awaken whose decayed attachment to the Stewart family was now a matter of such vital importance to the Stewart cause. Nor could Fergus perceive any obstacle to such a scheme. Waverley's attachment was evident; and as his person was handsome, and his taste apparently coincided with her own, he anticipated no opposition on the part of Flora. Indeed, between his ideas of patriarchal power, and those which he had acquired in France respecting the disposal of females in marriage, any opposition from his sister, dear as she was to him, would have been the last obstacle on which he would have calculated, even had the union been less eligible.

Influenced by these feelings, the Chief now led Waverley in quest of Miss Mac-Ivor, not without the hope that the present agitation of his guest's spirits might give him courage to cut short what Fergus termed the romance of the courtship. They found Flora, with her faithful attendants, Una and Cathleen, busied in preparing what appeared to Waverley to be white bridal favours. Disguising as well as he could the agitation of his mind, Waverley asked for what joyful occasion Miss Mac-Ivor made such ample preparation.

"It is for Fergus's bridal," she said, smiling.

"Indeed!" said Edward; "he has kept his secret well. I hope he will allow me to be his bride's-man."

"That is a man's office, but not yours, as Beatrice says," retorted Flora.

"And who is the fair lady, may I be permitted to ask, Miss Mac-Ivor?"

"Did not I tell you long since, that Fergus wooed no bride but Honour?" answered Flora.

---

1   "Nickname for the royalists who fought for Charles I during the civil wars"; in use by 1642, originally it was a derogatory term, denoting affiliation with Catholicism, foreign powers, and loose morals (*OCBH*, 177). Scott added the adjective "ancient" in the interleaved *Waverley* but it was replaced by "steady" in the *Magnum Opus Waverley*, presumably by Scott at proof stage in order to lend greater respect to the cavalier cause.

"And am I then incapable of being his assistant and counsellor in pursuit of honour?" said our hero, colouring deeply. "Do I rank so low in your opinion?"

"Far from it, Captain Waverley. I would to God you were of our determination! and made use of the expression which displeased you, soley

> Because you are not of our quality,
> But stand against us as an enemy."

"That time is past, sister," said Fergus; "and you may wish Edward Waverley (no longer captain) joy of being freed from the slavery to an usurper, implied in that sable and ill-omened emblem."

"Yes," said Waverley, undoing the cockade[1] from his hat, "it has pleased the king who bestowed this badge upon me, to resume it in a manner which leaves me little reason to regret his service."

"Thank God for that!" cried the enthusiast; "and O that they may be blind enough to treat every man of honour who serves them with the same indignity, that I may have less to sigh for when the struggle approaches!"

"And now, sister," said the Chieftain, "replace his cockade with one of a more lively colour. I think it was the fashion of the ladies of yore to arm and send forth their knights to high achievement."

"Not," replied the lady, "till the knight adventurer had well weighed the justice and the danger of the cause, Fergus. Mr Waverley is just now too much agitated by feelings of recent emotion, for me to press upon him a resolution of consequence."

Waverley felt half-alarmed at the thought of adopting the badge of what was by the majority of the kingdom esteemed rebellion, yet he could not disguise his chagrin at the coldness with which Flora parried her brother's hint. "Miss Mac-Ivor, I perceive, thinks the knight unworthy of her encouragement and favour," said he, somewhat bitterly.

"Not so, Mr Waverley," she replied, with great sweetness. "Why should I refuse my brother's valued friend a boon which I am distributing to his whole clan? Most willingly would I enlist every man of honour in the cause to which my brother has devoted himself. But Fergus has taken his measures with his eyes open. His life has been devoted to this cause from his cradle; with him its call is sacred, were it even a summons to the tomb. But how can I wish you, Mr Waverley,

---

1 "A ribbon, knot of ribbons, rosette, or the like, worn in the hat as a badge of office or party, or as part of a livery dress" (*OED*). The white cockade denoted the House of Stuart, the black leather cockade, the House of Hanover.

so new to the world, so far from every friend who might advise and ought to influence you,—in a moment too of sudden pique and indignation,—how can I wish you to plunge yourself at once into so desperate an enterprise?"

Fergus, who did not understand these delicacies, strode through the apartment biting his lip, and then, with a constrained smile, said, "Well, sister, I leave you to act your new character of mediator between the Elector of Hanover and the subjects of your lawful sovereign and benefactor," and left the room.

There was a painful pause, which was at length broken by Miss Mac-Ivor. "My brother is unjust," she said, "because he can bear no interruption that seems to thwart his loyal zeal."

"And do you not share his ardour?" asked Waverley.

"Do I not?" answered Flora—"God knows mine exceeds his, if that be possible. But I am not, like him, rapt by the bustle of military preparation, and the infinite detail necessary to the present undertaking, beyond consideration of the grand principles of justice and truth, on which our enterprise is grounded; and these, I am certain, can only be furthered by measures in themselves true and just. To operate upon your present feelings, my dear Mr Waverley, to induce you to an irretrievable step, of which you have not considered either the justice or the danger, is, in my poor judgment, neither the one nor the other."

"Incomparable Flora!" said Edward, taking her hand, "how much do I need such a monitor!"

"A better one by far," said Flora, gently withdrawing her hand, "Mr Waverley will always find in his own bosom, when he will give its small still voice leisure to be heard."

"No, Miss Mac-Ivor, I dare not hope it; a thousand circumstances of fatal self-indulgence have made me the creature rather of imagination than reason. Durst I but hope—could I but think—that you would deign to be to me that affectionate, that condescending friend, who would strengthen me to redeem my errors, my future life"—

"Hush, my dear sir! now you carry your joy at escaping the hands of a Jacobite recruiting officer to an unparalleled excess of gratitude."

"Nay, dear Flora, trifle with me no longer; you cannot mistake the meaning of those feelings which I have most involuntarily expressed; and since I have broken the barrier of silence, let me profit by my audacity.—Or may I, with your permission, mention to your brother"—

"Not for the world, Mr Waverley!"

"What am I to understand?" said Edward. "Is there any fatal bar—has any prepossession"—

"None, sir," answered Flora. "I owe it to myself to say, that I never yet saw the person, on whom I thought with reference to the present subject."

"The shortness of our acquaintance, perhaps—If Miss Mac-Ivor will deign to give me time"—

"I have not even that excuse. Captain Waverley's character is so open—is, in short, of that nature, that it cannot be misconstrued, either in its strength or its weakness."

"And for that weakness you despise me?" said Edward.

"Forgive me, Mr Waverley—and remember it is but within this half hour that there existed between us a barrier of a nature to me insurmountable, since I never could think of an officer in the service of the Elector of Hanover in any other light than as a casual acquaintance. Permit me then to arrange my ideas upon so unexpected a topic, and in less than an hour I will be ready to give you such reasons for the resolution I shall express, as may be satisfactory at least, if not pleasing to you." So saying, Flora withdrew, leaving Waverley to meditate upon the manner in which she had received his addresses.

Ere he could make up his mind whether to believe his suit had been acceptable or no, Fergus re-entered the apartment. "What, à la mort,[1] Waverley?" he cried. "Come down with me to the court, and you shall see a sight worth all the tirades of your romances. An hundred fire-locks, my friend, and as many broadswords, just arrived from good friends; and two or three hundred stout fellows almost fighting which shall first possess them.—But let me look at you closer. Why, a true Highlander would say you had been blighted by an evil eye.—Or can it be this silly girl that has thus blanked your spirit?—Never mind her, dear Edward; the wisest of her sex are fools in what regards the business of life."

"Indeed, my good friend," answered Waverley, "all that I can charge against your sister is, that she is too sensible, too reasonable."

"If that be all, I ensure you for a louis-d'or against the mood lasting four-and-twenty hours. No woman was ever steadily sensible for that period; and I will engage, if that will please you, Flora shall be as unreasonable to-morrow as any of her sex. You must learn, my dear Edward, to consider women *en mousquetaire*."[2] So saying, he seized Waverley's arm, and dragged him off to review his military preparations.

CHAPTER XXVII.
Upon the same Subject.

FERGUS MAC-IVOR had too much tact and delicacy to renew the subject which he had interrupted. His head was, or appeared to be, so full of guns, broadswords, bonnets, canteens, and tartan hose, that

---

1 To the death.
2 "In a soldier's way" (*PW*, 585).

Waverley could not for some time draw his attention to any other topic.

"Are you to take the field so soon, Fergus," he asked, "that you are making all these martial preparations?"

"When we have settled that you go with me, you shall know all; but otherwise, the knowledge might rather be prejudicial to you."

"But are you serious in your purpose, with such inferior forces, to rise against an established government? It is mere frenzy."

"*Laissez faire à Don Antoine.*[1] I shall take good care of myself. We shall at least use the compliment of Conan, who never got a stroke but he gave one. I would not, however," continued the Chieftain, "have you think me mad enough to stir till a favourable opportunity: I will not slip my dog before the game's afoot. But, once more, will you join with us, and you shall know all?"

"How can I?" said Waverley; "I, who have so lately held that commission which is now posting back to those that gave it? My accepting it implied a promise of fidelity, and an acknowledgment of the legality of the government."

"A rash promise," answered Fergus, "is not a steel handcuff; it may be shaken off, especially when it was given under deception, and has been repaid by insult. But if you cannot immediately make up your mind to a glorious revenge, go to England, and ere you cross the Tweed, you will hear tidings that will make the world ring; and if Sir Everard be the gallant old cavalier I have heard him described by some of our *honest* gentlemen of the year one thousand seven hundred and fifteen, he will find you a better horse-troop and a better cause than you have lost."

"But your sister, Fergus?"

"Out, hyperbolical fiend!" replied the Chief, laughing; "how vexest thou this man!—Speak'st thou of nothing but of ladies?"

"Nay, be serious, my dear friend," said Waverley; "I feel that the happiness of my future life must depend upon the answer which Miss Mac-Ivor shall make to what I ventured to tell her this morning."

"And is this your very sober earnest," said Fergus, more gravely, "or are we in the land of romance and fiction?"

"My earnest, undoubtedly. How could you suppose me jesting on such a subject?"

"Then, in very sober earnest," answered his friend, "I am very glad to hear it; and so highly do I think of Flora, that you are the only man in England for whom I would say so much.—But before you shake my hand so warmly, there is more to be considered.—Your own family—will they approve your connecting yourself with the sister of a high-born Highland beggar?"

---

1 Leave it to me (*PW*, 585).

"My uncle's situation," said Waverley, "his general opinions, and his uniform indulgence, entitle me to say, that birth and personal qualities are all he would look to in such a connexion. And where can I find both united in such excellence as in your sister?"

"O nowhere! *Cela va sans dire*,"[1] replied Fergus with a smile. "But your father will expect a father's prerogative in being consulted."

"Surely; but his late breach with the ruling powers removes all apprehension of objection on his part, especially as I am convinced that my uncle will be warm in my cause."

"Religion perhaps," said Fergus, "may make obstacles, though we are not bigotted Catholics."

"My grandmother was of the Church of Rome, and her religion was never objected to by my family.—Do not think of *my* friends, dear Fergus; let me rather have your influence where it may be more necessary to remove obstacles—I mean with your lovely sister."

"My lovely sister," replied Fergus, "like her loving brother, is very apt to have a pretty decisive will of her own, by which, in this case, you must be ruled; but you shall not want my interest, nor my counsel. And, in the first place, I will give you one hint. Loyalty is her ruling passion; and since she could spell an English book, she has been in love with the memory of the gallant Captain Wogan, who renounced the service of the usurper Cromwell to join the standard of Charles II., marched a handful of cavalry from London to the Highlands to join Middleton,[2] then in arms for the king, and at length died gloriously in the royal cause. Ask her to show you some verses she made on his history and fate; they have been much admired, I assure you. The next point is—I think I saw Flora go up towards the waterfall a short time since—follow, man, follow! Don't allow the garrison time to strengthen its purposes of resistance. *Alerte à la muraille!*[3] Seek Flora out, and learn her decision as soon as you can, and Cupid go with you, while I go to look over belts and cartouch-boxes."[4]

Waverley ascended the glen with an anxious and throbbing heart. Love, with all its romantic train of hopes, fears, and wishes, was mingled with other feelings of a nature less easily defined. He could not but remember how much this morning had changed his fate, and

---

1 That goes without saying (*LCD*).

2 Captain Edward Wogan first fought on the Parliamentarian side in the Civil War, but he then changed sides and soldiered for Charles II at the Battle of Worcester and then served under John Middleton, First Earl of Middleton (1608-74), in Scotland where Wogan died in 1654 in battle (not 1649 as Scott suggests), and is buried near Loch Tey (*OCBH*, 642; *OW*, 432).

3 "Quick, to the ramparts!" (*PW*, 585).

4 Cartridge boxes.

into what a complication of perplexity it was likely to plunge him. Sun-rise had seen him possessed of an esteemed rank in the honourable profession of arms, his father to all appearance rapidly rising in the favour of his sovereign;—all this had passed away like a dream— he himself was dishonoured, his father disgraced, and he had become involuntarily the confidant at least, if not the accomplice, of plans, dark, deep, and dangerous, which must infer either the subversion of the government he had so lately served, or the destruction of all who had participated in them. Should Flora even listen to his suit favourably, what prospect was there of its being brought to a happy termination, amid the tumult of an impending insurrection? Or how could he make the selfish request that she should leave Fergus, to whom she was so much attached, and, retiring with him to England, wait, as a distant spectator, the success of her brother's undertaking, or the ruin of all his hopes and fortunes?—Or, on the other hand, to engage himself, with no other aid than his single arm, in the dangerous and precipitate counsels of the Chieftain,—to be whirled along by him, the partaker of all his desperate and impetuous motions, renouncing almost the power of judging, or deciding upon the rectitude or prudence of his actions,—this was no pleasing prospect for the secret pride of Waverley to stoop to. And yet what other conclusion remained, saving the rejection of his addresses by Flora, an alternative not to be thought of in the present high-wrought state of his feelings, with any thing short of mental agony. Pondering the doubtful and dangerous prospect before him, he at length arrived near the cascade, where, as Fergus had augured, he found Flora seated.

She was quite alone, and as soon as she observed his approach, she rose, and came to meet him. Edward attempted to say something within the verge of ordinary compliment and conversation, but found himself unequal to the task. Flora seemed at first equally embarrassed, but recovered herself more speedily, and (an unfavourable augury for Waverley's suit) was the first to enter upon the subject of their last interview. "It is too important, in every point of view, Mr Waverley, to permit me to leave you in doubt of my sentiments."

"Do not speak them speedily," said Waverley, much agitated, "unless they are such as I fear, from your manner, I must not dare to anticipate. Let time—let my future conduct—let your brother's influence"—

"Forgive me, Mr Waverley," said Flora, her complexion a little heightened, but her voice firm and composed. "I should incur my own heavy censure, did I delay expressing my sincere conviction that I can never regard you otherwise than as a valued friend. I should do you the highest injustice did I conceal my sentiments for a moment. I see I distress you, and I grieve for it, but better now than later; and O, better a thousand times, Mr Waverley, that you should feel a present momentary disappointment, than the long and heart-sickening griefs which attend a rash and ill-assorted marriage!"

"Good God!" exclaimed Waverley, "why should you anticipate such consequences from a union, where birth is equal, where fortune is favourable, where, if I may venture to say so, the tastes are similar, where you allege no preference for another, where you even express a favourable opinion of him whom you reject?"

"Mr Waverley, I *have* that favourable opinion," answered Flora; "and so strongly, that though I would rather have been silent on the grounds of my resolution, you shall command them, if you exact such a mark of my esteem and confidence."

She sat down upon a fragment of rock, and Waverley, placing himself near her, anxiously pressed for the explanation she offered.

"I dare hardly," she said, "tell you the situation of my feelings, they are so different from those usually ascribed to young women at my period of life; and I dare hardly touch upon what I conjecture to be the nature of yours, lest I should give offence where I would willingly administer consolation. For myself, from my infancy till this day, I have had but one wish—the restoration of my royal benefactors to their rightful throne. It is impossible to express to you the devotion of my feelings to this single subject; and I will frankly confess, that it has so occupied my mind as to exclude every thought respecting what is called my own settlement in life. Let me but live to see the day of that happy restoration, and a Highland cottage, a French convent, or an English palace, will be alike indifferent to me."

"But, dearest Flora, how is your enthusiastic zeal for the exiled family inconsistent with my happiness?"

"Because you seek, or ought to seek, in the object of your attachment, a heart whose principal delight should be in augmenting your domestic felicity, and returning your affection, even to the height of romance. To a man of less keen sensibility, and less enthusiastic tenderness of disposition, Flora Mac-Ivor might give content, if not happiness; for, were the irrevocable words spoken, never would she be deficient in the duties which she vowed."

"And why,—why, Miss Mac-Ivor, should you think yourself a more valuable treasure to one who is less capable of loving, of admiring you, than to me?"

"Simply because the tone of our affections would be more in unison, and because his more blunted sensibility would not require the return of enthusiasm which I have not to bestow. But you, Mr Waverley, would, for ever refer to the idea of domestic happiness which your imagination is capable of painting, and whatever fell short of that ideal representation would be construed into coolness and indifference, while you might consider the enthusiasm with which I regarded the success of the royal family, as defrauding your affection of its due return."

"In other words, Miss Mac-Ivor, you cannot love me?" said her suitor dejectedly.

"I could esteem you, Mr Waverley, as much, perhaps more, than any man I have ever seen; but I cannot love you as you ought to be loved. O! do not, for your own sake, desire so hazardous an experiment! The woman whom you marry, ought to have affections and opinions moulded upon yours. Her studies ought to be your studies;—her wishes, her feelings, her hopes, her fears, should all mingle with yours. She should enhance your pleasures, share your sorrows, and cheer your melancholy."

"And why will not you, Miss Mac-Ivor, who can so well describe a happy union, why will not you be yourself the person you describe?"

"Is it possible you do not yet comprehend me?" answered Flora. "Have I not told you, that every keener sensation of my mind is bent exclusively towards an event, upon which, indeed, I have no power but those of my earnest prayers?"

"And might not the granting the suit I solicit," said Waverley, too earnest on his purpose to consider what he was about to say, "even advance the interest to which you have devoted yourself? My family is wealthy and powerful, inclined in principles to the Stewart race, and should a favourable opportunity"—

"A favourable opportunity!" said Flora, somewhat scornfully,—"Inclined in principles!—Can such lukewarm adherence be honourable to yourselves, or gratifying to your lawful sovereign?—Think, from my present feelings, what I should suffer when I held the place of member in a family, where the rights which I hold most sacred are subjected to cold discussion, and only deemed worthy of support when they shall appear on the point of triumphing without it!"

"Your doubts," quickly replied Waverley, "are unjust as far as concerns myself. The cause that I shall assert, I dare support through every danger, as undauntedly as the boldest who draws sword in its behalf."

"Of that," answered Flora, "I cannot doubt for a moment. But consult your own good sense and reason rather than a prepossession hastily adopted, probably only because you have met a young woman possessed of the usual accomplishments, in a sequestered and romantic situation. Let your part in this great and perilous drama rest upon conviction, and not on a hurried, and probably a temporary feeling."

Waverley attempted to reply, but his words failed him. Every sentiment that Flora had uttered vindicated the strength of his attachment; for even her loyalty, although wildly enthusiastic, was generous and noble, and disdained to avail itself of any indirect means of supporting the cause to which she was devoted.

After walking a little way in silence down the path, Flora thus resumed the conversation.—"One word more, Mr Waverley, ere we bid farewell to this topic for ever; and forgive my boldness if that word have the air of advice. My brother Fergus is anxious that you should join him in his present enterprise. But do not consent to this; you could not, by your single exertions, further his success, and you would inevitably share his fall, if it be God's pleasure that fall he must. Your character would also suffer irretrievably. Let me beg you will return to your own country; and, having publicly freed yourself from every tie to the usurping government, I trust you will see cause, and find opportunity, to serve your injured sovereign with effect, and stand forth, as your loyal ancestors, at the head of your natural followers and adherents, a worthy representative of the house of Waverley."

"And should I be so happy as thus to distinguish myself, might I not hope"—

"Forgive my interruption," said Flora. "The present time only is ours, and I can but explain to you with candour the feelings which I now entertain; how they might be altered by a train of events too favourable perhaps to be hoped for, it were in vain even to conjecture: only be assured, Mr Waverley, that, after my brother's honour and happiness, there is none which I shall more sincerely pray for than for yours."

With these words she parted from him, for they were now arrived where two paths separated. Waverley reached the castle amidst a medley of conflicting passions. He avoided any private interview with Fergus, as he did not find himself able either to encounter his raillery, or reply to his solicitations. The wild revelry of the feast, for Mac-Ivor kept open table for his clan, served in some degree to stun reflection. When their festivity was ended, he began to consider how he should again meet Miss Mac-Ivor after the painful and interesting explanation of the morning. But Flora did not appear. Fergus, whose eyes flashed when he was told by Cathleen that her mistress designed to keep her apartment that evening, went himself in quest of her; but apparently his remonstrances were in vain, for he returned with a heightened complexion, and manifest symptoms of displeasure. The rest of the evening passed on without any allusion, on the part of either Fergus or Waverley, to the subject which engrossed the reflections of the latter, and perhaps of both.

When retired to his own apartment, Edward endeavoured to sum up the business of the day. That the repulse he had received from Flora, would be persisted in for the present, there was not doubt. But could he hope for ultimate success in case circumstances permitted the renewal of his suit? Would the enthusiastic loyalty, which at this animating moment left no room for a softer passion, survive, at least in its engrossing force, the success or failure of the present political machinations? And if so, could he hope that the interest which she had acknowledged him to possess in her favour, might be improved into a warmer attachment? He taxed his memory to recall every word she had used, with the appropriate looks and gestures which had enforced them, and ended by finding himself in the same state of uncertainty. It was very late before sleep brought relief to the tumult of his mind, after the most painful and agitating day which he had ever passed.

CHAPTER XXVIII.
A Letter from Tully-Veolan.

IN the morning, when Waverley's troubled reflections had for some time given way to repose, there came music to his dreams, but not the voice of Selma.[1] He imagined himself transported back to Tully-Veolan, and that he heard Davie Gellatley singing in the court those matins[2] which used generally to be the first sounds that disturbed his repose while a guest of the Baron of Bradwardine. The notes which suggested this vision continued, and waxed louder, until Edward awoke in earnest. The illusion, however, did not seem entirely dispelled. The apartment was in the fortress of Ian nan Chaistel, but it was still the voice of Davie Gellatley that made the following lines resound under the window:—

> My heart's in the Highlands, my heart is not here,
> My heart's in the Highlands a-chasing the deer;
> A-chasing the wild deer, and following the roe,
> My heart's in the Highlands wherever I go.[ccc]

Curious to know what could have determined Mr Gellatley on an excursion of such unwonted extent, Edward began to dress himself in all haste, during which operation the minstrelsy of Davie changed its tune more than once:—

---

1 Peacefulness, though Lamont cites James MacPherson's "The Songs of Selma" as a possible reference and annotates it as "Highland minstrelsy" (*OW*, 432), while Hook explains it as "the gathering place of the bards in *Ossian*" (*PW*, 585).

2 "One of the canonical hours of the breviary; properly a midnight office, but sometimes recited at daybreak, and followed immediately by lauds" (*OED*).

There's nought in the Highlands but syboes[1] and leeks,
And lang-leggit callants gaun wanting the breeks;[2]
Wanting the breeks, and without hose and shoon,
But we'll a' win the breeks when King Jamie comes hame.[ddd]

By the time Waverley was dressed and had issued forth, David had associated himself with two or three of the numerous Highland loungers who always graced the gates of the castle with their presence, and was capering and dancing full merrily in the doubles and full career of a Scotch foursome reel,[3] to the music of his own whistling. In this double capacity of dancer and musician, he continued, until an idle piper, who observed his zeal, obeyed the unanimous call of *Seid suas* (*i.e.*, blow up), and relieved him from the latter part of his trouble. Young and old then mingled in the dance as they could find partners. The appearance of Waverley did not interrupt David's exercise, though he contrived, by grinning, nodding, and throwing one or two inclinations of the body into the graces with which he performed the Highland fling, to convey to our hero symptoms of recognition. Then, while busily employed in setting, whooping all the while, and snapping his fingers over his head, he of a sudden prolonged his side-step until it brought him to the place where Edward was standing, and, still keeping time to the music like Harlequin in a pantomime,[4] he thrust a letter into our hero's hand, and continued his saltation[5] without pause or intermission. Edward, who perceived that the address was in Rose's hand-writing, retired to peruse it, leaving the faithful bearer to continue his exercise until the piper or he should be tired out.

The contents of the letter greatly surprised him. It had originally commenced with, *Dear Sir*; but these words had been carefully erased, and the monosyllable, *Sir*, substituted in their place. The rest of the contents shall be given in Rose's own language.

---

1   "Young spring onions with the green stalk attached" (*OED*).
2   "Young lad; a somewhat irrisory [i.e., mocking] use of the old term gallant; a fine fellow" (*WSG*); "gaun" means "going" and "wanting the breeks" is "without trousers."
3   "A lively dance, chiefly associated with Scotland, usually danced by two couples [a foursome] facing each other, and describing a series of figures of eight" (*OED*).
4   John Rich took the character of Harlequin, "one of the principal stock characters of the Italian commedia dell'arte," and "incorporated the role into dance pantomimes based on the combination of a commedia plot and a classical fable. Harlequin was also the principal character of the slapstick pantomime form known as a harlequinade in England ..." (*EB*, 5:708).
5   "Leaping, bounding, or jumping" (*OED*).

"I fear I am using an improper freedom by intruding upon you, yet I cannot trust to any one else to let you know some things which have happened here, with which it seems necessary you should be acquainted. Forgive me, if I am wrong in what I am doing; for, alas! Mr Waverley, I have no better advice than that of my own feelings;— my dear father is gone from this place, and when he can return to my assistance and protection, God alone knows. You have probably heard, that in consequence of some troublesome news from the Highlands, warrants were sent out for apprehending several gentlemen in these parts, and, among others, my dear father. In spite of all my tears and entreaties that he would surrender himself to the government, he joined with Mr Falconer and some other gentlemen, and they have all gone northwards, with a body of about forty horsemen. So I am not so anxious concerning his immediate safety, as about what may follow afterwards, for these troubles are only beginning. But all this is nothing to you, Mr Waverley, only I thought you would be glad to learn that my father has escaped, in case you happen to have heard that he was in danger.

"The day after my father went off, there came a party of soldiers to Tully-Veolan, and behaved very rudely to Bailie Macwheeble; but the officer was very civil to me, only said his duty obliged him to search for arms and papers. My father had provided against this by taking away all the arms except the old useless things which hung in the hall, and he had put all his papers out of the way. But O! Mr Waverley, how shall I tell you, that they made strict inquiry after you, and asked when you had been at Tully-Veolan, and where you now were. The officer is gone back with his party, but a non-commissioned officer and four men remain as a sort of garrison in the house. They have hitherto behaved very well, as we are forced to keep them in good-humour. But these soldiers have hinted as if on your falling into their hands you would be in great danger; I cannot prevail on myself to write what wicked falsehoods they said, for I am sure they are falsehoods; but you will best judge what you ought to do. The party that returned carried off your servant prisoner, with your two horses, and every thing that you left at Tully-Veolan. I hope God will protect you, and that you will get safe home to England, where you used to tell me there was no military violence nor fighting among clans permitted, but every thing was done according to an equal law that protected all who were harmless and innocent. I hope you will exert your indulgence as to my boldness in writing to you, where it seems to me, though perhaps erroneously, that your safety and honour are concerned. I am sure—at least I think, my father would approve of my writing; for Mr Rubric is fled to his cousin's at the Duchran, to be out of danger from the soldiers and the Whigs, and Bailie Macwheeble does not like to meddle (he says) in other men's concerns, though I hope what may serve my father's friend at such a time as this, cannot be termed improper interference. Farewell, Captain Waverley! I shall probably never see you more; for it would be very improper to wish you to call at Tully-Veolan just now, even if these men were gone; but I will always remember with gratitude your kindness in assisting so poor a scholar as myself, and your attentions to my dear, dear father.

"I remain your obliged servant,
"ROSE COMYNE BRADWARDINE.

"P.S.—I hope you will send me a line by David Gellatley, just to say you have received this, and that you will take care of yourself; and forgive me if I entreat you, for your own sake, to join none of these unhappy cabals, but escape, as fast as possible, to your own fortunate country.—My compliments to my dear Flora, and to Glennaquoich. Is she not as handsome and accomplished as I described her?"

Thus concluded the letter of Rose Bradwardine, the contents of which both surprised and affected Waverley. That the Baron should fall under the suspicions of government, in consequence of the present stir among the partizans of the house of Stewart, seemed only the natural consequence of his political predilections; but how *he* himself should have been involved in such suspicions, conscious that until yesterday he had been free from harbouring a thought against the prosperity of the reigning family, seemed inexplicable. Both at Tully-Veolan and Glennaquoich, his hosts had respected his engagements with the existing government, and though enough passed by accidental innuendo that might induce him to reckon the Baron and the Chief among those disaffected gentlemen who were still numerous in Scotland, yet until his own connexion with the army had been broken off by the resumption of his commission, he had no reason to suppose that they nourished any immediate or hostile attempts against the present establishment. Still he was aware that unless he meant at once to embrace the proposal of Fergus Mac-Ivor, it would deeply concern him to leave the suspicious neighbourhood without delay, and repair where his conduct might undergo a satisfactory examination. Upon this he the rather determined, as Flora's advice favoured his doing so, and because he felt inexpressible repugnance at the idea of being accessary to the plague of civil war. Whatever were the original rights of the Stewarts, calm reflection told him, that, omitting the question how far James the Second could forfeit those of his posterity, he had, according to the united voice of the whole nation, justly forfeited his own. Since that period, four monarchs had reigned in peace and glory over Britain, sustaining and exalting the character of the nation abroad, and its liberties at home. Reason asked, was it worth while to disturb a government so long settled and established, and to plunge a kingdom into all the miseries of civil war, for the purpose of replacing upon the throne the descendants of a monarch by whom it had been wilfully forfeited? If, on the other hand, his own final conviction of the goodness of their cause, or the commands of his father or uncle, should recommend to him allegiance to the Stewarts, still it was necessary to clear his own character by showing that he had not, as seemed to be falsely insinuated, taken any step to this purpose, during his holding the commission of the reigning monarch.

The affectionate simplicity of Rose, and her anxiety for his safety,—his sense too of her unprotected state, and of the terror and actual dangers to which she might be exposed, made an impression upon his mind, and he instantly wrote to thank her in the kindest terms for her solicitude on his account, to express his earnest good wishes for her welfare and that of her father, and to assure her of his own safety. The feelings which this task excited were speedily lost in the necessity which he now saw of bidding farewell to Flora Mac-Ivor, perhaps for ever. The pang attending this reflection was inexpressible; for her high-minded elevation of character, her self-devotion to the cause which she had embraced, united to her scrupulous rectitude as to the means of serving it, had vindicated to his judgment the choice adopted by his passions. But time pressed, calumny was busy with his fame, and every hour's delay increased the power to injure it. His departure must be instant.

With this determination he sought out Fergus, and communicated to him the contents of Rose's letter, with his own resolution instantly to go to Edinburgh, and put into the hands of some one or other of those persons of influence to whom he had letters from his father, his exculpation from any charge which might be preferred against him.

"You run your head into the lion's mouth," answered Mac-Ivor. "You do not know the severity of a government harassed by just apprehensions, and a consciousness of their own illegality and insecurity. I shall have to deliver you from some dungeon in Stirling or Edinburgh Castle."

"My innocence, my rank, my father's intimacy with Lord M—, General G—, &c., will be a sufficient protection," said Waverley.

"You will find the contrary," replied the Chieftain; "these gentlemen will have enough to do about their own matters. Once more, will you take the plaid, and stay a little while with us among the mists and the crows, in the bravest cause ever sword was drawn in?"[eee]

"For many reasons, my dear Fergus, you must hold me excused."

"Well then," said Mac-Ivor, "I shall certainly find you exerting your poetical talents in elegies upon a prison, or your antiquarian researches in detecting the Oggam[fff] character, or some Punic hieroglyphic[1] upon the key-stones[2] of a vault, curiously arched. Or what say you to *un petit pendement bien joli*?[3] against which awkward ceremony I don't warrant you, should you meet a body of the armed west-country Whigs."

"And why should they use me so?" said Waverley.

"For a hundred good reasons," answered Fergus: "first, you are an Englishman; secondly, a gentleman; thirdly, a prelatist abjured;[4] and, fourthly, they have not had an opportunity to exercise their talents on such a subject this long while. But don't be cast down, beloved: all will be done in the fear of the Lord."

"Well, I must run my hazard."

"You are determined, then?"

"I am."

"Wilful will do't," said Fergus;—"but you cannot go on foot, and I shall want no horse, as I must march on foot at the head of the children of Ivor; you shall have brown Dermid."

"If you will sell him, I shall certainly be much obliged."

"If your proud English heart cannot be obliged by a gift or loan, I will not refuse money at the entrance of a campaign: his price is twenty guineas. [Remember, reader, it was Sixty Years since.] And when do you propose to depart?"

"The sooner the better," answered Waverley.

"You are right, since go you must, or rather, since go you will: I will take Flora's pony, and ride with you as far as Bally-Brough.—Callum Beg, see that our horses are ready, with a pony for yourself, to attend and carry Mr Waverley's baggage as far as — (naming a small town), where he can have a horse and guide to Edinburgh. Put on a Lowland dress, Callum, and see you keep your tongue close, if you would not have me cut it out: Mr Waverley rides Dermid." Then turning to Edward, "You will take leave of my sister?"

"Surely—that is, if Miss Mac-Ivor will honour me so far."

"Cathleen, let my sister know Mr Waverley wishes to bid her farewell before he leaves us.—But Rose Bradwardine, her situation must be thought of—I wish she were here. And why should she not?— There are but four red-coats at Tully-Veolan, and their muskets would be very useful to us."

To these broken remarks Edward made no answer; his ear indeed received them, but his soul was intent upon the expected entrance of

---

1 "Punic" means "belonging to Carthage; Carthaginian" (*OED*).

2 The key stone is "the stone at the summit of an arch which, being the last put in, is looked upon as locking the whole together" (*OED*).

3 "A pretty little hanging" (*PW*, 585).

4 Episcopalian renounced (*OED*).

Flora. The door opened.—It was but Cathleen, with her lady's excuse, and wishes for Captain Waverley's health and happiness.

CHAPTER XXIX.
Waverley's Reception in the Lowlands after his Highland Tour.

IT was noon when the two friends stood at the top of the pass of Bally-Brough. "I must go no farther," said Fergus Mac-Ivor, who during the journey had in vain endeavoured to raise his friend's spirits. "If my cross-grained[1] sister has any share in your dejection, trust me she thinks highly of you, though her present anxiety about the public cause prevents her listening to any other subject. Confide your interest to me; I will not betray it, providing you do not again assume that vile cockade."

"No fear of that, considering the manner in which it has been recalled. Adieu, Fergus; do not permit your sister to forget me."

"And adieu, Waverley; you may soon hear of her with a prouder title. Get home, write letters, and make friends as many and as fast as you can; there will speedily be unexpected guests on the coast of Suffolk,[2] or my news from France has deceived me."ggg

Thus parted the friends; Fergus returning back to his castle, while Edward, followed by Callum Beg, the latter transformed from point to point into a Low-country groom, proceeded to the little town of —.

Edward paced on under the painful and yet not altogether embittered feelings, which separation and uncertainty produce in the mind of a youthful lover. I am not sure if the ladies understand the full value of the influence of absence, nor do I think it wise to teach them, lest, like the Clelias and Mandanes[3] of yore, they should resume the humour of sending their lovers into banishment. Distance, in truth, produces in idea the same effect as in real perspective. Objects are softened, and rounded, and rendered doubly graceful; the harsher and more ordinary points of character are mellowed down, and those by which it is remembered are the more striking outlines that mark sublimity, grace, or beauty. There are mists too in the mental, as well as the natural horizon, to conceal what is less pleasing in distant objects, and there are happy lights, to stream in full glory upon those points which can profit by brilliant illumination.

Waverley forgot Flora Mac-Ivor's prejudices in her magnanimity,

---

1 Contrary.
2 On the east coast of England, the proposed landing place for French armies supporting Charles Edward Stuart.
3 Heroines of seventeenth-century French romances by Madeleine de Scudéry (1607-1701), *Clelie* and *Artamene, ou le Grand Cyrus*; these heroines somewhat capriciously test their lovers' resolve by sending them off on adventures.

and almost pardoned her indifference towards his affection, when he recollected the grand and decisive object which seemed to fill her whole soul. She, whose sense of duty so wholly engrossed her in the cause of a benefactor, what would be her feelings in favour of the happy individual who should be so fortunate as to awaken them? Then came the doubtful question, whether he might not be that happy man,—a question which fancy endeavoured to answer in the affirmative, by conjuring up all she had said in his praise, with the addition of a comment much more flattering than the text warranted. All that was commonplace, all that belonged to the every-day world, was melted away and obliterated in those dreams of imagination, which only remembered with advantage the points of grace and dignity that distinguished Flora from the generality of her sex, not the particulars which she held in common with them. Edward was, in short, in the fair way of creating a goddess out of a high-spirited, accomplished, and beautiful young woman; and the time was wasted in castle-building, until, at the descent of a steep hill, he saw beneath him the market-town of —.

The Highland politeness of Callum Beg—there are few nations, by the way, who can boast of so much natural politeness as the Highlanders[hhh]—the Highland civility of his attendant had not permitted him to disturb the reveries of our hero. But observing him rouse himself at the sight of the village, Callum pressed closer to his side, and hoped "when they cam to the public, his honour wad not say nothing about Vich Ian Vohr, for ta people were bitter Whigs, deil burst tem."

Waverley assured the prudent page that he would be cautious; and as he now distinguished, not indeed the ringing of bells, but the tinkling of something like a hammer against the side of an old mossy, green, inverted porridge-pot, that hung in an open booth, of the size and shape of a parrot's cage, erected to grace the east end of a building resembling an old barn, he asked Callum Beg if it were Sunday.

"Could na say just preceesely—Sunday seldom cam aboon the pass of Bally-Brough."

On entering the town, however, and advancing towards the most apparent public-house which presented itself, the numbers of old women, in tartan screens and red cloaks, who streamed from the barn-resembling building, debating, as they went, the comparative merits of the blessed youth Jabesh Rentowel, and that chosen vessel Maister Goukthrapple, induced Callum to assure his temporary master, "that it was either ta muckle Sunday hersell, or ta little government Sunday that they ca'd ta fast."[1]

---

1 The great Sunday itself, or the government Sunday, "one of the fast-days ... appointed by the [British] government" on which prayers were said for the defeat of the Jacobites (*PW*, 586).

On alighting at the sign of the Seven-branched Golden Candle-stick, which, for the further delectation of the guests, was graced with a short Hebrew motto, they were received by mine host, a tall thin puritanical figure, who seemed to debate with himself whether he ought to give shelter to those who travelled on such a day. Reflecting, however, in all probability, that he possessed the power of mulcting[1] them for this irregularity, a penalty which they might escape by passing into Gregor Duncanson's at the sign of the Highlander and the Hawick Gill, Mr Ebenezer Cruickshanks condescended to admit them into his dwelling.

To this sanctified person Waverley addressed his request, that he would procure him a guide, with a saddle-horse, to carry his portmanteau to Edinburgh.

"And whar may ye be coming from?" demanded mine host of the Candlestick.

"I have told you where I wish to go; I do not conceive any further information necessary either for the guide or his saddle-horse."

"Hem! Ahem!" returned he of the Candlestick, somewhat disconcerted at this rebuff. "It's the general fast, sir, and I cannot enter into ony carnal transactions on sic a day, when the people should be humbled, and the backsliders should return, as worthy Mr Goukthrapple said; and moreover when, as the precious Mr Jabesh Rentowel did weel observe, the land was mourning for covenants burnt, broken, and buried."

"My good friend," said Waverley, "if you cannot let me have a horse and guide, my servant shall seek them elsewhere."

"Aweel! Your servant?—and what for gangs he not forward wi' you himsell?"

Waverley had but very little of a captain of horse's spirit within him—I mean of that sort of spirit which I have been obliged to when I happened, in a mail-coach, or diligence, to meet some military man who has kindly taken upon him the disciplining of the waiters, and the taxing of reckonings. Some of this useful talent our hero had, however, acquired during his military service, and on this gross provocation it began seriously to arise, "Look ye, sir; I came here for my own accommodation, and not to answer impertinent questions. Either say you can, or cannot, get me what I want; I shall pursue my course in either case."

Mr Ebenezer Cruickshanks left the room with some indistinct muttering; but whether negative or acquiescent, Edward could not well distinguish. The hostess, a civil, quiet, laborious drudge, came to take

---

1 Punishing.

his orders for dinner, but declined to make answer on the subject of the horse and guide; for the Salique law,[1] it seems, extended to the stables of the Golden Candlestick.

From a window which overlooked the dark and narrow court in which Callum Beg rubbed down the horses after their journey, Waverley heard the following dialogue betwixt the subtle foot-page of Vich Ian Vohr and his landlord:

"Ye'll be frae the north, young man?" began the latter.

"And ye may say that," answered Callum.

"And ye'll hae ridden a lang way the day, it may weel be?"

"Sae lang, that I could weel tak a dram."

"Gudewife, bring the gill stoup."[2]

Here some compliments passed fitting the occasion, when my host of the Golden Candlestick, having, as he thought, opened his guest's heart by this hospitable propitiation, resumed his scrutiny.

"Ye'll no hae mickle better whisky than that aboon the Pass?"

"I am nae frae aboon the Pass."

"Ye're a Highlandman by your tongue?"

"Na; I am but just Aberdeen-a-way."

"And did your master come frae Aberdeen wi' you?"

"Ay—that's when I left it mysell," answered the cool and impenetrable Callum Beg.

"And what kind of gentleman is he?"

"I believe he is ane o' King George's state officers; at least he's aye for ganging on to the south, and he has a hantle siller, and never grudges ony thing till a poor body, or in the way of a lawing."[3]

"He wants a guide and a horse frae hence to Edinburgh?"

"Ay, and ye maun find it him forthwith."

"Ahem! It will be chargeable."[4]

"He cares na for that a bodle."[5]

"Aweel, Duncan—did ye say your name was Duncan, or Donald?"

"Na, man—Jamie—Jamie Steenson—I telt ye before."

This last undaunted parry altogether foiled Mr Cruickshanks, who, though not quite satisfied either with the reserve of the master, or the extreme readiness of the man, was contented to lay a tax on the reckoning and horse-hire, that might compound for his ungratified curios-

---

1 I.e., the Salic law, which specifies that only men may inherit wealth and power.

2 Wife, bring the cup containing a gill, "1/4 of a standard pint" (*OED*).

3 He's all for going on to the south, and he has a great deal of silver, and never begrudges anyone anything, even at the tavern (*WSG*).

4 Expensive.

5 He is not concerned about that.

ity. The circumstance of its being the fast day was not forgotten in the charge, which, on the whole, did not, however, amount to much more than double what in fairness it should have been.

Callum Beg soon after announced in person the ratification of this treaty, adding, "Ta auld deevil was ganging to ride wi' ta Duinhé-wassel hersell."

"That will not be very pleasant, Callum, nor altogether safe, for our host seems a person of great curiosity; but a traveller must submit to these inconveniences. Meanwhile, my good lad, here is a trifle for you to drink Vich Ian Vohr's health."

The hawk's eye of Callum flashed delight upon a golden guinea, with which these last words were accompanied. He hastened, not without a curse on the intricacies of a Saxon breeches pocket, or *spleuchan*,[1] as he called it, to deposit the treasure in his fob; and then, as if he conceived the benevolence called for some requital on his part, he gathered close up to Edward, with an expression of countenance peculiarly knowing, and spoke in an under tone, "If his honour thought ta auld deevil Whig carle was a bit dangerous, she could easily provide for him, and teil ane ta wiser."[2]

"How, and in what manner?"

"Her ain sell," replied Callum, "could wait for him a wee bit frae the toun, and kittle his quarters wi' her *skene-occle*."

"Skene-occle! what's that?"

Callum unbuttoned his coat, raised his left arm, and, with an emphatic nod, pointed to the hilt of a small dirk, snugly deposited under it, in the lining of his jacket. Waverley thought he had misunderstood his meaning; he gazed in his face, and discovered in Callum's very handsome, though embrowned features, just the degree of roguish malice with which a lad of the same age in England would have brought forward a plan for robbing an orchard.

"Good God, Callum, would you take the man's life?"

"Indeed," answered the young desperado, "and I think he has had just a lang enough lease o't, when he's for betraying honest folk, that come to spend siller at his public."

Edward saw nothing was to be gained by argument, and therefore contented himself with enjoining Callum to lay aside all practices against the person of Mr Ebenezer Cruickshanks; in which injunction the page seemed to acquiesce with an air of great indifference.

"Ta Duinhé-wassel might please himsell; ta auld rudas loon had never done Callum nae ill. But here's a bit line frae ta Tighearna, tat he bade me gie your honour ere I came back."

---

1 "A tobacco pouch, frequently used as a purse" (*OED*).
2 No one would be the wiser.

The letter from the Chief contained Flora's lines on the fate of Captain Wogan, whose enterprising character is so well drawn by Clarendon.[1] He had originally engaged in the service of the Parliament, but had abjured that party upon the execution of Charles I.; and upon hearing that the royal standard was set up by the Earl of Glencairn and General Middleton in the Highlands of Scotland, took leave of Charles II., who was then at Paris, passed into England, assembled a body of cavaliers in the neighbourhood of London, and traversed the kingdom, which had been so long under domination of the usurper, by marches conducted with such skill, dexterity, and spirit, that he safely united his handful of horsemen with the body of Highlanders then in arms. After several months of desultory warfare, in which Wogan's skill and courage gained him the highest reputation, he had the misfortune to be wounded in a dangerous manner, and no surgical assistance being within reach, he terminated his short but glorious career.

There were obvious reasons why the politic Chieftain was desirous to place the example of this young hero under the eye of Waverley, with whose romantic disposition it coincided so peculiarly. But his letter turned chiefly upon some trifling commissions which Waverley had promised to execute for him in England, and it was only toward the conclusion that Edward found these words:—"I owe Flora a grudge for refusing us her company yesterday; and as I am giving you the trouble of reading these lines, in order to keep in your memory your promise to procure me the fishing-tackle and cross-bow from London, I will enclose her verses on the Grave of Wogan. This I know will teaze her; for, to tell you the truth, I think her more in love with the memory of that dead hero, than she is likely to be with any living one, unless he shall tread a similar path. But English squires of our day keep their oak-trees to shelter their deer parks, or repair the losses of an evening at White's,[2] and neither invoke them to wreath their brows, nor shelter their graves. Let me hope for one brilliant exception in a dear friend, to whom I would most gladly give a dearer title."

The verses were inscribed,

TO AN OAK TREE,

In the Church-Yard of —, in the Highlands of Scotland, said to mark the grave of Captain Wogan, killed in 1649.

> EMBLEM of England's ancient faith,
> Full proudly may thy branches wave,

---

1 Edward Hyde, Earl of Clarendon (1609-74) wrote the *History of the Great Rebellion* (1702-04) about the English Civil War (*OCBH*, 215).

2 Gambling house in London.

Where loyalty lies low in death,
  And valour fills a timeless grave.

And thou, brave tenant of the tomb!
  Repine not if our clime deny,
Above thine honour'd sod to bloom,
  The flowerets of a milder sky.

These owe their birth to genial May;
  Beneath a fiercer sun they pine,
Before the winter storm decay—
  And can their worth be type of thine?

No! for, 'mid storms of Fate opposing,
  Still higher swell'd thy dauntless heart,
And, while Despair the scene was closing.
  Commenced thy brief but brilliant part.

'Twas then thou sought'st on Albyn's hill,[1]
  (When England's sons the strife resign'd)
A rugged race resisting still,
  And unsubdued though unrefined.

Thy death's hour heard no kindred wail,
  No holy knell thy requiem rung;
Thy mourners were the plaided Gael,
  Thy dirge the clamorous pibroch sung.

Yet, who, in Fortune's summer-shine
  To waste life's longest term away,
Would change that glorious dawn of thine,
  Though darken'd ere its noontide day?

Be thine the Tree whose dauntless boughs
  Brave summer's drought and winter's gloom!
Rome bound with oak her patriots' brows,
  As Albyn shadows Wogan's tomb.

Whatever might be the real merit of Flora Mac-Ivor's poetry, the enthusiasm which it intimated was well calculated to make a corresponding impression upon her lover. The lines were read—read again—then deposited in Waverley's bosom—then again drawn out,

---

1 Name for Scotland, esp. the Highlands, from Alba, the Gaelic for Scotland.

and read line by line, in a low and smothered voice, and with frequent pauses which prolonged the mental treat, as an epicure protracts, by sipping slowly, the enjoyment of a delicious beverage. The entrance of Mrs Cruickshanks, with the sublunary articles of dinner and wine, hardly interrupted this pantomime of affectionate enthusiasm.

At length the tall ungainly figure and ungracious visage of Ebenezer presented themselves. The upper part of his form, notwithstanding the season required no such defence, was shrouded in a large great-coat, belted over his under habiliments, and crested with a huge cowl of the same stuff, which, when drawn over the head and hat, completely overshadowed both, and being buttoned beneath the chin, was called a *trot-cozy*. His hand grasped a huge jockey-whip, garnished with brass mounting. His thin legs tenanted a pair of gambadoes,[1] fastened at the sides with rusty clasps. Thus accoutred, he stalked into the midst of the apartment, and announced his errand in brief phrase:—"Yer horses are ready."

"You go with me yourself then, landlord?"

"I do, as far as Perth; where ye may be supplied with a guide to Embro',[2] as your occasions shall require."

Thus saying, he placed under Waverley's eye the bill which he held in his hand; and at the same time, self-invited, filled a glass of wine, and drank devoutly to a blessing on their journey. Waverley stared at the man's impudence, but, as their connexion was to be short, and promised to be convenient, he made no observation upon it; and, having paid his reckoning, expressed his intention to depart immediately. He mounted Dermid accordingly, and sallied forth from the Golden Candlestick, followed by the puritanical figure we have described, after he had, at the expense of some time and difficulty, and by the assistance of a "louping-on-stane," or structure of masonry erected for the traveller's convenience in front of the house, elevated his person to the back of a long-backed, raw-boned, thin-gutted phantom of a broken-down blood-horse, on which Waverley's portmanteau was deposited. Our hero, though not in a very gay humour, could hardly help laughing at the appearance of his new squire, and at imagining the astonishment which his person and equipage would have excited at Waverley-Honour.

Edward's tendency to mirth did not escape mine host of the Candlestick, who, conscious of the cause, infused a double portion of souring into the pharasaical leaven of his countenance,[3] and resolved

---

1 "A kind of large boot or gaiter, attached to a saddle, to protect the rider's legs and feet from the wet or cold. In later use, sometimes applied to leather leggings or overalls fastened with clasps" (*OED*).

2 Edinburgh, capital of Scotland.

3 The inflexible, self-righteous expression on his face.

internally that, in one way or other, the young *Englisher* should pay dearly for the contempt with which he seemed to regard him. Callum also stood at the gate, and enjoyed, with undissembled glee, the ridiculous figure of Mr Cruickshanks. As Waverley passed him, he pulled off his hat respectfully, and, approaching the stirrup, bade him "Tak heed the auld Whig deevil played him nae cantrip."[1]

Waverley once more thanked, and bade him farewell, and then rode briskly onward, not sorry to be out of hearing of the shouts of the children, as they beheld old Ebenezer rise and sink in his stirrups, to avoid the concussions occasioned by a hard trot upon a half-paved street. The village of — was soon several miles behind him.

END OF VOLUME FIRST.

---

1 Trick.

WAVERLEY NOVELS,
VOL. II
WAVERLEY.

PRINTED FOR CADELL & COMPANY, EDINBURGH
AND SIMPKIN AND MARSHALL, LONDON.
1829

WAVERLEY;
OR,
'TIS SIXTY YEARS SINCE

––––––

Under which King, Bezonian? speak, or die!
Henry IV, Part II.

CHAPTER I.

Shows that the Loss of a Horse's Shoe may be a serious Inconvenience.

THE manner and air of Waverley, but, above all, the glittering contents of his purse, and the indifference with which he seemed to regard them, somewhat overawed his companion, and deterred him from making any attempts to enter upon conversation. His own reflections were moreover agitated by various surmises, and by plans of self-interest, with which these were intimately connected. The travellers journeyed, therefore, in silence, until it was interrupted by the annunciation, on the part of the guide, that his "naig had lost a fore-foot shoe, which, doubtless, his honour would consider it was his part to replace."

This was what lawyers call a *fishing question*, calculated to ascertain how far Waverley was disposed to submit to petty imposition. "My part to replace your horse's shoe, you rascal!" said Waverley, mistaking the purport of the intimation.

"Indubitably," answered Mr Cruickshanks; "though there was no preceese clause to that effect, it canna be expected that I am to pay for the casualties whilk may befall the puir naig while in your honour's service.—Nathless, if your honour"—

"O, you mean I am to pay the farrier; but where shall we find one?"

Rejoiced at discerning there would be no objection made on the part of his temporary master, Mr Cruickshanks assured him that Cairnvreckan,[1] a village which they were about to enter, was happy in an excellent blacksmith; "but as he was a professor, he would drive a nail for no man on the Sabbath, or kirk-fast,[2] unless it were in a case of absolute necessity, for which he always charged sixpence each shoe." The most important part of this communication, in the opinion of the speaker, made a very slight impression on the hearer, who only internally wondered what college this veterinary professor belonged to; not aware that the word was used to denote any person who pretended to uncommon sanctity of faith and manner.

As they entered the village of Cairnvreckan, they speedily distinguished the smith's house. Being also a *public*,[3] it was two stories high,

---

1   A fictional village, possibly modeled on Auchterarder or Methven (*OW*, 434).
2   A fast ordained by the church; "kirk" is the northern English and Scottish form of the word "church" (*OED*).
3   A public house, bar.

and proudly reared its crest, covered with grey slate, above the thatched hovels by which it was surrounded. The adjoining smithy betokened none of the Sabbatical silence and repose which Ebenezer had augured from the sanctity of his friend. On the contrary, hammer crashed and anvil rang, the bellows groaned, and the whole apparatus of Vulcan[1] appeared to be in full activity. Nor was the labour of a rural and pacific nature. The master smith, benempt,[2] as his sign intimated, John Muck-lewrath, with two assistants, toiled busily in arranging, repairing, and furbishing old muskets, pistols, and swords, which lay scattered around his work-shop in military confusion. The open shed, containing the forge, was crowded with persons who came and went as if receiving and communicating important news; and a single glance at the aspect of the people who traversed the street in haste, or stood assembled in groups, with eyes elevated, and hands uplifted, announced that some extraordinary intelligence was agitating the public mind of the municipality of Cairnvreckan. "There is some news," said mine host of the Candlestick, pushing his lantern-jawed visage and bare-boned nag rudely forward into the crowd—"there is some news; and if it please my Creator, I will forthwith obtain speirings[3] thereof."

Waverley, with better regulated curiosity than his attendant's, dismounted, and gave his horse to a boy who stood idling near. It arose, perhaps from the shyness of his character in early youth, that he felt dislike at applying to a stranger even for casual information, without previously glancing at his physiognomy and appearance. While he looked about in order to select the person with whom he would most willingly hold communication, the buzz around saved him in some degree the trouble of interrogatories. The names of Lochiel, Clanronald, Glengarry, and other distinguished Highland Chiefs, among whom Vich Ian Vohr was repeatedly mentioned, were as familiar in men's mouths as household words; and from the alarm generally expressed, he easily conceived that their descent into the Lowlands, at the head of their armed tribes, had either already taken place, or was instantly apprehended.

Ere Waverley could ask particulars, a strong, large-boned, hard-featured woman, about forty, dressed as if her clothes had been flung on with a pitchfork, her cheeks flushed with a scarlet red where they were not smutted with soot and lamp-black, jostled through the crowd, and, brandishing high a child of two years old, which she danced in her arms, without regard to its screams of terror, sang forth, with all her might,—

---

1 Vulcan was the Roman god of fire and metalworking (*OED*).
2 Named (*WSG*).
3 "Askings; answers to questions asked; information" (*WSG*).

> "Charlie is my darling, my darling, my darling,
> Charlie is my darling,
> > The young Chevalier!"[1]

"D'ye hear what's come ower ye now," continued the virago, "ye whingeing Whig carles?[2] D'ye hear wha's coming to cow yer cracks?[3]

> 'Little wot ye wha's coming,
> Little wot ye wha's coming,
> > A' the wild Macraws are coming.'"

The Vulcan of Cairnvreckan, who acknowledged his Venus in this exulting Bacchante,[4] regarded her with a grim and ire-foreboding countenance, while some of the senators[5] of the village hastened to interpose. "Whisht, gudewife; is this a time, or is this a day, to be singing your ranting fule sangs in?—a time when the wine of wrath is poured out without mixture in the cup of indignation, and a day when the land should give testimony against popery, and prelacy, and quakerism, and independency, and supremacy, and erastianism, and antinomianism, and a' the errors of the church?"[6]

"And that's a' your Whiggery," re-echoed the Jacobite heroine; "that's a' your Whiggery, and your presbytery, ye cut-lugged, graning carles![7] What! d'ye think the lads wi' the kilts will care for yer synods[8] and yer presbyteries,[9] and yer buttock-mail,[10] and yer stool o' repentance? Vengeance on the black face o't! many an honester woman's been set upon it than streeks doon beside ony Whig in the country. I mysell"—

Here John Mucklewrath, who dreaded her entering upon a detail of personal experience, interposed his matrimonial authority. "Gae

---

1 Song about Charles Edward Stuart by Lady Carolina Nairne (1766-1845) written well after the Jacobite rebellion of 1745.
2 You whining Whig fellows.
3 "Stop your boasting" (*WSG*).
4 A priestess or female worshiper of Bacchus (*OED*).
5 Old men (*OED*).
6 As Lamont notes, these are all "forms of belief inconsistent with strict presbyterianism" (*OW*, 434).
7 "Crop-eared," "groaning" fellows (*WSG*).
8 An assembly of the clergy of the presbyterian church (*OED*).
9 "A body or assembly of presbyters or elders, consisting of all the ministers ... " (*OED*).
10 "Fine imposed on fornication in lieu of sitting on the stool of repentance" (*WSG*).

hame, and be d— (that I should say sae[1]), and put on the sowens[2] for supper."

"And you, ye doil'd dotard,"[3] replied his gentle helpmate, her wrath, which had hitherto wandered abroad over the whole assembly, being at once and violently impelled into its natural channel, "*ye* stand there hammering dog-heads for fules that will never snap them at a Highlandman, instead of earning bread for your family, and shoeing this winsome young gentleman's horse that's just come frae the north! I'se warrant him nane of your whingeing[4] King George folk, but a gallant Gordon, at the least o' him."

The eyes of the assembly were now turned upon Waverley, who took the opportunity to beg the smith to shoe his guide's horse with all speed, as he wished to proceed on his journey;—for he had heard enough to make him sensible that there would be danger in delaying long in this place. The smith's eyes rested on him with a look of displeasure and suspicion, not lessened by the eagerness with which his wife enforced Waverley's mandate. "D'ye hear what the weel-favoured young gentleman says, ye drunken ne'er-do-good?"

"And what may your name be, sir?" quoth Mucklewrath.

"It is of no consequence to you, my friend, provided I pay your labour."

"But it may be of consequence to the state, sir," replied an old farmer, smelling strongly of whisky and peat-smoke; "and I doubt we maun delay your journey till you have seen the Laird."

"You certainly," said Waverley, haughtily, "will find it both difficult and dangerous to detain me, unless you can produce some proper authority."

There was a pause and a whisper among the crowd—"Secretary Murray"; "Lord Lewis Gordon";[5] "Maybe the Chevalier himsell!" Such were the surmises that passed hurriedly among them, and there was obviously an increased disposition to resist Waverley's departure. He attempted to argue mildly with them, but his voluntary ally, Mrs Mucklewrath, broke in upon and drowned his expostulations, taking his part with an abusive violence, which was all set down to Edward's

---

1 That I should say so.
2 "Flummery; blancmange, made of oatmeal which remains in the bran after bolting, converted into a subacid starch" (*WSG*).
3 "Dazed; stupid; doting" (*WSG*); "imbecile" (*OED*).
4 "Fawning and whining like a dog" (*WSG*).
5 John Murray (1717-77) was secretary to Charles Edward Stuart. Lord Lewis Gordon (?- 1754), as Lord Lieutenant of Aberdeen and Banff and Governor of Aberdeen, raised money and men for the Jacobite army in 1745, and fought at Inverurie (*OW*, 434).

account by those on whom it was bestowed. "*Ye'll* stop ony gentleman that's the Prince's freend?" for she too, though with other feelings, had adopted the general opinion respecting Waverley. "I daur ye to touch him," spreading abroad her long and muscular fingers, garnished with claws which a vulture might have envied. "I'll set my ten commandments in the face o' the first loon that lays a finger on him."

"Gae hame, gudewife," quoth the farmer aforesaid; "it wad better set you to be nursing the gudeman's bairns[1] than to be deaving[2] us here."

"*His* bairns?" retorted the Amazon, regarding her husband with a grin of ineffable contempt—"*His* bairns!

> 'O gin ye were dead, gudeman,
>   And a green turf on your head, gudeman!
> Then I wad ware my widowhood
>   Upon a ranting Highlandman.'"[3]

This canticle, which excited a suppressed titter among the younger part of the audience, totally overcame the patience of the taunted man of the anvil. "Deil be in me but I'll put this het gad down her throat!" cried he, in an ecstasy of wrath, snatching a bar from the forge; and he might have executed his threat, had he not been withheld by a part of the mob, while the rest endeavoured to force the termagant out of his presence.

Waverley meditated a retreat in the confusion, but his horse was nowhere to be seen. At length he observed, at some distance, his faithful attendant, Ebenezer, who, as soon as he had perceived the turn matters were likely to take, had withdrawn both horses from the press, and, mounted on the one, and holding the other, answered the loud and repeated calls of Waverley for his horse. "Na, na! if ye are nae friend to kirk and the king, and are detained as siccan[4] a person, ye maun answer to honest men of the country for breach of contract; and I maun keep the naig and the walise[5] for damage and expense, in respect my horse and mysell will lose to-morrow's day's-wark, besides the afternoon preaching."

Edward, out of patience, hemmed in and hustled by the rabble on every side, and every moment expecting personal violence, resolved to

---

1 Children (*WSG*).
2 Deafening (*WSG*).
3 David Herd, *Ancient and Modern Scottish Songs* (2 vols., 1776), ii, 207 (*OW*, 434).
4 Such (*WSG*).
5 "Saddlebags; portmanteau" (*WSG*).

try measures of intimidation, and at length drew a pocket-pistol, threatening, on the one hand, to shoot whomsoever dared to stop him, and, on the other, menacing Ebenezer with a similar doom, if he stirred a foot with the horses. The sapient Partridge[1] says, that one man with a pistol, is equal to a hundred unarmed, because, though he can shoot but one of the multitude, yet no one knows but that he himself may be that luckless individual. The *levy en masse* of Cairn-vreckan would therefore probably have given way, nor would Ebenezer, whose natural paleness had waxed three shades more cadaverous, have ventured to dispute a mandate so enforced, had not the Vulcan of the village, eager to discharge upon some more worthy object the fury which his helpmate had provoked, and not ill satisfied to find such an object in Waverley, rushed at him with the red-hot bar of iron, with such determination, as made the discharge of his pistol an act of self-defence. The unfortunate man fell; and while Edward, thrilled with a natural horror at the incident, neither had presence of mind to unsheathe his sword, not to draw his remaining pistol, the populace threw themselves upon him, disarmed him, and were about to use him with great violence, when the appearance of a venerable clergyman, the pastor of the parish, put a curb on their fury.

This worthy man (none of the Goukthrapples or Rentowels) maintained his character with the common people, although he preached the practical fruits of Christian faith, as well as its abstract tenets, and was respected by the higher orders, notwithstanding he declined soothing their speculative errors by converting the pulpit of the gospel into a school of heathen morality. Perhaps it is owing to this mixture of faith and practice in his doctrine, that, although his memory has formed a sort of era in the annals of Cairnvreckan, so that the parishioners, to denote what befell Sixty Years since, still say it happened "in good Mr Morton's time," I have never been able to discover which he belonged to, the evangelical, or the moderate party in the kirk. Nor do I hold the circumstance of much moment, since, in my own remembrance, the one was headed by an Erskine, the other by a Robertson.[iii]

Mr Morton had been alarmed by the discharge of the pistol, and the increasing hubbub around the smithy. His first attention, after he had directed the bystanders to detain Waverley, but to abstain from injuring him, was turned to the body of Mucklewrath, over which his wife, in a revulsion of feeling, was weeping, howling, and tearing her elf-locks, in a state little short of distraction. On raising up the smith, the first discovery was, that he was alive; and the next, that he was likely to live as long as if he had never heard the report of a pistol in

---

1 Character in Fielding's novel *Tom Jones* (1749), companion to young Tom who, like Edward Waverley, gets caught up in the Jacobite Rebellion of 1745.

his life. He had made a narrow escape, however; the bullet had grazed his head, and stunned him for a moment or two, which trance terror and confusion of spirit had prolonged somewhat longer. He now arose to demand vengeance on the person of Waverley, and with difficulty acquiesced in the proposal of Mr Morton, that he should be carried before the Laird, as a justice of peace, and placed at his disposal. The rest of the assistants unanimously agreed to the measure recommended; even Mrs Mucklewrath, who had begun to recover from her hysterics, whimpered forth, "She wadna say naething against what the minister proposed; he was e'en ower gude for his trade, and she hoped to see him wi' a dainty decent bishop's gown on his back; a comelier sight than your Geneva cloaks and bands,[1] I wis."

All controversy being thus laid aside, Waverley, escorted by the whole inhabitants of the village who were not bed-ridden, was conducted to the house of Cairnvreckan, which was about half a mile distant.

CHAPTER II.
An Examination.

MAJOR MELVILLE of Cairnvreckan, an elderly gentleman, who had spent his youth in the military service, received Mr Morton with great kindness, and our hero with civility, which the equivocal circumstances wherein Edward was placed rendered constrained and distant.

The nature of the smith's hurt was inquired into, and as the actual injury was likely to prove trifling, and the circumstances in which it was received rendered the infliction, on Edward's part, a natural act of self-defence, the Major conceived he might dismiss the matter, on Waverley's depositing in his hands a small sum for the benefit of the wounded person.

"I could wish, sir," continued the Major, "that my duty terminated here; but it is necessary that we should have some further inquiry into the cause of your journey through the country at this unfortunate and distracted time."

Mr Ebenezer Cruickshanks now stood forth, and communicated to the magistrate all he knew or suspected, from the reserve of Waverley, and the evasions of Callum Beg. The horse upon which Edward rode, he said, he knew to belong to Vich Ian Vohr, though he dared not tax

---

1 The typical outfit of a Presbyterian clergyman at this time consisted of a black gown and a white neckband. This manner of dress, according to Hook, was "introduced from Geneva in the sixteenth century," hence the term "Geneva cloaks" (*PW*, 586).

Edward's former attendant with the fact, lest he should have his house and stables burnt over his head some night by that godless gang, the Mac-Ivors. He concluded by exaggerating his own services to kirk and state, as having been the means, under God (as he modestly qualified the assertion), of attaching this suspicious and formidable delinquent. He intimated hopes of future reward, and of instant reimbursement for loss of time, and even of character, by travelling on the state business on the fast-day.

To this Major Melville answered, with great composure, that so far from claiming any merit in this affair, Mr Cruickshanks ought to deprecate the imposition of a very heavy fine for neglecting to lodge, in terms of recent proclamation, an account with the nearest magistrate of any stranger who came to his inn; that, as Mr Cruickshanks boasted so much of religion and loyalty, he should not impute this conduct to disaffection, but only suppose that his zeal for kirk and state had been lulled asleep by the opportunity of charging a stranger with double horse-hire; that, however, feeling himself incompetent to decide singly upon the conduct of a person of such importance, he should reserve it for consideration of the next quarter-sessions. Now our history for the present saith no more of him of the Candlestick, who wended dolorous and malcontent back to his own dwelling.

Major Melville then commanded the villagers to return to their homes, excepting two, who officiated as constables, and whom he directed to wait below. The apartment was thus cleared of every person but Mr Morton, whom the Major invited to remain; a sort of factor, who acted as clerk; and Waverley himself. There ensued a painful and embarrassed pause, till Major Melville, looking upon Waverley with much compassion, and often consulting a paper or memorandum which he held in his hand, requested to know his name.—"Edward Waverley."

"I thought so; late of the — dragoons, and nephew of Sir Everard Waverley of Waverley-Honour?"

"The same."

"Young gentleman, I am extremely sorry that this painful duty has fallen to my lot."

"Duty, Major Melville, renders apologies superfluous."

"True, sir; permit me, therefore, to ask you how your time has been disposed of since you obtained leave of absence from your regiment, several weeks ago, until the present moment?"

"My reply," said Waverley, "to so general a question must be guided by the nature of the charge which renders it necessary. I request to know what that charge is, and upon what authority I am forcibly detained to reply to it?"

"The charge, Mr Waverley, I grieve to say, is of a very high nature, and affects your character both as a soldier and a subject. In the former capacity, you are charged with spreading mutiny and rebellion among the men you commanded, and setting them the example of desertion, by prolonging your own absence from the regiment, contrary to express orders of your commanding officer. The civil crime of which you stand accused is that of high treason, and levying war against the king, the highest delinquency of which a subject can be guilty."

"And by what authority am I detained to reply to such heinous calumnies?"

"By one which you must not dispute, nor I disobey."

He handed to Waverley a warrant from the Supreme Criminal Court of Scotland, in full form, for apprehending and securing the person of Edward Waverley, Esq., suspected of treasonable practices, and other high crimes and misdemeanours.

The astonishment which Waverley expressed at this communication was imputed by Major Melville to conscious guilt, while Mr Morton was rather disposed to construe it into the surprise of innocence unjustly suspected. There was something true in both conjectures; for although Edward's mind acquitted him of the crime with which he was charged, yet a hasty review of his own conduct convinced him he might have great difficulty in establishing his innocence to the satisfaction of others.

"It is a very painful part of this painful business," said Major Melville, after a pause, "that, under so grave a charge, I must necessarily request to see such papers as you have on your person."

"You shall, sir, without reserve," said Edward, throwing his pocket-book and memorandums upon the table; "there is but one with which I could wish you would dispense."

"I am afraid, Mr Waverley, I can indulge you with no reservation."

"You shall see it then, sir; and as it can be of no service, I beg it may be returned."

He took from his bosom the lines he had that morning received, and presented them with the envelope. The Major perused them in silence, and directed his clerk to make a copy of them. He then wrapped the copy in the envelope, and placing it on the table before him, returned the original to Waverley, with an air of melancholy gravity.

After indulging the prisoner, for such our hero must now be considered, with what he thought a reasonable time for reflection, Major Melville resumed his examination, premising, that as Mr Waverley seemed to object to general questions, his interrogatories should be as specific as his information permitted. He then proceeded in his investigation, dictating, as he went on, the import of the questions and answers to the amanuensis, by whom it was written down.

"Did Mr Waverley know one Humphry Houghton, a non-commissioned officer in Gardiner's dragoons?"

"Certainly; he was sergeant of my troop, and son of a tenant of my uncle."

"Exactly—and had a considerable share of your confidence, and an influence among his comrades?"

"I had never occasion to repose confidence in a person of his description," answered Waverley. "I favoured Sergeant Houghton as a clever, active young fellow, and I believe his fellow-soldiers respected him accordingly."

"But you used through this man," answered Major Melville, "to communicate with such of your troop as were recruited upon Waverley-Honour?"

"Certainly; the poor fellows, finding themselves in a regiment chiefly composed of Scotch or Irish, looked up to me in any of their little distresses, and naturally made their countryman, and sergeant, their spokesman on such occasions."

"Sergeant Houghton's influence," continued the Major, "extended, then, particularly over those soldiers who followed you to the regiment from your uncle's estate?"

"Surely;—but what is that to the present purpose?"

"To that I am just coming, and I beseech your candid reply. Have you, since leaving the regiment, held any correspondence, direct or indirect, with this Sergeant Houghton?"

"I!—I hold correspondence with a man of his rank and situation!—How, or for what purpose?"

"That you are to explain;—but did you not, for example, send to him for some books?"

"You remind me of a trifling commission," said Waverley, "which I gave Sergeant Houghton, because my servant could not read. I do recollect I bade him, by letter, select some books, of which I sent him a list, and send them to me at Tully-Veolan."

"And of what description were those books?"

"They related almost entirely to elegant literature; they were designed for a lady's perusal."

"Were there not, Mr Waverley, treasonable tracts and pamphlets among them?"

"There were some political treatises, into which I hardly looked. They had been sent to me by the officiousness of a kind friend, whose heart is more to be esteemed than his prudence or political sagacity: they seemed to be dull compositions."

"That friend," continued the persevering inquirer, "was a Mr Pembroke, a nonjuring clergyman,[1] the author of two treasonable works, of which the manuscripts were found among your baggage?"

"But of which, I give you my honour as a gentleman," replied Waverley, "I never read six pages."

"I am not your judge, Mr Waverley; your examination will be transmitted elsewhere. And now to proceed—do you know a person that passes by the name of Wily Will, or Will Ruthven?"

"I never heard of such a name till this moment."

"Did you never through such a person, or any other person, communicate with Sergeant Humphry Houghton, instigating him to desert, with many of his comrades as he could seduce to join him, and unite with the Highlanders and other rebels now in arms under the command of the young Pretender?"

"I assure you I am not only entirely guiltless of the plot you have laid to my charge, but I detest it from the very bottom of my soul, nor would I be guilty of such treachery to gain a throne, either for myself or any other man alive."

"Yet when I consider this envelope in the handwriting of one of those misguided gentlemen who are now in arms against their country, and the verses which it enclosed, I cannot but find some analogy between the enterprise I have mentioned and the exploit of Wogan, which the writer seems to expect you should imitate."

Waverley was struck with the coincidence, but denied that the wishes or expectations of the letter-writer were to be regarded as proofs of a charge otherwise chimerical.

"But, if I am rightly informed, your time was spent, during your absence from the regiment, between the house of this Highland Chieftain, and that of Mr Bradwardine, of Bradwardine, also in arms for this unfortunate cause?"

"I do not mean to disguise it; but I do deny, most resolutely, being privy to any of their designs against the government."

"You do not, however, I presume, intend to deny, that you attended your host Glennaquoich to a rendezvous, where, under a pretence of a general hunting match, most of the accomplices of his treason were assembled to concert measures for taking arms?"

"I acknowledge having been at such a meeting," said Waverley; "but I neither heard nor saw any thing which could give it the character you affix to it."

---

1 "A beneficed Anglican clergyman who refused to take the Oaths of Allegiance and Supremacy to William and Mary and their successors after the Glorious Revolution of 1688" (*AHD*).

"From thence you proceeded," continued the magistrate, "with Glennaquoich and a part of his clan, to join the army of the young Pretender, and returned, after having paid your homage to him, to discipline and arm the remainder, and unite them to his bands on their way southward?"

"I never went with Glennaquoich on such an errand. I never so much as heard that the person whom you mention was in the country."

He then detailed the history of his misfortune at the hunting match, and added, that on his return he found himself suddenly deprived of his commission, and did not deny that he then, for the first time, observed symptoms which indicated a disposition in the Highlanders to take arms; but added, that having no inclination to join their cause, and no longer any reason for remaining in Scotland, he was now on his return to his native country, to which he had been summoned by those who had a right to direct his motions, as Major Melville would perceive from the letters on the table.

Major Melville accordingly perused the letters of Richard Waverley, of Sir Everard, and of Aunt Rachel; but the inferences he drew from them were different from what Waverley expected. They held the language of discontent with government, threw out no obscure hints of revenge, and that of poor Aunt Rachel, which plainly asserted the justice of the Stewart cause, was held to contain the open avowal of what the others only ventured to insinuate.

"Permit me another question, Mr Waverley," said Major Melville,— "Did you not receive repeated letters from your commanding-officer, warning you and commanding you to return to your post, and acquainting you with the use made of your name to spread discontent among your soldiers?"

"I never did, Major Melville. One letter, indeed, I received from him, containing a civil intimation of his wish that I would employ my leave of absence otherwise than in constant residence at Bradwardine, as to which, I own, I thought he was not called on to interfere; and, finally, I received, on the same day on which I observed myself superseded in the Gazette, a second letter from Colonel Gardiner, commanding me to join the regiment, an order which, owing to my absence, already mentioned and accounted for, I received too late to be obeyed. If there were any intermediate letters, and certainly from the Colonel's high character I think it probable that there were, they have never reached me."

"I have omitted, Mr Waverley," continued Major Melville, "to inquire after a matter of less consequence, but which has nevertheless been publicly talked of to your disadvantage. It is said, that a treasonable toast having been proposed in your hearing and presence, you, holding his majesty's commission, suffered the task of resenting it to devolve upon another gentleman of the company. This, sir, cannot be charged against you in a court of justice; but if, as I am informed, the officers of your regiment requested an explanation of such a rumour, as a gentleman and soldier, I cannot but be surprised that you did not afford it to them."

This was too much. Beset and pressed on every hand by accusations, in which gross falsehoods were blended with such circumstances of truth as could not fail to procure them credit,—alone, unfriended, and in a strange land, Waverley almost gave up his life and honour for lost, and, leaning his head upon his hand, resolutely refused to answer any further questions, since the fair and candid statement he had already made had only served to furnish arms against him.

Without expressing either surprise or displeasure at the change in Waverley's manner, Major Melville proceeded composedly to put several other queries to him. "What does it avail me to answer you?" said Edward, sullenly. "You appear convinced of my guilt, and wrest every reply I have made to support your own preconceived opinion. Enjoy your supposed triumph, then, and torment me no further. If I am capable of the cowardice and treachery your charge burdens me with, I am not worthy to be believed in any reply I can make to you. If I am not deserving of your suspicion—and God and my own conscience bear evidence with me that it is so—then I do not see why I should, by my candour, lend my accusers arms against my innocence. There is no reason I should answer a word more, and I am determined to abide by this resolution."[1] And again he resumed his posture of sullen and determined silence.

"Allow me," said the magistrate, "to remind you of one reason that may suggest the propriety of a candid and open confession. The inexperience of youth, Mr Waverley, lays it open to the plans of the more designing and artful; and one of your friends at least—I mean Mac-Ivor of Glennaquoich—ranks high in the latter class, as, from your apparent ingenuousness, youth, and unacquaintance with the manners of the Highlands, I should be disposed to place you among the former. In such a case, a false step, or error like yours, which I shall be happy to consider as involuntary, may be atoned for, and I would willingly act as intercessor. But as you must necessarily be acquainted

---

1 The *Interleaved Waverley* adds "and I am determined to ___" while the *Magnum Opus Waverley* continues the sentence with "to abide by this resolution," which seems to be not the ending Scott originally had in mind for this sentence though exactly where he was going is unclear since the *IW* is indecipherable.

with the strength of the individuals in this country who have assumed arms, with their means, and with their plans, I must expect you will merit this mediation on my part by a frank and candid avowal of all that has come to your knowledge upon these heads. In which case, I think I can venture to promise that a very short personal restraint will be the only ill consequence that can arise from your accession to these unhappy intrigues."

Waverley listened with great composure until the end of this exhortation, when, springing from his seat, with an energy he had not yet displayed, he replied, "Major Melville, since that is your name, I have hitherto answered your questions with candour, or declined them with temper, because their import concerned myself alone; but as you presume to esteem me mean enough to commence informer against others, who received me, whatever may be their public misconduct, as a guest and friend,—I declare to you that I consider your questions as an insult infinitely more offensive than your calumnious suspicions; and that, since my hard fortune permits me no other mode of resenting them than by verbal defiance, you should sooner have my heart out of my bosom, than a single syllable of information on subjects which I could only become acquainted with in the full confidence of unsuspecting hospitality."

Mr Morton and the Major looked at each other; and the former, who, in the course of the examination, had been repeatedly troubled with a sorry rheum,[1] had recourse to his snuff-box and his handkerchief.

"Mr Waverley," said the Major, "my present situation prohibits me alike from giving or receiving offence, and I will not protract a discussion which approaches to either. I am afraid I must sign a warrant for detaining you in custody, but this house shall for the present be your prison. I fear I cannot persuade you to accept a share of our supper?—(Edward shook his head)—but I will order refreshments in your apartment."

Our hero bowed and withdrew, under guard of the officers of justice, to a small but handsome room, where, declining all offers of food or wine, he flung himself on the bed, and, stupefied by the harassing events and mental fatigue of this miserable day, he sunk into a deep and heavy slumber. This was more than he himself could have expected; but it is mentioned of the North-American Indians, when at the stake of torture, that on the least intermission of agony, they will sleep until the fire is applied to awaken them.

---

1 Bad cold.

CHAPTER III.

A Conference, and the Consequence.

MAJOR MELVILLE had detained Mr Morton during his examination of Waverley, both because he thought he might derive assistance from his practical good sense and approved loyalty, and also because it was agreeable to have a witness of unimpeached candour and veracity to proceedings which touched the honour and safety of a young Englishman of high rank and family, and the expectant heir of a large fortune. Every step he knew would be rigorously canvassed, and it was his business to place the justice and integrity of his own conduct beyond the limits of question.

When Waverley retired, the laird and clergyman of Cairnvreckan sat down in silence to their evening meal. While the servants were in attendance, neither chose to say any thing on the circumstances which occupied their minds, and neither felt it easy to speak upon any other. The youth and apparent frankness of Waverley stood in strong contrast to the shades of suspicion which darkened around him, and he had a sort of naiveté and openness of demeanour, that seemed to belong to one unhackneyed in the ways of intrigue, and which pleaded highly in his favour.

Each mused over the particulars of the examination, and each viewed it through the medium of his own feelings. Both were men of ready and acute talent, and both were equally competent to combine various parts of evidence, and to deduce from them the necessary conclusions. But the wide difference of their habits and education often occasioned a great discrepancy in their respective deductions from admitted premises.

Major Melville had been versed in camps and cities; he was vigilant by profession, and cautious from experience, had met with much evil in the world, and therefore, though himself an upright magistrate and an honourable man, his opinions of others were always strict, and sometimes unjustly severe. Mr Morton, on the contrary, had passed from the literary pursuits of a college, where he was beloved by his companions, and respected by his teachers, to the ease and simplicity of his present charge, where his opportunities of witnessing evil were few, and never dwelt upon, but in order to encourage repentance and amendment; and where the love and respect of his parishioners repaid his affectionate zeal in their behalf, by endeavouring to disguise from him what they knew would give him the most acute pain, namely, their own occasional transgressions of the duties which it was the business of his life to recommend. Thus it was a common saying in the neighbourhood (though both were popular characters), that the laird knew only the ill in the parish, and the minister only the good.

A love of letters,[1] though kept in subordination to his clerical studies and duties, also distinguished the Pastor of Cairnvreckan, and had tinged his mind in earlier days with a slight feeling of romance, which no after incidents of real life had entirely dissipated. The early loss of an amiable young woman, whom he had married for love, and who was quickly followed to the grave by an only child, had also served, even after the lapse of many years, to soften a disposition naturally mild and contemplative. His feelings on the present occasion were therefore likely to differ from those of the severe disciplinarian, strict magistrate, and distrustful man of the world.

When the servants had withdrawn, the silence of both parties continued, until Major Melville, filling his glass, and pushing the bottle to Mr Morton, commenced.

"A distressing affair this, Mr Morton. I fear this youngster has brought himself within the compass of a halter."

"God forbid!" answered the clergyman.

"Marry, and amen," said the temporal magistrate; "but I think even your merciful logic will hardly deny the conclusion."

"Surely, Major," answered the clergyman, "I should hope it might be averted, for aught we have heard to-night?"

"Indeed!" replied Melville. "But, my good parson, you are one of those who would communicate to every criminal the benefit of clergy."

"Unquestionably I would: mercy and long-suffering are the grounds of the doctrine I am called to teach."

"True, religiously speaking; but mercy to a criminal may be gross injustice to the community. I don't speak of this young fellow in particular, who I heartily wish may be able to clear himself, for I like both his modesty and his spirit. But I fear he has rushed upon his fate."

"And why? Hundreds of misguided gentlemen are now in arms against the government, many, doubtless, upon principles which education and early prejudice have gilded with the names of patriotism and heroism;—Justice, when she selects her victims from such a multitude (for surely all will not be destroyed), must regard the moral motive. He whom ambition, or hope of personal advantage, has led to disturb the peace of a well-ordered government, let him fall a victim to the laws; but surely youth, misled by the wild visions of chivalry and imaginary loyalty, may plead for pardon."

"If visionary chivalry and imaginary loyalty come within the predicament of high treason," replied the magistrate, "I know no court

---

1 Literature.

in Christendom, my dear Mr Morton, where they can sue out their Habeas Corpus."[1]

"But I cannot see that this youth's guilt is at all established to my satisfaction," said the clergyman.

"Because your good-nature blinds your good sense," replied Major Melville. "Observe now: this young man, descended of a family of hereditary Jacobites, his uncle the leader of the Tory interest in the county of —, his father a disobliged and discontented courtier, his tutor a non-juror, and the author of two treasonable volumes—this youth, I say, enters into Gardiner's dragoons, bringing with him a body of young fellows from his uncle's estate, who have not stickled[2] at avowing, in their way, the high-church principles they learned at Waverley-Honour, in their disputes with their comrades. To these young men Waverley is unusually attentive; they are supplied with money beyond a soldier's wants, and inconsistent with his discipline; and are under the management of a favourite sergeant, through whom they hold an unusually close communication with their captain, and affect to consider themselves as independent of the other officers, and superior to their comrades."

"All this, my dear Major, is the natural consequence of their attachment to their young landlord, and of their finding themselves in a regiment levied chiefly in the north of Ireland and the west of Scotland, and of course among comrades disposed to quarrel with them, both as Englishmen, and as members of the Church of England."

"Well said, parson!" replied the magistrate.—"I would some of your synod heard you.—But let me go on. This young man obtains leave of absence, goes to Tully-Veolan—the principles of the Baron of Bradwardine are pretty well known, not to mention that this lad's uncle bought him off in the year fifteen;[3] he engages there in a brawl, in which he is said to have disgraced the commission he bore; Colonel Gardiner writes to him, first mildly, then more sharply—I think you will not doubt his having done so, since he says so; the mess invite him to explain the quarrel, in which he is said to have been involved; he neither replies to his commander nor his comrades. In the meanwhile, his soldiers become mutinous and disorderly, and at length, when the rumour of this unhappy rebellion becomes general, his favourite

---

1 The Habeas Corpus Act of 1689 legislated that the accused in England be given a trial within a reasonable amount of time or bail, except in treason or felony cases. In Scotland, this situation was covered by a similar act passed in 1701 (*OW*, 435).
2 Scrupled.
3 Refers to the 1715 Jacobite uprising, after which Sir Everard Waverley paid for the baron's freedom.

Sergeant Houghton, and another fellow, are detected in correspondence with a French emissary,[1] accredited, as he says, by Captain Waverley, who urges him, according to the men's confession, to desert with the troop and join their captain, who was with Prince Charles. In the meanwhile this trusty captain is, by his own admission, residing at Glennaquoich with the most active, subtle, and desperate Jacobite in Scotland; he goes with him at least as far as their famous hunting rendezvous, and I fear a little farther. Meanwhile two other summonses are sent him; one warning him of the disturbances in his troop, another peremptorily ordering him to repair to the regiment, which, indeed, common sense might have dictated, when he observed rebellion thickening all round him. He returns an absolute refusal, and throws up his commission."

"He had been already deprived of it," said Mr Morton.

"But he regrets," replied Melville, "that the measure had anticipated his resignation. His baggage is seized at his quarters, and at Tully-Veolan, and is found to contain a stock of pestilent jacobitical pamphlets, enough to poison a whole country, besides the unprinted lucubrations of his worthy friend and tutor Mr Pembroke."

"He says he never read them," answered the minister.

"In an ordinary case I should believe him," replied the magistrate, "for they are as stupid and pedantic in composition as mischievous in their tenets. But can you suppose any thing but value for the principles they maintain, would induce a young man of his age to lug such trash about with him? Then, when news arrives of the approach of the rebels, he sets out in a sort of disguise, refusing to tell his name; and, if yon old fanatic tell truth, attended by a very suspicious character, and mounted on a horse known to have belonged to Glennaquoich, and bearing on his person letters from his family expressing high rancour against the house of Brunswick, and a copy of verses in praise of one Wogan, who abjured the service of the Parliament to join the Highland insurgents, when in arms to restore the house of Stewart, with a body of English cavalry—the very counterpart of his own plot—and summed up with a 'Go thou and do likewise,' from that loyal subject, and most safe and peaceable character, Fergus Mac-Ivor of Glennaquoich, Vich Ian Vohr, and so forth. And, lastly," continued Major Melville, warming in the detail of his arguments, "where do we find this second edition of Cavalier Wogan? Why, truly, in the very track most proper for execution of his design, and pistoling the first of the king's subjects who ventures to question his intentions."

---

1 An agent sent by the French government to represent its interests.

Mr Morton prudently abstained from argument, which he perceived would only harden the magistrate in his opinion, and merely asked how he intended to dispose of the prisoner?

"It is a question of some difficulty, considering the state of the country," said Major Melville.

"Could you not detain him (being such a gentleman-like young man) here in your own house, out of harm's way, till this storm blow over?"

"My good friend," said Major Melville, "neither your house nor mine will be long out of harm's way, even were it legal to confine him here. I have just learned that the commander-in-chief,[1] who marched into the Highlands to seek out and disperse the insurgents, has declined giving them battle at Corryerick, and marched on northward with all the disposable force of government to Inverness, John-o'-Groat's House, or the devil, for what I know, leaving the road to the Low Country open and undefended to the Highland army."

"Good God!" said the clergyman. "Is the man a coward, a traitor, or an idiot?"

"None of the three, I believe," answered Melville. "Sir John has the common-place courage of a common soldier, is honest enough, does what he is commanded, and understands what is told him, but is as fit to act for himself in circumstances of importance, as I, my dear parson, to occupy your pulpit."

This important public intelligence naturally diverted the discourse from Waverley for some time; at length, however, the subject was resumed.

"I believe," said Major Melville, "that I must give this young man in charge to some of the detached parties of armed volunteers, who were lately sent out to overawe the disaffected districts. They are now recalled towards Stirling, and a small body comes this way to-morrow or next day, commanded by the westland man—what's his name?— You saw him, and said he was the very model of one of Cromwell's military saints."

"Gilfillan, the Cameronian," answered Mr Morton. "I wish the young gentleman may be safe with him. Strange things are done in the heat and hurry of minds in so agitating a crisis, and I fear Gilfillan is of a sect which has suffered persecution without learning mercy."

"He has only to lodge Mr Waverley in Stirling Castle," said the Major: "I will give injunctions to treat him well. I really cannot devise any better mode for securing him, and I fancy you would hardly advise me to encounter the responsibility of setting him at liberty."

---

1 Sir John Cope (d. 1760) was the commander of the Hanoverian Army.

"But you will have no objection to my seeing him to-morrow in private?" said the minister.

"None, certainly; your loyalty and character are my warrant. But with what view do you make the request?"

"Simply," replied Mr Morton, "to make the experiment whether he may not be brought to communicate to me some circumstances which may hereafter be useful to alleviate, if not to exculpate his conduct."

The friends now parted and retired to rest, each filled with the most anxious reflections on the state of the country.

CHAPTER IV.
A Confidant.

WAVERLEY awoke in the morning, from troubled dreams and unrefreshing slumbers, to a full consciousness of the horrors of his situation. How it might terminate he knew not. He might be delivered up to military law, which, in the midst of civil war, was not likely to be scrupulous in the choice of its victims, or the quality of the evidence. Nor did he feel much more comfortable at the thoughts of a trial before a Scottish court of justice, where he knew the laws and forms differed in many respects from those of England, and had been taught to believe, however erroneously, that the liberty and rights of the subject were less carefully protected. A sentiment of bitterness rose in his mind against the government, which he considered as the cause of his embarrassment and peril, and he cursed internally his scrupulous rejection of Mac-Ivor's invitation to accompany him to the field.

"Why did not I," he said to himself, "like other men of honour, take the earliest opportunity to welcome to Britain the descendant of her ancient kings, and lineal heir of her throne? Why did not I

> 'Unthread the rude eye of rebellion,
> And welcome home again discarded faith,
> Seek out Prince Charles, and fall before his feet?'[1]

All that has been recorded of excellence and worth in the house of Waverley has been founded upon their loyal faith to the house of Stewart. From the interpretation which this Scotch magistrate has put upon the letters of my uncle and father, it is plain that I ought to have understood them as marshalling me to the course of my ancestors; and it has been my gross dulness, joined to the obscurity of expression which they adopted for the sake of security, that has confounded my judge-

---

1 Shakespeare, *King John*, V.iv.11-13 (where "King John" replaces "Prince Charles").

ment. Had I yielded to the first generous impulse of indignation, when I learned that my honour was practised upon, how different had been my present situation! I had then been free and in arms, fighting, like my forefathers, for love, for loyalty, and for fame. And now I am here, netted and in the toils, at the disposal of a suspicious, stern, and cold-hearted man, perhaps to be turned over to the solitude of a dungeon, or the infamy of a public execution. O, Fergus! how true has your prophecy proved; and how speedy, how very speedy, has been its accomplishment!"

While Edward was ruminating on these painful subjects of contemplation, and very naturally, though not quite so justly, bestowing upon the reigning dynasty that blame which was due to chance, or, in part at least, to his own unreflecting conduct, Mr Morton availed himself of Major Melville's permission to pay him an early visit.

Waverley's first impulse was to intimate a desire that he might not be disturbed with questions or conversation; but he suppressed it upon observing the benevolent and reverend appearance of the clergyman who had rescued him from the immediate violence of the villagers.

"I believe, sir," said the unfortunate young man, "that in any other circumstances I should have had as much gratitude to express to you as the safety of my life may be worth; but such is the present tumult of my mind, and such is my anticipation of what I am yet likely to endure, that I can hardly offer you thanks for your interposition."

Mr Morton replied, that, far from making any claim upon his good opinion, his only wish and the sole purpose of his visit was to find out the means of deserving it. "My excellent friend, Major Melville," he continued, "has feelings and duties as a soldier and public functionary, by which I am not fettered; nor can I always coincide in opinions which he forms, perhaps with too little allowance for the imperfections of human nature." He paused, and then proceeded: "I do not intrude myself on your confidence, Mr Waverley, for the purpose of learning any circumstances, the knowledge of which can be prejudicial either to yourself or to others; but I own my earnest wish is, that you would intrust me with any particulars which could lead to your exculpation. I can solemnly assure you they will be deposited with a faithful, and, to the extent of his limited powers, a zealous agent."

"You are, sir, I presume, a Presbyterian clergyman?"—Mr Morton bowed—"Were I to be guided by the prepossessions of education, I might distrust your friendly professions in my case; but I have observed that similar prejudices are nourished in this country against your professional brethren of the Episcopal persuasion, and I am willing to believe them equally unfounded in both cases."

"Evil to him that thinks otherwise," said Mr Morton; "or who holds church government and ceremonies as the exclusive gage of Christian faith or moral virtue."

"But," continued Waverley, "I cannot perceive why I should trouble you with a detail of particulars, out of which, after revolving them as carefully as possible in my recollection, I find myself unable to explain much of what is charged against me. I know, indeed, that I am innocent, but I hardly see how I can hope to prove myself so."

"It is for that very reason, Mr Waverley," said the clergyman, "that I venture to solicit your confidence. My knowledge of individuals in this country is pretty general, and can upon occasion be extended. Your situation will, I fear, preclude your taking those active steps for recovering intelligence, or tracing imposture, which I would willingly undertake in your behalf; and if you are not benefited by my exertions, at least they cannot be prejudicial to you."

Waverley, after a few minutes' reflection, was convinced that his reposing confidence in Mr Morton, so far as he himself was concerned, could hurt neither Mr Bradwardine nor Fergus Mac-Ivor, both of whom had openly assumed arms against the government, and that it might possibly, if the professions of his new friend corresponded in sincerity with the earnestness of his expression, be of some service to himself. He therefore ran briefly over most of the events with which the reader is already acquainted, suppressing his attachment to Flora, and indeed neither mentioning her nor Rose Bradwardine in the course of his narrative.

Mr Morton seemed particularly struck with the account of Waverley's visit to Donald Bean Lean. "I am glad," he said, "you did not mention this circumstance to the Major. It is capable of great misconstruction on the part of those who do not consider the power of curiosity and the influence of romance as motives of youthful conduct. When I was a young man like you, Mr Waverley, any such hair-brained expedition (I beg your pardon for the expression) would have had inexpressible charms for me. But there are men in the world who will not believe that danger and fatigue are often incurred without any very adequate cause, and therefore who are sometimes led to assign motives of action entirely foreign to the truth. This man Bean Lean is renowned through the country as a sort of Robin Hood, and the stories which are told of his address and enterprise are the common tales of the winter fire-side. He certainly possesses talents beyond the rude sphere in which he moves; and, being neither destitute of ambition nor encumbered with scruples, he will probably attempt, by every means, to distinguish himself during the period of these unhappy commotions." Mr Morton then made a careful memorandum of the various particulars of Waverley's interview with Donald Bean, and the other circumstances which he had communicated.

The interest which this good man seemed to take in his misfortunes, above all, the full confidence he appeared to repose in his innocence, had the natural effect of softening Edward's heart, whom the coldness of Major Melville had taught to believe that the world was leagued to oppress him. He shook Mr Morton warmly by the hand, and, assuring him that his kindness and sympathy had relieved his mind of a heavy load, told him, that whatever might be his own fate, he belonged to a family who had both gratitude and the power of displaying it. The earnestness of his thanks called drops to the eyes of the worthy clergyman, who was doubly interested in the cause for which he had volunteered his services, by observing the genuine and undissembled feelings of his young friend.

Edward now enquired if Mr Morton knew what was likely to be his destination.

"Stirling Castle," replied his friend; "and so far I am well pleased for your sake, for the governor is a man of honour and humanity. But I am more doubtful of your treatment upon the road; Major Melville is involuntarily obliged to intrust the custody of your person to another."

"I am glad of it," answered Waverley. "I detest that cold-blooded calculating Scotch magistrate. I hope he and I shall never meet more: he had neither sympathy with my innocence nor with my wretchedness; and the petrifying accuracy with which he attended to every form of civility, while he tortured me by his questions, his suspicions, and his inferences, was as tormenting as the racks of the Inquisition. Do not vindicate him, my dear sir, for that I cannot bear with patience; tell me rather who is to have the charge of so important a state prisoner as I am."

"I believe a person called Gilfillan, one of the sect who are termed Cameronians."

"I never heard of them before."

"They claim," said the clergyman, "to represent the more strict and severe Presbyterians, who, in Charles Second's and James Second's days, refused to profit by the Toleration, or Indulgence, as it was called, which was extended to others of that religion. They held conventicles in the open fields, and being treated with great violence and cruelty by the Scottish government, more than once took arms during those reigns. They take their name from their leader, Richard Cameron."

"I recollect," said Waverley;—"but did not the triumph of Presbytery at the Revolution[1] extinguish that sect?"

"By no means," replied Morton; "that great event fell yet far short of what they proposed, which was nothing less than the complete

---

1 Refers to the "Glorious Revolution" when James II was exiled and his daughter, Mary, and her husband, William of Orange, took the throne of England and Scotland in 1688.

establishment of the Presbyterian Church, upon the grounds of the old Solemn League and Covenant. Indeed, I believe they scarce knew what they wanted; but being a numerous body of men, and not unacquainted with the use of arms, they kept themselves together as a separate party in the state, and at the time of the Union[1] had nearly formed a most unnatural league with their old enemies, the Jacobites, to oppose that important national measure. Since that time their numbers have gradually diminished; but a good many are still to be found in the western counties, and several, with a better temper than in 1707, have now taken arms for government. This person, whom they call Gifted Gilfillan, has been long a leader among them, and now heads a small party, which will pass here to-day, or to-morrow, on their march towards Stirling, under whose escort Major Melville proposes you shall travel. I would willingly speak to Gilfillan in your behalf; but, having deeply imbibed all the prejudices of his sect, and being of the same fierce disposition, he would pay little regard to the remonstrances of an Erastian divine,[2] as he would politely term me.—And now, farewell, my young friend; for the present, I must not weary out the Major's indulgence, that I may obtain his permission to visit you again in the course of the day."

CHAPTER V.
Things mend a little.

ABOUT noon, Mr Morton returned, and brought an invitation from Major Melville that Mr Waverley would honour him with his company to dinner, notwithstanding the unpleasant affair which detained him at Cairnvreckan, from which he should heartily rejoice to see Mr Waverley completely extricated. The truth was, that Mr Morton's favourable report and opinion had somewhat staggered the preconceptions of the old soldier concerning Edward's supposed accession to the mutiny in the regiment; and in the unfortunate state of the country, the mere suspicion of disaffection, or an inclination to join the insurgent Jacobites, might infer criminality indeed, but certainly not dishonour. Besides, a person whom the Major trusted had reported to him (though, as it proved, inaccurately), a contradiction of the agitating news of the preceding evening. According to this second edition of the intelligence, the Highlanders had withdrawn from the Lowland frontier with the purpose of following the army in their march to Inverness. The Major was at a loss, indeed, to reconcile his

---

1 Union between England and Scotland, 1707.
2 A minister who accepts the subordinate role of the ecclesiastical to the secular in the lives of his parishioners.

information with the well-known abilities of some of the gentlemen in the Highland army, yet it was the course which was likely to be most agreeable to others. He remembered the same policy had detained them in the north in the year 1715, and he anticipated a similar termination to the insurrection, as upon that occasion.

This news put him in such good-humour, that he readily acquiesced in Mr Morton's proposal to pay some hospitable attention to his unfortunate guest, and voluntarily added, he hoped the whole affair would prove a youthful *escapade*, which might be easily atoned by a short confinement. The kind mediator had some trouble to prevail on his young friend to accept the invitation. He dared not urge to him the real motive, which was a good-natured wish to secure a favourable report of Waverley's case from Major Melville to Governor Blakeney. He remarked, from the flashes of our hero's spirit, that touching upon this topic would be sure to defeat his purpose. He therefore pleaded, that the invitation argued the Major's disbelief of any part of the accusation which was inconsistent with Waverley's conduct as a soldier and man of honour, and that to decline his courtesy might be interpreted into a consciousness that it was unmerited. In short, he so far satisfied Edward that the manly and proper course was to meet the Major on easy terms, that, suppressing his strong dislike again to encounter his cold and punctilious civility, Waverley agreed to be guided by his new friend.

The meeting, at first, was stiff and formal enough. But Edward having accepted the invitation, and his mind being really soothed and relieved by the kindness of Morton, held himself bound to behave with ease, though he could not affect cordiality. The Major was somewhat of a *bon vivant*, and his wine was excellent. He told his old campaign stories, and displayed much knowledge of men and manners. Mr Morton had an internal fund of placid and quiet gaiety, which seldom failed to enliven any small party in which he found himself pleasantly seated. Waverley, whose life was a dream, gave ready way to the predominating impulse, and became the most lively of the party. He had at all times remarkable natural powers of conversation, though easily silenced by discouragement. On the present occasion, he piqued himself upon leaving on the minds of his companions a favourable impression of one who, under such disastrous circumstances, could sustain misfortunes with ease and gaiety. His spirits, though not unyielding, were abundantly elastic, and soon seconded his efforts. The trio were engaged in very lively discourse, apparently delighted with each other, and the kind host was pressing a third bottle of Burgundy, when the sound of a drum was heard at some distance. The Major, who, in the glee of an old soldier, had forgot the duties of a magistrate, cursed, with a muttered military oath, the circumstances which recalled him to his official functions. He rose and went towards the window, which commanded a very near view of the high-road, and he was followed by his guests.

The drum advanced, beating no measured martial tune, but a kind of rub-a-dub-dub, like that with which the fire-drum startles the slumbering artizans of a Scotch burgh.[1] It is the object of this history to do justice to all men; I must therefore record, in justice to the drummer, that he protested he could beat any known march or point of war known in the British army, and had accordingly commenced with "Dumbarton's Drums,"[2] when he was silenced by Gifted Gilfillan, the commander of the party, who refused to permit his followers to move to this profane, and even, as he said, persecutive tune, and commanded the drummer to beat the 119th Psalm.[3] As this was beyond the capacity of the drubber of sheepskin, he was fain to have recourse to the inoffensive row-dow-dow, as a harmless substitute for the sacred music which his instrument or skill were unable to achieve. This may be held a trifling anecdote, but the drummer in question was no less than town-drummer of Anderton. I remember his successor in office a member of that enlightened body, the British Convention:[4] be his memory, therefore, treated with due respect.

CHAPTER VI.
A Volunteer Sixty Years since.

ON hearing the unwelcome sound of the drum, Major Melville hastily opened a sashed door, and stepped out upon a sort of terrace which divided his house from the high-road from which the martial music proceeded. Waverley and his new friend followed him, though probably he would have dispensed with their attendance. They soon recognised in solemn march, first, the performer upon the drum; secondly,

---

1 The drum used to awaken Scottish townspeople in the event of a fire; also used to alert them to a military conflict—a call to arms.

2 A march, taking its name from George, Earl of Dumbarton, Colonel of the Royal Scots' regiment from 1645-88.

3 This psalm stresses the image of the road and the idea of staying the course God has set for one, and of God's light making the path clear even in darkness for the weary traveler.

4 Meeting in 1793 of the English and Scottish reform societies in Edinburgh. Such organizations were viewed by many as radical, and indeed, this meeting ended with the arrest of several of the societies' members. Scott's Tory or conservative leanings would have made such reform efforts unattractive, hence the ambivalent tone of the mention of the British Convention in this text (*PW*, 587).

a large flag of four compartments, on which were inscribed the words, COVENANT, KIRK, KING, KINGDOMS. The person who was honoured with this charge was followed by the commander of the party, a thin, dark, rigid-looking man, about sixty years old. The spiritual pride, which, in mine host of the Candlestick, mantled in a sort of supercilious hypocrisy, was, in this man's face, elevated and yet darkened by genuine and undoubting fanaticism. It was impossible to behold him without imagination placing him in some strange crisis, where religious zeal was the ruling principle. A martyr at the stake, a soldier in the field, a lonely and banished wanderer consoled by the intensity and supposed purity of his faith under every earthly privation; perhaps a persecuting inquisitor, as terrific in power as unyielding in adversity; any of these seemed congenial characters to this personage. With these high traits of energy, there was something in the affected precision and solemnity of his deportment and discourse, that bordered upon the ludicrous; so that, according to the mood of the spectator's mind, and the light under which Mr Gilfillan presented himself, one might have feared, admired, or laughed at him. His dress was that of a west-country peasant, of better materials indeed than that of the lower rank, but in no respect affecting either the mode of the age, or of the Scottish gentry at any period. His arms were a broadsword and pistols, which, from the antiquity of their appearance, might have seen the rout of Pentland, or Bothwell Brigg.[1]

As he came up a few steps to meet Major Melville, and touched solemnly, but slightly, his huge and overbrimmed blue bonnet, in answer to the Major, who had courteously raised a small triangular gold-laced hat, Waverley was irresistibly impressed with the idea that he beheld a leader of the Roundheads of yore, in conference with one of Marlborough's[2] captains.

The group of about thirty armed men who followed this gifted commander, was of a motley description. They were in ordinary Lowland dresses, of different colours, which, contrasted with the arms they bore, gave them an irregular and mobbish appearance; so much

---

1 The Pentland Rising occurred in 1666 when a group of covenanters who wanted Presbyterianism restored to Scotland occupied Dumfries in protest against laws requiring them to worship at parish churches or face fines. The uprising was squashed and many of the rebels executed. The battle of Bothwell Bridge in 1679 was another failed attempt on the part of covenanters to regain their rights to worship (OCBH, 116, 741).
2 A leader of Oliver Cromwell's Parliamentarian forces in the mid-seventeenth-century civil war speaking with a captain of John Churchill, Duke of Marlborough (1650-1722), who was an effective English general in the War of the Spanish Succession, 1701-13.

is the eye accustomed to connect uniformity of dress with the military character. In front were a few who apparently partook of their leader's enthusiasm; men obviously to be feared in combat where their natural courage was exalted by religious zeal. Others puffed and strutted, filled with the importance of carrying arms, and all the novelty of their situation, while the rest, apparently fatigued with their march, dragged their limbs listlessly along, or straggled from their companions to procure such refreshments as the neighbouring cottages and alehouses afforded.—Six grenadiers[1] of Ligonier's,[2] thought the Major to himself, as his mind reverted to his own military experience, would have sent all these fellows to the right about.

Greeting, however, Mr Gilfillan civilly, he requested to know if he had received the letter he had sent to him upon his march, and could undertake the charge of the state prisoner whom he there mentioned, as far as Stirling Castle. "Yea," was the concise reply of the Cameronian leader, in a voice which seemed to issue from the very *penetralia*[3] of his person.

"But your escort, Mr Gilfillan, is not so strong as I expected," said Major Melville.

"Some of the people," replied Gilfillan, "hungered and were athirst by the way, and tarried until their poor souls were refreshed with the word."

"I am sorry, sir," replied the Major, "you did not trust to your refreshing your men at Cairnvreckan; whatever my house contains is at the command of persons employed in the service."

"It was not of creature-comforts I spake," answered the Covenanter, regarding Major Melville with something like a smile of contempt; "howbeit, I thank you; but the people remained waiting upon the precious Mr Jabesh Rentowel, for the out-pouring of the afternoon exhortation."

"And have you, sir," said the Major, "when the rebels are about to spread themselves through this country, actually left a great part of your command at a field-preaching?"

Gilfillan again smiled scornfully as he made this indirect answer,—"Even thus are the children of this world wiser in their generation than the children of light!"

"However, sir," said the Major, "as you are to take charge of this gentleman to Stirling, and deliver him, with these papers, into the hands of Governor Blakeney, I beseech you to observe some rules of military discipline upon your march. For example, I would advise you

---

1 Foot soldiers in an elite unit, selected for their courage and strength.
2 John, Earl of Ligonier (1680-1770), one of Marlborough's soldiers.
3 Interior.

to keep your men more closely together, and that each, in his march, should cover his file-leader, instead of straggling like geese upon a common; and, for fear of surprise, I further recommend to you to form a small advance-party of your best men, with a single vidette[1] in front of the whole march, so that when you approach a village or a wood"—(Here the Major interrupted himself)—"But as I don't observe you listen to me, Mr Gilfillan, I suppose I need not give myself the trouble to say more upon the subject. You are a better judge, unquestionably, than I am, of the measures to be pursued; but one thing I would have you well aware of, that you are to treat this gentleman, your prisoner, with no rigour nor incivility, and are to subject him to no other restraint than is necessary for his security."

"I have looked into my commission," said Mr Gilfillan, "subscribed by a worthy and professing nobleman, William, Earl of Glencairn; nor do I find it therein set down that I am to receive any charges or commands anent[2] my doings from Major William Melville of Cairnvreckan."

Major Melville reddened even to the well-powdered ears which appeared beneath his neat military side-curls, the more so as he observed Mr Morton smile at the same moment. "Mr Gilfillan," he answered, with some asperity, "I beg ten thousand pardons for interfering with a person of your importance. I thought, however, that as you have been bred a grazier,[3] if I mistake not, there might be occasion to remind you of the difference between Highlanders and Highland cattle; and if you should happen to meet with any gentleman who has seen service, and is disposed to speak upon the subject, I should still imagine that listening to him would do you no sort of harm. But I have done, and have only once more to recommend this gentleman to your civility, as well as to your custody.—Mr Waverley, I am truly sorry we should part in this way; but I trust, when you are again in this country, I may have the opportunity to render Cairnvreckan more agreeable than circumstances have permitted on this occasion."

So saying, he shook our hero by the hand. Morton also took an affectionate farewell, and Waverley, having mounted his horse, with a musketeer leading it by the bridle, and a file upon each side to prevent his escape, set forward upon the march with Gilfillan and his party. Through the little village they were accompanied with the shouts of the children, who cried out, "Eh! see to the Southland gentleman, that's gaun to be hanged for shooting lang John Mucklewrath, the smith!"

---

1 Sentry on horseback sent out in advance of an army.
2 Respecting (*WSG*).
3 A person who grazes cattle (*AHD*).

CHAPTER VII.
An Incident.

THE dinner hour of Scotland Sixty Years since was two o'clock. It was therefore about four o'clock of a delightful autumn afternoon that Mr Gilfillan commenced his march, in hopes, although Stirling was eighteen miles distant, he might be able, by becoming a borrower of the night for an hour or two, to reach it that evening. He therefore put forth his strength, and marched stoutly along at the head of his followers, eyeing our hero from time to time, as if he longed to enter into controversy with him. At length, unable to resist the temptation, he slackened his pace till he was alongside of his prisoner's horse, and after marching a few steps in silence abreast of him, he suddenly asked,—"Can ye say wha the carle was wi' the black coat and the mousted head,[1] that was wi' the Laird of Cairnvreckan?"

"A Presbyterian clergyman," answered Waverley.

"Presbyterian!" answered Gilfillan contemptuously; "a wretched Erastian, or rather an obscured Prelatist,—a favourer of the black Indulgence; ane of thae dumb dogs that canna bark: they tell ower a clash o' terror and a clatter o' comfort in their sermons, without ony sense, or savour, or life.—Ye've been fed in siccan a fauld, belike?"[2]

"No; I am of the Church of England," said Waverley.

"And they're just neighbour-like," replied the Covenanter; "and nae wonder they gree[3] sae weel. Wha wad hae thought the goodly structure of the Kirk of Scotland, built up by our fathers in 1642, wad hae been defaced by carnal ends and the corruptions of the time;—ay, wha wad hae thought the carved work of the sanctuary would hae been sae soon cut down!"

To this lamentation, which one or two of the assistants chorussed with a deep groan, our hero thought it unnecessary to make any reply. Whereupon Mr Gilfillan, resolving that he should be a hearer at least, if not a disputant, proceeded in his Jeremiade.[4]

"And now is it wonderful, when, for lack of exercise anent the call to the service of the altar and the duty of the day, ministers fall into sinful compliances with patronage, and indemnities, and oaths, and bonds, and other corruptions,—is it wonderful, I say, that you, sir, and other sic-like unhappy persons, should labour to build up your auld Babel of iniquity, as in the bluidy persecuting saint-killing times? I

---

1 Cropped head of hair (*WSG*).
2 You've been a parishioner in such a church (*WSG*).
3 Agree.
4 "A literary work or speech expressing a bitter lament or a righteous prophecy of doom" (*AHD*).

trow, gin ye werena blinded wi' the graces and favours, and services and enjoyments, and employments and inheritances, of this wicked world, I could prove to you, by the Scripture, in what a filthy rag ye put your trust; and that your surplices, and your copes and vestments, are but cast-off garments of the muckle harlot, that sitteth upon seven hills, and drinketh of the cup of abomination. But, I trow, ye are deaf as adders upon that side of the head; ay, ye are deceived with her enchantments, and ye traffic with her merchandise, and ye are drunk with the cup of her fornication!"[1]

How much longer this military theologist might have continued his invective, in which he spared nobody but the scattered remnant of *hill-folk*, as he called them, is absolutely uncertain. His matter was copious, his voice powerful, and his memory strong; so that there was little chance of his ending his exhortation till the party had reached Stirling, had not his attention been attracted by a pedlar who had joined the march from a cross-road, and who sighed or groaned with great regularity at all fitting pauses of his homily.

"And what may ye be, friend?" said the Gifted Gilfillan.

"A puir pedlar, that's bound for Stirling, and craves the protection of your honour's party in these kittle[2] times. Ah! your honour has a notable faculty in searching and explaining the secret,—ay, the secret and obscure and incomprehensible causes of the backslidings of the land; ay, your honour touches the root o' the matter."

"Friend," said Gilfillan, with a more complacent voice than he had hitherto used, "honour not me. I do not go out to park-dikes, and to steadings,[3] and to market-towns, to have herds and cottars, and burghers pull off their bonnets to me as they do to Major Melville o' Cairn-vreckan, and ca' me laird, or captain, or honour;—no; my sma' means, whilk are not aboon twenty thousand merk, have had the blessing of increase, but the pride of my heart has not increased with them; nor do I delight to be called captain, though I have the subscribed commission of that gospel-searching nobleman, the Earl of Glencairn, in whilk I am so designated. While I live, I am and will be called Habakkuk Gilfillan, who will stand up for the standards of doctrine agreed on by the ance-famous Kirk of Scotland, before she trafficked with the accursed Achan,[4] while he has a plack[5] in his purse, or a drap o' bluid in his body."

---

1 These were some of the criticisms the Covenanters had of the Church of England and even of the more moderate arm of the Presbyterian Church.

2 "Ticklish, in all senses" (*WSG*).

3 Farms.

4 During the pillaging of Jericho, this Israelite stole, and was stoned to death as punishment. See Joshua 7:18-26 (*PW*, 588).

5 Halfpenny.

"Ah," said the pedlar, "I have seen your land about Mauchlin—a fertile spot! Your lines have fallen in pleasant places!—And siccan a breed o' cattle is not in ony laird's land in Scotland."

"Ye say right,—ye say right, friend," retorted Gilfillan eagerly, for he was not inaccessible to flattery upon this subject,—"Ye say right; they are the real Lancashire, and there's no the like o' them even at the Mains of Kilmaurs"; and he then entered into a discussion of their excellences, to which our readers will probably be as indifferent as our hero. After this excursion, the leader returned to his theological discussions, while the pedlar, less profound upon these mystic points, contented himself with groaning, and expressing his edification at suitable intervals.

"What a blessing it would be to the puir blinded popish nations among whom I hae sojourned, to have siccan a light to their paths! I hae been as far as Muscovia[1] in my sma' trading way, as a travelling merchant; and I hae been through France, and the Low Countries,[2] and a' Poland, and maist feck o'[3] Germany, and O! it would grieve your honour's soul to see the murmuring, and the singing, and massing, that's in the kirk, and the piping that's in the quire, and the heathenish dancing and dicing upon the Sabbath!"

This set Gilfillan off upon the Book of Sports and the Covenant, and the Engagers, and the Protestors, and the Whiggamore's Raid, and the Assembly of Divines at Westminster, and the Longer and Shorter Catechism, and the Excommunication at Torwood, and the slaughter of Archbishop Sharp.[4] This last topic, again, led him into the lawfulness of defensive arms, on which subject he uttered much more sense than could have been expected from some other parts of his harangue, and attracted even Waverley's attention, who had hitherto been lost in his own sad reflections. Mr Gilfillan then considered the lawfulness of a private man's standing forth as the avenger of public oppression, and as he was labouring with great earnestness the cause of Mas James Mitchell, who fired at the Archbishop of St Andrews some years before the prelate's assassination on Magus Muir,[5] an incident occurred which interrupted his harangue.

The rays of the sun were lingering on the very verge of the horizon,

---

1 Russia (*AHD*).

2 Belgium, the Netherlands, and Luxembourg (*AHD*).

3 Most part of.

4 James Sharp (1613-79), archbishop of St. Andrews, was assassinated by Covenanters.

5 In 1675, Mitchell confessed to the Scottish Privy Council that he had a few years earlier tried to kill Sharp. Sharp pursued him, and Mitchell was tried in 1678 and put to death (*OW*, 436).

as the party ascended a hollow and somewhat steep path, which led to the summit of a rising ground. The country was unenclosed, being part of a very extensive heath or common; but it was far from level, exhibiting in many places hollows filled with furze[1] and broom; in others, little dingles of stunted brushwood. A thicket of the latter description crowned the hill up which the party ascended. The foremost of the band, being the stoutest and most active, had pushed on, and, having surmounted the ascent, were out of ken for the present. Gilfillan, with the pedlar, and the small party who were Waverley's more immediate guard, were near the top of the ascent, and the remainder straggled after them at a considerable interval.

Such was the situation of matters, when the pedlar, missing, as he said, a little doggie which belonged to him, began to halt and whistle for the animal. This signal, repeated more than once, gave offence to the rigour of his companion, the rather because it appeared to indicate inattention to the treasures of theological and controversial knowledge which was pouring out for his edification. He therefore signified gruffly, that he could not waste his time in waiting for an useless cur.

"But if your honour wad consider the case of Tobit"—[2]

"Tobit!" exclaimed Gilfillan, with great heat; "Tobit and his dog baith are altogether heathenish and apocryphal, and none but a prelatist or a papist would draw them into question. I doubt I hae been mista'en in you, friend."

"Very likely," answered the pedlar, with great composure; "but ne'ertheless, I shall take leave to whistle again upon puir Bawty."

This last signal was answered in an unexpected manner; for six or eight stout Highlanders, who lurked among the copse and brushwood, sprung into the hollow way, and began to lay about them with their claymores. Gilfillan, unappalled at this undesirable apparition, cried out manfully, "The sword of the Lord and of Gideon!" and, drawing his broadsword, would probably have done as much credit to the good old cause as any of its doughty champions at Drumclog, when, behold! the pedlar, snatching a musket from the person who was next him, bestowed the butt of it with such emphasis on the head of his late instructor in the Cameronian creed, that he was forthwith levelled to the ground. In the confusion which ensued, the horse which bore our hero was shot by one of Gilfillan's party, as he discharged his firelock at random. Waverley fell with, and indeed under, the animal, and sustained some severe contusions. But he was almost instantly extricated from the fallen steed by two Highlanders, who, each seizing him by

---

1 Gorse bush, an "evergreen shrub with yellow flowers" growing throughout Europe (*OED*).

2 Tobit was the main character in the Book of Tobit from the Old Testament.

the arm, hurried him away from the scuffle and from the high-road. They ran with great speed, half supporting and half dragging our hero, who could, however, distinguish a few dropping shots[1] fired about the spot which he had left. This, as he afterwards learned, proceeded from Gilfillan's party, who had now assembled, the stragglers in front and rear having joined the others. At their approach the Highlanders drew off, but not before they had rifled Gilfillan and two of his people, who remained on the spot grievously wounded. A few shots were exchanged betwixt them and the Westlanders; but the latter, now without a commander, and apprehensive of a second ambush, did not make any serious effort to recover their prisoner, judging it more wise to proceed on their journey to Stirling, carrying with them their wounded captain and comrades.

CHAPTER VIII.
Waverley is still in Distress.

THE velocity, and indeed violence, with which Waverley was hurried along, nearly deprived him of sensation; for the injury he had received from his fall prevented him from aiding himself so effectually as he might otherwise have done. When this was observed by his conductors, they called to their aid two or three others of the party, and swathing our hero's body in one of their plaids, divided his weight by that means among them, and transported him at the same rapid rate as before, without any exertion of his own. They spoke little, and that in Gaelic; and did not slacken their pace till they had run nearly two miles, when they abated their extreme rapidity, but continued still to walk very fast, relieving each other occasionally.

Our hero now endeavoured to address them, but was only answered with "*Cha n'eil Beurl' agam,*" *i.e.*, "I have no English," being, as Waverley well knew, the constant reply of a Highlander, when he either does not understand, or does not choose to reply to, an Englishman or Lowlander. He then mentioned the name of Vich Ian Vohr, concluding that he was indebted to his friendship for his rescue from the clutches of Gifted Gilfillan; but neither did this produce any mark of recognition from his escort.

The twilight had given place to moonshine when the party halted upon the brink of a precipitous glen, which, as partly enlightened by the moon-beams, seemed full of trees and tangled brushwood. Two of the Highlanders dived into it by a small foot-path, as if to explore its recesses, and one of them returning in a few minutes, said something to his companions, who instantly raised their burden, and bore him,

---

1 A gunshot which is losing its velocity.

with great attention and care, down the narrow and abrupt descent. Notwithstanding their precautions, however, Waverley's person came more than once into contact, rudely enough, with the projecting stumps and branches which overhung the pathway.

At the bottom of the descent, and, as it seemed, by the side of a brook (for Waverley heard the rushing of a considerable body of water, although its stream was invisible in the darkness), the party again stopped before a small and rudely-constructed hovel. The door was open, and the inside of the premises appeared as uncomfortable and rude as its situation and exterior foreboded. There was no appearance of a floor of any kind; the roof seemed rent in several places; the walls were composed of loose stones and turf, and the thatch of branches of trees. The fire was in the centre, and filled the whole wigwam with smoke, which escaped as much through the door as by means of a circular aperture in the roof. An old Highland sibyl,[1] the only inhabitant of this forlorn mansion, appeared busy in the preparation of some food. By the light which the fire afforded, Waverley could discover that his attendants were not of the clan of Ivor, for Fergus was particularly strict in requiring from his followers that they should wear the tartan striped in the mode peculiar to their race; a mark of distinction anciently general through the Highlands, and still maintained by those Chiefs who were proud of their lineage, or jealous of their separate and exclusive authority.

Edward had lived at Glennaquoich long enough to be aware of a distinction which he had repeatedly heard noticed, and now satisfied that he had no interest with his attendants, he glanced a disconsolate eye around the interior of the cabin. The only furniture, excepting a washing-tub, and a wooden press, called in Scotland an *ambry*, sorely decayed, was a large wooden bed, planked, as is usual, all around, and opening by a sliding panel. In this recess the Highlanders deposited Waverley, after he had by signs declined any refreshment. His slumbers were broken and unrefreshing; strange visions passed before his eyes, and it required constant and reiterated efforts of mind to dispel them. Shivering, violent headache, and shooting pains in his limbs, succeeded these symptoms; and in the morning it was evident to his Highland attendants or guard, for he knew not in which light to consider them, that Waverley was quite unfit to travel.

After a long consultation among themselves, six of the party left the hut with their arms, leaving behind an old and a young man. The former addressed Waverley, and bathed the contusions, which swelling and livid colour now made conspicuous. His own portmanteau, which the Highlanders had not failed to bring off, supplied him with linen,

---

1 Woman prophet.

and, to his great surprise, was, with all its undiminished contents, freely resigned to his use. The bedding of his couch seemed clean and comfortable, and his aged attendant closed the door of the bed, for it had no curtain, after a few words of Gaelic, from which Waverley gathered that he exhorted him to repose. So behold our hero for a second time the patient of a Highland Esculapius, but in a situation much more uncomfortable than when he was the guest of the worthy Tomanrait.

The symptomatic fever which accompanied the injuries he had sustained, did not abate till the third day, when it gave way to the care of his attendants and the strength of his constitution, and he could now raise himself in his bed, though not without pain. He observed, however, that there was a great disinclination, on the part of the old woman who acted as his nurse, as well as on that of the elderly Highlander, to permit the door of the bed to be left open, so that he might amuse himself with observing their motions; and at length, after Waverley had repeatedly drawn open, and they had frequently shut, the hatchway of his cage, the old gentleman put an end to the contest, by securing it on the outside with a nail so effectually, that the door could not be drawn till this exterior impediment was removed.

While musing upon the cause of this contradictory spirit in persons whose conduct intimated no purpose of plunder, and who, in all other points, appeared to consult his welfare and his wishes, it occurred to our hero, that, during the worst crisis of his illness, a female figure, younger than his old Highland nurse, had appeared to flit around his couch. Of this, indeed, he had but a very indistinct recollection, but his suspicions were confirmed when, attentively listening, he often heard, in the course of the day, the voice of another female conversing in whispers with his attendant. Who could it be? And why should she apparently desire concealment? Fancy immediately roused herself, and turned to Flora Mac-Ivor. But after a short conflict between his eager desire to believe she was in his neighbourhood, guarding, like an angel of mercy, the couch of his sickness, Waverley was compelled to conclude that his conjecture was altogether improbable; since, to suppose she had left her comparatively safe situation at Glennaquoich to descend into the Low Country, now the seat of civil war, and to inhabit such a lurking-place as this, was a thing hardly to be imagined. Yet his heart bounded as he sometimes could distinctly hear the trip of a light female step glide to or from the door of the hut, or the suppressed sounds of a female voice, of softness and delicacy, hold dialogue with the hoarse inward croak of old Janet, for so he understood his antiquated attendant was denominated.

Having nothing else to amuse his solitude, he employed himself in contriving some plan to gratify his curiosity, in despite of the sedulous caution of Janet and the old Highland janizary,[1] for he had never seen the young fellow since the first morning. At length, upon accurate examination, the infirm state of his wooden prison-house appeared to supply the means of gratifying his curiosity, for out of a spot which was somewhat decayed he was able to extract a nail. Through this minute aperture he could perceive a female form, wrapped in a plaid, in the act of conversing with Janet. But, since the days of our grandmother Eve, the gratification of inordinate curiosity has generally borne its penalty in disappointment. The form was not that of Flora, nor was the face visible; and, to crown his vexation, while he laboured with the nail to enlarge the hole, that he might obtain a more complete view, a slight noise betrayed his purpose, and the object of his curiosity instantly disappeared; nor, so far as he could observe, did she again revisit the cottage.

All precautions to blockade his view were from that time abandoned, and he was not only permitted, but assisted, to rise, and quit what had been, in a literal sense, his couch of confinement. But he was not allowed to leave the hut; for the young Highlander had now rejoined his senior, and one or other was constantly on the watch. Whenever Waverley approached the cottage door, the sentinel upon duty civilly, but resolutely, placed himself against it and opposed his exit, accompanying his action with signs which seemed to imply there was danger in the attempt, and an enemy in the neighbourhood. Old Janet appeared anxious and upon the watch; and Waverley, who had not yet recovered strength enough to attempt to take his departure in spite of the opposition of his hosts, was under the necessity of remaining patient. His fare was, in every point of view, better than he could have conceived; for poultry, and even wine, were no strangers to his table. The Highlanders never presumed to eat with him, and, unless in the circumstance of watching him, treated him with great respect. His sole amusement was gazing from the window, or rather the shapeless aperture which was meant to answer the purpose of a window, upon a large and rough brook, which raged and foamed through a rocky channel, closely canopied with trees and bushes, about ten feet beneath the site of his house of captivity.

Upon the sixth day of his confinement, Waverley found himself so well, that he began to meditate his escape from this dull and miserable prison-house, thinking any risk which he might incur in the attempt preferable to the stupifying and intolerable uniformity of Janet's retirement. The question indeed occurred, whither he was to direct his

---

1 Highland warrior—a member of a group of elite, highly loyal supporters (*AHD*).

course when again at his own disposal. Two schemes seemed practicable, yet both attended with danger and difficulty. One was to go back to Glennaquoich, and join Fergus Mac-Ivor, by whom he was sure to be kindly received; and in the present state of his mind, the rigour with which he had been treated fully absolved him, in his own eyes, from his allegiance to the existing government. The other project was to endeavour to attain a Scottish seaport, and thence to take shipping for England. His mind wavered between these plans, and probably, if he had effected his escape in the manner he proposed, he would have been finally determined by the comparative facility by which either might have been executed. But his fortune had settled that he was not to be left to his option.

Upon the evening of the seventh day the door of the hut suddenly opened, and two Highlanders entered, whom Waverley recognised as having been a part of his original escort to this cottage. They conversed for a short time with the old man and his companion, and then made Waverley understand, by very significant signs, that he was to prepare to accompany them. This was a joyful communication. What had already passed during his confinement made it evident that no personal injury was designed to him; and his romantic spirit, having recovered during his repose much of that elasticity which anxiety, resentment, disappointment, and the mixture of unpleasant feelings excited by his late adventures had for a time subjugated, was now wearied with inaction. His passion for the wonderful, although it is the nature of such dispositions to be excited by that degree of danger which merely gives dignity to the feeling of the individual exposed to it, had sunk under the extraordinary and apparently insurmountable evils by which he appeared environed at Cairnvreckan. In fact, this compound of intense curiosity and exalted imagination forms a peculiar species of courage, which somewhat resembles the light usually carried by a miner,—sufficiently competent, indeed, to afford him guidance and comfort during the ordinary perils of his labour, but certain to be extinguished should he encounter the more formidable hazard of earth-damps or pestiferous vapours. It was now, however, once more rekindled, and with a throbbing mixture of hope, awe, and anxiety, Waverley watched the group before him, as those who were just arrived snatched a hasty meal, and the others assumed their arms, and made brief preparations for their departure.

As he sat in the smoky hut, at some distance from the fire, around which the others were crowded, he felt a gentle pressure upon his arm. He looked round.—It was Alice, the daughter of Donald Bean Lean. She showed him a packet of papers in such a manner that the motion was remarked by no one else, put her finger for a second to her lips, and passed on, as if to assist old Janet in packing Waverley's clothes in his portmanteau. It was obviously her wish that he should not seem to recognise her; yet she repeatedly looked back at him, as an opportunity occurred of doing so unobserved, and when she saw that he remarked what she did, she folded the packet with great address and speed in one of his shirts, which she deposited in the portmanteau.

Here then was fresh food for conjecture. Was Alice his unknown warden, and was this maiden of the cavern the tutelar genius that watched his bed during his sickness? Was he in the hands of her father? And if so, what was his purpose? Spoil, his usual object, seemed in this case neglected; for not only Waverley's property was restored, but his purse, which might have tempted this professional plunderer, had been all along suffered to remain in his possession. All this perhaps the packet might explain; but it was plain from Alice's manner that she desired he should consult it in secret. Nor did she again seek his eye after she had satisfied herself that her manœuvre was observed and understood. On the contrary, she shortly afterwards left the hut, and it was only as she tript out from the door, that, favoured by the obscurity, she gave Waverley a parting smile and nod of significance, ere she vanished in the dark glen.

The young Highlander was repeatedly dispatched by his comrades as if to collect intelligence. At length, when he had returned for the third or fourth time, the whole party arose, and made signs to our hero to accompany them. Before his departure, however, he shook hands with old Janet, who had been so sedulous in his behalf, and added substantial marks of his gratitude for her attendance.

"God bless you! God prosper you, Captain Waverley!" said Janet, in good Lowland Scotch, though he had never hitherto heard her utter a syllable, save in Gaelic. But the impatience of his attendants prohibited his asking any explanation.

CHAPTER IX.
A Nocturnal Adventure.

THERE was a moment's pause when the whole party had got out of the hut; and the Highlander who assumed the command, and who, in Waverley's awakened recollection, seemed to be the same tall figure who had acted as Donald Bean Lean's lieutenant, by whispers and signs imposed the strictest silence. He delivered to Edward a sword and steel pistol, and, pointing up the track, laid his hand on the hilt of his own claymore, as if to make him sensible they might have occasion to use force to make good their passage. He then placed himself at the head of the party, who moved up the pathway in single or Indian file, Waverley being placed nearest to their leader. He moved with great precaution, as if to avoid giving any alarm, and halted as soon as he came to the verge of the ascent. Waverley was soon sensible of the reason, for he heard at no great distance an English sentinel call out "All's well." The heavy sound sunk on the night-wind down the woody glen, and was answered by the echoes of its banks. A second, third, and fourth time the signal was repeated fainter and fainter, as if at a greater and greater distance. It was obvious that a party of soldiers were near, and upon their guard, though not sufficiently so to detect men skilful in every art of predatory warfare, like those with whom he now watched their ineffectual precautions.

When these sounds had died upon the silence of the night, the Highlanders began their march swiftly, yet with the most cautious silence. Waverley had little time, or indeed disposition, for observation, and could only discern that they passed at some distance from a large building, in the windows of which a light or two yet seemed to twinkle. A little farther on, the leading Highlander snuffed the wind like a setting spaniel, and then made a signal to his party again to halt. He stooped down upon all fours, wrapped up in his plaid, so as to be scarce distinguishable from the heathy ground on which he moved, and advanced in this posture to reconnoitre. In a short time he returned, and dismissed his attendants excepting one; and, intimating to Waverley that he must imitate his cautious mode of proceeding, all three crept forward on hands and knees.

After proceeding a greater way in this inconvenient manner than was at all comfortable to his knees and shins, Waverley perceived the smell of smoke, which probably had been much sooner distinguished by the more acute nasal organs of his guide. It proceeded from the corner of a low and ruinous sheep-fold, the walls of which were made of loose stones, as is usual in Scotland. Close by this low wall the Highlander guided Waverley, and, in order probably to make him sensible of his danger, or perhaps to obtain the full credit of his own dexterity, he intimated to him, by sign and example, that he might raise his head so as to peep into the sheep-fold. Waverley did so, and beheld an out-post of four or five soldiers lying by their watch-fire. They were all asleep, except the sentinel, who paced backwards and forwards with his firelock on his shoulder, which glanced red in the light of the fire as he crossed and re-crossed before it in his short walk, casting his eye frequently to that part of the heavens from which the moon, hitherto obscured by mist, seemed now about to make her appearance.

In the course of a minute or two, by one of those sudden changes of atmosphere incident to a mountainous country, a breeze arose, and swept before it the clouds which had covered the horizon, and the night planet poured her full effulgence upon a wide and blighted heath, skirted indeed with copse-wood and stunted trees in the quarter from which they had come, but open and bare to the observation of the sentinel in that to which their course tended. The wall of the sheep-fold indeed concealed them as they lay, but any advance beyond its shelter seemed impossible without certain discovery.

The Highlander eyed the blue vault, but far from blessing the useful light with Homer's, or rather Pope's, benighted peasant,[1] he muttered a Gaelic curse upon the unseasonable splendour of *Mac-Farlane's buat* (*i.e.*, lantern[iii]). He looked anxiously around for a few minutes, and then apparently took his resolution. Leaving his attendant with Waverley, after motioning to Edward to remain quiet, and giving his comrade directions in a brief whisper, he retreated, favoured by the irregularity of the ground, in the same direction and in the same manner as they had advanced. Edward, turning his head after him, could perceive him crawling on all fours with the dexterity of an Indian, availing himself of every bush and inequality to escape observation, and never passing over the more exposed parts of his track until the sentinel's back was turned from him. At length he reached the thickets and underwood which partly covered the moor in that direction, and probably extended to the verge of the glen where Waverley had been so long an inhabitant. The Highlander disappeared, but it was only for a few minutes, for he suddenly issued forth from a different part of the thicket, and advancing boldly upon the open heath, as if to invite discovery, he levelled his piece, and fired at the sentinel. A wound in the arm proved a disagreeable interruption to the poor fellow's meteorological observations, as well as to the tune of Nancy Dawson,[2] which he was whistling. He returned the fire ineffectually, and his comrades, starting up at the alarm, advanced alertly towards the spot from which the first shot had issued. The Highlander, after giving them a full view of his person, dived among the thickets, for his *ruse de guerre*[3] had now perfectly succeeded.

While the soldiers pursued the cause of their disturbance in one direction, Waverley, adopting the hint of his remaining attendant, made the best of his speed in that which his guide originally intended to pursue, and which now (the attention of the soldiers being drawn to a different quarter) was unobserved and unguarded. When they had run about a quarter of a mile, the brow of a rising ground, which they had surmounted, concealed them from further risk of observation. They still heard, however, at a distance, the shouts of the soldiers as they hallooed to each other upon the heath, and they could also hear the distant roll of a drum beating to arms in the same direction. But

---

1   Refers to Alexander Pope's translation of Homer's *Iliad*, VIII, 698.
2   A popular English tune, named after Nancy Dawson, a singer and dancer who died in 1767.
3   Military stratagem.

these hostile sounds were now far in their rear, and died away upon the breeze as they rapidly proceeded.

When they had walked about half an hour, still along open and waste ground of the same description, they came to the stump of an ancient oak, which, from its relics, appeared to have been at one time a tree of very large size. In an adjacent hollow they found several Highlanders, with a horse or two. They had not joined them above a few minutes, which Waverley's attendant employed, in all probability, in communicating the cause of their delay (for the words "Duncan Duroch" were often repeated), when Duncan himself appeared, out of breath indeed, and with all the symptoms of having run for his life, but laughing, and in high spirits at the success of the stratagem by which he had baffled his pursuers. This indeed Waverley could easily conceive might be a matter of no great difficulty to the active mountaineer, who was perfectly acquainted with the ground, and traced his course with a firmness and confidence to which his pursuers must have been strangers. The alarm which he excited seemed still to continue, for a dropping shot or two were heard at a great distance, which seemed to serve as an addition to the mirth of Duncan and his comrades.

The mountaineer now resumed the arms with which he had intrusted our hero, giving him to understand that the dangers of the journey were happily surmounted. Waverley was then mounted upon one of the horses, a change which the fatigue of the night and his recent illness rendered exceedingly acceptable. His portmanteau was placed on another pony, Duncan mounted a third, and they set forward at a round pace, accompanied by their escort. No other incident marked the course of that night's journey, and at the dawn of morning they attained the banks of a rapid river. The country around was at once fertile and romantic. Steep banks of wood were broken by corn fields, which this year presented an abundant harvest, already in a great measure cut down.

On the opposite bank of the river, and partly surrounded by a winding of its stream, stood a large and massive castle, the half-ruined turrets of which were already glittering in the first rays of the sun.^{kkk} It was in form an oblong square, of size sufficient to contain a large court in the centre. The towers at each angle of the square rose higher than the walls of the building, and were in their turn surmounted by turrets, differing in height, and irregular in shape. Upon one of these a sentinel watched, whose bonnet and plaid, streaming in the wind, declared him to be a Highlander, as a broad white ensign,[1] which floated from another tower, announced that the garrison was held by the insurgent adherents of the House of Stewart.

1 Flag.

Passing hastily through a small and mean town, where their appearance excited neither surprise nor curiosity in the few peasants whom the labours of the harvest began to summon from their repose, the party crossed an ancient and narrow bridge of several arches, and turning to the left, up an avenue of huge old sycamores, Waverley found himself in front of the gloomy yet picturesque structure which he had admired at a distance. A huge iron-grated door, which formed the exterior defence of the gateway, was already thrown back to receive them; and a second, heavily constructed of oak, and studded thickly with iron nails, being next opened, admitted them into the interior court-yard. A gentleman, dressed in the Highland garb, and having a white cockade in his bonnet, assisted Waverley to dismount from his horse, and with much courtesy bid him welcome to the castle.

The governor, for so we must term him,[1] having conducted Waverley to a half-ruinous apartment, where, however, there was a small camp-bed, and having offered him any refreshment which he desired, was then about to leave him.

"Will you not add to your civilities," said Waverley, after having made the usual acknowledgment, "by having the kindness to inform me where I am, and whether or not I am to consider myself as a prisoner?"

"I am not at liberty to be so explicit upon this subject as I could wish. Briefly, however, you are in the castle of Doune, in the district of Menteith, and in no danger whatever."

"And how am I assured of that?"

"By the honour of Donald Stewart, governor of the garrison, and lieutenant-colonel in the service of his Royal Highness Prince Charles Edward." So saying, he hastily left the apartment, as if to avoid further discussion.

Exhausted by the fatigues of the night, our hero now threw himself upon the bed, and was in a few minutes fast asleep.

CHAPTER X.
The Journey is continued.

BEFORE Waverley awakened from his repose, the day was far advanced, and he began to feel that he had passed many hours without food. This was soon supplied in form of a copious breakfast, but Colonel Stewart, as if wishing to avoid the queries of his guest, did not again present himself. His compliments were, however, delivered by a servant, with an offer to provide any thing in his power that could be

---

1 Donald Stewart, commander of the garrison.

useful to Captain Waverley on his journey, which he intimated would be continued that evening. To Waverley's further inquiries, the servant opposed the impenetrable barrier of real or affected ignorance and stupidity. He removed the table and provisions, and Waverley was again consigned to his own meditations.

As he contemplated the strangeness of his fortune, which seemed to delight in placing him at the disposal of others, without the power of directing his own motions, Edward's eye suddenly rested upon his portmanteau, which had been deposited in his apartment during his sleep. The mysterious appearance of Alice, in the cottage of the glen, immediately rushed upon his mind, and he was about to secure and examine the packet which she had deposited among his clothes, when the servant of Colonel Stewart again made his appearance, and took up the portmanteau upon his shoulders.

"May I not take out a change of linen, my friend?"

"Your honour sall get ane o' the Colonel's ain ruffled sarks, but this maun gang in the baggage-cart."

And so saying, he very coolly carried off the portmanteau, without waiting further remonstrance, leaving our hero in a state where disappointment and indignation struggled for the mastery. In a few minutes he heard a cart rumble out of the rugged court-yard, and made no doubt that he was now dispossessed, for a space at least, if not for ever, of the only documents which seemed to promise some light upon the dubious events which had of late influenced his destiny. With such melancholy thoughts he had to beguile about four or five hours of solitude.

When this space was elapsed, the trampling of horse was heard in the court-yard, and Colonel Stewart soon after made his appearance to request his guest to take some further refreshment before his departure. The offer was accepted, for a late breakfast had by no means left our hero incapable of doing honour to dinner, which was now presented. The conversation of his host was that of a plain country gentleman, mixed with some soldier-like sentiments and expressions. He cautiously avoided any reference to the military operations or civil politics of the time; and to Waverley's direct inquiries concerning some of these points, replied, that he was not at liberty to speak upon such topics.

When dinner was finished, the governor arose, and, wishing Edward a good journey, said, that having been informed by Waverley's servant that his baggage had been sent forward, he had taken the freedom to supply him with such changes of linen as he might find necessary, till he was again possessed of his own. With this compliment he disappeared. A servant acquainted Waverley an instant afterwards, that his horse was ready.

Upon this hint he descended into the court-yard, and found a trooper holding a saddled horse, on which he mounted, and sallied from the portal of Doune Castle, attended by about a score of armed men on horseback. These had less the appearance of regular soldiers than of individuals who had suddenly assumed arms from some pressing motive of unexpected emergency. Their uniform, which was blue and red, an affected imitation of that of French chasseurs,[1] was in many respects incomplete, and sate awkwardly upon those who wore it. Waverley's eye, accustomed to look at a well-disciplined regiment, could easily discover that the motions and habits of his escort were not those of trained soldiers, and that, although expert enough in the management of their horses, their skill was that of huntsmen or grooms, rather than of troopers. The horses were not trained to the regular pace so necessary to execute simultaneous and combined movements and formations; nor did they seem *bitted*[2] (as it is technically expressed) for the use of the sword. The men, however, were stout, hardy-looking fellows, and might be individually formidable as irregular cavalry. The commander of this small party was mounted upon an excellent hunter, and although dressed in uniform, his change of apparel did not prevent Waverley from recognising his old acquaintance, Mr Falconer of Balmawhapple.

Now, although the terms upon which Edward had parted with this gentleman were none of the most friendly, he would have sacrificed every recollection of their foolish quarrel, for the pleasure of enjoying once more the social intercourse of question and answer, from which he had been so long secluded. But apparently the remembrance of his defeat by the Baron of Bradwardine, of which Edward had been the unwilling cause, still rankled in the mind of the low-bred, and yet proud laird. He carefully avoided giving the least sign of recognition, riding doggedly at the head of his men, who, though scarce equal in numbers to a sergeant's party, were denominated Captain Falconer's troop, being preceded by a trumpet, which sounded from time to time, and a standard, borne by Cornet Falconer, the laird's younger brother. The lieutenant, an elderly man, had much the air of a low sportsman and boon companion; an expression of dry humour predominated in his countenance over features of a vulgar cast, which indicated habitual intemperance. His cocked hat was set knowingly upon one side of his head, and while he whistled the "Bob of Dumblain," under the influence of half a mutchkin[3] of brandy, he seemed to trot merrily forward, with a happy indifference to the state of the

---

1 "Light cavalry or infantry troops trained for rapid maneuvers" (*AHD*).

2 To place a bit in the mouth of a horse (*AHD*).

3 A "unit of liquid measure equal to 0.9 US pints" (*AHD*).

country, the conduct of the party, the end of the journey, and all other sublunary matters whatever.

From this wight,[1] who now and then dropped alongside of his horse, Waverley hoped to acquire some information, or at least to beguile the way with talk.

"A fine evening, sir," was Edward's salutation.

"Ow, ay, sir! a bra'[2] night," replied the lieutenant, in broad Scotch of the most vulgar description.

"And a fine harvest apparently," continued Waverley, following up his first attack.

"Ay, the aits will be got bravely in: but the farmers, deil burst them, and the corn-mongers, will make the auld price gude against them as has horses till keep."[3]

"You perhaps act as quarter-master,[4] sir?"

"Ay, quarter-master, riding-master, and lieutenant," answered this officer of all work. "And, to be sure, wha's fitter to look after the breaking and the keeping of the poor beasts than mysell, that bought and sold every ane o' them?"

"And pray, sir, if it be not too great a freedom, may I beg to know where we are going just now?"

"A fule's errand, I fear," answered this communicative personage.

"In that case," said Waverley, determined not to spare civility, "I should have thought a person of your appearance would not have been found on the road."

"Vera true, vera true, sir," replied the officer, "but every why has its wherefore. Ye maun ken, the laird there bought a' thir beasts frae me to munt his troop, and agreed to pay for them according to the necessities and prices of the time. But then he hadna the ready penny, and I hae been advised his bond will not be worth a boddle against the estate, and then I had a' my dealers to settle wi' at Martinmas;[5] and so as he very kindly offered me this commission, and as the auld *Fifteen*ˡˡˡ wad never help me to my siller for sending out naigs against the government, why, conscience! sir, I thought my best chance for payment was e'en to *gae out*ᵐᵐᵐ mysell; and ye may judge, sir, as I hae dealt a' my life in halters, I think na mickle o' putting my craig in peril of a St Johnstone's tippet."[6]

---

1 Human creature.
2 Splendid.
3 Yes, the oats will be gotten in, but the farmers, devil take them, and the corn-mongers, will make those who have horses to keep pay dearly for the oats (*WSG*).
4 "An officer responsible for food, clothing, and equipment of troops" (*AHD*).
5 November 11, feast of St. Martin of Tours.
6 I don't think much of putting my neck in peril of a halter, i.e., of being hanged.

"You are not, then, by profession a soldier?" said Waverley.

"Na, na; thank God," answered this doughty partisan, "I wasna bred at sae short a tether; I was brought up to hack and manger.[1] I was bred a horse-couper, sir; and if I might live to see you at Whitson-tryst, or at Stagshawbank, or the winter fair at Hawick,[2] and ye wanted a spanker[3] that would lead the field, I'se be caution I would serve ye easy; for Jamie Jinker was ne'er the lad to impose upon a gentleman. Ye're a gentleman, sir, and should ken a horse's points; ye see that through-ganging thing[4] that Balmawhapple's on; I selled her till him. She was bred out of Lick-the-Ladle, that wan the king's plate at Caverton-Edge, by Duke Hamilton's White-Foot," &c. &c. &c.

But as Jinker was entered full sail upon the pedigree of Balmawhapple's mare, having already got as far as great-grandsire and great-grand-dam, and while Waverley was watching for an opportunity to obtain from him intelligence of more interest, the noble captain checked his horse until they came up, and then, without directly appearing to notice Edward, said sternly to the genealogist, "I thought, lieutenant, my orders were preceese, that no one should speak to the prisoner?"

The metamorphosed horse-dealer was silenced of course, and slunk to the rear, where he consoled himself by entering into a vehement dispute upon the price of hay with a farmer, who had reluctantly followed his laird to the field, rather than give up his farm, whereof the lease had just expired. Waverley was therefore once more consigned to silence, foreseeing that further attempts at conversation with any of the party would only give Balmawhapple a wished-for opportunity to display the insolence of authority, and the sulky spite of a temper naturally dogged, and rendered more so by habits of low indulgence and the incense of servile adulation.

In about two hours' time, the party were near the Castle of Stirling, over whose battlements the union flag[5] was brightened as it waved in the evening sun. To shorten his journey, or perhaps to display his importance and insult the English garrison, Balmawhapple, inclining to the right, took his route through the royal park, which reaches to and surrounds the rock upon which the fortress is situated.

---

1 To "live at hack and manger" is to live in plenty, in comfort (*OED*).

2 Horse markets.

3 Horse of superior quality (*OED*).

4 Active, energetic (*OED*).

5 Lamont suggests this refers to the flag that was created when the crosses of St. Andrew and St. George were combined, after the Union of the Crowns in 1603 (*OW*, 438).

With a mind more at ease, Waverley could not have failed to admire the mixture of romance and beauty which renders interesting the scene through which he was now passing—the field which had been the scene of the tournaments of old—the rock from which the ladies beheld the contest, while each made vows for the success of some favourite knight—the towers of the Gothic church, where these vows might be paid—and, surmounting all, the fortress itself, at once a castle and palace, where valour received the prize from royalty, and knights and dames closed the evening amid the revelry of the dance, the song, and the feast. All these were objects fitted to arouse and interest a romantic imagination.

But Waverley had other objects of meditation, and an incident soon occurred of a nature to disturb meditation of any kind. Balmawhapple, in the pride of his heart, as he wheeled his little body of cavalry round the base of the castle, commanded his trumpet to sound a flourish, and his standard to be displayed. This insult produced apparently some sensation; for when the cavalcade was at such distance from the southern battery[1] as to admit of a gun being depressed so as to bear upon them, a flash of fire issued from one of the embrazures upon the rock; and ere the report with which it was attended could be heard, the rushing sound of a cannon-ball passed over Balmawhapple's head, and the bullet, burying itself in the ground at a few yards' distance, covered him with the earth which it drove up. There was no need to bid the party trudge. In fact, every man acting upon the impulse of the moment, soon brought Mr Jinker's steeds to show their mettle, and the cavaliers, retreating with more speed than regularity, never took to a trot, as the lieutenant afterwards observed, until an intervening eminence had secured them from any repetition of so undesirable a compliment on the part of Stirling Castle. I must do Balmawhapple, however, the justice to say, that he not only kept the rear of his troop, and laboured to maintain some order among them, but, in the height of his gallantry, answered the fire of the castle by discharging one of his horse-pistols at the battlements; although, the distance being nearly half a mile, I could never learn that this measure of retaliation was attended with any particular effect.

The travellers now passed the memorable field of Bannockburn,[2] and reached the Torwood, a place glorious or terrible to the recollections of the Scottish peasant, as the feats of Wallace, or the cruelties of

---

1 Cannons on the southern side of Stirling Castle.
2 Robert the Bruce defeated Edward II in 1314 there, thus establishing Scotland's independence from England.

Wude Willie Grime, predominate in his recollection.[1] At Falkirk,[2] a town formerly famous in Scottish history, and soon to be again distinguished as the scene of military events of importance, Balmawhapple proposed to halt and repose for the evening. This was performed with very little regard to military discipline, his worthy quarter-master being chiefly solicitous to discover where the best brandy might be come at. Sentinels were deemed unnecessary, and the only vigils performed were those of such of the party as could procure liquor. A few resolute men might easily have cut off the detachment; but of the inhabitants some were favourable, many indifferent, and the rest overawed. So nothing memorable occurred in the course of the evening, except that Waverley's rest was sorely interrupted by the revellers hallooing forth their Jacobite songs, without remorse or mitigation of voice.

Early in the morning they were again mounted, and on the road to Edinburgh, though the pallid visages of some of the troop betrayed that they had spent a night of sleepless debauchery. They halted at Linlithgow, distinguished by its ancient palace, which, Sixty Years since, was entire and habitable, and whose venerable ruins, *not quite Sixty Years since*, very narrowly escaped the unworthy fate of being converted into a barrack for French prisoners.[3] May repose and blessings attend the ashes of the patriotic statesman, who, amongst his last services to Scotland, interposed to prevent this profanation!

As they approached the metropolis of Scotland, through a champaign and cultivated country, the sounds of war began to be heard. The distant, yet distinct report of heavy cannon, fired at intervals, apprized Waverley that the work of destruction was going forward. Even Balmawhapple seemed moved to take some precautions, by sending an advanced party in front of his troop, keeping the main body in tolerable order, and moving steadily forward.

Marching in this manner they speedily reached an eminence, from which they could view Edinburgh stretching along the ridgy hill which slopes eastward from the Castle. The latter, being in a state of siege, or rather of blockade, by the northern insurgents, who had already occupied the town for two or three days, fired at intervals upon such

---

1 Wude Willie Grime was a farmer in Torwood, Stirlingshire, "supposed to have shot a man for trespassing" and was acquitted by reason of insanity (*PW*, 589).

2 Wallace "took refuge in Torwood after his defeat by Edward I" in 1298 at Falkirk (*PW*, 589).

3 Mary Queen of Scots was born in Linlithgow in 1542. In 1746 the palace burned while Hanoverian soldiers were within. Robert Blair, of Avountoun, refused to let the ruins be used as a barracks.

parties of Highlanders as exposed themselves, either on the main street, or elsewhere in the vicinity of the fortress. The morning being calm and fair, the effect of this dropping fire was to invest the Castle in wreaths of smoke, the edges of which dissipated slowly in the air, while the central veil was darkened ever and anon by fresh clouds poured forth from the battlements; the whole giving, by the partial concealment, an appearance of grandeur and gloom, rendered more terrific when Waverley reflected on the cause by which it was produced, and that each explosion might ring some brave man's knell.

Ere they approached the city, the partial cannonade had wholly ceased. Balmawhapple, however, having in his recollection the unfriendly greeting which his troop had received from the battery at Stirling, had apparently no wish to tempt the forbearance of the artillery of the Castle. He therefore left the direct road, and sweeping considerably to the southward, so as to keep out of the range of the cannon, approached the ancient palace of Holyrood,[1] without having entered the walls of the city. He then drew up his men in front of that venerable pile, and delivered Waverley to the custody of a guard of Highlanders, whose officer conducted him into the interior of the building.

A long, low, and ill-proportioned gallery, hung with pictures, affirmed to be the portraits of kings, who, if they ever flourished at all, lived several hundred years before the invention of painting in oil colours, served as a sort of guard chamber, or vestibule, to the apartments which the adventurous Charles Edward now occupied in the palace of his ancestors. Officers, both in the Highland and Lowland garb, passed and repassed in haste, or loitered in the hall, as if waiting for orders. Secretaries were engaged in making out passes, musters, and returns. All seemed busy, and earnestly intent upon something of importance; but Waverley was suffered to remain seated in the recess of a window, unnoticed by any one, in anxious reflection upon the crisis of his fate, which seemed now rapidly approaching.

CHAPTER XI.
An Old and a New Acquaintance.

WHILE he was deep sunk in his reverie, the rustle of tartans was heard behind him, a friendly arm clasped his shoulders, and a friendly voice exclaimed,

"Said the Highland prophet sooth? Or must second-sight go for nothing?"

Waverley turned, and was warmly embraced by Fergus Mac-Ivor. "A thousand welcomes to Holyrood, once more possessed by her

---

1 The royal residence in Edinburgh.

legitimate sovereign! Did I not say we should prosper, and that you would fall into the hands of the Philistines if you parted from us?"

"Dear Fergus!" said Waverley, eagerly returning his greeting, "it is long since I have heard a friend's voice. Where is Flora?"

"Safe, and a triumphant spectator of our success."

"In this place?" said Waverley.

"Ay, in this city at least," answered his friend, "and you shall see her; but first you must meet a friend whom you little think of, who has been frequent in his inquiries after you."

Thus saying, he dragged Waverley by the arm out of the guard chamber, and, ere he knew where he was conducted, Edward found himself in a presence-room, fitted up with some attempt at royal state.

A young man, wearing his own fair hair, distinguished by the dignity of his mien and the noble expression of his well-formed and regular features, advanced out of a circle of military gentlemen and Highland chiefs, by whom he was surrounded. In his easy and graceful manners Waverley afterwards thought he could have discovered his high birth and rank, although the star on his breast,[1] and the embroidered garter at his knee, had not appeared as its indications.

"Let me present to your Royal Highness," said Fergus, bowing profoundly—

"The descendant of one of the most ancient and loyal families in England," said the young Chevalier, interrupting him. "I beg your pardon for interrupting you, my dear Mac-Ivor; but no master of ceremonies is necessary to present a Waverley to a Stewart."

Thus saying, he extended his hand to Edward with the utmost courtesy, who could not, had he desired it, have avoided rendering the homage which seemed due to his rank, and was certainly the right of his birth. "I am sorry to understand, Mr Waverley, that, owing to circumstances which have been as yet but ill explained, you have suffered some restraint among my followers in Perthshire, and on your march here; but we are in such a situation that we hardly know our friends, and I am even at this moment uncertain whether I can have the pleasure of considering Mr Waverley as among mine."

He then paused for an instant; but before Edward could adjust a suitable reply, or even arrange his ideas as to its purport, the Prince took out a paper, and then proceeded:—"I should indeed have no doubts upon this subject, if I could trust to this proclamation, set forth by the friends of the Elector of Hanover, in which they rank Mr Waverley among the nobility and gentry who are menaced with the pains of high-treason for loyalty to their legitimate sovereign. But I desire to

---

1 John Home wrote that Charles Edward Stuart wore a star of the order of St. Andrew (*OW*, 438).

gain no adherents save from affection and conviction; and if Mr Waverley inclines to prosecute his journey to the south, or to join the forces of the Elector, he shall have my passport and free permission to do so; and I can only regret, that my present[1] power will not extend to protect him against the probable consequences of such a measure.— But," continued Charles Edward, after another short pause, "if Mr Waverley should, like his ancestor, Sir Nigel, determine to embrace a cause which has little to recommend it but its justice, and follow a prince who throws himself upon the affections of his people to recover the throne of his ancestors, or perish in the attempt, I can only say, that among these nobles and gentlemen he will find worthy associates in a gallant enterprise, and will follow a master who may be unfortunate, but, I trust, will never be ungrateful."

The politic Chieftain of the race of Ivor knew his advantage in introducing Waverley to this personal interview with the royal Adventurer. Unaccustomed to the address and manners of a polished court, in which Charles was eminently skilful, his words and his kindness penetrated the heart of our hero, and easily outweighed all prudential motives. To be thus personally solicited for assistance by a Prince, whose form and manners, as well as the spirit which he displayed in this singular enterprise, answered his ideas of a hero of romance; to be courted by him in the ancient halls of his paternal palace, recovered by the sword which he was already bending towards other conquests, gave Edward, in his own eyes, the dignity and importance which he had ceased to consider as his attributes. Rejected, slandered, and threatened upon the one side, he was irresistibly attracted to the cause which the prejudices of education, and the political principles of his family, had already recommended as the most just. These thoughts rushed through his mind like a torrent, sweeping before them every consideration of an opposite tendency,—the time, besides, admitted of no deliberation,—and Waverley, kneeling to Charles Edward, devoted his heart and sword to the vindication of his rights!

The Prince (for, although unfortunate in the faults and follies of his forefathers, we shall here, and elsewhere, give him the title due to his birth) raised Waverley from the ground, and embraced him with an expression of thanks too warm not to be genuine. He also thanked Fergus Mac-Ivor repeatedly for having brought him such an adherent, and presented Waverley to the various noblemen, chieftains, and officers who were about his person, as a young gentleman of the highest hopes and prospects, in whose bold and enthusiastic avowal of his

---

1 Scott added this adjective to the *Magnum Opus Waverley* to emphasize the transitory nature of Charles Edward Stuart's influence.

cause they might see an evidence of the sentiments of the English families of rank at this important crisis.[nnn] Indeed, this was a point much doubted among the adherents of the house of Stewart; and as a well-founded disbelief in the co-operation of the English Jacobites kept many Scottish men of rank from his standard, and diminished the courage of those who had joined it, nothing could be more seasonable for the Chevalier than the open declaration in his favour of the representative of the house of Waverley-Honour, so long known as cavaliers and royalists. This Fergus had foreseen from the beginning. He really loved Waverley, because their feelings and projects never thwarted each other; he hoped to see him united with Flora, and he rejoiced that they were effectually engaged in the same cause. But, as we before hinted, he also exulted as a politician in beholding secured to his party a partisan of such consequence; and he was far from being insensible to the personal importance which he himself gained with the Prince, from having so materially assisted in making the acquisition.

Charles Edward, on his part, seemed eager to show his attendants the value which he attached to his new adherent, by entering immediately, as in confidence, upon the circumstances of his situation. "You have been secluded so much from intelligence, Mr Waverley, from causes of which I am but indistinctly informed, that I presume you are even yet unacquainted with the important particulars of my present situation. You have, however, heard of my landing in the remote district of Moidart, with only seven attendants, and of the numerous chiefs and clans whose loyal enthusiasm at once placed a solitary adventurer at the head of a gallant army. You must also, I think, have learned, that the commander-in-chief of the Hanoverian Elector, Sir John Cope, marched into the Highlands at the head of a numerous and well-appointed military force, with the intention of giving us battle, but that his courage failed him when we were within three hours' march of each other, so that he fairly gave us the slip, and marched northward to Aberdeen, leaving the Low Country open and undefended. Not to lose so favourable an opportunity, I marched on to this metropolis, driving before me two regiments of horse, Gardiner's and Hamilton's, who had threatened to cut to pieces every Highlander that should venture to pass Stirling; and while discussions were carrying forward among the magistracy and citizens of Edinburgh, whether they should defend themselves or surrender, my good friend Lochiel (laying his hand on the shoulder of that gallant and accomplished chieftain) saved them the trouble of farther deliberation, by entering the gates with five hundred Camerons. Thus far, therefore, we have done well; but, in the meanwhile, this doughty general's nerves being braced by the keen air of Aberdeen, he has taken shipping for Dunbar, and I have just received certain information that he landed there yesterday. His purpose must unquestionably be, to march towards us to recover possession of the capital. Now there are two opinions in my council of war: one, that being inferior probably in numbers, and certainly in discipline and military appointments, not to mention our total want of artillery, and the weakness of our cavalry, it will be safest to fall back towards the mountains, and there protract the war until fresh succours arrive from France, and the whole body of the Highland clans shall have taken arms in our favour. The opposite opinion maintains, that a retrograde movement, in our circumstances, is certain to throw utter discredit on our arms and undertaking; and, far from gaining us new partisans, will be the means of disheartening those who have joined our standard. The officers who use these last arguments, among whom is your friend Fergus Mac-Ivor, maintain, that if the Highlanders are strangers to the usual military discipline of Europe, the soldiers whom they are to encounter are no less strangers to their peculiar and formidable mode of attack; that the attachment and courage of the chiefs and gentlemen are not to be doubted; and that as they will be in the midst of the enemy, their clansmen will as surely follow them; in fine, that having drawn the sword we should throw away the scabbard, and trust our cause to battle and to the God of Battles. Will Mr Waverley favour us with his opinion in these arduous circumstances?"

Waverley coloured high betwixt pleasure and modesty at the distinction implied in this question, and answered, with equal spirit and readiness, that he could not venture to offer an opinion as derived from military skill, but that the counsel would be far the most acceptable to him which should first afford him an opportunity to evince his zeal in his Royal Highness's service.

"Spoken like a Waverley!" answered Charles Edward; "and that you may hold rank in some degree corresponding to your name, allow me, instead of the captain's commission which you have lost, to offer you the brevet[1] rank of major in my service, with the advantage of acting as one of my aides-de-camp until you can be attached to a regiment, of which I hope several will be speedily embodied."

"Your Royal Highness will forgive me," answered Waverley (for his recollection turned to Balmawhapple and his scanty troop), "if I decline accepting any rank until the time and place where I may have interest enough to raise a sufficient body of men to make my command useful to your Royal Highness's service. In the meanwhile, I hope for your permission to serve as a volunteer under my friend Fergus Mac-Ivor."

---

1 Honorary.

"At least," said the Prince, who was obviously pleased with this proposal, "allow me the pleasure of arming you after the Highland fashion." With these words, he unbuckled the broadsword which he wore, the belt of which was plated with silver, and the steel basket-hilt richly and curiously inlaid. "The blade," said the Prince, "is a genuine Andrea Ferrara;[1] it has been a sort of heir-loom in our family; but I am convinced I put it into better hands than my own, and will add to it pistols of the same workmanship.—Colonel Mac-Ivor, you must have much to say to your friend; I will detain you no longer from your private conversation; but remember, we expect you both to attend us in the evening. It may be perhaps the last night we may enjoy in these halls, and as we go to the field with a clear conscience, we will spend the eve of battle merrily."

Thus licensed, the Chief and Waverley left the presence-chamber.

CHAPTER XII.
The Mystery begins to be cleared up.

"HOW do you like him?" was Fergus's first question, as they descended the large stone stair-case.

"A prince to live and die under," was Waverley's enthusiastic answer.

"I knew you would think so when you saw him, and I intended you should have met earlier, but was prevented by your sprain. And yet he has his foibles, or rather he has difficult cards to play, and his Irish officers,ᵒᵒᵒ who are much about him, are but sorry advisers,—they cannot discriminate among the numerous pretensions that are set up. Would you think it—I have been obliged for the present to suppress an earl's patent, granted for services rendered ten years ago, for fear of exciting the jealousy, forsooth, of C— and M—. But you were very right, Edward, to refuse the situation of aide-de-camp. There are two vacant, indeed, but Clanronald and Lochiel, and almost all of us, have requested one for young Aberchallader, and the Lowlanders and the Irish party are equally desirous to have the other for the Master of F—. Now if either of these candidates were to be superseded in your favour, you would make enemies. And then I am surprised that the prince should have offered you a majority, when he knows very well that nothing short of lieutenant-colonel will satisfy others, who cannot bring one hundred and fifty men to the field. 'But patience, cousin, and shuffle the cards!'[2] It is all very well for the present, and we must

---

1 See Scott's note dddd.
2 Cervantes, *Don Quixote*, Part II, Chapter 23.

have you properly equipped for the evening in your new costume; for, to say truth, your outward man is scarce fit for a court."

"Why," said Waverley, looking at his soiled dress, "my shooting jacket has seen service since we parted; but that, probably, you, my friend, know as well or better than I."

"You do my second-sight too much honour," said Fergus. "We were so busy, first with the scheme of giving battle to Cope, and afterwards with our operations in the Lowlands, that I could only give general directions to such of our people as were left in Perthshire to respect and protect you, should you come in their way. But let me hear the full story of your adventures, for they have reached us in a very partial and mutilated manner."

Waverley then detailed at length the circumstances with which the reader is already acquainted, to which Fergus listened with great attention. By this time they had reached the door of his quarters, which he had taken up in a small paved court, retiring from the street called the Canongate, at the house of a buxom widow of forty, who seemed to smile very graciously upon the handsome young Chief, she being a person with whom good looks and good-humour were sure to secure an interest, whatever might be the party's political opinions. Here Callum Beg received them with a smile of recognition. "Callum," said the Chief, "call Shemus an Snachad" (James of the Needle). This was the hereditary tailor of Vich Ian Vohr. "Shemus, Mr Waverley is to wear the *cath dath* (battle colour, or tartan); his trews must be ready in four hours. You know the measure of a well-made man: two double nails to the small of the leg"—

"Eleven from haunch to heel, seven round the waist—I give your honour leave to hang Shemus, if there's a pair of sheers in the Highlands that has a baulder sneck than her's ain at the *cumadh an truais*" (shape of the trews).

"Get a plaid of Mac-Ivor tartan, and sash," continued the Chieftain, "and a blue bonnet of the Prince's pattern, at Mr Mouat's in the Crames.[1] My short green coat, with silver lace and silver buttons, will fit him exactly, and I have never worn it. Tell Ensign Maccombich to pick out a handsome target from among mine. The Prince has given Mr Waverley broadsword and pistols, I will furnish him with a dirk and purse; add but a pair of low-heeled shoes, and then, my dear Edward (turning to him), you will be a complete son of Ivor."

These necessary directions given, the Chieftain resumed the subject of Waverley's adventures. "It is plain," he said, "that you have been in the custody of Donald Bean Lean. You must know that when I marched away my clan to join the Prince, I laid my injunctions on

1 Small shops in Edinburgh's High Street.

that worthy member of society to perform a certain piece of service, which done, he was to join me with all the force he could muster. But instead of doing so, the gentleman, finding the coast clear, thought it better to make war on his own account, and has scoured the country, plundering, I believe, both friend and foe, under prentence of levying black mail, sometimes as if by my authority, and sometimes (and be cursed to his consummate impudence) in his own great name! Upon my honour, if I live to see the cairn of Benmore again, I shall be tempted to hang that fellow! I recognise his hand particularly in the mode of your rescue from that canting rascal Gilfillan, and I have little doubt that Donald himself played the part of the pedlar on that occasion; but how he should not have plundered you, or put you to ransom, or availed himself in some way or other of your captivity for his own advantage, passes my judgment."

"When and how did you hear the intelligence of my confinement?" asked Waverley.

"The Prince himself told me," said Fergus, "and inquired very minutely into your history. He then mentioned your being at that moment in the power of one of our northern parties—you know I could not ask him to explain particulars—and requested my opinion about disposing of you. I recommended that you should be brought here as a prisoner, because I did not wish to prejudice you farther with the English government, in case you pursued your purpose of going southward. I knew nothing, you must recollect, of the charge brought against you of aiding and abetting high treason, which, I presume, had some share in changing your original plan. That sullen, good-for-nothing brute, Balmawhapple, was sent to escort you from Doune, with what he calls his troop of horse. As to his behaviour, in addition to his natural antipathy to every thing that resembles a gentleman, I presume his adventure with Bradwardine rankles in his recollection, the rather that I dare say his mode of telling that story contributed to the evil reports which reached your quondam[1] regiment."

"Very likely," said Waverley; "but now surely, my dear Fergus, you may find time to tell me something of Flora."

"Why," replied Fergus, "I can only tell you that she is well, and residing for the present with a relation in this city. I thought it better she should come here, as since our success a good many ladies of rank attend our military court; and I assure you, that there is a sort of consequence annexed to the near relative of such a person as Flora Mac-Ivor, and where there is such a justling of claims and requests, a man must use every fair means to enhance his importance."

---

1 Former.

There was something in this last sentence which grated on Waverley's feelings. He could not bear that Flora should be considered as conducing to her brother's preferment, by the admiration which she must unquestionably attract; and although it was in strict correspondence with many points of Fergus's character, it shocked him as selfish, and unworthy of his sister's high mind and his own independent pride. Fergus, to whom such manœuvres were familiar, as to one brought up at the French court, did not observe the unfavourable impression which he had unwarily made upon his friend's mind, and concluded by saying, "that they could hardly see Flora before the evening, when she would be at the concert and ball, with which the Prince's party were to be entertained. She and I had a quarrel about her not appearing to take leave of you. I am unwilling to renew it, by soliciting her to receive you this morning; and perhaps my doing so might not only be ineffectual, but prevent your meeting this evening."

While thus conversing, Waverley heard in the court, before the windows of the parlour, a well-known voice. "I aver to you, my worthy friend," said the speaker, "that it is a total dereliction of military discipline; and were you not as it were a *tyro*,[1] your purpose would deserve strong reprobation. For a prisoner of war is on no account to be coerced with fetters, or debinded *in ergastulo*,[2] as would have been the case had you put this gentleman into the pit of the peel-house[3] at Balmawhapple. I grant, indeed, that such a prisoner may for security be coerced *in carcere*, that is, in a public prison."

The growling voice of Balmawhapple was heard as taking leave in displeasure, but the word, "land-louper,"[4] alone was distinctly audible. He had disappeared before Waverley reached the house, in order to greet the worthy Baron of Bradwardine. The uniform in which he was now attired, a blue coat, namely, with gold lace, a scarlet waistcoat and breeches, and immense jack-boots, seemed to have added fresh stiffness and rigidity to his tall, perpendicular figure; and the consciousness of military command and authority had increased, in the same proportion, the self-importance of his demeanour, and dogmatism of his conversation.

He received Waverley with his usual kindness, and expressed immediate anxiety to hear an explanation of the circumstances attending the loss of his commission in Gardiner's dragoons; "not," he said, "that he had the least apprehension of his young friend having done aught

---

1 Beginner.
2 In a dungeon or private prison.
3 "A fortified house or tower of a kind constructed in the borderland of Scotland and England in the sixteenth century" (*AHD*).
4 A roving vagabond.

which could merit such ungenerous treatment as he had received from government, but because it was right and seemly that the Baron of Bradwardine should be, in point of trust and in point of power, fully able to refute all calumnies against the heir of Waverley-Honour, whom he had so much right to regard as his own son."

Fergus Mac-Ivor, who had now joined them, went hastily over the circumstances of Waverley's story, and concluded with the flattering reception he had met from the young Chevalier. The Baron listened in silence, and at the conclusion shook Waverley heartily by the hand, and congratulated him upon entering the service of his lawful Prince. "For," continued he, "although it has been justly held in all nations a matter of scandal and dishonour to infringe the *sacramentum militare*,[1] and that whether it was taken by each soldier singly, whilk the Romans denominated *per conjurationem*, or by one soldier in name of the rest, yet no one ever doubted that the allegiance so sworn was discharged by the *dimissio*, or discharging of a soldier, whose case would be as hard as that of colliers, salters, and other *adscripti glebæ*, or slaves of the soil, were it to be accounted otherwise. This is something like the brocard[2] expressed by the learned Sanchez in his work *De Jure-jurando*,[3] which you have questionless consulted upon this occasion. As for those who have calumniated you by leasing-making, I protest to Heaven I think they have justly incurred the penalty of the *Memnonia lex*, also called *Lex Rhemnia*, which is prelected upon by Tullius in his oration *In Verrem*.[4] I should have deemed, however, Mr Waverley, that before destining[5] yourself to any special service in the army of the Prince, ye might have inquired what rank the old Bradwardine held there, and whether he would not have been peculiarly happy to have had your services in the regiment of horse which he is now about to levy."

Edward eluded this reproach by pleading the necessity of giving an immediate answer to the Prince's proposal, and his uncertainty at the moment whether his friend the Baron was with the army, or engaged upon service elsewhere.

---

1 Soldier's oath of allegiance.

2 Principle.

3 Possibly Thomas Sanchez, S.J. (1550-1610), Spanish theologian, lawyer, and author (though according to Hook, he seems not to have written the text cited) (*PW*, 590).

4 "The Memnonian law dealt with the bringing of false accusations," according to Hook; he also points out that this law is not mentioned in the work cited (*PW*, 590), i.e., the *In Verrem* by the Roman orator Marcus Tullius Cicero (106-43 BCE).

5 Preordaining.

This punctilio being settled, Waverley made inquiry after Miss Brad-wardine, and was informed she had come to Edinburgh with Flora Mac-Ivor, under guard of a party of the Chieftain's men. This step was indeed necessary, Tully-Veolan having become a very un-pleasant, and even dangerous place of residence for an unprotected young lady, on account of its vicinity to the Highlands, and also to one or two villages, which, from aversion as much to the Caterans as zeal for presbytery, had declared themselves on the side of government, and formed irregular bodies of partisans, who had frequent skirmishes with the mountaineers, and sometimes attacked the houses of the Jacobite gentry in the braes, or frontier betwixt the mountain and plain.

"I would propose to you," continued the Baron, "to walk as far as my quarters in the Luckenbooths,[1] and to admire in your passage the High Street, whilk is, beyond a shadow of dubitation, finer than any street, whether in London or Paris. But Rose, poor thing, is sorely discomposed with the firing of the Castle, though I have proved to her from Blondel and Coehorn,[2] that it is impossible a bullet can reach these buildings; and, besides, I have it in charge from his Royal Highness to go to the camp, or leaguer of our army, to see that the men do *conclamare vasa*, that is, truss up their bag and baggage for to-morrow's march."

"That will be easily done by most of us," said Mac-Ivor, laughing.

"Craving your pardon, Colonel Mac-Ivor, not quite so easily as ye seem to opine. I grant most of your folk left the Highlands, expedited as it were, and free from the incumbrance of baggage; but it is unspeakable the quantity of useless sprechery[3] which they have col-lected on their march. I saw one fellow of yours (craving your pardon once more) with a pier-glass[4] upon his back."

"Ay," said Fergus, still in good-humour, "he would have told you, if you had questioned him, *a ganging foot is aye getting.*[5]—But come, my dear Baron, you know as well as I, that a hundred Uhlans,[6] or a single troop of Schmirschitz's Pandours,[7] would make more havoc in a country than the knight of the mirror and all the rest of our clans put together."

---

1 Row of "locked shops" and houses in the High Street, Edinburgh; taken down in 1817 (*OW*, 439).

2 François Blondel (1617-86) and Baron Menno Van Coehoorn (1641-1704) were military engineers (*OW*, 439).

3 Useless booty. Scott glosses "speagheries" as cattle lifting or "paltry booty of small articles" (*WSG*).

4 Mirror.

5 A walking foot is always looking for what it can get.

6 Member of cavalry, originally in the Polish army, then the German (*PW*, 590).

7 Croatian soldiers in the Austrian army with a reputation for brutality (*PW*, 590)

"And that is very true likewise," replied the Baron; "they are, as the heathen author says, *ferociores in aspectu, mitiores in actu*,[1] of a horrid and grim visage, but more benign in demeanour than their physiognomy or aspect might infer.—But I stand here talking to you two youngsters, when I should be in the King's Park."

"But you will dine with Waverley and me on your return? I assure you, Baron, though I can live like a Highlander when needs must, I remember my Paris education, and understand perfectly *faire la meilleure chère*."[2]

"And wha the deil doubts it," quoth the Baron, laughing, "when ye bring only the cookery, and the gude toun must furnish the materials?—Weel, I have some business in the toun too: But I'll join you at three, if the vivers can tarry so long."[3]

So saying, he took leave of his friends, and went to look after the charge which had been assigned him.

CHAPTER XIII.
A Soldier's Dinner.

JAMES OF THE NEEDLE was a man of his word, when whisky was no party to the contract; and upon this occasion Callum Beg, who still thought himself in Waverley's debt, since he had declined accepting compensation at the expense of mine Host of the Candlestick's person, took the opportunity of discharging the obligation, by mounting guard over the hereditary tailor of Sliochd nan Ivor; and, as he expressed himself, "targed him tightly" till the finishing of the job. To rid himself of this restraint, Shemus's needle flew through the tartan like lightning; and as the artist kept chanting some dreadful skirmish of Fin Macoul,[4] he accomplished at least three stitches to the death of every hero. The dress was, therefore, soon ready, for the short coat fitted the wearer, and the rest of the apparel required little adjustment.

Our hero having now fairly assumed the "garb of old Gaul," well calculated as it was to give an appearance of strength to a figure, which, though tall and well-made, was rather elegant than robust, I hope my fair readers will excuse him if he looked at himself in the mirror more than once, and could not help acknowledging that the reflection seemed that of a very handsome young fellow. In fact, there

---

1   "Fierce in appearance, in behavior mild" (*GW*).
2   "To make good cheer" (*PW*, 590).
3   If the food can last so long (*WSG*).
4   Fin Macoul was in Irish folklore "the greatest of all giants" (William Shepard Walsh, *A Handy Book of Curious Information* [Philadelphia: J.B. Lippincott, 1913], 426).

was no disguising it. His light-brown hair,—for he wore no periwig, notwithstanding the universal fashion of the time,—became the bonnet which surmounted it. His person promised firmness and agility, to which the ample folds of the tartan added an air of dignity. His blue eye seemed of that kind,

"Which melted in love, and which kindled in war";

and an air of bashfulness, which was in reality the effect of want of habitual intercourse with the world, gave interest to his features, without injuring their grace or intelligence.

"He's a pratty man—a very pratty man," said Evan Dhu (now Ensign Maccombich) to Fergus's buxom landlady.

"He's vera weel," said the Widow Flockhart, "but no naething sae weel-far'd as your colonel, ensign."

"I wasna comparing them," quoth Evan, "nor was I speaking about his being weel-favoured; but only that Mr Waverley looks clean-made and *deliver*,[1] and like a proper lad o' his quarters, that will not cry barley in a brulzie.[2] And, indeed, he's gleg aneuch[3] at the broadsword and target. I hae played wi' him mysell at Glennaquoich, and sae has Vich Ian Vohr, often of a Sunday afternoon."

"Lord forgie ye, Ensign Maccombich," said the alarmed Presbyterian; "I'm sure the colonel wad never do the like o' that!"

"Hout! hout! Mrs Flockhart," replied the ensign, "we're young blude, ye ken; and young saints, auld deils."

"But will ye fight wi' Sir John Cope the morn, Ensign Maccombich?" demanded Mrs Flockhart of her guest.

"Troth I'se ensure him, an he'll bide us,[4] Mrs Flockhart," replied the Gael.

"And will ye face thae tearing chields, the dragoons,[5] Ensign Maccombich?" again inquired the landlady.

"Claw for claw, as Conan said to Satan, Mrs Flockhart, and the deevil tak the shortest nails."

"And will the colonel venture on the bagganets[6] himsell?"

"Ye may swear it, Mrs Flockhart; the very first man will he be, by Saint Phedar."[7]

---

1 "Free in motion" (*WSG*).
2 "A cry among boys at their violent games for a truce" (*WSG*).
3 He's sharp enough (*WSG*).
4 In truth, I shall get a pledge from him and he'll stay with us.
5 Fierce cavalry soldiers.
6 Bayonets.
7 Peter, form of the Gaelic "Paeder."

"Merciful goodness! And if he's killed amang the red-coats!" exclaimed the soft-hearted widow.

"Troth, if it should sae befall, Mrs Flockhart, I ken ane that will no be living to weep for him. But we maun a' live the day, and have our dinner; and there's Vich Ian Vohr has packed his *dorlach*,[1] and Mr Waverley's wearied wi' majoring yonder afore the muckle pier-glass; and that grey auld stoor[2] carle, the Baron o' Bradwardine, that shot young Ronald of Ballenkeiroch, he's coming down the close[3] wi' that droghling coghling[4] bailie body they ca' Macwhupple, just like the Laird o' Kittlegab's French cook, wi' his turnspit doggie trindling ahint him, and I am as hungry as a gled, my bonny dow; sae bid Kate set on the broo', and do ye put on your pinners,[5] for ye ken Vich Ian Vohr winna sit down till ye be at the head o' the table;—and dinna forget the pint bottle o' brandy, my woman."

This hint produced dinner. Mrs Flockhart, smiling in her weeds[6] like the sun through a mist, took the head of the table, thinking within herself, perhaps, that she cared not how long the rebellion lasted, that brought her into company so much above her usual associates. She was supported by Waverley and the Baron, with the advantage of the Chieftain *vis-à-vis*. The men of peace and of war, that is, Bailie Macwheeble and Ensign Maccombich, after many profound congés to their superiors and each other, took their places on each side of the Chieftain. Their fare was excellent, time, place, and circumstances considered, and Fergus's spirits were extravagantly high. Regardless of danger, and sanguine from temper, youth, and ambition, he saw in imagination all his prospects crowned with success, and was totally indifferent to the probable alternative of a soldier's grave. The Baron apologized slightly for bringing Macwheeble. They had been providing, he said, for the expenses of the campaign. "And, by my faith," said the old man, "as I think this will be my last, so I just end where I began—I hae evermore found the sinews of war, as a learned author calls the *caisse militaire*, mair difficult to come by than either its flesh, blood, or bones."[7]

---

1 "Satchel of arrows; bundle; knapsack" (*WSG*).

2 Stubborn.

3 A narrow way or alley (*AHD*).

4 "Wheezing and blowing" (*WSG*).

5 A turnspit doggie is a "dog kept to turn the roasting-spit by running within a kind of tread wheel connected with it" (*OED*). His dog is trundling behind him; and I am as hungry as a kite, my bonny dove; so ask Kate to set on the soup, and put on your best cap with the lappets.

6 Black mourning clothes of a widow (*AHD*).

7 I have always found the money to support war, as a learned author calls the "military campaign fund," more difficult to come by than either its flesh, blood, or bones (soldiers) (*PW*, 590).

"What! have you raised our only efficient body of cavalry, and got ye none of the louis d'or out of the Doutelle, to help you?"[ppp]

"No, Glennaquoich; cleverer fellows have been before me."

"That's a scandal," said the young Highlander; "but you will share what is left of my subsidy: it will save you an anxious thought to-night, and will be all one to-morrow, for we shall all be provided for, one way or other, before the sun sets." Waverley, blushing deeply, but with great earnestness, pressed the same request.

"I thank ye baith, my good lads," said the Baron, "but I will not infringe upon your peculium.[1] Bailie Macwheeble has provided the sum which is necessary."

Here the Bailie shifted and fidgeted about in his seat, and appeared extremely uneasy. At length, after several preliminary hems, and much tautological[2] expression of his devotion to his honour's service, by night or day, living or dead, he began to insinuate, "that the Banks had removed a' their ready cash into the Castle; that, nae doubt, Sandie Goldie, the silversmith, would do mickle for his honour; but there was little time to get the wadset[3] made out; and, doubtless, if his honour Glennaquoich, or Mr Wauverley, could accommodate"—

"Let me hear of no such nonsense, sir," said the Baron, in a tone which rendered Macwheeble mute, "but proceed as we accorded before dinner, if it be your wish to remain in my service."

To this peremptory order the Bailie, though he felt as if condemned to suffer a transfusion of blood from his own veins into those of the Baron, did not presume to make any reply. After fidgeting a little while longer, however, he addressed himself to Glennaquoich, and told him, if his honour had mair ready siller than was sufficient for his occasions in the field, he could put it out at use for his honour in safe hands, and at great profit, at this time.

At this proposal Fergus laughed heartily, and answered, when he had recovered his breath,—"Many thanks, Bailie; but you must know, it is a general custom among us soldiers to make our landlady our banker.—Here, Mrs Flockhart," said he, taking four or five broad pieces out of a well-filled purse, and tossing the purse itself, with its remaining contents, into her apron, "these will serve my occasions; do you take the rest: be my banker if I live, and my executor if I die; but take care to give something to the Highland cailliachs[qqq] that shall cry the coronach loudest for the last Vich Ian Vohr."

"It is the *testamentum militare*," quoth the Baron, "whilk, amang the

---

1 Property.
2 Needless, repetitive, redundant (*AHD*).
3 Pledge (*WSG*).

Romans, was privilegiate to be nuncupative."[1] But the soft heart of Mrs Flockhart was melted within her at the Chieftain's speech; she set up a lamentable blubbering, and positively refused to touch the bequest, which Fergus was therefore obliged to resume.

"Well, then," said the Chief, "if I fall, it will go to the grenadier that knocks my brains out, and I shall take care he works hard for it."

Bailie Macwheeble was again tempted to put in his oar; for where cash was concerned, he did not willingly remain silent. "Perhaps he had better carry the gowd to Miss Mac-Ivor, in case of mortality, or accidents of war. It might tak the form of a *mortis causa* donation[2] in the young leddie's favour, and wad cost but the scrape of a pen to mak it out."

"The young lady," said Fergus, "should such an event happen, will have other matters to think of than these wretched louis-d'or."

"True—undeniable—there's nae doubt o' that; but your honour kens that a full sorrow"—

"Is endurable by most folk more easily than a hungry one?—True, Bailie, very true; and I believe there may even be some who would be consoled by such a reflection for the loss of the whole existing generation. But there is a sorrow which knows neither hunger nor thirst; and poor Flora"—He paused, and the whole company sympathized in his emotion.

The Baron's thoughts naturally reverted to the unprotected state of his daughter, and the big tear came to the veteran's eye. "If I fall, Macwheeble, you have all my papers and know all my affairs; be just to Rose."

The Bailie was a man of earthly mould, after all; a good deal of dirt and dross[3] about him, undoubtedly, but some kindly and just feelings he had, especially where the Baron or his young mistress were concerned. He set up a lamentable howl. "If that doleful day should come, while Duncan Macwheeble had a boddle,[4] it should be Miss Rose's. He wald scroll for a plack the sheet,[5] or she kenn'd what it was to want; if indeed a' the bonnie baronie o' Bradwardine and Tully-Veolan, with the fortalice and manor-place thereof (he kept sobbing

---

1 "Soldier's will and testament ... allowed to be oral rather than written" (*PW*, 590).

2 A "legal arrangement" whereby property is held by the grantee until the death of the grantor (*PW*, 590).

3 Commonplace, trivial (*AHD*).

4 A copper coin valued at the 6th part of an English penny, equal to two doits, or Scottish pennies" (*WSG*).

5 Would draft, or make a rough copy for a copper coin equivalent to the 3rd part of an English penny of the document (*WSG*).

and whining at every pause), tofts, crofts, mosses, muirs—outfield, infield—buildings—orchards—dovecots—with the right of net and coble[1] in the water and loch of Veolan—teinds,[2] parsonage and vicarage—annexis, connexis—rights of pasturage—fuel, feal,[3] and divot[4]—parts, pendicles,[5] and pertinents whatsoever—(here he had recourse to the end of his long cravat to wipe his eyes, which overflowed, in spite of him, at the ideas which this technical jargon conjured up)—all as more fully described in the proper evidents and titles thereof—and lying within the parish of Bradwardine, and the shire of Perth—if, as aforesaid, they must a' pass from my master's child to Inch-Grabbit, wha's a Whig and a Hanoverian, and be managed by his doer,[6] Jamie Howie, wha's no fit to be a birlieman, let be a bailie."—

The beginning of this lamentation really had something affecting, but the conclusion rendered laughter irresistible. "Never mind, Bailie," said Ensign Maccombich, "for the gude auld times of rugging and riving (pulling and tearing) are come back again, an' Sneckus Mac-Snackus (meaning, probably, annexis, connexis), and a' the rest of your friends, maun gie place to the langest claymore."[7]

"And that claymore shall be ours, Bailie," said the Chieftain, who saw that Macwheeble looked very blank at this intimation.

> "'Well give them the metal our mountain affords,
> Lillibulero,[8] bullen a la,
> And in place of broad-pieces, we'll pay with broadswords,
> Lero, lero, &c.
> With duns and with debts we will soon clear our score,
> Lillibulero, &c.
> For the man that's thus paid will crave payment no more,
> Lero, lero,' &c.[rrr]

But come, Bailie, be not cast down; drink your wine with a joyous heart; the Baron shall return safe and victorious to Tully-Veolan, and

---

1 Flat-bottomed rowboat (*AHD*).
2 Tithes.
3 Sod.
4 Thin sod for thatching (*WSG*).
5 "A small piece of ground or a cottage forming a dependent part of an estate" (*OED*).
6 Factor or agent, steward.
7 Must give way to the longest sword.
8 Song by Thomas Wharton, written in 1688, with music by Henry Purcell. Originally, it contained an anti-Catholic sentiment; in this version, there is an anti-Jacobite sentiment (*OW*, 441).

unite Killancureit's lairdship with his own, since the cowardly half-bred swine will not turn out for the Prince like a gentleman."

"To be sure, they lie maist ewest,"ˢˢˢ said the Bailie, wiping his eyes, "and should naturally fa' under the same factory."[1]

"And I," proceeded the Chieftain, "shall take care of myself, too; for you must know, I have to complete a good work here, by bringing Mrs Flockhart into the bosom of the Catholic church, or at least half way, and that is to your Episcopal meeting-house. O Baron! if you heard her fine counter-tenor admonishing Kate and Matty in the morning, you, who understand music, would tremble at the idea of hearing her shriek in the psalmody of Haddo's Hole."[2]

"Lord forgie you, colonel, how ye rin on! But I hope your honours will tak tea before ye gang to the palace, and I maun gang and mask it for you."[3]

So saying, Mrs Flockhart left the gentlemen to their own conversation, which, as might be supposed, turned chiefly upon the approaching events of the campaign.

CHAPTER XIV.
The Ball.

ENSIGN MACCOMBICH having gone to the Highland camp upon duty, and Bailie Macwheeble having retired to digest his dinner, and Evan Dhu's intimation of martial law, in some blind change-house, Waverley, with the Baron and the Chieftain, proceeded to Holyrood-House. The two last were in full tide of spirits, and the Baron rallied in his way our hero upon the handsome figure which his new dress displayed to advantage. "If you have any design upon the heart of a bonny Scotch lassie, I would premonish you,[4] when you address her, to remember and quote the words of Virgilius:—

'Nunc insanus amor duri me Martis in armis,
    Tela inter media atque adversos detinet hostes:'[5]

---

1 Financial agent (*OED*).
2 A small room at the north side of St. Giles Cathedral in Edinburgh in which Sir John Gordon of Haddo was imprisoned before his execution in 1644 for supporting Charles I (*Proceedings of the Society of Antiquaries of Scotland*, p. 289).
3 Make tea for you.
4 Warn you in advance (*AHD*).
5 "Now a mad passion for the stern god of war keeps me in arms surrounded by weapons and confronting foes," Virgil, *Eclogues* X, 44-45 (*PW*, 591).

Whilk verses Robertson of Struan, Chief of the Clan Donnochy[1] (unless the claims of Lude ought to be preferred *primo loco*), has thus elegantly rendered:

'For cruel love has gartan'd low my leg,
And clad my hurdies in a philabeg.'[2]

Although, indeed, ye wear the trews, a garment whilk I approve maist of the twa, as mair ancient and seemly."

"Or rather," said Fergus, "hear my song:

'She wadna hae a Lowland laird,
        Nor be an English lady;
But she's away with Duncan Græme,
        And he's row'd her in his plaidy.'"

By this time they reached the palace of Holyrood, and were announced respectively as they entered the apartments.

It is but too well known how many gentlemen of rank, education, and fortune, took a concern in the ill-fated and desperate undertaking of 1745. The ladies, also, of Scotland very generally espoused the cause of the gallant and handsome young Prince, who threw himself upon the mercy of his countrymen, rather like a hero of romance than a calculating politician. It is not, therefore, to be wondered that Edward, who had spent the greater part of his life in the solemn seclusion of Waverley-Honour, should have been dazzled at the liveliness and elegance of the scene now exhibited in the long-deserted halls of the Scottish palace. The accompaniments, indeed, fell short of splendour, being such as the confusion and hurry of the time admitted; still, however, the general effect was striking, and, the rank of the company considered, might well be called brilliant.

It was not long before the lover's eye discovered the object of his attachment. Flora Mac-Ivor was in the act of returning to her seat, near the top of the room, with Rose Bradwardine by her side. Among much elegance and beauty, they had attracted a great degree of the public attention, being certainly two of the handsomest women present. The Prince took much notice of both, particularly of Flora, with whom he danced; a preference which she probably owed to her foreign education, and command of the French and Italian languages.

When the bustle attending the conclusion of the dance permitted, Edward, almost intuitively, followed Fergus to the place where Miss

---

1   Alexander Robertson (1670-1749), Jacobite poet.
2   Clad my buttocks in a kilt (*WSG*).

Mac-Ivor was seated. The sensation of hope, with which he had nursed his affection in absence of the beloved object, seemed to vanish in her presence, and, like one striving to recover the particulars of a forgotten dream, he would have given the world at that moment to have recollected the grounds on which he had founded expectations which now seemed so delusive. He accompanied Fergus with downcast eyes, tingling ears, and the feelings of the criminal, who, while the melancholy cart moves slowly through the crowds that have assembled to behold his execution, receives no clear sensation either from the noise which fills his ears, or the tumult on which he casts his wandering look.

Flora seemed a little—a very little—affected and discomposed at his approach. "I bring you an adopted son of Ivor," said Fergus.

"And I receive him as a second brother," replied Flora.

There was a slight emphasis on the word, which would have escaped every ear but one that was feverish with apprehension. It was, however, distinctly marked, and, combined with her whole tone and manner, plainly intimated, "I will never think of Mr Waverley as a more intimate connexion." Edward stopped, bowed, and looked at Fergus, who bit his lip; a movement of anger, which proved that he also had put a sinister interpretation on the reception which his sister had given his friend. "This, then, is an end of my day-dream!" Such was Waverley's first thought, and it was so exquisitely painful as to banish from his cheek every drop of blood.

"Good God!" said Rose Bradwardine, "he is not yet recovered!"

These words, which she uttered with great emotion, were overheard by the Chevalier himself, who stepped hastily forward, and, taking Waverley by the hand, inquired kindly after his health, and added, that he wished to speak with him. By a strong and sudden effort, which the circumstances rendered indispensable, Waverley recovered himself so far as to follow the Chevalier in silence to a recess in the apartment.

Here the Prince detained him some time, asking various questions about the great Tory and Catholic families of England, their connexions, their influence, and the state of their affections towards the house of Stewart. To these queries Edward could not at any time have given more than general answers, and it may be supposed that, in the present state of his feelings, his responses were indistinct even to confusion. The Chevalier smiled once or twice at the incongruity of his replies, but continued the same style of conversation, although he found himself obliged to occupy the principal share of it, until he perceived that Waverley had recovered his presence of mind. It is probable that this long audience was partly meant to further the idea which the Prince desired should be entertained among his followers, that

Waverley was a character of political influence. But it appeared, from his concluding expressions, that he had a different and good-natured motive, personal to our hero, for prolonging the conference. "I cannot resist the temptation," he said, "of boasting of my own discretion as a lady's confidant. You see, Mr Waverley, that I know all, and I assure you I am deeply interested in the affair. But, my good young friend, you must put a more severe restraint upon your feelings. There are many here whose eyes can see as clearly as mine, but the prudence of whose tongues may not be equally trusted."

So saying, he turned easily away, and joined a circle of officers at a few paces' distance, leaving Waverley to meditate upon his parting expression, which, though not intelligible to him in its whole purport, was sufficiently so in the caution which the last word recommended. Making, therefore, an effort to show himself worthy of the interest which his new master had expressed, by instant obedience to his recommendation, he walked up to the spot where Flora and Miss Bradwardine were still seated, and having made his compliments to the latter, he succeeded, even beyond his own expectation, in entering into conversation upon general topics.

If, my dear reader, thou hast ever happened to take post-horses at —, or at — (one at least of which blanks, or more probably both, you will be able to fill up from an inn near your own residence), you must have observed, and doubtless with sympathetic pain, the reluctant agony with which the poor jades at first apply their galled necks to the collars of the harness. But when the irresistible arguments of the post-boy have prevailed upon them to proceed a mile or two, they will become callous to the first sensation; and being *warm in the harness*, as the said post-boy may term it, proceed as if their withers were altogether unwrung.[1] This simile so much corresponds with the state of Waverley's feelings in the course of this memorable evening, that I prefer it (especially as being, I trust, wholly original) to any more splendid illustration, with which Byshe's Art of Poetry[2] might supply me.

Exertion, like virtue, is its own reward; and our hero had, moreover, other stimulating motives for persevering in a display of affected composure and indifference to Flora's obvious unkindness. Pride, which supplies its caustic as an useful, though severe, remedy for the wounds of affection, came rapidly to his aid. Distinguished by the favour of a Prince; destined, he had room to hope, to play a conspicuous part in the revolution which awaited a mighty kingdom; excelling, probably, in mental acquirements, and equalling at least in personal accom-

---

1 As if the high part of the back of a horse was soundly whipped (*AHD*).
2 Edward Bysshe's *The Art of English Poetry* (1702).

plishments, most of the noble and distinguished persons with whom he was now ranked; young, wealthy, and high-born,—could he, or ought he, to droop beneath the frown of a capricious beauty?

> "O nymph, unrelenting and cold as thou art,
>   My bosom is proud as thine own."

With the feeling expressed in these beautiful lines (which, however, were not then written),[ttt] Waverley determined upon convincing Flora that he was not to be depressed by a rejection, in which his vanity whispered that perhaps she did her own prospects as much injustice as his. And, to aid this change of feeling, there lurked the secret and unacknowledged hope, that she might learn to prize his affection more highly, when she did not conceive it to be altogether within her own choice to attract or repulse it. There was a mystic tone of encouragement, also, in the Chevalier's words, though he feared they only referred to the wishes of Fergus in favour of an union between him and his sister. But the whole circumstances of time, place, and incident, combined at once to awaken his imagination, and to call upon him for a manly and decisive tone of conduct, leaving to fate to dispose of the issue. Should he appear to be the only one sad and disheartened on the eve of battle, how greedily would the tale be commented upon by the slander which had been already but too busy with his fame? Never, never, he internally resolved, shall my unprovoked enemies possess such an advantage over my reputation.

Under the influence of these mixed sensations, and cheered at times by a smile of intelligence and approbation from the Prince as he passed by the group, Waverley exerted his powers of fancy, animation, and eloquence, and attracted the general admiration of the company. The conversation gradually assumed the tone best qualified for the display of his talents and acquisitions. The gaiety of the evening was exalted in character, rather than checked, by the approaching dangers of the morrow. All nerves were strung for the future, and prepared to enjoy the present. This mood of mind is highly favourable for the exercise of the powers of imagination, for poetry, and for that eloquence which is allied to poetry. Waverley, as we have elsewhere observed, possessed at times a wonderful flow of rhetoric; and, on the present occasion, he touched more than once the higher notes of feeling, and then again ran off in a wild voluntary of fanciful mirth.[1] He was supported and excited by kindred spirits, who felt the same impulse of mood and time; and even those of more cold and calculating habits were hurried along by the torrent. Many ladies declined the dance,

---

1 A short piece of music, often improvised for a solo instrument (*AHD*).

which still went forward, and, under various pretences, joined the party to which the "handsome young Englishman" seemed to have attached himself. He was presented to several of the first rank, and his manners, which for the present were altogether free from the bashful restraint by which, in a moment of less excitation, they were usually clouded, gave universal delight.

Flora Mac-Ivor appeared to be the only female present who regarded him with a degree of coldness and reserve; yet even she could not suppress a sort of wonder at talents, which, in the course of their acquaintance, she had never seen displayed with equal brilliancy and impressive effect. I do not know whether she might not feel a momentary regret at having taken so decisive a resolution upon the addresses of a lover, who seemed fitted so well to fill a high place in the highest stations of society. Certainly she had hitherto accounted among the incurable deficiencies of Edward's disposition, the *mauvaise honte*,[1] which, as she had been educated in the first foreign circles, and was little acquainted with the shyness of English manners, was, in her opinion, too nearly related to timidity and imbecility of disposition. But if a passing wish occurred that Waverley could have rendered himself uniformly thus amiable and attractive, its influence was momentary; for circumstances had arisen since they met, which rendered, in her eyes, the resolution she had formed respecting him, final and irrevocable.

With opposite feelings, Rose Bradwardine bent her whole soul to listen. She felt a secret triumph at the public tribute paid to one, whose merit she had learned to prize too early and too fondly. Without a thought of jealousy, without a feeling of fear, pain, or doubt, and undisturbed by a single selfish consideration, she resigned herself to the pleasure of observing the general murmur of applause. When Waverley spoke, her ear was exclusively filled with his voice; when others answered, her eye took its turn of observation, and seemed to watch his reply. Perhaps the delight which she experienced in the course of that evening, though transient, and followed by much sorrow, was in its nature the most pure and disinterested which the human mind is capable of enjoying.

"Baron," said the Chevalier, "I would not trust my mistress in the company of your young friend. He is really, though perhaps somewhat romantic, one of the most fascinating young men whom I have ever seen."

"And by my honour, sir," replied the Baron, "the lad can sometimes be as dowff[2] as a sexagenary like myself. If your Royal Highness had

---

1   Embarrassment.
2   Dull (*WSG*).

seen him dreaming and dozing about the banks of Tully-Veolan like an hypochondriac person, or, as Burton's Anatomia[1] hath it, a phrenesiac or lethargic patient, you would wonder where he hath sae suddenly acquired all this fine sprack[2] festivity and jocularity."

"Truly," said Fergus Mac-Ivor, "I think it can only be the inspiration of the tartans; for, though Waverley be always a young fellow of sense and honour, I have hitherto often found him a very absent and inattentive companion."

"We are the more obliged to him," said the Prince, "for having reserved for this evening qualities which even such intimate friends had not discovered.—But come, gentlemen, the night advances, and the business of to-morrow must be early thought upon. Each take charge of his fair partner, and honour a small refreshment with your company."

He led the way to another suite of apartments, and assumed the seat and canopy at the head of a long range of tables, with an air of dignity mingled with courtesy, which well became his high birth and lofty pretensions. An hour had hardly flown away when the musicians played the signal for parting, so well known in Scotland.[uuu]

"Good night, then," said the Chevalier, rising; "Good night, and joy be with you!—Good night, fair ladies, who have so highly honoured a proscribed and banished Prince.—Good night, my brave friends; may the happiness we have this evening experienced be an omen of our return to these our paternal halls, speedily and in triumph, and of many and many future meetings of mirth and pleasure in the palace of Holyrood!"

When the Baron of Bradwardine afterwards mentioned this adieu of the Chevalier, he never failed to repeat, in a melancholy tone,

> "Audiit, et voti Phœbus succedere partem
> Mente dedit; partem volucres dispersit in auras";[3]

"which," as he added, "is weel rendered into English metre by my friend Bangour:[4]

> 'Ae half the prayer wi' Phœbus grace did find,
> The t'other half he whistled down the wind.'"

---

1 Robert Burton (1577-1640), *The Anatomy of Melancholy*.
2 Spruce, sprightly (*WSG*).
3 Virgil, *Aeneid*, xi, 794-95.
4 William Hamilton of Bangour (1704-54), a Scottish Jacobite poet who wrote "The Braes of Yarrow." Lamont suggests that although Scott attributes these lines to Hamilton, they have not been found in his works (*OW*, 442).

CHAPTER XV.
The March.

THE conflicting passions and exhausted feelings of Waverley had resigned him to late but sound repose. He was dreaming of Glennaquoich, and had transferred to the halls of Ian nan Chaistel the festal train which so lately graced those of Holyrood. The pibroch too was distinctly heard; and this at least was no delusion, for the "proud step of the chief piper" of the "chlain Mac-Ivor" was perambulating the court before the door of his Chieftain's quarters, and, as Mrs Flockhart, apparently no friend to his minstrelsy, was pleased to observe, "garring the very stane-and-lime wa's dingle wi' his screeching."[1] Of course it soon became too powerful for Waverley's dream, with which it had at first rather harmonized.

The sound of Callum's brogues in his apartment (for Mac-Ivor had again assigned Waverley to his care) was the next note of parting. "Winna yere honour bang up? Vich Ian Vohr and ta Prince are awa to the lang green glen ahint the clachan,[2] tat they ca' the King's Park,ᵛᵛᵛ and mony ane's on his ain shanks the day that will be carried on ither folk's ere night."

Waverley sprung up, and, with Callum's assistance and instructions, adjusted his tartans in proper costume. Callum told him also, "tat his leather *dorlach* wi' the lock on her was come frae Doune, and she was awa again in the wain wi' Vich Ian Vohr's walise."[3]

By this periphrasis Waverley readily apprehended his portmanteau was intended. He thought upon the mysterious packet of the maid of the cavern, which seemed always to escape him when within his very grasp. But this was no time for indulgence of curiosity; and having declined Mrs Flockhart's compliment of a *morning*, *i.e.*, a matutinal dram, being probably the only man in the Chevalier's army by whom such a courtesy would have been rejected, he made his adieus, and departed with Callum.

"Callum," said he, as they proceeded down a dirty close to gain the southern skirts of the Canongate, "what shall I do for a horse?"

"Ta deil ane ye maun think o'," said Callum. "Vich Ian Vohr's marching on foot at the head o' his kin (not to say ta Prince, wha does the like), wi' his target on his shoulder; and ye maun e'en be neighbour-like."

---

1 Causing the very mortar or cement of the buildings to ring with his screeching (*WSG*).
2 Behind the village.
3 His valise was in the farm wagon.

"And so I will, Callum—give me my target;—so, there we are fixed. How does it look?"

"Like the bra' Highlander tat's painted on the board afore the mickle change-house they ca' Luckie Middlemass's," answered Callum; meaning, I must observe, a high compliment, for, in his opinion, Luckie Middlemass's sign was an exquisite specimen of art. Waverley, however, not feeling the full force of this polite simile, asked him no farther questions.

Upon extricating themselves from the mean and dirty suburbs of the metropolis, and emerging into the open air, Waverley felt a renewal both of health and spirits, and turned his recollection with firmness upon the events of the preceding evening, and with hope and resolution towards those of the approaching day.

When he had surmounted a small craggy eminence, called St Leonard's Hill, the King's Park, or the hollow between the mountain of Arthur's Seat, and the rising grounds on which the southern part of Edinburgh is now built, lay beneath him, and displayed a singular and animating prospect. It was occupied by the army of the Highlanders, now in the act of preparing for their march. Waverley had already seen something of the kind at the hunting-match which he attended with Fergus Mac-Ivor; but this was on a scale of much greater magnitude, and incomparably deeper interest. The rocks, which formed the background of the scene, and the very sky itself, rang with the clang of the bagpipers, summoning forth, each with his appropriate pibroch, his chieftain and clan. The mountaineers, rousing themselves from their couch under the canopy of heaven, with the hum and bustle of a confused and irregular multitude, like bees alarmed and arming in their hives, seemed to possess all the pliability of movement fitted to execute military manœvres. Their motions appeared spontaneous and confused, but the result was order and regularity; so that a general must have praised the conclusion, though a martinet[1] might have ridiculed the method by which it was attained.

The sort of complicated medley created by the hasty arrangements of the various clans under their respective banners, for the purpose of getting into the order of march, was in itself a gay and lively spectacle. They had no tents to strike, having generally, and by choice, slept upon the open field, although the autumn was now waning, and the nights began to be frosty. For a little space, while they were getting into order, there was exhibited a changing, fluctuating, and confused appearance of waving tartans and floating plumes, and of banners displaying the proud gathering word of Clanronald, *Ganion Coheriga*—

---

1 A rigid military disciplinarian (*AHD*).

(Gainsay who dares); *Loch-Sloy*, the watchword of the Mac-Farlanes; *Forth, fortune, and fill the fetters*, the motto of the Marquis of Tullibardine; *Bydand*, that of Lord Lewis Gordon; and the appropriate signal words and emblems of many other chieftains and clans.

At length the mixed and wavering multitude arranged themselves into a narrow and dusky column of great length, stretching through the whole extent of the valley. In the front of the column the standard of the Chevalier was displayed, bearing a red cross upon a white ground, with the motto *Tandem Triumphans*.[1] The few cavalry, being chiefly Lowland gentry, with their domestic servants and retainers, formed the advanced guard of the army; and their standards, of which they had rather too many in respect of their numbers, were seen waving upon the extreme verge of the horizon. Many horsemen of this body, among whom Waverley accidentally remarked Balmawhapple, and his lieutenant, Jinker (which last, however, had been reduced, with several others, by the advice of the Baron of Bradwardine, to the situation of what he called reformed officers, or reformadoes), added to the liveliness, though by no means to the regularity, of the scene, by galloping their horses as fast forward as the press would permit,[2] to join their proper station in the van. The fascinations of the Circes of the High Street,[3] and the potations of strength with which they had been drenched over night, had probably detained these heroes within the walls of Edinburgh somewhat later than was consistent with their morning duty. Of such loiterers, the prudent took the longer and circuitous, but more open route, to attain their place in the march, by keeping at some distance from the infantry, and making their way through the enclosures to the right, at the expense of leaping over or pulling down the dry-stone fences. The irregular appearance and vanishing of these small parties of horsemen, as well as the confusion occasioned by those who endeavoured, though generally without effect, to press to the front through the crowd of Highlanders, maugre their curses, oaths, and opposition, added to the picturesque wildness, what it took from the military regularity, of the scene.

While Waverley gazed upon this remarkable spectacle, rendered yet more impressive by the occasional discharge of cannon-shot from the Castle at the Highland guards as they were withdrawn from its vicinity to join their main body, Callum, with his usual freedom of interference, reminded him that Vich Ian Vohr's folk were nearly at the head of the column of march which was still distant, and that "they would gang very fast after the cannon fired." Thus admonished, Waverley walked briskly

---

1 Triumphant in the end.
2 They moved forward as fast as the crowd would allow.
3 Prostitutes in Edinburgh.

forward, yet often casting a glance upon the darksome clouds of warriors who were collected before and beneath him. A nearer view, indeed, rather diminished the effect impressed on the mind by the more distant appearance of the army. The leading men of each clan were well armed with broadsword, target, and fusee,[1] to which all added the dirk, and most the steel pistol. But these consisted of gentlemen, that is, relations of the chief, however distant, and who had an immediate title to his countenance and protection. Finer and hardier men could not have been selected out of any army in Christendom; while the free and independent habits which each possessed, and which each was yet so well taught to subject to the command of his chief, and the peculiar mode of discipline adopted in Highland warfare, rendered them equally formidable by their individual courage and high spirit, and from their rational conviction of the necessity of acting in unison, and of giving their national mode of attack the fullest opportunity of success.

But, in a lower rank to these, there were found individuals of an inferior description, the common peasantry of the Highland country, who, although they did not allow themselves to be so called, and claimed often, with apparent truth, to be of more ancient descent than the masters whom they served, bore, nevertheless, the livery of extreme penury, being indifferently accoutred, and worse armed, half naked, stinted in growth, and miserable in aspect. Each important clan had some of those Helots[2] attached to them;—thus, the Mac-Couls, though tracing their descent from Comhal, the father of Finn or Fingal, were a sort of Gibeonites, or hereditary servants to the Stewarts of Appine; the Macbeths, descended from the unhappy monarch of that name, were subjects to the Morays, and clan Donnochy, or Robertsons of Athole; and many other examples might be given, were it not for the risk of hurting any pride of clanship which may yet be left, and thereby drawing a Highland tempest into the shop of my publisher. Now these same Helots, though forced into the field by the arbitrary authority of the chieftains under whom they hewed wood and drew water, were, in general, very sparingly fed, ill dressed, and worse armed. The latter circumstance was indeed owing chiefly to the general disarming act, which had been carried into effect ostensibly through the whole Highlands, although most of the chieftains contrived to elude its influence, by retaining the weapons of their own immediate clansmen, and delivering up those of less value, which they collected from these inferior satellites. It followed, as a matter of course, that, as we have already hinted, many of these poor fellows were brought to the field in a very wretched condition.

---

1 A combustible fuse for detonating explosives (*AHD*).

2 "Serfs of the Spartans who attended them in war" (*OW*, 442).

From this it happened, that, in bodies, the van of which were admirably well armed in their own fashion, the rear resembled actual banditti. Here was a pole-axe, there a sword without a scabbard; here a gun without a lock, there a scythe set strait upon a pole; and some had only their dirks, and bludgeons or stakes pulled out of hedges. The grim, uncombed, and wild appearance of these men, most of whom gazed with all the admiration of ignorance upon the most ordinary production of domestic art, created surprise in the Lowlands, but it also created terror. So little was the condition of the Highlands known at that late period,[1] that the character and appearance of their population, while thus sallying forth as military adventurers, conveyed to the south-country Lowlanders as much surprise as if an invasion of African Negroes, or Esquimaux Indians, had issued forth from the northern mountains of their own native country. It cannot therefore be wondered if Waverley, who had hitherto judged of the Highlanders generally, from the samples which the policy of Fergus had from time to time exhibited, should have felt damped and astonished at the daring attempt of a body not then exceeding four thousand men, and of whom not above half the number, at the utmost, were armed, to change the fate, and alter the dynasty, of the British kingdoms.

As he moved along the column, which still remained stationary, an iron gun, the only piece of artillery possessed by the army which meditated so important a revolution, was fired as the signal of march. The Chevalier had expressed a wish to leave this useless piece of ordnance behind him; but, to his surprise, the Highland chiefs interposed to solicit that it might accompany their march, pleading the prejudices of their followers, who, little accustomed to artillery, attached a degree of absurd importance to this field-piece, and expected it would contribute essentially to a victory which they could only owe to their own muskets and broadswords. Two or three French artillerymen were therefore appointed to the management of this military engine, which was drawn along by a string of Highland ponies, and was, after all, only used for the purpose of firing signals.[www]

No sooner was its voice heard upon the present occasion, than the whole line was in motion. A wild cry of joy from the advancing battalions rent the air, and was then lost in the shrill clangour of the bagpipes, as the sound of these, in their turn, was partially drowned by the heavy tread of so many men put at once into motion. The banners glittered and shook as they moved forward, and the horse hastened to occupy their station as the advanced guard, and to push on reconnoitring parties to ascertain and report the motions of the enemy.

---

1   Refers to the relative isolation of the Highlands and the resultant unfamiliarity of Lowlanders with the people living there.

They vanished from Waverley's eye as they wheeled round the base of Arthur's Seat, under the remarkable ridge of basaltic rocks which fronts the little lake of Duddingston.

The infantry followed in the same direction, regulating their pace by another body which occupied a road more to the southward. It cost Edward some exertion of activity to attain the place which Fergus's followers occupied in the line of march.

CHAPTER XVI.
An Incident gives rise to unavailing Reflections.

WHEN Waverley reached that part of the column which was filled by the clan of Mac-Ivor, they halted, formed, and received him with a triumphant flourish upon the bagpipes, and a loud shout of the men, most of whom knew him personally, and were delighted to see him in the dress of their country and of their sept. "You shout," said a Highlander of a neighbouring clan to Evan Dhu, "as if the Chieftain were just come to your head."

"*Mar e Bran is e a brathair,* If it be not Bran, it is Bran's brother," was the proverbial reply of Maccombich.[xxx]

"O, then, it is the handsome Sassenach Duinhé-wassel, that is to be married to Lady Flora?"

"That may be, or it may not be; and it is neither your matter nor mine, Gregor."

Fergus advanced to embrace the volunteer, and afford him a warm and hearty welcome; but he thought it necessary to apologize for the diminished numbers of his battalion (which did not exceed three hundred men), by observing, he had sent a good many out upon parties.

The real fact, however, was, that the defection of Donald Bean Lean had deprived him of at least thirty hardy fellows, whose services he had fully reckoned upon, and that many of his occasional adherents had been recalled by their several chiefs to the standards to which they most properly owed their allegiance. The rival chief of the great northern branch also of his own clan, had mustered his people, although he had not yet declared either for the government or for the Chevalier, and by his intrigues had in some degree diminished the force with which Fergus took the field. To make amends for these disappointments, it was universally admitted that the followers of Vich Ian Vohr, in point of appearance, equipment, arms, and dexterity in using them, equalled the most choice troops which followed the standard of Charles Edward. Old Ballenkeiroch acted as his major; and, with the other officers who had known Waverley when at Glennaquoich, gave our hero a cordial reception, as the sharer of their future dangers and expected honours.

The route pursued by the Highland army, after leaving the village of Duddingstone, was, for some time, the common post-road betwixt Edinburgh and Haddington, until they crossed the Esk, at Mussel-burgh, when, instead of keeping the low grounds towards the sea, they turned more inland, and occupied the brow of the eminence called Carberry Hill, a place already distinguished in Scottish history, as the spot where the lovely Mary surrendered herself to her insurgent sub-jects.[1] This direction was chosen because the Chevalier had received notice that the army of the government, arriving by sea from Aberdeen, had landed at Dunbar, and quartered the night before to the west of Haddington, with the intention of falling down towards the sea-side, and approaching Edinburgh by the lower coast-road. By keeping the height, which overhung that road in many places, it was hoped the Highlanders might find an opportunity of attacking them to advantage. The army therefore halted upon the ridge of Carberry Hill, both to refresh the soldiers, and as a central situation, from which their march could be directed to any point that the motions of the enemy might render most advisable. While they remained in this position, a messen-ger arrived in haste to desire Mac-Ivor to come to the Prince, adding, that their advanced post had had a skirmish with some of the enemy's cavalry, and that the Baron of Bradwardine had sent in a few prisoners.

Waverley walked forward out of the line to satisfy his curiosity, and soon observed five or six of the troopers, who, covered with dust, had galloped in to announce that the enemy were in full march westward along the coast. Passing still a little farther on, he was struck with a groan which issued from a hovel. He approached the spot, and heard a voice, in the provincial English of his native county, which endeav-oured, though frequently interrupted by pain, to repeat the Lord's Prayer. The voice of distress always found a ready answer in our hero's bosom. He entered the hovel, which seemed to be intended for what is called, in the pastoral counties of Scotland, a *smearing-house*;[2] and in its obscurity Edward could only at first discern a sort of red bundle; for those who had stripped the wounded man of his arms, and part of his clothes, had left him the dragoon-cloak in which he was enveloped.

"For the love of God," said the wounded man, as he heard Waver-ley's step, "give me a single drop of water!"

"You shall have it," answered Waverley, at the same time raising him in his arms, bearing him to the door of the hut, and giving him some drink from his flask.

---

1 The arrest of Mary Queen of Scots in 1567 took place at Carberry Hill after she had married Bothwell swiftly on the heels of the murder of her second husband, Darnley.

2 Place used for smearing sheep's wool with grease and tar (*OW*, 442).

"I should know that voice," said the man; but, looking on Waverley's dress with a bewildered look,—"no, this is not the young squire!"

This was the common phrase by which Edward was distinguished on the estate of Waverley-Honour, and the sound now thrilled to his heart with the thousand recollections which the well-known accents of his native country had already contributed to awaken. "Houghton!" he said, gazing on the ghastly features which death was fast disfiguring, "can this be you?"

"I never thought to hear an English voice again," said the wounded man; "they left me to live or die here as I could, when they found I would say nothing about the strength of the regiment. But, O squire! how could you stay from us so long, and let us be tempted by that fiend of the pit, Ruffin?—we should have followed you through flood and fire, to be sure."

"Ruffin! I assure you, Houghton, you have been vilely imposed upon."

"I often thought so," said Houghton, "though they showed us your very seal; and so Timms was shot, and I was reduced to the ranks."

"Do not exhaust your strength in speaking," said Edward; "I will get you a surgeon presently."

He saw Mac-Ivor approaching, who was now returning from headquarters, where he had attended a council of war, and hastened to meet him. "Brave news!" shouted the Chief; "we shall be at it in less than two hours. The Prince has put himself at the head of the advance, and, as he drew his sword, called out, 'My friends, I have thrown away the scabbard.' Come, Waverley, we move instantly."

"A moment,—a moment; this poor prisoner is dying;—where shall I find a surgeon?"

"Why, where should you? We have none, you know, but two or three French fellows, who, I believe, are little better than *garçons apothicaires*."[1]

"But the man will bleed to death."

"Poor fellow!" said Fergus, in a momentary fit of compassion; then instantly added, "But it will be a thousand men's fate before night; so come along."

"I cannot; I tell you he is a son of a tenant of my uncle's."

"O, if he's a follower of yours, he must be looked to; I'll send Callum to you; but *diaoul!—ceade millia molligheart*,"[2] continued the impatient Chieftain,—"what made an old soldier, like Bradwardine, send dying men here to cumber us?"

Callum came with his usual alertness; and, indeed, Waverley rather

---

1 Chemist's assistants (*GW*).
2 O the devil! A hundred thousand curses (*GW*).

gained than lost in the opinion of the Highlanders, by his anxiety about the wounded man. They would not have understood the general philanthropy, which rendered it almost impossible for Waverley to have passed any person in such distress; but, as apprehending that the sufferer was one of the *following,*[yyy] they unanimously allowed that Waverley's conduct was that of a kind and considerate chieftain, who merited the attachment of his people. In about a quarter of an hour poor Humphrey breathed his last, praying his young master, when he returned to Waverley-Honour, to be kind to old Job Houghton and his dame, and conjuring him not to fight with these wild petticoat-men against old England.

When his last breath was drawn, Waverley, who had beheld with sincere sorrow, and no slight tinge of remorse, the final agonies of mortality, now witnessed for the first time, commanded Callum to remove the body into the hut. This the young Highlander performed, not without examining the pockets of the defunct, which, however, he remarked had been pretty well spung'd.[1] He took the cloak, however, and proceeding with the provident caution of a spaniel hiding a bone, concealed it among some furze, and carefully marked the spot, observing, that if he chanced to return that way, it would be an excellent rokelay[2] for his auld mother Elspat.

It was by a considerable exertion that they regained their place in the marching column, which was now moving rapidly forward to occupy the high grounds above the village of Tranent, between which and the sea lay the purposed march of the opposite army.

This melancholy interview with his late sergeant forced many unavailing and painful reflections upon Waverley's mind. It was clear, from the confession of the man, that Colonel Gardiner's proceedings had been strictly warranted, and even rendered indispensable, by the steps taken in Edward's name to induce the soldiers of his troop to mutiny. The circumstance of the seal, he now, for the first time, recollected, and that he had lost it in the cavern of the robber, Bean Lean. That the artful villain had secured it, and used it as the means of carrying on an intrigue in the regiment for his own purposes, was sufficiently evident; and Edward had now little doubt that in the packet placed in his portmanteau by his daughter, he should find farther light upon his proceedings. In the meanwhile, the repeated expostulation of Houghton,—"Ah, squire, why did you leave us?" rung like a knell in his ears.

"Yes," he said, "I have indeed acted towards you with thoughtless cruelty. I brought you from your paternal fields, and the protection of

1 Pockets picked.
2 Short cloak.

a generous and kind landlord, and when I had subjected you to all the rigour of military discipline, I shunned to bear my own share of the burden, and wandered from the duties I had undertaken, leaving alike those whom it was my business to protect, and my own reputation, to suffer under the artifices of villainy. O, indolence and indecision of mind! if not in yourselves vices, to how much exquisite misery and mischief do you frequently prepare the way!"

CHAPTER XVII.
The Eve of Battle.

ALTHOUGH the Highlanders marched on very fast, the sun was declining when they arrived upon the brow of those high grounds which command an open and extensive plain stretching northward to the sea, on which are situated, but at a considerable distance from each other, the small villages of Seaton and Cockenzie, and the larger one of Preston. One of the low coast-roads to Edinburgh passed through this plain, issuing upon it from the enclosures of Seaton-House, and at the town or village of Preston again entering the defiles of an enclosed country. By this way the English general had chosen to approach the metropolis, both as most commodious for his cavalry, and being probably of opinion that, by doing so, he would meet in front with the Highlanders advancing from Edinburgh in the opposite direction. In this he was mistaken; for the sound judgment of the Chevalier, or of those to whose advice he listened, left the direct passage free, but occupied the strong ground by which it was over-looked and commanded.

When the Highlanders reached the heights above the plain described, they were immediately formed in array of battle along the brow of the hill. Almost at the same instant the van of the English appeared issuing from among the trees and enclosures of Seaton, with the purpose of occupying the level plain between the high ground and the sea; the space which divided the armies being only about half a mile in breadth. Waverley could plainly see the squadrons of dragoons issue, one after another, from the defiles, with their videttes in front, and form upon the plain, with their front opposed to that of the Prince's army. They were followed by a train of field-pieces, which, when they reached the flank of the dragoons, were also brought into line, and pointed against the heights. The march was continued by three or four regiments of infantry marching in open column, their fixed bayonets showing like successive hedges of steel, and their arms glancing like lightning, as, at a signal given, they also at once wheeled up, and were placed in direct opposition to the Highlanders. A second train of artillery, with another regiment of horse, closed the long march, and formed on the left flank of the infantry, the whole line facing southward.

While the English army went through these evolutions, the Highlanders showed equal promptitude and zeal for battle. As fast as the clans came upon the ridge which fronted their enemy, they were formed into line, so that both armies got into complete order of battle at the same moment. When this was accomplished, the Highlanders set up a tremendous yell, which was re-echoed by the heights behind them. The regulars, who were in high spirits, returned a loud shout of defiance, and fired one or two of their cannon upon an advanced post of the Highlanders. The latter displayed great earnestness to proceed instantly to the attack, Evan Dhu urging to Fergus, by way of argument, that "the *sidier roy* was tottering like an egg upon a staff, and that they had a' the vantage of the onset, for even a haggis[1] (God bless her!) could charge down hill."

But the ground through which the mountaineers must have descended, although not of great extent, was impracticable in its character, being not only marshy, but intersected with walls of dry stone, and traversed in its whole length by a very broad and deep ditch, circumstances which must have given the musketry of the regulars dreadful advantages, before the mountaineers could have used their swords, on which they were taught to rely. The authority of the commanders was therefore interposed to curb the impetuosity of the Highlanders, and only a few marksmen were sent down the descent to skirmish with the enemy's advanced posts, and to reconnoitre the ground.

Here then was a military spectacle of no ordinary interest, or usual occurrence. The two armies, so different in aspect and discipline, yet each admirably trained in its own peculiar mode of war, upon whose conflict the temporary fate at least of Scotland appeared to depend, now faced each other like two gladiators in the arena, each meditating upon the mode of attacking their enemy. The leading officers, and general's staff of each army, could be distinguished in front of their lines, busied with spy-glasses to watch each other's motions, and occupied in dispatching the orders and receiving the intelligence conveyed by the aides-de-camp and orderly men, who gave life to the scene by galloping along in different directions, as if the fate of the day depended upon the speed of their horses. The space between the armies was at times occupied by the partial and irregular contest of individual sharp-shooters, and a hat or bonnet was occasionally seen to fall, as a wounded man was borne off by his

---

1 A dish made with the intestines of a sheep, oatmeal, suet, onions, etc., boiled inside the sheep's stomach.

comrades. These, however, were but trifling skirmishes, for it suited the views of neither party to advance in that direction. From the neighbouring hamlets, the peasantry cautiously showed themselves, as if watching the issue of the expected engagement; and at no great distance in the bay were two square-rigged vessels, bearing the English flag, whose tops and yards were crowded with less timid spectators.

When this awful pause had lasted for a short time, Fergus, with another chieftain, received orders to detach their clans towards the village of Preston, in order to threaten the right flank of Cope's army, and compel him to a change of position. To enable him to execute these orders, the Chief of Glennaquoich occupied the churchyard of Tranent, a commanding situation, and a convenient place, as Evan Dhu remarked, "for any gentleman who might have the misfortune to be killed, and chanced to be curious about Christian burial." To check or dislodge this party, the English general detached two guns, escorted by a strong party of cavalry. They approached so near, that Waverley could plainly recognise the standard of the troop he had formerly commanded, and hear the trumpets and kettle-drums sound the signal of advance, which he had so often obeyed. He could hear, too, the well-known word given in the English dialect, by the equally well-distinguished voice of the commanding officer, for whom he had once felt so much respect. It was at that instant, that, looking around him, he saw the wild dress and appearance of his Highland associates, heard their whispers in an uncouth and unknown language, looked upon his own dress, so unlike that which he had worn from his infancy, and wished to awake from what seemed at the moment a dream, strange, horrible, and unnatural. "Good God!" he muttered, "am I then a traitor to my country, a renegade to my standard, and a foe, as that poor dying wretch expressed himself, to my native England!"

Ere he could digest or smother the recollection, the tall military form of his late commander came full in view, for the purpose of reconnoitring. "I can hit him now," said Callum, cautiously raising his fusee over the wall under which he lay couched, at scarce sixty yards' distance.

Edward felt as if he was about to see a parricide committed in his presence; for the venerable grey hair and striking countenance of the veteran recalled the almost paternal respect with which his officers universally regarded him. But ere he could say "Hold!" an aged Highlander, who lay beside Callum Beg, stopped his arm. "Spare your shot," said the seer, "his hour is not yet come. But let him beware of to-morrow—I see his winding-sheet high upon his breast."

Callum, flint to other considerations, was penetrable to superstition. He turned pale at the words of the *Taishatr*,[1] and recovered his piece. Colonel Gardiner, unconscious of the danger he had escaped, turned his horse round, and rode slowly back to the front of his regiment.

By this time the regular army had assumed a new line, with one flank inclined towards the sea, and the other resting upon the village of Preston; and, as similar difficulties occurred in attacking their new position, Fergus and the rest of the detachment were recalled to their former post. This alteration created the necessity of a corresponding change in General Cope's army, which was again brought into a line parallel with that of the Highlanders. In these manœuvres on both sides the day-light was nearly consumed, and both armies prepared to rest upon their arms for the night in the lines which they respectively occupied.

"There will be nothing done to-night," said Fergus to his friend Waverley; "ere we wrap ourselves in our plaids, let us go see what the Baron is doing in the rear of the line."

When they approached his post, they found the good old careful officer, after having sent out his night patrols, and posted his sentinels, engaged in reading the Evening Service of the Episcopal Church to the remainder of his troop. His voice was loud and sonorous, and though his spectacles upon his nose, and the appearance of Saunders Saunderson, in military array, performing the functions of clerk, had something ludicrous, yet the circumstances of danger in which they stood, the military costume of the audience, and the appearance of their horses, saddled and picquetted[2] behind them, gave an impressive and solemn effect to the office of devotion.

"I have confessed to-day, ere you were awake," whispered Fergus to Waverley; "yet I am not so strict a Catholic as to refuse to join in this good man's prayers."

Edward assented, and they remained till the Baron had concluded the service.

As he shut the book, "Now, lads," said he, "have at them in the morning, with heavy hands and light consciences." He then kindly greeted Mac-Ivor and Waverley, who requested to know his opinion of their situation. "Why, you know Tacitus saith, '*In rebus bellicis maxime dominatur Fortuna*,'[3] which is equiponderate with our vernacular adage, 'Luck can maist in the mellee.' But credit me, gentlemen, yon

---

1 A person who has second sight (*GW*).
2 Saddled and lined up ready for action (*AHD*).
3 "In matters of war Fortune mostly rules," Tacitus (c. 55-c. 117 CE), Roman historian (*PW*, 591).

man is not a deacon o' his craft. He damps the spirits of the poor lads he commands, by keeping them on the defensive, whilk of itself implies inferiority or fear. Now will they lie on their arms yonder, as anxious and as ill at ease as a toad under a harrow, while our men will be quite fresh and blithe for action in the morning. Well, good night.— One thing troubles me, but if to-morrow goes well off, I will consult you about it, Glennaquoich."—

"I could almost apply to Mr Bradwardine the character which Henry gives of Fluellen," said Waverley, as his friend and he walked towards their *bivouac*:[1]

> "Though it appears a little out of fashion,
> There is much care and valour in this 'Scotchman.'"[2]

"He has seen much service," answered Fergus, "and one is sometimes astonished to find how much nonsense and reason are mingled in his composition. I wonder what can be troubling his mind—probably something about Rose.—Hark! the English are setting their watch."

The roll of the drum and shrill accompaniment of the fifes swelled up the hill—died away—resumed its thunder—and was at length hushed. The trumpets and kettle-drums of the cavalry were next heard to perform the beautiful and wild point of war appropriated as a signal for that piece of nocturnal duty, and then finally sunk upon the wind with a shrill and mournful cadence.

The friends, who had now reached their post, stood and looked round them ere they lay down to rest. The western sky twinkled with stars, but a frost-mist, rising from the ocean, covered the eastern horizon, and rolled in white wreaths along the plain where the adverse army lay couched upon their arms. Their advanced posts were pushed as far as the side of the great ditch at the bottom of the descent, and had kindled large fires at different intervals, gleaming with obscure and hazy lustre through the heavy fog which encircled them with a doubtful halo.

The Highlanders, "thick as leaves in Valumbrosa,"[3] lay stretched upon the ridge of the hill, buried (excepting their sentinels) in the most profound repose. "How many of these brave fellows will sleep more soundly before to-morrow night, Fergus!" said Waverley, with an involuntary sigh.

---

1   Open-air camp.
2   Shakespeare, *Henry V*, IV.i.85-86; "Scotchman" is substituted for "Welshman" here.
3   From Milton's *Paradise Lost*, Book I, lines 302-03, referring to Satan and the other fallen angels in the pit of hell, Vallombrosa.

"You must not think of that," answered Fergus, whose ideas were entirely military. "You must only think of your sword, and by whom it was given. All other reflections are now TOO LATE."

With the opiate contained in this undeniable remark, Edward endeavoured to lull the tumult of his conflicting feelings. The Chieftain and he, combining their plaids, made a comfortable and warm couch. Callum, sitting down at their head (for it was his duty to watch upon the immediate person of the Chief), began a long mournful song in Gaelic, to a low and uniform tune, which, like the sound of the wind at a distance, soon lulled them to sleep.

CHAPTER XVIII.
The Conflict.

WHEN Fergus Mac-Ivor and his friend had slept for a few hours, they were awakened, and summoned to attend the Prince. The distant village-clock was heard to toll three as they hastened to the place where he lay. He was already surrounded by his principal officers and the chiefs of clans. A bundle of pease-straw,[1] which had been lately his couch, now served for his seat. Just as Fergus reached the circle, the consultation had broken up. "Courage, my brave friends!" said the Chevalier, "and each one put himself instantly at the head of his command; a faithful friend*zzz* has offered to guide us by a practicable, though narrow and circuitous route, which, sweeping to our right, traverses the broken ground and morass, and enables us to gain the firm and open plain, upon which the enemy are lying. This difficulty surmounted, Heaven and your good swords must do the rest."

The proposal spread unanimous joy, and each leader hastened to get his men in order with as little noise as possible. The army, moving by its right from off the ground on which they had rested, soon entered the path through the morass, conducting their march with astonishing silence and great rapidity. The mist had not risen to the higher grounds, so that for some time they had the advantage of starlight. But this was lost as the stars faded before approaching day, and the head of the marching column, continuing its descent, plunged as it were into the heavy ocean of fog, which rolled its white waves over the whole plain, and over the sea by which it was bounded. Some difficulties were now to be encountered, inseparable from darkness, a narrow, broken, and marshy path, and the necessity of preserving union in the march. These, however, were less inconvenient to Highlanders, from their habits of life, than they would have been to any other troops, and they continued a steady and swift movement.

---

1 Field of peas that has been cut.

As the clan of Ivor approached the firm ground, following the track of those who preceded them, the challenge of a patrol was heard through the mist, though they could not see the dragoon by whom it was made—"Who goes there?"

"Hush," cried Fergus, "hush! Let none answer, as he values his life.—Press forward"; and they continued their march with silence and rapidity.

The patrol fired his carabine[1] upon the body, and the report was instantly followed by the clang of his horse's feet as he galloped off. "*Hylax in limine latrat*,"[2] said the Baron of Bradwardine, who heard the shot; "that loon will give the alarm."

The clan of Fergus had now gained the firm plain, which had lately borne a large crop of corn. But the harvest was gathered in, and the expanse was unbroken by tree, bush, or interruption of any kind. The rest of the army were following fast, when they heard the drums of the enemy beat the general. Surprise, however, had made no part of their plan, so they were not disconcerted by this intimation that the foe was upon his guard and prepared to receive them. It only hastened their dispositions for the combat, which were very simple.

The Highland army, which now occupied the eastern end of the wide plain, or stubble field, so often referred to, was drawn up in two lines, extending from the morass towards the sea. The first was destined to charge the enemy, the second to act as a reserve. The few horse, whom the Prince headed in person, remained between the two lines. The Adventurer had intimated a resolution to charge in person at the head of his first line; but his purpose was deprecated by all around him, and he was with difficulty induced to abandon it.

Both lines were now moving forward, the first prepared for instant combat. The clans, of which it was composed, formed each a sort of separate phalanx, narrow in front, and in depth, ten, twelve, or fifteen files, according to the strength of the following. The best-armed and best-born, for the words were synonymous, were placed in front of each of these irregular subdivisions. The others in the rear shouldered forward the front, and by their pressure added both physical impulse, and additional ardour and confidence, to those who were first to encounter the danger.

"Down with your plaid, Waverley," cried Fergus, throwing off his own; "we'll win silks[3] for our tartans before the sun is above the sea."

The clansmen on every side stript their plaids, prepared their arms,

---

1 A lightweight rifle with a short barrel (*AHD*).

2 "Hylax barks at the gate"; Virgil, *Eclogues*, VIII, 107 (*PW*, 592).

3 Take off your tartan. "Silks" is "used allusively to indicate the rank of a king's counsel, marked by the right to wear a silk gown" (*OED*).

and there was an awful pause of about three minutes, during which the men, pulling off their bonnets, raised their faces to heaven, and uttered a short prayer; then pulled their bonnets over their brows, and began to move forward at first slowly. Waverley felt his heart at that moment throb as it would have burst from his bosom. It was not fear, it was not ardour,—it was a compound of both, a new and deeply energetic impulse, that with its first emotion chilled and astounded, then fevered and maddened his mind. The sounds around him combined to exalt his enthusiasm; the pipes played, and the clans rushed forward, each in its own dark column. As they advanced they mended their pace, and the muttering sounds of the men to each other began to swell into a wild cry.

At this moment, the sun, which was now risen above the horizon, dispelled the mist. The vapours rose like a curtain, and showed the two armies in the act of closing. The line of the regulars was formed directly fronting the attack of the Highlanders; it glittered with the appointments of a complete army, and was flanked by cavalry and artillery. But the sight impressed no terror on the assailants.

"Forward, sons of Ivor," cried their Chief, "or the Camerons will draw the first blood!"—They rushed on with a tremendous yell.

The rest is well known. The horse, who were commanded to charge the advancing Highlanders in the flank, received an irregular fire from their fusees as they ran on, and, seized with a disgraceful panic, wavered, halted, disbanded, and galloped from the field. The artillery-men, deserted by the cavalry, fled after discharging their pieces, and the Highlanders, who dropped their guns when fired, and drew their broadswords, rushed with headlong fury against the infantry.

It was at this moment of confusion and terror, that Waverley remarked an English officer, apparently of high rank, standing alone and unsupported by a field-piece, which, after the flight of the men by whom it was wrought, he had himself levelled and discharged against the clan of Mac-Ivor, the nearest group of Highlanders within his aim. Struck with his tall, martial figure, and eager to save him from inevitable destruction, Waverley outstripped for an instant even the speediest of the warriors, and, reaching the spot first, called to him to surrender. The officer replied by a thrust with his sword, which Waverley received in his target, and in turning it aside the Englishman's weapon broke. At the same time the battle-axe of Dugald Mahony was in the act of descending upon the officer's head. Waverley intercepted and prevented the blow, and the officer, perceiving further resistance unavailing, and struck with Edward's generous anxiety for his safety, resigned the fragment of his sword, and was committed by Waverley to Dugald, with strict charge to use him well, and not to pillage his person, promising him, at the same time, full indemnification for the spoil.

On Edward's right the battle for a few minutes raged fierce and thick. The English infantry, trained in the wars in Flanders, stood their ground with great courage. But their extended files were pierced and broken in many places by the close masses of the clans; and in the personal struggle which ensued, the nature of the Highlanders' weapons, and their extraordinary fierceness and activity, gave them a decided superiority over those who had been accustomed to trust much to their array and discipline, and felt that the one was broken and the other useless. Waverley, as he cast his eyes towards this scene of smoke and slaughter, observed Colonel Gardiner, deserted by his own soldiers in spite of all his attempts to rally them, yet spurring his horse through the field to take the command of a small body of infantry, who, with their backs arranged against the wall of his own park (for his house was close by the field of battle), continued a desperate and unavailing resistance. Waverley could perceive that he had already received many wounds, his clothes and saddle being marked with blood. To save this good and brave man, became the instant object of his most anxious exertions. But he could only witness his fall. Ere Edward could make his way among the Highlanders, who, furious and eager for spoil, now thronged upon each other, he saw his former commander brought from his horse by the blow of a scythe, and beheld him receive, while on the ground, more wounds than would have let out twenty lives. When Waverley came up, however, perception had not entirely fled. The dying warrior seemed to recognise Edward, for he fixed his eye upon him with an upbraiding, yet sorrowful look, and appeared to struggle for utterance. But he felt that death was dealing closely with him, and resigning his purpose, and folding his hands as if in devotion, he gave up his soul to his Creator. The look with which he regarded Waverley in his dying moments, did not strike him so deeply at that crisis of hurry and confusion, as when it recurred to his imagination at the distance of some time.[aaaa]

Loud shouts of triumph now echoed over the whole field. The battle was fought and won, and the whole baggage, artillery, and military stores of the regular army remained in possession of the victors. Never was a victory more complete. Scarce any escaped from the battle, excepting the cavalry, who had left it at the very onset, and even these were broken into different parties and scattered all over the country. So far as our tale is concerned, we have only to relate the fate of Balmawhapple, who, mounted on a horse as headstrong and stiffnecked as his rider, pursued the flight of the dragoons above four miles from the field of battle, when some dozen of the fugitives took heart of grace, turned round, and, cleaving his skull with their broadswords, satisfied the world that the unfortunate gentleman had actually brains, the end of his life thus giving proof of a fact greatly doubted during its progress. His death was lamented by few. Most of those who knew him agreed in the pithy observation of Ensign Maccombich, that there "was mair *tint* (lost) at Sheriff-Muir." His friend, Lieutenant Jinker, bent his eloquence only to exculpate his favourite mare from any share in contributing to the catastrophe. "He had tauld the laird a thousand times," he said, "that it was a burning shame to put a martingale upon the puir thing, when he would needs ride her wi' a curb of half a yard lang; and that he could na but bring himsell (not to say her) to some mischief, by flinging her down, or otherwise; whereas, if he had had a wee bit rinnin ring on the snaffle, she wad ha' rein'd as cannily as a cadger's pownie."

Such was the elegy of the Laird of Balmawhapple.[bbbb]

CHAPTER XIX.
An unexpected Embarrassment.

WHEN the battle was over, and all things coming into order, the Baron of Bradwardine, returning from the duty of the day, and having disposed those under his command in their proper stations, sought the Chieftain of Glennaquoich and his friend Edward Waverley. He found the former busied in determining disputes among his clansmen about points of precedence and deeds of valour, besides sundry high and doubtful questions concerning plunder. The most important of the last respected the property of a gold watch, which had once belonged to some unfortunate English officer. The party against whom judgment was awarded consoled himself by observing, "She (*i.e.*, the watch, which he took for a living animal) died the very night Vich Ian Vohr gave her to Murdoch"; the machine having, in fact, stopped for want of winding up.

It was just when this important question was decided, that the Baron of Bradwardine, with a careful and yet important expression of countenance, joined the two young men. He descended from his reeking charger, the care of which he recommended to one of his grooms. "I seldom ban, sir," said he to the man; "but if you play any of your hound's-foot tricks, and leave puir Berwick before he's sorted, to rin after spuilzie, deil be wi' me if I do not give your craig a thraw."[1] He then stroked with great complacency the animal which had borne him through the fatigues of the day, and having taken a tender leave of him,—"Weel, my good young friends, a glorious and decisive victory," said he; "but these loons of troopers fled ower soon. I should have

---

1   "I seldom curse, sir, ... but if you play any of your tricks, and leave poor Berwick before he's accommodated, to run after spoils, devil be with me if I don't give your neck a twist."

liked to have shown you the true points of the *prælium equestre*, or equestrian combat, whilk their cowardice has postponed, and which I hold to be the pride and terror of warfare. Weel, I have fought once more in this old quarrel, though I admit I could not be so far *ben*[1] as you lads, being that it was my point of duty to keep together our handful of horse. And no cavalier ought in any wise to begrudge honour that befalls his companions, even though they are ordered upon thrice his danger, whilk, another time, by the blessing of God, may be his own case.—But, Glennaquoich, and you, Mr Waverley, I pray ye to give me your best advice on a matter of mickle weight, and which deeply affects the honour of the house of Bradwardine.—I crave your pardon, Ensign Maccombich, and yours, Inveraughlin, and yours, Edderalshendrach, and yours, sir."

The last person he addressed was Ballenkeiroch, who, remembering the death of his son, loured on him with a look of savage defiance. The Baron, quick as lightning at taking umbrage, had already bent his brow, when Glennaquoich dragged his major from the spot, and remonstrated with him, in the authoritative tone of a chieftain, on the madness of reviving a quarrel in such a moment.

"The ground is cumbered with carcasses," said the old mountaineer, turning sullenly away; "*one more* would hardly have been kenn'd upon it; and if it wasna for yoursell, Vich Ian Vohr, that one should be Bradwardine's or mine."

The Chief soothed while he hurried him away; and then returned to the Baron. "It is Ballenkeiroch," he said, in an under and confidential voice, "father of the young man who fell eight years since in the unlucky affair at the Mains."

"Ah!" said the Baron, instantly relaxing the doubtful sternness in his features, "I can take mickle frae a man to whom I have unhappily rendered sic a displeasure as that. Ye were right to apprise me, Glennaquoich; he may look as black as midnight at Martinmas ere Cosmo Comyne Bradwardine shall say he does him wrang. Ah! I have nae male lineage, and I should bear with one I have made childless, though you are aware the blood-wit was made up to your ain satisfaction by assythment,[2] and that I have since expedited letters of slains.[3]—Weel, as I have said, I have no male issue, and yet it is needful that I maintain the honour of my house; and it is on that score I prayed ye for your peculiar and private attention."

---

1 Within.
2 "Legal reparation due from the killer to the heirs of a person killed" (*OW*, 444).
3 Letters from the relatives of people slain stating that they had received reparation and desired the murderer pardoned (*PW*, 592).

The two young men awaited to hear him, in anxious curiosity.

"I doubt na, lads," he proceeded, "but your education has been sae seen to, that ye understand the true nature of the feudal tenures?"[1]

Fergus, afraid of an endless dissertation, answered, "Intimately, Baron," and touched Waverley, as a signal to express no ignorance.

"And ye are aware, I doubt not, that the holding of the Barony of Bradwardine is of a nature alike honourable and peculiar, being blanch (which Craig opines ought to be Latinated *blancum*, or rather *francum*, a free holding), *pro servitio detrahendi, seu exuendi, caligas regis post battalliam*."[2] Here Fergus turned his falcon eye upon Edward, with an almost imperceptible rise of his eyebrow, to which his shoulders corresponded in the same degree of elevation. "Now, twa points of dubitation occur to me upon this topic. First, whether this service, or feudal homage, be at any event due to the person of the Prince, the words being, *per expressum, caligas* REGIS, the boots of the king himself; and I pray your opinion anent that particular before we proceed farther."

"Why, he is Prince Regent," answered Mac-Ivor, with laudable composure of countenance; "and in the court of France all the honours are rendered to the person of the Regent which are due to that of the King. Besides, were I to pull off either of their boots, I would render that service to the young Chevalier ten times more willingly than to his father."

"Ay, but I talk not of personal predilections. However, your authority is of great weight as to the usages of the court of France: and doubtless the Prince, as *alter ego*, may have a right to claim the *homagium* of the great tenants of the crown, since all faithful subjects are commanded, in the commission of regency, to respect him as the King's own person. Far, therefore, be it from me to diminish the lustre of his authority, by withholding this act of homage, so peculiarly calculated to give it splendour; for I question if the Emperor of Germany hath his boots taken off by a free baron of the empire. But here lieth the second difficulty.—The Prince wears no boots, but simply brogues and trews."

This last dilemma had almost disturbed Fergus's gravity.

"Why," said he, "you know, Baron, the proverb tells us, 'It's ill taking the breeks off a Highlandman,'—and the boots are here in the same predicament."

---

1 Control asserted over people during Feudalism; Scott, like many Scottish philosophers and historians, was interested in the study of feudalism (*OW*, 444).

2 Sir Thomas Craig (1538-1608), student of feudal law; "For the service of undoing and taking off the King's boots after battle" (*PW*, 592).

"The word *caligæ*, however," continued the Baron, "though I admit, that, by family tradition, and even in our ancient evidents, it is explained *lie* BOOTS, means, in its primitive sense, rather sandals; and Caius Cæsar, the nephew and successor of Caius Tiberius, received the agnomen of Caligula, *a caligulis, sive caligis levioribus, quibus adolescentior usus fuerat in exercitu Germanici patris sui.*[1] And the *caligæ* were also proper to the monastic bodies; for we read in an ancient Glossarium, upon the rule of St Benedict,[2] in the Abbey of St Amand, that *caligæ* were tied with latchets."

"That will apply to the brogues," said Fergus.

"It will so, my dear Glennaquoich, and the words are express; *Caligæ dictæ sunt ligantur; nam socci non ligantur, sed tantum intromittuntur;*[3] that is, *caligæ* are denominated from the ligatures, wherewith they are bound; whereas *socci*, which may be analogous to our mules, whilk the English denominate slippers, are only slipped upon the feet. The words of the charter are also alternative, *exuere, seu detrahere;* that is, to *undo*, as in the case of sandals or brogues; and to *pull off*, as we say vernacularly, concerning boots. Yet I would we had more light; but I fear there is little chance of finding hereabout any erudite author, *de re vestiaria.*"[4]

"I should doubt it very much," said the Chieftain, looking around on the straggling Highlanders, who were returning loaded with spoils of the slain, "though the *res vestiaria* itself seems to be in some request at present."

This remark coming within the Baron's idea of jocularity, he honoured it with a smile, but immediately resumed what to him appeared very serious business.

"Bailie Macwheeble indeed holds an opinion, that this honorary service is due, from its very nature, *si petatur tantum;*[5] only if his Royal Highness shall require of the great tenant of the crown to perform that personal duty; and indeed he pointed out the case in Dirleton's

---

1 Roman emperor before Caligula (43 BCE-37 CE). Lamont translates the Latin: "'from the light boots which he used to wear when young in the army of his father, Germanicus' (Seutonius, *Life of Caius*, 9)" and suggests that "Caius Tiberius is an (incorrect) reference to the Emperor Tiberius (AD 14-29), who was succeeded by his nephew Caligula (AD 29-37)" (*OW*, 444).

2 See chapter 55 of the Rule of St. Benedict, a book of precepts for monks written by St. Benedict of Nursia. St. Amandus founded the Abbey of St. Amand near Valenciennes in the seventh century (*OW*, 444).

3 Gaius Caesar received the name "Caligula" "from the small shoes worn in his youth when in the army of his father, Germanicus" (*PW*, 592).

4 Concerning clothes (*PW*, 592).

5 Only when called for (*PW*, 592).

Doubts and Queries,[1] Grippit *versus* Spicer, anent the eviction of an estate *ob non solutum canonem*,[2] that is, for non-payment of a feu-duty of three pepper-corns a-year, whilk were taxt to be worth seven-eigths of a penny Scots, in whilk the defender was assoilzied.[3] But I deem it safest, wi' your good favour, to place myself in the way of rendering the Prince this service, and to proffer performance thereof; and I shall cause the Bailie to attend with a schedule of a protest, whilk he has here prepared (taking out a paper), intimating, that if it shall be his Royal Highness's pleasure to accept of other assistance at pulling off his *caligæ*, (whether the same shall be rendered boots or brogues), save that of the said Baron of Bradwardine, who is in presence ready and willing to perform the same, it shall in no wise impinge upon or prejudice the right of the said Cosmo Comyne Bradwardine to perform the said service in future; nor shall it give any esquire, valet of the chamber, squire, or page, whose assistance it may please his Royal Highness to employ, any right, title, or ground, for evicting from the said Cosmo Comyne Bradwardine the estate and barony of Bradwardine, and others held as aforesaid, by the due and faithful performance thereof."

Fergus highly applauded this arrangement; and the Baron took a friendly leave of them, with a smile of contented importance upon his visage.

"Long live our dear friend, the Baron," exclaimed the Chief, as soon as he was out of hearing, "for the most absurd original that exists north of the Tweed! I wish to heaven I had recommended him to attend the circle this evening with a boot-ketch[4] under his arm. I think he might have adopted the suggestion, if it had been made with suitable gravity."

"And how can you take pleasure in making a man of his worth so ridiculous?"

"Begging pardon, my dear Waverley, you are as ridiculous as he. Why, do you not see that the man's whole mind is wrapped up in this ceremony? He has heard and thought of it since infancy, as the most august privilege and ceremony in the world; and I doubt not but the expected pleasure of performing it was a principal motive with him for taking up arms. Depend upon it, had I endeavoured to divert him from exposing himself, he would have treated me as an ignorant, conceited coxcomb,

---

1 *Dirleton's Doubts and Queries: Some Doubts and Questions in the Law of Scotland* (1698), written by Sir John Nisbet (1610-88).

2 Respecting the eviction of an estate due to the "legal condition not being observed" (*PW*, 592).

3 Acquitted (*WSG*).

4 A "boot-jack, a contrivance for pulling off boots" (*PW*, 592).

or perhaps might have taken a fancy to cut my throat; a pleasure which he once proposed to himself upon some point of etiquette, not half so important, in his eyes, as this matter of boots or brogues, or whatever the *caligæ* shall finally be pronounced by the learned. But I must go to headquarters, to prepare the Prince for this extraordinary scene. My information will be well taken, for it will give him a hearty laugh at present, and put him on his guard against laughing, when it might be very *mal-a-propos*. So, *au revoir*, my dear Waverley."

CHAPTER XX.
The English Prisoner.

THE first occupation of Waverley, after he departed from the Chieftain, was to go in quest of the officer whose life he had saved. He was guarded, along with his companions in misfortune, who were very numerous, in a gentleman's house near the field of battle.

On entering the room, where they stood crowded together, Waverley easily recognised the object of his visit, not only by the peculiar dignity of his appearance, but by the appendage of Dugald Mahony, with his battle-axe, who had stuck to him from the moment of his captivity, as if he had been skewered to his side. This close attendance was, perhaps, for the purpose of securing his promised reward from Edward, but it also operated to save the English gentleman from being plundered in the scene of general confusion; for Dugald sagaciously argued, that the amount of the salvage which he might be allowed, would be regulated by the state of the prisoner, when he should deliver him over to Waverley. He hastened to assure Waverley, therefore, with more words than he usually employed, that he had "keepit ta *sidier roy* haill, and that he wasna a plack the waur since the fery moment when his honour forbad her to gie him a bit clamhewit wi' her Lochaber-axe."

Waverley assured Dugald of a liberal recompence, and, approach-ing the English officer, expressed his anxiety to do any thing which might contribute to his convenience under his present unpleasant circumstances.

"I am not so inexperienced a soldier, sir," answered the Englishman, "as to complain of the fortune of war. I am only grieved to see those scenes acted in our own island, which I have often witnessed elsewhere with comparative indifference."

"Another such day as this," said Waverley, "and I trust the cause of your regrets will be removed, and all will again return to peace and order."

The officer smiled and shook his head. "I must not forget my situation so far as to attempt a formal confutation of that opinion; but, notwithstanding your success, and the valour which achieved it, you have undertaken a task to which your strength appears wholly inadequate."

At this moment Fergus pushed into the press.

"Come, Edward, come along; the Prince has gone to Pinkie-house[1] for the night; and we must follow, or lose the whole ceremony of the *caligae*. Your friend, the Baron, has been guilty of a great piece of cruelty; he has insisted upon dragging Bailie Macwheeble out to the field of battle. Now, you must know, the Bailie's greatest horror is an armed Highlander, or a loaded gun; and there he stands, listening to the Baron's instructions concerning the protest; ducking his head like a sea-gull at the report of every gun and pistol that our idle boys are firing upon the fields; and undergoing, by way of penance, at every symptom of flinching, a severe rebuke from his patron, who would not admit the discharge of a whole battery of cannon, within point-blank distance, as an apology for neglecting a discourse, in which the honour of his family is interested."

"But how has Mr Bradwardine got him to venture so far?" said Edward.

"Why, he had come as far as Musselburgh, I fancy, in hopes of making some of our wills; and the peremptory commands of the Baron dragged him forward to Preston after the battle was over. He complains of one or two of our ragamuffins having put him in peril of his life, by presenting their pieces[2] at him; but as they limited his ransom to an English penny, I don't think we need trouble the provost-martial upon that subject.—So, come along, Waverley."

"Waverley!" said the English officer, with great emotion; "the nephew of Sir Everard Waverley, of — shire?"

"The same, sir," replied our hero, somewhat surprised at the tone in which he was addressed.

"I am at once happy and grieved," said the prisoner, "to have met with you."

"I am ignorant, sir," answered Waverley, "how I have deserved so much interest."

"Did your uncle never mention a friend called Talbot?"

"I have heard him talk with great regard of such a person," replied Edward; "a colonel, I believe, in the army, and the husband of Lady Emily Blandeville; but I thought Colonel Talbot had been abroad."

"I am just returned," answered the officer; "and being in Scotland, thought it my duty to act where my services promised to be useful. Yes, Mr Waverley, I am that Colonel Talbot, the husband of the lady you have named; and I am proud to acknowledge, that I owe alike my pro-

---

1 The "seat of the Marquis of Tweeddale, on the road to Edinburgh south of Musselburgh" (*OW*, 445).
2 Weapons.

fessional rank and my domestic happiness to your generous and noble-minded relative. Good God! that I should find his nephew in such a dress, and engaged in such a cause!"

"Sir," said Fergus, haughtily, "the dress and cause are those of men of birth and honour."

"My situation forbids me to dispute your assertion," said Colonel Talbot; "otherwise it were no difficult matter to show, that neither courage nor pride of lineage can gild a bad cause. But, with Mr Waverley's permission, and yours, sir, if yours must also be asked, I would willingly speak a few words with him on affairs connected with his own family."

"Mr Waverley, sir, regulates his own motions.—You will follow me, I suppose, to Pinkie," said Fergus, turning to Edward, "when you have finished your discourse with this new acquaintance?" So saying, the Chief of Glennaquoich adjusted his plaid with rather more than his usual air of haughty assumption, and left the apartment.

The interest of Waverley readily procured for Colonel Talbot the freedom of adjourning to a large garden, belonging to his place of confinement. They walked a few paces in silence, Colonel Talbot apparently studying how to open what he had to say; at length he addressed Edward.

"Mr Waverley, you have this day saved my life; and yet I would to God that I had lost it, ere I had found you wearing the uniform and cockade of these men."

"I forgive your reproach, Colonel Talbot; it is well meant, and your education and prejudices render it natural. But there is nothing extraordinary in finding a man, whose honour has been publicly and unjustly assailed, in the situation which promised most fair to afford him satisfaction on his calumniators."

"I should rather say, in the situation most likely to confirm the reports which they have circulated," said Colonel Talbot, "by following the very line of conduct ascribed to you. Are you aware, Mr Waverley, of the infinite distress, and even danger, which your present conduct has occasioned to your nearest relatives?"

"Danger!"

"Yes, sir, danger. When I left England, your uncle and father had been obliged to find bail to answer a charge of treason, to which they were only admitted by the exertion of the most powerful interest. I came down to Scotland, with the sole purpose of rescuing you from the gulf into which you have precipitated yourself; nor can I estimate the consequences to your family, of your having openly joined the rebellion, since the very suspicion of your intention was so perilous to them. Most deeply do I regret, that I did not meet you before this last and fatal error."

"I am really ignorant," said Waverley, in a tone of reserve, "why Colonel Talbot should have taken so much trouble on my account."

"Mr Waverley," answered Talbot, "I am dull at apprehending irony; and therefore I shall answer your words according to their plain meaning. I am indebted to your uncle for benefits greater than those which a son owes to a father. I acknowledge to him the duty of a son; and as I know there is no manner in which I can requite his kindness so well as by serving you, I will serve you, if possible, whether you will permit me or no. The personal obligation which you have this day laid me under (although, in common estimation, as great as one human being can bestow on another), adds nothing to my zeal on your behalf; nor can that zeal be abated by any coolness with which you may please to receive it."

"Your intentions may be kind, sir," said Waverley, drily; "but your language is harsh, or at least peremptory."

"On my return to England," continued Colonel Talbot, "after long absence, I found your uncle, Sir Everard Waverley, in the custody of a king's messenger, in consequence of the suspicion brought upon him by your conduct. He is my oldest friend—how often shall I repeat it—my best benefactor! He sacrificed his own views of happiness to mine—he never uttered a word, he never harboured a thought, that benevolence itself might not have thought or spoken. I found this man in confinement, rendered harsher to him by his habits of life, his natural dignity of feeling, and—forgive me, Mr Waverley,—by the cause through which this calamity had come upon him. I cannot disguise from you my feelings upon this occasion; they were most painfully unfavourable to you. Having, by my family interest, which you probably know is not inconsiderable, succeeded in obtaining Sir Everard's release, I set out for Scotland. I saw Colonel Gardiner, a man whose fate alone is sufficient to render this insurrection for ever execrable. In the course of conversation with him, I found, that, from late circumstances, from a re-examination of the persons engaged in the mutiny, and from his original good opinion of your character, he was much softened towards you; and I doubted not, that if I could be so fortunate as to discover you, all might yet be well. But this unnatural rebellion has ruined all. I have, for the first time, in a long and active military life, seen Britons disgrace themselves by a panic flight, and that before a foe without either arms or discipline: and now I find the heir of my dearest friend—the son, I may say, of his affections—sharing a triumph, for which he ought the first to have blushed. Why should I lament Gardiner! His lot was happy, compared to mine!"

There was so much dignity in Colonel Talbot's manner, such a mixture of military pride and manly sorrow, and the news of Sir Everard's imprisonment was told in so deep a tone of feeling, that

Edward stood mortified, abashed, and distressed, in presence of the prisoner, who owed to him his life not many hours before. He was not sorry when Fergus interrupted their conference a second time.

"His Royal Highness commands Mr Waverley's attendance." Colonel Talbot threw upon Edward a reproachful glance, which did not escape the quick eye of the Highland Chief. "His *immediate* attendance," he repeated, with considerable emphasis. Waverley turned again towards the Colonel.

"We shall meet again," he said; "in the meanwhile, every possible accommodation"—

"I desire none," said the Colonel; "let me fare like the meanest of those brave men, who, on this day of calamity, have preferred wounds and captivity to flight; I would almost exchange places with one of those who have fallen, to know that my words have made a suitable impression on your mind."

"Let Colonel Talbot be carefully secured," said Fergus to the Highland officer, who commanded the guard over the prisoners; "it is the Prince's particular command; he is a prisoner of the utmost importance."

"But let him want no accommodation suitable to his rank," said Waverley.

"Consistent always with secure custody," reiterated Fergus. The officer signified his acquiescence in both commands, and Edward followed Fergus to the garden-gate, where Callum Beg, with three saddle-horses, awaited them. Turning his head, he saw Colonel Talbot re-conducted to his place of confinement by a file of Highlanders; he lingered on the threshold of the door, and made a signal with his hand towards Waverley, as if enforcing the language he had held towards him.

"Horses," said Fergus, as he mounted, "are now as plenty as blackberries; every man may have them for the catching. Come, let Callum adjust your stirrups, and let us to Pinkie-house^{cccc} as fast as these *ci-devant* dragoon-horses[1] choose to carry us."

CHAPTER XXI.
Rather unimportant.

"I WAS turned back," said Fergus to Edward, as they galloped from Preston to Pinkie-house, "by a message from the Prince. But, I suppose, you know the value of this most noble Colonel Talbot as a prisoner. He is held one of the best officers among the red-coats; a special friend and favourite of the Elector himself, and of that dread-

---

1 Horses formerly belonging to the dragoons.

ful hero, the Duke of Cumberland, who has been summoned from his triumphs at Fontenoy,[1] to come over and devour us poor Highlanders alive. Has he been telling you how the bells of St James's ring? Not 'turn again, Whittington,'[2] like those of Bow, in the days of yore?"

"Fergus!" said Waverley, with a reproachful look.

"Nay, I cannot tell what to make of you," answered the Chief of Mac-Ivor, "you are blown about with every wind of doctrine. Here have we gained a victory, unparalleled in history—and your behaviour is praised by every living mortal to the skies—and the Prince is eager to thank you in person—and all our beauties of the White Rose[3] are pulling caps for you,—and you, the *preux chevalier*[4] of the day, are stooping on your horse's neck like a butter-woman riding to market, and looking as black as a funeral!"

"I am sorry for poor Colonel Gardiner's death: he was once very kind to me."

"Why, then, be sorry for five minutes, and then be glad again; his chance to-day may be ours to-morrow; and what does it signify? The next best thing to victory is honourable death; but it is a *pis-aller*, and one would rather a foe had it than one's self."

"But Colonel Talbot has informed me that my father and uncle are both imprisoned by government on my account."

"We'll put in bail, my boy; old Andrew Ferrara[dddd] shall lodge his security; and I should like to see him put to justify it in Westminster-Hall!"

"Nay, they are already at liberty, upon bail of a more civic disposition."

"Then why is thy noble spirit cast down, Edward? Dost think that the Elector's ministers are such doves as to set their enemies at liberty at this critical moment, if they could or durst confine and punish them? Assure thyself that either they have no charge against your relations on which they can continue their imprisonment, or else they are afraid of our friends, the jolly cavaliers of old England. At any rate, you need not be apprehensive upon their account; and we will find some means of conveying to them assurances of your safety."

---

1 Hook points out the ironic tone of Fergus's phrase in that the Duke of Cumberland, such a scourge in the Highlands, led the Allied army to defeat at Fontenoy in May 1745, during the War of Austrian Succession (*PW*, 593).

2 What the bells of Bow Church in Cheapside were said to have told Richard (Dick) Whittington, future Lord Mayor of London, as he contemplated running away from his apprenticeship; he apparently listened to the bells and returned to his master (*OW*, 445).

3 The white rose was worn by those supportive of the Jacobite cause.

4 Prize nobleman.

Edward was silenced, but not satisfied, with these reasons. He had now been more than once shocked at the small degree of sympathy which Fergus exhibited for the feelings even of those whom he loved, if they did not correspond with his own mood at the time, and more especially if they thwarted him while earnest in a favourite pursuit. Fergus sometimes indeed observed, that he had offended Waverley, but, always intent upon some favourite plan or project of his own, he was never sufficiently aware of the extent or duration of his displeasure, so that the reiteration of these petty offences some-what cooled the volunteer's extreme attachment to his officer.

The Chevalier received Waverley with his usual favour, and paid him many compliments on his distinguished bravery. He then took him apart, made many inquiries concerning Colonel Talbot, and when he had received all the information which Edward was able to give concerning him and his connexions, he proceeded,—"I cannot but think, Mr Waverley, that since this gentleman is so particularly connected with our worthy and excellent friend, Sir Everard Waverley, and since his lady is of the house of Blandeville, whose devotion to the true and loyal principles of the Church of England is so generally known, the Colonel's own private sentiments cannot be unfavourable to us, whatever mask he may have assumed to accommodate himself to the times."

"If I am to judge from the language he this day held to me, I am under the necessity of differing widely from your Royal Highness."

"Well, it is worth making a trial at least. I therefore intrust you with the charge of Colonel Talbot, with power to act concerning him as you think most advisable; and I hope you will find means of ascertaining what are his real dispositions towards our Royal Father's restoration."

"I am convinced," said Waverley, bowing, "that if Colonel Talbot chooses to grant his parole, it may be securely depended upon; but if he refuses it, I trust your Royal Highness will devolve on some other person than the nephew of his friend, the task of laying him under the necessary restraint."

"I will trust him with no person but you," said the Prince, smiling, but peremptorily repeating his mandate; "it is of importance to my service that there should appear to be a good intelligence between you, even if you are unable to gain his confidence in earnest. You will therefore receive him into your quarters, and in case he declines giving his parole, you must apply for a proper guard. I beg you will go about this directly. We return to Edinburgh to-morrow."

Being thus remanded to the vicinity of Preston, Waverley lost the Baron of Bradwardine's solemn act of homage. So little, however, was he at this time in love with vanity, that he had quite forgotten the ceremony in which Fergus had laboured to engage his curiosity. But next day a formal Gazette was circulated, containing a detailed account of the battle of Gladsmuir, as the Highlanders chose to denominate their victory. It concluded with an account of the Court afterwards held by the Chevalier at Pinki-house, which contained this among other high-flown descriptive paragraphs:

"Since that fatal treaty which annihilates Scotland as an independent nation, it has not been our happiness to see her princes receive, and her nobles discharge, those acts of feudal homage, which, founded upon the splendid actions of Scottish valour, recall the memory of her early history, with the manly and chivalrous simplicity of the ties which united to the Crown the homage of the warriors by whom it was repeatedly upheld and defended. But on the evening of the 20th, our memories were refreshed with one of those ceremonies which belong to the ancient days of Scotland's glory. After the circle was formed, Cosmo Comyne Bradwardine, of that ilk, colonel in the service, &c. &c. &c. came before the Prince, attended by Mr D. Macwheeble, the Bailie of his ancient barony of Bradwardine (who, we understand, has been lately named a commissary), and, under form of instrument, claimed permission to perform, to the person of his Royal Highness, as representing his father, the service used and wont, for which, under a charter of Robert Bruce (of which the original was produced and inspected by the Masters of his Royal Highness's Chancery for the time being), the claimant held the barony of Bradwardine, and lands of Tully-Veolan. His claim being admitted and registered, his Royal Highness having placed his foot upon a cushion, the Baron of Bradwardine, kneeling upon his right knee, proceeded to undo the latchet of the brogue, or low-heeled Highland shoe, which our gallant young hero wears in compliment to his brave followers. When this was performed, his Royal Highness declared the ceremony completed; and embracing the gallant veteran, protested that nothing but compliance with an ordinance of Robert Bruce, could have induced him to receive even the symbolical performance of a menial office from hands which had fought so bravely to put the crown upon the head of his father. The Baron of Bradwardine then took instruments in the hands of Mr Commissary Macwheeble, bearing, that all points and circumstances of the act of homage had been *rite et solenniter acta et peracta*;[1] and a corresponding entry was made in the protocol of the Lord High Chamberlain, and in the record of Chancery. We understand that it is in contemplation of his Royal Highness, when his Majesty's pleasure can be known, to raise Colonel Bradwardine to the peerage, by the title of Viscount Bradwardine, of Bradwardine and Tully-Veolan, and that, in the meanwhile, his Royal

---

1 "Duly and solemnly executed and discharged" (*PW*, 593).

Highness, in his father's name and authority, has been pleased to grant him an honourable augmentation to his paternal coat of arms, being a budget or boot-jack,[1] disposed saltier-wise with a naked broadsword, to be borne in the dexter cantle of the shield; and, as an additional motto, on a scroll beneath, the words, 'Draw and draw off.'"

Were it not for the recollection of Fergus's raillery, thought Waverley to himself, when he had perused this long and grave document, how very tolerably would all this sound, and how little should I have thought of connecting it with any ludicrous idea! Well, after all, every thing has its fair, as well as its seamy side; and truly I do not see why the Baron's boot-jack may not stand as fair in heraldry as the water-buckets, waggons, cart-wheels, plough-socks, shuttles, candlesticks, and other ordinaries, conveying ideas of any thing save chivalry, which appear in the arms of some of our most ancient gentry.—This, however, is an episode in respect to the principal story.

When Waverley returned to Preston, and rejoined Colonel Talbot, he found him recovered from the strong and obvious emotions with which a concurrence of unpleasing events had affected him. He had regained his natural manner, which was that of an English gentleman and soldier, manly, open, and generous, but not unsusceptible of prejudice against those of a different country, or who opposed him in political tenets. When Waverley acquainted Colonel Talbot with the Chevalier's purpose to commit him to his charge, "I did not think to have owed so much obligation to that young gentleman," he said, "as is implied in this destination. I can at least cheerfully join in the prayer of the honest Presbyterian clergyman, that, as he has come among us seeking an earthly crown, his labours may be speedily rewarded with a heavenly one.eeee I shall willingly give my parole not to attempt an escape without your knowledge, since, in fact, it was to meet you that I came to Scotland; and I am glad it has happened even under this predicament. But I suppose we shall be but a short time together. Your Chevalier (that is a name we may both give to him), with his plaids and blue caps, will, I presume, be continuing his crusade southward?"

"Not as I hear; I believe the army makes some stay in Edinburgh, to collect reinforcements."

"And to besiege the Castle?" said Talbot, smiling sarcastically. "Well, unless my old commander, General Preston,[2] turn false metal,

---

1 The boot-jack is probably in the budget, a bag. "What follows are heraldic expressions meaning, roughly, crossing each other diagonally, and in the top right-hand corner of the shield" (*OW*, 446).

2 Earlier editions have "General Guest" rather than "General Preston"; Lamont glosses Preston as General George Preston (c. 1659-1748), deputy-governor of Edinburgh Castle (*OW*, 446).

or the Castle sink into the North Loch, events which I deem equally probable, I think we shall have some time to make up our acquaintance. I have a guess that this gallant Chevalier has a design that I should be your proselyte; and, as I wish you to be mine, there cannot be a more fair proposal, than to afford us fair conference together. But, as I spoke to-day under the influence of feelings I rarely give way to, I hope you will excuse my entering again upon controversy till we are somewhat better acquainted."

CHAPTER XXII.
Intrigues of Love and Politics.

IT is not necessary to record in these pages the triumphant entrance of the Chevalier into Edinburgh after the decisive affair of Preston. One circumstance, however, may be noticed, because it illustrates the high spirit of Flora Mac-Ivor. The Highlanders, by whom the Prince was surrounded, in the license and extravagance of this joyful moment, fired their pieces repeatedly, and one of these having been accidentally loaded with ball, the bullet grazed the young lady's temple as she waved her handkerchief from a balcony.[ffff] Fergus, who beheld the accident, was at her side in an instant; and, on seeing that the wound was trifling, he drew his broadsword, with the purpose of rushing down upon the man by whose carelessness she had incurred so much danger, when, holding him by the plaid, "Do not harm the poor fellow," she cried; "for heaven's sake, do not harm him! But thank God with me that the accident happened to Flora Mac-Ivor; for had it befallen a Whig, they would have pretended that the shot was fired on purpose."

Waverley escaped the alarm which this accident would have occasioned to him, as he was unavoidably delayed by the necessity of accompanying Colonel Talbot to Edinburgh.

They performed the journey together on horseback, and for some time, as if to sound each other's feelings and sentiments, they conversed upon general and ordinary topics.

When Waverley again entered upon the subject which he had most at heart, the situation, namely, of his father and his uncle, Colonel Talbot seemed now rather desirous to alleviate than to aggravate his anxiety. This appeared particularly to be the case when he heard Waverley's history, which he did not scruple to confide to him.

"And so," said the Colonel, "there has been no malice prepense, as lawyers, I think, term it, in this rash step of yours; and you have been trepanned into the service of this Italian knight-errant[1] by a few civil

---

1   "Trepanned" is trapped; Charles Edward Stuart's grandmother was Mary of Modena, an Italian princess, and he lived in Italy as a child.

speeches from him and one or two of his Highland recruiting ser-
geants? It is sadly foolish, to be sure, but not nearly so bad as I was led
to expect. However, you cannot desert, even from the Pretender, at
the present moment,—that seems impossible. But I have little doubt
that, in the dissensions incident to this heterogeneous mass of wild
and desperate men, some opportunity may arise, by availing yourself
of which, you may extricate yourself honourably from your rash
engagement before the bubble burst. If this can be managed, I would
have you go to a place of safety in Flanders, which I shall point out.
And I think I can secure your pardon from government after a few
months' residence abroad.

"I cannot permit you, Colonel Talbot," answered Waverley, "to
speak of any plan which turns on my deserting an enterprise in which
I may have engaged hastily, but certainly voluntarily, and with the
purpose of abiding the issue."

"Well," said Colonel Talbot, smiling, "leave me my thoughts and
hopes at least at liberty, if not my speech. But have you never examined your mysterious packet?"

"It is in my baggage," replied Edward; "we shall find it in
Edinburgh."

In Edinburgh they soon arrived. Waverley's quarters had been
assigned to him, by the Prince's express orders, in a handsome lodging,
where there was accommodation for Colonel Talbot. His first business
was to examine his portmanteau, and, after a very short search, out
tumbled the expected packet. Waverley opened it eagerly. Under a
blank cover, simply addressed to E. Waverley, Esq., he found a number
of open letters. The uppermost were two from Colonel Gardiner,
addressed to himself. The earliest in date was a kind and gentle remonstrance for neglect of the writer's advice, respecting the disposal of his
time during his leave of absence, the renewal of which, he reminded
Captain Waverley, would speedily expire. "Indeed," the letter proceeded, "had it been otherwise, the news from abroad, and my instructions from the War-office, must have compelled me to recall it, as there
is great danger, since the disaster in Flanders,[1] both of foreign invasion
and insurrection among the disaffected at home. I therefore entreat
you will repair, as soon as possible, to the head-quarters of the regiment; and I am concerned to add, that this is still the more necessary,
as there is some discontent in your troop, and I postpone enquiry into
particulars until I can have the advantage of your assistance."

---

1   On 31 May 1745, the Duke of Cumberland, leading English, Hanoverian,
    and Dutch soldiers, engaged with the French army under Marshal Saxe at
    Fontenoy in Flanders and were defeated, suffering devastating losses (*HEP*,
    IV, 160-61).

The second letter, dated eight days later, was in such a style as might have been expected from the Colonel's receiving no answer to the first. It reminded Waverley of his duty, as a man of honour, an officer, and a Briton; took notice of the increasing dissatisfaction of his men, and that some of them had been heard to hint, that their Captain encouraged and approved of their mutinous behaviour; and, finally, the writer expressed the utmost regret and surprise that he had not obeyed his commands by repairing to head-quarters, reminded him that his leave of absence had been recalled, and conjured him, in a style in which paternal remonstrance was mingled with military authority, to redeem his error by immediately joining his regiment. "That I may be certain," concluded the letter, "that this actually reaches you, I dispatch it by Corporal Tims, of your troop, with orders to deliver it into your own hand."

Upon reading these letters, Waverley, with great bitterness of feeling, was compelled to make the *amende honorable* to the memory of the brave and excellent writer; for surely, as Colonel Gardiner must have had every reason to conclude they had come safely to hand, less could not follow, on their being neglected, than that third and final summons, which Waverley actually received at Glennaquoich, though too late to obey it. And his being superseded, in consequence of his apparent neglect of this last command, was so far from being a harsh or severe proceeding, that it was plainly inevitable. The next letter he unfolded was from the Major of the regiment, acquainting him that a report, to the disadvantage of his reputation, was public in the country, stating, that one Mr Falconer of Ballihople, or some such name, had proposed, in his presence, a treasonable toast, which he permitted to pass in silence, although it was so gross an affront to the royal family, that a gentleman in company, not remarkable for his zeal for government, had nevertheless taken the matter up, and that, sup-posing the account true, Captain Waverley had thus suffered another, comparatively unconcerned, to resent an affront directed against him personally as an officer, and to go out with the person by whom it was offered. The Major concluded, that no one of Captain Waverley's brother officers could believe this scandalous story, but that it was necessarily their joint opinion that his own honour, equally with that of the regiment, depended upon its being instantly contradicted by his authority, &c. &c. &c.

"What do you think of all this?" said Colonel Talbot, to whom Waverley handed the letters after he had perused them.

"Think! it renders thought impossible. It is enough to drive me mad."

"Be calm, my young friend; let us see what are these dirty scrawls that follow."

The first was addressed, "For Master W. Ruffin These."—"Dear sur, sum of our yong gulpins[1] will not bite, thof I tuold them you shoed me the squoire's own seel. But Tims will deliver you the lettrs as desired, and tell ould Addem he gave them to squoir's hond, as to be sure yours is the same, and shall be ready for signal, and hoy for Hoy Church and Sachefrel,[2] as fadur sings at harvest-whome.[3]

 "Yours, deer Sur,
  "H.H.

"Poscriff. Do'e tell squoire we longs to heer from him, and has dootings about his not writing himself, and Lifetenant Bottler is smoky."[4]

"This Ruffin, I suppose, then, is your Donald of the Cavern, who has intercepted your letters, and carried on a correspondence with the poor devil Houghton, as if under your authority?"

"It seems too true. But who can Addem be?"

"Possibly Adam, for poor Gardiner, a sort of pun on his name."

The other letters were to the same purpose, and they soon received yet more complete light upon Donald Bean's machinations.

John Hodges, one of Waverley's servants, who had remained with the regiment, and had been taken at Preston, now made his appearance. He had sought out his master, with the purpose of again entering his service. From this fellow they learned, that some time after Waverley had gone from the head-quarters of the regiment, a pedlar, called Ruthven, Ruffin, or Rivane, known among the soldiers by the name of Wily Will, had made frequent visits to the town of Dundee. He appeared to possess plenty of money, sold his commodities very cheap, seemed always willing to treat his friends at the ale-house, and easily ingratiated himself with many of Waverley's troop, particularly Sergeant Houghton, and one Tims, also a non-commissioned officer. To these he unfolded, in Waverley's name, a plan for leaving the regiment and joining him in the Highlands, where report said the clans had already taken arms in great numbers. The men, who had been educated as Jacobites, so far as they had any opinion at all, and who knew their landlord, Sir Everard, had always been supposed to hold such

---

1 Gullible young people.

2 Henry Sacheverell (c. 1674-1724), a Tory high churchman who preached a sermon on Guy Fawkes Day, 1709, in which he "affirm[ed] ... the doctrine of passive obedience and condemn[ed] ... the toleration of dissenters," for which he was impeached (*OW*, 446).

3 Celebration after the harvest has been brought in.

4 Suspicious.

tenets, easily fell into the snare. That Waverley was at a distance in the Highlands, was received as a sufficient excuse for transmitting his letters through the medium of the pedlar; and the sight of his well-known seal seemed to authenticate the negotiations in his name, where writing might have been dangerous. The cabal, however, began to take air, from the premature mutinous language of those concerned. Wily Will justified his appellative; for, after suspicion arose, he was seen no more. When the Gazette appeared, in which Waverley was superseded, great part of his troop broke out into actual mutiny, but were surrounded and disarmed by the rest of the regiment. In consequence of the sentence of a court-martial, Houghton and Tims were condemned to be shot, but afterwards permitted to cast lots for life. Houghton, the survivor, showed much penitence, being convinced, from the rebukes and explanations of Colonel Gardiner, that he had really engaged in a very heinous crime. It is remarkable, that as soon as the poor fellow was satisfied of this, he became also convinced that the instigator had acted without authority from Edward, saying, "If it was dishonourable and against Old England, the squire could know nought about it; he never did, or thought to do, any thing dishonourable, no more didn't Sir Everard, nor none of them afore him, and in that belief he would live and die that Ruffin had done it all of his own head."

The strength of conviction with which he expressed himself upon this subject, as well as his assurances that the letters intended for Waverley had been delivered to Ruthven, made that revolution in Colonel Gardiner's opinion which he expressed to Talbot.

The reader has long since understood that Donald Bean Lean played the part of tempter on this occasion. His motives were shortly these. Of an active and intriguing spirit, he had been long employed as a subaltern[1] agent and spy by those in the confidence of the Chevalier, to an extent beyond what was suspected even by Fergus Mac-Ivor, whom, though obliged to him for protection, he regarded with fear and dislike. To success in this political department, he naturally looked for raising himself by some bold stroke above his present hazardous and precarious trade of rapine.[2] He was particularly employed in learning the strength of the regiments in Scotland, the character of the officers, &c., and had long had his eye upon Waverley's troop, as open to temptation. Donald even believed that Waverley himself was at bottom in the Stewart interest, which seemed confirmed by his long visit to the Jacobite Baron of Bradwardine. When, therefore, he came to his cave with one of Glennaquoich's attendants, the robber, who could never appreciate his real motive, which was mere curiosity, was so sanguine as to hope that his

---

1 Subordinate.
2 Practice of seizing and taking away by force the property of others (*OED*).

own talents were to be employed in some intrigue of consequence, under the auspices of this wealthy young Englishman. Nor was he undeceived by Waverley's neglecting all hints and openings afforded for explanation. His conduct passed for prudent reserve, and somewhat piqued Donald Bean, who, supposing himself left out of a secret where confidence promised to be advantageous, determined to have his share in the drama, whether a regular part were assigned him or not. For this purpose, during Waverley's sleep, he possessed himself of his seal, as a token to be used to any of the troopers whom he might discover to be possessed of the captain's confidence. His first journey to Dundee, the town where the regiment was quartered, undeceived him in his original supposition, but opened to him a new field of action. He knew there would be no service so well rewarded by the friends of the Chevalier, as seducing a part of the regular army to his standard. For this purpose he opened the machinations with which the reader is already acquainted, and which form a clew to all the intricacies and obscurities of the narrative previous to Waverley's leaving Glennaquoich.

By Colonel Talbot's advice, Waverley declined detaining in his service the lad whose evidence had thrown additional light on these intrigues. He represented to him it would be doing the man an injury to engage him in a desperate undertaking, and that, whatever should happen, his evidence would go some length, at least, in explaining the circumstances under which Waverley himself had embarked in it. Waverley therefore wrote a short state of what had happened, to his uncle and his father, cautioning them, however, in the present circumstances, not to attempt to answer his letter. Talbot then gave the young man a letter to the commander of one of the English vessels of war cruizing in the frith, requesting him to put the bearer ashore at Berwick, with a pass to proceed to — shire. He was then furnished with money to make an expeditious journey, and directed to get on board the ship by means of bribing a fishing-boat, which, as they afterwards learned, he easily effected.

Tired of the attendance of Callum Beg, who, he thought, had some disposition to act as a spy on his motions, Waverley hired as a servant a simple Edinburgh swain, who had mounted the white cockade in a fit of spleen and jealousy, because Jenny Jop had danced a whole night with Corporal Bullock of the Fusileers.

CHAPTER XXIII.
Intrigues of Society and Love.

COLONEL TALBOT became more kindly in his demeanour towards Waverley after the confidence he had reposed in him, and as they were necessarily much together, the character of the Colonel rose in Waverley's estimation. There seemed at first something harsh in his strong expressions of dislike and censure, although no one was in the general case more open to conviction. The habit of authority had also given his manners some peremptory hardness, notwithstanding the polish which they had received from his intimate acquaintance with the higher circles. As a specimen of the military character, he differed from all whom Waverley had as yet seen. The soldiership of the Baron of Bradwardine was marked by pedantry; that of Major Melville by a sort of martinet attention to the minutiæ and technicalities of discipline, rather suitable to one who was to manœuvre a battalion, than to him who was to command an army; the military spirit of Fergus was so much warped and blended with his plans and political views, that it was less that of a soldier than of a petty sovereign. But Colonel Talbot was in every point the English soldier. His whole soul was devoted to the service of his king and country, without feeling any pride in knowing the theory of his art with the Baron, or its practical minutiæ with the Major, or in applying his science to his own particular plans of ambition, like the Chieftain of Glennaquoich. Added to this, he was a man of extended knowledge and cultivated taste, although strongly tinged, as we have already observed, with those prejudices which are peculiarly English.

The character of Colonel Talbot dawned upon Edward by degrees; for the delay of the Highlanders in the fruitless siege of Edinburgh Castle occupied several weeks, during which Waverley had little to do, excepting to seek such amusement as society afforded. He would willingly have persuaded his new friend to become acquainted with some of his former intimates. But the Colonel, after one or two visits, shook his head, and declined farther experiment. Indeed he went farther, and characterized the Baron as the most intolerable formal pedant he had ever had the misfortune to meet with, and the Chief of Glennaquoich as a Frenchified Scotchman, possessing all the cunning and plausibility of the nation where he was educated, with the proud, vindictive, and turbulent humour of that of his birth. "If the devil," he said, "had sought out an agent expressly for the purpose of embroiling this miserable country, I do not think he could find a better than such a fellow as this, whose temper seems equally active, supple, and mischievous, and who is followed, and implicitly obeyed, by a gang of such cut-throats as those whom you are pleased to admire so much."

The ladies of the party did not escape his censure. He allowed that Flora Mac-Ivor was a fine woman, and Rose Bradwardine a pretty girl. But he alleged that the former destroyed the effect of her beauty by an affectation of the grand airs which she had probably seen practised in the mock court of St Germains.[1] As for Rose Bradwardine, he said it was impossible for any mortal to admire such a little uninformed thing, whose small portion of education was as ill adapted to her sex or youth, as if she had appeared with one of her father's old campaign-coats upon her person for her sole garment. Now much of this was mere spleen and prejudice in the excellent Colonel, with whom the white cockade on the breast, the white rose in the hair, and the Mac at the beginning of a name, would have made a devil out of an angel; and indeed he himself jocularly allowed, that he could not have endured Venus herself, if she had been announced in a drawing-room by the name of Miss Mac-Jupiter.

Waverley, it may easily be believed, looked upon these young ladies with very different eyes. During the period of the siege, he paid them almost daily visits, although he observed with regret that his suit made as little progress in the affections of the former, as the arms of the Chevalier in subduing the fortress. She maintained with rigour the rule she had laid down of treating him with indifference, without either affecting to avoid him, or to shun intercourse with him. Every word, every look, was strictly regulated to accord with her system, and neither the dejection of Waverley, nor the anger which Fergus scarcely suppressed, could extend Flora's attention to Edward beyond that which the most ordinary politeness demanded. On the other hand, Rose Bradwardine gradually rose in Waverley's opinion. He had several opportunities of remarking, that, as her extreme timidity wore off, her manners assumed a higher character; that the agitating circumstances of the stormy time seemed to call forth a certain dignity of feeling and expression, which he had not formerly observed; and that she omitted no opportunity within her reach to extend her knowledge and refine her taste.

Flora Mac-Ivor called Rose her pupil, and was attentive to assist her in her studies, and to fashion both her taste and her understanding. It might have been remarked by a very close observer, that in the presence of Waverley she was much more desirous to exhibit her friend's excellences than her own. But I must request of the reader to suppose, that this kind and disinterested purpose was concealed by the most cautious delicacy, studiously shunning the most distant approach to affectation. So that it was as unlike the usual exhibition

---

1   The mock court of St. Germains refers to James II/VII's court at St. Germain-en-Laye, which he was allowed by Louis XIV after the Glorious Revolution. As Lamont notes, "Flora would not have been old enough to remember the court at St. Germain" (*OW*, 446), since the court was dissolved in 1718.

of one pretty woman affecting to *proner*[1] another, as the friendship of David and Jonathan might be to the intimacy of two Bond-street loungers. The fact is, that though the effect was felt, the cause could hardly be observed. Each of the ladies, like two excellent actresses, were perfect in their parts, and performed them to the delight of the audience; and such being the case, it was almost impossible to discover that the elder constantly ceded to her friend that which was most suitable to her talents.

But to Waverley, Rose Bradwardine possessed an attraction which few men can resist, from the marked interest which she took in every thing that affected him. She was too young and too inexperienced to estimate the full force of the constant attention which she paid to him. Her father was too abstractedly immersed in learned and military discussions to observe her partiality, and Flora Mac-Ivor did not alarm her by remonstrance, because she saw in this line of conduct the most probable chance of her friend securing at length a return of affection.

The truth is, that in her first conversation after their meeting, Rose had discovered the state of her mind to that acute and intelligent friend, although she was not herself aware of it. From that time, Flora was not only determined upon the final rejection of Waverley's addresses, but became anxious that they should, if possible, be transferred to her friend. Nor was she less interested in this plan, though her brother had from time to time talked, as between jest and earnest, of paying his suit to Miss Bradwardine. She knew that Fergus had the true continental latitude of opinion respecting the institution of marriage, and would not have given his hand to an angel, unless for the purpose of strengthening his alliances, and increasing his influence and wealth. The Baron's whim of transferring his estate to the distant heir male, instead of his own daughter, was therefore likely to be an insurmountable obstacle to his entertaining any serious thoughts of Rose Bradwardine. Indeed, Fergus's brain was a perpetual workshop of scheme and intrigue, of every possible kind and description; while, like many a mechanic of more ingenuity than steadiness, he would often unexpectedly, and without any apparent motive, abandon one plan, and go earnestly to work upon another, which was either fresh from the forge of his imagination, or had at some former period been flung aside half finished. It was therefore often difficult to guess what line of conduct he might finally adopt upon any given occasion.

Although Flora was sincerely attached to her brother, whose high energies might indeed have commanded her admiration even without the ties which bound them together, she was by no means blind to his

---

1 Flatter.

faults, which she considered as dangerous to the hopes of any woman, who should found her ideas of a happy marriage in the peaceful enjoyment of domestic society, and the exchange of mutual and engrossing affection. The real disposition of Waverley, on the other hand, notwithstanding his dreams of tented fields and military honour, seemed exclusively domestic. He asked and received no share in the busy scenes which were constantly going on around him, and was rather annoyed than interested by the discussion of contending claims, rights, and interests, which often passed in his presence. All this pointed him out as the person formed to make happy a spirit like that of Rose, which corresponded with his own.

She remarked this point in Waverley's character one day while she sat with Miss Bradwardine. "His genius and elegant taste," answered Rose, "cannot be interested in such trifling discussions. What is it to him, for example, whether the Chief of the Macindallaghers, who has brought out only fifty men, should be a colonel or a captain? And how could Mr Waverley be supposed to interest himself in the violent altercation between your brother and young Corrinaschian, whether the post of honour is due to the eldest cadet of a clan or the youngest?"

"My dear Rose, if he were the hero you suppose him, he would interest himself in these matters, not indeed as important in themselves, but for the purpose of mediating between the ardent spirits who actually do make them the subject of discord. You saw when Corrinaschian raised his voice in great passion, and laid his hand upon his sword, Waverley lifted his head as if he had just awaked from a dream, and asked, with great composure, what the matter was."

"Well, and did not the laughter they fell into at his absence of mind, serve better to break off the dispute, than any thing he could have said to them?"

"True, my dear," answered Flora; "but not quite so creditably for Waverley as if he had brought them to their senses by force of reason."

"Would you have him peace-maker general between all the gunpowder Highlanders in the army? I beg your pardon, Flora, your brother, you know, is out of the question; he has more sense than half of them. But can you think the fierce, hot, furious spirits, of whose brawls we see much and hear more, and who terrify me out of my life every day in the world, are at all to be compared to Waverley?"

"I do not compare him with those uneducated men, my dear Rose. I only lament, that, with his talents and genius, he does not assume that place in society for which they eminently fit him, and that he does not lend their full impulse to the noble cause in which he has enlisted. Are there not Lochiel, and P—, and M—, and G—, all men of the highest education, as well as the first talents,—why will he not stoop like them to be alive and useful?—I often believe his zeal is frozen by that proud cold-blooded Englishman, whom he now lives with so much."

"Colonel Talbot?—he is a very disagreeable person, to be sure. He looks as if he thought no Scottish woman worth the trouble of handing her a cup of tea. But Waverley is so gentle, so well informed"—

"Yes," said Flora, smiling, "he can admire the moon, and quote a stanza from Tasso."

"Besides, you know how he fought," added Miss Bradwardine.

"For mere fighting," answered Flora, "I believe all men (that is, who deserve the name) are pretty much alike; there is generally more courage required to run away. They have besides, when confronted with each other, a certain instinct for strife, as we see in other male animals, such as dogs, bulls, and so forth. But high and perilous enterprise is not Waverley's forte. He would never have been his celebrated ancestor Sir Nigel, but only Sir Nigel's eulogist and poet. I will tell you where he will be at home, my dear, and in his place,—in the quiet circle of domestic happiness, lettered indolence, and elegant enjoyments, of Waverley-Honour. And he will refit the old library in the most exquisite Gothic taste, and garnish its shelves with the rarest and most valuable volumes;—and he will draw plans and landscapes, and write verses, and rear temples, and dig grottoes;—and he will stand in a clear summer night in the colonnade before the hall, and gaze on the deer as they stray in the moonlight, or lie shadowed by the boughs of the huge old fantastic oaks;—and he will repeat verses to his beautiful wife, who will hang upon his arm;—and he will be a happy man."

And she will be a happy woman, thought poor Rose. But she only sighed, and dropped the conversation.

CHAPTER XXIV.
Fergus, a Suitor.

WAVERLEY had, indeed, as he looked closer into the state of the Chevalier's Court, less reason to be satisfied with it. It contained, as they say an acorn includes all the ramifications of the future oak, as many seeds of *tracasserie*[1] and intrigue, as might have done honour to the Court of a large empire. Every person of consequence had some separate object, which he pursued with a fury that Waverley considered as altogether disproportioned to its importance. Almost all had their reasons for discontent, although the most legitimate was that of

---

1 Trickery.

the worthy old Baron, who was only distressed on account of the common cause.

"We shall hardly," said he one morning to Waverley, when they had been viewing the castle,—"we shall hardly gain the obsidional crown,[1] which you wot well was made of the roots or grain which takes root within the place besieged, or it may be of the herb woodbind, *paretaria*, or pellitory;[2] we shall not, I say, gain it by this same blockade or leaguer of Edinburgh Castle." For this opinion, he gave most learned and satisfactory reasons, that the reader may not care to hear repeated.

Having escaped from the old gentleman, Waverley went to Fergus's lodgings by appointment, to await his return from Holyrood-House. "I am to have a particular audience to-morrow," said Fergus to Waverley, overnight, "and you must meet me to wish me joy of the success which I securely anticipate."

The morrow came, and in the Chief's apartment he found Ensign Maccombich waiting to make report of his turn of duty in a sort of ditch which they had dug across the Castle-hill, and called a trench. In a short time the Chief's voice was heard on the stair in a tone of impatient fury:—"Callum,—why, Callum Beg,—Diaoul!" He entered the room with all the marks of a man agitated by a towering passion; and there were few upon whose features rage produced a more violent effect. The veins of his forehead swelled when he was in such agitation; his nostril became dilated; his cheek and eye inflamed; and his look that of a demoniac. These appearances of half-suppressed rage were the more frightful, because they were obviously caused by a strong effort to temper with discretion an almost ungovernable paroxysm of passion, and resulted from an internal conflict of the most dreadful kind, which agitated his whole frame of mortality.

As he entered the apartment, he unbuckled his broadsword, and throwing it down with such violence, that the weapon rolled to the other end of the room, "I know not what," he exclaimed, "withholds me from taking a solemn oath that I will never more draw it in his cause:—load my pistols, Callum, and bring them hither instantly;—instantly!" Callum, whom nothing ever startled, dismayed, or disconcerted, obeyed very cooly. Evan Dhu, upon whose brow the suspicion that his Chief had been insulted, called up a corresponding storm, swelled in sullen silence, awaiting to learn where or upon whom vengeance was to descend.

"So, Waverley, you are there," said the Chief, after a moment's rec-

---

1   The reward given by the Roman people to a Roman general or commander who delivered their town from siege (*GW*).

2   A wall-creeping plant.

ollection;—"Yes, I remember I asked you to share my triumph, and you have come to witness my—disappointment we shall call it." Evan now presented the written report he had in his hand, which Fergus threw from him with great passion. "I wish to God," he said, "the old den would tumble down upon the heads of the fools who attack, and the knaves who defend it! I see, Waverley, you think I am mad—leave us, Evan, but be within call."

"The Colonel's in an unco kippage,"[1] said Mrs Flockhart to Evan as he descended; "I wish he may be weel,—the very veins on his brent brow are swelled like whip-cord; wad he no tak something?"

"He usually lets blood for these fits," answered the Highland Ancient with great composure.

When this officer left the room, the Chieftain gradually reassumed some degree of composure. "I know, Waverley," he said, "that Colonel Talbot has persuaded you to curse ten times a-day your engagement with us;—nay, never deny it, for I am at this moment tempted to curse my own. Would you believe it, I made this very morning two suits to the Prince, and he has rejected them both; what do you think of it?"

"What can I think," answered Waverley, "till I know what your requests were?"

"Why, what signifies what they were, man? I tell you it was I that made them; I, to whom he owes more than to any three who have joined the standard; for I negotiated the whole business, and brought in all the Perthshire men when not one would have stirred. I am not likely, I think, to ask any thing very unreasonable, and if I did, they might have stretched a point.—Well, but you shall know all, now that I can draw my breath again with some freedom.—You remember my earl's patent; it is dated some years back, for services then rendered; and certainly my merit has not been diminished, to say the least, by my subsequent behaviour. Now, sir, I value this bauble of a coronet as little as you can, or any philosopher on earth; for I hold that the chief of such a clan as the Sliochd nan Ivor is superior in rank to any earl in Scotland. But I had a particular reason for assuming this cursed title at this time. You must know that I learned accidentally that the Prince has been pressing that old foolish Baron of Bradwardine to disinherit his male heir, or nineteenth or twentieth cousin, who has taken a command in the Elector of Hanover's militia, and to settle his estate upon your pretty little friend Rose; and this, as being the command of his king and overlord, who may alter the destination of a fief at pleasure, the old gentleman seems well reconciled to."

"And what becomes of the homage?"

1 Very violent passion (*WSG*).

"Curse the homage!—I believe Rose is to pull off the queen's slipper on her coronation-day, or some such trash. Well, sir, as Rose Bradwardine would always have made a suitable match for me, but for this idiotical predilection of her father for the heir-male, it occurred to me there now remained no obstacle, unless that the Baron might expect his daughter's husband to take the name of Bradwardine (which you know would be impossible in my case), and that this might be evaded by my assuming the title to which I had so good a right, and which, of course, would supersede that difficulty. If she was to be also Viscountess Bradwardine, in her own right, after her father's demise, so much the better; I could have no objection."

"But, Fergus," said Waverley, "I had no idea that you had any affection for Miss Bradwardine, and you are always sneering at her father."

"I have as much affection for Miss Bradwardine, my good friend, as I think it necessary to have for the future mistress of my family, and the mother of my children. She is a very pretty, intelligent girl, and is certainly of one of the very first Lowland families; and, with a little of Flora's instructions and forming, will make a very good figure. As to her father, he is an original, it is true, and an absurd one enough; but he has given such severe lessons to Sir Hew Halbert, that dear defunct the Laird of Balmawhapple, and others, that nobody dare laugh at him, so his absurdity goes for nothing. I tell you there could have been no earthly objection—none. I had settled the thing entirely in my own mind."

"But had you asked the Baron's consent," said Waverley, "or Rose's?"

"To what purpose? To have spoken to the Baron before I had assumed my title would have only provoked a premature and irritating discussion on the subject of the change of name, when, as Earl of Glennaquoich, I had only to propose to him to carry his d—d bear and boot-jack *party per pale*,[1] or in a scutcheon of pretence,[2] or in a separate shield perhaps—any way that would not blemish my own coat-of-arms. And as to Rose, I don't see what objection she could have made, if her father was satisfied."

"Perhaps the same that your sister makes to me, you being satisfied."

Fergus gave a broad stare at the comparison which this supposition implied, but cautiously suppressed the answer which rose to his tongue. "O, we should easily have arranged all that.—So, sir, I craved a private interview, and this morning was assigned; and I asked you to meet me here, thinking, like a fool, that I should want your counte-

1 "Dividing the shield vertically so that each coat occupies half of it" (*OW*, 447).
2 "A small shield bearing the wife's arms in the centre of the shield" (*OW*, 447).

nance as bride's-man.[1] Well—I state my pretensions—they are not denied—the promises so repeatedly made, and the patent granted—they are acknowledged. But I propose, as a natural consequence, to assume the rank which the patent bestowed.—I have the old story of the jealousy of C— and M— trumpt up against me.—I resist this pretext, and offer to procure their written acquiescence, in virtue of the date of my patent as prior to their silly claims.—I assure you I would have had such a consent from them, if it had been at the point of the sword. And then out comes the real truth; and he dares to tell me, to my face, that my patent must be suppressed for the present, for fear of disgusting that rascally coward and *faineant*[2]—(naming the rival chief of his own clan) who has no better title to be a chieftain than I to be Emperor of China; and who is pleased to shelter his dastardly reluctance to come out, agreeable to his promise twenty times pledged, under a pretended jealousy of the Prince's partiality to me. And, to leave this miserable driveller without a pretence for his cowardice, the Prince asks it as a personal favour of me, forsooth, not to press my just and reasonable request at this moment. After this, put your faith in princes!"

"And did your audience end here?"

"End? O no! I was determined to leave him no pretence for his ingratitude, and I therefore stated, with all the composure I could muster,—for I promise you I trembled with passion,—the particular reasons I had for wishing that his Royal Highness would impose upon me any other mode of exhibiting my duty and devotion, as my views in life made, what at any other time would have been a mere trifle, at this crisis a severe sacrifice; and then I explained to him my full plan."

"And what did the Prince answer?"

"Answer? Why—it is well it is written, Curse not the king, no, not in thy thought!—why, he answered, that truly he was glad I had made him my confidant, to prevent more grievous disappointment, for he could assure me, upon the word of a prince, that Miss Bradwardine's affections were engaged, and he was under a particular promise to favour them. 'So, my dear Fergus,' said he, with his most gracious cast of smile, 'as the marriage is utterly out of question, there need be no hurry, you know, about the earldom.' And so he glided off, and left me *planté la*."[3]

"And what did you do?"

"I'll tell you what I *could* have done at that moment—sold myself to the devil or the Elector, whichever offered the dearest revenge. How-

---

1 The bride's-man delivers the bride to the bridegroom (*OED*).

2 Sluggard (*PW*, 593).

3 Standing there.

ever I am now cool. I know he intends to marry her to some of his rascally Frenchmen, or his Irish officers, but I will watch them close; and let the man that would supplant me look well to himself.—*Bisogna coprirsi, Signor.*"[1]

After some further conversation, unnecessary to be detailed, Waverley took leave of the Chieftain, whose fury had now subsided into a deep and strong desire of vengeance, and returned home, scarce able to analyze the mixture of feelings which the narrative had awakened in his own bosom.

CHAPTER XXV.
"To one Thing constant never."

"I AM the very child of caprice," said Waverley to himself, as he bolted the door of his apartment, and paced it with hasty steps.—"What is it to me that Fergus Mac-Ivor should wish to marry Rose Bradwardine?—I love her not.—I might have been loved by her perhaps—but I rejected her simple, natural, and affecting attachment, instead of cherishing it into tenderness, and dedicated myself to one who will never love mortal man, unless old Warwick, the King-maker,[2] should rise from the dead. The Baron too—I would not have cared about his estate, and so the name would have been no stumbling-block. The devil might have taken the barren moors, and drawn off the royal *caligæ*, for any thing I would have minded. But, framed as she is for domestic affection and tenderness, for giving and receiving all those kind and quiet attentions which sweeten life to those who pass it together, she is sought by Fergus Mac-Ivor. He will not use her ill, to be sure—of that he is incapable—but he will neglect her after the first month; he will be too intent on subduing some rival chieftain, or circumventing some favourite at court, on gaining some heathy hill and lake, or adding to his bands some new troop of caterans, to inquire what she does, or how she amuses herself.

> 'And then will canker sorrow eat her bud,
> And chase the native beauty from her cheek;
> And she will look as hollow as a ghost,
> And dim and meagre as an ague fit,
> And so she'll die.'[3]

---

1 "Look out for yourself, Sir" (*PW*, 593).
2 Richard Neville, First Earl of Warwick (1428-71) was known as "the King-maker" because of his role in putting both Henry VI, a Lancastrian, and Edward IV, a Yorkist, on the English throne (*OCBH*, 968).
3 *King John* III.iv.82-86.

And such a catastrophe of the most gentle creature on earth might have been prevented, if Mr Edward Waverley had had his eyes!—Upon my word, I cannot understand how I thought Flora so much, that is, so *very* much, handsomer than Rose. She is taller indeed, and her manner more formed; but many people think Miss Bradwardine's more natural; and she is certainly much younger. I should think Flora is two years older than I am—I will look at them particularly this evening."

And with this resolution Waverley went to drink tea (as the fashion was Sixty Years since) at the house of a lady of quality, attached to the cause of the Chevalier, where he found, as he expected, both the ladies. All rose as he entered, but Flora immediately resumed her place, and the conversation in which she was engaged. Rose, on the contrary, almost imperceptibly made a little way in the crowded circle for his advancing the corner of a chair.—"Her manner, upon the whole, is most engaging," said Waverley to himself.

A dispute occurred whether the Gaelic or Italian language was most liquid, and best adapted for poetry: the opinion for the Gaelic, which probably might not have found supporters elsewhere, was here fiercely defended by seven Highland ladies, who talked at the top of their lungs, and screamed the company deaf, with examples of Celtic *euphonia*.[1] Flora, observing the Lowland ladies sneer at the comparison, produced some reasons to show that it was not altogether so absurd; but Rose, when asked for her opinion, gave it with animation in praise of Italian, which she had studied with Waverley's assistance. "She has a more correct ear than Flora, though a less accomplished musician," said Waverley to himself. "I suppose Miss Mac-Ivor will next compare Mac-Murrough nan Fonn[2] to Ariosto!"

Lastly, it so befell that the company differed whether Fergus should be asked to perform on the flute, at which he was an adept, or Waverley invited to read a play of Shakspeare; and the lady of the house good-humouredly undertook to collect the votes of the company for poetry or music, under the condition, that the gentleman whose talents were not laid under contribution that evening, should contribute them to enliven the next. It chanced that Rose had the casting vote. Now Flora, who seemed to impose it as a rule upon herself never to countenance any proposal which might seem to encourage Waverley, had voted for music, providing the Baron would take his violin to accompany Fergus. "I wish you joy of your taste, Miss Mac-Ivor," thought Edward, as they sought for his book. "I thought it better when

---

1 Euphony: the quality of having a pleasant sound.
2 Mac-Murrough of Fonn.

we were at Glennaquoich; but certainly the Baron is no great performer, and Shakspeare is worth listening to."

Romeo and Juliet was selected, and Edward read with taste, feeling, and spirit, several scenes from that play. All the company applauded with their hands, and many with their tears. Flora, to whom the drama was well known, was among the former; Rose, to whom it was altogether new, belonged to the latter class of admirers. "She has more feeling too," said Waverley, internally.

The conversation turning upon the incidents of the play, and upon the characters, Fergus declared that the only one worth naming, as a man of fashion and spirit, was Mercutio. "I could not," he said, "quite follow all his old-fashioned wit, but he must have been a very pretty fellow, according to the ideas of his time."

"And it was a shame," said Ensign Maccombich, who usually followed his Colonel everywhere, "for that Tibbert, or Taggart, or whatever was his name, to stick him under the other gentleman's arm while he was redding the fray."

The ladies, of course, declared loudly in favour of Romeo, but this opinion did not go undisputed. The mistress of the house, and several other ladies, severely reprobated the levity with which the hero transfers his affections from Rosalind to Juliet. Flora remained silent until her opinion was repeatedly requested, and then answered, she thought the circumstance objected to, not only reconcilable to nature, but such as in the highest degree evinced the art of the poet. "Romeo is described," said she, "as a young man, peculiarly susceptible of the softer passions; his love is at first fixed upon a woman who could afford it no return; this he repeatedly tells you,—

'From love's weak, childish bow she lives unharmed';[1]

and again,—

'She hath forsworn to love.'[2]

Now, as it was impossible that Romeo's love, supposing him a reasonable being, could continue to subsist without hope, the poet has, with great art, seized the moment when he was reduced actually to despair, to throw in his way an object more accomplished than her by whom he had been rejected, and who is disposed to repay his attachment. I can scarce conceive a situation more calculated to enhance the ardour of Romeo's affection for Juliet, than his being at once raised by her

---

1 Shakespeare, *Romeo and Juliet*, I.i.209.
2 Shakespeare, *Romeo and Juliet*, I.i.221.

from the state of drooping melancholy in which he appears first upon the scene, to the ecstatic state in which he exclaims—

> —'come what sorrow can,
> It cannot countervail the exchange of joy
> That one short moment gives me in her sight.'"[1]

"Good now, Miss Mac-Ivor," said a young lady of quality, "do you mean to cheat us out of our prerogative? Will you persuade us love cannot subsist without hope, or that the lover must become fickle if the lady is cruel? O fie! I did not expect such an unsentimental conclusion."

"A lover, my dear Lady Betty," said Flora, "may, I conceive, persevere in his suit under very discouraging circumstances. Affection can (now and then) withstand very severe storms of rigour, but not a long polar frost of downright indifference. Don't, even with *your* attractions, try the experiment upon any lover whose faith you value. Love will subsist on wonderfully little hope, but not altogether without it."

"It will be just like Duncan Mac-Girdie's mare," said Evan, "if your ladyships please; he wanted to use her by degrees to live without meat, and just as he had put her on a straw a-day, the poor thing died!"

Evan's illustration set the company a-laughing, and the discourse took a different turn. Shortly afterwards the party broke up, and Edward returned home, musing on what Flora had said. "I will love my Rosalind no more," said he; "she has given me a broad enough hint for that; and I will speak to her brother, and resign my suit. But for a Juliet—would it be handsome to interfere with Fergus's pretensions?—though it is impossible they can ever succeed: and should they miscarry, what then?—Why then *alors comme alors*."[2] And with this resolution, of being guided by circumstances, did our hero commit himself to repose.

CHAPTER XXVI.
A brave Man in Sorrow.

IF my fair readers should be of opinion that my hero's levity in love is altogether unpardonable, I must remind them, that all his griefs and difficulties did not arise from that sentimental source. Even the lyric poet, who complains so feelingly of the pains of love, could not forget, that, at the same time, he was "in debt and in drink," which, doubtless, were great aggravations of his distress. There were, indeed, whole days in which Waverley thought neither of Flora nor Rose Bradwar-

---

1 Shakespeare, *Romeo and Juliet*, II.vi.3-5.
2 So be it.

dine, but which were spent in melancholy conjectures on the probable state of matters at Waverley-Honour, and the dubious issue of the civil contest in which he was pledged. Colonel Talbot often engaged him in discussions upon the justice of the cause he had espoused. "Not," he said, "that it is possible for you to quit it at this present moment, for, come what will, you must stand by your rash engagement. But I wish you to be aware that the right is not with you; that you are fighting against the real interests of your country; and that you ought, as an Englishman and a patriot, to take the first opportunity to leave this unhappy expedition before the snow-ball melts."

In such political disputes, Waverley usually opposed the common arguments of his party, with which it is unnecessary to trouble the reader. But he had little to say when the Colonel urged him to compare the strength by which they had undertaken to overthrow the government, with that which was now assembling very rapidly for its support. To this statement Waverley had but one answer: "If the cause I have undertaken be perilous, there would be greater disgrace in abandoning it." And in his turn he generally silenced Colonel Talbot, and succeeded in changing the subject.

One night, when, after a long dispute of this nature, the friends had separated, and our hero had retired to bed, he was awakened about midnight by a suppressed groan. He started up and listened; it came from the apartment of Colonel Talbot, which was divided from his own by a wainscotted partition, with a door of communication. Waverley approached this door, and distinctly heard one or two deep-drawn sighs. What could be the matter? The Colonel had parted from him, apparently, in his usual state of spirits. He must have been taken suddenly ill. Under this impression, he opened the door of communication very gently, and perceived the Colonel, in his night-gown, seated by a table, on which lay a letter and picture. He raised his head hastily, as Edward stood uncertain whether to advance or retire, and Waverley perceived that his cheeks were stained with tears.

As if ashamed at being found giving way to such emotion, Colonel Talbot rose with apparent displeasure, and said, with some sternness, "I think, Mr Waverley, my own apartment, and the hour, might have secured even a prisoner against"—

"Do not say *intrusion*, Colonel Talbot; I heard you breathe hard, and feared you were ill; that alone could have induced me to break in upon you."

"I am well," said the Colonel, "perfectly well."

"But you are distressed," said Edward: "is there any thing can be done?"

"Nothing, Mr Waverley; I was only thinking of home, and some unpleasant occurrences there."

"Good God, my uncle!" exclaimed Waverley.

"No, it is a grief entirely my own. I am ashamed you should have seen it disarm me so much; but it must have its course at times, that it may be at others more decently supported. I would have kept it secret from you; for I think it will grieve you, and yet you can administer no consolation. But you have surprised me,—I see you are surprised yourself,—and I hate mystery. Read that letter."

The letter was from Colonel Talbot's sister, and in these words:

"I received yours, my dearest brother, by Hodges. Sir E.W. and Mr R. are still at large, but are not permitted to leave London. I wish to heaven I could give you as good an account of matters in the square. But the news of the unhappy affair at Preston came upon us, with the dreadful addition that you were among the fallen. You know Lady Emily's state of health, when your friendship for Sir E. induced you to leave her. She was much harassed with the sad accounts from Scotland of the rebellion having broken out; but kept up her spirits, as, she said, it became your wife, and for the sake of the future heir, so long hoped for in vain. Alas, my dear brother, these hopes are now ended! Notwithstanding all my watchful care, this unhappy rumour reached her without preparation. She was taken ill immediately; and the poor infant scarce survived its birth. Would to God this were all! But although the contradiction of the horrible report by your own letter has greatly revived her spirits, yet Dr— apprehends, I grieve to say, serious, and even dangerous, consequences to her health, especially from the uncertainty in which she must necessarily remain for some time, aggravated by the ideas she has formed of the ferocity of those with whom you are a prisoner.

"Do therefore, my dear brother, as soon as this reaches you, endeavour to gain your release, by parole, by ransom, or any way that is practicable. I do not exaggerate Lady Emily's state of health; but I must not—dare not—suppress the truth. Ever, my dear Philip, your most affectionate sister,

"LUCY TALBOT."

Edward stood motionless when he had perused this letter; for the conclusion was inevitable, that, by the Colonel's journey in quest of him, he had incurred this heavy calamity. It was severe enough, even in its irremediable part; for Colonel Talbot and Lady Emily, long without a family, had fondly exulted in the hopes which were now blasted. But this disappointment was nothing to the extent of the threatened evil; and Edward, with horror, regarded himself as the original cause of both.

Ere he could collect himself sufficiently to speak, Colonel Talbot had recovered his usual composure of manner, though his troubled eye denoted his mental agony.

"She is a woman, my young friend, who may justify even a soldier's tears." He reached him the miniature, exhibiting features which fully justified the eulogium; "and yet, God knows, what you see of her there is the least of the charms she possesses—possessed, I should perhaps say—but God's will be done."

"You must fly—you must fly instantly to her relief. It is not—it shall not be too late."

"Fly? How is it possible? I am a prisoner—upon parole."

"I am your keeper—I restore your parole—I am to answer for you."

"You cannot do so consistently with your duty; nor can I accept a discharge from you, with due regard to my own honour—you would be made responsible."

"I will answer it with my head, if necessary," said Waverley impetuously.[1] "I have been the unhappy cause of the loss of your child, make me not the murderer of your wife."

"No, my dear Edward," said Talbot, taking him kindly by the hand, "you are in no respect to blame; and if I concealed this domestic distress for two days, it was lest your sensibility should view it in that light. You could not think of me, hardly knew of my existence, when I left England in quest of you. It is a responsibility, Heaven knows, sufficiently heavy for mortality, that we must answer for the foreseen and direct result of our actions,—for their indirect and consequential operation, the great and good Being, who alone can foresee the dependence of human events on each other, hath not pronounced his frail creatures liable."

"But that you should have left Lady Emily," said Waverley, with much emotion, "in the situation of all others the most interesting to a husband, to seek a"—

"I only did my duty," answered Colonel Talbot, calmly, "and I do not, ought not, to regret it. If the path of gratitude and honour were always smooth and easy, there would be little merit in following it; but it moves often in contradiction to our interest and passions, and sometimes to our better affections. These are the trials of life, and this, though not the least bitter" (the tears came unbidden to his eyes), "is not the first which it has been my fate to encounter.—But we will talk of this to-morrow," he said, wringing Waverley's hands. "Good night; strive to forget it for a few hours. It will dawn, I think, by six, and it is now past two. Good night."

Edward retired, without trusting his voice with a reply.

---

1 Scott added adverbs to the dialogue tags in the conversation between Waverley and Talbot that follows in order to emphasize Waverley's emotionalism in contrast to Talbot's maturity.

CHAPTER XXVII.
Exertion.

WHEN Colonel Talbot entered the breakfast-parlour next morning, he learned from Waverley's servant that our hero had been abroad at an early hour, and was not yet returned. The morning was well advanced before he again appeared. He arrived out of breath, but with an air of joy that astonished Colonel Talbot.

"There," said he, throwing a paper on the table, "there is my morning's work.—Alick, pack up the Colonel's clothes. Make haste, make haste."

The Colonel examined the paper with astonishment. It was a pass from the Chevalier to Colonel Talbot, to repair to Leith, or any other port in possession of his Royal Highness's troops, and there to embark for England or elsewhere, at his free pleasure; he only giving his parole of honour not to bear arms against the house of Stewart for the space of a twelvemonth.

"In the name of God," said the Colonel, his eyes sparkling with eagerness, "how did you obtain this?"

"I was at the Chevalier's levee as soon as he usually rises. He was gone to the camp at Duddingston. I pursued him thither; asked and obtained an audience—but I will tell you not a word more, unless I see you begin to pack."

"Before I know whether I can avail myself of this passport, or how it was obtained?"

"O, you can take out the things again, you know.—Now I see you busy, I will go on. When I first mentioned your name, his eyes sparkled almost as bright as yours did two minutes since. 'Had you,' he earnestly asked, 'shown any sentiments favourable to his cause?' 'Not in the least, nor was there any hope you would do so.' His countenance fell. I requested your freedom. 'Impossible,' he said;—'your importance, as a friend and confidant of such and such personages, made my request altogether extravagant.' I told him my own story and yours; and asked him to judge what my feelings must be by his own. He has a heart, and a kind one, Colonel Talbot, you may say what you please. He took a sheet of paper, and wrote the pass with his own hand. 'I will not trust myself with my council,' he said; 'they will argue me out of what is right. I will not endure that a friend, valued as I value you, should be loaded with the painful reflections which must afflict you in case of further misfortune in Colonel Talbot's family; nor will I keep a brave enemy a prisoner under such circumstances. Besides,' said he, 'I think I can justify myself to my prudent advisers, by pleading the good effect such lenity will produce on the minds of the great English families with whom Colonel Talbot is connected.'"

"There the politician peeped out," said the Colonel.

"Well, at least he concluded like a king's son:— 'Take the passport; I have added a condition for form's sake; but if the Colonel objects to it, let him depart without giving any parole whatever. I come here to war with men, but not to distress or endanger women.'"

"Well, I never thought to have been so much indebted to the Pretend—"

"To the Prince," said Waverley, smiling.

"To the Chevalier," said the Colonel; "it is a good travelling name, and which we may both freely use. Did he say any thing more?"

"Only asked if there was any thing else he could oblige me in; and when I replied in the negative, he shook me by the hand, and wished all his followers were as considerate, since some friends of mine not only asked all he had to bestow, but many things which were entirely out of his power, or that of the greatest sovereign upon earth. Indeed, he said, no prince seemed, in the eyes of his followers, so like the Deity as himself, if you were to judge from the extravagant requests which they daily preferred to him."

"Poor young gentleman," said the Colonel, "I suppose he begins to feel the difficulties of his situation. Well, dear Waverley, this is more than kind, and shall not be forgotten while Philip Talbot can remember any thing. My life—pshaw—let Emily thank you for that—this is a favour worth fifty lives. I cannot hesitate on giving my parole in the circumstances: there it is—(he wrote it out in form).—And now, how am I to get off?"

"All that is settled: your baggage is packed, my horses wait, and a boat has been engaged, by the Prince's permission, to put you on board the Fox frigate. I sent a messenger down to Leith on purpose."

"That will do excellently well. Captain Beaver is my particular friend: he will put me ashore at Berwick or Shields, from whence I can ride post to London;—and you must intrust me with the packet of papers which you recovered by means of your Miss Bean Lean. I may have an opportunity of using them to your advantage.—But I see your Highland friend, Glen— what do you call his barbarous name? And his orderly with him—I must not call him his orderly cut-throat any more, I suppose. See how he walks as if the world were his own, with the bonnet on one side of his head, and his plaid puffed out across his breast! I should like now to meet that youth where my hands were not tied: I would tame his pride, or he should tame mine."

"For shame, Colonel Talbot! You swell at sight of tartan, as the bull is said to do at scarlet. You and Mac-Ivor have some points not much unlike, so far as national prejudice is concerned."

The latter part of this discourse took place in the street. They passed the Chief, the Colonel and he sternly and punctiliously greeting each other, like two duellists before they take their ground. It was evident the dislike was mutual. "I never see that surly fellow that dogs his heels," said the Colonel, after he had mounted his horse, "but he reminds me of lines I have somewhere heard—upon the stage, I think:

> —— 'Close behind him
> Stalks sullen Bertram, like a sorcerer's fiend,
> Pressing to be employed.'"[1]

"I assure you, Colonel," said Waverley, "that you judge too harshly of the Highlanders."

"Not a whit, not a whit; I cannot spare them a jot; I cannot bate them an ace.[2] Let them stay in their own barren mountains, and puff and swell, and hang their bonnets on the horns of the moon, if they have a mind; but what business have they to come where people wear breeches, and speak an intelligible language?—I mean intelligible in comparison to their gibberish, for even the Lowlanders talk a kind of English little better than the Negroes in Jamaica. I could pity the Pr—, I mean the Chevalier himself, for having so many desperadoes about him. And they learn their trade so early. There is a kind of subaltern imp, for example, a sort of sucking devil, whom your friend Glena— Glenamuck there, has sometimes in his train. To look at him, he is about fifteen years; but he is a century old in mischief and villainy. He was playing at quoits[3] the other day in the court; a gentleman, a decent-looking person enough, came past, and as a quoit hit his shin, he lifted his cane: but my young bravo whips out his pistol, like Beau Clincher in the Trip to the Jubilee,[4] and had not a scream of *Gardez l'eau*,[5] from an upper window, set all parties a scampering for fear of the inevitable consequences, the poor gentleman would have lost his life by the hands of that little cockatrice."

"A fine character you'll give Scotland upon your return, Colonel Talbot."

"O, Justice Shallow," said the Colonel, "will save me the trouble— 'Barren, barren, beggars all, beggars all. Marry, good air,'[6]—and that

---

1 From Charles Maturin's (1782-1824) *Bertram* (1816).

2 Obsolete expression of incredulity (*OED*).

3 Game wherein a quoit (metal or stone disc) is aimed at a pin stuck in the ground, and is intended to fall with the ring surrounding it (*OED*).

4 A character in *The Constant Couple, or, A Trip to the Jubilee* (1700), by George Farquhar (1678-1707).

5 Watch out for the contents of the chamber pot being dumped from the window above the street into the kennel, or gutter below.

6 Shakespeare, *Henry IV, Part II*, V.iii.7-8.

only when you are fairly out of Edinburgh, and not yet come to Leith, as is our case at present."

In a short time they arrived at the seaport:—

> "The boat rock'd at the pier of Leith,
> Full loud the wind blew down the ferry;
> The ship rode at the Berwick Law"—[1]

"Farewell, Colonel; may you find all as you would wish it! Perhaps we may meet sooner than you expect: they talk of an immediate route to England."

"Tell me nothing of that," said Talbot; "I wish to carry no news of your motions."

"Simply, then, adieu. Say, with a thousand kind greetings, all that is dutiful and affectionate to Sir Everard and Aunt Rachel.—Think of me as kindly as you can—speak of me as indulgently as your conscience will permit, and once more adieu."

"And adieu, my dear Waverley; many, many thanks for your kindness. Unplaid yourself on the first opportunity. I shall ever think on you with gratitude, and the worst of my censure shall be, *Que diable alloit il faire dans cette galere?*"[2]

And thus they parted, Colonel Talbot going on board of the boat, and Waverley returning to Edinburgh.

CHAPTER XXVIII.
The March.

IT is not our purpose to intrude upon the province of history. We shall therefore only remind our readers, that about the beginning of November the Young Chevalier, at the head of about six thousand men at the utmost, resolved to peril his cause on an attempt to penetrate into the centre of England, although aware of the mighty preparations which were made for his reception. They set forward on this crusade in weather which would have rendered any other troops incapable of marching, but which in reality gave these active mountaineers advantages over a less hardy enemy. In defiance of a superior army lying upon the Borders, under Field-Marshal Wade,[3] they besieged

---

1 Robert Burns, "The Silver Tassie."
2 "What the devil was he doing there?"—said by Geronte in Molière's *Les Fourberies de Scapin* (*PW*, 594).
3 Field-Marshal George Wade (1673-1748) commanded the Hanoverian army in Newcastle during the Jacobite Rebellion of 1745 (*OCBH*, 960).

and took Carlisle, and soon afterwards prosecuted their daring march to the southward.

As Colonel Mac-Ivor's regiment marched in the van of the clans, he and Waverley, who now equalled any Highlander in the endurance of fatigue, and was become somewhat acquainted with their language, were perpetually at its head. They marked the progress of the army, however, with very different eyes. Fergus, all air and fire, and confident against the world in arms, measured nothing but that every step was a yard nearer London. He neither asked, expected, nor desired any aid, except that of the clans, to place the Stewarts once more on the throne; and when by chance a few adherents joined the standard, he always considered them in the light of new claimants upon the favours of the future monarch, who, he concluded, must therefore subtract for their gratification so much of the bounty which ought to be shared among his Highland followers.

Edward's views were very different. He could not but observe, that in those towns in which they proclaimed James the Third, "no man cried, God bless him." The mob stared and listened, heartless, stupified, and dull, but gave few signs even of that boisterous spirit, which induces them to shout upon all occasions, for the mere exercise of their most sweet voices. The Jacobites had been taught to believe that the north-western counties abounded with wealthy squires and hardy yeomen, devoted to the cause of the White Rose. But of the wealthier Tories they saw little. Some fled from their houses, some feigned themselves sick, some surrendered themselves to the government as suspected persons. Of such as remained, the ignorant gazed with astonishment, mixed with horror and aversion, at the wild appearance, unknown language, and singular garb, of the Scottish clans. And to the more prudent, their scanty numbers, apparent deficiency in discipline, and poverty of equipment, seemed certain tokens of the calamitous termination of their rash undertaking. Thus the few who joined them were such as bigotry of political principle blinded to consequences, or whose broken fortunes induced to hazard all on a risk so desperate.

The Baron of Bradwardine being asked what he thought of these recruits, took a long pinch of snuff, and answered drily, "that he could not but have an excellent opinion of them, since they resembled precisely the followers who attached themselves to the good King David at the cave of Adullam;[1] *videlicet*, every one that was in distress, and every one that was in debt, and every one that was discontented, which the vulgate renders bitter of soul; and doubtless," he said, "they will prove mighty men of their hands, and there is much need that they should, for I have seen many a sour look cast upon us."

---

1   1 Samuel 22:1-2.

But none of these considerations moved Fergus. He admired the luxuriant beauty of the country, and the situation of many of the seats which they passed. "Is Waverley-Honour like that house, Edward?"

"It is one-half larger."

"Is your uncle's park as fine a one as that?"

"It is three times as extensive, and rather resembles a forest than a mere park."

"Flora will be a happy woman."

"I hope Miss Mac-Ivor will have much reason for happiness, unconnected with Waverley-Honour."

"I hope so too; but, to be mistress of such a place, will be a pretty addition to the sum total."

"An addition, the want of which, I trust, will be amply supplied by some other means."

"How," said Fergus, stopping short, and turning upon Waverley— "How am I to understand that, Mr Waverley?—Had I the pleasure to hear you aright?"

"Perfectly right, Fergus."

"And I am to understand that you no longer desire my alliance, and my sister's hand?"

"Your sister has refused mine," said Waverley, "both directly, and by all the usual means by which ladies repress undesired attentions."

"I have no idea," answered the Chieftain, "of a lady dismissing or a gentleman withdrawing his suit, after it has been approved of by her legal guardian, without giving him an opportunity of talking the matter over with the lady. You did not, I suppose, expect my sister to drop into your mouth like a ripe plum, the first moment you chose to open it?"

"As to the lady's title to dismiss her lover, Colonel," replied Edward, "it is a point which you must argue with her, as I am ignorant of the customs of the Highlands in that particular. But as to my title to acquiesce in a rejection from her without an appeal to your interest, I will tell you plainly, without meaning to undervalue Miss Mac-Ivor's admitted beauty and accomplishments, that I would not take the hand of an angel, with an empire for her dowry, if her consent were extorted by the importunity of friends and guardians, and did not flow from her own free inclination."

"An angel, with the dowry of an empire," repeated Fergus, in a tone of bitter irony, "is not very likely to be pressed upon a — shire squire. But, sir," changing his tone, "if Flora Mac-Ivor have not the dowry of an empire, she is *my* sister; and that is sufficient at least to secure her against being treated with any thing approaching to levity."

"She is Flora Mac-Ivor, sir," said Waverley, with firmness, "which to me, were I capable of treating *any* woman with levity, would be a more effectual protection."

The brow of the Chieftain was now fully clouded, but Edward felt too indignant at the unreasonable tone which he had adopted, to avert the storm by the least concession. They both stood still while this short dialogue passed, and Fergus seemed half disposed to say something more violent, but, by a strong effort, suppressed his passion, and, turning his face forward, walked sullenly on. As they had always hitherto walked together, and almost constantly side by side, Waverley pursued his course silently in the same direction, determined to let the Chief take his own time in recovering the good-humour which he had so unreasonably discarded, and firm in his resolution not to bate him an inch of dignity.

After they had marched on in this sullen manner about a mile, Fergus resumed the discourse in a different tone. "I believe I was warm, my dear Edward, but you provoke me with your want of knowledge of the world. You have taken pet at some of Flora's prudery, or high-flying notions of loyalty, and now, like a child, you quarrel with the plaything you have been crying for, and beat me, your faithful keeper, because my arm cannot reach to Edinburgh to hand it to you. I am sure, if I was passionate, the mortification of losing the alliance of such a friend, after your arrangement had been the talk of both the Highlands and Lowlands, and that without so much as knowing why or wherefore, might well provoke calmer blood than mine. I shall write to Edinburgh, and put all to rights; that is, if you desire I should do so; as indeed I cannot suppose that your good opinion of Flora, it being such as you have often expressed to me, can be at once laid aside."

"Colonel Mac-Ivor," said Edward, who had no mind to be hurried farther or faster than he chose, in a matter which he had already considered as broken off, "I am fully sensible of the value of your good offices; and certainly, by your zeal on my behalf in such an affair, you do me no small honour. But as Miss Mac-Ivor has made her election freely and voluntarily, and as all my attentions in Edinburgh were received with more than coldness, I cannot, in justice either to her or myself, consent that she should again be harassed upon this topic. I would have mentioned this to you some time since, but you saw the footing upon which we stood together, and must have understood it. Had I thought otherwise, I would have earlier spoken; but I had a natural reluctance to enter upon a subject so painful to us both."

"O, very well, Mr Waverley," said Fergus, haughtily, "the thing is at an end. I have no occasion to press my sister upon any man."

"Nor have I any occasion to court repeated rejection from the same young lady," answered Edward, in the same tone.

"I shall make due inquiry, however," said the Chieftain, without noticing the interruption, "and learn what my sister thinks of all this: we will then see whether it is to end here."

"Respecting such inquiries, you will of course be guided by your own judgment," said Waverley. "It is, I am aware, impossible Miss Mac-Ivor can change her mind; and were such an unsupposable case to happen, it is certain I will not change mine. I only mention this to prevent any possibility of future misconstruction."

Gladly at this moment would Mac-Ivor have put their quarrel to a personal arbitrement;[1] his eye flashed fire, and he measured Edward as if to choose where he might best plant a mortal wound. But although we do not now quarrel according to the modes and figures of Caranza or Vincent Saviola,[2] no one knew better than Fergus that there must be some decent pretext for a mortal duel. For instance, you may challenge a man for treading on your corn in a crowd, or for pushing you up to the wall, or for taking your seat in the theatre; but the modern code of honour will not permit you to found a quarrel upon your right of compelling a man to continue addresses to a female relative, which the fair lady has already refused. So that Fergus was compelled to stomach this supposed affront, until the whirligig of time, whose motion he promised himself he would watch most sedulously, should bring about an opportunity of revenge.

Waverley's servant always led a saddle-horse for him in the rear of the battalion to which he was attached, though his master seldom rode. But now, incensed at the domineering and unreasonable conduct of his late friend, he fell behind the column, and mounted his horse, resolving to seek the Baron of Bradwardine, and request permission to volunteer in his troop, instead of the Mac-Ivor regiment.

A happy time of it I should have had, thought he, after he was mounted, to have been so closely allied to this superb specimen of pride and self-opinion and passion. A colonel! Why, he should have been a generalissimo. A petty chief of three or four hundred men! His pride might suffice for the Cham of Tartary—the Grand Seignior—the Great Mogul![3] I am well free of him. Were Flora an angel, she would bring with her a second Lucifer of ambition and wrath for a brother-in-law.—

The Baron, whose learning (like Sancho's jests while in the Sierra Morena)[4] seemed to grow mouldy for want of exercise, joyfully embraced the opportunity of Waverley's offering his service in his reg-

---

1 Arbitration.
2 Jeronimo de Carranza (d. 1600) was a Spanish soldier who wrote *La Philosophia de Las Armas* (1569); Vincent Saviola was an Italian author who is remembered for his autobiography.
3 Genghis Khan (1162-1227), Mongol leader.
4 Cervantes, *Don Quixote*, Part I, Book III, Chapters IX-XII. The Sierra Morena was a "wild and inhospitable region of Southern Spain" (*PW*, 595).

iment, to bring it into some exertion. The good-natured old gentleman, however, laboured to effect a reconciliation between the two quondam friends.[1] Fergus turned a cold ear to his remonstrances, though he gave them a respectful hearing; and as for Waverley, he saw no reason why he should be the first in courting a renewal of the intimacy which the Chieftain had so unreasonably disturbed. The Baron then mentioned the matter to the Prince, who, anxious to prevent quarrels in his little army, declared, he would himself remonstrate with Colonel Mac-Ivor on the unreasonableness of his conduct. But, in the hurry of their march, it was a day or two before he had an opportunity to exert his influence in the manner proposed.

In the meanwhile, Waverley turned the instructions he had received while in Gardiner's dragoons to some account, and assisted the Baron in his command as a sort of adjutant. *"Parmi les aveugles un borgne est roi,"*[2] says the French proverb; and the cavalry, which consisted chiefly of Lowland gentlemen, their tenants and servants, formed a high opinion of Waverley's skill, and a great attachment to his person. This was indeed partly owing to the satisfaction which they felt at the distinguished English volunteer's leaving the Highlanders to rank among them; for there was a latent grudge between the horse and foot, not only owing to the difference of the services, but because most of the gentlemen, living near the Highlands, had at one time or other had quarrels with the tribes in their vicinity, and all of them looked with a jealous eye on the Highlanders' avowed pretensions to superior valour, and utility in the Prince's service.

CHAPTER XXIX.
The Confusion of King Agramant's Camp.

IT was Waverley's custom sometimes to ride a little apart from the main body, to look at any object of curiosity which occurred on the march. They were now in Lancashire, when, attracted by a castellated old hall, he left the squadron for half an hour, to take a survey and slight sketch of it. As he returned down the avenue, he was met by Ensign Maccombich. This man had contracted a sort of regard for Edward since the day of his first seeing him at Tully-Veolan, and introducing him to the Highlands. He seemed to loiter, as if on purpose to meet with our hero. Yet, as he passed him, he only approached his stirrup, and pronounced the single word, "Beware!" and then walked swiftly on, shunning all further communication.

---

1 Two former friends.
2 "Among the blind a one-eyed man is king" (*OW*, 448).

Edward, somewhat surprised at this hint, followed with his eyes the course of Evan, who speedily disappeared among the trees. His servant, Alick Polwarth, who was in attendance, also looked after the Highlander, and then riding up close to his master, said,

"The ne'er be in me, sir, if I think you're safe amang thae Highland rinthereouts."[1]

"What do you mean, Alick?" said Waverley.

"The Mac-Ivors, sir, hae gotten it into their heads, that ye hae affronted their young leddy, Miss Flora; and I hae heard mae than ane say, they wadna tak muckle to mak a black-cock[2] o' ye; and ye ken weel eneugh there's mony o' them wadna mind a bawbee[3] the weising a ball through the Prince himsell, an the Chief gae them the wink—or whether he did or no, if they thought it a thing that would please him when it was dune."

Waverley, though confident that Fergus Mac-Ivor was incapable of such treachery, was by no means equally sure of the forbearance of his followers. He knew, that where the honour of the Chief or his family was supposed to be touched, the happiest man would be he that could first avenge the stigma; and he had often heard them quote a proverb, "That the best revenge was the most speedy and most safe." Coupling this with the hint of Evan, he judged it most prudent to set spurs to his horse, and ride briskly back to the squadron. Ere he reached the end of the long avenue, however, a ball whistled past him, and the report of a pistol was heard.

"It was that deevil's buckie,[4] Callum Beg," said Alick; "I saw him whisk away through amang the reises."[5]

Edward, justly incensed at this act of treachery, galloped out of the avenue, and observed the battalion of Mac-Ivor at some distance moving along the common, in which it terminated. He also saw an individual running very fast to join the party; this he concluded was the intended assassin, who, by leaping an enclosure, might easily make a much shorter path to the main body than he could find on horseback. Unable to contain himself, he commanded Alick to go to the Baron of Bradwardine, who was at the head of his regiment about half a mile in front, and acquaint him with what had happened. He himself immediately rode up to Fergus's regiment. The Chief himself was in the act of joining them. He was on horseback, having returned from

---

1 The devil take me, sir, if I think you're safe among the Highland vagabonds (*WSG*; *OW*, 448).
2 Male of the black grouse.
3 Half-penny.
4 "A mischievous madcap that has an evil twist in his character" (*WSG*).
5 Shrubs (*WSG*).

waiting on the Prince. On perceiving Edward approaching, he put his horse in motion towards him.

"Colonel Mac-Ivor," said Waverley, without any farther salutation, "I have to inform you, that one of your people has this instant fired at me from a lurking-place."

"As that," answered Mac-Ivor, "excepting the circumstance of a lurking place, is a pleasure which I presently propose to myself, I should be glad to know which of my clansmen dared to anticipate me."

"I shall certainly be at your command whenever you please;—the gentleman who took your office upon himself is your page there, Callum Beg."

"Stand forth from the ranks, Callum! Did you fire at Mr Waverley?"

"No," answered the unblushing Callum.

"You did," said Alick Polwarth, who was already returned, having met a trooper by whom he dispatched an account of what was going forward to the Baron of Bradwardine, while he himself returned to his master at full gallop, neither sparing the rowels[1] of his spurs, nor the sides of his horse. "You did; I saw you as plainly as I ever saw the auld kirk at Coudingham."[2]

"You lie," replied Callum, with his usual impenetrable obstinacy. The combat between the knights would certainly, as in the days of chivalry, have been preceded by an encounter between the squires (for Alick was a stout-hearted Merseman, and feared the bow of Cupid far more than a Highlander's dirk or claymore), but Fergus, with his usual tone of decision, demanded Callum's pistol. The cock was down, the pan and muzzle were black with the smoke; it had been that instant fired.

"Take that," said Fergus, striking the boy upon the head with the heavy pistol-butt with his whole force,—"take that for acting without orders, and lying to disguise it." Callum received the blow without appearing to flinch from it, and fell without sign of life. "Stand still, upon your lives!" said Fergus to the rest of the clan; "I blow out the brains of the first man who interferes between Mr Waverley and me." They stood motionless; Evan Dhu alone showed symptoms of vexation and anxiety. Callum lay on the ground bleeding copiously, but no one ventured to give him any assistance. It seemed as if he had gotten his death-blow.

"And now for you, Mr Waverley; please to turn your horse twenty yards with me upon the common." Waverley complied; and Fergus,

---

1 "A small stellar wheel or disk with sharp radial points and capable of rotation, forming the extremity of a spur" (*OED*).

2 Church at Coldingham, Berwickshire (*OW*, 448).

confronting him when they were a little way from the line of march, said, with great affected coolness, "I could not but wonder, sir, at the fickleness of taste which you were pleased to express the other day. But it was not an angel, as you justly observed, who had charms for you, unless she brought an empire for her fortune. I have now an excellent commentary upon that obscure text."

"I am at a loss even to guess at your meaning, Colonel Mac-Ivor, unless it seems plain that you intend to fasten a quarrel upon me."

"Your affected ignorance shall not serve you, sir. The Prince,—the Prince himself, has acquainted me with your manœuvres. I little thought that your engagements with Miss Bradwardine were the reason of your breaking off your intended match with my sister. I suppose the information that the Baron had altered the destination of his estate, was quite a sufficient reason for slighting your friend's sister, and carrying off your friend's mistress."

"Did the Prince tell you I was engaged to Miss Bradwardine?" said Waverley. "Impossible."

"He did, sir," answered Mac-Ivor; "so, either draw and defend yourself, or resign your pretensions to the lady."

"This is absolute madness," exclaimed Waverley, "or some strange mistake!"

"O! No evasion! Draw your sword!" said the infuriated Chieftain,—his own already unsheathed.

"Must I fight in a madman's quarrel?"

"Then give up now, and for ever, all pretensions to Miss Bradwardine's hand."

"What title have you," cried Waverley, utterly losing command of himself,—"what title have you, or any man living, to dictate such terms to me?" And he also drew his sword.

At this moment, the Baron of Bradwardine, followed by several of his troop, came up on the spur, some from curiosity, others to take part in the quarrel, which they indistinctly understood had broken out between the Mac-Ivors and their corps. The clan, seeing them approach, put themselves in motion to support their Chieftain, and a scene of confusion commenced, which seemed likely to terminate in bloodshed. A hundred tongues were in motion at once. The Baron lectured, the Chieftain stormed, the Highlanders screamed in Gaelic, the horsemen cursed and swore in Lowland Scotch. At length matters came to such a pass, that the Baron threatened to charge the Mac-Ivors unless they resumed their ranks, and many of them, in return, presented their fire-arms at him and the other troopers. The confusion was privately fostered by old Ballenkeiroch, who made no doubt that his own day of vengeance was arrived, when, behold! a cry arose of

"Room! make way! *place à Monseigneur! place à Monseigneur!*"[1] This announced the approach of the Prince, who came up with a party of Fitz-James's foreign dragoons that acted as his body guard. His arrival produced some degree of order. The Highlanders re-assumed their ranks, the cavalry fell in and formed squadron, and the Baron and Chieftain were silent.

The Prince called them and Waverley before him. Having heard the original cause of the quarrel through the villainy of Callum Beg, he ordered him into custody of the provost-marshal for immediate execution, in the event of his surviving the chastisement inflicted by his Chieftain. Fergus, however, in a tone betwixt claiming a right and asking a favour, requested he might be left to his disposal, and promised his punishment should be exemplary. To deny this might have seemed to encroach on the patriarchal authority of the Chieftains, of which they were very jealous, and they were not persons to be disobliged. Callum was therefore left to the justice of his own tribe.

The Prince next demanded to know the new cause of quarrel between Colonel Mac-Ivor and Waverley. There was a pause. Both gentlemen found the presence of the Baron of Bradwardine (for by this time all three had approached the Chevalier by his command) an insurmountable barrier against entering upon a subject where the name of his daughter must unavoidably be mentioned. They turned their eyes on the ground, with looks in which shame and embarrassment were mingled with displeasure. The Prince, who had been educated amongst the discontented and mutinous spirits of the court of St Germains, where feuds of every kind were the daily subject of solicitude to the dethroned sovereign, had served his apprenticeship, as old Frederick of Prussia would have said, to the trade of royalty. To promote or restore concord among his followers was indispensable. Accordingly he took his measures.

"Monsieur de Beaujeu!"

"Monseigneur!" said a very handsome French cavalry officer, who was in attendance.

"Ayez la bonté d'alligner ces montagnards là, ainsi que la cavalerie, s'il vous plait, et de les remettre à la marche. Vous parlez si bien l'Anglois, cela ne vous donneroit pas beaucoup de peine."[2]

"Ah! pas de tout, Monseigneur," replied Mons. le Compte de Beaujeu, his head bending down to the neck of his little prancing

---

1 Make way for his highness.
2 Have the goodness to combine the Highlanders there as well as the cavalry, if you please, to begin again the march. You speak English well, do not trouble yourself.

highly managed charger. Accordingly he *piaffed*[1] away, in high spirits and confidence, to the head of Fergus's regiment, although understanding not a word of Gaelic, and very little English.

"Messieurs les sauvages Ecossois—dat is—gentilmans savages, have the goodness d'arranger vous."

The clan, comprehending the order more from the gesture than the words, and seeing the Prince himself present, hastened to dress their ranks.

"Ah! ver well! dat is fort bien!" said the Count de Beaujeu. "Gentilmans sauvages—mais, très bien.—Eh bien!—Qu'est ce que vous appellez visage, Monsieur?" (to a lounging trooper who stood by him). "Ah, oui! *face.*—Je vous remercie, Monsieur.—Gentilshommes, have de goodness to make de face to de right par file, dat is, by files.— Marsh!—Mais, très bien—encore, Messieurs; il faut vous mettre à la marche.... Marchez donc, au nom de Dieu, parceque j'ai oublié le mot Anglois—mais vous étes des braves gens, et me comprenez très bien."[2]

The Count next hastened to put the cavalry in motion. "Gentilmans cavalry, you must fall in.—Ah! par ma foi, I did not say fall off! I am a fear de little gross fat gentilman is moche hurt. Ah, mon Dieu! C'est le Commissaire qui nous a apporté les prémières nouvelles de ce maudit fracas. Je suis trop faché, Monsieur!"[3]

But poor Macwheeble, who, with a sword stuck across him, and a white cockade as large as a pancake, now figured in the character of a commissary, being overturned in the bustle occasioned by the troopers hastening to get themselves in order in the Prince's presence, before he could rally his galloway,[4] slunk to the rear amid the unrestrained laughter of the spectators.

"Eh bien, Messieurs, wheel to de right—Ah! dat is it!—Eh, Monsieur de Bradwardine, ayez la bonté de vous mettre à la tête de votre régiment, car, par Dieu, je n'en puis plus!"[5]

The Baron of Bradwardine was obliged to go to the assistance of Monsieur de Beaujeu, after he had fairly expended his few English military phrases. One purpose of the Chevalier was thus answered. The other he proposed was, that in the eagerness to hear and com-

---

1 Strutted.
2 Again, gentlemen; it is necessary to put you to the march ... March, then, in the name of God, because I forget the English word—but you are brave men, and understand me very well.
3 Oh, my God! It was the Commissaire who brought us the first news of this awful disturbance. I am too angry, Sir!
4 Small-sized riding horse (*OED*).
5 Have the goodness to stand at the head of your regiment, because, by God, I can't any longer.

prehend commands issued through such an indistinct medium in his own presence, the thoughts of the soldiers in both corps might get a current different from the angry channel in which they were flowing at the time.

Charles Edward was no sooner left with the Chieftain and Waverley, the rest of his attendants being at some distance, than he said, "If I owed less to your disinterested friendship, I could be most seriously angry with both of you for this very extraordinary and causeless broil, at a moment when my father's service so decidedly demands the most perfect unanimity. But the worst of my situation is, that my very best friends hold they have liberty to ruin themselves, as well as the cause they are engaged in, upon the slightest caprice."

Both the young men protested their resolution to submit every difference to his arbitration. "Indeed," said Edward, "I hardly know of what I am accused. I sought Colonel Mac-Ivor merely to mention to him that I had narrowly escaped assassination at the hand of his immediate dependent, a dastardly revenge, which I knew him to be incapable of authorising. As to the cause for which he is disposed to fasten a quarrel upon me, I am ignorant of it, unless it be that he accuses me, most unjustly, of having engaged the affections of a young lady in prejudice of his pretensions."

"If there is an error," said the Chieftain, "it arises from a conversation which I held this morning with his Royal Highness himself."

"With me?" said the Chevalier; "how can Colonel Mac-Ivor have so far misunderstood me?"

He then led Fergus aside, and, after five minutes' earnest conversation, spurred his horse towards Edward. "Is it possible—nay, ride up, Colonel, for I desire no secrets.—Is it possible, Mr Waverley, that I am mistaken in supposing that you are an accepted lover of Miss Bradwardine? A fact of which I was by circumstances, though not by communication from you, so absolutely convinced, that I alleged it to Vich Ian Vohr this morning as a reason why, without offence to him, you might not continue to be ambitious of an alliance, which to an unengaged person, even though once repulsed, holds out too many charms to be lightly laid aside."

"Your Royal Highness," said Waverley, "must have founded on circumstances altogether unknown to me, when you did me the distinguished honour of supposing me an accepted lover of Miss Bradwardine. I feel the distinction implied in the supposition, but I have no title to it. For the rest, my confidence in my own merit is too justly slight to admit of my hoping for success in any quarter after positive rejection."

The Chevalier was silent for a moment, looking steadily at them both, and then said, "Upon my word, Mr Waverley, you are a less happy man than I conceived I had very good reason to believe you. But now, gentlemen, allow me to be umpire in this matter, not as Prince Regent, but as Charles Stewart, a brother adventurer with you in the same gallant cause. Lay my pretensions to be obeyed by you entirely out of view, and consider your own honour, and how far it is well, or becoming, to give our enemies the advantage, and our friends the scandal, of showing that, few as we are, we are not united. And forgive me if I add, that the names of the ladies who have been mentioned, crave more respect from us all than to be made themes of discord."

He took Fergus a little apart, and spoke to him very earnestly for two or three minutes, and then returning to Waverley, said, "I believe I have satisfied Colonel Mac-Ivor, that his resentment was founded upon a misconception, to which, indeed, I myself gave rise; and I trust Mr Waverley is too generous to harbour any recollection of what is past, when I assure him that such is the case.—You must state this matter properly to your clan, Vich Ian Vohr, to prevent a recurrence of their precipitate violence." Fergus bowed. "And now, gentlemen, let me have the pleasure to see you shake hands."

They advanced coldly, and with measured steps, each apparently reluctant to appear most forward in concession. They did, however, shake hands, and parted, taking a respectful leave of the Chevalier.

Charles Edward[gggg] then rode to the head of the Mac-Ivors, threw himself from his horse, begged a drink out of old Ballenkeiroch's cantine, and marched about half a mile along with them, inquiring into the history and connexions of Sliochd nan Ivor, adroitly using the few words of Gaelic he possessed, and affecting a great desire to learn it more thoroughly. He then mounted his horse once more, and galloped to the Baron's cavalry, which was in front, halted them, and examined their accoutrements and state of discipline; took notice of the principal gentlemen, and even of the cadets; inquired after their ladies, and commended their horses; rode about an hour with the Baron of Bradwardine, and endured three long stories about Field-Marshal the Duke of Berwick.

"Ah, Beaujeu, mon cher ami," said he as he returned to his usual place in the line of march, "que mon métier de prince errant est ennuyant, par fois. Mais, courage! c'est le grand jeu, après tout."[1]

CHAPTER XXX.
A Skirmish.

THE reader need hardly be reminded, that, after a council of war held at Derby on the 5th of December, the Highlanders relinquished their

---

1 Ah, good sport, my dear friend, ... my profession of prince errant is boring, but courage: it is the grand game after all.

desperate attempt to penetrate farther into England, and, greatly to the dissatisfaction of their young and daring leader, positively determined to return northward. They commenced their retreat accordingly, and, by the extreme celerity of their movements, outstripped the motions of the Duke of Cumberland, who now pursued them with a very large body of cavalry.

This retreat was a virtual resignation of their towering hopes. None had been so sanguine as Fergus Mac-Ivor; none, consequently, was so cruelly mortified at the change of measures. He argued, or rather remonstrated, with the utmost vehemence at the council of war; and, when his opinion was rejected, shed tears of grief and indignation. From that moment his whole manner was so much altered, that he could scarcely have been recognised for the same soaring and ardent spirit, for whom the whole earth seemed too narrow but a week before. The retreat had continued for several days, when Edward, to his surprise, early on the 12th of December, received a visit from the Chieftain in his quarters, in a hamlet about half way between Shap and Penrith.

Having had no intercourse with the Chieftain since their rupture, Edward waited with some anxiety an explanation of this unexpected visit; nor could he help being surprised, and somewhat shocked, with the change in his appearance. His eye had lost much of its fire; his cheek was hollow, his voice was languid, even his gait seemed less firm and elastic than it was wont; and his dress, to which he used to be particularly attentive, was now carelessly flung about him. He invited Edward to walk out with him by the little river in the vicinity; and smiled in a melancholy manner when he observed him take down and buckle on his sword.

As soon as they were in a wild sequestered path by the side of the stream, the Chief broke out,—"Our fine adventure is now totally ruined, Waverley, and I wish to know what you intend to do:—nay, never stare at me, man. I tell you I received a packet from my sister yesterday, and, had I got the information it contains sooner, it would have prevented a quarrel, which I am always vexed when I think of. In a letter written after our dispute, I acquainted her with the cause of it; and she now replies to me, that she never had, nor could have, any purpose of giving you encouragement; so that it seems I have acted like a madman.—Poor Flora! She writes in high spirits; what a change will the news of this unhappy retreat make in her state of mind!"

Waverley, who was really much affected by the deep tone of melancholy with which Fergus spoke, affectionately entreated him to banish from his remembrance any unkindness which had arisen between them, and they once more shook hands, but now with sincere cordiality. Fergus again inquired of Waverley what he intended to do. "Had you not better leave this luckless army, and get down before us into Scotland, and embark for the Continent from some of the eastern ports that are still in our possession? When you are out of the kingdom, your friends will easily negotiate your pardon; and, to tell you the truth, I wish you would carry Rose Bradwardine with you as your wife, and take Flora also under your joint protection."—Edward looked surprised.—"She loves you, and I believe you love her, though, perhaps, you have not found it out, for you are not celebrated for knowing your own mind very pointedly." He said this with a sort of smile.

"How," answered Edward, "can you advise me to desert the expedition in which we are all embarked?"

"Embarked?" said Fergus; "the vessel is going to pieces, and it is full time for all who can, to get into the long-boat and leave her."

"Why, what will other gentlemen do?" answered Waverley, "and why did the Highland Chiefs consent to this retreat, if it is so ruinous?"

"O," replied Mac-Ivor, "they think that, as on former occasions, the heading, hanging, and forfeiting, will chiefly fall to the lot of the Lowland gentry; that they will be left secure in their poverty and their fastnesses, there, according to their proverb, 'to listen to the wind upon the hill till the waters abate.' But they will be disappointed; they have been too often troublesome to be so repeatedly passed over, and this time John Bull[1] has been too heartily frightened to recover his good-humour for some time. The Hanoverian ministers always deserved to be hanged for rascals; but now, if they get the power in their hands,—as, sooner or later, they must, since there is neither rising in England nor assistance from France,—they will deserve the gallows as fools, if they leave a single clan in the Highlands in a situation to be again troublesome to government. Ay, they will make root-and-branch-work,[2] I warrant them."

"And while you recommend flight to me," said Edward,—"a counsel which I would rather die than embrace,—what are your own views?"

"O," answered Fergus, with a melancholy air, "my fate is settled. Dead or captive I must be before to-morrow."

"What do you mean by that, my friend?" said Edward. "The enemy is still a day's march in our rear, and if he comes up, we are still strong enough to keep him in check. Remember Gladsmuir."

---

1 John Bull is England. John Arbuthnot, a Scottish writer living in London, first created the character of the honest, sober Bull for his pamphlet series *Law is a Bottomless Pit* (1713) (*OCBH*, 536).

2 A radical policy or reform involving the total abolition of some existing institution (*OED*).

"What I tell you is true notwithstanding, so far as I am individually concerned."

"Upon what authority can you found so melancholy a prediction?" asked Waverley.

"On one which never failed a person of my house. I have seen," he said, lowering his voice, "I have seen the Bodach Glas."

"Bodach Glas?"

"Yes: have you been so long at Glennaquoich, and never heard of the Grey Spectre? Though indeed there is a certain reluctance among us to mention him."

"No, never."

"Ah! it would have been a tale for poor Flora to have told you. Or, if that hill were Benmore, and that long blue lake, which you see just winding towards yon mountainous country, were Loch Tay, or my own Loch an Ri, the tale would be better suited with scenery. However, let us sit down on this knoll; even Saddleback and Ulswater will suit what I have to say better than the English hedgerows, enclosures, and farm-houses. You must know, then, that when my ancestor, Ian nan Chais-tel, wasted Northumberland, there was associated with him in the expedition a sort of Southland Chief, or captain of a band of Lowlan-ders, called Halbert Hall. In their return through the Cheviots,[1] they quarrelled about the division of the great booty they had acquired, and came from words to blows. The Lowlanders were cut off to a man, and their chief fell the last, covered with wounds by the sword of my ances-tor. Since that time, his spirit has crossed the Vich Ian Vohr of the day when any great disaster was impending, but especially before approaching death. My father saw him twice; once before he was made prisoner at Sheriff-Muir; another time on the morning of the day on which he died."

"How can you, my dear Fergus, tell such nonsense with a grave face?"

"I do not ask you to believe it; but I tell you the truth, ascertained by three hundred years' experience at least, and last night by my own eyes."

"The particulars, for heaven's sake!" said Waverley, with eagerness.

"I will, on condition you will not attempt a jest on the subject.—Since this unhappy retreat commenced, I have scarce ever been able to sleep for thinking of my clan, and of this poor Prince, whom they are leading back like a dog in a string, whether he will or no, and of the downfall of my family. Last night I felt so feverish that I left my quarters, and walked out, in hopes the keen frosty air would brace my nerves—I cannot tell how much I dislike going on, for I know you will

---

1 The Cheviot Hills, on the border of England and Scotland.

hardly believe me. However—I crossed a small footbridge, and kept walking backwards and forwards, when I observed with surprise, by the clear moonlight, a tall figure in a grey plaid, such as shepherds wear in the south of Scotland, which, move at what pace I would, kept regularly about four yards before me."

"You saw a Cumberland peasant in his ordinary dress, probably."

"No: I thought so at first, and was astonished at the man's audacity in daring to dog me. I called to him, but received no answer. I felt an anxious throbbing at my heart, and to ascertain what I dreaded, I stood still, and turned myself on the same spot successively to the four points of the compass.—By Heaven, Edward, turn where I would, the figure was instantly before my eyes, at precisely the same distance! I was then convinced it was the Bodach Glas. My hair bristled, and my knees shook. I manned myself, however, and determined to return to my quarters. My ghastly visitant glided before me (for I cannot say he walked), until he reached the foot-bridge: there he stopped, and turned full round. I must either wade the river, or pass him as close as I am to you. A desperate courage, founded on the belief that my death was near, made me resolve to make my way in despite of him. I made the sign of the cross, drew my sword, and uttered, 'In the name of God, Evil Spirit, give place!' 'Vich Ian Vohr,' it said, in a voice that made my very blood curdle, 'beware of to-morrow!' It seemed at that moment not half a yard from my sword's point; but the words were no sooner spoken than it was gone, and nothing appeared further to obstruct my passage. I got home, and threw myself on my bed, where I spent a few hours heavily enough; and this morning, as no enemy was reported to be near us, I took my horse, and rode forward to make up matters with you. I would not willingly fall until I am in charity with a wronged friend."

Edward had little doubt that this phantom was the operation of an exhausted frame and depressed spirits, working on the belief common to all Highlanders in such superstitions. He did not the less pity Fergus, for whom, in his present distress, he felt all his former regard revive. With the view of diverting his mind from these gloomy images, he offered, with the Baron's permission, which he knew he could readily obtain, to remain in his quarters till Fergus's corps should come up, and then to march with them as usual. The Chief seemed much pleased, yet hesitated to accept the offer.

"We are, you know, in the rear,—the post of danger in a retreat."

"And therefore the post of honour."

"Well," replied the Chieftain, "let Alick have your horse in readiness, in case we should be over-matched, and I shall be delighted to have your company once more."

The rear-guard were late in making their appearance, having been delayed by various accidents, and by the badness of the roads. At length they entered the hamlet. When Waverley joined the clan Mac-Ivor, arm-in-arm with their Chieftain, all the resentment they had entertained against him seemed blown off at once. Evan Dhu received him with a grin of congratulation; and even Callum, who was running about as active as ever, pale indeed, and with a great patch on his head, appeared delighted to see him.

"That gallows-bird's skull," said Fergus, "must be harder than marble: the lock of the pistol was actually broken."

"How could you strike so young a lad so hard?" said Waverley, with some interest.

"Why, if I did not strike hard sometimes, the rascals would forget themselves."

They were now in full march, every caution being taken to prevent surprise. Fergus's people, and a fine clan regiment from Badenoch, commanded by Cluny Mac-Pherson, had the rear. They had passed a large open moor, and were entering into the enclosures which surround a small village called Clifton. The winter sun had set, and Edward began to rally Fergus upon the false predictions of the Grey Spirit. "The ides of March are not past," said Mac-Ivor, with a smile; when, suddenly casting his eyes back on the moor, a large body of cavalry was indistinctly seen to hover upon its brown and dark surface. To line the enclosures facing the open ground, and the road by which the enemy must move from it upon the village, was the work of a short time. While these manœuvres were accomplishing, night sunk down, dark and gloomy, though the moon was at full. Sometimes, however, she gleamed forth a dubious light upon the scene of action.

The Highlanders did not long remain undisturbed in the defensive position they had adopted. Favoured by the night, one large body of dismounted dragoons attempted to force the enclosures, while another, equally strong, strove to penetrate by the high-road. Both were received by such a heavy fire as disconcerted their ranks, and effectually checked their progress. Unsatisfied with the advantage thus gained, Fergus, to whose ardent spirit the approach of danger seemed to restore all its elasticity, drawing his sword, and calling out "Claymore!"[1] encouraged his men, by voice and example, to break through the hedge which divided them, and rush down upon the enemy. Mingling with the dismounted dragoons, they forced them, at the sword-point, to fly to the open moor, where a considerable number were cut to pieces. But the moon, which suddenly shone out, showed to the English the small number of assailants, disordered by their own success. Two squadrons of horse moving to the support of their com-

---

1 "The word for attacking sword in hand" according to Scott, in *Tales of a Grandfather* (OW, 450).

panions, the Highlanders endeavoured to recover the enclosures. But several of them, amongst others their brave Chieftain, were cut off and surrounded before they could effect their purpose. Waverley, looking eagerly for Fergus, from whom, as well as from the retreating body of his followers, he had been separated in the darkness and tumult, saw him, with Evan Dhu and Callum, defending themselves desperately against a dozen of horsemen, who were hewing at them with their long broadswords. The moon was again at that moment totally over-clouded, and Edward, in the obscurity, could neither bring aid to his friends, nor discover which way lay his own road to rejoin the rear-guard. After once or twice narrowly escaping being slain or made prisoner by parties of the cavalry whom he encountered in the darkness, he at length reached an enclosure, and, clambering over it, concluded himself in safety, and on the way to the Highland forces, whose pipes he heard at some distance. For Fergus hardly a hope remained, unless that he might be made prisoner. Revolving his fate with sorrow and anxiety, the superstition of the Bodach Glas recurred to Edward's recollection, and he said to himself, with internal surprise, "what, can the devil speak truth?"hhhh

CHAPTER XXXI.
Chapter of Accidents.

EDWARD was in a most unpleasant and dangerous situation. He soon lost the sound of the bagpipes; and, what was yet more unpleasant, when, after searching long in vain, and scrambling through many enclosures, he at length approached the highroad, he learned, from the unwelcome noise of kettle-drums and trumpets, that the English cavalry now occupied it, and consequently were between him and the Highlanders. Precluded, therefore, from advancing in a straight direction, he resolved to avoid the English military, and endeavour to join his friends by making a circuit to the left, for which a beaten path, deviating from the main road in that direction, seemed to afford facilities. The path was muddy, and the night dark and cold; but even these inconveniences were hardly felt amidst the apprehensions which falling into the hands of the King's forces reasonably excited in his bosom.

After walking about three miles, he at length reached a hamlet. Conscious that the common people were in general unfavourable to the cause he had espoused, yet desirous, if possible, to procure a horse and guide to Penrith, where he hoped to find the rear, if not the main body, of the Chevalier's army, he approached the alehouse of the place. There was a great noise within: he paused to listen. A round English oath or two, and the burden of a campaign song, convinced him the hamlet also was occupied by the Duke of Cumberland's soldiers. Endeavouring to retire from it as softly as possible, and blessing the obscurity which hitherto he had murmured against, Waverley groped his way the best he could along a small paling, which seemed the boundary of some cottage garden. As he reached the gate of this little enclosure, his outstretched hand was grasped by that of a female, whose voice at the same time uttered, "Edward, is't thou, man?"

Here is some unlucky mistake, thought Edward, struggling, but gently, to disengage himself.

"Naen o' thy foun, now, man, or the red cwoats will hear thee; they hae been houlerying and poulerying every ane that past alehouse door this noight to make them drive their waggons and sick loike. Come into feyther's, or they'll do ho a mischief."

A good hint, thought Waverley, following the girl through the little garden into a brick-paved kitchen, where she set herself to kindle a match at an expiring fire, and with the match to light a candle. She had no sooner looked on Edward, than she dropped the light, with a shrill scream of "O feyther, feyther!"

The father, thus invoked, speedily appeared—a sturdy old farmer, in a pair of leather breeches, and boots pulled on without stockings, having just started from his bed; the rest of his dress was only a Westmoreland statesman's[1] robe-de-chambre,—that is, his shirt. His figure was displayed to advantage, by a candle which he bore in his left hand; in his right he brandished a poker.

"What hast ho here, wench?"

"O!" cried the poor girl, almost going off in hysterics, "I thought it was Ned Williams, and it is one of the plaid-men."

"And what was thee ganging to do wi' Ned Williams at this time o' noight?" To this, which was, perhaps, one of the numerous class of questions more easily asked than answered, the rosy-cheeked damsel made no reply, but continued sobbing and wringing her hands.

"And thee, lad, dost ho know that the dragoons be a town? Dost ho know that, mon? Ad, they'll sliver thee loike a turnip, mon."

"I know my life is in great danger," said Waverley, "but if you can assist me, I will reward you handsomely. I am no Scotchman, but an unfortunate English gentleman."

"Be ho Scot or no," said the honest farmer, "I wish thou hadst kept the other side of the hallan.[2] But since thou art here, Jacob Jopson will betray no man's bluid; and the plaids were gay canny,[3] and did not do so much mischief when they were here yesterday." Accordingly, he set

---

1 "Small landholder who did his own farming" (*WSG*).
2 "Partition between the door of a cottage and the fireplace" (*WSG*).
3 Pretty skillful; prudent; lucky; trustworthy (*WSG*).

seriously about sheltering and refreshing our hero for the night. The fire was speedily rekindled, but with precaution against its light being seen from without. The jolly yeoman cut a rasher of bacon, which Cicely soon broiled, and her father added a swingeing tankard of his best ale. It was settled, that Edward should remain there till the troops marched in the morning, then hire or buy a horse from the farmer, and, with the best directions that could be obtained, endeavour to overtake his friends. A clean, though coarse bed, received him after the fatigues of this unhappy day.

With the morning arrived the news that the Highlanders had evacuated Penrith, and marched off towards Carlisle; that the Duke of Cumberland was in possession of Penrith, and that detachments of his army covered the roads in every direction. To attempt to get through undiscovered would be an act of the most frantic temerity. Ned Williams (the right Edward) was now called to council by Cicely and her father. Ned, who perhaps did not care that his handsome namesake should remain too long in the same house with his sweetheart, for fear of fresh mistakes, proposed that Waverley, exchanging his uniform and plaid for the dress of the country, should go with him to his father's farm near Ulswater, and remain in that undisturbed retirement until the military movements in the country should have ceased to render his departure hazardous. A price was also agreed upon, at which the stranger might board with Farmer Williams, if he thought proper, till he could depart with safety. It was of moderate amount; the distress of his situation, among this honest and simple-hearted race, being considered as no reason for increasing their demand.

The necessary articles of dress were accordingly procured, and, by following by-paths, known to the young farmer, they hoped to escape any unpleasant rencontre. A recompense for their hospitality was refused peremptorily by old Jopson and his cherry-cheeked daughter; a kiss paid the one, and a hearty shake of the hand the other. Both seemed anxious for their guest's safety, and took leave of him with kind wishes.

In the course of their route, Edward, with his guide, traversed those fields which the night before had been the scene of action. A brief gleam of December's sun shone sadly on the broad heath, which, towards the spot where the great north-west road entered the enclosures of Lord Lonsdale's property, exhibited dead bodies of men and horses, and the usual companions of war, a number of carrion-crows, hawks, and ravens.

"And this, then, was thy last field," said Waverley to himself, his eye filling at the recollection of the many splendid points of Fergus's character, and of their former intimacy, all his passions and imperfections forgotten—"here fell the last Vich Ian Vohr, on a nameless heath; and in an obscure night-skirmish was quenched that ardent spirit, who thought it little to cut a way for his master to the British throne! Ambition, policy, bravery, all far beyond their sphere, here learned the fate of mortals. The sole support, too, of a sister, whose spirit, as proud and unbending, was even more exalted than thine own; here ended all thy hopes for Flora, and the long and valued line which it was thy boast to raise yet more highly by thy adventurous valour!"

As these ideas pressed on Waverley's mind, he resolved to go upon the open heath, and search if, among the slain, he could discover the body of his friend, with the pious intention of procuring for him the last rites of sepulture.[1] The timorous young man who accompanied him remonstrated upon the danger of the attempt, but Edward was determined. The followers of the camp had already stripped the dead of all they could carry away; but the country-people, unused to scenes of blood, had not yet approached the field of action, though some stood fearfully gazing at a distance. About sixty or seventy dragoons lay slain within the first enclosure, upon the high road, and on the open moor. Of the Highlanders, not above a dozen had fallen, chiefly those who, venturing too far on the moor, could not regain the strong ground. He could not find the body of Fergus among the slain. On a little knoll, separated from the others, lay the carcasses of three English dragoons, two horses, and the page Callum Beg, whose hard skull a trooper's broadsword had, at length, effectually cloven. It was possible his clan had carried off the body of Fergus; but it was also possible he had escaped, especially as Evan Dhu, who would never leave his Chief, was not found among the dead; or he might be prisoner, and the less formidable denunciation inferred from the appearance of the Bodach Glas might have proved the true one. The approach of a party, sent for the purpose of compelling the country-people to bury the dead, and who had already assembled several peasants for that purpose, now obliged Edward to rejoin his guide, who awaited him in great anxiety and fear under shade of the plantations.

After leaving this field of death, the rest of their journey was happily accomplished. At the house of Farmer Williams, Edward passed for a young kinsman, educated for the church, who was come to reside there till the civil tumults permitted him to pass through the country. This silenced suspicion among the kind and simple yeomanry of Cumberland, and accounted sufficiently for the grave manners and retired habits of the new guest. The precaution became more necessary than Waverley had anticipated, as a variety of incidents prolonged his stay at Fasthwaite, as the farm was called.

---

1 Burial (*OED*).

A tremendous fall of snow rendered his departure impossible for more than ten days. When the roads began to become a little practicable, they successively received news of the retreat of the Chevalier into Scotland; then, that he had abandoned the frontiers, retiring upon Glasgow; and that the Duke of Cumberland had formed the siege of Carlisle. His army, therefore, cut off all possibility of Waverley's escaping into Scotland in that direction. On the eastern border, Marshal Wade, with a large force, was advancing upon Edinburgh, and all along the frontier, parties of militia, volunteers, and partisans, were in arms to suppress insurrection, and apprehend such stragglers from the Highland army as had been left in England. The surrender of Carlisle, and the severity with which the rebel garrison were threatened, soon formed an additional reason against venturing upon a solitary and hopeless journey through a hostile country and a large army, to carry the assistance of a single sword to a cause which seemed altogether desperate.

In this lonely and secluded situation, without the advantage of company or conversation with men of cultivated minds, the arguments of Colonel Talbot often recurred to the mind of our hero. A still more anxious recollection haunted his slumbers—it was the dying look and gesture of Colonel Gardiner. Most devoutly did he hope, as the rarely occurring post brought news of skirmishes with various success, that it might never again be his lot to draw his sword in civil conflict. Then his mind turned to the supposed death of Fergus, to the desolate situation of Flora, and, with yet more tender recollection, to that of Rose Bradwardine, who was destitute of the devoted enthusiasm of loyalty, which, to her friend, hallowed and exalted misfortune. These reveries he was permitted to enjoy, undisturbed by queries or interruption; and it was in many a winter walk by the shores of Ulswater, that he acquired a more complete mastery of a spirit tamed by adversity, than his former experience had given him; and that he felt himself entitled to say firmly, though perhaps with a sigh, that the romance of his life was ended, and that its real history had now commenced. He was soon called upon to justify his pretensions by reason and philosophy.

CHAPTER XXXII.
A Journey to London.

THE family at Fasthwaite were soon attached to Edward. He had, indeed, that gentleness and urbanity which almost universally attracts corresponding kindness; and to their simple ideas his learning gave him consequence, and his sorrows interest. The last he ascribed, evasively, to the loss of a brother in the skirmish near Clifton; and in that primitive state of society, where the ties of affection were highly deemed of, his continued depression excited sympathy, but not surprise.

In the end of January, his more lively powers were called out by the happy union of Edward Williams, the son of his host, with Cicely Jopson. Our hero would not cloud with sorrow the festivity attending the wedding of two persons to whom he was so highly obliged. He therefore exerted himself, danced, sung, played at the various games of the day, and was the blithest of the company. The next morning, however, he had more serious matters to think of.

The clergyman who had married the young couple was so much pleased with the supposed student of divinity, that he came next day from Penrith on purpose to pay him a visit. This might have been a puzzling chapter had he entered into any examination of our hero's supposed theological studies; but fortunately he loved better to hear and communicate the news of the day. He brought with him two or three old newspapers, in one of which Edward found a piece of intelligence that soon rendered him deaf to every word which the Reverend Mr Twigtythe was saying upon the news from the north, and the prospect of the Duke's speedily overtaking and crushing the rebels. This was an article in these, or nearly these words:

"Died at his house, in Hill Street, Berkeley-Square, upon the 10th inst. Richard Waverley, Esq., second son of Sir Giles Waverley of Waverley-Honour, &c. &c. He died of a lingering disorder, augmented by the unpleasant predicament of suspicion in which he stood, having been obliged to find bail to a high amount, to meet an impending accusation of high-treason. An accusation of the same grave crime hangs over his elder brother, Sir Everard Waverley, the representative of that ancient family; and we understand the day of his trial will be fixed early in the next month, unless Edward Waverley, son of the deceased Richard, and heir to the Baronet, shall surrender himself to justice. In that case, we are assured it is his Majesty's gracious purpose to drop further proceedings upon the charge against Sir Everard. This unfortunate young gentleman is ascertained to have been in arms in the Pretender's service, and to have marched along with the Highland troops into England. But he has not been heard of since the skirmish at Clifton, on the 18th December last."

Such was this distracting paragraph.—"Good God!" exclaimed Waverley, "am I then a parracide?—Impossible! My father, who never showed the affection of a father while he lived, cannot have been so much affected by my supposed death as to hasten his own; no, I will not believe it,—it were distraction to entertain for a moment such a horrible idea. But it were, if possible, worse than parricide to suffer any danger to hang over my noble and generous uncle, who has ever been more to me than a father, if such evil can be averted by any sacrifice on my part!"

While these reflections passed like the stings of scorpions through Waverley's sensorium, the worthy divine was startled in a long disquisition on the battle of Falkirk by the ghastliness which they communicated to his looks, and asked him if he was ill? Fortunately the bride, all smirk and blush, had just entered the room. Mrs Williams was none of the brightest of women, but she was good-natured, and readily concluding that Edward had been shocked by disagreeable news in the papers, interfered so judiciously, that, without exciting suspicion, she drew off Mr Twigtythe's attention, and engaged it until he soon after took his leave. Waverley then explained to his friends, that he was under the necessity of going to London with as little delay as possible.

One cause of delay, however, did occur, to which Waverley had been very little accustomed. His purse, though well stocked when he first went to Tully-Veolan, had not been reinforced since that period; and although his life since had not been of a nature to exhaust it hastily, for he had lived chiefly with his friends or with the army, yet he found, that, after settling with his kind landlord, he should be too poor to encounter the expense of travelling post. The best course, therefore, seemed to be, to get into the great north road about Boroughbridge, and there take a place in the Northern Diligence, a huge old-fashioned tub, drawn by three horses, which completed the journey from Edinburgh to London (God willing, as the advertisement expressed it) in three weeks. Our hero, therefore, took an affectionate farewell of his Cumberland friends, whose kindness he promised never to forget, and tacitly hoped one day to acknowledge, by substantial proofs of gratitude. After some petty difficulties and vexatious delays, and after putting his dress into a shape better befitting his rank, though perfectly plain and simple, he accomplished crossing the country, and found himself in the desired vehicle *vis-à-vis* to Mrs Nosebag, the lady of Lieutenant Nosebag, adjutant and riding-master of the — dragoons, a jolly woman of about fifty, wearing a blue habit, faced with scarlet, and grasping a silver-mounted horse-whip.

This lady was one of those active members of society who take upon them *faire le frais de conversation*.[1] She had just returned from the north, and informed Edward how nearly her regiment had cut the petticoat people into ribands at Falkirk, "only somehow there was one of those nasty, awkward marshes, that they are never without in Scotland, I think, and so our poor dear little regiment suffered something, as my Nosebag says, in that unsatisfactory affair. You, sir, have served

---

1 "To keep up the conversation" (*PW*, 595).

in the dragoons?" Waverley was taken so much at unawares, that he acquiesced.

"O, I knew it at once; I saw you were military from your air, and I was sure you could be none of the foot-wobblers, as my Nosebag calls them. What regiment, pray?" Here was a delightful question. Waverley, however, justly concluded that this good lady had the whole army-list by heart; and, to avoid detection by adhering to truth, answered, "Gardiner's dragoons, ma'am; but I have retired some time."

"O aye, those as won the race at the battle of Preston, as my Nosebag says. Pray, sir, were you there?"

"I was so unfortunate, madam," he replied, "as to witness that engagement."

"And that was a misfortune that few of Gardiner's stood to witness, I believe, sir—ha! ha! ha! I beg your pardon; but a soldier's wife loves a joke."

Devil confound you, thought Waverley; what infernal luck has penned me up with this inquisitive hag!

Fortunately the good lady did not stick long to one subject. "We are coming to Ferrybridge, now," she said, "where there was a party of *ours* left to support the beadles, and constables, and justices, and these sort of creatures that are examining papers and stopping rebels, and all that." They were hardly in the inn before she dragged Waverley to the window, exclaiming, "Yonder comes Corporal Bridoon, of our poor dear troop; he's coming with the constable man; Bridoon's one of my lambs, as Nosebag calls 'em. Come, Mr — a—a,—pray, what's your name, sir?"

"Butler, ma'am," said Waverley, resolved rather to make free with the name of a former fellow-officer, than run the risk of detection by inventing one not to be found in the regiment.

"O, you got a troop lately, when that shabby fellow, Waverley, went over to the rebels? Lord, I wish our old cross Captain Crump would go over to the rebels, that Nosebag might get the troop!—Lord, what can Bridoon be standing swinging on the bridge for? I'll be hanged if he a'nt hazy, as Nosebag says.—Come, sir, as you and I belong to the service, we'll go put the rascal in mind of his duty."

Waverley, with feelings more easily conceived than described, saw himself obliged to follow this doughty female commander. The gallant trooper was as like a lamb as a drunk corporal of dragoons, about six feet high, with very broad shoulders, and very thin legs, not to mention a great scar across his nose, could well be. Mrs Nosebag addressed him with something which, if not an oath, sounded very like one, and commanded him to attend to his duty. "You be d—d for a —," commenced the gallant cavalier; but, looking up in order to suit the action to the words, and also to enforce the epithet which he meditated, with an adjective applicable to the party, he recognised the speaker, made his military salam, and altered his tone.—"Lord love your handsome face, Madam Nosebag, is it you? Why, if a poor fellow does happen to fire a slug of a morning, I am sure you were never the lady to bring him to harm."

"Well, you rascallion, go, mind your duty; this gentleman and I belong to the service; but be sure you look after that shy cock in the slouched hat that sits in the corner of the coach. I believe he's one of the rebels in disguise."

"D—n her gooseberry wig," said the corporal, when she was out of hearing, "that gimlet-eyed jade—mother adjutant, as we call her—is a greater plague to the regiment than prevot-marshal, sergeant-major, and old Hubble-de-Shuff, the colonel, into the bargain.—Come, Master Constable, let's see if this shy cock, as she calls him (who, by the way, was a Quaker from Leeds, with whom Mrs Nosebag had had some tart argument on the legality of bearing arms), will stand godfather to a sup of brandy, for your Yorkshire ale is cold on my stomach."

The vivacity of this good lady, as it helped Edward out of this scrape, was like to have drawn him into one or two others. In every town where they stopped, she wished to examine the corps de garde,[1] if there was one, and once very narrowly missed introducing Waverley to a recruiting-sergeant of his own regiment. Then she Captain'd and Butler'd him till he was almost mad with vexation and anxiety; and never was he more rejoiced in his life at the termination of a journey, than when the arrival of the coach in London freed him from the attentions of Madam Nosebag.

CHAPTER XXXIII.
What's to be done next?

IT was twilight when they arrived in town; and having shaken off his companions, and walked through a good many streets, to avoid the possibility of being traced by them, Edward took a hackney-coach and drove to Colonel Talbot's house, in one of the principal squares at the west end of the town. That gentleman, by the death of relations, had succeeded since his marriage to a large fortune, possessed considerable political interest, and lived in what is called great style.

When Waverley knocked at his door, he found it at first difficult to procure admittance, but at length was shown into an apartment where the Colonel was at table. Lady Emily, whose very beautiful features were still pallid from indisposition, sate opposite to him. The instant he heard Waverley's voice, he started up and embraced him. "Frank

---

1 "The small body of soldiers, stationed on guard or as sentinels" (*OED*).

Stanley, my dear boy, how d'ye do?—Emily, my love, this is young Stanley."

The blood started to the lady's cheek as she gave Waverley a reception, in which courtesy was mingled with kindness, while her trembling hand and faltering voice showed how much she was startled and discomposed. Dinner was hastily replaced, and while Waverley was engaged in refreshing himself, the Colonel proceeded—"I wonder you have come here, Frank; the doctors tell me the air of London is very bad for your complaints. You should not have risked it. But I am delighted to see you, and so is Emily, though I fear we must not reckon upon your staying long."

"Some particular business brought me up," muttered Waverley.

"I supposed so, but I sha'nt allow you to stay long.—Spontoon" (to an elderly military-looking servant out of livery), "take away these things, and answer the bell yourself, if I ring. Don't let any of the other fellows disturb us.—My nephew and I have business to talk of."

When the servants had retired, "In the name of God, Waverley, what has brought you here? It may be as much as your life is worth."

"Dear Mr Waverley," said Lady Emily, "to whom I owe so much more than acknowledgments can ever pay, how could you be so rash?"

"My father—my uncle—this paragraph,"—he handed the paper to Colonel Talbot.

"I wish to heaven these scoundrels were condemned to be squeezed to death in their own presses," said Talbot. "I am told there are not less than a dozen of their papers now published in town, and no wonder that they are obliged to invent lies to find sale for their journals. It is true, however, my dear Edward, that you have lost your father; but as to this flourish of his unpleasant situation having grated upon his spirits, and hurt his health—the truth is—for though it is harsh to say so now, yet it will relieve your mind from the idea of weighty responsibility—the truth then is, that Mr Richard Waverley, through this whole business, showed great want of sensibility, both to your situation and that of your uncle; and the last time I saw him, he told me, with great glee, that as I was so good as to take charge of your interests, he had thought it best to patch up a separate negotiation for himself, and make his peace with government through some channels which former connexions left still open to him."

"And my uncle, my dear uncle?"

"Is in no danger whatever. It is true (looking at the date of the paper) there was a foolish report some time ago to the purport here quoted, but it is entirely false. Sir Everard is gone down to Waverley-Honour, freed from all uneasiness, unless upon your own account. But you are in peril yourself—your name is in every proclamation—warrants are out to apprehend you. How and when did you come here?"

Edward told his story at length, suppressing his quarrel with Fergus; for, being himself partial to Highlanders, he did not wish to give any advantage to the Colonel's national prejudice against them.

"Are you sure it was your friend Glen's foot-boy you saw dead in Clifton Moor?"

"Quite positive."

"Then that little limb of the devil has cheated the gallows, for cut-throat was written in his face; though" (turning to Lady Emily) "it was a very handsome face too.—But for you, Edward, I wish you would go down again to Cumberland, or rather I wish you had never stirred from thence, for there is an embargo in all the seaports, and a strict search for the adherents of the Pretender; and the tongue of that con-founded woman will wag in her head like the clack of a mill, till somehow or other she will detect Captain Butler to be a feigned per-sonage."

"Do you know any thing," asked Waverley, "of my fellow-traveller?"

"Her husband was my sergeant-major for six years; she was a buxom widow, with a little money—he married her—was steady, and got on by being a good drill. I must send Spontoon to see what she is about; he will find her out among the old regimental connexions. To-morrow you must be indisposed, and keep your room from fatigue. Lady Emily is to be your nurse, and Spontoon and I your attendants. You bear the name of a near relation of mine, whom none of my present people ever saw, except Spontoon, so there will be no imme-diate danger. So pray feel your head ache and your eyes grow heavy as soon as possible, that you may be put upon the sick list; and, Emily, do you order an apartment for Frank Stanley, with all the attentions which an invalid may require."

In the morning the Colonel visited his guest. "Now," said he, "I have some good news for you. Your reputation as a gentleman and officer is effectually cleared of neglect of duty, and accession to the mutiny in Gardiner's regiment. I have had a correspondence on this subject with a very zealous friend of yours, your Scottish parson, Morton; his first letter was addressed to Sir Everard; but I relieved the good Baronet of the trouble of answering it. You must know, that your free-booting acquaintance, Donald of the Cave, has at length fallen into the hands of the Philistines. He was driving off the cattle of a certain proprietor, called Killan—something or other—"

"Killancureit?"

"The same—now the gentleman being, it seems, a great farmer, and having a special value for his breed of cattle, being, moreover, rather of a timid disposition, had got a party of soldiers to protect his property. So Donald run his head unawares into the lion's mouth, and was defeated and made prisoner. Being ordered for execution, his conscience was assailed on the one hand by a Catholic priest, on the other by your friend Morton. He repulsed the Catholic chiefly on account of the doctrine of extreme unction, which this economical gentleman considered as an excessive waste of oil. So his conversion from a state of impenitence fell to Mr Morton's share, who, I dare say, acquitted himself excellently, though, I suppose, Donald made but a queer kind of Christian after all. He confessed, however, before a magistrate, one Major Melville, who seems to have been a correct, friendly sort of person, his full intrigue with Houghton, explaining particularly how it was carried on, and fully acquitting you of the least accession to it. He also mentioned his rescuing you from the hands of the volunteer officer, and sending you, by orders of the Pret—Chevalier, I mean—as a prisoner to Doune, from whence he understood you were carried prisoner to Edinburgh. These are particulars which cannot but tell in your favour. He hinted that he had been employed to deliver and protect you, and rewarded for doing so; but he would not confess by whom, alleging, that though he would not have minded breaking any ordinary oath to satisfy the curiosity of Mr Morton, to whose pious admonitions he owed so much, yet, in the present case, he had been sworn to silence upon the edge of his dirk,[iiii] which, it seems, constituted, in his opinion, an inviolable obligation."

"And what is become of him?"

"Oh, he was hanged at Stirling after the rebels raised the siege, with his lieutenant, and four plaids besides; he having the advantage of a gallows more lofty than his friends."

"Well, I have little cause either to regret or rejoice at his death; and yet he has done me both good and harm to a very considerable extent."

"His confession, at least, will serve you materially, since it wipes from your character all those suspicions which gave the accusation against you a complexion of a nature different from that with which so many unfortunate gentlemen, now, or lately, in arms against the government, may be justly charged. Their treason—I must give it its name, though you participate in its guilt—is an action arising from mistaken virtue, and therefore cannot be classed as a disgrace, though it be doubtless highly criminal. Where the guilty are so numerous, clemency must be extended to far the greater number; and I have little doubt of procuring a remission for you, providing we can keep you out of the claws of justice, till she has selected and gorged upon her victims; for in this, as in other cases, it will be according to the vulgar proverb, "First come, first served." Besides, government are desirous at present to intimidate the English Jacobites, among whom they can find few examples for punishment. This is a vindictive and timid feeling which will soon wear off, for, of all nations, the English are least blood-thirsty by nature. But it exists at present, and you must, therefore, be kept out of the way in the mean time."

Now entered Spontoon with an anxious countenance. By his regimental acquaintances he had traced out Madam Nosebag, and found her full of ire, fuss, and fidget, at discovery of an imposter, who had travelled from the north with her under the assumed name of Captain Butler of Gardiner's dragoons. She was going to lodge an information on the subject, to have him sought for as an emissary of the Pretender; but Spontoon (an old soldier), while he pretended to approve, contrived to make her delay her intention. No time, however, was to be lost: the accuracy of this good dame's description might probably lead to the discovery that Waverley was the pretended Captain Butler; an identification fraught with danger to Edward, perhaps to his uncle, and even to Colonel Talbot. Which way to direct his course was now, therefore, the question.

"To Scotland," said Waverley.

"To Scotland?" said the Colonel; "with what purpose?—not to engage again with the rebels, I hope?"

"No—I considered my campaign ended, when, after all my efforts, I could not rejoin them; and now, by all accounts, they are gone to make a winter campaign in the Highlands, where such adherents as I am would rather be burdensome than useful. Indeed, it seems likely that they only prolong the war to place the Chevalier's person out of danger, and then to make some terms for themselves. To burden them with my presence would merely add another party, whom they would not give up, and could not defend. I understand they left almost all their English adherents in garrison at Carlisle, for that very reason:— and on a more general view, Colonel, to confess the truth, though it may lower me in your opinion, I am heartily tired of the trade in war, and am, as Fletcher's Humorous Lieutenant[1] says, 'even as weary of this fighting'"—

"Fighting! pooh, what have you seen but a skirmish or two?—Ah! if you saw war on the grand scale—sixty or a hundred thousand men in the field on each side!"

"I am not at all curious, Colonel.—Enough, says our homely proverb, is as good as a feast. The plumed troops and the big war used to enchant me in poetry; but the night marches, vigils, couches under the wintry sky, and such accompaniments of the glorious trade, are not at all to my taste in practice:—then for dry blows, I had *my* fill of fighting at Clifton, where I escaped by a hair's-breadth half a dozen times; and you, I should think"—. He stopped.

---

1   John Fletcher (1579-1625), *The Humorous Lieutenant,* produced 1619 (*PW,* 596).

"Had enough of it at Preston? you mean to say," answered the Colonel, laughing; "but ''tis my vocation, Hal.'"[1]

"It is not mine though," said Waverley; "and having honourably got rid of the sword, which I drew only as a volunteer, I am quite satisfied with my military experience, and shall be in no hurry to take it up again."

"I am very glad you are of that mind,—but then what would you do in the north?"

"In the first place, there are some seaports on the eastern coast of Scotland still in the hands of the Chevalier's friends; should I gain any of them, I can easily embark for the Continent."

"Good—your second reason?"

"Why, to speak the very truth, there is a person in Scotland upon whom I now find my happiness depends more than I was always aware, and about whose situation I am very anxious."

"Then Emily was right, and there is a love affair in the case after all?—And which of these two pretty Scotchwomen, whom you insisted upon my admiring, is the distinguished fair? Not Miss Glen— I hope."

"No."

"Ah, pass for the other; simplicity may be improved, but pride and conceit never. Well, I don't discourage you; I think it will please Sir Everard, from what he said when I jested with him about it; only I hope that intolerable papa, with his brogue, and his snuff, and his Latin, and his insufferable long stories about the Duke of Berwick, will find it necessary hereafter to be an inhabitant of foreign parts. But as to the daughter, though I think you might find as fitting a match in England, yet if your heart be really set upon this Scotch rose-bud, why the Baronet has a great opinion of her father and of his family, and he wishes much to see you married and settled, both for your own sake and for that of the three ermines passant, which may otherwise pass away altogether. But I will bring you his mind fully upon the subject, since you are debarred correspondence for the present, for I think you will not be long in Scotland before me."

"Indeed! and what can induce you to think of returning to Scotland? No relenting longings towards the land of mountains and floods, I am afraid."

"None, on my word; but Emily's health is now, thank God, re-established, and, to tell you the truth, I have little hopes of concluding the business which I have at present most at heart, until I can have a personal interview with his Royal Highness the Commander-in-Chief; for, as Fluellen says, 'the duke doth love me well, and I thank heaven I have deserved some love at his hands.'[2] I am now going out for an

---

1 Shakespeare, *Henry IV, Part I*, I.ii.116. Falstaff to Prince Hal.
2 Shakespeare, *Henry V*, III.vi.23-25.

hour or two to arrange matters for your departure; your liberty extends to the next room, Lady Emily's parlour, where you will find her when you are disposed for music, reading, or conversation. We have taken measures to exclude all servants but Spontoon, who is as true as steel."

In about two hours Colonel Talbot returned, and found his young friend conversing with his lady; she pleased with his manners and information, and he delighted at being restored, though but for a moment, to the society of his own rank, from which he had been for some time excluded.

"And now," said the Colonel, "hear my arrangements, for there is little time to lose. This youngster, Edward Waverley, alias Williams, alias Captain Butler, must continue to pass by his fourth *alias* of Francis Stanley, my nephew: he shall set out to-morrow for the North, and the chariot shall take him the first two stages. Spontoon shall then attend him; and they shall ride post as far as Huntingdon; and the presence of Spontoon, well known on the road as my servant, will check all disposition to enquiry. At Huntingdon you will meet the real Frank Stanley. He is studying at Cambridge; but, a little while ago, doubtful if Emily's health would permit me to go down to the North myself, I procured him a passport from the secretary of state's office to go in my stead. As he went chiefly to look after you, his journey is now unnecessary. He knows your story; you will dine together at Huntingdon; and perhaps your wise heads may hit upon some plan for removing or diminishing the danger of your farther progress northward. And now (taking out a morocco case), let me put you in funds for the campaign."

"I am ashamed, my dear Colonel,"—

"Nay," said Colonel Talbot, "you should command my purse in any event; but this money is your own. Your father, considering the chance of your being attainted, left me his trustee for your advantage. So that you are worth above £15,000, besides Brerewood Lodge—a very independent person, I promise you. There are bills here for £200; any larger sum you may have, or credit abroad, as soon as your motions require it."

The first use which occurred to Waverley of his newly-acquired wealth, was to write to honest Farmer Jopson, requesting his acceptance of a silver tankard on the part of his friend Williams, who had not forgotten the night of the eighteenth December last. He begged him at the same time carefully to preserve for him his Highland garb and accoutrements, particularly the arms, curious in themselves, and to which the friendship of the donors gave additional value. Lady Emily undertook to find some suitable token of remembrance, likely to flatter the vanity and please the taste of Mrs Williams; and the

Colonel, who was a kind of farmer, promised to send the Ulswater patriarch an excellent team of horses for cart and plough.

One happy day Waverley spent in London; and, travelling in the manner projected, he met with Frank Stanley at Huntingdon. The two young men were acquainted in a minute.

"I can read my uncle's riddle," said Stanley; "the cautious old soldier did not care to hint to me that I might hand over to you this passport, which I have no occasion for; but if it should afterwards come out as the rattle-pated trick of a young Cantab,[1] *cela ne tire à rien.*[2] You are therefore to be Francis Stanley, with this passport." This proposal appeared in effect to alleviate a great part of the difficulties which Edward must otherwise have encountered at every turn; and accordingly he scrupled not to avail himself of it, the more especially as he had discarded all political purposes from his present journey, and could not be accused of furthering machinations against the government while travelling under protection of the secretary's passport.

The day passed merrily away. The young student was inquisitive about Waverley's campaigns, and the manners of the Highlands, and Edward was obliged to satisfy his curiosity by whistling a pibroch, dancing a strathspey, and singing a Highland song. The next morning Stanley rode a stage northward with his new friend, and parted from him with great reluctance, upon the remonstrances of Spontoon, who, accustomed to submit to discipline, was rigid in enforcing it.

CHAPTER XXXIV.
Desolation.

WAVERLEY riding post, as was the usual fashion of the period, without any adventure save one or two queries, which the talisman of his passport sufficiently answered, reached the borders of Scotland. Here he heard the tidings of the decisive battle of Culloden. It was no more than he had long expected, though the success of Falkirk had thrown a faint and setting gleam over the arms of the Chevalier. Yet it came upon him like a shock, by which he was for a time altogether unmanned. The generous, the courteous, the noble-minded Adventurer, was then a fugitive, with a price upon his head; his adherents, so brave, so enthusiastic, so faithful, were dead, imprisoned, or exiled. Where, now, was the exalted and high-souled Fergus, if, indeed, he had survived the night at Clifton? Where the pure-hearted and primitive Baron of Bradwardine, whose foibles seemed foils to set off the

---

1 Empty-headed trick of a young man from Cambridge University (*OED*).
2 "That does not matter" (*PW*, 596).

disinterestedness of his disposition, the genuine goodness of his heart, and his unshaken courage? Those who clung for support to these fallen columns, Rose and Flora, where were they to be sought, and in what distress must not the loss of their natural protectors have involved them? Of Flora, he thought with the regard of a brother for a sister; of Rose, with a sensation yet more deep and tender. It might be still his fate to supply the want of those guardians they had lost. Agitated by these thoughts he precipitated his journey.

When he arrived in Edinburgh, where his inquiries must necessarily commence, he felt the full difficulty of his situation. Many inhabitants of that city had seen and known him as Edward Waverley; how, then, could he avail himself of a passport as Francis Stanley? He resolved, therefore, to avoid all company, and to move northward as soon as possible. He was, however, obliged to wait a day or two in expectation of a letter from Colonel Talbot, and he was also to leave his own address, under his feigned character, at a place agreed upon. With this latter purpose he sallied out in the dusk through the well-known streets, carefully shunning observation, but in vain: one of the first persons whom he met at once recognised him. It was Mrs Flockhart, Fergus Mac-Ivor's good-humoured landlady.

"Gude guide us, Mr Waverley, is this you? Na, ye needna be feared for me. I wad betray nae gentleman in your circumstances—eh, lack-a-day! lack-a-day! here's a change o' markets; how merry Colonel Mac-Ivor and you used to be in our house!" And the good-natured widow shed a few natural tears. As there was no resisting her claim of acquaintance, Waverley acknowledged it with a good grace, as well as the danger of his own situation. "As it's near the darkening, sir, wad ye just step in by to our house, and tak a dish o' tea? And I am sure if ye like to sleep in the little room, I wad tak care ye are no disturbed, and naebody wad ken ye; for Kate and Matty, the limmers,[1] gaed aff wi' twa o 'Hawley's dragoons, and I hae twa new queans[2] instead o' them."

Waverley accepted her invitation, and engaged her lodging for a night or two, satisfied he should be safer in the house of this simple creature than anywhere else. When he entered the parlour, his heart swelled to see Fergus's bonnet, with the white cockade, hanging beside the little mirror.

"Ay," said Mrs Flockhart, sighing, as she observed the direction of his eyes, "the puir Colonel bought a new ane just the day before they marched, and I winna let them tak that ane doun, but just to brush it

---

1 Loose women (*WSG*).
2 Wenches (*WSG*).

ilka day mysell; and whiles I look at it till I just think I hear him cry to Callum to bring him his bonnet, as he used to do when he was ganging out.—It's unco silly—the neighbours ca' me a Jacobite—but they may say their say—I am sure it's no for that—but he was as kind-hearted a gentleman as ever lived, and as weel-fa'rd[1] too. Oh, d'ye ken, sir, when he is to suffer?"

"Suffer! Good heaven!—Why, where is he?"

"Eh, Lord's sake! d'ye no ken? The poor Hieland body, Dugald Mahony, cam here a while syne, wi' ane o' his arms cuttit off, and a sair clour in the head[2]—ye'll mind Dugald, he carried aye an axe on his shouther—and he cam here just begging, as I may say, for something to eat. Aweel, he tauld us the Chief, as they ca'd him (but I aye ca' him the Colonel), and Ensign Maccombich, that ye mind weel, were ta'en somewhere beside the English border, when it was sae dark that his folk never missed him till it was ower late, and they were like to gang clean daft. And he said that little Callum Beg (he was a bauld mischievous callant that), and your honour, were killed that same night in the tuilzie,[3] and mony mae braw men. But he grat[4] when he spak o' the Colonel, ye never saw the like. And now the word gangs the Colonel is to be tried, and to suffer wi' them that were ta'en at Carlisle."

"And his sister?"

"Ay, that they ca'd the Lady Flora—weel, she's away up to Carlisle to him, and lives wi' some grand Papist lady thereabouts to be near him."

"And," said Edward, "the other young lady?"

"Whilk other? I ken only of ae sister the Colonel had."

"I mean Miss Bradwardine," said Edward.

"Ou, ay; the laird's daughter," said his landlady. "She was a very bonny lassie, poor thing, but far shyer than Lady Flora."

"Where is she, for God's sake?"

"Ou, wha kens where ony o' them is now? Puir things, they're sair ta'en doun for their white cockades and their white roses; but she gaed north to her father's in Perthshire, when the government troops cam back to Edinbro'. There was some pretty men amang them, and ane Major Whacker was quartered on me, a very ceevil gentleman,—but O, Mr Waverley, he was naething sae weel fa'rd as the puir Colonel."

"Do you know what is become of Miss Bradwardine's father?"

---

1 Well-favored (*GW*).
2 A sore bump on the head (*GW*).
3 Scuffle (*WSG*).
4 Cried (*WSG*).

"The auld laird? Na, naebody kens that; but they say he fought very hard in that bluidy battle at Inverness; and Deacon Clank, the white-iron smith, says, that the government folk are sair agane him for having been *out* twice; and troth he might hae ta'en warning, but there's nae fule like an auld fule—the puir Colonel was only out ance."

Such conversation contained almost all the good-natured widow knew of the fate of her late lodgers and acquaintances; but it was enough to determine Edward, at all hazards, to proceed instantly to Tully-Veolan, where he concluded he should see, or at least hear something of Rose. He therefore left a letter for Colonel Talbot at the place agreed upon, signed by his assumed name, and giving for his address the post-town next to the Baron's residence.

From Edinburgh to Perth he took post-horses, resolving to make the rest of his journey on foot; a mode of travelling to which he was partial, and which had the advantage of permitting a deviation from the road when he saw parties of military at a distance. His campaign had considerably strengthened his constitution, and improved his habits of enduring fatigue. His baggage he sent before him as opportunity occurred.

As he advanced northward, the traces of war became visible. Broken carriages, dead horses, unroofed cottages, trees felled for palisades, and bridges destroyed, or only partially repaired,—all indicated the movements of hostile armies. In those places where the gentry were attached to the Stewart cause, their houses seemed dismantled or deserted, the usual course of what may be called ornamental labour was totally interrupted, and the inhabitants were seen gliding about, with fear, sorrow, and dejection on their faces.

It was evening when he approached the village of Tully-Veolan, with feelings and sentiments—how different from those which attended his first entrance! Then, life was so new to him, that a dull or disagreeable day was one of the greatest misfortunes which his imagination anticipated, and it seemed to him that his time ought only to be consecrated to elegant or amusing study, and relieved by social or youthful frolic. Now, how changed! How saddened, yet how elevated was his character, within the course of a very few months! Danger and misfortune are rapid, though severe teachers. "A sadder and a wiser man," he felt, in internal confidence and mental dignity, a compensation for the gay dreams which, in his case, experience had so rapidly dissolved.

As he approached the village, he saw, with surprise and anxiety, that a party of soldiers were quartered near it, and, what was worse, that they seemed stationary there. This he conjectured from a few tents which he beheld glimmering upon what was called the Common Moor. To avoid the risk of being stopped and questioned in a place where he was so likely to be recognised, he made a large circuit, altogether avoiding the hamlet, and approaching the upper gate of the avenue by a by-path well known to him. A single glance announced that great changes had taken place. One half of the gate, entirely destroyed, and split up for firewood, lay in piles, ready to be taken away; the other swung uselessly about upon its loosened hinges. The battlements above the gate were broken and thrown down, and the carved Bears, which were said to have done sentinel's duty upon the top for centuries, now, hurled from their posts, lay among the rubbish. The avenue was cruelly wasted. Several large trees were felled and left lying across the path; and the cattle of the villagers, and the more rude hoofs of dragoon horses, had poached into black mud the verdant turf which Waverley had so much admired.

Upon entering the court-yard, Edward saw the fears realized which these circumstances had excited. The place had been sacked by the King's troops, who, in wanton mischief, had even attempted to burn it; and though the thickness of the walls had resisted the fire, unless to a partial extent, the stables and out-houses were totally consumed. The towers and pinnacles of the main building were scorched and blackened; the pavement of the court broken and shattered; the doors torn down entirely, or hanging by a single hinge; the windows dashed in and demolished, and the court strewed with articles of furniture broken into fragments. The accessaries of ancient distinction, to which the Baron, in the pride of his heart, had attached so much importance and veneration, were treated with peculiar contumely. The fountain was demolished, and the spring, which had supplied it, now flooded the court-yard. The stone-basin seemed to be destined for a drinking-trough for cattle, from the manner in which it was arranged upon the ground. The whole tribe of Bears, large and small, had experienced as little favour as those at the head of the avenue, and one or two of the family pictures, which seemed to have served as targets for the soldiers, lay on the ground in tatters. With an aching heart, as may well be imagined, Edward viewed this wreck of a mansion so respected. But his anxiety to learn the fate of the proprietors, and his fears as to what that fate might be, increased with every step. When he entered upon the terrace, new scenes of desolation were visible. The balustrade was broken down, the walls destroyed, the borders overgrown with weeds, and the fruit-trees cut down or grubbed up. In one copartment of this old-fashioned garden were two immense horse-chestnut trees, of whose size the Baron was particularly vain: too lazy, perhaps, to cut them down, the spoilers, with malevolent ingenuity, had mined them, and placed a quantity of gunpowder in the cavity. One had been shivered to pieces by the explosion, and the fragments lay scattered around, encumbering the ground it had so long shadowed. The other mine had been more partial in its effect. About one-fourth of the trunk of the tree was torn from the mass, which, mutilated and defaced on the one side, still spread on the other its ample and undiminished boughs.[jjjj]

Amid these general marks of ravage, there were some which more particularly addressed the feelings of Waverley. Viewing the front of the building, thus wasted and defaced, his eyes naturally sought the little balcony which more properly belonged to Rose's apartment—her *troisième*, or rather *cinquième étage*.[1] It was easily discovered, for beneath it lay the stage-flowers and shrubs, with which it was her pride to decorate it, and which had been hurled from the bartizan:[2] several of her books were mingled with broken flower-pots and other remnants. Among these, Waverley distinguished one of his own, a small copy of Ariosto, and gathered it as a treasure, though wasted by the wind and rain.

While, plunged in the sad reflections which the scene excited, he was looking around for some one who might explain the fate of the inhabitants, he heard a voice from the interior of the building singing, in well-remembered accents, an old Scottish song:

> "They came upon us in the night,
> And brake my bower and slew my knight:
> My servants a' for life did flee,
> And left us in extremitie.
>
> They slew my knight, to me sae dear;
> They slew my knight, and drave his gear;[kkkk]
> The moon may set, the sun may rise,
> But a deadly sleep has closed his eyes."

Alas, thought Edward, is it thou? Poor helpless being, art thou alone left, to gibber and moan, and fill with thy wild and unconnected scraps of minstrelsy the halls that protected thee?—He then called, first low, and then louder, "Davie—Davie Gellatley!"

The poor simpleton showed himself from among the ruins of a sort of green-house, that once terminated what was called the Terrace-walk, but at first sight of a stranger retreated, as if in terror. Waverley, remembering his habits, began to whistle a tune to which he was partial, which Davie had expressed great pleasure in listening to, and had picked up from him by the ear. Our hero's minstrelsy no more

---

1 Third or rather fifth floor.
2 Battlement (*WSG*).

equalled that of Blondel,[1] than poor Davie resembled Cœur de Lion; but the melody had the same effect, of producing recognition. Davie again stole from his lurking-place, but timidly, while Waverley, afraid of frightening him, stood making the most encouraging signals he could devise.—"It's his ghaist," muttered Davie; yet, coming nearer, he seemed to acknowledge his living acquaintance. The poor fool himself appeared the ghost of what he had been. The peculiar dress in which he had been attired in better days, showed only miserable rags of its whimsical finery, the lack of which was oddly supplied by the remnants of tapestried hangings, window-curtains, and shreds of pictures, with which he had bedizened his tatters. His face, too, had lost its vacant and careless air, and the poor creature looked hollow-eyed, meagre, half-starved, and nervous to a pitiable degree. After long hesitation, he at length approached Waverley with some confidence, stared him sadly in the face, and said, "A' dead and gane—a' dead and gane."

"Who are dead?" said Waverley, forgetting the incapacity of Davie to hold any connected discourse.

"Baron—and Bailie—and Saunders Saunderson—and Lady Rose, that sang sae sweet—A' dead and gane—dead and gane;

> But follow, follow me,
> While glow-worms light the lea,
> I'll show ye where the dead should be—
> > Each in his shroud,
> > While winds pipe loud,
> > And the red moon peeps dim through the cloud.
> Follow, follow me;
> Brave should he be
> That treads by night the dead man's lea."

With these words, chanted in a wild and earnest tone, he made a sign to Waverley to follow him, and walked rapidly towards the bottom of the garden, tracing the bank of the stream, which, it may be remembered, was its eastern boundary. Edward, over whom an involuntary shuddering stole at the import of his words, followed him in some hope of an explanation. As the house was evidently deserted, he could not expect to find among the ruins any more rational informer.

---

1 "A troubadour; in legend a friend and follower of Richard, Coeur de Lion." According to legend, he found Richard in the Castle of Durrenstein on the Danube by whistling a stanza of a song they'd jointly composed, and Richard whistled the next stanza (PW, 596).

Davie, walking very fast, soon reached the extremity of the garden, and scrambled over the ruins of the wall that once had divided it from the wooded glen in which the old Tower of Tully-Veolan was situated. He then jumped down into the bed of the stream, and, followed by Waverley, proceeded at a great pace, climbing over some fragments of rock, and turning with difficulty round others. They passed beneath the ruins of the castle; Waverley followed, keeping up with his guide with difficulty, for the twilight began to fall. Following the descent of the stream a little lower, he totally lost him, but a twinkling light, which he now discovered among the tangled copse-wood and bushes, seemed a surer guide. He soon pursued a very uncouth path; and by its guidance at length reached the door of a wretched hut. A fierce barking of dogs was at first heard, but it stilled at his approach. A voice sounded from within, and he held it most prudent to listen before he advanced.

"Wha hast thou brought here, thou unsonsy[1] villain, thou?" said an old woman, apparently in great indignation. He heard Davie Gellatley, in answer, whistle a part of the tune by which he had recalled himself to the simpleton's memory, and had now no hesitation to knock at the door. There was a dead silence instantly within, except the deep growling of the dogs; and he next heard the mistress of the hut approach the door, not probably for the sake of undoing a latch, but of fastening a bolt. To prevent this, Waverley lifted the latch himself.

In front was an old wretched-looking woman, exclaiming, "Wha comes into folk's houses in this gate, at this time o' the night?" On one side, two grim and half-starved deer greyhounds laid aside their ferocity at his appearance, and seemed to recognise him. On the other side, half concealed by the open door, yet apparently seeking that concealment reluctantly, with a cocked pistol in his right hand, and his left in the act of drawing another from his belt, stood a tall bony gaunt figure in the remnants of a faded uniform, and a beard of three weeks' growth.

It was the Baron of Bradwardine.—It is unnecessary to add, that he threw aside his weapon, and greeted Waverley with a hearty embrace.

CHAPTER XXXV.
Comparing of Notes.

THE Baron's story was short, when divested of the adages and common-places, Latin, English, and Scotch, with which his erudition garnished it. He insisted much upon his grief at the loss of Edward

---

1 Luckless (*OW*, 451).

and of Glennaquoich, fought the fields of Falkirk and Culloden, and related how, after all was lost in the last battle, he had returned home, under the idea of more easily finding shelter among his own tenants, and on his own estate, than elsewhere. A party of soldiers had been sent to lay waste his property, for clemency was not the order of the day. Their proceedings, however, were checked by an order from the civil court. The estate, it was found, might not be forfeited to the crown, to the prejudice of Malcolm Bradwardine of Inch-Grabbit, the heir-male, whose claim could not be prejudiced by the Baron's attainder, as deriving no right through him, and who, therefore, like other heirs of entail in the same situation, entered upon possession. But, unlike many in similar circumstances, the new laird speedily showed that he intended utterly to exclude his predecessor from all benefit or advantage in the estate, and that it was his purpose to avail himself of the old Baron's evil fortune to the full extent. This was the more ungenerous, as it was generally known, that, from a romantic idea of not prejudicing this young man's right as heir-male, the Baron had refrained from settling his estate on his daughter.

This selfish injustice was resented by the country people, who were partial to their old master, and irritated against his successor. In the Baron's own words, "The matter did not coincide with the feelings of the commons of Bradwardine, Mr Waverley; and the tenants were slack and repugnant in payment of their mails and duties; and when my kinsman came to the village wi' the new factor, Mr James Howie, to lift the rents, some wanchancy[1] person—I suspect John Heatherblutter, the auld game-keeper, that was out wi' me in the year fifteen—fired a shot at him in the gloaming, whereby he was so affrighted, that I may say with Tullius in Catilinam, *Abiit, evasit, erupit, effugit.*[2] He fled, sir, as one may say, incontinent to Stirling. And now he hath advertised the estate for sale, being himself the last substitute in the entail.—And if I were to lament about sic matters, this would grieve me mair than its passing from my immediate possession, whilk, by the course of nature, must have happened in a few years. Whereas now it passes from the lineage that should have possessed it in *sæcula sæculorum.*[3] But God's will be done, *humana perpessi sumus.*[4] Sir John of Bradwardine—Black Sir John, as he is called—who was the common ancestor of our house and the Inch-Grabbits, little thought

---

1 Unlucky (*WSG*).
2 The correct quotation is: "abiit, excessit, evasit, erupit": "varying terms to express haste, secrecy, and energy of the flight" (*GW*). From Cicero, *In Catilinam*, II, I, I.
3 "Age without end" (*OW*, 452).
4 "We have borne all that man can inflict upon us" (*GW*).

such a person would have sprung from his loins. Meantime, he has accused me to some of the *primates*, the rulers for the time, as if I were a cut-throat, and an abettor of bravoes and assassinates, and coupe-jarrets.[1] And they have sent soldiers here to abide on the estate, and hunt me like a partridge upon the mountains, as Scripture says of good King David, or like our valiant Sir William Wallace,—not that I bring myself into comparison with either.—I thought, when I heard you at the door, they had driven the auld deer to his den at last; and so I e'en proposed to die at bay, like a buck of the first head.—But now, Janet, canna ye gie us something for supper?"

"Ou ay, sir, I'll brander[2] the moor-fowl that John Heatherblutter brought in this morning; and ye see puir Davie's roasting the black hen's eggs.—I daur say, Mr Wauverley, ye never kend that a' the eggs that were sae weel roasted at supper in the Ha'-house were aye turned by our Davie?—There's no the like o' him ony gate for powtering[3] wi' his fingers amang the het peat-ashes, and roasting eggs." Davie all this while lay with his nose almost in the fire, nuzzling among the ashes, kicking his heels, mumbling to himself, turning the eggs as they lay in the hot embers, as if to confute the proverb, that "there goes reason to roasting of eggs," and justify the eulogium which poor Janet poured out upon

"Him whom she loved, her idiot boy."[4]

"Davie's no sae silly as folk tak him for, Mr Wauverley; he wadna hae brought you here unless he had kend ye was a friend to his Honour—indeed the very dogs kend ye, Mr Wauverley, for ye was aye kind to beast and body.—I can tell you a story o' Davie, wi' his Honour's leave: his Honour, ye see, being under hiding in thae sair times—the mair's the pity—he lies a' day, and whiles a' night, in the cove in the dern hag; but though it's a bieldy eneugh bit, and the auld gudeman o' Corse-Cleugh has panged it wi' a kemple o' strae amaist, yet when the country's quiet, and the night very cauld, his Honour whiles creeps doun here to get a warm at the ingle, and a sleep amang the blankets, and gangs awa in the morning. And so, ae morning, siccan a fright as I got! Twa unlucky red-coats were up for black-fishing, or some siccan ploy—for the neb o' them's never out o' mischief—and they just got a glisk o' his Honour as he gaed into the wood, and banged aff a gun at him. I out like a jer-

---

1 "Those who disable by hamstringing" (*OW*, 452).
2 Broil (*GW*).
3 "Groping among the ashes" (*WSG*).
4 William Wordsworth, "The Idiot Boy" (1798), line 16.

falcon,[1] and cried,—'Wad they shoot an honest woman's poor innocent bairn?' And I fleyt at them, and threepit it was my son; and they
damned and swuir at me that it was the auld rebel, as the villains
ca'd his Honour; and Davie was in the wood, and heard the tuilzie,
and he, just out o' his ain head, got up the auld grey mantle that his
Honour had flung off him to gang the faster, and he cam out o' the
very same bit o' the wood, majoring and looking about sae like his
Honour, that they were clean beguiled, and thought they had letten
aff their gun at crack-brained Sawney, as they ca' him; and they gae
me saxpence, and twa saumon fish, to say naething about it.—Na,
na, Davie's no just like other folk, puir fallow; but he's no sae silly
as folk tak him for.—But, to be sure, how can we do eneugh for his
Honour, when we and ours have lived on his ground this twa
hundred years; and when he keepit my puir Jamie at school and
college, and even at the Ha'-house, till he gaed to a better place; and
when he saved me frae being ta'en to Perth as a witch—Lord forgi'e
them that would touch sic a puir silly auld body!—and has maintained puir Davie at heck and manger maist feck o' his life?"

Waverley at length found an opportunity to interrupt Janet's narrative, by an inquiry after Miss Bradwardine.

"She's weel and safe, thank God! at the Duchran," answered the
Baron; "the laird's distantly related to us, and more nearly to my chaplain, Mr Rubrick; and, though he be of Whig principles, yet he's not
forgetful of auld friendship at this time. The Bailie's doing what he can
to save something out of the wreck for puir Rose; but I doubt, I doubt,
I shall never see her again, for I maun lay my banes in some far
country."

"Hout na, your Honour," said old Janet, "ye were just as ill aff in
the feifteen, and got the bonnie baronie back, an' a'.—And now the
eggs is ready, and the muir-cock's brandered, and there's ilk ane a
trencher and some saut, and the heel o' the white loaf that cam frae
the Bailie's; and there's plenty o' brandy in the greybeard that Luckie
Maclearie sent doun, and winna ye be suppered like princes?"

"I wish one Prince, at least, of our acquaintance, may be no worse
off," said the Baron to Waverley, who joined him in cordial hopes for
the safety of the unfortunate Chevalier.

They then began to talk of their future prospects. The Baron's plan
was very simple. It was, to escape to France, where, by the interest of
his old friends, he hoped to get some military employment, of which
he still conceived himself capable. He invited Waverley to go with him,

---

1   Obsolete for Gerfalcon, "a large falcon, especially one used to fly at herons"
    (*OED*).

a proposal in which he acquiesced, providing the interest of Colonel Talbot should fail in procuring his pardon. Tacitly he hoped the Baron would sanction his addresses to Rose, and give him a right to assist him in his exile; but he forbore to speak on this subject until his own fate should be decided. They then talked of Glennaquoich, for whom the Baron expressed great anxiety, although, he observed, he was "the very Achilles of Horatius Flaccus,—

Impiger, iracundus, inexorabilis, acer.[1]

Which," he continued, "has been thus rendered (vernacularly) by Struan Robertson:[2]

A fiery etter-cap, a fractious chiel,
As het as ginger, and as stieve as steel."

Flora had a large and unqualified share of the good old man's sympathy.

It was now wearing late. Old Janet got into some kind of kennel behind the hallan; Davie had been long asleep and snoring between Ban and Buscar. These dogs had followed him to the hut after the mansion-house was deserted, and there constantly resided; and their ferocity, with the old woman's reputation of being a witch, contributed a good deal to keep visitors from the glen. With this view, Bailie Macwheeble provided Janet underhand with meal for their maintenance, and also with little articles of luxury for his patron's use, in supplying which much precaution was necessarily used. After some compliments, the Baron occupied his usual couch, and Waverley reclined in an easy chair of tattered velvet, which had once garnished the state bed-room of Tully-Veolan (for the furniture of this mansion was now scattered through all the cottages in the vicinity), and went to sleep as comfortably as if he had been in a bed of down.

CHAPTER XXXVI.
More Explanation.

WITH the first dawn of day, old Janet was scuttling about the house to wake the Baron, who usually slept sound and heavily.

"I must go back," he said to Waverley, "to my cove; will you walk down the glen wi' me?"

---

1 From Horace, *Ars Poetica*, 121: "active, irascible, inexorable, keen" (*PW*, 597).
2 Robertson of Struan (1668-1749); according to Lamont, this quotation may not be from Robertson's work (*OW*, 452).

They went out together, and followed a narrow and entangled foot-path, which the occasional passage of anglers, or wood-cutters, had traced by the side of the stream. On their way, the Baron explained to Waverley, that he would be under no danger in remaining a day or two at Tully-Veolan, and even in being seen walking about, if he used the precaution of pretending that he was looking at the estate as agent or surveyor for an English gentleman, who designed to be purchaser. With this view, he recommended to him to visit the Bailie, who still lived at the factor's house, called Little Veolan, about a mile from the village, though he was to remove at next term. Stanley's passport would be an answer to the officer who commanded the military; and as to any of the country people who might recognise Waverley, the Baron assured him he was in no danger of being betrayed by them.

"I believe," said the old man, "half the people of the barony know that their poor auld laird is somewhere hereabout; for I see they do not suffer a single bairn to come here a bird-nesting; a practice, whilk, when I was in full possession of my power as baron, I was unable totally to inhibit. Nay, I often find bits of things in my way, that the poor bodies, God help them! leave there, because they think they may be useful to me. I hope they will get a wiser master, and as kind a one as I was."

A natural sigh closed the sentence; but the quiet equanimity with which the Baron endured his misfortunes, had something in it vener-able and even sublime. There was no fruitless repining, no turbid melancholy; he bore his lot, and the hardships which it involved, with a good-humoured, though serious composure, and used no violent language against the prevailing party.

"I did what I thought my duty," said the good old man, "and ques-tionless they are doing what they think theirs. It grieves me sometimes to look upon these blackened walls of the house of my ancestors; but doubtless officers cannot always keep the soldier's hand from depre-dation and spuilzie; and Gustavus Adolphus[1] himself, as ye may read in Colonel Munro[2] his Expedition with the worthy Scotch regiment called Mackay's regiment, did often permit it.—Indeed I have myself seen as sad sights as Tully-Veolan now is, when I served with the Marechal Duke of Berwick. To be sure we may say with Virgilius

---

1 King of Sweden (1594-1637). Hook describes him as a "warrior king," actively participating in the Thirty Years' War in Germany, 1618-48 (*PW*, 597).

2 Col. Robert Munro (d. 1680), a Scot who fought in the English Civil War, author of *Monro His Expedition with the Worthy Scots Regiment, Called MacKeye's Regiment*, pub. 1637 (*OW*, 452).

Maro, *Fuimus Troes*[1]—and there's the end of an auld sang.[2] But houses and families and men have a' stood lang eneugh when they have stood till they fall with honour; and now I hae gotten a house that is not unlike a *domus ultima*"[3]—they were now standing below a steep rock. "We poor Jacobites," continued the Baron, looking up, "are now like the conies in Holy Scripture[4] (which the great traveller Pococke[5] calleth Jerboa), a feeble people, that make our abode in the rocks. So, fare you well, my good lad, till we meet at Janet's in the even; for I must get into my Patmos,[6] which is no easy matter for my auld stiff limbs."

With that he began to ascend the rock, striding, with the help of his hands, from one precarious footstep to another, till he got about half way up, where two or three bushes concealed the mouth of a hole, resembling an oven, into which the Baron insinuated, first his head and shoulders, and then, by slow gradation, the rest of his long body; his legs and feet finally disappearing, coiled up like a huge snake entering his retreat, or a long pedigree introduced with care and difficulty into the narrow pigeon-hole of an old cabinet. Waverley had the curiosity to clamber up and look in upon him in his den, as the lurking-place might well be termed. Upon the whole, he looked not unlike that ingenious puzzle, called *a reel in a bottle*,[7] the marvel of children (and of some grown people too, myself for one), who can neither comprehend the mystery how it has got in, or how it is to be taken out. The cave was very narrow, too low in the roof to admit of his standing, or almost of his sitting up, though he made some awkward attempts at the latter posture. His sole amusement was the perusal of his old friend Titus Livius, varied by occasionally scratching Latin proverbs and texts of Scripture with his knife on the roof and walls of his fortalice, which were of sand-stone. As the cave was dry, and filled with clean straw and withered fern, "it made," as he said, coiling himself up with an air of snugness and comfort which contrasted strangely with his situation, "unless when the wind was due north, a very passable *gite*[8] for an old soldier." Neither, as he observed, was he without sentries for the purpose of reconnoitring. Davie and

1   "We are Trojans no longer"; Virgil, *Aeneid* II, 325 (*PW*, 597).
2   Allusion to the Union of 1707 between England and Scotland.
3   Last home; tomb (*PW*, 597).
4   Proverbs 30:26 (*OW*, 453).
5   Richard Pococke (1704-65), bishop of Ossory, who wrote *Description of the East* (1743) and *Description of Palestine* (1745).
6   Greek island where, legend has it, St. John the Divine lived in a cave.
7   On the model of a ship in a bottle; a reel is a spool-like instrument.
8   "Splendid ... lodging place" (*OED*).

his mother were constantly on the watch, to discover and avert danger; and it was singular what instances of address seemed dictated by the instinctive attachment of the poor simpleton, when his patron's safety was concerned.

With Janet, Edward now sought an interview. He had recognised her at first sight as the old woman who had nursed him during his sickness after his delivery from Gifted Gilfillan. The hut also, though a little repaired, and somewhat better furnished, was certainly the place of his confinement; and he now recollected on the common moor of Tully-Veolan the trunk of a large decayed tree, called the *trysting-tree*, which he had no doubt was the same at which the Highlanders rendezvoused on that memorable night. All this he had combined in his imagination the night before; but reasons, which may probably occur to the reader, prevented him from catechising Janet in the presence of the Baron.

He now commenced the task in good earnest; and the first question was, Who was the young lady that visited the hut during his illness? Janet paused for a little; and then observed that to keep the secret now, would neither do good nor ill to any body.

"It was just a leddy, that hasna her equal in the world—Miss Rose Bradwardine!"

"Then Miss Rose was probably also the author of my deliverance," inferred Waverley, delighted at the confirmation of an idea which local circumstances had already induced him to entertain.

"I wot weel, Mr Wauverley, and that was she e'en; but sair, sair angry and affronted wad she hae been, puir thing, if she had thought ye had been ever to ken a word about the matter; for she gar'd me speak aye Gaelic when ye was in hearing, to mak ye trow we were in the Hielands. I can speak it weil eneugh, for my mother was a Hieland woman."

A few more questions now brought out the whole mystery respecting Waverley's deliverance from the bondage in which he left Cairnvreckan. Never did music sound sweeter to an amateur, than the drowsy tautology, with which old Janet detailed every circumstance, thrilled upon the ears of Waverley. But my reader is not a lover, and I must spare his patience, by attempting to condense within reasonable compass, the narrative which old Janet spread through a harangue of nearly two hours.

When Waverley communicated to Fergus the letter he had received from Rose Bradwardine, by Davie Gellatley, giving an account of Tully-Veolan being occupied by a small party of soldiers, that circumstance had struck upon the busy and active mind of the Chieftain. Eager to distress and narrow the posts of the enemy, desirous to prevent their establishing a garrison so near him, and willing also to oblige the Baron,—for he often had the idea of marriage with Rose floating through his brain,—he resolved to send some of his people to drive out the red-coats, and to bring Rose to Glennaquoich. But just as he had ordered Evan with a small party on this duty, the news of Cope's having marched into the Highlands to meet and disperse the forces of the Chevalier, ere they came to a head, obliged him to join the standard with his whole forces.

He sent to order Donald Bean to attend him; but that cautious freebooter, who well understood the value of a separate command, instead of joining, sent various apologies which the pressure of the times compelled Fergus to admit as current, though not without the internal resolution of being revenged on him for his procrastination, time and place convenient. However, as he could not amend the matter, he issued orders to Donald to descend into the Low Country, drive the soldiers from Tully-Veolan, and, paying all respect to the mansion of the Baron, to take his abode somewhere near it, for protection of his daughter and family, and to harass and drive away any of the armed volunteers, or small parties of military, which he might find moving about the vicinity.

As this charge formed a sort of roving commission, which Donald proposed to interpret in the way most advantageous to himself, as he was relieved from the immediate terrors of Fergus, and as he had, from former secret services, some interest in the councils of the Chevalier, he resolved to make hay while the sun shone. He achieved, without difficulty, the task of driving the soldiers from Tully-Veolan; but although he did not venture to encroach upon the interior of the family, or to disturb Miss Rose, being unwilling to make himself a powerful enemy in the Chevalier's army,

"For well he knew the Baron's wrath was deadly";

yet he set about to raise contributions and exactions upon the tenantry, and otherwise to turn the war to his own advantage. Meanwhile he mounted the white cockade, and waited upon Rose with a pretext of great devotion for the service in which her father was engaged, and many apologies for the freedom he must necessarily use for the support of his people. It was at this moment that Rose learned, by open-mouthed fame, with all sorts of exaggeration, that Waverley had killed the smith at Cairnvreckan, in an attempt to arrest him; had been cast into a dungeon by Major Melville of Cairnvreckan, and was to be executed by martial law within three days. In the agony which these tidings excited, she proposed to Donald Bean the rescue of the prisoner. It was the very sort of service which he was desirous to undertake, judging it might constitute a merit of such a nature as would make amends for any peccadilloes which he might be guilty of in the country. He had the art, however, pleading all the while duty and discipline, to hold off, until poor Rose, in the extremity of her distress, offered to bribe him to the enterprise with some valuable jewels which had been her mother's.

Donald Bean, who had served in France, knew, and perhaps overestimated, the value of these trinkets. But he also perceived Rose's apprehensions of its being discovered that she had parted with her jewels for Waverley's liberation. Resolved this scruple should not part him and the treasure, he voluntarily offered to take an oath that he would never mention Miss Rose's share in the transaction; and foreseeing convenience in keeping the oath, and no probable advantage in breaking it, he took the engagement—in order, as he told his lieutenant, to deal handsomely by the young lady—in the only mode and form which, by a mental paction[1] with himself, he considered as binding—he swore secrecy upon his drawn dirk. He was the more especially moved to this act of good faith by some attentions that Miss Bradwardine showed to his daughter Alice, which, while they gained the heart of the mountain damsel, highly gratified the pride of her father. Alice, who could now speak a little English, was very communicative in return for Rose's kindness, readily confided to her the whole papers respecting the intrigue with Gardiner's regiment, of which she was the depositary, and as readily undertook, at her instance, to restore them to Waverley without her father's knowledge. "For they may oblige the bonnie young lady and the handsome young gentleman," said Alice, "and what use has my father for a whin bits o' scarted paper?"[2]

The reader is aware that she took an opportunity of executing this purpose on the eve of Waverley's leaving the glen.

How Donald executed his enterprise, the reader is aware. But the expulsion of the military from Tully-Veolan had given alarm, and, while he was lying in wait for Gilfillan, a strong party, such as Donald did not care to face, was sent to drive back the insurgents in their turn, to encamp there, and to protect the country. The officer, a gentleman and a disciplinarian, neither intruded himself on Miss Bradwardine, whose unprotected situation he respected, nor permitted his soldiers to commit any breach of discipline. He formed a little camp, upon an eminence, near the house of Tully-Veolan, and placed proper guards at the passes in the vicinity. This unwelcome news reached Donald Bean Lean as he was returning to Tully-Veolan. Determined, however, to obtain the guerdon[3] of his labour, he resolved, since approach to

---

1 Bargain (*OED*).
2 A number of bits of pen-scratched paper.
3 Reward (*OED*).

Tully-Veolan was impossible, to deposit his prisoner in Janet's cottage, a place, the very existence of which could hardly have been suspected even by those who had long lived in the vicinity, unless they had been guided thither, and which was utterly unknown to Waverley himself. This effected, he claimed and received his reward. Waverley's illness was an event which deranged all their calculations. Donald was obliged to leave the neighbourhood with his people, and to seek more free course for his adventures elsewhere. At Rose's earnest entreaty, he left an old man, a herbalist, who was supposed to understand a little of medicine, to attend Waverley during his illness.

In the meanwhile, new and fearful doubts started in Rose's mind. They were suggested by old Janet, who insisted, that a reward having been offered for the apprehension of Waverley, and his own personal effects being so valuable, there was no saying to what breach of faith Donald might be tempted. In an agony of grief and terror, Rose took the daring resolution of explaining to the Prince himself the danger in which Mr Waverley stood, judging that, both as a politician, and a man of honour and humanity, Charles Edward would interest himself to prevent his falling into the hands of the opposite party. This letter she at first thought of sending anonymously, but naturally feared it would not, in that case, be credited. She therefore subscribed her name, though with reluctance and terror, and consigned it in charge to a young man, who, at leaving his farm to join the Chevalier's army, made it his petition to her to have some sort of credentials to the Adventurer, from whom he hoped to obtain a commission.

The letter reached Charles Edward on his descent to the Low-lands, and, aware of the political importance of having it supposed that he was in correspondence with the English Jacobites, he caused the most positive orders to be transmitted to Donald Bean Lean, to transmit Waverley, safe and uninjured, in person or effects, to the governor of Doune Castle. The freebooter durst not disobey, for the army of the Prince was now so near him that punishment might have followed; besides, he was a politician as well as a robber, and was unwilling to cancel the interest created through former secret serv-ices, by being refractory on this occasion. He therefore made a virtue of necessity, and transmitted orders to his lieutenant to convey Edward to Doune, which was safely accomplished in the mode men-tioned in a former chapter. The governor of Doune was directed to send him to Edinburgh as a prisoner, because the Prince was appre-hensive that Waverley, if set at liberty, might have resumed his purpose of returning to England, without affording him an opportu-nity of a personal interview. In this, indeed, he acted by the advice of the Chieftain of Glennaquoich, with whom it may be remembered the Chevalier communicated upon the mode of disposing of

Edward, though without telling him how he came to learn the place of his confinement.

This, indeed, Charles Edward considered as a lady's secret; for although Rose's letter was couched in the most cautious and general terms, and professed to be written merely from motives of humanity, and zeal for the Prince's service, yet she expressed so anxious a wish that she should not be known to have interfered, that the Chevalier was induced to suspect the deep interest which she took in Waverley's safety. This conjecture, which was well founded, led, however, to false inferences. For the emotion which Edward displayed on approaching Flora and Rose at the ball of Holyrood, was placed by the Chevalier to the account of the latter; and he concluded that the Baron's views about the settlement of his property, or some such obstacle, thwarted their mutual inclinations. Common fame, it is true, frequently gave Waverley to Miss Mac-Ivor; but the Prince knew that common fame is very prodigal in such gifts; and, watching attentively the behaviour of the ladies towards Waverley, he had no doubt that the young Englishman had no interest with Flora, and was beloved by Rose Bradwardine. Desirous to bind Waverley to his service, and wishing also to do a kind and friendly action, the Prince next assailed the Baron on the subject of settling his estate upon his daughter. Mr Bradwardine acquiesced; but the consequence was, that Fergus was immediately induced to prefer his double suit for a wife and an earldom, which the Prince rejected in the manner we have seen. The Chevalier, constantly engaged in his own multiplied affairs, had not hitherto sought any explanation with Waverley, though often meaning to do so. But after Fergus's declaration, he saw the necessity of appearing neutral between the rivals, devoutly hoping that the matter, which now seemed fraught with the seeds of strife, might be permitted to lie over till the termination of the expedition. When on the march to Derby, Fergus, being questioned concerning his quarrel with Waverley, alleged as the cause, that Edward was desirous of retracting the suit he had made to his sister, the Chevalier plainly told him, that he had himself observed Miss Mac-Ivor's behaviour to Waverley, and that he was convinced Fergus was under the influence of a mistake in judging of Waverley's conduct, who, he had every reason to believe, was engaged to Miss Bradwardine. The quarrel which ensued between Edward and the chieftain is, I hope, still in the remembrance of the reader. These circumstances will serve to explain such points of our narrative as, according to the custom of story-tellers, we deemed it fit to leave unexplained, for the purpose of exciting the reader's curiosity.

When Janet had once finished the leading facts of this narrative, Waverley was easily enabled to apply the clew which they afforded, to other mazes of the labyrinth in which he had been engaged. To Rose

Bradwardine, then, he owed the life which he now thought he could willingly have laid down to serve her. A little reflection convinced him, however, that to live for her sake was more convenient and agreeable, and that, being possessed of independence, she might share it with him either in foreign countries or in his own. The pleasure of being allied to a man of the Baron's high worth, and who was so much valued by his uncle Sir Everard, was also an agreeable consideration, had any thing been wanting to recommend the match. His absurdities, which had appeared grotesquely ludicrous during his prosperity, seemed, in the sunset of his fortune, to be harmonized and assimilated with the noble features of his character, so as to add peculiarity without exciting ridicule. His mind occupied with such projects of future happiness, Edward sought Little Veolan, the habitation of Mr Duncan Macwheeble.

CHAPTER XXXVII.
Now is Cupid a child of conscience—he makes restitution.
—SHAKSPEARE.[1]

MR DUNCAN MACWHEEBLE, no longer Commissary or Bailie, though still enjoying the empty name of the latter dignity, had escaped proscription by an early secession from the insurgent party, and by his insignificance.

Edward found him in his office, immersed among papers and accounts. Before him was a large bicker of oatmeal-porridge, and at the side thereof, a horn-spoon and a bottle of two-penny. Eagerly running his eye over a voluminous law-paper, he from time to time shovelled an immense spoonful of these nutritive viands into his capacious mouth. A pot-bellied Dutch bottle of brandy which stood by, intimated either that this honest limb of the law had taken his *morning* already, or that he meant to season his porridge with such digestive; or perhaps both circumstances might reasonably be inferred. His night-cap and morning-gown had whilome[2] been of tartan, but, equally cautious and frugal, the honest Bailie had got them dyed black, lest their original ill-omened colour might remind his visitors of his unlucky excursion to Derby. To sum up the picture, his face was daubed with snuff up to the eyes, and his fingers with ink up to the knuckles. He looked dubiously at Waverley as he approached the little green rail which fenced his desk and stool from the approach of the vulgar. Nothing could give the Bailie more annoyance than the idea of his acquaintance being claimed by any of the unfortunate gentlemen,

---

1 *Merry Wives of Windsor*, V.v.32.
2 At some time past (*OED*).

who were now so much more likely to need assistance than to afford profit. But this was the rich young Englishman—who knew what might be his situation?—he was the Baron's friend too—what was to be done?

While these reflections gave an air of absurd perplexity to the poor man's visage, Waverley, reflecting on the communication he was about to make to him, of a nature so ridiculously contrasted with the appearance of the individual, could not help bursting out a-laughing, as he checked the propensity to exclaim with Syphax,—

> "Cato's a proper person to intrust
> A love-tale with."[1]

As Mr Macwheeble had no idea of any person laughing heartily, who was either encircled by peril or oppressed by poverty, the hilarity of Edward's countenance greatly relieved the embarrassment of his own, and, giving him a tolerably hearty welcome to Little Veolan, he asked what he would choose for breakfast. His visitor had, in the first place, something for his private ear, and begged leave to bolt the door. Duncan by no means liked this precaution, which savoured of danger to be apprehended; but he could not now draw back.

Convinced he might trust this man, as he could make it his interest to be faithful, Edward communicated his present situation and future schemes to Macwheeble. The wily agent listened with apprehension when he found Waverley was still in a state of proscription—was somewhat comforted by learning that he had a passport—rubbed his hands with glee when he mentioned the amount of his present fortune—opened huge eyes when he heard the brilliancy of his future expectations—but when he expressed his intention to share them with Miss Rose Bradwardine, ecstacy had almost deprived the honest man of his senses. The Bailie started from his three-footed stool like the Pythoness from her tripod;[2] flung his best wig out of the window, because the block on which it was placed stood in the way of his career; chucked his cap to the ceiling, caught it as it fell; whistled Tullochgorum;[3] danced a Highland fling with inimitable grace and agility, and then threw himself exhausted into a chair, exclaiming, "Lady Wauverley!—ten thousand a-year, the least penny!—Lord preserve my poor understanding!"—

"Amen with all my heart," said Waverley; "but now, Mr Macwheeble, let us proceed to business." This word had somewhat a sedative

---

1 Joseph Addison, *Cato* (1713), II.vi.10-11.
2 In Greek mythology, the Pythoness was priestess of Apollo, who spoke the Delphic oracles while seated on a tripod in the temple (*PW*, 597).
3 A reel.

effect, but the Bailie's head, as he expressed himself, was still "in the bees." He mended his pen, however, marked half a dozen sheets of paper with an ample marginal fold, whipped down Dallas of St Martin's Styles from a shelf, where that venerable work roosted with Stair's Institutions, Dirleton's Doubts, Balfour's Practiques,[1] and a parcel of old account-books—opened the volume at the article Contract of Marriage, and prepared to make what he called a "sma' minute, to prevent parties frae resiling."[2]

With some difficulty, Waverley made him comprehend that he was going a little too fast. He explained to him that he should want his assistance, in the first place, to make his residence safe for the time, by writing to the officer at Tully-Veolan, that Mr Stanley, an English gentleman nearly related to Colonel Talbot, was upon a visit of business at Mr Macwheeble's, and, knowing the state of the country, had sent his passport for Captain Foster's inspection. This produced a polite answer from the officer, with an invitation to Mr Stanley to dine with him, which was declined (as may easily be supposed), under pretence of business.

Waverley's next request was, that Mr Macwheeble would dispatch a man and horse to —, the post-town at which Colonel Talbot was to address him, with directions to wait there until the post should bring a letter for Mr Stanley, and then to forward it to Little Veolan with all speed. In a moment, the Bailie was in search of his apprentice (or servitor, as he was called Sixty Years since), Jock Scriever, and in not much greater space of time, Jock was on the back of the white pony.

"Tak care ye guide him weel, sir, for he's aye been short in the wind since—a hem—Lord be gude to me! (in a low voice), I was gaun to come out wi'—since I rode whip and spur to fetch the Chevalier to redd[3] Mr Wauverley and Vich Ian Vohr; and an uncanny coup I gat for my pains.[4]—Lord forgie your honour! I might hae broken my neck—but throth it was in a venture, mae ways nor ane; but this makes amends for a'. Lady Wauverley!—ten thousand a-year!—Lord be gude unto me!"

---

1 *System of Stiles, As now Practised within the Kingdom of Scotland* by George Dallas of St. Martin's, in Rosshire, published 1667, used in the practice of Scottish law; *The Institutions of Law of Scotland* by James Dalrymple, Viscount Stair, published 1681; *Some Doubts and Questions in the Law ... of Scotland* by John Nisbet, Lord Dirleton, published in 1698; and *Practicks* by Sir James Balfour, published 1754 (*OW*, 453).

2 "A short written record of the agreement to prevent parties from withdrawing" (*PW*, 598).

3 Advise (*WSG*).

4 A dangerous turn over (*WSG*).

"But you forget, Mr Macwheeble, we want the Baron's consent—the lady's— "

"Never fear, I'se be caution for them—I'se gie you my personal warrandice[1]—ten thousand a-year! It dings Balmawhapple out and out—a year's rent's worth a' Balmawhapple, fee and life-rent! Lord make us thankful!"

To turn the current of his feelings, Edward inquired if he had heard any thing lately of the Chieftain of Glennaquoich?

"Not one word," answered Macwheeble, "but that he was still in Carlisle Castle, and was soon to be panelled[2] for his life. I dinna wish the young gentleman ill," he said, "but I hope that they that hae got him will keep him, and no let him back to this Hieland border to plague us wi' black mail, and a' manner o' violent, wrongous, and masterfu' oppression and spoliation, both by himself and others of his causing, sending, and hounding out; and he couldna tak care o' the siller when he had gotten it neither, but flang it a' into yon idle quean's lap at Edinburgh—but light come light gane. For my part, I never wish to see a kilt in the country again, nor a red coat, nor a gun, for that matter, unless it were to shoot a paitrick:[3]—they're a' tarr'd wi' ae stick. And when they have done ye wrang, even when ye hae gotten decreet of spuilzie, oppression, and violent profits against them, what better are ye?—they hae na a plack to pay ye; ye need never extract it."

With such discourse, and the intervening topics of business, the time passed until dinner, Macwheeble meanwhile promising to devise some mode of introducing Edward at the Duchran, where Rose at present resided, without risk of danger or suspicion; which seemed no very easy task, since the laird was a very zealous friend to government. The poultry-yard had been laid under requisition, and cockyleeky[4] and Scotch collops[5] soon reeked in the Bailie's little parlour. The landlord's corkscrew was just introduced into the muzzle of a pint-bottle of claret (cribbed possibly from the cellars of Tully-Veolan), when the sight of the grey pony, passing the window at full trot, induced the Bailie, but with due precaution, to place it aside for the moment. Enter Jock Scriever with a packet for Mr Stanley; it is Colonel Talbot's seal; and Edward's fingers tremble as he undoes it. Two official papers, folded, signed, and sealed in all formality, drop out. They were hastily picked up by the Bailie, who had a natural respect for every thing

---

1   "A guarantee, an undertaking to secure another against risk" in Scots Law (*OED*).
2   On trial (*OED*).
3   Partridge (*WSG*).
4   "Leek soup in which a cock has been boiled" (*WSG*).
5   Steaks.

resembling a deed, and, glancing slily on their titles, his eyes, or rather spectacles, are greeted with "Protection by his Royal Highness to the person of Cosmo Comyne Bradwardine, Esq., of that ilk, commonly called Baron of Bradwardine, forfeited for his accession to the late rebellion." The other proves to be a protection of the same tenor in favour of Edward Waverley, Esq. Colonel Talbot's letter was in these words:—

"MY DEAR EDWARD,

"I am just arrived here, and yet I have finished my business; it has cost me some trouble though, as you shall hear. I waited upon his Royal Highness immediately on my arrival, and found him in no very good humour for my purpose. Three or four Scotch gentlemen were just leaving his levee. After he had expressed himself to me very courteously; 'Would you think it,' he said, 'Talbot, here have been half a dozen of the most respectable gentlemen, and best friends to government north of the Forth, Major Melville of Cairnvreckan, Rubrick of Duchran, and others, who have fairly wrung from me, by their downright importunity, a present protection, and the promise of a future pardon, for that stubborn old rebel whom they call Baron of Bradwardine. They allege that his high personal character, and the clemency which he showed to such of our people as fell into the rebels' hands, should weigh in his favour; especially as the loss of his estate is likely to be a severe enough punishment. Rubrick has undertaken to keep him at his own house till things are settled in the country; but it's a little hard to be forced in a manner to pardon such a mortal enemy to the House of Brunswick.' This was no favourable moment for opening my business; however, I said I was rejoiced to learn that his Royal Highness was in the course of granting such requests, as it emboldened me to present one of the like nature in my own name. He was very angry, but I persisted; I mentioned the uniform support of our three votes in the house, touched modestly on services abroad, though valuable only in his Royal Highness's having been pleased to kindly accept them, and founded pretty strongly on his own expressions of friendship and good-will. He was embarrassed, but obstinate. I hinted the policy of detaching, on all future occasions, the heir of such a fortune as your uncle's from the machinations of the disaffected. But I made no impression. I mentioned the obligations which I lay under to Sir Everard, and to you personally, and claimed, as the sole reward of my services, that he would be pleased to afford me the means of evincing my gratitude. I perceived that he still meditated a refusal, and, taking my commission from my pocket, I said (as a last resource), that as his Royal Highness did not, under these pressing circumstances, think me worthy of a favour which he had not scrupled to grant to other gentlemen, whose services I could hardly judge more important than my own, I must beg leave to deposit, with all humility, my commission in his Royal Highness's hands, and to retire from the service. He was not prepared for this; he told me to take up my commission; said some handsome things of my services, and granted my request. You are therefore once more a free man, and I have promised for you that you will be a good boy in future, and remember what you owe to the lenity of government. Thus you see *my* prince can be as generous as *yours*. I do not pretend, indeed, that he confers a favour with all the foreign graces and compliments of your Chevalier errant; but he has a plain English manner, and the evident reluctance with which he grants your request, indicates the sacrifice which he makes of his own inclination to your wishes. My friend, the adjutant-general, has procured me a duplicate of the Baron's protection (the original being in Major Melville's possession), which I send to you, as I know that if you can find him you will have pleasure in being the first to communicate the joyful intelligence. He will of course repair to the Duchran without loss of time, there to ride quarantine for a few weeks. As for you, I give you leave to escort him thither, and to stay a week there, as I understand a certain fair lady is in that quarter. And I have the pleasure to tell you, that whatever progress you can make in her good graces will be highly agreeable to Sir Everard and Mrs Rachel, who will never believe your views and prospects settled, and the three ermines passant in actual safety, until you present them with a Mrs Edward Waverley. Now, certain love-affairs of my own—a good many years since—interrupted some measures which were then proposed in favour of the three ermines passant; so I am bound in honour to make them amends. Therefore make good use of your time, for, when your week is expired, it will be necessary that you go to London to plead your pardon in the law courts.

"Ever, dear Waverley, yours most truly,
"PHILIP TALBOT."

CHAPTER XXXVIII.
Happy's the wooing
That's not long a-doing.[1]

WHEN the first rapturous sensation occasioned by these excellent tidings had somewhat subsided, Edward proposed instantly to go down to the glen to acquaint the Baron with their import. But the

---

1 "Lo heare the man that must of loue complaine," ll. 26-27, in *The Paradise of Dainty Devices* (1576-1606), ed. H.E. Rollins, 1927, p. 71 (*OW*, 454).

cautious Bailie justly observed, that if the Baron were to appear instantly in public, the tenantry and villagers might become riotous in expressing their joy, and give offence to "the powers that be," a sort of persons for whom the Bailie always had unlimited respect. He therefore proposed that Mr Waverley should go to Janet Gellatley's, and bring the Baron up under cloud of night to Little Veolan, where he might once more enjoy the luxury of a good bed. In the meanwhile, he said, he himself would go to Captain Foster, and show him the Baron's protection, and obtain his countenance for harbouring him that night, and he would have horses ready on the morrow to set him on his way to the Duchran along with Mr Stanley, "whilk denomination, I apprehend, your honour will for the present retain," said the Bailie.

"Certainly, Mr Macwheeble; but will you not go down to the glen yourself in the evening to meet your patron?"

"That I wad wi' a' my heart; and mickle obliged to your honour for putting me in mind o' my bounden duty. But it will be past sunset afore I get back frae the Captain's, and at these unsonsy hours the glen has a bad name—there's something no that canny about auld Janet Gellatley. The Laird he'll no believe thae things, but he was aye ower rash and venturesome—and feared neither man nor deevil—and sae's seen o't. But right sure am I Sir George Mackenyie says, that no divine can doubt there are witches, since the Bible says thou shalt not suffer them to live; and that no lawyer in Scotland can doubt it, since it is punishable with death by our law.[1] So there's baith law and gospel for it. An his honour winna believe the Leviticus,[2] he might aye believe the Statute-book—but he may tak his ain way o't; it's a' ane to Duncan Macwheeble. However, I shall send to ask up auld Janet this e'en; it's best no to lightly them that have that character—and we'll want Davie to turn the spit, for I'll gar[3] Eppie put down a fat goose to the fire for your honours to your supper."

When it was near sunset, Waverley hastened to the hut; and he could not but allow that superstition had chosen no improper locality, or unfit object, for the foundation of her fantastic terrors. It resembled exactly the description of Spenser:

---

1 Sir George Mackenyie (1636-91) was Lord Advocate of Scotland, a lawyer and author of *Laws and Customs of Scotland in Matters Criminal* (1674) in which the laws regarding witches are clarified. Lamont notes that "Prosecutions for witchcraft were not prohibited until 1735, although they had not taken place for some years" (*OW*, 454).
2 See Exodus 22:18.
3 Make (*WSG*).

> "There, in a gloomy hollow glen, she found
>   A little cottage built of sticks and reeds,
> In homely wise, and wall'd with sods around,
>   In which a witch did dwell in loathly weeds,
> And wilful want, all careless of her needs;
>   So choosing solitary to abide
> Far from all neighbours, that her devilish deeds,
>   And hellish arts, from people she might hide,
> And hurt far off, unknown, whomsoever she espied."[1]

He entered the cottage with these verses in his memory. Poor old Janet, bent double with age, and bleared with peat-smoke, was tottering about the hut with a birch broom, muttering to herself as she endeavoured to make her hearth and floor a little clean for the reception of her expected guests. Waverley's step made her start, look up, and fall a-trembling, so much had her nerves been on the rack for her patron's safety. With difficulty Waverley made her comprehend that the Baron was now safe from personal danger; and when her mind had admitted that joyful news, it was equally hard to make her believe that he was not to enter again upon possession of his estate. "It behoved[2] to be," she said, "he wad get it back again; naebody wad be sae gripple[3] as to tak his gear[4] after they had gi'en him a pardon: and for that Inch-Grabbit, I could whiles wish mysell a witch for his sake, if I werena feared the Enemy wad tak me at my word." Waverley then gave her some money, and promised that her fidelity should be rewarded. "How can I be rewarded, sir, sae weel, as just to see my auld maister and Miss Rose come back and bruik[5] their ain?"

Waverley now took leave of Janet, and soon stood beneath the Baron's Patmos. At a low whistle, he observed the veteran peeping out to reconnoitre, like an old badger with his head out of his hole. "Ye hae come rather early, my good lad," said he, descending; "I question if the redcoats hae beat the tattoo yet, and we're not safe till then."

"Good news cannot be told too soon," said Waverley; and with infinite joy communicated to him the happy tidings. The old man stood for a moment in silent devotion, then exclaimed, "Praise be to God!—I shall see my bairn again."

"And never, I hope, to part with her more," said Waverley.

---

1   Spenser, *Faerie Queene*, Book III, canto VII, st. 6 (*PW*, 598).
2   "To have use for or need of; to require" (*OED*).
3   "Griping; greedy; avaricious" (*WSG*).
4   "Goods; dress; equipment" (*WSG*).
5   "Use; wear; enjoy" (*WSG*).

"I trust in God, not, unless it be to win the means of supporting her; for my things are but in a bruckle[1] state;—but what signifies warld's[2] gear?"

"And if," said Waverley modestly, "there were a situation in life which would put Miss Bradwardine beyond the uncertainty of fortune, and in the rank to which she was born, would you object to it, my dear Baron, because it would make one of your friends the happiest man in the world?" The Baron turned, and looked at him with great earnestness. "Yes," continued Edward, "I shall not consider my sentence of banishment as repealed, unless you will give me permission to accompany you to the Duchran, and"—

The Baron seemed collecting all his dignity to make a suitable reply to what, at another time, he would have treated as the propounding a treaty of alliance between the houses of Bradwardine and Waverley. But his efforts were in vain; the father was too mighty for the Baron; the pride of birth and rank were swept away;—in the joyful surprise, a slight convulsion passed rapidly over his features as he gave way to the feelings of nature, threw his arms around Waverley's neck, and sobbed out,—"My son, my son! If I had been to search the world, I would have made my choice here." Edward returned the embrace with great sympathy of feeling, and for a little while they both kept silence. At length it was broken by Edward. "But Miss Bradwardine?"

"She had never a will but her old father's; besides, you are a likely youth, of honest principles, and high birth; no, she never had any other will than mine, and in my proudest days I could not have wished a mair eligible espousal for her than the nephew of my excellent old friend, Sir Everard.—But I hope, young man, ye deal na rashly in this matter? I hope ye hae secured the approbation of your ain friends and allies, particularly of your uncle, who is *in loco parentis*? Ah! we maun tak heed o' that." Edward assured him that Sir Everard would think himself highly honoured in the flattering reception his proposal had met with, and that it had his entire approbation; in evidence of which, he put Colonel Talbot's letter into the Baron's hand. The Baron read it with great attention. "Sir Everard," he said, "always despised wealth in comparison of honour and birth; and indeed he hath no occasion to court the *Diva Pecunia*.[3] Yet I now wish, since this Malcolm turns out such a parricide,[4] for I can call him no better, as to think of alienating the family inheritance—I now wish (his eyes fixed on a part of

---

1 "Brickle, brittle, ticklish" (*WSG*).
2 "Worldly" (*OED*).
3 Goddess of money (*OED*).
4 By selling the Bradwardine estate, Malcolm undermines the patriarchy, thus committing a figurative "parracide."

the roof which was visible above the trees) that I could have left Rose the auld hurley-house,[1] and the riggs[2] belanging to it.—And yet," said he, resuming more cheerfully, "it's may be as weel as it is; for, as Baron of Bradwardine, I might have thought it my duty to insist upon certain compliances respecting name and bearings, whilk now, as a landless laird wi' a tocherless daughter,[3] no one can blame me for departing from."

Now, Heaven be praised! thought Edward, that Sir Everard does not hear these scruples! The three ermines passant and rampant bear would certainly have gone together by the ears.—He then, with all the ardour of a young lover, assured the Baron, that he sought for his happiness only in Rose's heart and hand, and thought himself as happy in her father's simple approbation, as if he had settled an earldom upon his daughter.

They now reached Little Veolan. The goose was smoking on the table, and the Bailie brandished his knife and fork. A joyous greeting took place between him and his patron. The kitchen, too, had its company. Auld Janet was established at the ingle-nook;[4] Davie had turned the spit to his immortal honour; and even Ban and Buscar, in the liberality of Macwheeble's joy, had been stuffed to the throat with food, and now lay snoring on the floor.

The next day conducted the Baron and his young friend to the Duchran, where the former was expected, in consequence of the success of the nearly unanimous application of the Scottish friends of government in his favour. This had been so general and so powerful, that it was almost thought his estate might have been saved, had it not passed into the rapacious hands of his unworthy kinsman, whose right, arising out of the Baron's attainder, could not be affected by a pardon from the crown. The old gentleman, however, said, with his usual spirit, he was more gratified by the hold he possessed in the good opinion of his neighbours, than he would have been in being "rehabilitated and restored *in integrum,* had it been found practicable."

We shall not attempt to describe the meeting of the father and daughter,—loving each other so affectionately, and separated under such perilous circumstances. Still less shall we attempt to analyze the deep blush of Rose, at receiving the compliments of Waverley, or stop to inquire whether she had any curiosity respecting the particular cause of his journey to Scotland at that period. We shall not even trouble the reader with the hum-drum details of a courtship Sixty

---

1   "Literally *last house*; as the house now stands, or as it was last built" (*WSG*).
2   "Ridge of land; course; path" (*WSG*).
3   Daughter with no dowry to accompany her into marriage.
4   Fireside (*WSG*).

Years since. It is enough to say, that, under so strict a martinet as the Baron, all things were conducted in due form. He took upon himself, the morning after their arrival, the task of announcing the proposal of Waverley to Rose, which she heard with a proper degree of maiden timidity. Fame does, however, say, that Waverley had, the evening before, found five minutes to apprize her of what was coming, while the rest of the company were looking at three twisted serpents, which formed a *jet d'eau* in the garden.

My fair readers will judge for themselves; but, for my part, I cannot conceive how so important an affair could be communicated in so short a space of time; at least, it certainly took a full hour in the Baron's mode of conveying it.

Waverley was now considered as a received lover in all the forms. He was made, by dint of smirking and nodding on the part of the lady of the house, to sit next Miss Bradwardine at dinner, to be Miss Bradwardine's partner at cards. If he came into the room, she of the four Miss Rubricks who chanced to be next Rose, was sure to recollect that her thimble, or her scissors, were at the other end of the room, in order to leave the seat nearest to Miss Bradwardine vacant for his occupation. And sometimes, if papa and mamma were not in the way to keep them on their good behaviour, the misses would titter a little. The old Laird of Duchran would also have his occasional jest, and the old lady her remark. Even the Baron could not refrain; but here Rose escaped every embarrassment but that of conjecture, for his wit was usually couched in a Latin quotation. The very footmen sometimes grinned too broadly, the maid-servants giggled mayhap too loud, and a provoking air of intelligence seemed to pervade the whole family. Alice Bean, the pretty maid of the cavern, who, after her father's *misfortune*, as she called it, had attended Rose as fille-de-chambre, smiled and smirked with the best of them. Rose and Edward, however, endured all these little vexatious circumstances as other folks have done before and since, and probably contrived to obtain some indemnification, since they are not supposed, on the whole, to have been particularly unhappy during Waverley's six days' stay at the Duchran.

It was finally arranged that Edward should go to Waverley-Honour to make the necessary arrangements for his marriage, thence to London to take the proper measures for pleading his pardon, and return as soon as possible to claim the hand of his plighted bride. He also intended in his journey to visit Colonel Talbot; but, above all, it was his most important object to learn the fate of the unfortunate Chief of Glennaquoich; to visit him at Carlisle, and to try whether any thing could be done for procuring, if not a pardon, a commutation at least, or alleviation, of the punishment to which he was almost certain of being condemned; and, in case of the worst, to offer the miserable Flora an asylum with Rose, or otherwise to assist her views in any mode which might seem possible. The fate of Fergus seemed hard to be averted. Edward had already striven to interest his friend, Colonel Talbot, in his behalf; but had been given distinctly to understand, by his reply, that his credit in matters of that nature was totally exhausted.

The Colonel was still in Edinburgh, and proposed to wait there for some months upon business confided to him by the Duke of Cumberland. He was to be joined by Lady Emily, to whom easy travelling and goat's whey were recommended, and who was to journey northward, under the escort of Francis Stanley. Edward, therefore, met the Colonel at Edinburgh, who wished him joy in the kindest manner on his approaching happiness, and cheerfully undertook many commissions which our hero was necessarily obliged to delegate to his charge. But on the subject of Fergus he was inexorable. He satisfied Edward, indeed, that his interference would be unavailing; but, besides, Colonel Talbot owned that he could not conscientiously use any influence in favour of that unfortunate gentleman. "Justice," he said, "which demanded some penalty of those who had wrapped the whole nation in fear and in mourning, could not perhaps have selected a fitter victim. He came to the field with the fullest light upon the nature of his attempt. He had studied and understood the subject. His father's fate could not intimidate him; the lenity of the laws which had restored to him his father's property and rights could not melt him. That he was brave, generous, and possessed many good qualities, only rendered him the more dangerous; that he was enlightened and accomplished, made his crime the less excusable; that he was an enthusiast in a wrong cause, only made him the more fit to be its martyr. Above all, he had been the means of bringing many hundreds of men into the field, who, without him, would never have broken the peace of the country.

"I repeat it," said the Colonel, "though Heaven knows with a heart distressed for him as an individual, that this young gentleman has studied and fully understood the desperate game which he has played. He threw for life or death, a coronet or a coffin; and he cannot now be permitted, with justice to the country, to draw stakes because the dice have gone against him."

Such was the reasoning of those times, held even by brave and humane men towards a vanquished enemy. Let us devoutly hope, that, in this respect at least, we shall never see the scenes, or hold the sentiments, that were general in Britain Sixty Years since.

CHAPTER XXXIX.

To-morrow? O that's sudden!—Spare him, spare him![1]

—SHAKSPEARE.

EDWARD, attended by his former servant Alick Polwarth, who had re-entered his service at Edinburgh, reached Carlisle while the commission of Oyer and Terminer[2] on his unfortunate associates was yet sitting. He had pushed forward in haste, not, alas! with the most distant hope of saving Fergus, but to see him for the last time. I ought to have mentioned, that he had furnished funds for the defence of the prisoners in the most liberal manner, as soon as he heard that the day of trial was fixed. A solicitor, and the first counsel, accordingly attended; but it was upon the same footing on which the first physicians are usually summoned to the bedside of some dying man of rank; the doctors to take the advantage of some incalculable chance of an exertion of nature—the lawyers to avail themselves of the barely possible occurrence of some legal flaw. Edward pressed into the court, which was extremely crowded; but by his arriving from the north, and his extreme eagerness and agitation, it was supposed he was a relation of the prisoners, and people made way for him. It was the third sitting of the court, and there were two men at the bar. The verdict of GUILTY was already pronounced. Edward just glanced at the bar during the momentous pause which ensued. There was no mistaking the stately form and noble features of Fergus Mac-Ivor, although his dress was squalid, and his countenance tinged with the sickly yellow hue of long and close imprisonment. By his side was Evan Maccombich. Edward felt sick and dizzy as he gazed on them; but he was recalled to himself as the Clerk of Arraigns pronounced the solemn words: "Fergus Mac-Ivor of Glennaquoich, otherwise called Vich Ian Vohr, and Evan Mac-Ivor, in the Dhu of Tarrascleugh, otherwise called Evan Dhu, otherwise called Evan Maccombich, or Evan Dhu Maccombich—you, and each of you, stand attainted of high treason. What have you to say for yourselves why the Court should not pronounce judgment against you, that you die according to law?"

Fergus, as the presiding Judge was putting on the fatal cap of judgment, placed his own bonnet upon his head, regarded him with a steadfast and stern look, and replied in a firm voice, "I cannot let this numerous audience suppose that to such an appeal I have no answer to make. But what I have to say, you would not bear to hear, for my

---

1 *Measure for Measure,* II.ii.83.
2 "A commission of judges to try criminal cases" (*PW*, 598).

defence would be your condemnation. Proceed, then, in the name of God, to do what is permitted to you. Yesterday, and the day before, you have condemned loyal and honourable blood to be poured forth like water. Spare not mine. Were that of all my ancestors in my veins, I would have peril'd it in this quarrel." He resumed his seat, and refused again to rise.

Evan Maccombich looked at him with great earnestness, and, rising up, seemed anxious to speak; but the confusion of the court, and the perplexity arising from thinking in a language different from that in which he was to express himself, kept him silent. There was a murmur of compassion among the spectators, from the idea that the poor fellow intended to plead the influence of his superior as an excuse for his crime. The Judge commanded silence, and encouraged Evan to proceed.

"I was only ganging to say, my lord," said Evan, in what he meant to be an insinuating manner, "that if your excellent honour, and the honourable Court, would let Vich Ian Vohr go free just this once, and let him gae back to France, and no to trouble King George's government again, that ony six o' the very best of his clan will be willing to be justified in his stead; and if you'll just let me gae down to Glennaquoich, I'll fetch them up to ye mysell, to head or hang, and you may begin wi' me the very first man."

Notwithstanding the solemnity of the occasion, a sort of laugh was heard in the court at the extraordinary nature of the proposal. The Judge checked this indecency, and Evan, looking sternly around, when the murmur abated, "If the Saxon gentlemen are laughing," he said, "because a poor man, such as me, thinks my life, or the life of six of my degree, is worth that of Vich Ian Vohr, it's like enough they may be very right; but if they laugh because they think I would not keep my word, and come back to redeem him, I can tell them they ken neither the heart of a Hielandman, nor the honour of a gentleman."

There was no farther inclination to laugh among the audience, and a dead silence ensued.

The Judge then pronounced upon both prisoners the sentence of the law of high treason, with all its horrible accompaniments. The execution was appointed for the ensuing day. "For you, Fergus Mac-Ivor," continued the Judge, "I can hold out no hope of mercy. You must prepare against tomorrow for your last sufferings here, and your great audit hereafter."

"I desire nothing else, my lord," answered Fergus, in the same manly and firm tone.

The hard eyes of Evan, which had been perpetually bent on his Chief, were moistened with a tear. "For you, poor ignorant man," continued the Judge, "who, following the ideas in which you have been educated, have this day given us a striking example how the loyalty due to the king and state alone, is, from your unhappy ideas of clanship, transferred to some ambitious individual, who ends by making you the tool of his crimes—for you, I say, I feel so much compassion, that if you can make up your mind to petition for grace, I will endeavour to procure it for you. Otherwise—"

"Grace me no grace," said Evan; "since you are to shed Vich Ian Vohr's blood, the only favour I would accept from you, is—to bid them loose my hands and gie me my claymore, and bide you just a minute sitting where you are!"

"Remove the prisoners," said the Judge; "his blood be upon his own head."

Almost stupified with his feelings, Edward found that the rush of the crowd had conveyed him out into the street, ere he knew what he was doing. His immediate wish was to see and speak with Fergus once more. He applied at the Castle where his unfortunate friend was confined, but was refused admittance. "The High Sheriff," a non-commissioned officer said, "had requested of the governor that none should be admitted to see the prisoner excepting his confessor and his sister."

"And where was Miss Mac-Ivor?" They gave him the direction. It was the house of a respectable Catholic family near Carlisle.

Repulsed from the gate of the Castle, and not venturing to make application to the High Sheriff or Judges in his own unpopular name, he had recourse to the solicitor who came down in Fergus's behalf. This gentleman told him, that it was thought the public mind was in danger of being debauched by the account of the last moments of these persons, as given by the friends of the Pretender; that there had been a resolution, therefore, to exclude all such persons as had not the plea of near kindred for attending upon them. Yet, he promised (to oblige the heir of Waverley-Honour) to get him an order for admittance to the prisoner the next morning, before his irons were knocked off for execution.

Is it of Fergus Mac-Ivor they speak thus, thought Waverley, or do I dream? Of Fergus, the bold, the chivalrous, the free-minded? The lofty chieftain of a tribe devoted to him? Is it he, that I have seen lead the chase and head the attack,—the brave, the active, the young, the noble, the love of ladies, and the theme of song,—is it he who is ironed like a malefactor; who is to be dragged on a hurdle to the common gallows; to die a lingering and cruel death, and to be mangled by the hand of the most outcast of wretches? Evil indeed was the spectre, that boded such a fate as this to the brave Chief of Glennaquoich!

With a faltering voice he requested the solicitor to find means to warn Fergus of his intended visit, should he obtain permission to make it. He then turned away from him, and, returning to the inn, wrote a scarcely intelligible note to Flora Mac-Ivor, intimating his purpose to wait upon her that evening. The messenger brought back a letter in Flora's beautiful Italian hand, which seemed scarce to tremble even under this load of misery. "Miss Flora Mac-Ivor," the letter bore, "could not refuse to see the dearest friend of her dear brother, even in her present circumstances of unparalleled distress."

When Edward reached Miss Mac-Ivor's present place of abode, he was instantly admitted. In a large and gloomy tapestried apartment, Flora was seated by a latticed window, sewing what seemed to be a garment of white flannel. At a little distance sat an elderly woman, apparently a foreigner, and of a religious order. She was reading in a book of Catholic devotion, but when Waverley entered, laid it on a table and left the room. Flora rose to receive him, and stretched out her hand, but neither ventured to attempt speech. Her fine complexion was totally gone; her person considerably emaciated; and her face and hands as white as the purest statuary marble, forming a strong contrast with her sable dress and jet-black hair. Yet, amid these marks of distress, there was nothing negligent or ill-arranged about her attire; even her hair, though totally without ornament, was disposed with her usual attention to neatness. The first words she uttered were, "Have you seen him?"

"Alas, no," answered Waverley, "I have been refused admittance."

"It accords with the rest," she said; "but we must submit. Shall you obtain leave, do you suppose?"

"For—for—to-morrow," said Waverley; but muttering the last word so faintly that it was almost unintelligible.

"Ay, then or never," said Flora, "until"—she added, looking upward, "the time when, I trust, we shall all meet. But I hope you will see him while earth yet bears him. He always loved you at his heart, though—but it is vain to talk of the past."

"Vain indeed!" echoed Waverley.

"Or even of the future, my good friend," said Flora, "so far as earthly events are concerned; for how often have I pictured to myself the strong possibility of this horrid issue, and tasked myself to consider how I could support my part; and yet how far has all my anticipation fallen short of the unimaginable bitterness of this hour!"

"Dear Flora, if your strength of mind"—

"Ay, there it is," she answered, somewhat wildly; "there is, Mr Waverley, there is a busy devil at my heart, that whispers—but it were madness to listen to it—that the strength of mind on which Flora prided herself has murdered her brother!"

"Good God! how can you give utterance to a thought so shocking?"

"Ay, is it not so? But yet it haunts me like a phantom; I know it is unsubstantial and vain; but it *will* be present; will intrude its horrors on my mind; will whisper that my brother, as volatile as ardent, would have divided his energies amid a hundred objects. It was I who taught him to concentrate them, and to gage all on this dreadful and desperate cast. Oh that I could recollect that I had but once said to him, 'He that striketh with the sword shall die by the sword'; that I had but once said, Remain at home; reserve yourself, your vassals, your life, for enterprises within the reach of man. But O, Mr Waverley, I spurred his fiery temper, and half of his ruin at least lies with his sister!"

The horrid idea which she had intimated, Edward endeavoured to combat by every incoherent argument that occurred to him. He recalled to her the principles on which both thought it their duty to act, and in which they had been educated.

"Do not think I have forgotten them," she said, looking up, with eager quickness; "I do not regret his attempt, because it was wrong! O no! on that point I am armed; but because it was impossible it could end otherwise than thus."

"Yet it did not always seem so desperate and hazardous as it was; and it would have been chosen by the bold spirit of Fergus, whether you had approved it or no; your counsels only served to give unity and consistence to his conduct; to dignify, but not to precipitate, his resolution." Flora had soon ceased to listen to Edward, and was again intent upon her needle-work.

"Do you remember," she said, looking up with a ghastly smile, "you once found me making Fergus's bride-favours, and now I am sewing his bridal-garment. Our friends here," she continued, with suppressed emotion, "are to give hallowed earth in their chapel to the bloody relics of the last Vich Ian Vohr. But they will not all rest together; no—his head!—I shall not have the last miserable consolation of kissing the cold lips of my dear, dear Fergus!"

The unfortunate Flora here, after one or two hysterical sobs, fainted in her chair. The lady, who had been attending in the anteroom, now entered hastily, and begged Edward to leave the room, but not the house.

When he was recalled, after the space of nearly half an hour, he found that, by a strong effort, Miss Mac-Ivor had greatly composed herself. It was then he ventured to urge Miss Bradwardine's claim, to be considered as an adopted sister, and empowered to assist her plans for the future.

"I have had a letter from my dear Rose," she replied, "to the same purpose. Sorrow is selfish and engrossing, or I would have written to express, that, even in my own despair, I felt a gleam of pleasure at learning her happy prospects, and at hearing that the good old Baron has escaped the general wreck. Give this to my dearest Rose; it is her poor

Flora's only ornament of value, and was the gift of a princess." She put into his hands a case, containing the chain of diamonds with which she used to decorate her hair. "To me it is in future useless. The kindness of my friends has secured me a retreat in the convent of the Scottish Benedictine nuns in Paris. To-morrow—if indeed I can survive to-morrow—I set forward on my journey with this venerable sister. And now, Mr Waverley, adieu! May you be as happy with Rose as your amiable dispositions deserve; and think sometimes on the friends you have lost. Do not attempt to see me again; it would be mistaken kindness."

She gave him her hand, on which Edward shed a torrent of tears, and, with a faltering step, withdrew from the apartment, and returned to the town of Carlisle. At the inn, he found a letter from his law friend, intimating, that he would be admitted to Fergus next morning, as soon as the Castle gates were opened, and permitted to remain with him till the arrival of the Sheriff gave signal for the fatal procession.

CHAPTER XL.
——— A darker departure is near,
The death drum is muffled, and sable the bier.[1]
—CAMPBELL.

AFTER a sleepless night, the first dawn of morning found Waverley on the esplanade in front of the old Gothic gate of Carlisle Castle. But he paced it long in every direction, before the hour when, according to the rules of the garrison, the gates were opened, and the drawbridge lowered. He produced his order to the sergeant of the guard, and was admitted.

The place of Fergus's confinement was a gloomy and vaulted apartment in the central part of the Castle; a huge old tower, supposed to be of great antiquity, and surrounded by outworks,[2] seemingly of Henry VIII.'s time, or somewhat later. The grating of the large old-fashioned bars and bolts, withdrawn for the purpose of admitting Edward, was answered by the clash of chains, as the unfortunate Chieftain, strongly and heavily fettered, shuffled along the stone floor of his prison, to fling himself into his friend's arms.

"My dear Edward," he said, in a firm and even cheerful voice, "this is truly kind. I hear of your approaching happiness with the highest pleasure. And how does Rose? and how is our old whimsical friend the Baron? Well, I trust, since I see you at freedom.—And how will you settle precedence between the three ermines passant and the bear and boot-jack?"

---

1 From the ballad "Lochiel's Warning" by Thomas Campbell (1777-1844).
2 Fortifications.

"How, O how, my dear Fergus, can you talk of such things at such a moment!"

"Why, we have entered Carlisle with happier auspices, to be sure—on the 16th of November last, for example, when we marched in, side by side, and hoisted the white flag on these ancient towers. But I am no boy, to sit down and weep, because the luck has gone against me. I knew the stake which I risked; we played the game boldly, and the forfeit shall be paid manfully. And now, since my time is short, let me come to the questions that interest me most—the Prince? has he escaped the bloodhounds?"

"He has, and is in safety."

"Praised be God for that! Tell me the particulars of his escape."

Waverley communicated that remarkable history, so far as it had then transpired, to which Fergus listened with deep interest. He then asked after several other friends; and made many minute inquiries concerning the fate of his own clansmen. They had suffered less than other tribes who had been engaged in the affair; for, having in a great measure dispersed and returned home after the captivity of their Chieftain, according to the universal custom of the Highlanders, they were not in arms when the insurrection was finally suppressed, and consequently were treated with less rigour. This Fergus heard with great satisfaction.

"You are rich," he said, "Waverley, and you are generous. When you hear of these poor Mac-Ivors being distressed about their miserable possessions by some harsh overseer or agent of government, remember you have worn their tartan, and are an adopted son of their race. The Baron, who knows our manners, and lives near our country, will apprize you of the time and means to be their protector. Will you promise this to the last Vich Ian Vohr?"

Edward, as may well be believed, pledged his word; which he afterwards so amply redeemed, that his memory still lives in these glens by the name of the Friend of the Sons of Ivor.

"Would to God," continued the Chieftain, "I could bequeath to you my rights to the love and obedience of this primitive and brave race:—or at least, as I have striven to do, persuade poor Evan to accept of his life upon their terms; and be to you, what he has been to me, the kindest,—the bravest,—the most devoted—"

The tears which his own fate could not draw forth, fell fast for that of his foster-brother.

"But," said he, drying them, "that cannot be. You cannot be to them Vich Ian Vohr; and these three magic words," said he, half smiling, "are the only *Open Sesame* to their feelings and sympathies, and poor Evan must attend his foster-brother in death, as he has done through his whole life."

"And I am sure," said Maccombich, raising himself from the floor, on which, for fear of interrupting their conversation, he had lain so still, that, in the obscurity of the apartment, Edward was not aware of his presence,—"I am sure Evan never desired or deserved a better end than just to die with his Chieftain."

"And now," said Fergus, "while we are upon the subject of clanship—what think you now of the prediction of the Bodach Glas?"—Then, before Edward could answer, "I saw him again last night—he stood in the slip of moonshine, which fell from that high and narrow window, towards my bed. Why should I fear him, I thought—to-morrow, long ere this time, I shall be as immaterial as he. 'False Spirit,' I said, 'art thou come to close thy walks on earth, and to enjoy thy triumph in the fall of the last descendant of thine enemy!' The spectre seemed to beckon and to smile, as he faded from my sight. What do you think of it?—I asked the same question of the priest, who is a good and sensible man; he admitted that the church allowed that such apparitions were possible, but urged me not to permit my mind to dwell upon it, as imagination plays us such strange tricks. What do you think of it?"

"Much as your confessor," said Waverley, willing to avoid dispute upon such a point at such a moment. A tap at the door now announced that good man, and Edward retired while he administered to both prisoners the last rites of religion, in the mode which the Church of Rome prescribes.

In about an hour he was re-admitted; soon after, a file of soldiers entered with a blacksmith, who struck the fetters from the legs of the prisoners.

"You see the compliment they pay to our Highland strength and courage—we have lain chained here like wild beasts, till our legs are cramped into palsy, and when they free us, they send six soldiers with loaded muskets to prevent our taking the castle by storm!"

Edward afterwards learned that these severe precautions had been taken in consequence of a desperate attempt of the prisoners to escape, in which they had very nearly succeeded.

Shortly afterwards the drums of the garrison beat to arms. "This is the last turn-out," said Fergus, "that I shall hear and obey. And now, my dear, dear Edward, ere we part let us speak of Flora—a subject which awakes the tenderest feeling that yet thrills within me."

"We part not *here*!" said Waverley.

"O yes, we do; you must come no farther. Not that I fear what is to follow for myself," he said proudly: "Nature has her tortures as well as art; and how happy should we think the man who escapes from the throes of a mortal and painful disorder, in the space of a short half hour? And this matter, spin it out as they will, cannot last longer. But what a dying man can suffer firmly, may kill a living friend to look upon.—This same law of high treason," he continued, with astonishing firmness and composure, "is one of the blessings, Edward, with which your free country has accommodated poor old Scotland—her own jurisprudence, as I have heard, was much milder. But I suppose one day or other—when there are no longer any wild Highlanders to benefit by its tender mercies—they will blot it from their records, as levelling them with a nation of cannibals. The mummery, too, of exposing the senseless head—they have not the wit to grace mine with a paper coronet; there would be some satire in that, Edward. I hope they will set it on the Scotch gate though, that I may look, even after death, to the blue hills of my own country, which I love so dearly. The Baron would have added,

'Moritur, et moriens dulces reminiscitur Argos.'"[1]

A bustle, and the sound of wheels and horses' feet, was now heard in the court-yard of the Castle. "As I have told you why you must not follow me, and these sounds admonish me that my time flies fast, tell me how you found poor Flora?"

Waverley, with a voice interrupted by suffocating sensations, gave some account of the state of her mind.

"Poor Flora!" answered the Chief, "she could have borne her own sentence of death, but not mine. You, Waverley, will soon know the happiness of mutual affection in the married state—long, long may Rose and you enjoy it!—but you can never know the purity of feeling which combines two orphans, like Flora and me, left alone as it were in the world, and being all in all to each other from our very infancy. But her strong sense of duty, and predominant feeling of loyalty, will give new nerve to her mind after the immediate and acute sensation of this parting has passed away. She will then think of Fergus as of the heroes of our race, upon whose deeds she loved to dwell."

"Shall she not see you then?" asked Waverley. "She seemed to expect it."

"A necessary deceit will spare her the last dreadful parting. I could not part with her without tears, and I cannot bear that these men should think they have power to extort them. She was made to believe she would see me at a later hour, and this letter, which my confessor will deliver, will apprize her that all is over."

An officer now appeared, and intimated that the High Sheriff and his attendants waited before the gate of the Castle, to claim the bodies of Fergus Mac-Ivor and Evan Maccombich. "I come," said Fergus.

---

1 "Dies and dying thinks of dear Argos"; Virgil, *Aeneid* X, 782 (*PW*, 599).

Accordingly, supporting Edward by the arm, and followed by Evan Dhu and the priest, he moved down the stairs of the tower, the soldiers bringing up the rear. The court was occupied by a squadron of dragoons and a battalion of infantry, drawn up in hollow square. Within their ranks was the sledge, or hurdle, on which the prisoners were to be drawn to the place of execution, about a mile distant from Carlisle. It was painted black, and drawn by a white horse. At one end of the vehicle sat the Executioner, a horrid-looking fellow, as beseemed his trade, with the broad axe in his hand; at the other end, next the horse, was an empty seat for two persons. Through the deep and dark Gothic arch-way, that opened on the drawbridge, were seen on horseback the High Sheriff and his attendants, whom the etiquette betwixt the civil and military powers did not permit to come farther. "This is well GOT UP for a closing scene," said Fergus, smiling disdainfully as he gazed around upon the apparatus of terror. Evan Dhu exclaimed with some eagerness, after looking at the dragoons, "These are the very chields that galloped off at Gladsmuir, before we could kill a dozen o' them. They look bold enough now, however." The priest entreated him to be silent.

The sledge now approached, and Fergus, turning round, embraced Waverley, kissed him on each side of the face, and stepped nimbly into his place. Evan sat down by his side. The priest was to follow in a carriage belonging to his patron, the Catholic gentleman at whose house Flora resided. As Fergus waved his hand to Edward, the ranks closed around the sledge, and the whole procession began to move forward. There was a momentary stop at the gate-way, while the governor of the Castle and the High Sheriff went through a short ceremony, the military officer there delivering over the persons of the criminals to the civil power. "God save King George!" said the High Sheriff. When the formality concluded, Fergus stood erect in the sledge, and, with a firm and steady voice, replied, "God save King *James*!" These were the last words which Waverley heard him speak.

The procession resumed its march, and the sledge vanished from beneath the portal, under which it had stopped for an instant. The dead-march was then heard, and its melancholy sounds were mingled with those of a muffled peal, tolled from the neighbouring cathedral. The sound of the military music died away as the procession moved on; the sullen clang of the bells was soon heard to sound alone.

The last of the soldiers had now disappeared from under the vaulted arch-way through which they had been filing for several minutes; the court-yard was now totally empty, but Waverley still stood there as if stupified, his eyes fixed upon the dark pass where he had so lately seen the last glimpse of his friend. At length, a female servant of the governor's, struck with compassion at the stupified misery which his countenance expressed, asked him if he would not walk into her master's house and sit down? She was obliged to repeat her question twice ere he comprehended her, but at length it recalled him to himself. Declining the courtesy by a hasty gesture, he pulled his hat over his eyes, and, leaving the Castle, walked as swiftly as he could through the empty streets, till he regained his inn, then rushed into an apartment, and bolted the door.

In about an hour and a half, which seemed an age of unutterable suspense, the sound of the drums and fifes, performing a lively air, and the confused murmur of the crowd which now filled the streets, so lately deserted, apprised him that all was finished, and that the military populace were returning from the dreadful scene. I will not attempt to describe his sensations.

In the evening the priest made him a visit, and informed him that he did so by directions of his deceased friend, to assure him that Fergus Mac-Ivor had died as he lived, and remembered his friendship to the last. He added, he had also seen Flora, whose state of mind seemed more composed since all was over. With her, and sister Theresa, the priest proposed next day to leave Carlisle, for the nearest seaport from which they could embark for France. Waverley forced on this good man a ring of some value, and a sum of money to be employed (as he thought might gratify Flora) in the services of the Catholic church, for the memory of his friend. "*Fungarque inani munere*,"[1] he repeated, as the ecclesiastic retired. "Yet why not class these acts of remembrance with other honours, with which affection, in all sects, pursues the memory of the dead?"

The next morning ere day-light he took leave of the town of Carlisle, promising to himself never again to enter its walls. He dared hardly look back towards the Gothic battlements of the fortified gate under which he passed, for the place is surrounded with an old wall. "They're no there," said Alick Polwarth, who guessed the cause of the dubious look which Waverley cast backward, and who, with the vulgar appetite for the horrible, was master of each detail of the butchery,—"the heads are ower the Scotch yate, as they ca' it. It's a great pity of Evan Dhu, who was a very weel-meaning, good-natured man, to be a Hielandman; and indeed so was the Laird o' Glennaquoich too, for that matter, when he wasna in ane o' his tirrivies."[2]

---

1 "And perform the empty service"; Virgil, *Aeneid* VI, 885 (*PW*, 599).
2 Tantrums (*WSG*).

CHAPTER XLI.
Dulce Domum.[1]

THE impression of horror with which Waverley left Carlisle softened by degrees into melancholy, a gradation which was accelerated by the painful, yet soothing, task of writing to Rose; and, while he could not suppress his own feelings of the calamity, he endeavoured to place it in a light which might grieve her, without shocking her imagination. The picture which he drew for her benefit he gradually familiarized to his own mind, and his next letters were more cheerful, and referred to the prospects of peace and happiness which lay before them. Yet, though his first horrible sensations had sunk into melancholy, Edward had reached his native country before he could, as usual on former occasions, look round for enjoyment upon the face of nature.

He then, for the first time since leaving Edinburgh, began to experience that pleasure which almost all feel who return to a verdant, populous, and highly cultivated country, from scenes of waste desolation, or of solitary and melancholy grandeur. But how were those feelings enhanced when he entered on the domain so long possessed by his forefathers; recognised the old oaks of Waverley-Chace; thought with what delight he should introduce Rose to all his favourite haunts; beheld at length the towers of the venerable hall arise above the woods which embowered it, and finally threw himself into the arms of the venerable relations to whom he owed so much duty and affection!

The happiness of their meeting was not tarnished by a single word of reproach. On the contrary, whatever pain Sir Everard and Mrs Rachel had felt during Waverley's perilous engagement with the young Chevalier, it assorted too well with the principles in which they had been brought up, to incur reprobation, or even censure. Colonel Talbot also had smoothed the way, with great address, for Edward's favourable reception, by dwelling upon his gallant behaviour in the military character, particularly his bravery and generosity at Preston; until, warmed at the idea of their nephew's engaging in single combat, making prisoner, and saving from slaughter, so distinguished an officer as the Colonel himself, the imagination of the Baronet and his sister ranked the exploits of Edward with those of Wilibert, Hildebrand, and Nigel, the vaunted heroes of their line.

The appearance of Waverley, embrowned by exercise, and dignified by the habits of military discipline, had acquired an athletic and hardy character, which not only verified the Colonel's narration, but surprised and delighted all the inhabitants of Waverley-Honour. They crowded to see, to hear him, and to sing his praises. Mr Pembroke,

---

1 "Home sweet home" (*PW*, 599).

who secretly extolled his spirit and courage in embracing the genuine cause of the Church of England, censured his pupil gently, nevertheless, for being so careless of his manuscripts, which indeed, he said, had occasioned him some personal inconvenience, as, upon the Baronet's being arrested by a king's messenger, he had deemed it prudent to retire to a concealment called "The Priest's Hole," from the use it had been put to in former days; where, he assured our hero, the butler had thought it safe to venture with food only once in the day, so that he had been repeatedly compelled to dine upon victuals either absolutely cold, or, what was worse, only half warm, not to mention that sometimes his bed had not been arranged for two days together. Waverley's mind involuntarily turned to the Patmos of the Baron of Bradwardine, who was well pleased with Janet's fare, and a few bunches of straw stowed in a cleft in the front of a sand-cliff; but he made no remarks upon the contrast which could only mortify his worthy tutor.

All was now in a bustle to prepare for the nuptials of Edward, an event to which the good old Baronet and Mrs Rachel looked forward as if to the renewal of their own youth. The match, as Colonel Talbot had intimated, had seemed to them in the highest degree eligible, having every recommendation but wealth, of which they themselves had more than enough. Mr Clippurse was, therefore, summoned to Waverley-Honour, under better auspices than at the commencement of our story. But Mr Clippurse came not alone; for, being now stricken in years, he had associated with him a nephew, a younger vulture (as our English Juvenal,[1] who tells the tale of Swallow the attorney, might have called him), and they now carried on business as Messrs Clippurse and Hookem. These worthy gentlemen had directions to make the necessary settlements on the most splendid scale of liberality, as if Edward were to wed a peeress in her own right, with her paternal estate tacked to the fringe of her ermine.

But before entering upon a subject of proverbial delay, I must remind my reader of the progress of a stone rolled down hill by an idle truant boy (a pastime at which I was myself expert in my more juvenile years): it moves at first slowly, avoiding by inflection every obstacle of the least importance; but when it has attained its full impulse, and draws near the conclusion of its career, it smokes and thunders down, taking a rood at every spring,[2] clearing hedge and ditch like a

---

1 Swallow is a character in *The Borough*, Letter VI by George Crabbe (1754-1832), who wrote in the biting manner of the Roman satirist, Juvenal (*PW*, 599).

2 Taking a measure of land, "properly containing 40 square poles or perches, but varying locally" (*OED*).

Yorkshire huntsman, and becoming most furiously rapid in its course when it is nearest to being consigned to rest for ever. Even such is the course of a narrative, like that which you are perusing. The earlier events are studiously dwelt upon, that you, kind reader, may be introduced to the character rather by narrative, than by the duller medium of direct description; but when the story draws near its close, we hurry over the circumstances, however important, which your imagination must have forestalled, and leave you to suppose those things, which it would be abusing your patience to relate at length.

We are, therefore, so far from attempting to trace the dull progress of Messrs Clippurse and Hookem, or that of their worthy official brethren, who had the charge of suing out the pardons of Edward Waverley and his intended father-in-law, that we can but touch upon matters more attractive. The mutual epistles, for example, which were exchanged between Sir Everard and the Baron upon this occasion, though matchless specimens of eloquence in their way, must be consigned to merciless oblivion. Nor can I tell you at length, how worthy Aunt Rachel, not without a delicate and affectionate allusion to the circumstances which had transferred Rose's maternal diamonds to the hands of Donald Bean Lean, stocked her casket with a set of jewels that a duchess might have envied. Moreover, the reader will have the goodness to imagine that Job Houghton and his dame were suitably provided for, although they could never be persuaded that their son fell otherwise than fighting by the young squire's side; so that Alick, who, as a lover of truth, had made many needless attempts to expound the real circumstances to them, was finally ordered to say not a word more upon the subject. He indemnified himself, however, by the liberal allowance of desperate battles, grisly executions, and raw-head and bloody-bone stories, with which he astonished the servants'-hall.

But although these important matters may be briefly told in narrative, like a newspaper report of a Chancery suit, yet, with all the urgency which Waverley could use, the real time which the law proceedings occupied, joined to the delay occasioned by the mode of travelling at that period, rendered it considerably more than two months ere Waverley, having left England, alighted once more at the mansion of the Laird of Duchran to claim the hand of his plighted bride.

The day of his marriage was fixed for the sixth after his arrival. The Baron of Bradwardine, with whom bridals, christenings, and funerals, were festivals of high and solemn import, felt a little hurt, that, including the family of the Duchran, and all the immediate vicinity who had title to be present on such an occasion, there could not be above thirty persons collected. "When he was married," he observed, "three hundred horse of gentlemen born, besides servants, and some score or two of Highland lairds, who never got on horseback, were present on the occasion."

But his pride found some consolation in reflecting, that he and his son-in-law having been so lately in arms against government, it might give matter of reasonable fear and offence to the ruling powers, if they were to collect together the kith, kin, and allies of their houses, arrayed in effeir of war,[1] as was the ancient custom of Scotland on these occasions.—"And, without dubitation," he concluded with a sigh, "many of those who would have rejoiced most freely upon these joyful espousals, are either gone to a better place, or are now exiles from their native land."

The marriage took place on the appointed day. The Reverend Mr Rubrick, kinsman to the proprietor of the hospitable mansion where it was solemnized, and chaplain to the Baron of Bradwardine, had the satisfaction to unite their hands; and Frank Stanley acted as bridesman, having joined Edward with that view soon after his arrival. Lady Emily and Colonel Talbot had proposed being present; but Lady Emily's health, when the day approached, was found inadequate to the journey. In amends, it was arranged that Edward Waverley and his lady, who, with the Baron, proposed an immediate journey to Waverley-Honour, should, in their way, spend a few days at an estate which Colonel Talbot had been tempted to purchase in Scotland as a very great bargain, and at which he proposed to reside for some time.

CHAPTER XLII.
"This is no mine ain house, I ken by the bigging o't."[2]
—*Old Song.*

THE nuptial party travelled in great style. There was a coach and six after the newest pattern, which Sir Everard had presented to his nephew, that dazzled with its splendour the eyes of one half of Scotland; there was the family coach of Mr Rubrick;—both these were crowded with ladies, and there were gentlemen on horseback, with their servants, to the number of a round score.[3] Nevertheless, without having the fear of famine before his eyes, Bailie Macwheeble met them in the road, to entreat that they would pass by his house at Little Veolan. The Baron stared, and said his son and he would certainly ride by Little Veolan, and pay their compliments to the Bailie, but could not think of bringing with them the "haill *comitatus nuptialis*, or mat-

---

1   Warlike guise (*WSG*).

2   Song found in David Herd's *Ancient and Modern Scottish Songs*, 2 vols. (1776), II, 217 (*OW*, 456). The translation is "This is not my own house; I know by the building of it."

3   Twenty.

rimonial procession." He added, "that, as he understood that the barony had been sold by its unworthy possessor, he was glad to see his old friend Duncan had regained his situation under the new *Dominus*, or proprietor." The Bailie ducked, bowed, and fidgeted, and then again insisted upon his invitation; until the Baron, though rather piqued at the pertinacity of his instances, could not nevertheless refuse to consent, without making evident sensations which he was anxious to conceal.

He fell into a deep study as they approached the top of the avenue, and was only startled from it by observing that the battlements were replaced, the ruins cleared away, and (most wonderful of all) that the two great stone bears, those mutilated Dagons of his idolatry, had resumed their posts over the gateway. "Now this new proprietor," said he to Edward, "has shown mair *gusto*, as the Italians call it, in the short time he has had this domain, than that hound Malcolm, though I bred him here mysell, has acquired *vita adhuc durante*.[1]—And now I talk of hounds, is not yon Ban and Buscar, who come scouping[2] up the avenue with Davie Gellatley?"

"I vote we should go to meet them, sir," said Waverley, "for I believe the present master of the house is Colonel Talbot, who will expect to see us. We hesitated to mention to you at first that he had purchased your ancient patrimonial property, and even yet, if you do not incline to visit him, we can pass on to the Bailie's."

The Baron had occasion for all his magnanimity. However, he drew a long breath, took a long snuff, and observed, since they had brought him so far, he could not pass the Colonel's gate, and he would be happy to see the new master of his old tenants. He alighted accordingly, as did the other gentlemen and ladies;—he gave his arm to his daughter, and as they descended the avenue, pointed out to her how speedily the "*Diva Pecunia* of the Southron—their tutelary deity, he might call her—had removed the marks of spoliation."

In truth, not only had the felled trees been removed, but, their stumps being grubbed up, and the earth round them levelled and sown with grass, every mark of devastation, unless to an eye intimately acquainted with the spot, was already totally obliterated. There was a similar reformation in the outward man of Davie Gellatley, who met them, every now and then stopping to admire the new suit which graced his person, in the same colours as formerly, but bedizened fine enough to have served Touchstone[3] himself. He danced up with his usual ungainly frolics, first to the Baron, and then to Rose, passing his

1 As long as life lasts (*GW*).
2 "Moving hastily; running, scampering" (*WSG*).
3 The fool in Shakespeare's *As You Like It*.

hands over his clothes, crying, "*Bra', bra', Davie*," and scarce able to sing a bar to an end of his thousand-and-one songs, for the breathless extravagance of his joy. The dogs also acknowledged their old master with a thousand gambols. "Upon my conscience, Rose," ejaculated the Baron, "the gratitude o' thae dumb brutes, and of that puir innocent, brings the tears into my auld een, while that schellum[1] Malcolm—but I'm obliged to Colonel Talbot for putting my hounds into such good condition, and likewise for puir Davie. But, Rose, my dear, we must not permit them to be a life-rent burden upon the estate."[2]

As he spoke, Lady Emily, leaning upon the arm of her husband, met the party at the lower gate, with a thousand welcomes. After the ceremony of introduction had been gone through, much abridged by the ease and excellent breeding of Lady Emily, she apologized for having used a little art to wile them back to a place which might awaken some painful reflections.—"But as it was to change masters, we were very desirous that the Baron"—

"Mr Bradwardine, madam, if you please," said the old gentleman.

"Mr Bradwardine, then, and Mr Waverley, should see what we have done towards restoring the mansion of your fathers to its former state."

The Baron answered with a low bow. Indeed, when he entered the court, excepting that the heavy stables, which had been burnt down, were replaced by buildings of a lighter and more picturesque appearance, all seemed as much as possible restored to the state in which he had left it when he assumed arms some months before. The pigeon-house was replenished; the fountain played with its usual activity, and not only the Bear who predominated over its basin, but all the other Bears whatsoever, were replaced on their several stations, and renewed or repaired with so much care, that they bore no tokens of the violence which had so lately descended upon them. While these minutiæ had been so heedfully attended to, it is scarce necessary to add, that the house itself had been thoroughly repaired, as well as the gardens, with the strictest attention to maintain the original character of both, and to remove, as far as possible, all appearance of the ravage they had sustained. The Baron gazed in silent wonder; at length he addressed Colonel Talbot.

"While I acknowledge my obligation to you, sir, for the restoration of the badge of our family, I cannot but marvel that you have nowhere established your own crest, whilk is, I believe, a mastiff, anciently called a talbot; as the poet has it,

---

1 Rogue (*WSG*).
2 "The rights of one with a life interest" in an estate (*PW*, 598).

A talbot strong—a sturdy tyke.

At least such a dog is the crest of the martial and renowned Earls of Shrewsbury, to whom your family are probably blood relations."

"I believe," said the Colonel, smiling, "our dogs are whelps of the same litter—for my part, if crests were to dispute precedence, I should be apt to let them, as the proverb says, 'fight dog, fight bear.'"

As he made this speech, at which the Baron took another long pinch of snuff, they had entered the house, that is, the Baron, Rose, and Lady Emily, with young Stanley and the Bailie, for Edward and the rest of the party remained on the terrace, to examine a new green-house stocked with the finest plants. The Baron resumed his favourite topic: "however it may please you to derogate from the honour of your burgonet, Colonel Talbot, which is doubtless your humour, as I have seen in other gentlemen of birth and honour in your country, I must again repeat it as a most ancient and distinguished bearing, as well as that of my young friend Francis Stanley, which is the eagle and child."

"The bird and bantling they call it in Derbyshire, sir," said Stanley.

"Ye're a daft callant, sir," said the Baron, who had a great liking to this young man, perhaps because he sometimes teazed him.—"Ye're a daft callant, and I must correct you some of these days," shaking his great brown fist at him. "But what I meant to say, Colonel Talbot, is, that yours is an ancient *prosapia*, or descent, and since you have law-fully and justly acquired the estate for you and yours, which I have lost for me and mine, I wish it may remain in your name as many centuries as it has done in that of the late proprietor's."

"That," answered the Colonel, "is very handsome, Mr Bradwar-dine, indeed."

"And yet, sir, I cannot but marvel that you, Colonel, whom I noted to have so much of the *amor patriæ*,[1] when we met in Edinburgh, as even to vilipend[2] other countries, should have chosen to establish your Lares, or household gods, *procul a patriæ finibus*,[3] and in a manner to expatriate yourself."

"Why really, Baron, I do not see why, to keep the secret of these foolish boys, Waverley and Stanley, and of my wife, who is no wiser, one old soldier should continue to impose upon another. You must know then that I have so much of that same prejudice in favour of my native country, that the sum of money which I advanced to the seller of this extensive barony has only purchased for me a box in — shire, called Brerewood Lodge, with about two hundred and fifty acres of

---

1 Love of country.
2 Slander (*GW*).
3 "Far away from the borders of your own country" (*PW*, 599).

land, the chief merit of which is, that it is within a very few miles of Waverley-Honour."

"And who, then, in the name of Heaven, has bought this property?"

"That," said the Colonel, "it is this gentleman's profession to explain."

The Bailie, whom this reference regarded, and who had all this while shifted from one foot to another with great impatience, "like a hen," as he afterwards said, "upon a het girdle";[1] and chuckling, he might have added, like the said hen in all the glory of laying an egg,— now pushed forward. "That I can, that I can, your Honour"; drawing from his pocket a budget of papers, and untying the red tape with a hand trembling with eagerness. "Here is the disposition and assignation, by Malcolm Bradwardine of Inch-Grabbit, regularly signed and tested in terms of the statute, whereby, for a certain sum of sterling money presently contented and paid to him, he has disponed,[2] alienated, and conveyed, the whole estate and barony of Bradwardine, Tully-Veolan, and others, with the fortalice and manor-place"—

"For God's sake, to the point, sir; I have all that by heart," said the Colonel.

"To Cosmo Comyne Bradwardine, Esq." pursued the Bailie, "his heirs and assignees, simply and irredeemably—to be held either *a me vel de me*"[3]—

"Pray read short, sir."

"On the conscience of an honest man, Colonel, I read as short as is consistent with style.—Under the burden and reservation always"—

"Mr Macwheeble, this would outlast a Russian winter—give me leave. In short, Mr Bradwardine, your family estate is your own once more in full property, and at your absolute disposal, but only burdened with the sum advanced to re-purchase it, which I understand is utterly disproportioned to its value."

"An auld sang—an auld sang, if it please your honours," cried the Bailie, rubbing his hands; "look at the rental book."

"Which sum being advanced by Mr Edward Waverley, chiefly from the price of his father's property which I bought from him, is secured to his lady your daughter, and her family by this marriage."

"It is a catholic security,"[4] shouted the Bailie, "to Rose Comyne Bradwardine *alias* Wauverley, in liferent, and the children of the said

---

1 Hot griddle: "an iron plate for firing cakes on" (*WSG*).

2 Assigned (*GW*).

3 "By me directly or indirectly through my heirs" (*PW*, 599).

4 "'When a real security extends over several estates, on one of which there are other securities, the debt of the catholic security falls to be paid ratably from all' according to Bell's *Principles of the Laws of Scotland*" (*PW*, 599).

marriage, in fee; and I made up a wee bit minute of an ante-nuptial contract, *intuitu matrimonij*,[1] so it cannot be subject to reduction hereafter, as a donation *inter virum et uxorem*."[2]

It is difficult to say whether the worthy Baron was most delighted with the restitution of his family property, or with the delicacy and generosity that left him unfettered to pursue his purpose in disposing of it after his death, and which avoided, as much as possible, even the appearance of laying him under pecuniary obligation. When his first pause of joy and astonishment was over, his thoughts turned to the unworthy heir-male, who, he pronounced, had sold his birth-right, like Esau, for a mess o' pottage.[3]

"But wha cookit the parritch for him?" exclaimed the Bailie; "I wad like to ken that;—wha, but your honour's to command, Duncan Macwheeble? His honour, young Mr Wauverley, put it a' into my hand frae the beginning—frae the first calling o' the summons, as I may say. I circumvented them—I played at bogle about the bush[4] wi' them—I cajolled them; and if I havena gien Inch-Grabbit and Jamie Howie a bonnie begunk,[5] they ken themselves. Him a writer! I didna gae slapdash to them wi' our young bra' bridegroom, to gar them haud up the market: na, na; I scared them wi' our wild tenantry, and the Mac-Ivors, that are but ill settled yet, till they durstna on ony errand whatsoever gang ower the door-stane after gloaming, for fear John Heatherblutter, or some siccan dare-the-deil, should tak a baff[6] at them: then, on the other hand, I beflumm'd[7] them wi' Colonel Talbot—wad they offer to keep up the price again' the Duke's friend? Did they na ken wha was master? Had they na seen eneugh, by the sad example of mony a puir misguided unhappy body"—

"Who went to Derby, for example, Mr Macwheeble?" said the Colonel to him, aside.

"O whisht, Colonel, for the love o' God! let that flee stick i' the wa'.[8] There were mony good folk at Derby; and it's ill speaking of halters,"—with a sly cast of his eye toward the Baron, who was in a deep reverie.

---

1 In prospect of marriage (*PW*, 599).
2 A gift made by a husband to his wife before marriage (which makes it non-revocable) (*OW*, 456).
3 Genesis 25:29-34 (*PW*, 600).
4 Play hide and seek; a bogle is a "bugbear" (*WSG*).
5 Nice trick (*WSG*).
6 Blow (*WSG*).
7 Flattered (*WSG*).
8 Let that fly stick on the wall.

Starting out of it at once, he took Macwheeble by the button, and led him into one of the deep window recesses, whence only fragments of their conversation reached the rest of the party. It certainly related to stamp-paper and parchment; for no other subject, even from the mouth of his patron, and he, once more, an efficient one, could have arrested so deeply the Bailie's reverent and absorbed attention.

"I understand your honour perfectly; it can be dune as easy as taking out a decreet in absence."[1]

"To her and him, after my demise, and to their heirs-male,—but preferring the second son, if God shall bless them with two, who is to carry the name and arms of Bradwardine of that Ilk, without any other name or armorial bearings whatsoever."

"Tut, your honour!" whispered the Bailie, "I'll make a slight jotting the morn; it will cost but a charter of resignation *in favorem*;[2] and I'll hae it ready for the next term in Exchequer."

Their private conversation ended, the Baron was now summoned to do the honours of Tully-Veolan to new guests. These were, Major Melville of Cairnvreckan, and the Reverend Mr Morton, followed by two or three others of the Baron's acquaintances, who had been made privy to his having again acquired the estate of his fathers. The shouts of the villagers were also heard beneath in the court-yard; for Saunders Saunderson, who had kept the secret for several days with laudable prudence, had unloosed his tongue upon beholding the arrival of the carriages.

But, while Edward received Major Melville with politeness, and the clergyman with the most affectionate and grateful kindness, his father-in-law looked a little awkward, as uncertain how he should answer the necessary claims of hospitality to his guests, and forward the festivity of his tenants. Lady Emily relieved him, by intimating, that, though she must be an indifferent representative of Mrs Edward Waverley in many respects, she hoped the Baron would approve of the entertainment she had ordered, in expectation of so many guests; and that they would find such other accommodations provided, as might in some degree support the ancient hospitality of Tully-Veolan. It is impossible to describe the pleasure which this assurance gave the Baron, who, with an air of gallantry half appertaining to the stiff Scottish laird, and half to the officer in the French service, offered his arm to the fair speaker, and led the way in something between a stride and a minuet step, into the large dining parlour, followed by all the rest of the good company.

---

1   "A court judgement allowing land to pass from one vassal to another" (*PW*, 600).
2   "The charter allowing the transfer of land from one vassal to another had to be obtained from the appropriate feudal superior" (*PW*, 600).

By dint of Saunderson's directions and exertions, all here, as well as in the other apartments, had been disposed as much as possible according to the old arrangement; and where new movables had been necessary, they had been selected in the same character with the old furniture. There was one addition to this fine old apartment, however, which drew tears into the Baron's eyes. It was a large and spirited painting, representing Fergus Mac-Ivor and Waverley in their Highland dress, the scene a wild, rocky, and mountainous pass, down which the clan were descending in the background. It was taken from a spirited sketch, drawn while they were in Edinburgh by a young man of high genius, and had been painted on a full-length scale by an eminent London artist. Raeburn[1] himself (whose Highland Chiefs do all but walk out of the canvass) could not have done more justice to the subject; and the ardent, fiery, and impetuous character of the unfortunate Chief of Glennaquoich was finely contrasted with the contemplative, fanciful, and enthusiastic expression of his happier friend. Beside this painting hung the arms which Waverley had borne in the unfortunate civil war. The whole piece was beheld with admiration, and deeper feelings.

Men must, however, eat, in spite both of sentiment and vertu; and the Baron, while he assumed the lower end of the table, insisted that Lady Emily should do the honours of the head, that they might, he said, set a meet example to the *young folk*. After a pause of deliberation, employed in adjusting in his own brain the precedence between the Presbyterian kirk and Episcopal church of Scotland, he requested Mr Morton, as the stranger, would crave a blessing, observing that Mr Rubrick, who was at *home*, would return thanks for the distinguished mercies it had been his lot to experience. The dinner was excellent. Saunderson attended in full costume, with all the former domestics, who had been collected, excepting one or two, that had not been heard of since the affair of Culloden. The cellars were stocked with wine which was pronounced to be superb, and it had been contrived that the Bear of the Fountain, in the court-yard, should (for that night only) play excellent brandy punch for the benefit of the lower orders.

When the dinner was over, the Baron, about to propose a toast, cast a somewhat sorrowful look upon the side-board, which, however, exhibited much of his plate, that had either been secreted, or purchased by neighbouring gentlemen from the soldiery, and by them gladly restored to the original owner.

"In the late times," he said, "those must be thankful who have saved life and land; yet when I am about to pronounce this toast, I cannot

---

1 Sir Henry Raeburn (1756-1823), Scottish portrait painter who painted several portraits of Scott. See the portrait on p. 2 of this edition.

but regret an old heir-loom, Lady Emily—a *poculum potatorium*,[1] Colonel Talbot"—

Here the Baron's elbow was gently touched by his Major Domo, and, turning round, he beheld, in the hands of Alexander ab Alexandro, the celebrated cup of Saint Duthac, the Blessed Bear of Bradwardine! I question if the recovery of his estate afforded him more rapture. "By my honour," he said, "one might almost believe in brownies and fairies, Lady Emily, when your ladyship is in presence!"

"I am truly happy," said Colonel Talbot, "that, by the recovery of this piece of family antiquity, it has fallen within my power to give you some token of my deep interest in all that concerns my young friend Edward. But that you may not suspect Lady Emily for a sorceress, or me for a conjuror, which is no joke in Scotland, I must tell you that Frank Stanley, your friend, who has been seized with a tartan fever ever since he heard Edward's tales of old Scottish manners, happened to describe to us at second hand this remarkable cup. My servant, Spontoon, who, like a true old soldier, observes every thing and says little, gave me afterwards to understand that he thought he had seen the piece of plate Mr Stanley mentioned, in the possession of a certain Mrs Nosebag, who, having been originally the helpmate of a pawnbroker, had found opportunity, during the late unpleasant scenes in Scotland, to trade a little in her old line, and so became the depositary of the more valuable part of the spoil of half the army. You may believe the cup was speedily recovered; and it will give me very great pleasure if you allow me to suppose, that its value is not diminished by having been restored through my means."

A tear mingled with the wine which the Baron filled, as he proposed a cup of gratitude to Colonel Talbot, and "The Prosperity of the united Houses of Waverley-Honour and Bradwardine!"—

It only remains for me to say, that as no wish was ever uttered with more affectionate sincerity, there are few which, allowing for the necessary mutability of human events, have been, upon the whole, more happily fulfilled.

CHAPTER XLIII.
A Postscript, which should have been a Preface.

OUR journey is now finished, gentle reader; and if your patience has accompanied me through these sheets, the contract is, on your part, strictly fulfilled. Yet, like the driver who has received his full hire, I still linger near you, and make, with becoming diffidence, a trifling additional claim upon your bounty and good nature. You are as free,

---

1 Cup.

however, to shut the volume of the one petitioner, as to close your door in the face of the other.

This should have been a prefatory chapter, but for two reasons: first, that most novel readers, as my own conscience reminds me, are apt to be guilty of the sin of omission respecting that same matter of prefaces; secondly, that it is a general custom with that class of students, to begin with the last chapter of a work; so that, after all, these remarks, being introduced last in order, have still the best chance to be read in their proper place.

There is no European nation, which, within the course of half a century, or little more, has undergone so complete a change as this kingdom of Scotland. The effects of the insurrection of 1745,—the destruction of the patriarchal power of the Highland chiefs,—the abolition of the heritable jurisdictions of the Lowland nobility and barons,—the total eradication of the Jacobite party, which, averse to intermingle with the English, or adopt their customs, long continued to pride themselves upon maintaining ancient Scottish manners and customs,—commenced this innovation. The gradual influx of wealth, and extension of commerce, have since united to render the present people of Scotland a class of beings as different from their grandfathers, as the existing English are from those of Queen Elizabeth's time. The political and economical effects of these changes have been traced by Lord Selkirk[1] with great precision and accuracy. But the change, though steadily and rapidly progressive, has, nevertheless, been gradual; and, like those who drift down the stream of a deep and smooth river, we are not aware of the progress we have made until we fix our eye on the now distant point from which we have drifted. Such of the present generation as can recollect the last twenty or twenty-five years of the eighteenth century, will be fully sensible of the truth of this statement; especially if their acquaintance and connexions lay among those, who, in my younger time, were facetiously called "folks of the old leaven,"[2] who still cherished a lingering, though hopeless attachment, to the house of Stewart. This race has now almost entirely vanished from the land, and with it, doubtless, much absurd political prejudice; but also, many living examples of singular and disinterested attachment to the principles of loyalty which they received from their fathers, and of old Scottish faith, hospitality, worth, and honour.

It was my accidental lot, though not born a Highlander (which may be an apology for much bad Gaelic) to reside, during my childhood and youth, among persons of the above description; and now, for the

---

1   Thomas Douglas, Earl of Selkirk, *Observations on the Present State of the Highlands of Scotland*, 1805.
2   Corinthians 5: 6-7.

purpose of preserving some idea of the ancient manners of which I have witnessed the almost total extinction, I have embodied in imaginary scenes, and ascribed to fictitious characters, a part of the incidents which I then received from those who were actors in them. Indeed, the most romantic parts of this narrative are precisely those which have a foundation in fact. The exchange of mutual protection between a Highland gentleman and an officer of rank in the king's service, together with the spirited manner in which the latter asserted his right to return the favour he had received, is literally true. The accident by a musket-shot, and the heroic reply imputed to Flora, relate to a lady of rank not long deceased. And scarce a gentleman who was "in hiding," after the battle of Culloden, but could tell a tale of strange concealments, and of wild and hair's-breadth 'scapes, as extraordinary as any which I have ascribed to my heroes. Of this, the escape of Charles Edward himself, as the most prominent, is the most striking example. The accounts of the battle of Preston and skirmish at Clifton, are taken from the narrative of intelligent eye-witnesses, and corrected from the History of the Rebellion by the late venerable author of Douglas.[1] The Lowland Scottish gentlemen, and the subordinate characters, are not given as individual portraits, but are drawn from the general habits of the period, of which I have witnessed some remnants in my younger days, and partly gathered from tradition.

It has been my object to describe these persons, not by a caricatured and exaggerated use of the national dialect, but by their habits, manners, and feelings; so as in some distant degree to emulate the admirable Irish portraits drawn by Miss Edgeworth, so different from the "Teagues" and "dear joys," who so long, with the most perfect family resemblance to each other, occupied the drama and the novel.[2]

I feel no confidence, however, in the manner in which I have executed my purpose. Indeed, so little was I satisfied with my production, that I laid it aside in an unfinished state, and only found it again by mere accident among other waste papers in an old cabinet, the drawers of which I was rummaging, in order to accommodate a friend with some fishing tackle, after it had been mislaid for several years. Two works upon similar subjects, by female authors, whose genius is highly creditable to their country, have appeared in the interval; I mean Mrs Hamilton's Glenburnie, and the late account of Highland

---

1 *A History of the Rebellion of '45* (1756) by John Home (1722-1808).

2 Maria Edgeworth (1767-1849), Anglo-Irish novelist, is credited with writing the first National novel, *Castle Rackrent* (1800), in which her treatment of the Irish character countered the simplistic, stereotypical views previously presented (the "Teagues" and "old joys"). For further information on Edgeworth's relationship with Scott, see the Introduction.

Superstitions. But the first is confined to the rural habits of Scotland, of which it has given a picture with striking and impressive fidelity; and the traditional records of the respectable and ingenious Mrs Grant of Laggan,[1] are of a nature distinct from the fictitious narrative which I have here attempted.

I would willingly persuade myself, that the preceding work will not be found altogether uninteresting. To elder persons it will recall scenes and characters familiar to their youth; and to the rising generation the tale may present some idea of the manners of their forefathers.

Yet I heartily wish that the task of tracing the evanescent manners of his own country had employed the pen of the only man in Scotland who could have done it justice,—of him so eminently distinguished in elegant literature, and whose sketches of Colonel Caustic and Umphraville[2] are perfectly blended with the finer traits of national character. I should in that case have had more pleasure as a reader, than I shall ever feel in the pride of a successful author, should these sheets confer upon me that envied distinction. And as I have inverted the usual arrangement, placing these remarks at the end of the work to which they refer, I will venture on a second violation of form, by closing the whole with a Dedication;

THESE VOLUMES
BEING RESPECTFULLY INSCRIBED
TO
OUR SCOTTISH ADDISON,[3]
HENRY MACKENZIE,
BY
AN UNKNOWN ADMIRER
OF
HIS GENIUS.

END OF WAVERLEY.

---

1 *The Cottagers of Glenburnie* (1808) by Elizabeth Hamilton (1758-1816), and *Essays on the Superstitions of the Highlanders of Scotland* (1811) by Anne Grant of Laggan (1755-1838). For excerpts from each, see Appendices D2-3.

2 Henry Mackenzie (1745-1831), author of *The Man of Feeling* (1771); Colonel Caustic is a character in *The Lounger* (1785); Umphraville appears in Mackenzie's *The Mirror* (1779).

3 *The Oxford Companion to English Literature,* ed. Margaret Drabble, 5th ed., suggests that Henry Mackenzie's novel, *The Man of Feeling* (1771), presents the "refined and gentle hero ... in a series of sketches loosely woven together, somewhat in the manner of [Joseph] Addison's essays on Sir Roger de Coverley" (603).

Scott's Notes to *Waverley*, Volumes One and Two[1]

a. A homely metrical narrative of the events of the period, which contains some striking particulars, and is still a great favourite with the lower classes, gives a very correct statement of the behaviour of the mountaineers respecting this same military license; and as the verses are little known, and contain some good sense, we venture to insert them.

THE AUTHOR'S ADDRESS TO ALL IN GENERAL.

Now, gentle readers, I have let you ken
My very thoughts, from heart to pen,
'Tis needless for to conten'
   Or yet controule,
For there's not a word o't I can men'—
   So ye must thole.

For on both sides, some were not good;
I saw them murd'ring in cold blood,
Not the gentlemen, but wild and rude,
   The baser sort,
Who to the wounded had no mood
   But murd'ring sport!

Ev'n both at Preston and Falkirk,
That fatal night ere it grew mirk,
Piercing the wounded with their durk,
   Caused many cry!
Such pity's shown from Savage and Turk
   As peace to die.

A woe be to such hot zeal,
To smite the wounded on the fiell!
It's just they got such groats in kail,
   who do the same.
It only teaches cruelty's real
   To them again.

I've seen the men call'd Highland Rogues,
With Lowland men make *shangs*[2] a brogs,[3]
Sup kail and brose, and fling the cogs

---

1 The following notes, with the exception of f. and tt., were added for the *Magnum Opus Waverley* edition (see A Note on the Text).
2 A shang or shangan is "a stick cleft at one end for putting on a dog's tail" (*OED*).
3 Small sticks.

Out at the door,
Take cocks, hens, sheep, and hogs,
    And pay nought for.

I saw a Highlander, 'twas right drole,
With a string of puddings hung on a pole,
Whip'd o'er his shoulder, skipped like a fole,
        Caus'd Maggy bann,
Lap o'er the midden and midden-hole,
        And aff he ran.

When check'd for this, they'd often tell ye—
Indeed *her nainsell's*[1] a tume belly;
You'll no gie't wanting bought, nor sell me;
        Hersell will hae't;
Go tell King Shorge, and Shordy's Willie,
        I'll hae a meat.

I saw the soldiers at Linton-brig,
Because the man was not a Whig,
Of meat and drink leave not a skig,
        Within his door;
They burnt his very hat and wig,
        And thump'd him sore.

And through the Highlands they were so rude,
As leave them neither clothes nor food,
Then burnt their houses to conclude;
        'Twas tit for tat.
How can *her nainsell* e'er be good,
        To think on that?

And after all, O, shame and grief!
To use some worse than murd'ring thief,
Their very gentleman and chief,
        Unhumanly!
Like Popish tortures, I believe,
        Such cruelty.

 Ev'n what was act on open stage
At Carlisle, in the hottest rage,
When mercy was clapt in a cage,
        And pity dead,
Such cruelty approv'd by every age,
        I shook my head.

---

1 One's own self. "A phrase attributed to Highlanders in place of the first
   personal pronoun, and hence used as a designation for a Highlander" (*OED*).

So many to curse, so few to pray,
And some aloud huzza did cry;
They cursed the Rebel Scots that day,
            As they'd been nowt
Brought up for slaughter, as that way
            Too many rowt.

Therefore, alas! dear countrymen,
O never do the like again,
To thirst for vengeance, never ben'
            Your gun nor pa',
But with the English e'en borrow and len',
            Let anger fa'.

Their boasts and bullying, not worth a louse,
As our King's the best about the house.
'Tis ay good to be sober and douce,
            To live in peace;
For many, I see, for being o'er crouse,
            Gets broken face.

b. Alas! That attire, respectable and gentlemanlike in 1805, or thereabouts, is
   now as antiquated as the Author of WAVERLEY has himself become since
   that period! The reader of fashion will please to fill up the costume with an
   embroidered waistcoat of purple velvet or silk, and a coat of whatever colour
   he pleases.
c. Where the Chevalier Saint George, or, as he was termed, the Old Pretender,
   held his exiled court, as his situation compelled him to shift his place of residence.
d. Long the oracle of the country gentlemen of the high Tory party. The ancient
   News-Letter was written in manuscript and copied by clerks, who addressed
   the copies to the subscribers. The politician by whom they were compiled
   picked up his intelligence at Coffee-houses, and often pleaded for an additional gratuity, in consideration of the extra expense attached to frequenting
   such places of fashionable resort.
e. There is a family legend to this purpose, belonging to the knightly family of
   Bradshaigh, the proprietors of Haigh-hall, in Lancashire, where, I have been
   told, the event is recorded on a painted glass window. The German ballad of
   the Noble Moringer turns upon a similar topic. But undoubtedly many such
   incidents may have taken place, where, the distance being great and the intercourse infrequent, false reports concerning the fate of absent Crusaders must
   have been commonly circulated, and sometimes perhaps rather hastily credited at home.
f. See Hoppner's tale of the Seven Lovers.

g. These Introductory Chapters have been a good deal censured as tedious and unnecessary. Yet there are circumstances recorded in them which the author has not been able to persuade himself to retract or cancel.

h. The attachment to this classic was, it is said, actually displayed, in the manner mentioned in the text, by an unfortunate Jacobite in that unhappy period. He escaped from the jail in which he was confined for a hasty trial and certain condemnation, and was retaken as he hovered around the place in which he had been imprisoned, for which he could give no better reason than the hope of recovering his favourite *Titus Livius*. I am sorry to add, that the simplicity of such a character was found to form no apology for his guilt as a rebel, and that he was condemned and executed.

i. Nicholas Amhurst [1697-1742], a noted political writer, who conducted for many years a paper called the Craftsman, under the assumed name of Caleb D'Anvers. He was devoted to the Tory interest, and seconded, with much ability, the attacks of Pulteney on Sir Robert Walpole.[1] He died in 1742, neglected by his great patrons, and in the most miserable circumstances.

"Amhurst survived the downfall of Walpole's power, and had reason to expect a reward for his labours. If we excuse Bolingbroke,[2] who had only saved the shipwreck of his fortunes, we shall be at a loss to justify Pulteney, who could with ease have given this man a considerable income. The utmost of his generosity to Amhurst, that I ever heard of, was a hogshead of claret! He died, it is supposed, of a broken heart; and was buried at the charge of his honest printer, Richard Francklin."—(*Lord Chesterfield's Characters Reviewed*, p. 42.)

j. I have now given in the text, the full name of this gallant and excellent man, and proceed to copy the account of his remarkable conversion, as related by Dr. Doddridge.

"This memorable event," says the pious writer, "happened towards the middle of July 1719. The major had spent the evening (and, if I mistake not, it was the Sabbath) in some gay company, and had an unhappy assignation with a married woman, whom he was to attend exactly at twelve. The company broke up about eleven; and not judging it convenient to anticipate the time appointed, he went into his chamber to kill the tedious hour, perhaps with some amusing book, or some other way. But it very accidentally happened, that he took up a religious book, which his good mother or aunt had, without his knowledge, slipped into his portmanteau. It was called, if I remember the

---

1 William Pulteney, first earl of Bath (1684-1764), initially supported Sir Robert Walpole, first earl of Orford (1676-1745), but when Walpole did not offer him a position in his Whig government, he attacked the prime minister in 1725 in print (*OCBH*, 780, 964).

2 Henry St. John Bolingbroke, First Viscount (1678-1751), served in a variety of capacities, including Tory MP and secretary of war, and negotiated the Peace of Utrecht in 1713. Impeached and exiled, he became secretary of state to the Old Pretender, James Francis Edward Stuart, at his court in France; he returned to England in 1723 and opposed Walpole through his political writings (*OCBH*, 112).

title exactly, The Christian Soldier, or Heaven taken by Storm, and it was written by Mr. Thomas Watson. Guessing by the title of it that he would find some phrases of his own profession spiritualized in a manner which he thought might afford him some diversion, he resolved to dip into it; but he took no serious notice of any thing it had in it; and yet while this book was in his hand, an impression was made upon his mind (perhaps God only knows how) which drew after it a train of the most important and happy consequences. He thought he saw an unusual blaze of light fall upon the book which he was reading, which he at first imagined might happen by some accident in the candle; but lifting up his eyes, he apprehended to his extreme amazement, that there was before him, as it were suspended in the air, a visible representation of the Lord Jesus Christ upon the cross, surrounded on all sides with a glory; and was impressed, as if a voice, or something equivalent to a voice, had come to him, to this effect, (for he was not confident as to the words), 'Oh, sinner! did I suffer this for thee, and are these thy returns!' Struck with so amazing a phenomenon as this, there remained hardly any life in him, so that he sunk down in the arm-chair in which he sat, and continued, he knew not how long, insensible."

"With regard to this vision," says the ingenious Dr Hibbert, "the appearance of our Saviour on the cross, and the awful words repeated, can be considered in no other light than as so many recollected images of the mind, which, probably, had their origin in the language of some urgent appeal to repentance, that the colonel might have casually read, or heard delivered. From what cause, however, such ideas were rendered as vivid as actual impressions, we have no information to be depended upon. This vision was certainly attended with one of the most important of consequences, connected with the Christian dispensation—the conversion of a sinner. And hence no single narrative has, perhaps, done more to confirm the superstitious opinion that apparitions of this awful kind cannot arise without a divine fiat." Dr Hibbert adds, in a note—"A short time before the vision, Colonel Gardiner had received a severe fall from his horse. Did the brain receive some slight degree of injury from the accident, so as to predispose him to this spiritual illusion?"—(*Hibbert's Philosophy of Apparitions*, Edinburgh, 1824, p. 190.)

k. The courtesy of an invitation to partake a traveller's meal, or at least that of being invited to share whatever liquor the guest called for, was expected by certain old landlords in Scotland even in the youth of the author. In requital, mine host was always furnished with the news of the country, and was probably a little of a humourist to boot. The devolution of the whole actual business and drudgery of the inn upon the poor gudewife, was very common among the Scottish Bonifaces.[1] There was in ancient times, in the city of Edinburgh, a gentleman of good family, who condescended, in order to gain a livelihood, to become the nominal keeper of a coffeehouse, one of the first places of the kind which had been opened in the Scottish metropolis. As usual, it was entirely managed by the careful and industrious Mrs. B—; while

---

1 "The name of the jovial innkeeper in Farquhar's *Beaux Strategem* (1707); whence taken as the generic proper name of innkeepers ..." (*OED*).

her husband amused himself with field sports, without troubling his head about the matter. Once upon a time the premises having taken fire, the husband was met, walking up the High Street loaded with his guns and fishing-rods, and replied calmly to some one who enquired after his wife, "that the poor woman was trying to save a parcel of crockery, and some trumpery-books"; the last being those which served her to conduct the business of the house.

There were many elderly gentlemen in the author's younger days, who still held it part of the amusement of a journey "to parley with mine host," who often resembled, in his quaint humour, mine Host of the Garter in the Merry Wives of Windsor; or Blague of the George in the Merry Devil of Edmonton.[1] Sometimes the landlady took her share of entertaining the company. In either case the omitting to pay them due attention gave displeasure, and perhaps brought down a smart jest, as on the following occasion:—

A jolly dame who, not "Sixty Years since," kept the principal caravansary[2] at Greenlaw, in Berwickshire, had the honour to receive under her roof a very worthy clergyman, with three sons of the same profession, each having a cure of souls; be it said in passing, none of the reverend party were reckoned powerful in the pulpit. After dinner was over, the worthy senior, in the pride of his heart, asked Mrs Buchan whether she ever had had such a party in her house before. "Here sit I," he said, "a placed minister of the Kirk of Scotland, and here sit my three sons, each a placed minister of the same kirk.—Confess, Luckie Buchan, you never had such a party in your house before." The question was not premised by any invitation to sit down and take a glass of wine or the like, so Mrs B. answered dryly, "Indeed, sir, I cannot just say that ever I had such a party in my house before, except once in the forty-five, when I had a Highland piper here, with his three sons, all Highland pipers; *and deil a spring they could play amang them.*

l. There is no particular mansion described under the name of Tully-Veolan; but the peculiarities of the description occur in various old Scottish Seats. The House of Warrender upon Bruntsfield Links, and that of Old Ravelston, belonging, the former to Sir George Warrender, the latter to Sir Alexander Keith, have both contributed several hints to the description in the text. The House of Dean, near Edinburgh, has also some points of resemblance with Tully-Veolan. The author has, however, been informed, that the House of Grandtully resembles that of the Baron of Bradwardine still more than any of the above.

m. At Ravelston may be seen such a garden, which the taste of the proprietor, the author's friend and kinsman, Sir Alexander Keith, Knight Mareschal, has judiciously preserved. That, as well as the house, is, however, of smaller dimensions than the Baron of Bradwardine's mansion and garden are presumed to have been.

---

1 *The Merry Devil of Edmonton*, a romantic comedy, was published in 1608. Its authorship is unknown, though it has been attributed to Drayton (*OCEL*, 642).

2 A caravansary is "a kind of inn in Eastern countries where caravans put up, being a large quadrangular building with a spacious court in the middle" (*OED*).

n. This is a genuine ancient fragment, with some alteration in the two last lines.

o. I am ignorant how long the ancient and established custom of keeping fools has been disused in England. Swift writes an epitaph on the Earl of Suffolk's fool,—

"Whose name was Dickie Pearce."[1]

In Scotland the custom subsisted till late in the last century; at Glammis Castle, is preserved the dress of one of the jesters, very handsome, and ornamented with many bells. It is not above thirty years since such a character stood by the sideboard of a nobleman of the first rank in Scotland, and occasionally mixed in the conversation, till he carried the joke rather too far, in making proposals to one of the young ladies of the family, and publishing the bans betwixt her and himself in the public church.

p. After the Revolution of 1688, and on some occasions when the spirit of the Presbyterians had been unusually animated against their opponents, the Episcopal clergymen, who were chiefly non-jurors, were exposed to be mobbed, as we should now say, or *rabbled*, as the phrase then went, to expiate their political heresies. But notwithstanding that the Presbyterians had the persecution in Charles II., and his brother's time, to exasperate them, there was little mischief done beyond the kind of petty violence mentioned in the text.

q. Southey's Madoc.[2]

r. I may here mention, that the fashion of compotation described in the text, was still occasionally practised in Scotland, in the author's youth. A company, after having taken leave of their host, often went to finish the evening at the clachan or village, in "womb of tavern." Their entertainer always accompanied them to take the stirrup-cup, which often occasioned a long and late revel.

The *Poculum Potatorium* [drinking cup] of the valiant Baron, his blessed Bear, has a prototype at the fine old castle of Glammis, so rich in memorials of ancient times; it is a massive beaker of silver, double gilt, moulded into the shape of a lion, and holding about an English pint of wine. The form alludes to the family name of Strathmore, which is Lyon, and, when exhibited, the cup must necessarily be emptied to the Earl's health. The author ought perhaps to be ashamed of recording that he has had the honour of swallowing the contents of the Lion; and the recollection of the feat served to suggest the story of the Bear of Bradwardine. In the family of Scott of Thirlestane (not Thirlestane in the Forest, but the place of the same name in Roxburghshire) was long preserved a cup of the same kind, in the form of a jack-boot. Each guest was obliged to empty this at his departure. If the guest's name was Scott, the necessity was doubly imperative.

When the landlord of an inn presented his guests with *deoch an doruis*, that is, the drink at the door, or the stirrup-cup, the draught was not charged in the reckoning. On this point a learned Bailie of the town of Forfar pronounced a very sound judgement.

---

1 Jonathan Swift, "Epitaph in Berkeley Church-Yard, Gloucestershire," *The Poetical Works of Jonathan Swift*, ed. John Mitford (Boston: Riverside, 1879), vol. 1, p. 414.

2 *Madoc* (1805), a narrative poem by Romantic poet Robert Southey (1774-1843).

A., an ale-wife in Forfar, had brewed her "peck of malt," and set the liquor out of doors to cool; the cow of B., a neighbour of A., chanced to come by, and seeing the good beverage, was allured to taste it, and finally to drink it up. When A. came to take in her liquor, she found her tub empty, and from the cow's staggering and staring, so as to betray her intemperance, she easily divined the mode in which her "browst" had disappeared. To take vengeance on Crummie's ribs with a stick, was her first effort. The roaring of the cow brought B., her master, who remonstrated with his angry neighbour, and received in reply a demand for the value of the ale which Crummie had drunk up. B. refused payment, and was conveyed before C., the Bailie, or sitting Magistrate. He heard the case patiently; and then demanded of the plaintiff A., whether the cow had sat down to her potation, or taken it standing. The plaintiff answered, she had not seen the deed committed, but she supposed the cow drank the ale while standing on her feet; adding, that had she been near, she would have made her use them to some purpose. The Bailie, on this admission, solemnly adjudged the cow's drink to be *deoch an doruis*—a stirrup-cup, for which no charge could be made, without violating the ancient hospitality of Scotland.

s. This has been censured as an anachronism; and it must be confessed that agriculture of this kind was unknown to the Scotch Sixty Years since.

t. *Suum cuique.* This snatch of a ballad was composed by Andrew MacDonald, the ingenious and unfortunate author of Vimonda.

u. The learned in cookery dissent from the Baron of Bradwardine, and hold the roe venison dry and indifferent food, unless when dressed in soup and Scotch collops.

v. A bare-footed Highland lad is called a gillie-wet-foot. Gillie, in general, means servant or attendant.

w. The Baron ought to have remembered that the joyous Allan literally drew his blood from the house of the noble Earl, whom he terms—

> Dalhousie of an old descent,
> My stoup, my pride, my ornament.

x. The story last told was said to have happened in the south of Scotland; but— *cedant arma togæ*[1]—and let the gown have its dues. It was an old clergyman, who had wisdom and firmness enough to resist the panic which seized his brethren, who was the means of rescuing a poor insane creature from the cruel fate which would otherwise have overtaken her. The accounts of the trials for witchcraft form one of the most deplorable chapters in Scottish story.

y. Although canting heraldry is generally reprobated, it seems nevertheless to have been adopted in the arms and mottos of many honourable families. Thus the motto of the Vernons, *Ver non semper viret*, is a perfect pun, and so is that of the Onslows, *Festina lente.*[2] The *Periissem ni per-iissem* of the Anstruthers is liable to a similar objection. One of that ancient race, finding that an antago-

---

1 Lamont translates this as "Let arms yield to the gown," and notes it is from Cicero's *De Officiis* I, xxii, 77 (*OW*, 423).

2 The Vernons' motto, *ver non semper viret*, or "Spring is not always green"; *Vernon semper viret* offers the opposite: "Vernon always flourishes." The Onslows' motto, *festina lente*, means to hasten slowly.

nist, with whom he had fixed a friendly meeting, was determined to take the opportunity of assassinating him, prevented the hazard by dashing out his brains with a battle-axe. Two sturdy arms, brandishing such a weapon, form the usual crest of the family, with the above motto—*Periissem ni periissem*—(I had died, unless I had gone through with it).

z.   A *creagh* was an incursion for plunder, termed on the Borders a *raid*.

aa.   *Sornars* may be translated sturdy beggars, more especially indicating those unwelcome visitors who exact lodgings and victuals by force, or something approaching to it.

bb.   Mac-Donald of Barrisdale, one of the very last Highland gentlemen who carried on the plundering system to any great extent, was a scholar and a well-bred gentleman. He engraved on his broadswords the well-known lines—

> *Hae tibi erunt artes—pacisque imponere morem,*
> *Parcere subjectis, et debellare superbos.*

Indeed, the levying of black mail, was, before the 1745, practised by several chiefs of very high rank, who, in doing so, contended that they were lending the laws the assistance of their arms and swords, and affording a protection which could not be obtained from the magistracy in the disturbed state of the country. The author has seen a Memoir of Mac-Pherson of Cluny, Chief of that ancient clan, from which it appears that he levied protection-money to a very large amount, which was willingly paid even by some of his most powerful neighbours. A gentleman of this clan hearing a clergyman hold forth to his congregation on the crime of theft, interrupted the preacher to assure him, he might leave the enforcement of such doctrines to Cluny Mac-Pherson, whose broadsword would put a stop to theft sooner than all the sermons of all the ministers of the Synod.

cc.   The Town-guard of Edinburgh were, till a late period, armed with this weapon when on their police-duty. There was a hook at the back of the axe, which the ancient Highlanders used to assist them to climb over walls, fixing the hook upon it, and raising themselves by the handle. The axe, which was also much used by the natives, is supposed to have been introduced into both countries from Scandinavia.

dd.   It is not the weeping birch, the most common species in the Highlands, but the woolly-leaved Lowland birch, that is distinguished by this fragrance.

ee.   An adventure, very similar to what is here stated, actually befell the late Mr Abercromby of Tullibody, grandfather of the present Lord Abercromby, and father of the celebrated Sir Ralph. When this gentleman, who lived to a very advanced period of life, first settled in Stirlingshire, his cattle were repeatedly driven off by the celebrated Rob Roy, or some of his gang; and at length he was obliged, after obtaining a proper safe-conduct, to make the cateran such a visit as that of Waverley to Bean Lean in the text. Rob received him with much courtesy, and made many apologies for the accident, which must have happened, he said, through some mistake. Mr Abercromby was regaled with collops from two of his own cattle, which were hung up by the heels in the cavern, and was dismissed in perfect safety, after having agreed to pay in future a small sum of black mail, in consideration of which Rob Roy not only undertook to forbear his herds in future, but to replace any that should be stolen from him by other freebooters. Mr Abercromby said, Rob Roy affected to consider him as a friend to the Jacobite interest, and a sincere enemy to the Union. Neither of these circumstances were true; but the laird thought it quite unnecessary to undeceive his Highland host at the risk of bringing on a political dispute in such a situation. This anecdote I received many years since (about 1792), from the mouth of the venerable gentleman who was concerned in it.

ff.   This was the regale presented by Rob Roy to the Laird of Tullibody.

gg.   This celebrated gibbet was, in the memory of the last generation, still standing at the western end of the town of Crieff, in Perthshire. Why it was called the *kind* gallows, we are unable to inform the reader with certainty; but it is alleged that the Highlanders used to touch their bonnets as they passed a place, which had been fatal to many of their countrymen, with the ejaculation—"God bless her nain sell, and the Tiel tamn you!" It may therefore have been called kind, as being a sort of native or kindred place of doom to those who suffered there, as in fulfilment of a natural destiny.

hh.   The story of the bridegroom carried off by Caterans, on his bridal-day, is taken from one which was told to the author by the late Laird of Mac-Nab, many years since. To carry off persons from the Lowlands, and to put them to ransom, was a common practice with the wild Highlanders, as it is said to be at the present day with the banditti in the South of Italy. Upon the occasion alluded to, a party of Caterans carried off the bridegroom, and secreted him in some cave near the mountain of Schihallion. The young man caught the small-pox before his ransom could be agreed on; and whether it was the fine cool air of the place, or the want of medical attendance, Mac-Nab did not pretend to be positive; but so it was, that the prisoner recovered, his ransom was paid, and he was restored to his friends and bride, but always considered the Highland robbers as having saved his life, by their treatment of his malady.

ii.   The Scotch are liberal in computing their land and liquor; the Scottish pint corresponds to two English quarts. As for their coin, every one knows the couplet—

How can the rogues pretend to sense?—
Their pound is only twenty pence.

jj.   This happened on many occasions. Indeed, it was not till after the total destruction of the clan influence, after 1745, that purchasers could be found, who offered a fair price for the estates forfeited in 1715, which were then brought to sale by the creditors of the York Buildings Company, who had purchased the whole or greater part from government at a very small price. Even so late as the period first mentioned, the prejudices of the public in favour of the heirs of the forfeited families threw various impediments in the way of intending purchasers of such property.

kk.   This sort of political game ascribed to Mac-Ivor was in reality played by several Highland chiefs, the celebrated Lord Lovat[1] in particular, who used

---

1   Simon Fraser, Lord Lovat (1667-1747), Scottish chief, fought for both Jacobite and Hanoverian sides at different times in his career, somewhat self-

that kind of finesse to the uttermost. The Laird of Mac—[1] was also captain of an independent company, but valued the sweets of present pay too well to incur the risk of losing them in the Jacobite cause. His martial consort raised his clan, and headed it, in 1745. But the chief himself would have nothing to do with king-making, declaring himself for that monarch, and no other, who gave the Laird of Mac— "half-a-guinea the day, and half-a-guinea the morn."

ll.   In explanation of the military exercise observed at the Castle of Glennaquoich, the author begs to remark, that the Highlanders were not only well practised in the use of the broadsword, firelock, and most of the manly sports and trials of strength common throughout Scotland, but also used a peculiar sort of drill, suited to their own dress and mode of warfare. There were, for instance, different modes of disposing the plaid, one when on a peaceful journey, another when danger was apprehended; one way of enveloping themselves in it when expecting undisturbed repose, and another which enabled them to start up with sword and pistol in hand on the slightest alarm.

Previous to 1720, or thereabouts, the belted plaid was universally worn, in which the portion which surrounded the middle of the wearer, and that which was flung around his shoulders, were all of the same piece of tartan. In a desperate onset, all was thrown away, and the clan charged bare beneath the doublet, save for an artificial arrangement of the shirt, which, like that of the Irish, was always ample, and for the sporran-mollach, or goat's-skin purse.

The manner of handling the pistol and dirk was also part of the Highland manual exercise, which the author has seen gone through by men who had learned it in their youth.

mm. Pork, or swine's flesh, in any shape, was, till of late years, much abominated by the Scotch, nor is it yet a favourite food amongst them. King Jamie carried this prejudice to England, and is known to have abhorred pork almost as much as he did tobacco. Ben Jonson[2] has recorded this peculiarity, where the gipsy in a masque, examining the king's hand, says,

————you should by this line
Love a horse, and a hound, but no part of a swine.
The Gipsies Metamorphosed.[3]

James's own proposed banquet for the Devil, was a loin of pork and a poll of ling, with a pipe of tobacco for digestion.

---

servingly. In 1715, he took the government side and gained a pardon for past indiscretions; in 1745, his son and clan fought for Charles Edward Stuart, while Lovat himself claimed loyalty to the government in London. This two-timing caught up with him and he was beheaded in 1747 as a Jacobite.

1 Lamont suggests this is the Laird of Mackintosh (*OW*, 427).

2 English dramatist and poet (1572/3-1637).

3 From Ben Jonson's *A Masque of the Metamorphosed Gipsies*, first performed 1621 (*The Works of Ben Jonson*, ed. William Gifford [London: Edward Moxon, 1853], p. 620).

nn. In the number of persons of all ranks who assembled at the same table, though by no means to discuss the same fare, the Highland chiefs only retained a custom which had been formerly universally observed throughout Scotland. "I myself," says the traveller, Fynes Morrison,[1] in the end of Queen Elizabeth's reign, the scene being the Lowlands of Scotland, "was at a knight's house, who had many servants to attend him, that brought in his meat with their heads covered with blue caps, the table being more than half furnished with great platters of porridge, each having a little piece of sodden meat. And when the table was served, the servants did sit down with us; but the upper mess, instead of porridge, had a pullet, with some prunes in the broth."—(*Travels*, p. 155.)

Till within this last century, the farmers, even of a respectable condition, dined with their work-people. The difference betwixt those of high degree, was ascertained by the place of the party above or below the salt, or, sometimes, by a line drawn with chalk on the dining table. Lord Lovat, who knew well how to feed the vanity, and restrain the appetites, of his clansmen, allowed each sturdy Fraser, who had the slightest pretensions to be a Duinhé-wassel, the full honour of the sitting, but, at the same time, took care that his young kinsmen did not acquire at his table any taste for outlandish luxuries. His lordship was always ready with some honourable apology, why foreign wines and French brandy, delicacies which he conceived might sap the hardy habits of his cousins, should not circulate past an assigned point on the table.

oo. In the Irish ballads, relating to Fion, (the Fingal of MacPherson),[2] there occurs, as in the primitive poetry of most nations, a cycle of heroes, each of whom has some distinguishing attribute; upon these qualities, and the adventures of those possessing them, many proverbs are formed, which are still current in the Highlands. Among other characters, Conan is distinguished as in some respects a kind of Thersites,[3] but brave and daring even to rashness. He had made a vow that he would never take a blow without returning it; and having, like other heroes of antiquity, descended to the infernal regions, he received a cuff from the Arch-fiend, who presided there, which he instantly returned, using the expression in the text. Sometimes the proverb is worded thus:—"Claw for claw, and the devil take the shortest nails, as Conan said to the devil."

pp. The Highland poet almost always was an improvisatore. Captain Burt met one of them at Lovat's table.

qq. The description of the waterfall mentioned in this chapter is taken from that of Ledeard, at the farm so called on the northern side of Lochard, and near the head of the Lake, four or five miles from Aberfoyle. It is upon a

---

1 Fynes Morrison (1566-1630), English traveler and writer, published *An Itinerary* in 1617, a record of his travels throughout Europe.

2 Fingal was the "hero of Celtic song and legend. His exploits form the connecting link of the Ossian poems" (*OW*, 430).

3 Son of Agrius, boorish, obscene soldier chastised by Odysseus and Achilles. A slave in Shakespeare's *Troilus and Cressida*, I.iii.

small scale, but otherwise one of the most exquisite cascades it is possible to behold. The appearance of Flora with the harp, as described, has been justly censured as too theatrical and affected for the lady-like simplicity of her character. But something may be allowed to her French education, in which point and striking effect always make a considerable object.

rr.   The young and daring Adventurer, Charles Edward, landed at Glenaladale, in Moidart, and displayed his standard in the valley of Glenfinnan, mustering around it the Mac-Donalds, the Camerons, and other less numerous clans, whom he had prevailed on to join him. There is a monument erected on the spot, with a Latin inscription by the late Doctor Gregory.

ss.   The Marquis of Tullibardine's elder brother, who, long exiled, returned to Scotland with Charles Edward in 1745.

tt.   Good sooth, I reck nought of your Helicon;
    Drink water whoso will, in faith I will drink none.

uu.   This ancient Gaelic ditty is still well known, both in the Highlands and in Ireland. It was translated into English, and published, if I mistake not, under the auspices of the facetious Tom D'Urfey,[1] by the title of "Colley, my Cow."

vv.   The thrust from the tynes, or branches, of the stag's horns, were accounted far more dangerous than those of the boar's tusk:—
    If thou be hurt with horn of stag, it brings thee to thy bier,[2]
    But barber's hand shall boar's hurt heal; thereof have thou no fear.

ww.   This garb, which resembled the dress often put on children in Scotland, called a polonie (i.e., polonaise), is a very ancient modification of the Highland garb. It was, in fact, the hauberk or shirt of mail, only composed of cloth instead of rings of armour.

xx.   Old Highlanders will still make the *deasil* around those whom they wish well to. To go round a person in the opposite direction, or *wither-shins* (German for *wider-shīns*), is unlucky, and a sort of incantation.

yy.   This metrical spell, or something very like it, is preserved by Reginald Scott, in his work on Witchcraft.

zz.   On the morrow they made their biers
    of birch and hazel grey.
              Chevy Chase.[3]

aaa.   The author has been sometimes accused of confounding fiction with reality. He therefore thinks it necessary to state, that the circumstance of the hunting described in the text as preparatory to the insurrection of 1745, is, so far as he knows, entirely imaginary. But it is well known such a great

---

1   English satirical dramatist and songster (1653-1723).
2   "To bring to the grave or to death ... " (*OED*).
3   "The Ballad of Chevy Chase," an early English ballad (c. fifteenth century) about the conflict between the English Percy and the Scottish Douglas, and the tragic outcome of their confrontation: Percy insists on hunting over the border in Scotland, despite the fact that the land belongs to Douglas; Douglas and his men confront the Earl of Northumberland and his party, and at the end of the skirmish, both leaders are dead.

hunting was held in the Forest of Brae-Mar, under the auspices of the Earl of Mar, as preparatory to the Rebellion of 1715; and most of the Highland chieftains who afterwards engaged in that civil commotion were present on this occasion.

bbb. Corresponding to the Lowland saying, "Mony ane speirs the gate they ken fu' weel."

ccc. These lines form the burden of an old song to which Burns[1] wrote additional verses.

ddd. These lines are also ancient, and I believe to the tune of

We'll never hae peace till Jamie comes hame;

to which Burns likewise wrote some verses.

eee. A Highland rhyme on Glencairn's Expedition, in 1650, has these lines—

"We'll bide a while among ta crows,
We'll wiske ta sword and bend ta bows."

fff. The Oggam is a species of the old Irish character. This idea of the correspondence betwixt the Celtic and Punic, founded on a scene in Plautus was not started till General Vallancey set up his theory, long after the date of Fergus Mac-Ivor.[2]

ggg. The sanguine Jacobites, during the eventful years 1745-46, kept up the spirits of their party by the rumour of descents from France on behalf of the Chevalier St George.

hhh. The Highlander, in former times, had always a high idea of his own gentility, and was anxious to impress the same upon those with whom he conversed. His language abounded in the phrases of courtesy and compliment; and the habit of carrying arms, and mixing with those who did so, made it particularly desirable they should use cautious politeness in their intercourse with each other.

iii. The Rev. John Erskine, D.D. [1721-1803], an eminent Scottish divine, and a most excellent man, headed the Evangelical party in the Church of Scot-

---

1 Robert Burns (1759-96), Scottish poet. As well as writing his own poetry, Burns spent much of his career collecting and editing old Scottish songs for various miscellanies, including *The Scots Musical Museum* and *Select Scottish Airs*, for which he went into the Highlands looking for songs. He wrote in both eighteenth-century standard English and in Scots, sometimes mixing the two in his work. Like Scott, Burns was also much influenced by Henry Mackenzie's *Man of Feeling*.

2 Titus Maccius Plautus (c. 254-184 BCE), Roman comic poet and dramatist specializing in middle- and lower-class characters. General Charles Vallencey (1721-1812), co-founder of the Royal Irish Academy, "initiated the scholarship of Ogam" (<http://www.pgil-eirdatas.org>). The "theory" he advanced was that Ireland's ancient civilization was sophisticated and complex, and he based this on its language, which he found paralleled that of other highly civilized cultures, such as China, Iran, and Phoenicia. See his *Grammar of the Iberno-Celtic or Irish Language* (1773); in *Collectionea de Rebus Hibernicus*, he gave a Phoenico-Gaelic interpretation of the Carthaginian speech in Plautus's *Poenuluis*.

land at the time when the celebrated Dr Robertson, the historian, was the leader of the Moderate party. These two distinguished persons were colleagues in the Old Grey Friars' Church, Edinburgh; and, however much they differed in church politics, preserved the most perfect harmony as private friends, and as clergymen serving the same cure.[1]

jjj. The clan of Mac-Farlane, occupying the fastnesses [Fortresses][2] of the western side of Loch Lomond, were great depredators on the Low Country, and as their excursions were made usually by night, the moon was proverbially called their lantern. Their celebrated pibroch of *Hoggil nam Bo*,[3] which is the name of their gathering tune, intimates similar practices,—the sense being:—

> We are bound to drive the bullocks,
> All by hollows, hirsts and hillocks,
> Through the sleet, and through the rain.
> When the moon is beaming low
> On frozen lake and hills of snow,
> Bold and heartily we go;
> And all for little gain.

kkk. This noble ruin is dear to my recollection, from associations which have been long and painfully broken. It holds a commanding station on the banks of the river Teith, and has been one of the largest castles in Scotland. Murdock, Duke of Albany,[4] the founder of this stately pile, was beheaded on the Castle-hill of Stirling, from which he might see the towers of Doune, the monument of his fallen greatness.

In 1745-46, as stated in the text, a garrison on the part of the Chevalier was put into the castle, then less ruinous than at present. It was commanded by Mr Stewart of Balloch, as governor for Prince Charles; he was a man of property near Callander. This castle became at that time the actual scene of a romantic escape made by John Home, the author of Douglas, and some other prisoners, who, having been taken at the battle of Falkirk, were confined there by the insurgents. The poet, who had in his own mind a large stock of that romantic and enthusiastic spirit of adventure, which he has described as animating the youthful hero of his drama, devised and undertook the perilous enterprise of escaping from his prison. He inspired his companions with his sentiments, and when every attempt at open force

---

1 Parish.

2 Claire Lamont notes that Scott visited Doune for the first time in 1793, and heard the story of Home's escape from the castle where he'd been held prisoner after the battle of Falkirk in which the Hanoverian army was defeated by Prince Charles's forces in 1746 (*OW*, 437).

3 Further information on this pibroch can be found in *The Celtic Monthly*, iii (Nov. 1894): 39, and C.S. Thomason, *Ceol Mor* (1900), 131 (*OW*, 437).

4 Murdac Steward, second duke of Albany (c. 1362-1425), cousin of James I, imprisoned with him for 13 years in the Tower of London and at Windsor, oversaw James I's coronation at Scone, but was arrested soon thereafter at James's command and beheaded on his orders.

was deemed hopeless, they resolved to twist their bed-clothes into ropes, and thus to descend. Four persons, with Home himself, reached the ground in safety. But the rope broke with the fifth, who was a tall lusty man. The sixth was Thomas Barrow, a brave young Englishman, a particular friend of Home's. Determined to take the risk, even in such unfavourable circumstances, Barrow committed himself to the broken rope, slid down it as far as it could assist him, and then let himself drop. His friend beneath succeeded in breaking his fall. Nevertheless, he dislocated his ankle, and had several of his ribs broken. His companions, however, were able to bear him off in safety.

The Highlanders next morning sought for their prisoners, with great activity. An old gentleman told the author, he remembered seeing the commander Stewart,

> Bloody with spurring, fiery red with haste,

riding furiously through the country in quest of the fugitives.

lll.   The Judges of the Supreme Court of Session in Scotland are proverbially termed, among the country people, The Fifteen.

mmm. To *go out*, or *to have been out*, in Scotland, was a conventional phrase similar to that of the Irish respecting a man having been *up*, both having reference to an individual who had been engaged in insurrection. It was accounted ill-breeding in Scotland, about forty years since, to use the phrase *rebellion* or *rebel*, which might be interpreted by some of the parties present as a personal insult. It was also esteemed more polite even for stanch Whigs to denominate Charles Edward the Chevalier, than to speak of him as the Pretender; and this kind of accommodating courtesy was usually observed in society where individuals of each party mixed on friendly terms.

nnn.   The Jacobite sentiments were general among the western counties, and in Wales. But although the great families of the Wynnes, the Wyndhams, and others, had come under an actual obligation to join Prince Charles if he should land, they had done so under the express stipulation, that he should be assisted by an auxiliary army of French, without which they foresaw the enterprise would be desperate. Wishing well to his cause, therefore, and watching an opportunity to join him, they did not, nevertheless, think themselves bound in honour to do so, as he was only supported by a body of wild mountaineers, speaking an uncouth dialect, and wearing a singular dress. The race up to Derby struck them with more dread than admiration. But it was difficult to say what the effect might have been, had either the battle of Preston or Falkirk been fought and won during the advance into England.

ooo.   Divisions early showed themselves in the Chevalier's little army, not only amongst the independent chieftains, who were far too proud to brook subjection to each other, but betwixt the Scotch, and Charles's governor O'Sullivan, an Irishman by birth, who, with some of his countrymen bred in the Irish-Brigade in the service of the King of France, had an influence with the Adventurer, much resented by the Highlanders, who were sensible that their own clans made the chief or rather the only strength of his enterprise. There was a feud, also, between Lord George Murray, and

John Murray of Broughton, the Prince's secretary, whose disunion greatly embarrassed the affairs of the Adventurer. In general, a thousand different pretensions divided their little army, and finally contributed in no small degree to its overthrow.

ppp.   The Doutelle was an armed vessel, which brought a small supply of money and arms from France for the use of the insurgents.

qqq.   Old women, on whom devolved the duty of lamenting for the dead, which the Irish call *Keenning*.

rrr.   These lines, or something like them, occur in an old Magazine of the period.

sss.   *i.e.*, Contiguous.

ttt.   They occur in Miss Seward's fine verses, beginning—
"To thy rocks, stormy Lannow, adieu."[1]

uuu.   Which is, or was wont to be, the old air of "Good night and joy be wi' you a'!"

vvv.   The main body of the Highland army encamped, or rather bivouacked, in that part of the King's Park which lies towards the village of Duddingston.

www.   This circumstance, which is historical, as well as the description that precedes it, will remind the reader of the war of La Vendée, in which the royalists, consisting chiefly of insurgent peasantry, attached a prodigious and even superstitious interest to the possession of a piece of brass ordnance, which they called Marie Jeane.

The Highlanders of an early period were afraid of cannon, with the noise and effect of which they were totally unacquainted. It was by means of three or four small pieces of artillery, that the Earls of Huntly and Errol, in James VI.'s time, gained a great victory at Glenlivat, over a numerous Highland army, commanded by the Earl of Argyle. At the battle of the Bridge of Dee, General Middleton obtained by his artillery a similar success, the Highlanders not being able to stand the discharge of *Musket's-Mother*, which was the name they bestowed on great-guns. In an old ballad on the battle of the Bridge of Dee,[2] these verses occur:—

> The Highlandmen are pretty men
>   For handling sword and shield,
> But yet they are but simple men
>   To stand a stricken field.
>
> The Highlandmen are pretty men
>   For target and claymore,
> But yet they are but naked men
>   To face the cannon's roar.

---

1   Anna Seward (1742-1809); the lines are from "Song" in *The Poetical Works of Anna Seward*, edited by Walter Scott, 1810 (I, 158).

2   A battle between Royalist forces and Covenanters in 1639, won by the Highlanders.

For the cannon's roar on a summer night
    Like thunder in the air;
Was never man in Highland garb
    Would face the cannon fair.

But the Highlanders of 1745 had got far beyond the simplicity of their forefathers, and showed throughout the whole war how little they dreaded artillery, although the common people still attached some consequence to the possession of the field-piece, which led to this disquisition.

xxx. Bran, the well-known dog of Fingal, is often the theme of Highland proverb as well as song.

yyy. *Scottice* for followers.

zzz. The faithful friend who pointed out the pass by which the Highlanders moved from Tranent to Seaton, was Robert Anderson, junior, of Whitburgh, a gentleman of property in East Lothian.[1] He had been interrogated by the Lord George Murray concerning the possibility of crossing the uncouth and marshy piece of ground which divided the armies, and which he described as impracticable. When dismissed, he recollected that there was a circuitous path leading eastward through the marsh into the plain, by which the Highlanders might turn the flank of Sir John Cope's position, without being exposed to the enemy's fire. Having mentioned his opinion to Mr Hepburn of Keith, who instantly saw its importance, he was encouraged by that gentleman to awake Lord George Murray, and communicate the idea to him. Lord George received the information with grateful thanks, and instantly awakened Prince Charles, who was sleeping in the field with a bunch of pease under his head. The Adventurer received with alacrity the news that there was a possibility of bringing an excellently provided army to a decisive battle with his own irregular forces. His joy on the occasion was not very consistent with the charge of cowardice brought against him by Chevalier Johnstone, a discontented follower, whose Memoirs possess at least as much of a romantic as a historical character.[2] Even by the account of the Chevalier himself, the Prince was at the head of the second line of the Highland army during the battle, of which he says, "It was gained with such rapidity, that in the second line, where I was still by the side of the Prince, we saw no other enemy than those who were lying on the ground killed and wounded, *though we were not more than fifty paces behind our first line, running always as fast as we could to overtake them.*"

This passage in the Chevalier's Memoirs places the Prince within fifty paces of the heat of the battle, a position which would never have been the choice of one unwilling to take a share of its dangers. Indeed, unless

---

1 According to Lamont, this first portion of Scott's note, dealing with Robert Anderson, Jr., of Whitburgh, is from John Home's *The History of the Rebellion in the Year 1745* (1802), 114 (*OW*, 443).

2 James Johnstone (1719-1800), aide-de-camp to Charles Edward Stuart. Wrote *Memoirs of the Rebellion in 1745 and 1746*, published in 1820.

the chiefs had complied with the young Adventurer's proposal to lead the van in person, it does not appear that he could have been deeper in the action.

aaaa.   The death of this good Christian and gallant man is thus given by his affectionate biographer, Dr Doddridge, from the evidence of eye-witnesses:—

"He continued all night under arms, wrapped in his cloak, and generally sheltered under a rick of barley, which happened to be in the field. About three in the morning he called his domestic servants to him, of which there were four in waiting. He dismissed three of them with most affectionate Christian advice, and such solemn charges relating to the performance of their duty, and the care of their souls, as seemed plainly to intimate that he apprehended it was at least very probable he was taking his last farewell of them. There is great reason to believe that he spent the little remainder of the time, which could not be much above an hour, in those devout exercises of soul which had been so long habitual to him, and to which so many circumstances did then concur to call him. The army was alarmed by break of day, by the noise of the rebels' approach, and the attack was made before sunrise, yet when it was light enough to discern what passed. As soon as the enemy came within gun-shot they made a furious fire; and it is said that the dragoons which constituted the left wing, immediately fled. The Colonel at the beginning of the onset, which in the whole lasted but a few minutes, received a wound by a bullet in his left breast, which made him give a sudden spring in his saddle; upon which his servant, who led the horse, would have persuaded him to retreat, but he said it was only a wound in the flesh, and fought on, though he presently after received a shot in his right thigh. In the meantime, it was discerned that some of the enemy fell by him, and particularly one man, who had made him a treacherous visit but a few days before, with great profession of zeal for the present establishment.

"Events of this kind pass in less time than the description of them can be written, or than it can be read. The Colonel was for a few moments supported by his men, and particularly by that worthy person Lieutenant-Colonel Whitney, who was shot through the arm here, and a few months after fell nobly at the battle of Falkirk, and by Lieutenant West, a man of distinguished bravery, as also by about fifteen dragoons, who stood by him to the last. But after a faint fire, the regiment in general was seized with a panic; and though their Colonel and some other gallant officers did what they could to rally them once or twice, they at last took a precipitate flight. And just in the moment when Colonel Gardiner seemed to be making a pause to deliberate what duty required him to do in such circumstances, an accident happened, which must, I think, in the judgement of every worthy and generous man, be allowed a sufficient apology for exposing his life to so great hazard, when his regiment had left him. He saw a party of the foot, who were then bravely fighting near him, and whom he was ordered to support, had no officer to head them; upon which he said eagerly, in the hearing of the person from whom I had this account, 'These brave fellows will be cut to pieces for want of a commander,' or words to that effect; which while he was speaking, he rode up to them and cried out, 'Fire on, my lads, and fear nothing.' But just as the words were out of his mouth, a Highlander advanced towards him with a scythe fastened to a long pole, with which he gave him so dreadful a wound on his right arm, that his sword dropped out of his hand; and at the same time several others coming about him while he was thus dreadfully entangled with that cruel weapon, he was dragged off from his horse. The moment he fell, another Highlander, who, if the king's evidence at Carlisle may be credited, (as I know not why they should not, though the unhappy creature died denying it), was one Mac-Naught, who was executed about a year after, gave him a stroke either with a broadsword or a Lochaber-axe (for my informant could not exactly distinguish) on the hinder part of his head, which was the mortal blow. All that his faithful attendant saw further at this time was, that as his hat was falling off, he took it in his left hand and waved it as a signal to him to retreat, and added, what were the last words he ever heard him speak, 'Take care of yourself;' upon which the servant retired."

Some remarkable Passages in the Life of Colonel James Gardiner, by P. Doddridge, D.D. London, 1747, p. 187.

I may remark on this extract, that it confirms the account given in the text of the resistance offered by some of the English infantry. Surprised by a force of peculiar and unusual description, their opposition could not be long or formidable, especially as they were deserted by the cavalry, and those who undertook to manage the artillery. But although the affair was soon decided, I have always understood that many of the infantry showed an inclination to do their duty.

bbbb. It is scarcely necessary to say that the character of this brutal young Laird is entirely imaginary. A gentleman, however, who resembled Balmawhapple in the article of courage only, fell at Preston in the manner described. A Perthshire gentleman of high honour and respectability, one of the handful of cavalry who followed the fortunes of Charles Edward, pursued the fugitive dragoons almost alone till near Saint Clement's Wells, where the efforts of some of the officers had prevailed on a few of them to make a momentary stand. Perceiving at this moment that they were pursued by only one man and a couple of servants, they turned upon him and cut him down with their swords. I remember, when a child, sitting on his grave, where the grass long grew rank and green, distinguishing it from the rest of the field. A female of the family then residing at Saint Clement's Wells used to tell me the tragedy of which she had been an eye-witness, and showed me in evidence one of the silver clasps of the unfortunate gentleman's waistcoat.

cccc. Charles Edward took up his quarters after the battle at Pinkie-house, adjoining to Musselburgh.

dddd. The name of Andrea de Ferrara[1] is inscribed on all the Scottish broadswords which are accounted of peculiar excellence. Who this artist

---

1 According to Lamont, "Andrea Ferrara was a North Italian swordsmith of the late sixteenth century. His name became a mark of quality for Scotsmen in

was, what were his fortunes, and when he flourished, have hitherto defied the research of antiquaries; only it is in general believed that Andrea de Ferrara was a Spanish or Italian artificer, brought over by James the IV. or V. to instruct the Scots in the manufacture of sword blades. Most barbarous nations excel in the fabrication of arms; and the Scots had attained great proficiency in forging swords, so early as the field of Pinkie; at which period the historian Patten describes them as "all notably broad and thin, universally made to slice, and of such exceeding good temper, that as I never saw any so good, so I think it hard to devise better."— (*Account of Somerset's Expedition*)

It may be observed, that the best and most genuine Andrea Ferraras have a crown marked on the blades.

eeee.   The clergyman's name was Mac-Vicar. Protected by the cannon of the Castle, he preached every Sunday in the West Kirk, while the Highlanders were in possession of Edinburgh; and it was in presence of some of the Jacobites that he prayed for Prince Charles Edward in the terms quoted in the text.

ffff.   The incident here said to have happened to Flora Mac-Ivor, actually befell Miss Nairne, a lady with whom the author had the pleasure of being acquainted. As the Highland army rushed into Edinburgh, Miss Nairne, like other ladies who approved of their cause, stood waving her handkerchief from a balcony, when a ball from a Highlander's musket, which was discharged by accident, grazed her forehead. "Thank God," said she, the instant she recovered, "that the accident happened to me, whose principles are known. Had it befallen a Whig, they would have said it was done on purpose."

gggg.   The Author of Waverley has been charged with painting the young Adventurer in colours more amiable than his character deserved. But having known many individuals who were near his person, he has been described according to the light in which those eye-witnesses saw his temper and qualifications. Something must be allowed, no doubt, to the natural exaggerations of those who remembered him as the bold and adventurous Prince, in whose cause they had braved death and ruin; but is their evidence to give place entirely to that of a single malcontent?

I have already noticed the imputations thrown by the Chevalier Johnstone on the Prince's courage. But some part at least of that gentleman's tale is purely romantic. It would not, for instance, be supposed, that at the time he is favouring us with the highly wrought account of his amour with the adorable Peggie, the Chevalier Johnstone was a married man, whose grandchild is now alive, or that the whole circumstantial story concerning the outrageous vengeance taken by Gordon of Abbachie on a Presbyterian clergyman, is entirely apocryphal. At the same time it may be admitted, that the Prince, like others of his family, did not esteem the

---

the seventeenth and eighteenth centuries, and many Scots swords bear his name, but it is doubted whether any of them are in fact his work ... since the forging of trade-marks was not uncommon" (*OW*, 445).

services done him by his adherents so highly as he ought. Educated in high ideas of his hereditary right, he has been supposed to have held every exertion and sacrifice made in his cause as too much the duty of the person making it, to merit extravagant gratitude on his part. Dr King's evidence (which his leaving the Jacobite interest renders somewhat doubtful) goes to strengthen this opinion.[1]

The ingenious editor of Johnstone's Memoirs[2] has quoted a story said to be told by Helvetius, stating that Prince Charles Edward, far from voluntarily embarking on his daring expedition, was literally bound hand and foot, and to which he seems disposed to yield credit. Now, it being a fact as well known as any in his history, and, so far as I know, entirely undisputed, that the Prince's personal entreaties and urgency positively forced Boisdale and Lochiel into insurrection, when they were earnestly desirous that he would put off his attempt until he could obtain a sufficient force from France, it will be very difficult to reconcile his alleged reluctance to undertake the expedition, with his desperately insisting on carrying on the rising into effect, against the advice and entreaty of his most powerful and most sage partizans. Surely a man who had been carried bound on board the vessel which brought him to so desperate an enterprise, would have taken the opportunity afforded by the reluctance of his partisans, to return to France in safety.

It is averred in Johnstone's Memoirs, that Charles Edward left the field of Culloden without doing the utmost to dispute the victory; and, to give the evidence on both sides, there is in existence the more trust-worthy testimony of Lord Elcho,[3] who states, that he himself earnestly exhorted the Prince to charge at the head of the left wing, which was entire, and retrieve the day or die with honour. And on his counsel being declined, Lord Elcho took leave of him with a bitter execration, swearing he would never look on his face again, and kept his word.

On the other hand, it seems to have to have been the opinion of almost all the other officers, that the day was irretrievably lost, one wing of the Highlanders being entirely routed, the rest of the army out-numbered, out-flanked, and in a condition totally hopeless. In this situation of things, the Irish officers who surrounded Charles's person interfered to force him off the field. A cornet who was close to the Prince, left a strong attestation, that he had seen Sir Thomas Sheridan[4] seize the bridle of his horse, and turn him round. There is some discrepancy of evidence; but the

---

1 William King (1685-1763), leader of the Jacobites at Oxford until 1761 when he left off support of the group (*OW*, 449).

2 Johnstone's *Memoirs of the Rebellion of 1745 and 1746*, edited by "J.B." Johnstone's depiction of Charles Edward Stuart was the opposite of Scott's more attractive version (*OW*, 449).

3 David Wemyss, Lord Elcho (1721-87), wrote *A Short Account of the Affairs of Scotland in the Years 1744, 1745, 1746*, published finally in 1907.

4 Lord Thomas Sheridan was an Irish Roman Catholic, tutor to Charles Edward Stuart, and trusted officer in his army.

opinion of Lord Elcho, a man of fiery temper, and desperate at the ruin which he beheld impending, cannot fairly be taken, in prejudice of a character for courage which is intimated by the nature of the enterprise itself, by the Prince's eagerness to fight on all occasions, by his determination to advance from Derby to London, and by the presence of mind which he manifested during the romantic perils of his escape. The author is far from claiming for this unfortunate person the praise due to splendid talents; but he continues to be of opinion, that at the period of his enterprise, he had a mind capable of facing danger and aspiring to fame.

That Charles Edward had the advantages of a graceful presence, courtesy, and an address and manner becoming his station, the author never heard disputed by any who approached his person, nor does he conceive that these qualities are overcharged in the present attempt to sketch his portrait.[1] The following extracts corroborative of the general opinion respecting the Prince's amiable disposition, are taken from a manuscript account of his romantic expedition, by James Maxwell of Kirkconnell, of which I possess a copy, by the friendship of J. Menzies, Esq. of Pitfoddells. The author, though partial to the Prince, whom he faithfully followed, seems to have been a fair and candid man, and well acquainted with the intrigues among the Adventurer's council:—

"Every body was mightily taken with the Prince's figure and personal behaviour. There was but one voice about them. Those whom interest or prejudice made a runaway to his cause, could not help acknowledging that they wished him well in all other respects, and could hardly blame him for his present undertaking. Sundry things had concurred to raise his character to the highest pitch, besides the greatness of the enterprise, and the conduct that had hitherto appeared in the execution of it. There were several instances of good-nature and humanity that had made a great impression on peoples' minds. I shall confine myself to two or three. Immediately after the battle, as the Prince was riding along the ground that Cope's army had occupied a few minutes before, one of the officers came up to congratulate him, and said, pointing to the killed, 'Sir, there are your enemies at your feet.' The Prince, far from exulting, expressed a great deal of compassion for his father's deluded subjects, whom he declared he was heartily sorry to see in that posture. Next day, while the Prince was at Pinkie-House, a citizen of Edinburgh came to make some representation to Secretary Murray about the tents that city was ordered to furnish against a certain day. Murray happened to be out of the way, which the Prince hearing of, called to have the gentleman brought to him, saying, he would rather dispatch the business, whatever it was, himself, than have the gentleman wait, which he did, by granting every thing that was asked. So much affability in a young prince, flushed with victory, drew encomiums even from his enemies. But what gave the people the highest idea of him, was the negative he gave to a thing that very nearly

---

1   The remaining text of the note does not appear in the *Interleaved Waverley*, and was therefore added at proof stage for the *Magnum Opus* edition.

concerned his interest, and upon which the success of his enterprise perhaps depended. It was proposed to send one of the prisoners to London, to demand of that court a cartel for the exchange of prisoners taken, and to be taken, during this war, and to intimate that a refusal would be looked upon as a resolution on their part to give no quarter. It was visible a cartel would be of great advantage to the Prince's affairs; his friends would be more ready to declare for him if they had nothing to fear but the chance of war in the field; and if the court of London refused to settle a cartel,[1] the Prince was authorised to treat his prisoners in the same manner the Elector of Hanover was determined to treat such of the Prince's friends as might fall into his hands: it was urged that a few examples would compel the court of London to comply. It was to be presumed that the officers of the English army would make a point of it. They had never engaged in the service, but upon such terms as are in use among all civilized nations, and it could be no stain upon their honour to lay down their commissions if these terms were not observed, and that owing to the obstinacy of their own Prince. Though this scheme was plausible, and represented as very important, the Prince could never be brought into it; it was below him, he said, to make empty threats, and he would never put such as those into execution; he would never in cold blood take away lives which he had saved in heat of action, at the peril of his own. These were not the only proofs of good nature the Prince gave about this time. Every day produced something new of this kind. These things softened the rigour of a military government, which was only imputed to the necessity of his affairs, and which he endeavoured to make as gentle and easy as possible."

It has been said, that the Prince sometimes exacted more state and ceremonial than seemed to suit his condition; but, on the other hand, some strictness of etiquette was altogether indispensable where he must otherwise have been exposed to general intrusion. He could also endure, with a good grace, the retorts which his affectation of ceremony sometimes exposed him to. It is said, for example, that Grant of Glenmoriston having made a hasty march to join Charles, at the head of his clan, rushed into the Prince's presence at Holyrood, with unceremonious haste, without having attended to the duties of the toilet. The Prince received him kindly, but not without a hint that a previous interview with the barber might not have been wholly unnecessary. "It is not beardless boys," answered the displeased Chief, "who are to do your Royal Highness's turn." The Chevalier took the rebuke in good part.

On the whole, if Prince Charles had concluded his life soon after his miraculous escape, his character in history must have stood very high. As it was, his station is amongst those, a certain brilliant portion of whose life forms a remarkable contrast to all which precedes, and all which follows it. The following account of the skirmish at Clifton is extracted from the manuscript Memoirs of Evan Macpherson of Cluny, Chief of the clan

hhhh.

---

1 "A written challenge, a letter of defiance" (*OED*).

Macpherson, who had the merit of supporting the principal brunt of that spirited affair. The Memoirs appear to have been composed about 1755, only ten years after the action had taken place. They were written in France, where that gallant Chief resided in exile, which accounts for some Gallicisms which occur in the narrative.[1]

"In the Prince's return from Derby back towards Scotland, my Lord George Murray, Lieutenant-General, cheerfully charg'd himself with the command of the rear; a post, which, altho' honourable, was attended with great danger, many difficulties, and no small fatigue: for the Prince being apprehensive that his retreat to Scotland might be cut off by Marischall Wade, who lay to the northward of him with an armie much supperior to what H.R.H. had, while the Duke of Comberland with his whole cavalrie followed hard in the rear, was obliged to hasten his marches. It was not, therefore, possible for the artilirie to march so fast as the Prince's army, in the depth of winter, extremely bad weather, and the worst roads in England; so Lord George Murray was obliged often to continue his marches long after it was dark almost every night, while at the same time he had frequent allarms and disturbances from the Duke of Comberland's advanc'd parties. Towards the evening of the twentie-eight December 1745, the Prince entered the town of Penrith, in the Province of Comberland. But as Lord George Murray could not bring up the artilirie so fast as he wou'd have wish'd, he was oblig'd to pass the night six miles short of that town, together with the regiment of MacDonel of Glengarrie, which that day happened to have the arrear guard. The Prince, in order to refresh his armie, and to give My Lord George and the artilirie time to come up, resolved to sejour the 29th at Penrith; so ordered his little army to appear in the morning under arms, in order to be reviewed, and to know in what manner the numbers stood from his haveing entered England. It did not at that time amount to 5000 foot in all, with about 400 cavalrie, compos'd of the noblesse who serv'd as volunteers, part of whom form'd a first troop of guards for the Prince, under the command of My Lord Elchoe, now Comte de Weems, who, being proscribed, is presently in France. Another part formed a second troup of guards under the command of My Lord Balmirino, who was beheaded at the Tower of London. A third part serv'd under My Lord le Comte de Kilmarnock, who was likewise beheaded at the Tower. A fourth part serv'd under My Lord Pitsligow, who is also proscribed; which cavalrie, tho' very few in numbers, being all Noblesse, were very brave, and of infinite advantage to the foot, not only in the day of battle, but in serving as advanced guards on the several marches, and in patroling dureing the night on the different roads which led towards the towns where the army happened to quarter.

"While this small army was out in a body on the 29th December, upon a riseing ground to the northward of Penrith, passing review, Mons. de Cluny, with his tribe, was ordered to the Bridge of Clifton, about a mile

---

1   The remaining text of the note does not appear in the *Interleaved Waverley*, and was therefore added at proof stage for the *Magnum Opus* edition.

to southward of Penrith, after having pass'd in review before Mons. Pat-
tullo, who was charged with the inspection of the troops, and was likeways
Quarter Master General of the army, and is now in France. They
remained under arms at the Bridge, waiting the arrival of My Lord
George Murray with the artilirie, whom Mons. de Cluny had orders to
cover in passing the bridge. They arrived about sunsett closly pursued by
the Duke of Comberland with the whole body of his cavalrie, reckoned
upwards of 3000 strong, about a thousand of whom, as near as might be
computed, dismounted, in order to cut off the passage of the artilirie
towards the bridge, while the Duke and the others remained on horseback
in order to attack the rear. My Lord George Murray advanced, and
although he found Mons. de Cluny and his tribe in good spirits under
arms, yet the circumstance appear'd extremely delicate. The numbers
were vastly unequall, and the attack seem'd very dangerous; so My Lord
George declin'd giving orders to such time as he ask'd Mons. de Cluny's
oppinion. 'I will attack them with all my heart,' says Mons. de Cluny, 'if
you order me.' 'I do order it then,' answered My Lord George, and immediately went on himself along with Mons. de Cluny, and fought sword in
hand on foot, at the head of the single tribe of Macphersons. They in a
moment made their way through a strong hedge of thorns, under the
cover whereof the cavalrie had taken their station, in the strugle of passing
which hedge My Lord George Murray, being dressed *en montagnard*, as all
the army were, lost his bonet and wig; so continued to fight bear-headed
during the action. They at first made a brisk discharge of their fire arms
on the enemy, then attacked them with their sabres, and made a great
slaughter a considerable time, which obliged Comberland and his cavalrie
to fly with precipitation and in great confusion; in so much, that if the
Prince had been provided in a sufficient number of cavalrie to have taken
advantage of the disorder, it is beyond question that the Duke of
Comberland and the bulk of his cavalrie had been taken prisoners. By this
time it was so dark that it was not possible to view or number the slain
who filled all the ditches which happened to be on the ground where they
stood. But it was computed that, besides those who went off wounded,
upwards of a hundred at least were left on the spot, among whom was
Colonel Honywood, who commanded the dismounted cavalrie, whose
sabre of considerable value Mons. de Cluny brought off and still pre-
serves; and his tribe lykeways brought off many arms;—the Colonel was
afterwards taken up, and, his wounds being dress'd, with great difficultie
recovered. Mons. de Cluny lost only in the action twelve men, of whom
some haveing been only wounded, fell afterwards into the hands of the
enemy, and were sent as slaves to America, whence several of them
returned, and one of them is now in France, a sergeant in the Regiment
of Royal Scots. How soon the accounts of the enemies approach had
reached the Prince, H.R.H. had immediately ordered Mi—Lord le Comte
de Nairne, Brigadier, who, being proscribed, is now in France, with the
three batalions of the Duke of Athol, the batalion of the Duke of Perth,
and some other troups under his command, in order to support Cluny,
and to bring off the artilirie. But the action was intirely over, before the

Comte de Nairne, with his command, cou'd reach nigh to the place. They therefore return'd all to Penrith, and the artilirie marched up in good order. Nor did the Duke of Comberland ever afterwards dare to come within a day's march of the Prince and his army dureing the course of all that retreat, which was conducted with great prudence and safety when in some manner surrounded by enemies.

iiii. As the heathen deities contracted an indelible obligation if they swore by Styx,[1] the Scottish Highlanders had usually some peculiar solemnity attached to an oath, which they intended should be binding on them. Very frequently it consisted in laying their hand, as they swore, on their own drawn dirk; which dagger, becoming a party to the transaction, was invoked to punish any breach of faith. But by whatever ritual the oath was sanctioned, the party was extremely desirous to keep secret what the especial oath was, which he considered irrevocable. This was a matter of great convenience, as he felt no scruple in breaking his asseveration, when made in any other form than that which he accounted as peculiarly solemn; and therefore readily granted any engagement which bound him no longer than he inclined. Whereas, if the oath which he accounted inviolable was once publicly known, no party with whom he might have occasion to contract, would have rested satisfied with any other. Louis XI. of France practised the same sophistry, for he also had a peculiar species of oath, the only one which he was ever known to respect, and which, therefore, he was very unwilling to pledge. The only engagement which that wily tyrant accounted binding upon him, was an oath by the Holy Cross of Saint Lo d'Angers, which contained a portion of the True Cross. If he prevaricated after taking his oath, Louis believed he should die within the year. The Constable Saint Paul, being invited to a personal conference with Louis, refused to meet the king unless he would agree to ensure him safe conduct under sanction of this oath. But, says Comines, the king replied, he would never again pledge that engagement to mortal man, though he was willing to take any other oath which could be devised. The treaty was broken off, therefore, after much chaffering concerning the nature of the vow which Louis was to take. Such is the difference between the dictates of superstition and those of conscience.

jjjj. A pair of chestnut trees, destroyed, the one entirely, and the other in part, by such a mischievous and wanton act of revenge, grew at Invergarry Castle, the fastness of MacDonald of Glengarry.

kkkk. The first three couplets are from an old ballad, called the Border Widow's Lament.[2]

---

1 In Greek mythology, Styx "is a river in the underworld over which the souls of the dead were ferried by Charon" (*WD*).

2 "The Lament of the Border Widow" in Scott's *Minstrelsy of the Scottish Border*, 2nd ed., 1803 (*OW*, 451).

Appendix A: Selected Reviews of Waverley (1814-31)

1. From the *Quarterly Review*, July 1814 [John Wilson Croker]

[Gary Kelly notes that though Scott contributed toward founding the *Quarterly Review*, a voice for Tory views, in order to "counterbalance the Whig *Edinburgh Review* ..." in 1809, he "had close ties with the *Edinburgh Review*—a sign of his ability to get along with men of differing political and cultural values" (*DLB*, 282).]

We have had so many occasions to invite our reader's attention to that species of composition called Novels, and have so often stated our general views of the principles of this very agreeable branch of literature, that we shall venture on the consideration of our present subject with but a few observations, and those applicable to a class of novels, of which it is a favourable specimen.

The earlier novelists wrote at periods when society was not perfectly formed, and we find that their picture of life was an embodying of their own conceptions of the "*beau idéal.*"—Heroes all generosity and ladies all chastity, exalted above the vulgarities of society and nature, maintain, through eternal folios, their visionary virtues, without the stain of any moral frailty, or the degradation of any human necessities. But this high-flown style went out of fashion as the great mass of mankind became more informed of each other's feelings and concerns, and as a nearer intercourse taught them that the real course of human life is a conflict of duty and desire, of virtue and passion, of right and wrong; in the description of which it is difficult to say whether uniform virtue or unredeemed vice would be in the greater degree tedious and absurd.

The novelists next endeavoured to exhibit a general view of society. The characters in Gil Blas[1] and Tom Jones[2] are not individuals so much as specimens of the human race; and these delightful works have been, are, and ever will be popular, because they present lively and accurate delineations of the workings of the human soul, and that every man who reads them is obliged to confess to himself, that in

---

1   *Gil Blas*, or *Histoire de Gil Blas de Santillane*, was a picaresque novel written by Alain-Rene Lesage (1668-1747) and published between 1715 and 1735 in France.
2   *The History of Tom Jones*, also a picaresque novel, was written by Henry Fielding (1707-54) and published in London in 1749.

similar circumstances with the personages of Le Sage and Fielding, he would probably have acted in the way in which they are described to have done.

From this species the transition to a third was natural. The first class was theory—it was improved into a *generic* description, and that again led the way to a more particular classification—a copying not of man in general, but of men of a peculiar nation, profession, or temper, or, to go a step further—of *individuals*.

Thus Alcander[1] and Cyrus[2] could never have existed in human society—they are neither French, nor English, nor Italian, because it is only allegorically that they are *men*. Tom Jones might have been a Frenchman, and Gil Blas an Englishman, because the essence of their characters is human nature, and the personal situation of the individual is almost indifferent to the success of the object which the author proposed to himself: while, on the other hand, the characters of the most popular novels of later times are Irish, or Scotch, or French, and not in the abstract *men*.—The general operations of nature are circumscribed to her effects on an individual character, and the modern novels of this class, compared with the broad and noble style of the earlier writers, may be considered as Dutch pictures, delightful in their vivid and minute details of common life, wonderfully entertaining to the close observer of peculiarities, and highly creditable to the accuracy, observation, and humour of the painter, but exciting none of those more exalted feelings, giving none of those higher views of the human soul which delight and exalt the mind of the spectator of Raphael,[3] Correggio,[4] or Murillo.[5]

But as in a gallery we are glad to see every style of excellence, and are ready to amuse ourselves with Teniers[6] and Gerard Dow,[7] so we derive great pleasure from the congenial delineations of Castle Rackrent[8] and Waverley; and we are well assured that any reader who is qualified to judge of the illustration we have borrowed from a sister art, will not accuse us of undervaluing, by this comparison, either Miss

---

1 Hero of *The Amorous Conquests of the Great Alcander*, a romance, published in 1685 and written by the French novelist Gatien Courtilz de Sandras (1644-1712).

2 Hero of the romance *Artamenes; or, The Grand Cyrus* by French novelist Madeleine de Scudéry (1607-1701), published from 1649-53.

3 Raphael Sanzio (1483-1520), an Italian painter and architect.

4 Antonio de Correggio (1489-1534), an Italian painter.

5 Bartolome Esteban Murillo (1618-82), Spanish painter.

6 David Teniers the Younger (1610-90), Flemish artist.

7 Gerard Dow or Dew, Gerrit Dou (1613-75), Dutch painter.

8 *Castle Rackrent* (1800) by Maria Edgeworth (1767-1849), a national novel.

Edgeworth or the ingenious author of the work now under consideration. We mean only to say, that the line of writing which they have
adopted is less comprehensive and less sublime, but not that it is less
entertaining or less useful than that of their predecessors. On the contrary, so far as utility constitutes merit in a novel, we have no hesitation in preferring the moderns to their predecessors. We do not believe
that any man or woman was ever improved in morals or manners by
the reading of Tom Jones or Peregrine Pickle,[1] though we are confident that many have profited by the Tales of Fashionable Life,[2] and
the Cottagers of Glenburnie.[3]

We have heard Waverley called a Scotch Castle Rack-rent; and we
have ourselves alluded to a certain resemblance between these
works; but we must beg leave to explain that the resemblance consists only in this, that the one is a description of the peculiarities of
Scottish manners as the other is of those of Ireland; and that we are
far from placing on the same level the merits and qualities of the
works. Waverley is of a much higher strain, and may be safely placed
far above the amusing vulgarity of Castle Rack-rent, and by the side
of Ennui or the Absentee, the best undoubtedly of Miss Edgeworth's
compositions....

We shall conclude this article, which has grown to an immoderate
length, by observing what, indeed, our readers must have already discovered, that Waverley, who gives his name to the story, is far from
being its hero, and that in truth the interest and merit of the work is
derived, not from any of the ordinary qualities of a novel, but from the
truth of its facts, and the accuracy of its delineations.

We confess that we have, speaking generally, a great objection to
what may be called historical romance, in which real and fictitious
personages, and actual and fabulous events are mixed together to the
utter confusion of the reader, and the unsettling of all accurate recollections of past transactions; and we cannot but wish that the
ingenious and intelligent author of Waverley had rather employed
himself in recording *historically* the character and transactions of his
countrymen *Sixty Years since*, than in writing a work, which, though
it may be, in its facts, almost true, and in its delineations perfectly
accurate, will yet, in sixty years *hence*, be regarded, or rather, probably, *disregarded*, as a *mere* romance, and the gratuitous invention of a
facetious fancy.

---

1 *Peregrine Pickle* (1751) by Tobias Smollett (1721-71).
2 *Tales of Fashionable Life* (1809-12) by Maria Edgeworth, in 6 vols., containing
  her novels the *Absentee* and *Ennui*.
3 *The Cottagers of Glenburnie* (1808) by Scottish novelist Elizabeth Hamilton
  (1758-1816). See Appendix D2 for an excerpt.

2. From the *Scots Magazine*, July 1814

Romance, certainly, in the present age, is the species of composition which has assumed the greatest variety of forms. There seems to have arisen among the present class of readers, a desire to have some instruction blended with their amusement ... Perhaps, among these various stories, none are more pleasing than those which undertake to delineate the peculiarities of national manners. The public have been amused by such representations, relative to our sister island, from the pens of several of the most distinguished writers of the age. Of late, Scottish manners have been undertaken; and though not perhaps altogether so strongly marked, they still contain very sufficient room for curious or comic observation. Some of the old national failings, of which traces still remain among the lower orders, have been exposed by Mrs. Hamilton[1] with uncommon force, spirit, and humour. The present volumes undertake a somewhat loftier theme, and more remote from our daily observation.—The picture, however, is drawn with a very masterly hand. And, according to every information which we can collect or obtain, it is characterized by the strictest truth, though presenting features which almost surpass the wildness of romance. To many readers it may appear impossible, that the period of sixty years should have produced a change so wonderful, as that Scotland should then have presented scenes which now appear as strange as those which pass in New Holland[2] ... In the Lowlands, indeed, the change, though sensible, has been by no means so miraculous; but in the mountainous districts, it is otherwise. The current of civilization, flowing from the south, had, at that time, made [little] impression *there*. All the feudal ... ideas, extinct in every other country, reigned here with a sway almost undiminished. The aspect which they then presented is fresh in the memory of tradition, and has doubtless been described to the author by living witnesses. An opportunity is thus given to paint, not only what the Highlands were sixty years ago, but in some degree what all Europe was, at the distance of three centuries. [Here follow lengthy extracts from the novel.]

From this slight sketch, and from the specimens given, our readers must feel this to be a work decidedly original, and possessing strong claims to public attention. Report assigns it to the most admired poet of the age;[3] a subject on which we have in vain sought for any precise information. The internal evidence does not certainly contradict the

---

1 Elizabeth Hamilton, Scottish novelist. See previous note.
2 Australia was known as New Holland.
3 I.e., Scott.

assertion; and we see no reason that even such a writer could have, to disown a performance like the present.

3. From the *British Critic*, August 1814

There is a certain gratification felt in introducing two distinguished personages to each other, although it may be ascertained, from various circumstances, that they must necessarily have been soon acquainted, without the formality of the said introduction. Such a gratification will be ours in the present instance: we request permission, therefore, to introduce "Waverley, or 'Tis Sixty Years since," a publication which has already excited considerable interest in the sister kingdom, to the literary world on this side of the Tweed. It is with the more satisfaction that we undertake this duty, as it is an office which but seldom falls to the share of the conductors of a critical journal to execute. So rapid is the circulation of those works, to which the public attention has been by anticipation directed, that it is our province rather to confirm or correct a judgment already formed, than to direct it to a new and undiscovered object. Where however an opportunity occurs of performing our duty in this latter respect, we undertake it with pleasure, because commendation is generally its end; and it is with peculiar pleasure that we undertake it in the present instance, because we are assured that in such commendation the public will coincide. We have now the start both of general curiosity and general opinion; lest therefore we should lose the vantage ground, we shall proceed in the execution of our duty, and present to the public a work, in which, before many weeks are passed, they will feel a very lively interest.

A very short time has elapsed, since this publication made its appearance in Edinburgh, and though it came into the world in the modest garb of anonymous obscurity, the northern literati are unanimous, as we understand, in ascribing part of it at least to the pen of W. Scott. As that gentleman has too much good sense to play the coquet with the world, we understand that he perseveres in a formal denial of the charge; though from all we can learn, the *not guilty* which he pleads to the indictment, proceeds almost as faintly from his mouth, as from the tongue of a notorious offender at the bar of the Old Bailey.[1] Of the circumstances which form the external evidence in proof of this charge, we must of course be supposed essentially ignorant, as we in the south can have no opportunity of entering into the secret history of the literary world in the north; nor if we had, should we attempt to

---

1 Now the Central Criminal Court of England in London, constructed during the Middle Ages.

enter into its detail, as to the generality of our readers it could afford neither amusement nor interest. In the internal evidence alone we can feel a concern, and, such as it is, we shall present it to our readers, that they may be enabled to form their opinions upon the same ground with ourselves. We shall only add, that upon this evidence principally the tale in question has been ascribed to our favourite poet, as before it was actually presented to the public in Edinburgh, no expectation had been formed of the appearance of such a work.

The time which the author has chosen for the historical part of his tale, is a period to which no Briton can look back without the strongest emotions, and the most anxious interest. It is the year 1745, the last fatal year when the blood of our countrymen was spilt on its own shores, when Briton met Briton on his native land. It has pleased Providence, in his mercy to this favoured country, for a space of now nearly seventy years, to secure it not only from the invasions of foreign foes, but to preserve it from the still more fearful and deadly scenes of civil commotion. By the restoration of peace to the whole European world, a mighty machine of national strength is suddenly diverted from those external objects to which it has been so long and so powerfully directed; it is our earnest hope, as it is our most confident trust, that its gigantic force may not, by an unnatural revulsion, be turned inwardly upon itself, and that the same energies which blessed us with victory, and crowned us with glory in our operations abroad, may not inflame us with the ardour of contention, nor curse us with the spirit of discord at home.—May the peace, which our exertions in the cause of all that is great and good have purchased and secured to the world around us, descend "twice blessed" upon our native land. If the history of those bloody days, which is embodied in this tale, shall by an early and awful warning inspire the nation with a jealous vigilance against the very first symptoms of their recurrence, we shall consider that not even the light pages of fiction have trifled in vain....

We have thus given a short sketch of the story, which is in itself too interesting for an abridgement, and too replete with varied incident to bear the rapidity of a dry detail. If, however, from our imperfect outline, we shall have induced the reader to enjoy the full colouring in the original, we shall not have failed in our desire of discovering to his mind a source of valuable and legitimate amusement.

We are unwilling to consider this publication in the light of a common novel, whose fate it is to be devoured with rapidity for the day, and to be afterwards forgotten for ever; but as a vehicle of curious accurate information upon a subject which must at all times demand our attention—the history and manners of a very large and renowned portion of the inhabitants of these islands; of a race who, within these few years, have vanished from the face of their native land, but have left their names and their actions behind them as monuments of spirited independence, and of intrepid loyalty to that unfortunate family, who now with their brave defenders are for ever gone. We would recommend this tale, as faithfully embodying the lives, the manners, and the opinions of this departed race, and as affording those features of ancient days, which no man probably, besides its author, has had the means to collect, the desire to preserve, or the power to pourtray. This tale should be ranked in the same class with the Arabian nights' entertainments, in which the story, however it may for a moment engage the attention, is but of little consequence, in proportion to the faithful picture which they present of the manners and customs of the east.

... Let those who are engaged in forming the minds of youth of this country not disdain to receive a hint even from the trifling pages of a novel, and let those who are placed under their care, as they value both themselves and their best hopes, learn from the character of Waverley early to distrust that inordinate self-confidence, and that over-bearing petulance, which teaches them to despise that order, that labour, and that discipline of the mind, which can alone secure to them the full completion of their ambitious views. The most fatal enemies to the bright prospects of future distinction are the ramblings of superficial enquiry, and the pride of conceited indolence.

The religious opinions expressed in the course of the tale are few, but of those few we fully approve. The loyalty and strength of the political sentiments clearly prove their author to be a man of a sound and vigorous mind, whose talents have not been lowered, nor whose spirit debased by the flimsy theories and the mawkish speculations of modern metaphysical politics. The humourous and happy adaptation of legal terms shew no moderate acquaintance with the arena of the law, and a perpetual allusion to the English and the Latin classics no common share of scholarship and of taste.

That there are faults in the work we cannot deny, and some glaring errors, which we could heartily wish in a second edition were altered or erased, as they have a tendency to lessen the permanent value of the work, and to place it in the scale of a more common production. The pieces of intelligence which are represented as appearing in the newspapers, savour much more of modern manners, than "sixty years since"; such as the supersession of Waverley in the form of a paragraph ...

... There is here and there a tendency to caricature and broad farce, which we are persuaded that the good taste of the author himself will discover, and his good sense will correct. Of the poetry which is interspersed we can speak in the highest terms....

If the testimony of this witness be not sufficient to work conviction in the reader's mind as to the name of the author, he will find still fuller testimony in other poems, which we have not room to extract.

Whoever may be the author of the prose, we strongly suspect that the poetry at least was written by W. Scott; if our conjecture is unfounded, we congratulate the world on the appearance of a new poet, whose genius bears so striking a resemblance to their old favourite. Respecting the prose, we own that our suspicions are very strong of Walter Scott, as in very few besides himself are united that strength of feeling, that richness of anecdote, that store of historical knowledge, that accuracy of legal information, and above all, those high constitutional principles which dignify and adorn the mind of that original and native poet.

We ought to have before observed, that to justify the second name, "'Tis sixty years since," the author informs us that this tale was written in the year 1805; of this we have no reason to doubt; the first sketches were probably drawn at that period, although, from the use of certain cant words of the present year, such as *tact, bivouacking,* ... we are of opinion that the finishing stroke has been but very lately applied.

4. From the *Antijacobin Review and Magazine*, September 1814

It has long been our wish to see those days revived when writers of genius, information, and talents, did not think their time wasted, nor their labour misemployed, in the composition of *Novels*. It was then believed that something more was wanting to exhibit a correct delineation of life and manners, with a view to produce a moral effect, than the art of weaving an intricate story, of bringing forward ludicrous characters, and of exhibiting a multitude of improbable incidents. All these, it was known, might be easily produced by a mind uninstructed in any system of ethics, and even most imperfectly versed in the ways of the world. Fielding, Smollet, Graves,[1] Brooke,[2] Lenox,[3] Mackenzie,[4] and many others, dignified, by their productions, the art of Novel-writing, and raised it high in the estimation of the rational and well-informed part of the world. From their time, till within the last few years, with very few exceptions indeed, nothing, in the shape of a novel, has been produced which can be read with pleasure or advan-

---

1 Richard Graves (1715-1804), English novelist and minister, author of *The Spiritual Quixote* (1772).
2 Frances Brooke (1724-89), English novelist, author of *The History of Emily Montague* (1769).
3 Charlotte Lennox (1720-1804), English novelist, author of *The Female Quixote* (1752).
4 Henry Mackenzie (1745-1831), Scottish novelist, author of *The Man of Feeling* (1771).

tage, while shoals of compositions bearing the name, have issued from the London presses, which have tended to exhibit the national character in a contemptible point of view, and which have had no small effect in relaxing the vigour of moral principles in the younger part of the present generation.

Among the novellists of the present day, the female writers have borne away the palm;—and of those who are known, Mrs. West[1] is, unquestionably, entitled to the highest praise; as her novels are, generally speaking, highly interesting, and as the author suffers no fair opportunity for the inculcation of religious and moral principle to escape her. Miss Edgeworth ranks high in point of talent, and in knowledge of the world—but there is scarcely a production of her pen, of which any reader could conjecture, on reading it, whether it was written by a pagan or a christian. For works of imagination, strongly marked by genius, and distinguished beyond all others for strong descriptive powers, Mrs. Ratcliffe[2] stands eminently conspicuous. The anonymous authors of *Self-control*,[3] and of *Things by their right Names*,[4] but more especially the last, deserve to be classed among the very best writers of novels. Miss Hamilton, too, must not be forgotten in the enumeration of those literary characters who have successfully laboured to restore this species of writing to some portion of its pristine fame. Surely, notwithstanding the general discredit cast upon novel-writing, it affords as ample a scope for the exercise of intellectual strength, and for the display of diversified talent, as almost any other species of composition; while it is fully as capable of being rendered a vehicle for useful information, and moral instruction.

It is with real pleasure, then, that we take up a novel, written by a man or woman of sense, talent, and knowledge. And such pleasure we have derived from the perusal of the novel before us; the scene of which is laid chiefly in Scotland, and during the rebellion in 1745; a period, affording great opportunities for the delineation of interesting characters, for the relation of affecting incidents, and for the inculcation of good principles. At the same time, however, it must be observed, that the writer takes upon himself a task of peculiar delicacy, and attended with peculiar difficulty. For though the period is too remote for prejudices to operate, or animosity to survive, with any degree of formidable strength; though the parties personally interested

---

1 Jane West (1758-1852), English novelist, author of *A Tale of the Times* (1799).
2 Ann Radcliffe (1764-1823), English novelist, author of *The Mysteries of Udolpho* (1794).
3 *Self-Control* (1811) by English novelist Mary Brunton (1778-1818).
4 *Things by Their Right Names* (1812) by English novelist Frances Jacson (1754-1842).

in the transactions of that day have all, or nearly all, been consigned to "that bourne from which no traveller returns"; and though no remnant is left of the unhappy House of Stuart, to rouze jealousy, or to excite apprehensions; there are certain feelings still alive, and a certain vigilance still awake, which render the avowal of a partiality for certain principles, and certain politics, though not unsafe, at least unpleasant and invidious. The author, however, has performed this difficult task with considerable skill and ability, steering clear of every thing which could give offence to the reigning family, and yet not disgracing himself by the sacrifice of truth, or by the abject servility of a time-serving parasite. Perhaps there are no men more entitled to respect, than those who, at the period referred to, actuated by a spirit of persevering loyalty, however misapplied or wrongly-directed, risked their fortunes and their lives, in a most unequal and nearly desperate contest, in support of their principles and of what they conceived to be their duty....

The story is well-told, the incidents are interesting, and the sentiments good. The book is evidently the production of a Scotchman, and public report has ascribed it to the pen of Mr. Walter Scott. Whether it be his or not, it is a work which would do no discredit to his reputation. It is, naturally enough, replete with Scotticisms, and with expressions unintelligible to Englishmen; but as it was very well intended for circulation in Scotland (to which country the sale of the first edition was almost wholly confined) no fault could be found with it on that account, though it is a formidable objection to an English reader. The manners of Scotland are ably pourtrayed; and very considerable talent is exhibited in the structure and conduct of the plot, incidents, and catastrophe. The author, indeed, talks of persons charged with high treason in England being admitted to bail, which would be perfectly illegal, and therefore impracticable; speaks of *prejudices exclusively English,* without reason and without authority; and betrays some few prejudices of his own, which, however, are highly excusable.

5. From the *Scourge*, October 1814

The poetical character of Walter Scott is duly appreciated, and generally understood. The fluency of his verse, the beauty of his descriptive passages, the sublimity of his more vigorous efforts, and the pure and irresistible pathos of his tender and amatory effusions, have commanded the admiration, and awakened the enthusiasm of the most determined enemies to his frequent violations of the laws of criticism, and his obstrusive offences against good taste. But his character as a writer of prose is yet undetermined and ambiguous. The learning and good sense which he displayed in the incidental comments, contained in the Minstrelsy of the Scottish Border, would have elevated a more prudent writer to the highest eminence of criticism ...

Were we to deduce our opinion from internal evidence, we should decide against the claims of Mr. Scott, to the composition of Waverley. It abounds indeed with the peculiar knowledge which characterizes the poetical effusion of that gentleman; and displays a minute and even technical acquaintance with the scenery, the manners, and the history of the Scottish highlands, but it is at the same time pervaded by a tone of sober and rational reflection; by a scholastic precision, and an aptitude for classical comment and quotation, of which he has exhibited no evidence in his former productions, and which appears to be utterly inconsistent with his habits of study, and the features of his mind. The poetry and the prose of Mr. Scott have seldom been distinguished by the minute delineation of conflicting passions, by the skilful development of character, or the felicitous portraiture of individual habits. But the author of Waverley at once delights and instructs the reader by the most exquisite delineation of those peculiarities of temper, habit, and intellectual power, which interest in proportion to the difficulty of their execution. In one respect, indeed, Mr. Scott, and the author whose production we are now examining, bear a close resemblance, and are on the most perfect level with each other. They both excel in their description of local scenery, and their acquaintance with the general aspect of ancient manners. The description of the architectural structures as they existed "sixty years since," are only equalled in accuracy and beauty by the rapid but vigorous and hasty sketches of the glen, the mountain, the loch, the cavern, and various combinations of sublime, beautiful, and picturesque scenery, which, even at the present time, awake the astonishment, and soothe the passions of the observer, and were then to be viewed in all the grandeur of uncultivated magnificence....

6. From the *Edinburgh Review*, November 1814 [Francis Jeffrey]

It is wonderful what genius and adherence to nature will do, in spite of all disadvantages. Here is a thing obviously very hastily, and, in many places, very unskillfully written—composed, one half of it, in a dialect unintelligible to four-fifths of the reading population of the country—relating to a period too recent to be romantic, and too far gone by to be familiar—and published, moreover, in a quarter of the island where materials and talents for novel-writing have been supposed to be equally wanting; and yet, by the mere force and truth and vivacity of its colouring, already casting the whole tribe of ordinary novels into the shade, and taking its place rather with the most popular of our modern poems, than with the rubbish of provincial romances.

The secret of this success, we take it, is merely that the author is a person of genius; and that he has, notwithstanding, had virtue enough to be true to nature throughout, and to content himself, even in the marvellous parts of his story, with copying from actual existences, rather than from the phantasms of his own imagination.

... The object of the work before us, was evidently to present a faithful and animated picture of the manners and state of society that prevailed in this northern part of the island, in the earlier part of the last century; and the author has judiciously fixed upon the era of the Rebellion in 1745, not only as enriching his pages with the interest inseparably attached to the narration of such occurrences, but as affording a fair opportunity for bringing out all the contrasted principles and habits which distinguished the different classes of persons who then divided the country, and formed among them the basis of almost all that was peculiar in the national character.... [A]nd one great source of the interest which the volumes before us undoubtedly possess, is to be sought in the surprise that is excited by discovering, that in our own country, and almost in our own age, manners and characters existed, and were conspicuous, which we had been accustomed to consider as belonging to remote antiquity, or extravagant romance.

The way in which they are here represented must satisfy every reader, we think, by an inward *tact* and conviction, that the delineation has been made from actual experience and observation;—experience and observation employed perhaps only on a few surviving relics and specimens of what was familiar a little earlier—but generalized from instances sufficiently numerous and complete, to warrant all that may have been added to the portrait:—And indeed the records and vestiges of the more extraordinary parts of the representation are still sufficiently abundant, to satisfy all who have the means of consulting them, as to the perfect accuracy of the picture....

Though that narrative is always lively and easy, however, we think the great charm of the work consists in the characters and descriptions ...

... The worst part of the book by far is that portion of the first volume which contains the history of the hero's residence in England—and next to it is the laborious, tardy, and obscure explanation of some puzzling occurrences in the story, which the reader would, in general, be much better pleased to be permitted to forget—and which are neither well explained after all, nor at all worth explaining. The passages in which the author speaks in his own person, and assumes the smart and flippant style of modern makers of paragraphs, are also considerably below mediocrity—and form a strange and humiliating contrast with the force and freedom of his manner when engaged in those dramatic or picturesque representations to which his genius so decidedly inclines.

There has been much speculation, at least in this quarter of the island, about the author of this singular performance—and certainly it is not easy to conjecture why it is still anonymous.—Judging by internal evidence, to which alone we pretend to have access, we should not scruple to ascribe it to the highest of those authors to whom it has been assigned by the sagacious conjectures of the public;—and this at least we will venture to say, that if it be indeed the work of an author hitherto unknown, Mr Scott would do well to look to his laurels, and to rouse himself for a sturdier competition than any he has yet had to encounter.

7. From the *Monthly Review*, November 1814

The Memoirs of the Count de Grammont[1] have generally, of late years, been classed in point of authenticity among the fairy-tales of their lively and intelligent author; and, supposing that not a syllable of them were strictly true, the work itself would scarcely be the less historically valuable. This remark, we fear, cannot be made with respect to Voltaire's Charles XII;[2] which, though it contains a number of well-established and important truths, is nevertheless, to all purposes of historical utility, as mere a romance as those of Florian[3] and Marmontel.[4] The difference lies in this circumstance: Count Hamilton's stories are the vivid reflections of the character, customs, and opinions of that class and period of society to which they refer; while the facts related by the patriarch of Ferney[5] are coloured according to the dictates of his own fancy, and dressed out for ornament and effect. Whoever be the author of Waverley, and most of our readers probably know that it is attributed to Mr. Walter Scott, he is an historian of the former order; and those, who regard a knowledge of the motives and principles of actions as more worthy of attainment than the chronological succession of those actions themselves, will acquire a much larger share of such information from the perusal of these volumes than from all the tomes of Smol-

---

1 *Memoirs of the Count de Grammont* (1713) by Anthony Hamilton (1646-1720).
2 *Histoire de Charles XII* (1731) by François-Marie Arouet (Voltaire) (1694-1778).
3 Jean-Pierre Claris de Florian (1755-94), French poet and romance writer.
4 Jean-François Marmontel (1723-99), French historian and writer.
5 Voltaire, who built a chateau in Ferney, France.

lett, Belsham,[1] and Adolphus.[2] The frame of the picture is fiction: but the delineation itself is as correct, minute, and spirited a copy of nature as ever came from the hands of an artist.

... Such is the bare outline of a tale which has little of the ordinary attractions of a novel to recommend it, and which will therefore probably disappoint all those readers who take it up at a circulating library.... It is strictly an historical romance, and yet scarcely belongs to any class of composition usually decorated with that title. Neither is it a picture of existing manners, and therefore not to be placed by the side of *Ennui* or the *Cottagers of Glenburnie*. In short, without wasting any more time in saying what it is *not*, we shall proceed by a few extracts to shew what it *is*, having already prepared the way for them by our sketch of the leading incidents with which they are introduced. One word more, however, before we begin. It is evident that, if a portrait of a living object be valuable only as it is taken from the existing reality, that of one long since dead cannot be worth a farthing unless it be copied from some original memorial. It is therefore not with a view to disparage the author of this superior performance, but by way of compliment to our own sagacity, that we record our discovery that most of the descriptions of local manners and customs, and some strong touches of character, to be found in these volumes, may be traced to a publication intitled "Letters from a Gentleman in the North of Scotland to his Friend in London," printed in the year 1754, but professing to have been written several years sooner. That entertaining work contains, indeed, as we believe, the only authentic contemporaneous delineation of the peculiarities which it intends to describe; and when we add that the author of "*The Lady of the Lake*" has expressed his acknowledgements to it for some of the most striking features of that romantic poem, the circumstance may serve at once to justify the author of Waverley in the use which he has made of the same materials, and to strengthen the very prevalent opinion as to the identity of the poet and the historian. It does not become *us* to express any decisive judgment on a point which the author has perseveringly involved in deep obscurity: but the hint which we have just afforded, coupled with the spirit of the work itself, as developed in the passages which we now proceed to quote, will give our readers all the means of determining for themselves that we can communicate.

... It is not one of the least merits of this very uncommon production, that all the subordinate characters are touched with the same dis-

---

1   Thomas Belsham (1750-1829), English minister and writer.
2   John Adolphus (1768-1845), London lawyer and writer, author of *The History of England*.

criminating force which so strongly marks their principals; and that, in this manner, almost every variety of station and interest, such as it existed at the period under review, is successively brought before the mind of the reader in colours vivid as the original.

... A few oversights, we think, we have detected in the conduct of the story, which ought not to remain unnoticed. For example, the age of Stanley and Lady Emily does not seem well to accord with the circumstances of their union, as related in the commencement of the work; and we are not quite satisfied that Edward should have been so easily reconciled to the barbarous and stubborn prejudices, which preclude even the office of intercession for his gallant friend and companion in arms.

The pieces of poetry, which are not very profusely scattered through these volumes, can scarcely fail to be ascribed to Mr. Scott, whatever may be judged of the body of the work. In point of comparative merit, we should class them neither with the highest nor with the meanest effusions of his lyric minstrelsy.

8. From the *Critical Review*, March 1815

This romance, lavishly extolled by the Scotch reviewers, is attributed to the pen of Walter Scott. Why a poet of established fame, should dwindle into a scribbler of novels, we cannot tell. At all events, we are not among his flatterers, and candidly affirm, we neither like the work nor the subject; but the name of Walter Scott claims attention....

We are well inclined to accord to Waverly [sic] the praise which criticism, divested of prejudice, and uninfluenced by public or private bias, can warrant. Had the work been less national, (we are speaking of novel or romance) and divested of its endless Scotch idioms, Gaelic allusions, scraps of Latin, and a ridiculous French character expunged, we think it would have proved as acceptable to English novel readers, as it must doubtless be to those on the other side of the Tweed. Every part, intelligible to us, is certainly written with much ability, and the characters are well discriminated: yet, as we have already intimated, the main incidents are merely the rebellion of 1745, treated "novel wise."

9. From the *London Magazine*, June 1829

[The final two reviews are of the *Magnum Opus Waverley*.]

We think this is a mistake. Not in a pecuniary point of view, certainly,—for we doubt not its sale will be enormous.—But it is nothing short of a blunder as regards the ultimate fame of the Author of Waverley,—and we thought that Sir Walter had been sagacious enough to know it. What we mean is this. To go behind the scenes prevents real enjoyment of the play....

In like manner we think that Sir Walter has been unwise, in letting us see the machinery of his scenery—which from the front had so beautiful an effect—and shewing as some of the reality of characters which, as he had put them upon the scene, were so admirable in their several natures. Why would not he leave—not well but, admirably— alone? Why shew us the warp and woof of that tapestry which, in its unbetrayed state, was so perfect?

And now to consider more directly the work before us. The more we consider it, the more we really regret its publication. After what we have said, we shall not be considered luke-warm admirers of this great writer. He has given us gratification in every shape;—in his liveliness,—in his stronger and broader mirth,—in the graceful and *piquant* tone of his direct narrative—in the startling rapidity of his almost visible pictures of action, and the almost unequalled reality of his descriptions of external nature. Still more have we admired and felt his power of portraying every variation of human character, as well arising from the natural disposition and gifts, as from the circumstances of situation and event. In the rendering the effects of these two causes combined, he is unrivalled. Lastly, we thank him for his admirable representations of the passions and feelings, which form at once the most attractive and beneficial subjects of human contemplation. Of the more lofty and the fiercer, his portraitures are magnificent and vivid; but we confess that the delineations for which we are the most grateful, are his exquisite touches of what is fond, and simple, and pure, and generous, and tender.

It is because we feel these qualities to be so perfectly brought into action as the books exist, that we are reluctant to enter into their analysis. Nay, we do not even enjoy the exposition which Sir Walter makes of the progress of his mind during his literary career. It is certainly curious in a metaphysical point of view—but we still feel that it lessens the general effect, which was "one and indivisible" in our minds; and, moreover, in the talking of self, always so difficult, we do not think Sir Walter has struck upon the happiest tone.

...The part of this preface which has pleased us the least is that in which Sir Walter talks of the incognito. He says a great deal, and tells us nothing. The original cause must always have been manifest—the dread, namely, of compromising the poet's reputation: but to that which has always appeared to us the only enigmatical part of the business, Sir Walter gives no solution. We mean why, when the fame of the novelist even eclipsed, greatly in fact—in desert incalculably—that of the poet, why did he not at once declare—"They are one?"

... We now come to the annotations upon "Waverley" itself.... We cannot find it our hearts to abet Sir Walter's mis-deeds by quoting many of his notes. We do not want affidavits to the truth to nature of his incidents, still less of his characters; and, to continue the legal metaphor, the plain narrative by the counsel is far more interesting than the question-and-answer work of the witness. And in these books, he must be more than a sceptic who needs any evidence at all after he has read the statement.

... There is only one other note we shall mention, and we think Sir Walter has been highly imprudent in printing it. We allude to his answers to the accusations of his portrait of Charles Edward being highly flattered. Every one of Sir Walter's historical knowledge must know that so it is—and others, who know it too, will perhaps tell the public so one of these days. We do not allude to the doubt as to his personal courage—we believe he had his fair share of that universal male quality—but he was narrow-minded, and selfish; and his later life—especially after his marriage—*proves* him to have been brutally careless of the welfare of others, and exclusively attentive to his own.

The illustrations of these volumes are poor. It would give us great pleasure if Flora M'Ivor could see how she is represented singing at the fountain. It would have this effect from her being one of our favourite aversions. Her mind is masculine, and that is enough to ruin a woman for ever in the estimation of those who know what a woman is. Let the mind be as strong, in its pure sense, as you please—but if it lack feminine delicacy, *hélas*!

... We have done—and that as we began. *Nous chantons toujours notre refrein.*[1]—We feel convinced that the reality of the Fictions will be seriously injured by the introduction of the reality of the Facts.

10. From the *North American Review*, April 1831

The edition of Scott's novels, which we have undertaken to notice, is one which has received the final revision of the author; and he has taken advantage of it to communicate to the world historical facts, on which the incidents and characters in his works are founded. We can well imagine that he did this with a sort of triumph; for it shows that he drew from nothing but the ocean-spring of his own imagination. A few notes relative to matters of fact, are acceptable enough as illustrations; but the traditions which he brings forward as containing the

---

1 Hélas: "alas"; nous chantons toujours notre refrein: "we always sing our refrain."

suggestions of such characters as Meg Merrilies,[1] Madge Wildfire,[2] and others, evidently would not help a poor fancy, and would do little more than embarrass a strong one. Altogether we think they might as well have been reserved; for such an air of vivid reality attaches to his descriptions, that we think all his events and characters as if they had really existed. We are rather vexed at being told, on the best authority, that they are nothing more than life-like fictions; we almost say as Bentley did of Horace,[3] "Yea, if he were now here and swore it, I would not believe him."

In Waverley, there is little taken from tradition, though the whole story, otherwise loosely constructed, is held together by that thread of history which is known to all. The Chevalier is a historical character; a young prince, who believed that his father had the same right to his kingdom that others have to their estates; and who, if he had been told at the moment of invasion that the majority of the nation had a right, and were disposed to reject him, would have replied, that this question was the one to be decided. The author has painted the character of this young prince in bright colors, and the evidence of facts bears him out in so doing. It is not surprising that a dethroned and discrowned sovereign, or one who has seen that hope, which is brighter than a crown, deferred and destroyed, should fall into excesses in exile, poverty and humiliation, to which, in better days, he was a stranger. This was evidently the case with Charles Edward. In the days of Waverley, he was a brave and romantic young adventurer, who, so long as his prosperity lasted, possessed the attachment of all about him, but who, as usual, found enough to act the hyæna as soon as he was fallen. The evidence of Dr. King[4] against him, is that of a disappointed partisan, who deserted his cause. If he were as spiritless and enervated as he is often represented, it seems difficult to account for his return to England in 1759, which seems to have been putting his head into the lion's mouth. Historians do not mention this last and most hopeless endeavor; but Dr. King testifies, that Charles Edward actually visited London in disguise; and we remember a conversation in Boswell's Tour to the Hebrides,[5] in which a chieftan stated to Dr. Johnson, that the Chevalier was at that time in England. The romance of Redgauntlet is founded on this incident, which involved no serious conse-

---

1   Character in Scott's novel *Guy Mannering* (1815).
2   Character in Scott's novel *The Heart of Midlothian* (1818).
3   Richard Bentley (1662-1742), English theologian and classicist, editor of the works of Horace.
4   Dr. William King (1685-1763), memoirist.
5   James Boswell traveled to his native Scotland with his friend, Samuel Johnson, and published *Journal of a Tour to the Hebrides* (1785).

quences. We have no doubt, then, that Charles Edward, though afterwards miserably changed, was in youth what Scott describes him.

This is the character in which the novelist was aided by the history of the times, and it strikes every reader as precisely the one in which no such aid was needed. It might have been drawn by a very inferior hand. But the Baron of Bradwardine, with his pedantry and ancestral vanity, so oddly mingled with good sense, courage, and generous feeling; Fergus, whose noble bearing on the memorable trial, makes us forget how fiery and unreasonable he had been; Evan, whose attachment to his chieftain had become a part of his nature; Baillie Macwheeble, who pauses in the moment of capture, to set down a "sma' minute" to make matters sure; the high-souled and lovely Flora; the equally lovely and gentle Rose, are all creations of the author's genius. It seems to us, that the want of interest complained of in the character of Waverley, arises from its truth to nature. What more natural, than that one educated as he had been, should be acted upon by the force of circumstances? They know little of human nature, who think that such a character cannot have much that is high and manly to redeem its failings and errors.

... And no doubt many a narrative might be drawn to the letter from real life, which critics would pronounce decidedly unnatural, for the same reason which makes a French connoisseur think a tragedy of Addison more natural than Shakespeare's; because he has an idea of what nature requires firmly fixed in his mind, and compares every thing with this in preference to real life, thinking that if it be not nature, it is something better than nature....

... At some future time we may resume the subject, and if we do nothing more, may save some readers the trouble of picking out the information which Scott has given with respect to the materials which have suggested his scenes and characters. All such information only shows how little he needs to borrow, or rather how much he overpays; for whenever he takes a scene from history, he repairs its faded colors, sets it in a proper light, and gives it a force and reality which it never had before.

For this reason, among others, we are glad to see this edition. Such works should be in a cheap and accessible form; families may read them with instruction as well as pleasure; we lament the want of discrimination amounting to folly, which sets down all works that bear the name of novels as if they came under the same description, and warns us against reading novels as if they were not as various in moral and intellectual character as all other productions of the mind. There are novels which have an extensive circulation among us, and are not a little admired by the very young, which are vile as respects moral sentiment, and contemptible in their literary pretensions; those who degrade Scott to the level of such writers not only libel him, but they injure the cause which they profess to have at heart; for some novels will be read, and if they tell their children that such works are all alike, their children will be as likely to choose the worse as the better, believing that equal injustice is done to all by such sweeping condemnation.... It is like the French revolutionary practice of taking off the prisoner, and investigating the merits of his sentence at the next convenient time.

One thing we would suggest to all concerned in publishing future editions of these novels. Nothing can be more unsatisfactory than the prints which they afford us. When we see a sketch of a scene, which has impressed itself on our minds like those of Shakespeare and Scott, we are sure to be disappointed; for, however good in itself, it is not what we expected and wished to see. Let any one look at the prints of Nicol Jarvie with his red-hot coulter, or Duncan of Knockdunder at the table, and he will feel that such attempts are provoking; these poor efforts to represent the scene, only serve to disturb our vivid imaginations. Any one who wishes to illustrate these novels, should give representations of the scenes described in them; the sketch of the Grassmarket in this edition, is worth all the rest of the prints put together; it is not every one who can visit Rob Roy's cave, and millions would be grateful to any artist who should furnish such views, to give compactness and unity in their minds to the author's local descriptions.

Appendix B: The Union of 1707

1. Jonathan Swift, "Verses Said to Be Written on the Union (1707)," *The Works of Dr Jonathan Swift, Dean of St Patrick's Dublin*, vol. 7 (Edinburgh: G. Hamilton, J. Balfour, & L. Hunter, 1757)

The Queen[1] has lately lost a part
Of her *entirely-English* heart,
For want of which, by way of botch,
She piec'd it up again with Scotch.
Bless'd revolution, which creates
Divided hearts, united states!
See how the double nation lies;
Like a rich coat with skirts of frize:
As if a man in making posies
Should bundle thistles up with roses.
Who ever yet a union saw
Of kingdoms without faith or law?
Henceforward let no statesman dare
A kingdom to a ship compare;
Lest he should call our commonweal
A vessel with a double keel;
Which, just like ours, new rigg'd and mann'd,
And got about a league from land,
By change of wind to leeward side,
The pilot knew not how to guide.
So tossing faction will o'erwhelm
Our crazy double-bottom'd realm.

2. From Daniel Defoe, *A Tour Thro' the Whole Island of Great Britain* (1724-27) (London: D. Browne et al., 1761)

[Katherine Penovich, in "From 'Revolution Principles' to Union: Daniel Defoe's Intervention in the Scottish Debate," calls Defoe "England's primary pro-Union pamphleteer" (232). She notes that Defoe left London in September, 1706, "posing and for the most part passing as an English businessman in search of economic opportunity in Edinburgh"—a necessary disguise as relations between Scotland and England had "deteriorated into rash belligerence" (228). The real

---

1 Queen Anne (1665-1714) of England, Scotland, and Ireland.

purpose of his trip, however, according to Penovich, was to "advance the cause of the Union" (228). He traveled in Scotland for fifteen months, writing essays "in support of the treaty both before and after its ratification, gathering intelligence for the English ministry and materials for his ... *History of the Union of Great Britain*" (228). In addition, Murray Pittock contends that in his travels through Scotland and in his *Tour*, Defoe "stoked" Scottish fears "of being alienized and marooned on the periphery of Britain"(*Inventing and Resisting Britain*, 31). Indeed, at the time, writers who opposed the union, including Spreul, Black, and Fletcher, charged that Defoe and others hired by the English government in London "grossly exaggeraged the benefits of the English trade" (Lenman, *An Economic History of Modern Scotland 1660-1976*, 56). In his biography of Defoe, Scott wrote that not surprisingly Defoe was no "great favorite in Scotland: ... it is not wonderful that, where almost the whole nation was decidedly averse to the union, a character like De Foe, sent thither to promote it by all means, direct and indirect, should be regarded with dislike, and even exposed to the damage of assassination...." (qtd. in P. Scott, *Walter Scott and Scotland*, 76).]

Before I describe, in my own Way, this frightful Country, it is fit to observe that *Scotland* may be divided into four Districts, which I have not seen any of our Geographers do before me; yet, I believe, may not be an improper Measurement for such as would form a just idea of the Whole in their Minds:

1. The *South-Land*, or that Part of *Scotland* South of the River *Tay*, drawing a Line from the *Tay*, about *Perth*, to *Lochlomond*, and down to *Dunbarton*, and the Bank of *Clyde*.
2. The *Middle*, or *Midland*, being all the Country from the *Tay* and the *Loughlomond*, North to the Lake of *Ness* and *Aber*, including a long Slope to the South, taking in the Western *Highland* of *Argyle* and *Lorn*, and the Isles of *Isla* and *Jura*.
3. The *Northland*, being all the Country beyond *Inverness*, and the *Lough*, or River *Ness*, North, drawing the Line over the narrow Space of *Glengary*, between the *Ness* and *Aber*, and bounded by them both from the Eastern to the Western Sea.
4. The *Islands*, being all the Western and Northern Islands, the *Hebrides*, *Sky*, *Orkneys*, and other Isles of *Shetland*.

According to this Description, having passed the Bridge over the River *Ness*, I am entered on the third Division of *Scotland*, call'd the *Northland*.... It must be owned, here are but few Towns; the People live, dispersed in Clans, under a kind of Vassalage, submitting to their Lords as their lawful Monarchs, and many of them acknowledge no other; tho' this too is in a manner got over, and the Clans are less dependent on their Chiefs, than they used to be, by virtue of an Act of Parliament made for that purpose.

Their Employment is chiefly Hunting, for their Food; though they also breed large Quantities of Black Cattle, with which they pay their Lairds, or Leaders, the Rent of the Lands. These Cattle are driven annually to *England* to be sold, and are bought up chiefly in the Counties of *Norfolk*, *Suffolk*, and *Essex*; as I have mentioned in several Places in my *Tour*....

In our attempt to come down to the Southward by the Coast of *Tayne*, and the Shire of *Ross*, we should have been extremely disappointed, and perhaps have been obliged to get a Ship or Bark, to have carried us round the Isle of *Sky* into *Lochaber*, had it not been for the extraordinary Courtesy of some of the Gentlemen of the Country ...

We have nothing now remaining for a full Survey of *Scotland*, but the Western Part of the middle Division of it; and this, though a large Country, yet affords not an equal Variety with the Eastern Part of the same Division.

To traverse the Remainder of this Country, I must begin upon the *Upper Tay*, as we may justly call it, where I left off, when I turned away East; and here we have, in especial manner, the Countries of *Badenach*, *Athol*, and *Braidalbin*: this is an hilly Country properly; but as it is watered by the *Tay*, and many other pleasant Rivers, which fall into it, there are several fruitful Valleys interspersed among the Hills; nor are even the *Highlands* themselves, or the *Highlanders* the Inhabitants, any thing so wild, untaught, or untractable, as we have been made to believe; and as are to be found in the North-land Division, that is to say, in *Strathnavern*, *Ross*, *Tayne*, &c. ...

As I have given Accounts of several public Charities, and other laudable Institutions, in the Southern Parts of *Britain*, it would be inexcusable not to mention the Society in *Scotland* for propagating Christian Knowledge in the *Highlands*, it being one of the worthiest Designs of the present Age, ... and as it will comprise a Description of the said *Highlands*, and of the *Scots* Islands, we cannot insert it in a more proper Place. It is comprehended in a Letter, written *June* 1739, from a Gentleman, who is a great Encourager of this noble Institution, to his Friend; and is as follows:

The Extent of the *Highlands* of *Scotland* is much greater than has commonly been imagined. From the *Mull* of *Kintyre* to *Faro-head* in *Strathnavern* is more than 200 Miles in a strait Line from South to North; and from *Faro-head* to *John o'Grot's* House, is above 60 Miles along the North and Northern Coast of the Continent.

Besides, there is a vast Number of inhabited Islands, of which some are both large and populous: for Instance; *Jura* is 24 Miles Long; *Isla* 16; *Mull* 24; *Sky* 48; *Long Island*, comprehending *Bara*, *Southuist*, *Northuist*, and *Lewis*; 100 and many others, from two to twelve Miles in Length. The Isles of *Orkney* and *Zetland* [Shetland] are to be considered by themselves; for to *Orkney* alone belong 33 inhabited Islands, one of which is 24 Miles, and another 12, in Length. In *Zetland* there are about 30 inhabited Islands, some of which are six, others seven Miles long. Many of these Islands lie at considerable Distances from the Continent, and from one another, and are in Extent about one half of *Scotland*.

In this large Track of Country Ignorance and Superstition greatly prevail: in some Places, the Remains even of Paganism are still to be found; and in many others, the Reformation from Popery has never yet obtained. The Parishes where Ministers are settled, are commonly of very great Extent, some 30, 40, 50 Miles long; and generally divided by impassable Mountains and Lakes; so that most of the Inhabitants, being destitute of all Means of Knowledge, and without any Schools to educate their Children, are intirely ignorant of the Principles of Religion and Viture; live in idleness and Poverty; have no Notion of Industry, or Sense of Liberty; are subject to the Command of their Popish disaffected Chieftains; who have always opposed the propagating Christian Knowledge, and the *English* Tongue, that they might with less Difficulty keep their miserable Vassals in a slavish Dependence. The poorer Sort have only the *Irish* Tongue, and little Correspondence with the civilized Parts of the Nation; and only come among them to pillage the more industrious Inhabitants. They are brought up in Principles of Tyranny and arbitrary Government; depend upon foreign Papists, as their main Support, and the native *Irish*, as their best Correspondents and Allies. This has been the source of all the Rebellions and Insurrections in that Country since the Revolution.

On the other hand, they are naturally of a quick Genius, of great bodily Strength, inured to Hardship. Their Country is commodiously situated for the noblest Fishery in the World; of which our Neighbours have made immense Profit. They have Mines and Woods, and great Quantity of Black Cattle, and vast Tracts of improveable Land; which lie waste for want of Industry in the People, and not considering the Advantage of their Situation. They are a numerous and prolific People; and, if reformed in their Principles and Manners, and usefully employed, might be made a considerable Accession of Power and Wealth to *Great Britain*. Some Clans of *Highlanders*, well instructed in the Arts of War, and well affected to the Government, would make as able and formidable a

Body for their Country's Defence, as *Great Britain*, or *Switzerland*, or any Part of *Europe*, are able to produce ...

3. From Daniel Defoe, *A Review of the State of the British Nation*, vol. 4, no. 21, 1707

Saturday, 29 March 1707
[The New Union]

... I have a long Time dwelt on the Subject of a Union; I have happily seen it transacted in the Kingdom of *Scotland*; I have seen it carry'd on there thro' innumerable Oppositions, both publick and private, peaceable and unpeaceable; I have seen it perfected there, and ratify'd, sent up to *England*, debated, oppos'd, and at last pass'd in both houses, and having obtained the Royal Assent, I have the Pleasure, just while I am writing these Lines, to hear the Guns proclaiming the happy Conjunction from *Edinburgh* Castle.

And tho' it brings an unsatisfying childish Custom in Play, and exposes me to a vain, and truly ridiculous Saying in *England*, *As the Fool thinks, &c.*, yet 'tis impossible to put the lively Sound of the Cannon just now firing, into any other Note to my Ear than the articulate Expression of UNION, UNION.

Strange power of Imagination, strange incoherence of Circumstances that fills the Mind so with the thing, that it makes even the thunder of Warlike engines cry Peace; and what is made to divide and destroy, speaks out the Language of this Glorious Conjunction!

I have hardly Room to introduce the various Contemplations of the Consequences of this mighty Transaction; 'tis a Sea of universal Improvement, every Day it discovers new Mines of Treasure, and when I launch out in the Bark of my own Imagination, I every Minute discover new Success, new Advantages, and the approaching Happiness of both Kingdoms.

Nor am I an idle Spectator here; I have told *Scotland* of Improvements in Trade, Wealth, and Shipping, that shall accrue to them on the happy Conclusion of this Affair, and I am pleas'd doubly with this, that I am like to be one of the first Men, that shall give them the Pleasure of the Experiment.

I have told them of the improvement of their Coal Trade, and 'tis their own Fault if they do not particularly engage 20 or 25 Sail of Ships immediately from England on that Work.

I have told them of the Improvement of their Salt, and I am now contracting for *English* Merchants, for Scots Salt, to the Value of above 10,000 pounds per Annum.

I have told them of Linen Manufactures, and I have now above 100 poor Families at Work, by my Procuring and Direction, for the making such Sorts of Linen, and in such Manner as never was made here before, and as no Person in the Trade will believe could be made here, till they see it.

This has been my Employment in *Scotland*, and this my Endeavour to do that Nation Service, and convince them by the Practice, that what I have said of the Union, has more Weight in it, than some have endeavour'd to perswade them.

Those, that have charged me with Missions and Commissions, from neither they nor I know who, shall blush at their Rashness, and be asham'd for reflecting on a Man, come hither on purpose to do them Good.

Have I had a hand in the Union—Have I been maltreated by the Tongues of the violent, threaten'd to be murther'd, and insulted, because I have pleaded for it, and pressed you to....

I plead no merit, I do not raise the Value of what I have done; and I know some, that are gone to *London* to sollicit the Reward of what they have had no hand in, I might have said, are gone to claim the Merit, of what I have been the single Author of—But as this has been the constant Way of the World with me, so I have no Repinings on that Account; nor am I pleading any other Merit than that I may have it wrote on my Grave, that I did my Duty in promoting the Union, and consequently the Happiness of these Nations ...

4. **"The Union." From** *The Jacobite Relics of Scotland; Being the Songs, Airs, and Legends of the Adherents to the House of Stuart*, **collected and edited by James Hogg (Edinburgh: William Blackwell; and London: T. Cadell and W. Davies, 1819)**

Now fy let us a' to the treaty,
  For there will be wonders there,
For Scotland is to be a bride, sir,
  And wed to the Earl of Stair.[1]
There's Queensberry, Seafield, and Mar, sir,
  And Mor__ton comes in, by the bye;
There's London, and Le—ven, and Weenns, sir,
  And Suth-er-land, fre-quent-ly dry.

There's Roseberry, Glasgow, and Duplin,
  And Lord Archibald Campbell, and Ross;

---

1 John Dalrymple, First Earl of Stair (1648-1707), played a key role in promoting the union, as did the men whose names follow in the poem.

The president, Francis Montgomery,
  Wha ambles like ony paced horse.
There's Johnstoun, Dan Campbell, and Ross, lad,
  Whom the court hath had still on their hench;
There's solid Pitmedden and Forgland,
  Wha design'd jumping on to the bench.

There's Ormistoun and Tillicoultrie,
  And Smollett for the town of Dumbarton;
There's Arniston, too, and Carnwathie,
  Put in by his uncle, L. Wharton;
There's Grant, and young Pennicook, sir,
  Hugh Montgomery, and Davy Dalrymple;
There's one who will surely bear bouk, sir,
  Prestongrange, who indeed is not simple.

Now the Lord bless the jimp one-and-thirty,
  If they prove not traitors in fact,
But see that their bride be well drest, sir,
  Or the devil take all the pack.
May the devil take all the hale pack, sir,
  Away on his back with a bang;
Then well may our new-buskit bridie
  For her own first wooer think lang.

Appendix C: The Jacobite Rebellion of 1745

1. Tobias Smollett, "Tears of Scotland." From *The Poetical Works of Johnson, Parnell, Gray, and Smollett*, ed. Rev. George Gilfillan (Edinburgh: James Nichol; London: James Nisbet; and Dublin: W. Robertson, 1855)

[As in his novel *Humphry Clinker* (1771), Smollett is concerned in this poem to champion the rural pleasures of the country of his birth, but the elegiac tone to this poem, written in 1746 after the failure of the Jacobite Rebellion, suggests Smollett's nationalist sympathies are yet too impassioned to allow him the more balanced perspective on the union between England and Scotland he achieves in the later work. Interestingly, Smollett sees the rebellion as a civil war, as some of the Jacobite songs of the era do as well.]

[Written in the Year 1746.]

Mourn, hapless Caledonia! mourn
Thy banish'd peace, thy laurels torn!
Thy sons, for valour long renown'd,
Lie slaughter'd on their native ground;
Thy hospitable roofs no more
Invite the stranger to the door;
In smoky ruins sunk they lie,
The monuments of cruelty.

The wretched owner sees afar
His all become the prey of war;
Bethinks him of his babes and wife,
Then smites his breast and curses life.
Thy swains are famish'd on the rocks,
Where once they fed their wanton flocks:
Thy ravish'd virgins shriek in vein;
Thy infants perish on the plain.

What boots it, then, in every clime,
Through the wide-spreading waste of Time,
Thy martial glory, crown'd with praise,
Still shone with undiminish'd blaze?

Thy towering spirit now is broke,
Thy neck is bended to the yoke.
What foreign arms could never quell,
By civil rage and rancour fell.

The rural pipe and merry lay
No more shall cheer the happy day;
No social scenes of gay delight
Beguile the dreary winter night.
No strains but those of sorrow flow,
And nought be heard but sounds of woe,
While the pale phantoms of the slain
Glide nightly o'er the silent plain.
Oh! baneful cause, oh! fatal morn,
Accursed to ages yet unborn!
The sons against their father stood,
The parent shed his children's blood.
Yet, when the rage of battle ceased,
The victor's soul was not appeased:
The naked and forlorn must feel
Devouring flames and murdering steel!

The pious mother, doom'd to death,
Forsaken wanders o'er the heath,
The bleak wind whistles round her head,
Her helpless orphans cry for bread;
Bereft of shelter, food, and friend,
She views the shades of night descend,
And, stretch'd beneath the inclement skies,
Weeps o'er her tender babes, and dies.

While the warm blood bedews my veins,
And unimpair'd remembrance reigns,
Resentment of my country's fate,
Within my filial breast shall beat;
And, spite of her insulting foe,
My sympathising verse shall flow:
Mourn, hapless Caledonia! mourn
Thy banish'd peace, thy laurels torn!

2. Songs from *The Jacobite Relics of Scotland; Being the Songs, Airs, and Legends, of the Adherents to the House of Stuart*, collected and edited by James Hogg (Edinburgh: William Blackwood; and London: T. Cadell and W. Davies, 1819)

[Jacobite songs caught the excitement of Charles Edward Stuart's coming, registered the hope that coming inspired in many that positive change was in the offing, and fueled the fire of rebellious sentiments. Those written much after the '45, such as Lady Nairne's "Charlie Is My Darling," celebrated, in Bruce Lenman's words, "certain Jacobite sentiments, but not the critical or subversive ones," during Britain's wars with France (*Jacobite Contemporary Documents*, 257). This "sentimental Jacobitism" stressed the strengths Scotland brought to Britain's defense. Pittock argues in *The Invention of Scotland* that the reinvigoration of these Jacobite songs by such folk groups as the Corries in the years leading up to the 1979 Devolution Referendum looks back beyond sentiment to the earlier purpose of the songs, as a call to arms of sorts, and a recognition that the spirit of past actions, even failed actions, can positively encourage present endeavors. While the 1979 Referendum did not pass, the 1999 one did, and Scotland's parliament once again is in place in Edinburgh.]

a. "Here's to the King, Sir"

Here's to the chieftains
Of the Scots Highland clans;
They've done it mair than ance,
    And will do't again.
        Fill up your bumpers[1] high, &c.

When you hear the trumpets sound
Tutti tatti to the drum,
Up your swords, and down your gun,
    And to the loons again.
        Fill up your bumpers high, &c.

Here's to the king o' Swedes,
Fresh laurels crown his head!
Pox on every sneaking blade
    That winna do't again!
        Fill up your bumpers high, &c.

---

1 "A cup or glass of wine, etc., filled to the brim, esp. when drunk as a toast" (*OED*).

But to make a' things right, now,
He that drinks maun fight too,
To shew his heart's upright too,
    And that he'll do't again.
        Fill up your bumpers high, &c.

b. "The King shall enjoy his own again"

There's neither Swallow, Dove, nor Dade,
Can soar more high, or deeper wade,
Or show more reasons from the stars,
What causes peace, what causes wars.
    The man in the moon
    May wear out his shoon,
By running after Charles' wain;
    But all to no end,
    For the times will never mend
Till the king shall enjoy his own again.

For forty years our royal throne
Has been his father's and his own,
Nor is there any one but he,
With right can there a sharer be;
    For who better may
    Our high sceptre sway,
Than he whose right it is to reign:
    Then look for no peace,
    For the wars will never cease
Till the king shall enjoy his own again.

Though for a time we see Whitehall[1]
With cobwebs hanging on the wall,
Instead of gold and silver bright,
That glanc'd with splendour day and night,
    With rich perfume
    In every room,
All to delight that princely train;
    These again shall be,
    When the time we see
That the king shall enjoy his own again.

---

1 Main residence of English rulers in London from 1530 to 1698, when fire
  destroyed it.

...Then far upon the northern hill,
My hope shall cast her anchor still,
Until I see some peaceful dove
Bring home the branch I dearly love;
    And there will I wait
    Till the waters abate,
Which now surround my swimming brain,
    For rejoice will never I,
    Till I hear the joyful cry,
That the king enjoys his own again.

3. Songs from *Jacobite Songs and Ballads*, ed. Gilbert S. Mac-Quoid (London: Walter Scott, 1887)

a. "Maclean's Welcome"

Come o'er the stream, Charlie, dear Charlie, brave Charlie,
    Come o'er the stream, Charlie, and dine with Maclean;
And though you be weary, we'll make your heart cheery,
    And welcome our Charlie and his loyal train.
We'll bring down the track deer, we'll bring down the black steer,
    The lamb from the bracken and doe from the glen;
The salt sea we'll harry, and bring to our Charlie,
    The cream from the bothy and curd from the pen.
    Come o'er the stream, Charlie, dear Charlie, brave Charlie,
    Come o'er the stream, Charlie, and dine with Maclean;
And though you be weary, we'll make your heart cheery,
    And welcome our Charlie and his loyal train.

And you shall drink freely the dews of Glen-Sheerly,
    That stream in the star-light when kings do not ken;
And deep be your meed of the wine that is red,
    To drink to your sire and his friend the Maclean.
    Come o'er the stream, Charlie, dear Charlie, brave Charlie,
    Come o'er the stream, Charlie, and dine with Maclean;
And though you be weary, we'll make your heart cheery,
    And welcome our Charlie and his loyal train.

If aught will invite you, or more will delight you,
    'Tis ready, a troop of our bold Highlandmen
Shall range on the heather with bonnet and feather,
    Strong arms and broad claymores three hundred and ten.

b. "Will he no come back again"

Royal Charlie's now awa,
 Safely owre the friendly main;
Mony a heart will break in twa,
 Should he ne'er come back again.
  Will you no come back again?
  Will you no come back again?
  Better lo'ed you'll never be,
  And will you no come back again?

Mony a traitor 'mang the isles
 Brak the band o' nature's law;
Mony a traitor, wi' his wiles,
 Sought to swear his life awa.
  Will he no come back again?
  Will he no come back again?
  Better lo'ed he'll never be,
  And will he no come back again?

The hills he trode were a' his ain,
 And bed beneath the birken tree;
The bush that hid him on the plain,
 There's none on earth can claim but he.
  Will he no come back again? etc.

Whene'er I hear the blackbird sing,
 Unto the e'ening sinking down,
Or merle that makes the woods to ring,
 To me they hae nae ither soun',
  Than, Will he no come back again? etc.

Mony a gallant sodger fought,
 Mony a gallant chief did fa';
Death itself were dearly bought,
 A' for Scotland's king and law.
  Will he no come back again? etc.

Sweet the lay rock's note and lang,
 Lilting wildly up the glen;
And aye the o'ercome o' the sang
 Is, "Will he no come back again?"
  Will he no come back again? etc.

c. "O'er the Water to Charlie"

Come boat me o'er, come row me o'er,
    Come boat me o'er to Charlie;
I'll gie John Ross anither bawbee[1]
    To ferry me o'er to Charlie.
        We'll o'er the water, we'll o'er the sea,
            We'll o'er the water to Charlie;
        Come weel, come woe, we'll gather and go,
            And live or die wi' Charlie.

It's weel I lo'e my Charlie's name,
    Though some there be abhor him;
But O to see Auld Nick gaun hame,
    And Charlie's faes before him!
        We'll o'er the water, etc.

I swear by moon and stars sae bright,
    And sun that glances early,
If I had twenty thousand lives,
    I'd gie them a' for Charlie.
        We'll o'er the water, etc.

I ance had sons, but now hae nane;
    I bred them toiling sairly;
And I wad bear them a' again,
    And lose them a' for Charlie;
        We'll o'er the water, we'll o'er the sea,
            We'll o'er the water to Charlie;
        Come weel, come woe, we'll gather and go,
            And live or die wi' Charlie.

4. From Henry Fielding, *The History of the Present Rebellion in Scotland* (London: Printed for M. Cooper, 1745)

[Leith Davis, in *Acts of Union*, notes that the "literary battle to write the history" of the Jacobite Rebellion was "extensive" (49), and that Fielding's journalism of the period charts his concern with readers' apathetic responses to the unrest. He recognized their willingness to be persuaded by various narratives of the rebellion, whether these were based on fact or fiction. Brian McCrea contends that "the '45

---

1   A Scottish halfpenny.

was 'the definitive event in [Fielding's] political life,' forcing him to articulate 'the old Whig principles' in reaction to the political apathy around him" (qtd. in Davis, 51). While his pamphlets and his *History*, an excerpt of which is printed below, were "typical of anti-Jacobite propaganda at that time," they also "foreshadow a later interest in the political uses of fiction" (Davis 51). Davis notes that while the subtitle of Fielding's *History* suggests the work benefitted from the eyewitness accounts of a James MacPherson, the *Caledonian Mercury*, a pro-Jacobite paper, on 28 October 1745, "claimed there 'never was an officer of the Name of Macpherson in the Prince's Army'"; this suggests that the following piece should be read with some caution, not as fact, but as a fiction that gives quite a different picture of Charles Edward Stuart's army—disciplined, adept, Catholic—than Scott's depiction of the rebels as a raggle-taggle band of poorly armed and trained warriors in *Waverley*.]

THE HISTORY of the PRESENT REBELLION in SCOTLAND
From the Departure of the Pretender's Son from *Rome*,
down to the present Time.
In which is
A full ACCOUNT of the Conduct of this Young Invader, from his first Arrival in *Scotland;* with the several Progresses he made there; and likewise a very particular RELATION of the Battle of *Preston*, with an exact List of the Slain, Wounded, and Prisoners, on both Sides.

Taken from the Relation of Mr. JAMES MACPHERSON, who was an Eye-Witness of the Whole, and who took the first Opportunity of leaving the Rebels, into whose Service he was forced, and in which he had a Captain's Commission.

* * *

The present Rebellion is a Matter of such Consequence to this Country, and must so seriously engage the Attention of every *Briton* who hath the least Regard either to his own real Good, or the Welfare of his Posterity, that I shall make no Apology for the present Undertaking; in which my Reader may be assured, that as the utmost Pains have been taken to procure the best Intelligence, so he may safely rely on the Truth of the Facts related.

The Pretender's eldest Son *Charles*, who is now in the twenty-fifth Year of his Age, having, in the Beginning of the Summer, taken a solemn Leave of his Father at *Rome*, and in the Presence of the Pope and Cardinals, having made a solemn Vow that he would never forsake his Religion; set out with one *Patrick Graham* his Confessor, the Marquis of *Tullibardine*, General *Mackdonell*, and some other Attendants, amongst which is one Mr. *Fisher*, a person who some Years ago murdered his Friend Mr. *Darby* in the Temple, for which he hath a Pardon under the Pretender's Sign Manual, and is advanced to the Post of Major in the Highland Army.

Having past thro' *France* by Land, and visited the *French* King in his Camp, from whom he obtained five Independent Companies, besides a large Quantity of Arms, and a Ship of War, together with further Promises of future Assistance, he departed for *Brest*; where the aforesaid Soldiers and Arms being put on board, in the Beginning of *August* they sailed out of that Harbour; the Pretender's Son himself, together with those Attendants who accompanied him from *Rome*, being embarked in a small Vessel.

They had not been long at Sea before they met with one of our Men of War, between whom and the *Frenchman* a very sharp Engagement ensued; in which both Ships suffered extremely, and the latter was so entirely disabled, that she was obliged to put back into *Brest*.

During this Engagement, the small Vessel which carried the Pretender's Son escaped, and made immediately for the Western Coast of *Scotland*. No *English* Man of War being at that Time in those Seas, they cruized for some Days off the Islands of *Bara* and *Ust*, and at last stood in for the Coast of *Lochaber*, and on the 10th of *August* in the Evening landed between the Islands of *Mull* and *Skie*.

One *Macpherson*, whose Hut stood about a Mile from the Seashore, seeing these People land, had the Curiosity to advance towards them, and was told by one of his Countrymen that came with them who they were, and particularly, that the young Man was the Prince of *Wales* and the Son of his King. *Charles* presently came up to him, and giving him a *French* Pistole, asked him if he would not bear Arms for his King and Country, to which *Macpherson* readily answered he would, and then *Charles* very graciously held forth his Hand for him to kiss, which he accordingly did.

The young Pretender then threw himself on the Ground, and kiss'd it, after which his Confessor cut a Turf and presented it to him, saying, *In the Name of the most holy and infallible Pope, I present thee this as Regent for thy Father, and do hereby, by virtue of the full Powers to me delegated, invest the most puissant* James III. *with the Possession and Rule of the Kingdom of* Great Britain; *which he is to hold at the Will and Pleasure of the Holy See. Dost thou therefore, in his Name, accept the Government of these Realms, on the Condition of fighting the Cause of our holy Mother the Church, to the utter Extirpation of the Persons of Hereticks; and wilt thou persevere manfully in the same, 'till the Blood of Hereticks shall be washed away from the Face of the Earth?*

The Young Pretender on his Knees received the Turf from the Hand of his Confessor, and faithfully promised in his Father's Name to fulfil all that had been enjoined him....

Charles spent three Days in visiting the several Huts of these Highlanders; amongst whom he distributed his Money very liberally, so that by the End of the third Day, he had enlisted upwards of 70 in his Party. He delivered them Arms, (for he had Arms with him for 500 Men only) a sufficient Number for 6500 having miscarried in the *French* Man of War.

On the 14th of *August* the Marquis of *Tullibardin*, and two other of the *Scottish* Chiefs returned with a Body of above 300 of the Clans, who were immediately disposed into a Regiment, and called, *The Royal Regiment of Highland Guards.* The Command of which was given to the Marquis, one *Mackay* was made Lieutenant Colonel, and Mr. *Fisher* Major. The Captains and inferior Officers were chosen out of the Clans.

This Regiment was no sooner formed, than the utmost Diligence was made use of to discipline them, and instruct them in the Use of Arms. Nor was much less Diligence used by the Confessor, assisted by another Priest whose Name was *Fraser*, to instruct them in the *Roman* Catholic Religion, and this with such Success, that upwards of 200 of these ignorant People were converted in less than a Fortnight.

The Government no sooner received Advice of the landing of the Pretender's Son in *Scotland*, than immediately a Proclamation was published, with a Reward of *L.30000* for the apprehending him. And at the same Time, an Order was issued for all the Officers of his Majesty's Land Forces in *Great Britain* to repair to their respective Posts.

The Regiments which at that Time lay in the North were Colonel *Gardiner's* and *Hamilton's* Dragoons, together with the Regiments of Foot of *Lascelles, Murray, Guise,* and *Lee.* These were ordered to march directly towards *Stirling*, where they were to encamp under the Command of Lieutenant General Sir *John Cope.*

... By the 20th of *August,* before which time the two other Chiefs were returned with their Clans, the Army of the Rebels were increased to the Number of 1200. They then proceeded to form two other Regiments, one of which was commanded by General *Mackdonell,* and the other by the Pretender's Son himself.

On the 22d, having made themselves Tents, they marched a few Miles, and encamped on a Hill, (for before this Time they kept in separate Companies, at some Distance from each other, in order to avoid Discovery) a Strategem which had so good an Effect, that whoever recollects the Accounts which the News Papers gave us of the first Landing of the Pretender, must remember with what Incertainty they spoke of a few Men being landed in the West of *Scotland*, who were sometimes Gentlemen from *Ireland* hunting, and sometimes were quite vanished, every subsequent Account actually contradicting the former; so that few except the most credulous, gave any Belief to it....

However, the Alarm of their Success daily encreasing in *England*, and the Numbers which from Time to Time joined them giving a very just Cause of Uneasiness to our Ministry here, the General receiv'd peremptory Orders to march forwards, which he did; and in the mean Time the Rebels gave him the slip, and on the 29th march'd towards *Perth*, the Duke of that Name leading the Van, *Charles* marching in the Centre, and General *Macdonell* in the Rear. This Evening they were join'd by Lord *George Murray*, Brother of the Duke of *Athol*, and by three other Gentlemen, one of whom is Brother to an Earl.

On the 30th, they marched no more than three Miles, on Advice that the King's Forces, under the Command of his Excellency Lieutenant-General Sir *John Cope*, was marching towards them. However, this afterwards proved a false Rumour. *Charles* express'd great Bravery on this Occasion; and shewing a Medal which he wore on his Right Arm, said, *he feared nothing while he had the Protection of that holy Relique.* And indeed the greater Part of the Army, who were now Catholics (so well had the Priests, who were now likewise encreased in Number, bestowed their Time, and so plentifully had they bestowed their Reliques) seemed to rely more, some on an old Tooth, others on a Lock of Hair, and others on some such Bawble, for Protection, than on their Swords: Not that they neglected the human Means of strengthening themselves; on the contrary, they spent at least twelve Hours in every Day in the Exercise of their Arms, to their Instructions in which the few Officers they had addicted themselves incessantly. *Charles* himself was constantly busied either in this, or his Devotions; which last occupied a full third Part of his Time.

... The Duke of *Perth* summoned many of his Tenants to meet him at *Blair*, and bring with them all the Rent they owed him, on Pain of being treated with the utmost Severity. He likewise ordered as many of them as could procure Arms to furnish themselves therewith, and bring them along with them: Most of these obeyed his Summons, and produced him all the Money and Arms in their Power. But instead of discharging these poor Wretches, after they had delivered him their Rent (and some of them more than was due) he insisted on their bearing Arms in the Pretender's Cause.

... This Duke of *Perth*, notwithstanding the apparent Cruelty of this Action, is a Man of good Character, and hath formerly behaved himself like a worthy and good natur'd Gentleman: But such is the Nature of this Cause, and of the Spirit with which it is conducted; headed by a young, rash, ambitious, fiery Zealot, under the absolute

Government and Guidance of furious, enraged Priests, who breathe nothing but Blood and Desolation, and have so effectually breath'd their horrid Principles into the poor wild Wretches under their Influence and Command, that the whole Army, according to *Macpherson*, and others who have seen it, is liker to a Legion of Devils than of Men. May God confine them to their own Borders, or, if they attempt to overleap them, inspire this Nation with a Spirit sufficient soon to drive them out of her own Bowels, in which they would quickly become the most violent and mortal Disease.

... At this Time the Alarm grew very high in *London*. On the 9th, his Majesty published a Proclamation for disarming Papists and Nonjurors, and for commanding all Papists and reputed Papists to depart from the Cities of *London* and *Westminster*, and from within ten Miles from the same; and for confining Papists and reputed Papists to their Habitations, and for putting in Execution the Laws against Riots and Rioters.

And now Addresses of the most loyal and zealous Kind began to flock in from all corporate Bodies in the Kingdom, in which the City of *London*, the Court of Lieutenancy, and the whole Body of Merchants, led the Way: All these were conceived in the strongest Terms of Loyalty, and expressing a true Sense of the Dangers with which these Kingdoms were threatned by Popery and arbitrary Power. All People began to think of arming themselves in the Cause of the Public; and several Noblemen, who have since put it in Execution, took out Commissions to raise Regiments for the public Service.

... On the 13th, they again marched at Day-break, and in the Morning passed the Frith at the Ford of *Frews*, five Miles above *Stirling*. Here *Charles* attempting to give an extraordinary Instance of his Bravery, by passing the Water first, and mistaking the Ford, very narrowly escaped drowning, from which he was preserved by Lieutenant *Duncan Madson*, who at the Hazard of his own Life rescued him from the Waves.

... In the Evening, some of those who had attended the Pretender's Son into the Town, returned into the Camp, and gave an Account to the Rebels there of the Reception which *Charles* and his Friends had met with; and which (whether it arose from Fear or Favour I will not determine) was much more to his Satisfaction than he expected. Indeed, had the City been inclined to have made a vigorous Resistance, it would have been very difficult, if not impossible, for the Pretender's Forces to have taken it in any reasonable Time; especially as they daily expected a Visit from Sir *John Cope*, and who, it was said, was to have been greatly strengthened with a Regiment from the Townsmen of *Edinburgh*. This Success, therefore, (to whatever Treachery it was owing) greatly elated the whole Party, especially the Priests, who failed not to ascribe it to the Favour of Heaven, as they again deriv'd that Favour from the Prevalence of their own Prayers.

... The Rebels (as the Guards, &c.) within the Town, were now not much better supplied than those without, the Provision which the People cared to afford them being almost totally exhausted the first Day, and the neighbouring Country having before been pretty well drained by the Prudence of General *Guest*. Some of the most violent desired to be led on to the Assault of the Castle, though almost impregnable by Nature, and well furnished with Cannon, Ammunition and Men. This Attempt was too romantic and impossible, to receive any Countenance from their Commanders: And it was then with the utmost Difficulty that they were restrained from plundering the whole Town; however, the Consideration that they were their own Countrymen somewhat allayed their Fury, though it did not entirely prevent all Disorders; and many Violences were in spite of the superior Officers committed, as well on the Persons as Properties of the Inhabitants, both Men and Women; for all of whom (except those concerned in the Treachery of delivering up the Town) the Reader will have a just Compassion. God forbid that any City of *England* should ever be exposed to the same Danger, to all the Rapine and Cruelty which such a Banditti of Ruffians, when let loose by their Commanders, nay, even encouraged by them, would without Mercy commit; a Scene of Misery more easy to conceive, than pleasant to describe; and of which, without my undergoing that irksome Task, the Reader may have an adequate Idea, by perusing the History of any one popish Conquest.

About Three in the Morning the Rebels began to move, and turn'd at first Eastward and marched about a Mile in Length, then facing about to the Left they formed themselves in five Columns; in which Posture they advanced towards Sir *John Cope*, *Charles* himself taking Possession of a neighbouring Hill, from which he might survey the whole Action.

... The extreme Column of the Rebels, which were to the Right, having advanced 'till they were opposite the Cannon, which consisted only of six small Field Pieces, immediately faced about, and ran with the utmost Violence up to the Mouths of the Cannon, which by an extreme Neglect of those whose Duty it was, not however to be in the least charged on the General, never fired on them once: It was then that the brave Colonel *Gardiner* ordered his Dragoons to charge them in Flank, which Service he could not prevail on them to perform; but having given them a single Discharge of their Fire-Arms, they immediately turned about, and like Men struck with a sudden Panic, ran away.

The Colonel having in vain attempted to rally them, (as did Lord *Loudon*, who threw himself at their Head, and charged the Rebels) on a sudden quitted his Horse, and charged with the Foot, who being attacked with great Fury by the Highlanders, and seeing themselves deserted by the Horse, after having made two irregular Fires, which did very little Execution, many of them threw down their Arms, and turned their Backs to the Enemy.

All was now in general Confusion: Poor Colonel *Gardiner*, and those few brave Officers that stood their Ground, fell a Victim to the Rage of the Enemy, who finding no longer Resistance, fell to the most inhuman Butchery, with which having somewhat tired themselves, they proceeded to make Prisoners of all those, who survived the blunted Edge of their Swords ...

5. From Walter Scott, *Redgauntlet. A Tale of the Eighteenth Century* (New York: Printed by James and John Harper for Evert Duyckinck, Collins & Co., Collins & Hannay, E. Bliss & K. White, A.T. Goodrich, Wm. B. Gilley, George Long, and H.I. Megary, 1824)

[*Redgauntlet*, published ten years after *Waverley*, describes Charles Edward Stuart's final departure from Scotland. The extent to which Charles's failure to return the Stuart monarchy to power means an end not only to his cause, but also to that of Scottish nationalism, is unclear, but the tone of the ending of this novel is much bleaker than *Waverley*'s.]

... The last heir of the Stewarts leaned on Redgauntlet's arm as they walked towards the beach; for the ground was rough, and he no longer possessed the elasticity of limb and of spirit which had, twenty years before, carried him over many a Highland hill, as light as one of their native deer. His adherents followed, looking on the ground, their feelings struggling against the dictates of their reason.

... They arrived at the place of embarkation. The Prince stood a moment with folded arms, and looked around him in deep silence. A paper was then slipped into his hands—he looked at it, and said, "I find the two friends I have left at Fairladies are apprised of my destination, and propose to embark from Bowness. I presume this will not be an infringement of the conditions under which you have acted?"

"Certainly not," answered General Campbell; "they shall have all facility to join you."

"I wish, then," said Charles, "only another companion.—Redgauntlet, the air of this country is as hostile to you as it is to me. These gentlemen have made their peace, or rather they have done nothing to break it. But you—come you, and share my home where chance shall cast it. We shall never see these shores again; but we will talk of them, and of our disconcerted bull-fight."

"I follow you, sire, through life," said Redgauntlet, "as I would have followed you to death. Permit me one moment."

The Prince then looked round, and seeing the abashed countenances of his other adherents bent upon the ground, he hastened to say, "Do not think that you, gentlemen, have obliged me less because your zeal was mingled with prudence, entertained, I am sure, more on my own account, and on that of your country, than from selfish apprehensions."

He stepped from one to another, and, amid sobs and bursting tears, received the adieus of the last remnant which had hitherto supported his lofty pretensions, and addressed them individually with accents of tenderness and affection.

The General drew a little aloof, and signed to Redgauntlet to speak with him while this scene proceeded. "It is now all over," he said, "and Jacobite will be henceforward no longer a party-name. When you tire of foreign parts, and wish to make your peace, let me know. Your restless zeal alone has impeded your pardon hitherto."

"And now I shall not need it," said Redgauntlet. "I leave England for ever; but I am not displeased that you should hear my family adieus.—Nephew, come hither. In presence of General Campbell, I tell you, that though to breed you up in my own political opinions has been for many years my anxious wish, I am now glad that it could not be accomplished. You pass under the service of the reigning Monarch without the necessity of changing your allegiance—a change, however," he added, looking around him, "which sits more easy on honourable men than I could have anticipated; but some wear the badge of their loyalty on the sleeve, and others in the heart.—You will, from henceforth, be uncontrolled master of all the property of which forfeiture could not deprive your father—of all that belonged to him,—excepting this, his good sword, (laying his hand on the weapon he wore) which shall never fight for the House of Hanover; and as my hand will never draw weapon more, I shall sink it forty fathoms deep in the wide ocean. Bless you, young man. If I have dealt harshly with you, forgive me. I had set my whole desires on one point,—God knows, with no selfish purpose; and I am justly punished by this final termination of my views, for having been too little scrupulous in the means by which I pursued them—Niece, farewell, and may God bless you also!"

...The unfortunate Charles Edward had now given his last adieus to his downcast adherents. He made a sign with his hand to Redgauntlet, who came to assist him into the skiff. General Campbell also offered his assistance; the rest appearing too much affected by the scene which had taken place to prevent him.

"You are not sorry, General, to do me this last act of courtesy," said the Chevalier; "and, on my part, I thank you for it. You have taught me the principle on which men on the scaffold feel forgiveness and kindness even for their executioner.—Farewell!"

They were seated in the boat, which presently pulled off from the land. The Oxford divine broke out into a loud benediction, in terms which General Campbell was too generous to criticize at the time, or to remember afterwards;—nay, it is said, that Whig and Campbell as he was, he could not help joining in the universal Amen which resounded from the shore.

Appendix D: Scottish Folklore and Legend in Contemporary Literature

1. From James Macpherson, "The Battle of Lora." From *The Poems of Ossian*, vol. 2 (London: J.D. Dewick for Lackington, Allen, and Co., 1803)

[James Macpherson (1736-96) was born in Kingussie, Scotland, and published *Fingal, an Ancient Epic Poem in Six Books*, in 1762. Macpherson claimed the work was a translation of the ancient Scottish bard, Ossian; however, the manuscripts he said were originals were proven in 1805 by the Scottish novelist Henry Mackenzie and others to be instead doctored versions of Gaelic poems. Despite Macpherson's duplicity, *Poems by Ossian*, of which "The Battle of Lora" is one, were extremely popular throughout Britain, but especially in Scotland where the work engendered national pride.]

The
BATTLE of LORA:
A POEM.

ARGUMENT

Fingal, at his return from Ireland, after he had expelled Swaran from that kingdom, made a feast to all his heroes: he forgot to invite Ma-Ronnan and Aldo, two chiefs, who had not been along with him in his expedition. They resented his neglect; and went over to Erragon, king of Sora, a country of Scandinavia, the declared enemy of Fingal. The valor of Aldo soon gained him a great reputation in Sora; and Lorma, the beautiful wife of Erragon, fell in love with him. He found means to escape with her, and to come to Fingal, who resided then in Selma, on the western coast. Erragon invaded Scotland, and was slain in battle by Gaul the son of Morni, after he had rejected terms of peace offered him by Fingal. In this war Aldo fell, in a single combat, by the hands of his rival Erragon, and the unfortunate Lorma afterward died of grief.

Son of the distant land, who dwellest in the secret cell! do I hear the sounds of thy grove? or, is it thy voice of songs? The torrent was loud in my ear; but I heard a tuneful voice. Dost thou praise the chiefs of thy land; or the spirits of the wind? But, lonely dweller of rocks! look thou on that heathy plain. Thou seest green tombs, with their rank, whistling grass: with their stones of mossy heads. Thou seest them, son of the rock, but Ossian's eyes have failed.

A mountain-stream comes roaring down, and sends its waters round a green hill. Four mossy stones, in the midst of withered grass, rear their heads on the top. Two trees, which the storms have bent, spread their whistling branches around. This is thy dwelling, Erragon; this thy narrow house: the sound of thy shells have been long forgot in Sora. Thy shield is become dark in thy hall. Erragon, king of ships! chief of distant Sora! how hast thou fallen on our mountains? How is the mighty low? Son of the secret cell! dost thou delight in songs? Hear the battle of Lora. The sound of its steel is long since past. So thunder on the darkened hill roars, and is no more. The sun returns with his silent beams. The glittering rocks, and green heads of the mountains smile.

The bay of Cona received our ships from Erin's rolling waves. Our white sheets hung loose to the masts. The boisterous winds roared behind the groves of Morven. The horn of the king is sounded; the deer start from their rocks. Our arrows flew in the woods. The feast of the hill is spread. Our joy was great on our rocks, for the fall of the terrible Swaran. Two heroes were forgot at our feast. The rage of their bosoms burned. They rolled their red eyes in secret. The sigh bursts from their breasts. They were seen to talk together, and to throw their spears on the earth. They were two dark clouds, in the midst of our joy; like pillars of mist on the settled sea. They glitter to the sun, but the mariners fear a storm.

"Raise my white sails," said Ma-ronnan, "raise them to the winds of the west. Let us rush, O Aldo! through the foam of the northern wave. We are forgot at the feast: but our arms have been red in blood. Let us leave the hills of Fingal, and serve the king of Sora. His countenance is fierce. War darkens round his spear. Let us be renowned, O Aldo, in the battles of other lands!"

They took their swords, their shields of thongs. They rushed to Lumar's resounding bay. They came to Sora's haughty king, the chief of bounding steeds. Erragon had returned from the chace. His spear was red in blood. He bent his dark face to the ground; and whistled as he went. He took the strangers to his feasts; they fought and conquered in his wars.

Aldo returned with his fame towards Sora's lofty walls. From her tower looked the spouse of Erragon, the humid, rolling eyes of Lorma. Her yellow hair flies on the wind of the ocean. Her white breast heaves, like snow on heath; when the gentle winds arise, and slowly move it in the light. She saw young Aldo, like the beam of Sora's setting sun. Her soft heart sighed. Tears filled her eyes. Her white arm supported her head. Three days she sat within the hall, and covered her grief with joy. On the fourth, she fled with the hero along the troubled sea. They came to Cona's mossy towers, to Fingal, king of spears.

"Aldo of the heart of pride!" said Fingal, rising in wrath: "shall I defend thee from the rage of Sora's injured king? Who will now receive my people into their halls! Who will give the feast of strangers, since Aldo, of the little soul, has dishonoured my name in Sora? Go to thy hills, thou feeble hand! Go: hide thee in caves. Mournful is the battle we must fight, with Sora's gloomy king. Spirit of the noble Trenmor! when will Fingal cease to fight? I was born in the midst of battles, and my steps must move in blood to the tomb. But my hand did not injure the weak, my steel did not touch the feeble in arms. I behold thy tempests, O Morven! which will overturn my halls; when my children are dead in battle, and none remains to dwell in Selma. They will the feeble come, but they will not know my tomb. My renown is only in song. My deeds shall be as a dream to future times!"

His people gathered around Erragon, as the storms round the ghost of night; when he calls them, from the top of Morven, and prepares to pour them on the land of the stranger. He came to the shore of Cona. He sent his bard to the king; to demand the combat of thousands; or the land of many hills! Fingal sat in his hall with the friends of his youth around him. The young heroes were at the chace, far distant in the desert. The grey-haired chiefs talked of other times; of the actions of their youth ...

... The king of Morven sat on his hill. The sun-beam of battle flew on the wind. The friends of his youth are near, with all their waving locks of age. Joy rose in the hero's eyes when he beheld his sons in war; when he saw us amidst the lightning of swords, mindful of the deeds of our fathers. Erragon came on, in his strength, like the roar of a winter stream. The battle falls around his steps: death dimly stalks along by his side!

"Who comes," said Fingal, "like the bounding roe, like the hart of echoing Cona? His shield glitters on his side. The clang of his armour is mournful. He meets with Erragon in the strife! Behold the battle of the chiefs! It is like the contending of ghosts in a gloomy storm. But fallest thou, son of the hill, and is thy white bosom stained with blood? Weep, unhappy Lorma, Aldo is no more!" The king took the spear of his strength. He was sad for the fall of Aldo. He bent his deathful eyes on the foe; but Gaul met the king of Sora. Who can relate the fight of the chiefs? The mighty stranger fell!

"Sons of Cona!" Fingal cried aloud, "stop the hand of death. Mighty was he that is low! Much is he mourned in Sora! The stranger will come towards his hall, and wonder why it is so silent. The king is fallen, O stranger. The joy of his house is ceased. Listen to the sound of his woods. Perhaps his ghost is murmuring there! But he is far distant, on Morven, beneath the sword of a foreign foe." Such were the words of Fingal, when the bard raised the song of peace. We stopped our uplifted swords. We spared the feeble foe. We laid Erragon in a tomb. I raised the voice of grief. The clouds of night came rolling down. The ghost of Erragon appeared to some. His face was cloudy and dark; an half-formed sigh is in his breast. "Blest be thy soul, O king of Sora! thine arm was terrible in war!" ...

2. From Elizabeth Hamilton, *The Cottagers of Glenburnie* (Edinburgh: J. Ballantyne, 1808)

[Ian Duncan, in *Scott's Shadow: The Novel in Romantic Edinburgh*, finds Hamilton's novel to be "exemplary of the Scottish school of domestic national fiction" (79). Certainly, in his "A Postscript, that should have been a Preface," the last chapter of *Waverley*, Scott acknowledges that Hamilton's novel treats a similar subject, though it is "confined to the rural habits of Scotland, of which it has given a picture with striking and impressive fidelity" (452). Duncan notes that *The Cottagers of Glenburnie* was the "first Scottish novel published in Edinburgh." Its realistic Scottish setting and depiction of "regional manners" establish it as one of the earliest examples of "national fiction before *Waverley*" (71).]

CHAP. VI.
Domestic Sketches.—Picture of Glenburnie.—View of a Scotch Cottage in the last century.

... They had not proceeded many paces, until they were struck with admiration at the uncommon wildness of the scene, which now opened to their view. The rocks which seemed to guard the entrance of the Glen, were abrupt and savage, and approached so near each other, that one could suppose them to have been riven asunder, to give a passage to the clear stream which flowed between them. As they advanced, the hills receded on either side, making room for meadows, and corn fields, through which the rapid burn pursued its way, in many a fantastic maze.
... The road which winded along the foot of the hills, on the north side of the Glen, owed as little to art as any country road in the kingdom. It was very narrow, and much encumbered by loose stones, brought down from the hills above, by the winter torrents.
Mrs Mason and Mary were so enchanted by the change of scenery, which was incessantly unfolding to their view, that they made no complaints of the slowness of their progress, nor did they much regret being

obliged to stop a few minutes at a time, where they found so much to amuse and to delight them. But Mr Stewart had no patience at meeting with obstructions, which with a little pains could have been so easily obviated; and as he walked by the side of the car, expatiated upon the indolence of the people of the Glen, who, though they had no other road to the market, could contentedly go on from year to year, without making an effort to repair it. "How little trouble would it cost," said he, "to throw the smaller of these loose stones in these holes and ruts, and to remove the larger ones to the side, where they would form a fence between the road and the hill. There are enough of idle boys in the Glen to effect all this, by working at it for one hour a week during the summer. But then their fathers must unite in setting them to work; and there is not one in the Glen, who would not sooner have his horses lamed, and his carts torn to pieces, than have his son employed in a work that would benefit his neighbours as much as himself!"

... Our party drove off, and at every turning of the road, expressed fresh admiration at the increasing beauty of the scene. Towards the top of the Glen, the hills seemed to meet; the rocks became more frequent, and more prominent, sometimes standing naked and exposed, and sometimes peeping over the tops of the rowan tree and weeping birch, which grew in great abundance on all the steepy banks. At length the village appeared in view. It consisted of about twenty or thirty thatched cottages, which, but for their chimneys, and the smoke that issued from them, might have passed for so many stables or hog sties, so little had they to distinguish them as the abodes of man. That one horse, at least, was the inhabitant of every dwelling, there was no room to doubt, as every door could not only boast its dunghill, but had a small cart tilted up on its end directly before it; which cart, though often broken, and always dirty, seemed ostentatiously displayed as a proof of wealth.

... At length Mrs MacClarty came in, all out of breath, followed by her daughters, two big girls of eleven and thirteen years of age. She welcomed Mrs Mason and her friends with great kindness, and made many apologies for being in no better order to receive them; but said, that both her gudeman and her thought that her cusine would have staid at Gowan-brae till after the fair, as they were too far off at Glenburnie to think of going to it; though it would, to be sure, be only natural for Mrs Mason to like to see all the grand sights that were to be seen there; for, to be sure, she would gang many places before she saw the like. Mrs Mason smiled, and assured her she would have more pleasure in looking at the fine view from her door, than in all the sights at the fair.

"Ay, it's a bonny piece of corn to be sure," returned Mrs MacClarty, with great simplicity; "but then, what with the trees, and rocks, and wimplings o' the burn, we have nae room to make parks of ony size."

"But were your trees, and rocks, and wimplings of the burn, all removed," said Mr Stewart, "then your prospect would be worth looking at, Mrs MacClarty! would it not?"

Though Mr Stewart's irony was lost upon the good-woman, it produced a laugh among the young folks, which she, however, did not resent, but immediately fell to busying herself in sweeping in the hearth, and adding turf to the fire, in order to make the kettle boil for tea.

"I think," said Miss Mary, "you might make your daughters save you that trouble;" looking at the two girls, who stood all this time leaning against the wall.

"O poor things," said their mother, "they have not been used to it; they have eneugh of time for wark yet."

"Depend upon it," said Mrs Mason, "young people can never begin too soon; your eldest daughter there will soon be as tall as yourself."

"Indeed she's a stately growth," said Mrs MacClarty, pleased with the observation; "and Jenny there is little ahint her; but what are they but bairns yet for a' that! In time, I warrant, they'll do weel eneugh. Meg can milk a cow as weel as I can do, when she likes."

"And does she not always like to do all she can?" said Mrs Mason.

"O, we manna complain," returned the mother, "she does weel eneugh."

The gawky girl now began to rub the wall up and down with her dirty fingers; but happily the wall was of too dusky a hue to be easily stained. And here let us remark the advantage which our cottages in general possess over those of our southern neighbours; theirs being so whitened up, that no one can have the comfort of laying a dirty hand upon them, without leaving the impression; an inconvenience which reduces people in that station, to the necessity of learning to stand upon their legs, without the assistance of their hands; whereas in our country, custom has rendered the hands in standing at a door, or in going up or down a stair, no less necessary than the feet, as may be plainly seen in the finger marks which meet one's eyes in all directions.

Some learned authors have indeed adduced this propensity, in support of the theory which teaches, that mankind originally walked upon all fours, and that standing erect is an outrage on the laws of nature; while others, willing to trace it to a more honourable source, contend, that as the propensity evidently prevails chiefly among those, who are conscious of being able to transmit the colour of their hands to the objects on which they place them, it is decidedly an impulse of genius, and in all probability derived from our Pictish ancestors, whose passion for painting is well known to have been great and universal.

3 From Anne MacVicar Grant, *Essays on the Superstitions of the Highlanders of Scotland: To Which Are Added, Translations from the Gaelic; and Letters Connected With Those Formerly Published*, vol. 1 (London: Longman, Hurst, Rees, Orme, and Brown, 1811)

[In his "A Postscript, which should have been a Preface," Scott recognizes Anne Grant's *Essays on the Superstitions of the Highlanders of Scotland*, published in 1811, as a precursor, albeit non-fiction, of *Waverley* in its rendering of "traditional records" (452). Ina Ferris, in "Melancholy, Memory, and the 'Narrative Situation' of History in Post-Enlightenment Scotland" suggests that, like *Waverley*, Grant's essays call attention not to a Jacobite theme but to the Highland Clearances as a theme, "the problem not so much of past as of passing things" (82), and finds that "a similar sense of break and attenuation in the social bond informs" her work as well as his. Like Scott, Grant recognizes the necessity of progress but is concerned with the cost of exile from one's home; Ferris suggests that "the historical genres emerged out of that tension" (83).]

ESSAY I
On the Superstitions of the Highlands, their Origin, and Tendency.

When nations, in the progress of knowledge and refinement, have arrived at a high state of cultivation, and are thus enabled to take extensive views of life and manners, from the height to which they have attained, they begin to look with a mixture of contempt and self-gratulation on those wider regions still inhabited by tribes, as rude and barbarous as their own ancestors have been at a remoter period.

Among others, slowly advancing in gradual progression from rudeness to refinement, we find much to excite our wonder and compassion; yet often feel ourselves compelled to stoop from all the pride of science, to bestow our tribute of esteem or admiration on the talents that sometimes illuminate the gloom of ignorance, or the mild affections and faithful attachments that sometimes endear the abodes of humble simplicity.

The comparison between an uncivilized and highly illuminated people, must certainly be very much in favour of the latter. We should cultivate the garden to very little purpose, if its productions were not more beautiful and more abundant than those of the wilderness. Yet the natural taste that leads us to wander and to speculate with a kind of nameless pleasure among the wildest recesses of the forest or the fell, does not abate, but exalt our delight in the fertility and beauty of cultivated scenes: On the contrary, the pleasure is heightened by contrast.

The analogy betwixt the sensations I have been describing, and the intellectual pleasure derived from contemplating the human mind in its native state, opposed to that to which the highest culture can exalt it, holds very closely. Were we to land on some savage island, where the foot of man has never trod, nor his hand removed incumbrance or opened access, we should be harrassed with fears and perplexed with intricacies. The tangled luxuriancy of a thorny wild would obstruct our path; and from the gloom of the impenetrable thicket, the lurking tiger, or the envenomed serpent would seem ready to spring; and at least haunt the startled imagination.

... But among a people, whose progress towards civilization, is so far advanced, that the feelings of the heart, and the powers of the imagination have been called forth, preceding the light of science, as the morning star and the dusky dawn do the effulgence of the sun ... the mind finds something to dwell on that is soothing and satisfactory. We contemplate nations in the state, with a feeling like that which every unspoilt mind derives from the innocent prattle of such children as are not confined in artificial trammels, but allowed to express their own thoughts in their own words. We feel all the comparative consciousness, that we can think deeper, and express ourselves better; yet, making the due allowances, we wonder how they think so soundly, and speak so well.

To this wonder is added the never failing charm of simplicity, and the delight we take in detecting the first motions as they arise in the untutored breast; and assisting the retrograde view, we love to indulge of our own feelings and opinions, during that guileless period.

These nearly resemble the general motives, that prompts us to explore with a curiosity, ardent and not useless, the characters and manners of nations such as I have described. The philosopher and politician may be stimulated in their researches by many other causes; but these are the leading sentiments of those who merely wish to be pleased and informed.

Whoever has observed the very great pains taken by men of capacious mind and enlightened curiosity, to trace the progress of mind in remote and uncivilized countries, as well as through the remote and obscure periods of local history or natural records, must wonder at our countrymen in particular. Their diligent search of what is remote, and in a great measure unattainable in the history of mind and manners, and total neglect of what is obvious and within reach, nay, concealed in the recesses of their native country,—is not merely strange, but altogether unaccountable. They have bewildered themselves in endless and fruitless researches, regarding the ancient Scythians and modern Tartars, the Belgae, the Gauls, the Goths, the more modern Danes. I speak at random, and merely repeat a string of names of which I know very little, and they cannot know very much. In the mean time, their curiosity seems very moderately excited by the greatest of possible curiosities—even by the remains of the most ancient, unmingled, and original people in Europe: of a people who, surrounded by strangers, have preserved for a series of ages, which no records can trace, their national spirit, their national language, their national habits, their national poetry, and, above all, their national mode of thinking and expressing their thoughts; their stile of manners, and strain of conversation, and still more their local traditions, and family genealogies in one uninterrupted series.

Why has not this wide field for speculation been explored. Why have the lovers of useful knowledge neglected to dig into a mine so rich in science; even that most valuable science, the knowledge of human nature.

But the lovers of this coy science, have too long delayed to follow her to her retreat. In the deep recesses of our Alpine glens, they might have wooed and won the nymph who presides over the hidden treasures of antique lore. In the Celtic Muse, they would have found an Egeria,[1] who would have enlightened them by her mystic counsels, and told them the secrets of other times, now doomed to long oblivion. Now it is too late.

"Tha, caimine Malmhine gu dian."[2]

The fair form, where inspiration has for so many ages, awaked the bard, animated the hero, and soothed the lover, is fast gliding into the mist of obscurity, and will soon be no more than a remembered dream, "When the hunter awakes from his noon-day slumber, and has heard in his vision the spirits of the hill."

The neglect of pretenders to science, in omitting to acquire a language, through which so much is to be known, and the apparent indifference of natives, in not producing at an earlier period, in the light of a more current language, the hidden treasures of their own, seems equally unaccountable.

---

1 A fourth-century Spanish nun who wrote of her pilgrimage to Mount Sinai and other holy places.
2 The literal translation of these words is, "The steps of Malvina drew near." But the metaphorical signification is more properly, The steps of Malvina are departing—they drew near to the awful forms of her fathers, to the "Cloudy Tabernacles," of souls escaped from suffering and from sorrow. [Grant's note]

One who, like the writer of these pages, is not absolutely a native, nor entirely a stranger, but has added the observant curiosity of the latter to the facilities of enquiry enjoyed by the former, might best, if otherwise qualified, explain this paradox....

Select Bibliography and Works Cited

Abbey, Cherie, and Janet Mullane, eds. *Nineteenth-Century Literature Criticism.* Vol. 15. Detroit: Gale Research Co., 1993.

Alexander, J.H. "Descriptive Guide to the Interleaved Set." *Scott's Interleaved Waverley Novels: the 'Magnum Opus.'* Ed. Iain Gordon Brown. [Oxford]: Pergamon Books, 1987.

Beiderwell, Bruce. "The Reasoning of Those Times: Scott's *Waverley* and the Problem of Punishment." *Clio* 15.1 (1985): 15-30.

Butler, Marilyn. "Introduction." *Castle Rackrent.* By Maria Edgeworth. London: Penguin, 1992.

——. *Maria Edgeworth: A Literary Biography.* Oxford: Clarendon P., 1972.

Butler, R.F. "Maria Edgeworth and Sir Walter Scott, Unpublished Letters, 1823." *Review of English Studies,* new series 9.33 (1958): 23-40.

Buzard, James. "Translation and Tourism: Scott's *Waverley* and the Rendering of Culture." *The Yale Journal of Criticism: Interpretation in the Humanities* 8 (1995): 31-59.

Colley, Linda. *Britons: Forging the Nation 1707-1837.* New Haven, CT: Yale UP, 1992.

Craig, David. *Scottish Literature and the Scottish People 1680-1830.* London: Chatto and Windus, 1961.

Crawford, Robert. *Devolving English Literature.* Edinburgh: Edinburgh UP, 2000.

Daiches, David. *Sir Walter Scott and His World.* New York: Viking, 1971.

Davis, Leith. *Acts of Union: Scotland and the Literary Negotiation of the British Nation 1707-1830.* Stanford, CA: Stanford UP, 1998.

Devine, T.M. *The Scottish Nation, A History 1700-2000.* New York: Viking, 1999.

Ferris, Ina. *The Achievement of Literary Authority: Gender, History, and the* Waverley *Novels.* Ithaca, NY: Cornell UP, 1991.

——. "Melancholy, Memory, and the 'Narrative Sit.' of History in Post-Enlightenment Scotland." *Scotland and the Borders of Romanticism.* Ed. Leith Davis, Ian Duncan, and Janet Sorensen. Cambridge: Cambridge UP, 2004.

Finlay, Richard. "Caledonia or North Britain? Scottish Identity in the Eighteenth Century." *Image and Identity.* Ed. Dauvit Broun, et al. Edinburgh: John Donald Publishers, 1998.

——. "Controlling the Past: Scottish Historiography and Scottish Identity in the Nineteenth and Twentieth Centuries." *Scottish Affairs* 9 (Autumn 1994): 127-42.

Garside, Peter. "Dating *Waverley*'s Early Chapters." *The Bibliotheck* 13.3 (1986): 61-81.

——. "Popular Fiction and National Tale: Hidden Origins of Scott's *Waverley*." *Nineteenth-Century Literature* 46.1 (1991): 30-53.

Harvie, Christopher. "Scott and the Image of Scotland." *Patriotism: The Making and Unmaking of British National Identity*. Ed. Raphael Samuel. Vol. III: "National Fictions." London: Routledge, 1989.

Hayden, John, ed. *Scott: The Critical Heritage*. New York: Barnes and Noble, 1970.

Hollingsworth, Brian. "Completing the 'Union': Edgeworth's *The Absentee* and Scott the Novelist." *Scott in Carnival*. Ed. J.H. Alexander and David Hewitt. Aberdeen: Association for Scottish Literary Studies, 1993.

Kelly, Gary. "Maria Edgeworth." *Dictionary of Literary Biography: British Romantic Novelists 1789-1832*. Vol. 116. Detroit: Gale Research Co., 1992.

Kerr, James. *Fiction against History: Scott as Storyteller*. Cambridge: Cambridge UP, 1989.

Kidd, Colin. *Subverting Scotland's Past*. Cambridge: Cambridge UP, 1993.

Kiely, Robert. *The Romantic Novel in England*. Cambridge, MA: Harvard UP, 1979.

Lamont, Claire. "Jacobite Songs as Intertexts in *Waverley* and *The Highland Widow*." *Scott in Carnival*. Ed. J.H. Alexander and David Hewitt. Aberdeen: Association for Scottish Literary Studies, 1993.

Lenman, Bruce. *An Economic History of Modern Scotland 1660-1976*. Hamden, CT: Archon, 1977.

——. "Union, Jacobitism, and Enlightenment." *Why Scottish History Matters*. Ed. Rosalind Mitchison. London: The Saltire Society, 1997.

Lockhart, J.G. *The Life of Sir Walter Scott*. 5 vols. New York: Thomas Y. Crowell and Co., 1870.

Lukacs, Georg. *The Historical Novel*. Lincoln: U of Nebraska P, 1983.

Mackie, J.D. *A History of Scotland*. 2nd ed. Rev. Bruce Lenman and Geoffrey Parker. London: Penguin, 1978.

McCrone, David, Angela Morris, and Richard Kiely. *Scotland—The Brand*. Edinburgh: Edinburgh UP, 1995.

Millgate, Jane. "The Interleaved Waverley Novels." *Scott's Interleaved*

Waverley Novels: the 'Magnum Opus.' Ed. Iain Gordon Brown. [Oxford]: Pergamon Books, 1987.

——. *Scott's Last Edition.* Edinburgh: Edinburgh UP, 1997.

Moretti, Franco. *Atlas of the European Novel.* London: Verso, 1998.

Penovich, Katherine. "From 'Revolution Principles' to Union: Daniel Defoe's Intervention in the Scottish Debate." *A Union for Empire.* Ed. John Robertson. Cambridge: Cambridge UP, 1995.

Pittock, Murray. *Inventing and Resisting Britain.* New York: St. Martin's P, 1997.

——. *The Invention of Scotland.* London: Routledge, 1991.

Raven, James. "Britain, 1750-1830." *The Novel.* Vol. 1. Ed. Franco Moretti. Princeton, NJ: Princeton UP, 2006.

Robertson, John. "Union, State, and Empire: The Britain of 1707 in its European Setting." *An Imperial State at War.* Ed. Lawrence Stone. New York: Routledge, 1994.

Ross, Alexander. *The Imprint of the Picturesque in Nineteenth-Century British Fiction.* Waterloo, ON: Wilfrid Laurier UP, 1986.

St. Clair, William. *The Reading Nation in the Romantic Period.* Cambridge: Cambridge UP, 2004.

Scott, Paul. *Walter Scott and Scotland.* London: The Saltire Society, 1994.

Scott, Sir Walter. "General Preface." *Waverley Novels.* Vol. 1. Edinburgh: Cadell, 1829.

——. *Journal.* New York: Harper and Brothers, 1891.

——. *The Malachi Letters. Romantic Period Writings 1798-1832: An Anthology.* Ed. Zachary Leader and Ian Haywood. London: Routledge, 1998 [1826].

——. *Tales of a Grandfather.* Vol. III. Philadelphia: Porter and Coates, 1829.

——. *Waverley.* Ed. Andrew Lang. Boston: Estes and Lauriat, 1893.

——. *Waverley.* Ed. Andrew Hook. London: Penguin, 1985 [1972].

——. *Waverley.* Ed. Claire Lamont. Oxford: Oxford UP, 1986.

Stein, Richard. "Historical Fiction and the Implied Reader: Scott and Iser." *Novel* 14.3 (Spring 1981): 213-31.

Trumpener, Katie. *Bardic Nationalism.* Princeton, NJ: Princeton UP, 1997.

Vakil, Cyrus. "Walter Scott and the Historicism of Scottish Enlightenment Philosophical History." *Scott in Carnival.* Ed. J.H. Alexander and David Hewitt. Aberdeen: Association for Scottish Literary Studies, 1993.

Williams, Ioan. *Sir Walter Scott on Novelists and Fiction.* London: Routledge and Kegan Paul, 1968.